Also by **Scott Sigler**

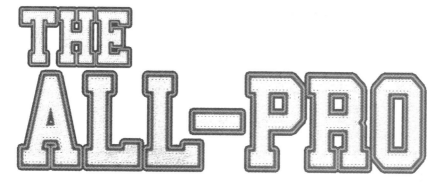

Galactic Football League: Book Three

Scott Sigler

ENTERTAINMENT

THE ALL-PRO
(The Galactic Football League Series, Book III)

Published in the United States by Empty Set Entertainment

For more information, email info@emptyset.com

Library of Congress Cataloging-in-Publication Data
Sigler, Scott
    The All-Pro/ Scott Sigler.
    p. cm
    1. Science Fiction — Fiction   2. Sports — Fiction
Library of Congress Control Number: 2011904462

ISBN: 978-0-983-19633-4

Printed in the United States of America

Book design by Donna Mugavero at Sheer Brick Studio
Cover design by Scott E. Pond at Scott E. Pond Designs
Cover art (figure) by Adrian Bogart at Punch Designs

First paperback edition MARCH 2014

*This book is dedicated to
Terry Bradshaw,
my first football hero.*

*This book is dedicated to
the Orange and the Black —
the greatest fans in the galaxy.*

Acknowledgments

Gridiron greats, who line up to play every damn Sunday:

A "Future Hall-of-Famer" Kovacs
publisher, ally, warrior to the core

Donna "Chalkboard" Mugavero
interior book design

Scott "Big Fish" Pond
color insert design

John "The Franchise" Vizcarra
continuity coach

Adrian "The Bruiser" Bogart
cover alien art

Rob "Moo" Otto
football analyst

Irv "Coach" Sigler
playbook consultant

Special Thanks

Team Dark Øverlord:

Arioch Morningstar
audio production

Carmen Wellman
Siglerpedia Czar

Author's Note

Oh, hello there. I didn't see you hanging around, waiting patiently for this book. That's a lie. Of course I saw you, you stalker.

A brief timeline note for THE ALL-PRO. If you read THE STARTER, an article at the end of that novel reported the results of the 2683 Tier Two Tournament. The Orbiting Death won the T2 Tourney, beating the Texas Earthlings in the championship game. That earned both teams promotion to Tier One, where you will see them play in this book.

As THE ALL-PRO opens, however, the T2 Tournament has not yet happened. That article about the Orbiting Death's tourney win? That was a *flash forward*, a little sneak peek to set up a primary rivalry for the Ionath Krakens.

In the pages you are about to read, our story begins with Quentin scouting for players at the Tier Three Tournament, also known as the "Two Weeks of Hell." This tournament happens three months after the 2683 Tier One season that you read about in THE STARTER and right before the beginning of the Tier Two season.

Am I confusing the bejezus out of you? Here, this might help:

THE STARTER:
    Tier One Season: Jan. 2, 2683, to May 22, 2683

THE ALL-PRO: (off-season for Quentin & Co.)
    Tier Three Tournament: Aug. 14, 2683, to Aug. 28, 2683
    Tier Two Regular Season: Aug. 28, 2683, to Dec. 25, 2683

THE ALL-PRO: (in-season for Quentin & Co.)
    Tier One Preseason: Jan. 1, 2684, to Jan. 22, 2684
    Tier One Regular Season: Jan. 27, 2684, to April 20, 2684
    Tier One Postseason: April 27, 2684, to May 11, 2684

I hope that clears things up. Now, enjoy the book, drop and give me twenty and *run the plays that I call!*

BOOK ONE:
THE OFF-SEASON
April 23, 2683, to
December 31, 2683

**Transcript from the "Galaxy's Greatest Sports Show
with Dan, Akbar, and Tarat the Smasher"**

DAN: Hello again, sports fans. I am the semi-mystical being known
as Dan *the Man* Gianni, once again bringing you the most
stunning show the universe has witnessed since the Big Bang.
With me as always, Hall-of-Fame linebacker Tarat the Smasher and my lil' buddy, Akbar Smith.

TARAT: Thank you, Dan.

AKBAR: *Lil' buddy*? Are you kidding?

DAN: No need to thank me, Akbar. Everyone in broadcasting needs
a great nickname.

AKBAR: And your great nickname is *Dan the Man*? That's the best
you got?

TARAT: Well, we can't all have names like *Smasher*, lil' buddy.

DAN: Hey! Was that humor out of Tarat? Fantastic.

AKBAR: Tarat, how many times do I have to tell you to not encour-
age him?

TARAT: But I thought it was good to offer Humans encouragement.

DAN: Never mind him, Tarat. Let's get into the news. The Tier Three Tournament is underway. We're through the first round of the famed *Two Weeks of Hell*.

TARAT: My money is on the Achnad Archangels.

AKBAR: I'm going with the Kull Conquerors.

DAN: You're both wrong, wrong and ... oh wait ... I have a memo here ... yes, it says *wrong*! The Pittsburgh Steelers are the cream of the Tier Three crop this year and they'll bring the Homestead Cup back to Earth for the first time in a decade.

AKBAR: The Steelers? You're crazy. And what the hell is a *steeler*, anyway?

TARAT: A steeler is someone who practices theft, Akbar. And Dan, with a statement like that, I have to question the validity of your decision-making process.

DAN: Both of you, shush it. We're not going to dwell on Tier Three, because the real story is free agency for the upcoming 2684 Tier One season. You guys know how this works. Tier One finishes, which takes us to the Two Weeks of Hell for Tier Three and when *that* finishes we have the Tier Two season. With Tier One season finished and the Wabash Wolfpack crowned champs, we immediately jump into the free agency window. Teams can sign any player who is not under contract.

AKBAR: Sure, but we won't see any big signings for another few weeks, Dan. Players have to feel things out.

DAN: Wrong, fish-breath! This just in. The Galaxy's Greatest Sports Show is the first with the story — Rick Renaud, formerly with the New Rodina Astronauts and the top free-agent quarterback in all of football, just signed with the Yall Criminals.

TARAT: The Criminals got Renaud? That is a big move.

AKBAR: That instantly makes them contenders again. Last year, they were six-and-six, but in '82, they were eleven-and-one and favored to win it all before they lost to the To Pirates in the semi-finals.

TARAT: They only lost that game because quarterback Morite

Whittmore was hurt in the second quarter. The Criminals were ahead when that happened.

DAN: Well, we'll see what the Yall Criminals can do now that they have their man. Renaud's deal is eighteen megacredits a season for six seasons, one hundred eight megacredits total, forty-eight of those guaranteed. That's forty-eight *million* credits, guaranteed, even if he doesn't play a down for the Criminals. That makes him the highest-paid player in the history of the GFL. We know the rules committee is looking into a salary cap for 2686, which means the 2685 season could be the last year where a team can pay whatever it wants to land a player. With Renaud defining what a quarterback can make, what does that mean for free-agent quarterbacks at the *end* of the 2684 season, heading into 2685, which might well be the last year of monster contracts?

AKBAR: And by *free-agent quarterbacks next year*, you're referring to Quentin Barnes?

DAN: Who else? His contract with the Krakens is up after the 2684 season. There will be no other major QBs on the market. Sure, Frank Zimmer is available, but even if the To Pirates don't re-sign him—

TARAT: Which won't happen unless the Pirates want bloody riots all across the Ki Empire.

AKBAR: Try across the whole damn *galaxy*.

DAN: Right. Zimmer and the Pirates are one and the same. Not signing him means great loss of life and also general sadness among many. Like I was saying, even if Zimmer is available, no one is going to pay him top dollar with his age and history of concussions. Don Pine's contract with Ionath is also up at the end of 2684, but he's also *old* and he's not even starting for the Krakens. The young-gun quarterbacks, like Themala's Gavin Warren and the Orbiting Death's Condor Adrienne, are either tied up in long-term contracts or protected for two years due to promotion from Tier Two to Tier One. Barnes is a free agent, he'll only be *twenty* in Earth years and he's shaping up to be a superstar.

AKBAR: You know, Renaud averaged 315 passing yards per game and Barnes averaged 268 when he played the entire game. Barnes isn't *that* far behind the best quarterback in football right now. For all the great roster moves made by Gredok the Splithead, he messed up by not signing Barnes to a long-term deal.

TARAT: I think Barnes will carry some animosity at being paid league minimum for two years.

DAN: But will Gredok make Barnes the highest-paid player in the league? Will he lock him up?

AKBAR: If he doesn't do it, someone will. The Bartel Water Bugs need a QB. And sooner or later, the Pirates need to replace Zimmer.

TARAT: And my sources tell me that the Mars Planets have new investors. They badly want to return to Tier One and are willing to spend the money to get there.

DAN: But would Barnes drop to a Tier Two team if the five time GFL champion To Pirates are willing to make him Zimmer's heir? I don't think so.

TARAT: Humans are obsessed with finances, Dan. There is no limit to what your species will do when money is part of the equation.

AKBAR: And let's not forget the gangland factor. As far as we know, someone will strong-arm Barnes into signing. Anna Villani did that with Condor Adrienne.

DAN: Hey now, Akbar, let's not go making wild accusations.

AKBAR: What the hell do you mean *wild accusations*?

TARAT: That means a baseless claim or an assertion that lacks facts or supporting evidence, Akbar.

AKBAR: Thanks, Tarat. You're always so helpful. Why don't you have another spider snack? Do you guys think that Condor Adrienne walked away from the Whitok Pioneers and signed with the Orbiting Death just *because*?

DAN: Akbar, you can't deny that Villani is putting together an impressive team. Adrienne? Yalla the Biter at linebacker? And Chooch Motumbo at running back to replace Ju Tweedy?

AKBAR: Don't you mean replace *the murderer?*

DAN: I mean *replace Ju Tweedy*, Akbar. There is no evidence that Ju killed Grace McDermot.

AKBAR: And I've got a wormhole to sell you.

TARAT: But there is no such thing as a wormhole.

AKBAR: Exactly.

DAN: Anyway, Villani's spending the bucks to make a run at Tier One. She locked up Adrienne, which means that after the upcoming 2684 Tier One season, Barnes is going to be the biggest catch on the market.

TARAT: He should get an agent.

AKBAR: No kidding. Barnes makes league minimum. And have you seen his commercials? The Miller Lager commercial is awful. The kid can't act at all.

TARAT: I thought the commercial was very informative about the benefits of the product.

DAN: Oh, for crying out loud. The only other commercial he did was that one for Sayed Luxury Yachts. Barnes didn't say anything, just stood there looking all quarterback-ish. He should do more like that.

AKBAR: Maybe he should just worry about football. Let's be honest — he pulled the Krakens out of the fire last year and stayed in Tier One, but he hasn't proven anything other than he can sling the ball if his offensive line gives him time. We have to see if he's focused this year.

DAN: If he's focused? Why wouldn't he be dialed in like a laser?

TARAT: My sources say he's spending time with Somalia Midori, the singer of the band Trench Warfare. Apparently, her appearance is what you Humans would call *distracting.*

AKBAR: Distracting? Yeah, that's a good word for it.

DAN: You can say that again. That is, if you're into 6-foot-6 supermodels with legs up to the moon. But to each their own. You know what? Let's go to the callers. Can Barnes handle his newfound celebrity and elevate the Krakens to a playoff team? Line three from Wilson 6, you're on the Space. *Go!*

CALLER: Yeah, I hope Barnes loses focus this year, so that New

Rodina can get him cheap. Rick Renaud's betrayal left us hurting this year. Renaud should be shot!

TARAT: I think that is a bit extreme for leaving a team. For fumbling the ball, it is acceptable, but not for leaving a team.

DAN: The New Rodina Astronauts have about as much of a chance
at signing Barnes as I have at stealing Somalia Midori away
from him. Two words: *not gonna happen.* Next call, line five
from Alimum, you're on the Space. *Go!*

From *The Ionath City Gazette*

GFL Names 2683 All-Pro Team

by TOYAT THE INQUISITIVE

NEW YORK CITY, EARTH, PLANETARY UNION — GFL Commissioner Rob Froese today announced the 2683 All-Pro selections. This elite group is well represented by the Orange and the Black. Dominant left tackle Kill-O-Yowet and defensive end Aleksandar Michnik were named among the league's best at their positions.

Kill-O and Michnik became Ionath's first Tier One All-Pro players since 2675, when Moog-A-Vero earned the honor, also at left tackle. The Krakens were relegated to Tier Two at the end of the 2676 season. The 2683 campaign was the Krakens' first Tier One outing in seven seasons of play.

Quarterback Rick Renaud was named the league's most valuable player on the heels of his 11-1 season with the New Rodina Astronauts. Renaud threw for 3,780 yards, a new single-season record for twelve games and averaged 315 per game with 27 touchdowns and 9 interceptions. Renaud led the Astros to the GFL championship game, where they lost 23-17 in a double-overtime thriller to the Wabash Wolfpack.

This is the last season that the All-Pro selections are announced after the Galaxy Bowl. Beginning in the upcoming 2684 season, the All-Pro team will be named at the end of Week Thirteen, right before the playoffs begin.

OFFENSE

Quarterback
Rick Renaud
New Rodina Astronauts

Gavin Warren
Themala Dreadnaughts

Frank Zimmer
To Pirates

Running back
Don Dennis
Themala Dreadnaughts

Jack Townsend
Yall Criminals

Stephen Schacknies
New Rodina Astronauts

Fullback
Ralph Schmeer
Wabash Wolfpack

Kahn-En-Roll
New Rodina Astronauts

Wide receiver
Atlanta
New Rodina Astronauts

Angoon
Isis Ice Storm

Victoria
To Pirates

Naksup
Wabash Wolfpack

Tight end
Brandon Rowe
Alimum Armada

Rich Evanko
New Rodina Astronauts

Tackle
Kill-O-Yowet
Ionath Krakens

Maik-De-Jong
Neptune Scarlet Fliers

Steve Henry
Alimum Armada

Guard
Lor-En-Zen
Jupiter Jacks

Al-E-Rand
Bord Brigands

Mik-Gar-E
Sheb Stalkers

Center
Graham Harting
To Pirates

Kola-Kow-Ski
D'Kow War Dogs

DEFENSE

Defensive end

Ryan Nossek
Isis Ice Storm

Steve Owens
D'Kow War Dogs

Aleksandar Michnik
Ionath Krakens

Interior lineman

Stephen Wardop
Wabash Wolfpack

Gum-Aw-Pin
Sala Intrigue

Cian-Mac-Man
Lu Juggernauts

Outside linebacker

Douglas Glisson
New Rodina Astronauts

Richard Damge
To Pirates

Jan Dennison
Neptune Scarlet Fliers

Inside/Middle linebacker

Mike Dowell
Jang Atom Smashers

Chaka the Brutal
Isis Ice Storm

Cornerback

Xuchang
Jupiter Jacks

Matsumoto
Mars Planets

Smileyberg
Coranadillana Cloud Killers

Free/Strong safety

Cairns
Shorah Warlords

Ciudad Juarez
To Pirates

Tulsa
Neptune Scarlet Fliers

SPECIAL TEAMS

Punter: Ryan Allen
Chillich Spider-Bears

Place kicker: Shi-Ki-Kill
Coranadillana Cloud Killers

Kick returner: Chetumal
Hittoni Hullwalkers

COACH OF THE YEAR

Alan Roark
Wabash Wolfpack

LEAGUE MVP

Rick Renaud
New Rodina Astronauts

2

AUGUST 2683

QUENTIN BARNES WALKED DOWN the stone steps of Smithwicks Arena. Another Sunday, another packed stadium.

But this time, he was just a spectator.

He headed for the best seats in the house — lower level, against the glass, at the midfield line. Two burly HeavyG guards walked in front of him. Just behind him walked John Tweedy and Rebecca Montagne. Behind them, two additional guards. Heads turned as the group descended. Some of those heads were for Quentin, he knew, because his face had become more than just a little bit famous during the recent 2683 Tier One season. Only *some* of the looks were for him, however, because most heads turned to stare at the woman walking by his side.

The 6-foot-6, blue-skinned, spike-mohawked lead singer of Trench Warfare — Somalia Midori.

His date.

"Quentin, this is wild-wild," she said. Somalia looked around the stadium's shallow bowl, taking in the strangely dressed League of Planets natives. "You take a girl out for bloodsport? Such a classy-flashy act."

He wasn't sure if she was being genuine or sarcastic. He was never really sure with her. But it was only their second date. He had yet to figure out the nuances of her sense of humor. Any time he wasn't sure what she meant, though, just one look at her made all the confusion worthwhile — perfect blue skin, a tall, blonde mohawk sure to block the view of anyone sitting behind her, an outfit that would barely qualify as undergarments back on Micovi. The singer of his favorite band of all time and she was *his date* to Dinolition.

Quentin felt a fist pound his left shoulder, hard enough to hurt, hard enough to almost make him tumble down the stadium's tan stone steps. Quentin didn't react with violence, however, or even a hint of surprise — when John Tweedy was your best friend, you were going to get hit all the time for just about any reason conceivable. John was what people called *excitable*.

"Q!" John screamed, practically in Quentin's ear. "Thanks again for the tickets. This is going to be great!"

Quentin hoped so. He had to admit, this was pretty exciting. He hadn't been a spectator at a non-football sporting event since leaving Micovi. He'd seen plenty of football games, for certain, traipsing around the galaxy with Krakens head coach Hokor the Hookchest for Tier Two and Tier Three ballgames, scouting for players that might fill a spot on the Krakens' 2684 roster. Sometimes team owner Gredok the Splithead came along, sometimes backup quarterback Donald Pine.

The hunt for players was what had brought Quentin here, to Wilson 6, for the Tier Three tournament. The two-week tournament hosted games mostly in the big football cities: Jang, Hittoni and Einstein. The Jang Atom Smashers and the Hittoni Hullwalkers played in Tier One, while the Wilson 6 Physicists were a Tier Two team from the city of Einstein. Dinolition, on the other hand? You only found that fringe sport way out in the Wastes.

The two guards in front stopped at the bottom of the sandstone stairs. They turned their backs to the clear, twenty foot high enclosure, then gestured to the right, along the row of fold-down seats. Beyond the high crysteel walls, Quentin saw the dirt playing field some ten feet below.

He went down the row first, followed by Somalia, then Rebecca and John. It still felt weird to get the star treatment, even a bit uncomfortable, but he suspected that he'd get used to it pretty fast. Free transport to the Wastes, four on-the-glass tickets to the spectacle that was Dinolition, full personal security and four-star hotel accommodations? Yeah, stardom had some perks.

John sat for only a second before he stood — wild eyes wide and grinning mouth open — to shout over the top of Rebecca and Somalia. "Holy *crap*, Q! On the shucking *glass*? Do you have any idea how *awesome* this is going to be?"

"I hope so," Quentin said. He wasn't as excited as John — no one ever was, about anything — but Quentin was still pretty fired up. He'd seen holocasts of Dinolition's insanity, but word was you had to see a match in person to really appreciate the carnage.

If it hadn't been for an invitation from the Dinolition Commissioner and the commissioner's promises of high security, Quentin would have never thought to attend this match. He didn't travel much. When he did, it certainly wasn't out in the open like this, as a celebrity.

The people who had bombed the Ionath Krakens' victory parade eight months earlier could still be out there. Gredok had "taken care of" the cell directly responsible for that lethal attack, but no one knew if there was a bigger organization behind it, possibly plotting another attempt on Quentin's life. If, indeed, Quentin had been the actual target. Such threats reduced the desire to travel, to go anywhere that involved a crowd.

But the Dinolition invite had come from the top. Even Gredok the Splithead, owner of the Krakens franchise, had looked into the trip and declared it safe. Relatively, anyway — their team bus, the *Touchback*, was the only truly safe place for Quentin and his fellow Krakens.

Quentin would have had the trip checked out by his private detective, Frederico Esteban Giuseppe Gonzaga, but Fred hadn't been heard from since halfway through the Tier One season some seven weeks ago. Frederico was supposedly off searching for Quentin's family. Quentin didn't know if the hunt was successful, didn't have any information at all, really, save for Fred's pay that came out of Quentin's bank account every week.

When the Dinolition invitation had come in, Quentin couldn't think of a better person to take along than his teammate and friend, the deadly John Tweedy, Ionath's starting middle linebacker. John loved *all* sports, really, but seemed extra-special-crazy for Dinolition. Quentin had planned on inviting Coach Hokor, since they were all on Wilson 6 for the same scouting trip, but the second John learned there was a total of four tickets, he asked if he could bring Rebecca.

Becca "The Wrecka" Montagne, the Krakens starting fullback and girlfriend of John Tweedy. Becca was an excellent blocker, smart and she caught everything thrown her way. She had taken over the starting slot from veteran Paul Pierson near the end of the Tier One season. Off of the playing field, however, Quentin couldn't stand the HeavyG woman. She didn't *get* football, didn't *get* that it was a violent game and that sentients got hurt, sentients died. The look on John's face, however — so excited, so eager — had made Quentin say *sure, bring her along.*

That, of course, left Quentin needing a date of his own. A check of touring schedules resulted in a wonderful coincidence — Trench Warfare was playing five shows on Wilson 6. A call to Somalia's management resulted in an instant date.

Quentin reached his open seat. Seats in most stadiums barely accommodated his 7-foot-tall, 380-pound body, but this one was quite comfortable. The League of Planets had more HeavyG citizens than any other government. Laws prohibiting racism ensured that the massive Human variants weren't discriminated against with Human-sized facilities.

Somalia sat in the seat on his right. Graceful and athletic, she curled her long legs up onto the seat and slid her sinewy arms around Quentin's right bicep. Quentin was aware of sentients taking pictures, shooting holos — that had happened on their first date, a dinner in Ionath City. The paparazzi had come out of the woodwork. Quentin had no idea how the camera crews found out so quickly, but that was their business and they were probably very good at it. The experience had made dinner quite uncomfortable — he didn't like the attention. He was already nervous enough dating a superstar. Dozens of cameras stalking his every move made it even worse. Pictures and holos of the couple hit hundreds of networks before the appetizer was even served.

The Dinolition crowd consisted mostly of modded Humans and minority HeavyG. Plenty of Quyth Leaders, Warriors and Workers dotted the stands, as did several well dressed Ki. Very few Sklorno were in attendance — the species was not welcome on League of Planets worlds.

To Quentin's left sat an overweight Human with a long, white beard. The man dressed in the strange, slightly fuzzy clothing preferred by League citizens. Quentin quickly looked him up and down, searching for any protrusions that might show the handle of a knife, the shape of a gun. He saw nothing.

Quentin turned to look at the people behind him, giving them the same once-over. Some of the spectators recognized him, smiled at him, the expression people have when they unexpectedly find themselves near someone famous. Quentin's eyes paused on the person directly behind him, a Human teenager not more than sixteen.

The kid's eyes narrowed in anger.

Quentin's body tensed. Was the kid strapped with a suicide bomb? Normally, Quentin would just run, but that wasn't an option with Somalia, Becca and John sitting right there.

The kid sneered. "What are you lookin' at, butt-nugget? Turn around. And by the way, the Krakens suck."

Quentin's gaze dropped to the boy's shirt — white, with the boot-print logo of the Hittoni Hullwalkers, a team the Krakens played every year.

The kid was just a football fan.

Quentin felt the stress ease away. "Good luck to your Hullwalkers this year."

"In all games but one," John Tweedy said. John had turned around in his seat. He stared at the boy. John had a full-body, subdermal tattoo that let him flash colors, images and words anywhere on his skin. He usually used it to scroll messages across his face. This time, his forehead read: I'M PUTTING THE HULLCRAPPERS IN A SHALLOW GRAVE, SO START DIGGING NOW AND SAVE US ALL SOME TIME.

"John, knock it off," Quentin said. "He's just a kid."

John shrugged. "He's gotta grow up sometime. Hey, kid, you're going to watch the match all nice-like and not bother my friend, right?"

The kid's eyes widened as he looked at John Tweedy. Quentin was quite a bit bigger than John, but perhaps people just feared linebackers more than quarterbacks.

"Sure," the kid said quietly. "Yeah. All nice-like. Sure."

The scene was a little embarrassing, but the fact that John hadn't come over the seat and started a brawl made Quentin count his lucky stars.

Movement from out in the wide, circular arena drew Quentin's attention. On the dirt oval's far side, the arena walls receded. A hover-platform slid out, floated to midfield. On the platform was a tall wheel split into twenty pie-like sections, each a different color. In front of the wheel stood three Humans and two HeavyG, all holding long, brass trumpets that gleamed in the noonday sun. Red banners dangled from the trumpets, banners that matched the trumpeters' red, gold-braided uniforms. A small, Human woman stood off to the side. She wore a yellow dress with silver stripes that complemented her silver boots, gloves and tiara. Quite the spectacle.

Quentin leaned forward to look to his right, to John Tweedy. When he did, Quentin locked eyes with Rebecca — she had been staring at him, an expression of narrow-eyed anger on her face. She instantly looked away.

"John," Quentin said. "What's going on?"

"Opening ceremonies," John said. "Pageantry and all that."

The trumpeters ripped out a short bit of music that echoed from the speakerfilm lining the stadium walls. Smithwicks Arena wasn't as large as the Krakens' home field. Ionath Stadium seated 185,000 screaming fans, while Smithwicks held maybe 40,000 at most. The playing area was larger and rounder than a football field, the size used for some obscure sport called *cricket*. At the ends of the oblong stadium, fifteen rows of seats were cut away to make room for ornate, thirty foot high double doors.

John pounded on the glass.

"Here it comes, Q! Time for the big boys." The words PALEONTOLOGY ROCKS danced on John's face.

The trumpet music stopped. The woman in the loud, yellow dress spoke, her voice magnified by the sound system.

"Welcome to *Die … no … litionnnnnn!*"

She waited for the crowd roar to die down. "I am your host and league commissioner, Rachel Guestford. This contest is a three-round affair with a 10,000 total kilo weight limit. No replacement mounts allowed. And now, your contestants. Hailing from Roughland on Rodina, with a record of seven wins and two losses, I give you, the Roughland Ridgebacks!"

The big double doors to Quentin's left opened. He knew what was supposed to come out, yet when it did, he could barely believe his eyes.

"High One," Quentin said. "Oh … my."

A giant, lizard-looking creature, covered from head to toe in gleaming, red armor. It stomped out of the doors, head low, powerful legs carrying it forward. A long tail trailed behind, parallel to and ten feet above the ground. Behind this huge creature's head rode a Human wearing ornate armor of black and red. The Human sat in a leather saddle and carried a long, black lance. The monster walked forward. Its jockey raised the lance high, saluting the crowd.

High above midfield, a holoscreen flared to life. Quentin saw a close-up of the huge animal and its jockey — a squat man covered head-to-toe in high-tech armor that was designed to look ancient, lined with runes and scrolls and filigree. Various holologos advertising dozens of products blazed from the armor's curved skin. He looked as decorated by endorsements as the Essadari rocket-sleds of the racing leagues. Above the image of monster and jockey, Quentin saw the red and black logo for the jockey's team, the Roughland Ridgebacks.

Text scrolled out below the images.

POUGHKEEPSIE PETE, CAPTAIN, RIDGEBACKS

And below that:

TYRANNOSAURUS REX, 6,432 KILOS

John pounded the glass even harder. "That's Pete! Come on, Pete! Eat someone!"

Quentin remembered John's description of Poughkeepsie Pete. The Human stood all of three feet tall. Hard to tell when he was on the back of a shucking red-armored dinosaur, that was for sure.

Pete's mount walked out fifty yards, halfway to the center of the arena, then stopped.

"He's always on Old Bess," John said. "That's his favorite ride. I can't wait to see what he brings out with him."

As if on queue, more red-armored dinosaurs strode out of the doors. Three fast- and lethal-looking creatures, much smaller than the T. rex. Quentin thought he saw feathers sticking out from spots in the red armor, from the short arms and from between head-armor plates. He looked up to the overhead holo.

TONY KOESTER / BEISHANLONG GRANDIS / 542 KILOS

CRITTER CLARK / GALLIMIMUS BULLATUS / 501 KILOS

IAN BAHAS / ACHILLOBATOR GIGANTUS / 709 KILOS

"John, why are those so much smaller?"

"They're speedsters," John said. "You never know what game will come up on the wheel, Q. You only get ten thousand kilos total weight for all three rounds. Twenty games, different strategies for each game, sometimes you need mass, sometimes you need speed, sometimes both. Just wait and see."

The trumpets blared anew, as did Rachel Guestford.

"And their opponent," she said. "Hailing from The Reef in the outer reaches, I give you the Reef Stompers!"

The big doors at the opposite end swung open. Giant, *blue*-armored creatures strode out. These looked more like huge, six-legged spiders, or perhaps six-legged crabs — and all had one eye.

"Eww," Somalia said. "Those are just *disgusting*."

The first creature's lance-wielding jockey didn't look Human. Quentin looked up to the holodisplay. The image showed a spinning logo for the Reef Stompers. Below that, a live image of a blue-armored Quyth Leader rider.

SABAT THE NIFTY, CAPTAIN, STOMPERS

The Leader caste dominated Quyth culture. Even though they were all of three feet tall, they controlled both the Worker and Warrior castes. The Warriors on the Krakens roster were all six feet or taller, around four hundred pounds. Like the Warriors, Leaders had two legs — thighs that pointed up and back, forelegs that angled forward and down, kind of like a frog. The body rose up from those low hips. Two large middle arms extended from the sides, ending in clumsy hands good for hitting or walking on all-fours. The real dexterous work came from the pedipalps — limbs that stuck out from the bottom of the head, below the species' single eye. On a Warrior, the pedipalps were as thick and muscular as a Human arm. On a Leader, however, the limbs looked thin, more suitable for delicate work. A Leader's softball-sized eye looked huge in its head, while the larger Warrior's baseball-sized eye stayed mostly hidden behind thick ridges of chitin. Other than those differences, the Warriors had hard-chitin skin, while fur covered the Leaders. Workers were somewhere in the middle on all counts — about four feet tall, thickly built for manual labor.

Quentin had never seen a Leader participate in any athletic event, let alone wear armor into a dangerous contest. And *The Reef*? He'd never heard of it.

"Somalia, where did the announcer say the Stompers were from again?"

"A crazy place," she said. "The Reef is a huge-huge artifact on the galaxy's edge. Bigger than four or five planets combined or something. We played a show out there."

"Galaxy's *edge*? How many punches to reach that?"

Somalia's eyes narrowed as she thought. Quentin found the look incredibly attractive.

"Twenty-four, I think," she said. "Yeah, twenty-four punches, one way. Took us three weeks of travel to get there."

By Quentin's count, that would be forty-eight punches worth

of motion sickness. Not a good time. "That's a really long trip. How many shows did you play?"

"Just the one."

"You did *forty-eight* punches for a *single* show?"

"We played a private party for Mary Garrett. She's rich-rich like we could never taste. We made more money on that show than the rest of the tour combined."

Somalia, it seemed, traveled even more than Quentin did. Endless trips through punch-space to perform in front of thousands of sentients. In that regard, they had much in common.

The holodisplay zoomed out to give a larger view of the spiderish monstrosity. It had to be twenty feet high, with a mouth full of long, inwardly curved teeth. Quentin realized that the creature really only had four legs — the other two were pedipalps, perhaps five feet long and tipped with claws the size of butcher knives.

NIGHTMARE BEAST, 6,871 KILOS

"Damn, that's big," Quentin said. His eyes flicked to the scratched crysteel walls, a small part of him wondering if they actually could restrain such big beasts.

Two smaller creatures walked out of the double doors. Four long legs supported a thick body with a stubby neck extended up from the front. Shorter pedipalp arms hung from the sides of a sleek, one-eyed head.

POTOL THE HALF-WIT / SPIDER-BEAR / 614 KILOS

YOPAT THE CRAZED / SPIDER-BEAR / 734 KILOS

"Sweet!" John shouted. He stood up in his seat and pounded his fists against the crysteel. "Come on, Pete! Eat those ticks up!"

The racial insult drew glares from the Quyth Warriors, Workers and Leaders, seated nearby, but none of them said a word.

The two teams of horrific mounts lined up on either side of the floating platform. The wheel started spinning. A hush fell over the crowd. A stiff flapper at the top of the wheel *clacked* against posts ringing the wheel's outer edge, the sound magnified by the stadium's speakerfilm. The *clacks* slowed as the wheel did, until the top flapper pointed to a slice labeled DISMOUNT.

John jumped up and down. "*Super*-sweet! You'll like this one,

Q. The goal is to tear the other jockeys off their mounts. Last team with a mounted jockey wins."

The trumpeters let out a *bah-bah-bahhhh* blast. Monsters from both teams returned to the wall near their respective doors. The wheel platform slid back across the field and into its space below the rows of fans. Arena walls slid back into place.

The game was about to begin.

"Q, get ready," John said. "Get ready for some *Dino-shucking-lition!*"

Quentin nodded but wasn't sure if he was ready at all. The city of New Rodina wasn't that far away — what if one of these creatures ran wild through the streets? There would be panic, carnage.

The trumpets sounded another five notes, *bah-bah-bah-bah, BAHHHH!* and the match was on. The Tyrannosaurus rex rushed straight forward. Its speedy teammates sprinted single file to the right, following the oblong wall's long curve. Their path would bring them directly under Quentin's seat. The blue-armored Stompers seemed to pause for a second, reminding Quentin of the way he looked at a defense just before the snap, then they shot forward, monsters scuttling on four huge legs. The Nightmare Beast led the charge, flanked on either side by the two Spider-Bears.

John slapped the glass. "They're going after Pete! Come on, Pete! Take 'em out!"

Pete's Tyrannosaur closed the distance, its big body moving with a grace and speed Quentin hadn't thought possible for a creature of that size. The two smaller Quyth mounts ran ahead of their bigger teammate, first angling out, then back in to attack Pete's flanks. Quentin saw the red-armored Ridgeback speedsters break off from the wall, running three abreast, trying to come in from the rear but they would be too late. While he'd never seen the game, Quentin instantly understood what had happened — the Ridgebacks had split up, hoping to draw the smaller Quyth mounts away from Pete. The Stompers hadn't taken the bait — instead, they focused their attack on the now-isolated T. rex.

Would they take Pete out right away?

The two largest creatures on the pitch came hurtling at each other. As the smaller Quyth mounts closed in from the sides, Quentin saw the big Nightmare Beast slow, just a bit, almost flinching away from the impact.

Lances snapped off of hard armor. The Tyrannosaur lowered its head and smashed into the Nightmare Beast, a high-speed concussion of armor and flesh some 12,000 kilos strong. The crowd roared in satisfaction, a blood-lust scream similar to what Quentin heard when he was on a football field. Bits of armor, both Ridgeback-red and Stomper-blue, broke off and flew like brightly colored shrapnel, falling to the pitch and skidding across the dirt surface.

The Nightmare Beast stumbled to the side. The T. rex struck, opening its gaping mouth and reaching for the blue-armored jockey. Such *speed* from something so *big*. Quentin's breath locked in his chest.

John screamed in time with the rabid crowd: "*Eat him up, eat him up, rah-rah-rah!*"

Mouth wide, wet-white teeth flashing in the afternoon sun, the T. rex's jaws bit down on the Quyth Leader jockey. Just as they closed, Quentin saw the Quyth Leader's blue armor *shift*, compressing somehow into a smaller, rounder shape. The T. rex's teeth snapped together and the Quyth Leader vanished somewhere inside that huge mouth.

The two smaller Spider-Bears attacked. One jumped at the T. rex's throat, wide mouth and curved jaws punching into the red neck-armor. The other Spider-Bear went high, leaping fifteen feet into the air to land on the T. rex's back. Four long legs bowed out at the joints, lowering the creature's center of gravity and letting it scramble up the moving T. rex's long neck.

"Pete, look out!" John screamed as if the jockey could hear him ninety meters away over the roar of forty thousand fans.

Pete reached down to the side of his saddle and pulled something free. He stood and turned, his feet balancing on the saddle, one hand holding the T. rex's reins, the other holding a war-hammer almost as big as he was.

The scene held Quentin fast — the T. rex thrashing from left to right, a Spider-Bear trying to cling to its neck from below, a second

Spider-Bear rushing up its back to attack an armored little man brandishing a hammer.

Pedipalps reached for Pete, who suddenly dove to the left, *off* the T. rex. Quentin expected him to plummet twenty feet to the ground, but Pete was still holding the reins. The motion brought Pete swinging underneath, left hand holding the reins, right hand swinging the hammer. The hammer's big head *smashed* into the dangling Spider-Bear's rider, knocking him off his mount to crash to the pitch below.

John jumped up and down. "That's two! One more!"

It had all happened in the span of a few seconds, from the first crash to Pete's action-hero swing. The Ridgeback speedsters closed in, two of them actually leaping up onto the T. rex's back to attack the Spider-Bear still crawling up the big neck. With almost a thousand kilos on its back and a red-armored midget swinging from its reins, the T. rex stood tall and let out a roar that made Quentin's stomach quiver. The Spider-Bear tried to cling tight, to hang on to the suddenly vertical neck, but both red-armored speedsters bit down on its legs and dragged it free. Armor spinning and blue blood spurting in long streaks, the three smaller creatures crashed hard to the dirt pitch. The impact seemed to stun mounts and jockeys alike.

The third Ridgeback speedster, however, had been waiting. It closed in like a blur, bit down on the blue-armored rider and yanked him out of his saddle. A flick of the head sent the Quyth Leader flying thirty feet into the air. A fall like that could easily kill a sentient, but at the apex, Quentin saw the Leader's armor shift into a blue ball. As that ball plummeted toward the ground, it slowed, small, hidden rockets shooting out little cones of flame. It hit without much velocity, then rolled to a stop.

"This is *horrible*," Somalia said. "I love it! Becca, do you like the game?"

Becca gave a polite smile, shook her head. "Not sure this is for me. Quite impressive, though, I'll say that."

Trumpets sounded, the crowd bellowed.

"First round to the Ridgebacks," an announcer called, accompanied by a four-note blast from the trumpets. "Both teams return to your section to await the next spin."

Quentin felt a fist hit his shoulder. John had somehow reached across both Becca and Somalia without touching either one.

"Q! What did you think? Awesome, right?"

Quentin shook his head. "John, that was horrible. That big lizard thing killed that Leader! This isn't a *sport*, it's barbaric."

John laughed. "Q, it's okay. Armor turtles up when a jockey is in danger."

Quentin again gazed out to the pitch. Sure enough, the Quyth Leader's armor shifted again. The blue ball seemed to *unfold* and the tiny Quyth Leader stood. His Spider-Bear mount, trailing a stream of blood from its legs, scuttled over to him, picked him up with its pedipalps and placed him back in the saddle. Jockey and mount then ran back to their side of the pitch to await the next spin.

"See?" John said. "He's fine. They'll patch up his mount's legs as best they can, then go at it for the second round."

"But what about the first one?" Quentin said. "John, Pete's mount *swallowed* him!"

John nodded. "Yeah, sure, he got munched. He's out of the game. His backup has to come in and take over. But don't worry, Q, Pete's ride will poop him out in a few hours."

"He'll what?"

"Poop him out."

"*Poop* him out?"

"Yeah, sure. That or puke him up. Jockey armor has like two day's worth of oxygen, Q. Just enjoy the next spin."

Quentin eased back in his chair. He felt Somalia's fingers tighten in his own. Even with her there, he wasn't enjoying the show. It was just so ... *brutal*. Was this how some sentients felt when he played football? When players were knocked out, had limbs torn off ... even *died*? And yet, just like when he played, the crowd ate up every last minute of it. Was this gladiator sport really any different than his?

"Hey, Mister Barnes."

The voice came from behind. The kid with the Hullwalkers shirt. Quentin turned. "Yeah?"

"Sorry about calling you a butt-nugget. Would you sign my messageboard?" The kid offered a small board that already projected a floating image of Quentin's face, a picture the kid had just taken while Quentin was watching the action down in the pit.

People thought they could take a picture of him whenever they wanted? Did he have no privacy?

No, he did not. Not anymore. At least not while playing in the GFL.

"Sure, kid," Quentin said and took the board. He started to sign with the tip of his pointer finger when the image on the messageboard wavered. It changed from a picture to words.

FREDERICO SAYS YOU SHOULD GO TO THE BATHROOM, RIGHT NOW. THE OUT-OF-ORDER ONE.

Quentin stared at the board. He'd been sitting here, watching the match for what, a half-hour? And this kid had been a plant from square one?

"Are you gonna sign it, or what?"

Quentin looked up. The kid kept a perfect poker face. Quentin looked back down to see that the message was gone. His picture was back again, with a space for him to sign.

"Yeah, sure." Quentin signed his name. He handed back the board.

"Thanks," the kid said. "And the Krakens still suck."

Quentin nodded, then excused himself to Somalia. He walked to the steps. Two security guards stood up as well.

"Need something, Mister Barnes?"

"Bathroom," Quentin said.

The security guard put his wrist near his mouth and mumbled something. He nodded at Quentin. "Right this way, sir."

The guard walked up the sandstone steps. Quentin followed, the second security guard right behind him.

• • •

THE FIRST SECURITY GUARD came out of the bathroom, stepping over the yellow tape running between two orange cones.

"All clear," he said. "Janitor is in there, but I patted him down. He's just fixing something. He's clean. Go on in, Mister Barnes, we'll keep an eye out for you."

"Thanks." Quentin stepped over the yellow tape and walked in. From far behind him, down in the stadium, he heard the roar of the bloodthirsty crowd and wondered who had been eaten.

Inside the bathroom, he saw the janitor repairing a nannite hand-cleaning machine. The wall-mounted device hung open, various parts and tanks sitting on towels on the tile floor.

If Quentin hadn't known Frederico was the janitor, he would have never recognized the man. When in his normal state, Frederico was six feet tall, about two hundred pounds and in his mid-thirties. He always looked like he'd just stepped out of a tough-guy detective holo. The bearded, slouched-over schlub in the bathroom, however, looked like he was pushing fifty and would need a crane to help him stand up straight.

"Excuse me," Quentin said. "I need to use the facilities."

The bearded janitor looked up, saw Quentin, then looked around the bathroom, checking to make sure no one else had crept in. Normally, even while in disguise, Frederico looked confident, calm. Now, however, his eyes carried a haunted look, as if there were someone — or some*thing* — stalking him.

It had been months since Quentin had seen this man. Months that Frederico had supposedly been out hunting for Quentin's family. Had the search finally produced results?

"You surprise me," Quentin said. "I thought this Dinolition thing was legit, but you set up the tickets?"

Frederico shrugged. "Rachel Guestford owes me a favor or three. I had to contact you while you were away from Ionath, make sure no one knew I was trying to reach you."

That didn't sound good. Only John Tweedy knew Frederico was working for Quentin. Frederico and Quentin both wanted to keep that information away from Gredok the Splithead.

"Fred, are you okay? I know how much you like to play dress-up and all, but is something wrong?"

The janitor nodded. "Yeah. Someone doesn't want me to find out about your family. I've spent the last few weeks ducking some pretty heavy hitters."

Heavy hitters. And who could that be? The same group that bombed the victory parade? Or maybe sentients who worked for the owner of the Ionath Krakens?

"Who were they? Gredok's gang?"

Frederico shook his head. "I wish I knew. I can't say for sure if they're his goons. And they're not the only ones. That little reporter piece of fluff was also on Micovi, digging away."

"Piece of fluff? You mean Yolanda Davenport?"

Frederico nodded. "That's the one. I was at Micovi Stadium, seeing if the Raiders had any info on your past. She was there."

"Did she see you?"

Fred laughed. "Quentin, please. I'm a professional."

"What was she doing on Micovi?"

"Digging into the history of Quentin Barnes, just like me. Just like the heavies I ran into."

"She find anything?"

"I don't know," Frederico said. "I don't think she found much. She seemed to be looking for real specific stuff, stuff about your time with the Raiders, not about your childhood. The hitters, on the other hand? They wanted the same info I found. They always seemed to be just a step behind me."

"So … you *did* find something?" Quentin waited for him to speak, but the man seemed to have trouble finding the words. "Well? Come on, Fred. Out with it."

Frederico looked at the ground, shrugged his shoulders. "You *sure* you want this, Quentin?"

It had to be bad news. But was it *all* bad news? Was Quentin really alone? He took a breath, let it out slowly and tried to brace himself for the words.

"Yes. I want to know. All of it."

"Okay," Fred said. "I managed to find a family record based on DNA. I used some of your blood."

"You didn't ask me for my blood."

Frederico shrugged. "You're religious. Who knows what you superstitious primitives think is sacred?"

"I bleed all the time on the field, Fred. You really assume I would think blood is sacred?"

"There's no logic in religion, Quentin. Anyway, if you said *no*, I would have been out of an option, so I went with it."

"And where, exactly, did you get my blood?"

"Nanocyte patch back in Ionath Stadium," Frederico said. "Not hard to come by, Quentin. As you mentioned, you bleed a lot. You knew a guy on Micovi named Sam Sargsyan? Ran a bar-becue restaurant?"

Sam Sargsyan. *Mister Sam.* That brought back memories. "Yeah, what's he got to do with it?"

"Nothing," Frederico said. "I met him though. He said you liked to eat. A lot."

"I weigh almost four hundred pounds, Fred. Of course I eat a lot. You're stalling. Come on, tell me."

Fred chewed on his lip for a second, then nodded. "You're right, I'm stalling. The Purist Nation records are scattershot at best. Their technology is about four hundred years behind every-one else's, but I found the death record for your older brother."

Quentin nodded. No news there. When Quentin had been five, he'd watched his brother hang for the horrendous crime of steal-ing bread.

"Turns out your name isn't *Barnes*," Fred said. "At least, not originally. Looks like your family changed names. I'm not sure why."

"So what's my real name?"

"Carbonaro," Fred said. "I found it on your brother's death record."

Carbonaro. Quentin wasn't even Quentin Barnes? He'd never heard the name Carbonaro before. Maybe that was his birth name, but he'd been Barnes all his life and would continue to be so.

"Your brother's death record led me to your mother and father," Frederico said. "I could find no official death record of your father."

Quentin felt a stab of excitement in his chest, but he tempered it — no record of death did *not* mean his father was alive. "What's my father's name?"

"Cillian Carbonaro."

A name. Such a simple thing and yet it made the man somehow real. There was no proof that Quentin's father was dead. He might be out there. Maybe.

"That's a start," Quentin said. "And my mother?"

Frederico paused, then shook his head slowly. "Her name was Constance Carbonaro."

Wisps of memory bubbled up. A woman with tight, curly, black hair. Smiling down at him. Quentin couldn't quite form her face. His *mother*.

"And she's … "

He couldn't say the words.

"She's dead, Quentin. I found her record. It's accurate, no question. I'm sorry."

Quentin had felt elation at learning his father's fate was unknown. The news of his mother made that feeling fade, then sink. His mother. *Gone*. The woman he suddenly remembered: young, too young to have children but that was how it went on Micovi — children by fourteen, or you were a sinner. There were other memories, little bits and pieces that didn't connect — brief recollections of being held, being talked to in a voice that made the monsters go away, a voice that made everything all right.

"There's more," Frederico said. "You told me about your brother, but you said you didn't have any other siblings."

Quentin nodded, finding it was hard to move even that much. The remote possibility that his father *might* not have died on Micovi couldn't blur the hammer-thud pain of knowing his mother was gone forever. Everything felt heavy. It even hurt a little to breathe.

"Why did you tell me that?" Frederico asked. "Why didn't you tell me you had a sister?"

Quentin stared at the smaller man. The words didn't seem to make sense. "I ... I don't have a sister."

Frederico smiled. "Well, if the records are accurate, you do. Jeanine Carbonaro. She's about ten years older than you. She would have been about fifteen the time your brother died."

A sister? That couldn't be true. But what if it was? The sluggish feeling brought on by the knowledge of his mother expanded, spread, a creeping sensation that more bad news was about to hit home.

"And my ... my *sister's* record?" Quentin said. "Did you find a death record on her?"

Frederico shook his head. "Don't get too excited, okay? Just because I didn't find a death record doesn't mean—"

"Doesn't mean that she's alive, I know. I get it, Frederico, you can stop repeating that, okay?"

Frederico nodded. "Right, sorry. It's just ... well, you wouldn't be much of a poker player, Quentin. I can see the hope in your face."

"We're not playing poker." Quentin could hide expressions when he needed to, when he wanted to. Enough to even fool Gredok the Splithead, a sentient who could read your body temperature, your pulse. The game of manipulation ran rampant through all things GFL. Quentin had committed himself to learning that game, mastering it.

"It's the eyes," Frederico said. "A dead giveaway every time."

"You're not going to start talking about how pretty my eyes are again, are you?"

Frederico smiled, shook his head. "No, not at all. To tell you the truth, when we first met I did that just to get a rise out of you. You're okay-looking by the numbers, but you're really not my type."

"I wish I could say I was offended by that."

The roar of the crowd made them both look at the door.

Frederico nodded. "You need to get back to your date. If you want, I'll keep looking for more info."

"I do," Quentin said. "Just find whatever you can. Even ... even death records give me some idea, you know?"

Frederico nodded, then turned his attention back to the nan-nite machine. He was probably going to actually repair it. That struck Quentin as an odd touch for a meeting that took this much effort to set up, but Frederico seemed to be all about the details.

Quentin turned and walked out of the bathroom. The two guards were waiting for him.

"Everything okay, Mister Barnes?"

"Yeah, fine. Had some New Rodina food this morning, it caught up with me is all. Let's head back down."

The guard nodded. "Yes sir, Mister Barnes. We missed the second round. The wheel picked *Four Laps* and the Stompers took it. They just spun the wheel for round three — it's *Capture the Flag*, my favorite. You'll love it, Mister Barnes. This one is *really* bloody."

Quentin let the guards walk him back down the steps. Compared to the first round of Dinolition, he could only imagine what *really* bloody could mean.

NOTHING IN THE GALAXY could possibly be as exciting as playing football. Just *watching* it, however, proved a surprisingly close second. Quentin had no emotional involvement in the T3 Tourney championship game between the Mathara Manglers and the Achnad Archangels. He wasn't rooting for anyone, didn't know a player on either team, and yet his heart pounded as time ticked away. Fourth quarter, Achnad up 13-10. He was on the edge of his seat.

Affectionately known as the "Two Weeks of Hell," the single-elimination tournament featured thirty-two teams playing games every three days until a sole champion remained. In that two weeks, thirty games had been played across the League of Planets' five worlds and two net colonies. The championship game, of course, took place in the crown jewel of the system's football stadiums, the Shipyard — home field of the three-time GFL champion Hittoni Hullwalkers. Quentin would be back in this very stadium in Week Four of the Tier One season, some six months away.

Like every football-crazed kid, he'd dreamed of playing in the Shipyard, just like he'd dreamed of playing in To Pirates Stadium and the galaxy's other gridiron meccas. This year, however, one dream, one stadium, rose above all others:

The Tomb of the Virilli.

Home field of the Yall Criminals.

Not because Ionath played at Yall in Week Two in the showcase that was Monday Night Football, but because this year the stadium hosted the sport's ultimate game — Galaxy Bowl XXVI, where the GFL champion would be crowned.

Where Quentin and his teammates would join the ranks of legends.

But that conquest was many months away and would not happen without adding some fresh blood to the Krakens roster. That meant scouting the Tier Three Tourney, looking for players that Gredok might sign.

What little he'd seen of Hittoni stunned him, everything from the towering buildings to the three decks of grav-roads to the citizens. So many different Human variants. Some were modified so heavily they would have never been allowed on a football field — skin colors, grafts, implants, cybernetics, countless thousands who seemed to treat the Human body as a canvas or a lump of clay to be beautified according to a myriad of personal tastes. That was the League of Planets for you, the technological capital of civilization. When it came to building ships or building bodies, the League stood above all others.

Hittoni wasn't as densely populated as the insanity he'd seen on the Sklorno world of Alimum. Quentin had been there during the Tier One season for the Krakens' game against the Armada, seen a planet with eighty billion sentients, a city with five billion sentients packed in tight.

Hittoni, by comparison, had just over a billion in the massive area considered the "city proper." But while Alimum was far more congested, Quentin hadn't left the private, guarded areas of the football stadium. Hittoni was a Human planet — mostly blue-skinned Humans, true, but Humans nonetheless — and as such,

Quentin had enjoyed a rare semi-anonymous walk around the stadium as if he were just another sports fan.

The stadium itself was a museum documenting the history of space travel. The League of Planets had collected many ancient pre-punch drive vessels. These floated free on grav-pads lining the stadium concourse. Quentin, Hokor and John Tweedy had walked a slow lap around the Shipyard, looking at priceless relics with names like *Pioneer, Challenger, Ikaros, Sputnik, Voyager, Helios, Shenzou, Aurora, Jaxa* and more. Quentin found it fascinating that the birth of football and the birth of Human spaceflight had occurred within just a few decades of each other.

Coincidence? He didn't think so.

He'd been recognized several times on the walk around the concourse. It was a football stadium, after all. Once his League-appointed bodyguards allowed the fans to approach, Quentin signed every messageboard thrust his way. Many fans asked Hokor as well, but the coach didn't like to talk to anyone and had the guards keep everyone away. Hokor, it seemed, harbored more fear from the victory parade bombing than Quentin did.

The bombing wasn't far from the minds of the Creterakians, that was for sure. The small, winged creatures flew overhead in multiple flocks of five, ten, even twenty. There were far more than Quentin had ever seen before, even back on Micovi during his PNFL days. The creatures ruled here, in the League of Planets, just like they did in most of the galaxy. Bodies roughly the size and shape of a football with a flat, two-foot-long tail that paralleled the ground. Two pair of foot-long arms, stacked on top of each other: the bottom arms held the ever-present entropic rifles, the top arms flapped madly, flying via the veined membrane that ran from the tiny hands all the way back to the tip of the tail. And then those disgusting heads: three pair of eyes — one pair that sat on either side of the head, looking out to the left and right; one pair up front, letting them see all before them; and one pair looking *down*, giving them a perfect view of the ground beneath. Their skin held various shades of red, usually with splotches of pink or purple.

You could always tell the military Creterakians apart from the civilians. Military wore the black or silver uniforms of the Empire; some wore the white uniforms of GFL Security. Civilians, on the other hand, wore garish outfits with clashing colors, insane patterns and — usually — flashing lights of some kind. Shizzle, the Krakens' Creterakian translator, was famous for his abhorrent taste in clothes.

The stadium walk had ended with an elevator ride to a luxury box, where Quentin and the others sat in a large seat and looked down at the white field far below. Dark blue lines and numbers looked almost black under the domed stadium's bright lights. As the teams battled, Quentin focused on the player he'd decided he just had to have — Sklorno wide receiver Cheboygan.

"Barnes," Hokor said, "I'm still not sold on Cheboygan. She's good, but she'd be our fourth receiver at best and she's not that fast. What about Cofferville or Minas Gerais? Both of those receivers have timed their 30-yard dash in the upper tenth percentile of all Tier Three players."

Quentin shook his head. "I've already got speed, Coach. Hawick and Milford are blazers. I want ball-control, I want receivers who can catch anything I throw at them, *and* who can live through the season." The female Sklorno bodies had evolved for speed, speed and more speed. Muscular thighs rose back and up, narrow forelegs pointed forward and down to connect with long, flexible feet — these grasshopper-like limbs made the species the fastest sentients in the galaxy. The legs supported a narrow, vertical trunk of a body that bent back in a slight curve, ending in the Sklorno's strange head. At the front of the small head, near the neck, two long raspers that could curl up hidden behind a chin plate or dangle down to the ground, revealing thousands of tiny rasper teeth. Above the chin plate, a dense crop of coarse, black hairs around four long eye stalks. The eye stalks moved separately, letting a Sklorno see everything around her. Below the chin plate, on the body, were the long, muscular tentacles that reached out like boneless snakes to snag footballs out of the air.

The physiology alone was strange enough to begin with even

without the Sklorno's coloration — which was no coloration at all. Clear skin showed fluttering, translucent muscles, transparent blood coursing through them, all wrapped around black bones that looked blurred and out of focus from the tissue surrounding them.

Cheboygan's clear skin was mostly hidden, of course, by her light green and yellow Manglers uniform and helmet. She was bigger than most Sklorno receivers, her stats said she was stronger, and there were more factors that made Quentin want her on the Krakens' roster.

"Coach, her speed isn't top-shelf, but she's still plenty damn fast," Quentin said. "Did you check out her mass-to-speed score and her density rating?"

John looked up from his double serving of chili fries. The words *density rating* seemed to leave a bad taste in his mouth.

"Huh? Q, what kind of stat is that? You mean her strength?"

"Not her *strength*, John. Mass, her density. How, uh, tightly compacted she is."

"You mean if she's fat?"

Quentin shook his head. "No, not that. The more mass she has, the bigger hits she can take. Combine her mass with her speed, or her *velocity*, and you get her force. That means if I throw to her over the middle while she's moving, she has more *force* than a linebacker like you."

"Screw that," John said. "I'm made of mega-force. *Super*-mega force, even. I'll knock her right the hell out."

"Yes, John, of course you will. But not all linebackers are stone-bred monstrosities like you."

"And cultured." John pointed with a chili-covered fry for emphasis. "That part comes from Ma."

Quentin nodded. "And cultured. Anyway, the more *force* the receiver has, I think the better suited she is to catching passes over the middle. Defenses don't have to worry about Milford or Hawick running those routes because they don't have enough mass to take those hits without getting hurt. Right now, I can only throw short over the middle to our tight ends or our running backs. I want more options. Force equals mass times acceleration, so I want lots of force."

John popped the greasy fry into his mouth. He chewed with his mouth open and kept talking. "Mass? Acceleration? Sounds to me like you've been hanging out with that nerd Kimberlin again. He trying to make you all smart and stuff?"

"He's tutoring me," Quentin said. "So what?"

John rolled his eyes. YOU CAN'T TEACH AN OLD DOG SPILLED MILK scrolled across his forehead. "You're a football player, Q. How about you worry about *football*? I mean, do you even have an agent yet?"

Quentin shook his head. "No, but I'm supposed to meet with Yitzhak's agent when I get back to Ionath. Guy's name is Danny Lundy."

John's right hand turned into an emphatic fist. "Lundy is my agent, Q! He's the man. He'll tear the tongue out of anyone who gets in your way."

"Good to know."

"Anyway, Q, you should just focus on football. You don't need all this physics crap. Just trust your eyes. Stop trying to be something you're not."

Quentin looked back down to the field. *Something he was not?* What did that mean? Was he supposed to stay ignorant just because he played football? No, no way. Kimberlin had promised that knowledge would *add* to Quentin's ability to lead the Krakens to a championship, not *distract* from it. Studying was hard work. Kimberlin demanded perfect scores, but at least some of the knowledge seemed promising. Physics, in particular. In the past six weeks of tutoring, Quentin had learned about things like mass, force, velocity and conservation of momentum. He knew the actual reason why little players bounced off of big players. He knew why tacklers needed a low center of gravity and why he was putting his receivers' lives at risk if he threw too high — something called *torque*. He understood how air density impacted the flight of a pass.

The knowledge was amazing. Kimberlin also wanted to teach

useless stuff like history, but some of the species biology might prove helpful. Quentin was willing to learn anything if that knowledge would give him the edge he needed to claim the GFL title. If John didn't need such knowledge, that was John's business, but Quentin refused to feel bad about expanding his brain.

Down on the field, the light green and yellow Manglers broke the huddle and lined up. The Archangels — white jerseys and turquoise helmets showing the dirt, blood and damage of a nearly complete game — dug in, trying to protect their slim 13-10 lead. Every player on that field knew that scouts from hundreds of upper tier teams were watching, and they played accordingly.

Hokor quickly activated a palm-up display on his pedipalp, then clicked through the interface until a slowly spinning display of Cheboygan appeared.

"Eight feet tall, three hundred sixty pounds," Hokor said. "Unusually large for a Sklorno. She's slow, though."

"Slow for a Sklorno," Quentin said. "That means she's still faster than Starcher or Ju Tweedy. All that size, moving at high speed? Coach, that's money."

Hokor looked at the stats some more, then down to the field. "I am not sure, Barnes. Speed kills."

The Manglers quarterback took the snap and dropped back. Lights played off of a light green jersey with yellow letters and numbers, the light green helmet with a yellow saw logo on the side. Cheboygan, wearing the Sklorno version of the same uniform, ran downfield ten yards, then angled for the deep middle on a post pattern. She drew double coverage, opening up the shallow middle on a crossing route. Quentin watched the ball sail through the air, hitting receiver Manzhouli fifteen yards downfield and almost directly over center. She bobbled it, reached up for it, then flew backward as a white-and-turquoise-clad Archangel defensive back put a shoulder pad in her chest.

Manzhouli fell hard, skidded, but didn't get up. The game ground to a halt as a medsled slid out of the tunnel and moved toward the prone player. Quentin checked the roster — the player who delivered the hit was number 72, a defensive tackle's number.

Tim Crawford. Quentin watched the replay, saw that Crawford had dropped off the line into coverage and closed quickly.

"Coach, did you see that?"

"Of course," Hokor said. "Crawford is on my list of players that we want. That Mathara quarterback is throwing too high, exposing his receivers to damage. Sklorno just aren't durable enough. This is the title game, and this is the third receiver the Manglers have lost.

"That's why I want Cheboygan, Coach. You see my point?"

Hokor's pedipalps twitched, his three sets of antennae circled. "Barnes, most quarterbacks go for pure speed and catching ability."

"I'm not most quarterbacks. I want a team that can take a punch in the mouth and keep on coming."

The medsled hovered over Manzhouli, lowered thousands of nano-fiber filaments that wrapped around her, lifted her without adjusting her position. The sled slid off the field, taking her to the locker-room tunnel. Quentin watched the Mathara sidelines. He expected a Sklorno to run out and replace Manzhouli, but instead, a Quyth Warrior trotted onto the field.

A light-green uniformed Quyth Warrior the likes of which Quentin had never seen. Six foot three or so, probably three hundred sixty pounds, this Warrior's legs and middle arms looked the same as those of any member of his caste. His pedipalps, however, were long — so long they could touch the ground while he was standing straight upright.

John started laughing and slapping his thigh. Half-chewed chili fries shot out of his mouth to land on the luxury box counter. "Lookit the 'palps on that one! What a little mutie!" IXNAY ON THE DNA scrolled across his face.

Hokor made a noise Quentin had never heard, kind a half-spit, half-cough. "Disgusting," the coach said. "That abomination shouldn't be allowed to live, let alone allowed to play."

Quentin called up his own palm-up display, scanning through the Manglers roster until he found the Warrior. He was the sixth receiver on the depth chart — Tara the Freak.

The Manglers broke the huddle and lined up. Quentin felt a buzzing inside his chest, the feeling that he was about to discover something before anyone else did. Tara lined up in the slot, about three yards to the right of the offensive line. A Sklorno wide receiver lined up outside of him, almost to the sidelines.

"Coach?" Quentin said. "What do you mean, *abomination*?"

"Just look at those pedipalps," Hokor said. "Tara is *imperfect*. He is a mutant. He should be eliminated. Why his *Shamakath* allows him to live is beyond me."

Quentin had never heard a Quyth Leader talk so hatefully about his own kind before.

The ball snapped, the Manglers quarterback dropped back. Cheboygan again sprinted downfield on a post pattern, her big body again drawing double coverage.

Instead of running, Tara turned sideways, tucked into a ball and *rolled* — the Quyth Warrior's strange form of sprinting. At ten yards downfield, he popped out of the roll only long enough to change direction, tucking again before rolling left on a crossing pattern.

Tim Crawford, the Archangels defensive tackle that had knocked Manzhouli out of the game, again dropped back into short coverage. Tara popped out of the roll and looked back for the ball. Another poorly thrown pass, the ball *again* several feet too high. Tara's mutant pedipalps reached up for the catch — the big blur of turquoise and white slammed into Tara's exposed midsection, bending the Quyth Warrior in half.

The world-class collision drew an *ohhhh* from the crowd. Quentin watched the two players hit the ground. Watched, and saw that Tara had come down with the ball.

A hit like *that*, and he made the catch?

"Coach," Quentin said.

"No," Hokor said.

Tim Crawford was slow to stand. Tara, on the other hand, popped right up. A hit that might have killed a Sklorno, and Tara sprang up as if he'd done nothing more hurtful than trip over a shoelace onto a big feather pillow.

"*Coach*," Quentin said.

"Absolutely *not*," Hokor said.

"But Coach, he—"

"*No!* I will not have that … that … *freak* wearing a Krakens uniform, and that is final!"

Quentin looked at the diminutive Quyth Leader and tried not to laugh. Hokor's black-striped yellow fur had puffed up, making him look all soft and fuzzy. Such a display might make Hokor look frightening to a Quyth Warrior, but to a Human, it just made him look cute.

"Whatever you say, Coach. Just take it easy, okay? You want one of John's chili fries?"

John helpfully reached out a fry covered in glistening, wet-brown chili and melted cheese.

Hokor looked at it, then shivered. "Humans. The things you will eat."

Hokor's fur slowly lowered back to its normal, silky-flat state. Quentin didn't need to rock the boat at the moment, but he'd seen something that he couldn't *un*-see. The Krakens needed toughness, durability — if that's what a mutant freak provided, then that's what the Krakens would sign.

3

SEPTEMBER 2683

WITH THE TIER THREE TOURNAMENT COMPLETE, Quentin, John and Hokor returned to Ionath on Quentin's yacht, the *Hypatia*. Before leaving Wilson 6, however, Quentin had caught another Trench Warfare concert with John. After the concert, Quentin had said goodbye to Somalia. Her last kiss had been amazing. The way she pressed her body up against his, the things she had whispered in his ear.

It had been a long cruise home. Plenty of time to review holos of the various prospects they'd targeted. John had his heart set on landing a defensive end named Rich Palmer, who played for the Venus Vultures. Quentin hadn't seen the man play. He'd been busy watching other games and focusing on offensive players.

Quentin wanted two players in particular. Getting his way would require some of that poker face that Frederico didn't seem to think Quentin possessed.

Quentin did. And he would use it now. Sitting in Hokor's office on the *Touchback*'s 18th deck, he talked with Hokor, Gredok the Splithead, Messal the Efficient and Don Pine. This was their final meeting before Gredok went out to try and sign new rook-

ies, before he engaged in bidding wars, negotiations or any other nefarious tactics required to bolster the Krakens' ranks. The
Touchback was mostly empty — it was the off-season, and players were either down on the planet or off in their home systems.
Aside from Q, just the sentients who would decide the future of
the Ionath Krakens' roster and a skeleton crew helping Captain
Kate Cheevers maintain the ship.

Hokor sat behind his desk. His desktop showed several three-
inch-high holographic players in a close-up of on-field action. Stats
floated beside the players. Off to Hokor's right, Gredok sat in a
chair custom-made to his small dimensions. Messal the Efficient
stood next to Gredok. Quentin and Don sat in chairs in front of
Hokor's desk.

"So, we can get her?" Quentin said. "We can get Cheboygan?"

He spoke to Gredok, but it was really a numbers-crunching
question. Messal the Efficient worked a palm-up display, ripping
through numbers faster than Quentin could track. Messal's duties,
it seemed, encompassed far more than keeping the *Touchback* neat
and orderly.

Everyone waited for Messal's answer. A Quyth Worker, Messal
had the same back-folded legs, middle arms, single eye and pedipalp structure shared by Leaders and Warriors. Workers were taller than Leaders, with muscle-knotted pedipalp arms well suited to
manual labor. Subservient in every way, Quyth Workers deferred
to Leaders, Warriors, even members of other species.

Holotanks behind Hokor showed several players wearing a
myriad of Tier Three colors. The Krakens had set their sights on
eight candidates. They probably wouldn't get them all, but Gredok
would land at least half.

Messal looked up. "Table fluctuations indicate we will have
the finances to sign our top priorities — receiver Cheboygan, defensive back Gladwin, defensive tackle Tim Crawford and the
half-breed defensive end Rich Palmer. Second priorities are defensive back Cooperstown, outside linebacker Cody Bowyer and linebacker Regat the Unobtrusive."

Don nodded, satisfied. "If we get them all, that really bolsters our defense. We need depth at defensive back. Too bad about Standish getting pregnant."

Don was right about that. The Krakens' four starting defensive backs — strong safety Davenport, free safety Perth, cornerback Berea and cornerback Wahiawa, who had taken over the starting job from Stockbridge — were decent players, but the Sklorno backing them up weren't nearly as talented.

"Are you guys *sure* Standish is gone?" Quentin said. "I mean, so she got knocked up, so what?"

"Her body will permanently change," Don said. "By the time she's recovered from dropping that egg sac, she'll be a step slower than *you*. If a Sklorno gets pregnant, her career is over."

Last year, Standish had been the team's backup right cornerback, assigned with the task of covering the opposition's receivers. She saw little playing time, but when she'd been in the game she'd done her job well. Losing her hurt, but it was better than losing Wahiawa or Berea, the starting cornerbacks. The saying went that you were only as good as your bench — the Krakens had to grab rookies to fill that gap.

"Then I hope we get Gladwin and Cooperstown," Quentin said. "Defense has enough problems as it is."

"We'll get them," Hokor said. "Then we are all in agreement?" He asked that out of courtesy. The final decisions were his. Only Gredok, the team owner, could overrule him. Gredok had to keep a running balance between personnel needs versus team finances.

Finances — that was where Quentin would make his play.

"There's one more," Quentin said. "I want Tara the Freak from the Mathara Manglers."

Coach Hokor's black-striped fur fluffed up. "I told you, Barnes, absolutely *not*."

Quentin leaned forward in his chair, rested his elbows on Hokor's desk. "Why not, Coach? Because he *looks funny*?"

Hokor slammed his pedipalp fists down on his desk. "He does not just *look funny*, Barnes! He is *malformed*!"

"You don't seem to have anything against Rich Palmer. He's half-Human, half-HeavyG."

"He's your kind," Hokor said. "No one cares how ugly you all are. We Quyth do care about failed genetic lines. He is called Tara the *Freak* for a reason!"

Quentin leaned back, threw his hands up in frustration. "Oh, *no*! Oh, High One, he is *malformed*! What's going to happen? His long pedipalp arms are suddenly going to pop off his head, grab a hatchet and chase us around like some horror-holo?"

Quentin felt a hand on his right shoulder.

"Q," Don said. "There's more to it than that."

It was all Quentin could to not to slap Don's hand away. "The guy can catch the ball," Quentin said. "He can run routes over the middle. He can take hits. When he's in the game, linebackers will have to cover him, have to watch for him, and that opens up other areas of the field. What *more to it* is there?"

"Much more," Gredok said.

Whenever the Quyth Leader spoke, those around him listened carefully. Gredok's black fur looked impeccably groomed — silky, shiny, smooth. He wore an outfit of spun silver, burnished so it wasn't reflective enough to compete with the red and blue jewels that formed patterns of a solar system across his chest. Dozens of bracelets hung from both sets of wrists. As usual, Gredok's attire screamed *money* and *prestige*.

"Barnes," Gredok said, "you've been studying with Kimberlin, have you not?"

Quentin nodded.

"And have you learned about the Quyth culture?"

"A little. Lately I've been focused on physics, some galactic history, that kind of thing."

"Well, then allow me to edify you," Gredok said. His voice rang with calm control, the voice of a sentient who got what he wanted without yelling, without showing emotion. "Hokor told me of your interest in this player. I had my scouts look into him. It is amazing that Tara was not killed when he came out of the egg sac."

"What? Kill him when he's a *baby*?" Such barbarism, and yet everyone called Quentin's home system of the Purist Nation *primitive*.

"The malformed are usually killed by their Leader," Gredok

said. "I myself killed two of my brothers once we had hatched and I saw that they were imperfect."

Gredok, a killer from the time he could walk. Quentin shouldn't have been surprised, but such cut-throat behavior shocked him regardless.

"Why would you kill your own family?"

"It is related to breeding, Barnes. A prospective female will examine not only the Leader with which she might have progeny, but also that Leader's Worker and Warrior sac-mates. This gives her better knowledge of the Leader's larger genetic makeup, and what their offspring may turn out to be. If she sees imperfections in the genetic stock, she will simply choose another Leader with which to breed."

"You killed your own *brothers*," Quentin said. Quentin would have given anything to have his brother back, anything to find his sister, and Gredok had killed two of his own? Sometimes it was hard to accept other cultures as equals — evil was evil, no matter how you tried to justify it.

"I did," Gredok said. "And I am not alone. That is why you don't see many mutations in the Quyth culture. Tara is the only survivor of his brood. Some viral contamination in his egg sac, it seems. He's been an outcast all his life."

Hokor waved his hands across a three-inch holo of Cheboygan. She vanished. He tapped a few icons, replacing her with a holo of Tara the Freak. Tara's long pedipalp arms drew everyone's attention.

"Tara is the only Quyth Warrior on the Manglers' roster," Hokor said. "That is why he can play in Mathara. We have four Warrior players."

"So Tara would be our fifth," Quentin said. "So what?"

Gredok's left-middle pincer played with the bracelets on his right pedipalp. "You ask why an obvious prospect like Tara is available? Because Tier Two and Tier One teams know he is ... Pine, what is the word you use to describe a player whose team-unity disruption factor outweighs his or her on-field benefit?"

"Locker-room poison," Pine said.

A touch of orange swirled across Gredok's large cornea.

Quentin knew that expression — Gredok found something humorous. "Yes," the Leader said. "*Poison*. How appropriate."

"So no one wants him," Quentin said.

"Correct," Hokor said. "No one wants the mutation."

Quentin looked around the room. He'd based his strategy on this moment, knowing he'd have to make his play at the last second and convince Gredok just before the team owner headed out to battle for players.

"No one wants him," Quentin said. "That means he's affordable."

Gredok said nothing, but his eye swirled with a touch of light red.

"Messal," Quentin said, "what is Tara's salary?"

"One hundred thousand," Massal said. "We'd have to pay at least double that to the Manglers as a transfer fee."

Quentin nodded. Time to play his hand. "So let me see if I get this right. We have a player who can help this team. A player who can take hits and is highly resistant to injury. A player who can catch spit in the wind. A player who we can have for a transfer fee of two hundred thousand, and sign him at the Tier One *minimum* salary, probably for a three-year contract. And we're going let him go because he has long arms?"

Hokor banged on his desktop again. "You don't understand! The other Warriors will not accept it!"

Quentin shrugged. "Huh. So our Warriors decide who plays for the Krakens and who does not? And here I would have thought their *Shamakath* made those decisions."

The office fell silent. Hokor's fur fell flat. He sat back down in his little chair. Don Pine looked away, but Quentin stared right at Gredok, waiting for a response.

Quentin saw more threads of a light red flow across Gredok's eye. Light red, the color of friendship, appreciation, or — in this context, Quentin guessed — respect.

"Barnes makes a good point," Gredok said. "I will look further into this Tara the Freak. If I choose to sign him, the other Warriors will support the decision."

Don shook his head. "No, they won't. No disrespect, Gredok, but this is a mistake."

Quentin turned on Don. "That's exactly what you said about George Starcher. How did he turn out?"

Don leaned back. "George is fine, *so far*. But if you bothered to do any research before you made these emotional decisions, Q, you'd know George is *always* fine for the first season with a new team."

"It's different this time," Quentin said. "He knows this is his last chance."

Don shrugged. "I hope you're right. And I hope you're right about Tara, but I know you're not."

Quentin waved his hands in annoyance. Don Pine was one of the greats, but he was also old and jaded. So pessimistic!

Quentin turned to face the team owner. "Gredok, forget this *looking into* stuff — are you going to sign Tara the Freak, or not?"

Out of the corner of his eye, Quentin saw Hokor's fur ruffle, saw the Coach's eye swirl with threads of black and dark blue. There was no way around the disrespect of appealing to the team owner and overruling the head Coach. Don didn't want Tara, Hokor didn't want Tara, but that didn't matter. Quentin would not allow prejudice or racism to determine who suited up in the Orange and the Black.

"Yes," Gredok said. "We will sign Tara."

Hokor stood up, fur fluffed out full length. "But *Shamakath*! You can't—"

"I *can't*?" Gredok let the word hang.

Hokor paused, then his fur fell halfway to flat. His eye flooded with the green of anxiety — he had overstepped his bounds. Hokor ran a pedipalp over his six antennae. "My apologies, *Shamakath*. Of course, the final decision is yours."

Gredok stood. "The decision *is* mine. And the responsibility, Barnes, is yours. Prepare yourself for an adverse reaction from your Warrior teammates. If you can't make the other Warriors accept Tara, I will cut him. I am willing to gamble based on your instincts, but we are too close to a championship team to tolerate ongoing disruptions."

Quentin nodded. "I agree."

"You *agree*?" Gredok said. "How nice for you."

They filtered out of the office, leaving Hokor to keep flipping through player holos.

Quentin had just taken more control over the franchise, and at Hokor's expense. Quentin would make it up to him. Once Tara started catching passes over the middle, Coach would see, and everything would work out.

4

OCTOBER 2683

Transcript of broadcast from Galactic News Network

"Yes, Brad, I'm at Planet Yall in the Sklorno Dynasty, near the scene of tragedy. Flight 894-B, a ship loaded with some fifty thousand Sklorno, exploded near dawn, local time, killing every sentient aboard. This is the worst maritime disaster in this area since the Creterakian conflict."

"Tom, was this an accident or was it foul play?"

"Well, Brad, that very question is on the minds of investigators from both the Sklorno Dynasty and the Creterakian Empire. A punch-drive explosion caused the disaster. There is no indication of weapons fired at the ship. Investigators are confident the explosion was internal, although it is as yet unknown if that explosion was accidental or if it was sabotage. A group called the Purist Liberation Front has claimed responsibility for the blast, but Creterakian officials say that is unlikely and that the terrorist organization is simply trying to take the credit."

"Tom, any statement from the Purist Nation?"

"Yes, Brad, the Grand Mullah herself stated that the Purist

Nation had nothing to do with the disaster, although she did say that since all the lives lost were, quote, *of demonic descent, the deaths were clear evidence of God's direct interaction in the universe*, end quote."

"So if it's not a Purist sect, Tom, who would the suspects be?"

"Well, Brad, Creterakian officials think that if it was sabotage, the Zoroastrian Guild has to be behind it."

"The Zoroastrian Guild being that shadowy organization dedicated to overthrowing the Creterakian Empire's control of several systems, of course."

"That's right, Brad, but what scares experts isn't the Creterakian analysis, but rather the Sklorno Dynasty's growing opinion that the culprit is, in fact, the Prawatt Jihad itself. Yall is only a few short light-years away from the Prawatt/Sklorno border. If the Sklorno believe the Prawatt are responsible for this bombing, there could be major ramifications."

"Is that due to the Sklorno/Prawatt War of 2556, Tom?"

"That and more, Brad. That war lasted two years and cost millions of lives on both sides. It ended without a clear winner, but the Prawatt navy was so weakened that it lost the planet Yewalla to the Rewall Association in 2559. Many think the Jihad still blame the Sklorno for the loss of that valuable world. The Sklorno Dynasty is part of Creterakian-controlled space, but the Jihad was never conquered during the Takeover. While no official contact has been conducted with the hostile Prawatt in some forty years, experts are confident the Jihad possesses the galaxy's third-largest navy, behind only the Creterakian Empire and the Quyth Concordia."

"But Tom, the Sklorno Dynasty has no navy of its own. So what's the fear?"

"Brad, there are 269 billion sentient beings in the Dynasty, most of whom are very hostile to the occupying Creterakian garrisons. Experts estimate the number of interstellar-capable craft at some 200 million. The Sklorno are a religious race, capable of unifying and acting upon a central belief in very short order. If the majority of Sklorno decide the Prawatt Jihad is at fault and want to attack, there is no way the Creterakians can stop that many ships. If *any* Sklorno ships attack Prawatt space, the Prawatt will view that as an act of war *by the Creterakians*, because the Creterakians control Sklorno space. While it is unlikely, it is realistic to say we're looking at the possible start of a fifth galactic war."

"That sounds like a very complicated situation, Tom."

"Brad, it certainly is. We'll continue to monitor the investigation of Flight 894-B. For GNN, this is Tom Skivvers, signing off."

5

NOVEMBER 2683

THE OFF-SEASON SEEMED to last forever. After scouting players, Quentin started to go stir-crazy without football. With two months until the season began, he decided to visit the *Touchback* while it was in for repairs at the mind-bogglingly huge dry dock know as the *CAS Linus Torvalds*.

If there wasn't such a big planet behind it, the *Torvalds'* size would seem almost incomprehensible. Jupiter, of course, was a massive planet. One of the largest in any populated system. Red and orange swirling stripes reminded Quentin of jawbreakers, the only candy he could afford when he'd been a kid back on Micovi. A jawbreaker could last days, even weeks if you only worked on it a little each night. The few times he had enough money to eat his fill, he'd spend a bit extra on one of those treats.

Dozens of glowing lights far off in the distance showed the many stations of the Jupiter Net Colony, the string of constructs in orbit around the great gas giant. To think this had once been a lifeless planet seemed strange — now 275 million sentients living aboard some 7,000 vessels made Jupiter's orbit their home.

Quentin's GFL immunity meant he could take his yacht anywhere in Creterakian-controlled space. That included the Planetary Union. No shuttle necessary this time out, as the *Hypatia* itself could fly right inside the *Torvalds*. Well, the visiting crew could fly it in, anyway. Quentin had to take on boarders and cede control of his yacht so that it could be steered inside. He stood in his salon, watching the *Hypatia* fly through a portal so big his yacht looked like a pea dropped into a big bucket. The portal led through the *Torvalds'* hull, walls so massive their thickness was at least ten times the *Hypatia's* length.

Inside, an empty space so vast it was difficult to comprehend. You could fit an entire football stadium in here. No, four, maybe five stadiums. Lining the *Torvalds'* interior, he saw long pier-arms holding the colorful team busses of other GFL franchises: red hull with white-trimmed blue stars of the Texas Earthlings; brown with long yellow-trimmed maroon stripes belonging to the Themala Dreadnaughts; the gold, copper and silver ship of the Jupiter Jacks; and a half-dozen more. The size of the *Torvalds* made these ships look like the toys of a small child.

And there, the orange hull of the *Touchback*. His temporary pilot flew the *Hypatia* close to the Krakens' team bus. The *Touchback's* landing bay doors were open — a strange site indeed, as they usually opened to the emptiness of space. The inside of the *Torvalds*, however, had its own atmosphere.

For two straight seasons, Quentin had spent the majority of his time on the *Touchback* — either alone in his quarters or surrounded by teammates in the locker room, the dining area, or the practice field. The ship seemed a living thing, a small town whose population was dedicated to preparing for games.

The Tier One preseason would begin on January 1, 2684. Just two months away. Then, the *Touchback* would again ring with the laughter of players, resonate with the crash of armor hitting armor on the practice field, and — of course — echo with the angry, amplified voice of Coach Hokor the Hookchest. But in November? During the off-season? The *Touchback* seemed like a ghost ship.

Last season he'd become aware of the support staff that helped run the Krakens franchise, a staff that Gredok did not allow to interact with the players. Quentin had spent most of his life in a stratified society, where the working class of Micovi catered to the religious aristocracy. He had hated that life, hated feeling like he was second class, like he wasn't as good because he didn't have rank, position or money. He wouldn't allow others to see him the way he once saw the Micovi elite.

The *Hypatia* shuddered slightly as it docked. The *Torvalds* crew led him to his own small landing bay, where a floating supply platform carried him through the *Touchback*'s open bay doors. Waiting inside for him were two women in orange uniforms, seams done in pinstripe black. The woman on the right, a short brunette, held a messageboard. Her uniform looked like her hair — neat, pressed, immaculate.

The woman on the left he recognized from in-ship messages and broadcasts, even though despite two years aboard he'd never actually met her face to face — Captain Kate Cheevers. She was the taller of the two, but more unkempt. Her uniform was unbuttoned down the chest, the left flap flopping open and showing a black T-shirt beneath. Dirty-blonde hair spilled down her back. The flash of three small, gold loops through her left nostril caught the room lights, as did two smaller ones pierced through her right eyebrow. She wore no makeup on her pink skin. Thin lips crinkled at the corners, the mark of a woman who frequently wears an easy smile. Quentin had heard the Captain was hot, and those rumors were dead-on. Knee-high black boots accentuated legs that were probably quite nice under the orange pants. The thing that caught his eye most of all, however, was the gun belt, angling down from her left hip to her right thigh. The handle of a firearm led into a black leather holster.

Quentin stepped off the supply platform.

"Mister Barnes," Captain Kate said. "A pleasure to meet you." She extended her hand, and he shook it. Rough skin. Working-class skin.

"Captain. Please call me Quentin."

She winked, a motion that seemed to make her whole head twitch to the right. "You don't want me to call you *Elder*?"

Quentin laughed uncomfortably. "No, please don't. I hate that."

Captain Kate gestured to the other woman. "This is Sayeeda. She's part of the crew. Sayeeda is overseeing landing bay door repairs while I take you on the tour.

Sayeeda offered her tiny hand, which seemed to vanished when Quentin shook it.

"Nice to meet you," she said. "I asked the Captain if I could say hi. I'm a fan."

"Thanks," Quentin said. "Hopefully, we'll give you a lot to cheer about this year."

Sayeeda nodded, then walked to the bay's right side. Quentin saw where she was going — toward a GFL-sized Human in grease-smeared coveralls.

"Hey, is that George Starcher?"

Captain Kate nodded. "It is."

"What the hell is he doing? Is he fixing something?"

"He didn't have anything to do in the off-season, so he wanted to join the repair crew," Kate said. "He used to be in the Planetary Union navy. You didn't know that?"

Quentin shook his head. "No, I had no idea."

"So, you've never met me, you haven't seen most of our ship, and you don't even know if your teammates are veterans. You don't know much, do you?"

Wow, this woman didn't mince words. "Hey, I'm here now, aren't I?"

Kate pursed her lips, then nodded. "Fair enough. And that's way more than most of your teammates have done. The ship crew is basically considered to be second class to all you fancy football players. Ready for your tour?"

"Yes." Quentin's eyes once again strayed to her firearm.

She saw him looking. "Checking out the help?"

Quentin's eyes snapped up. "Oh, uh, no! No, I'm just ... "

"The gun?"

He nodded. "Yeah, is that real?"

She smiled. Something haughty in that smile, something so

self-confident it bordered on arrogance. She pulled the pistol and offered it butt-first. "Yeah, it's real. You want to touch it?"

Quentin held up his hands. "No thanks."

"Don't like guns?"

"No, I don't. I've never even held one."

She laughed and holstered the pistol with practiced ease. "Good man. And as long as you're under my watch, you'll never have to. Captain Kate will keep you safe, pretty thing." She gave her head-twitch wink.

"Uh ... "

"Let's go. You're nice to look at, quarterback, but even in the off-season I have a lot to do. Let's show you around."

She started on the bridge. It surprised Quentin how small it was, nothing more than a fairly large room packed with holo-tanks. It could hold only about ten, maybe twelve sentients comfortably, which wasn't bad considering the bridge crew numbered five, including Captain Kate. Big crysteel windows lined three sides of the bridge, providing a view of the *Torvalds'* vast interior and the other ships docked miles away. A glowing, holographic *Touchback* dominated the center of the bridge. Four workstations sat almost under the hologram, two on the left, two on the right. Two chairs sat empty. Two men, dressed in the crew's orange uniforms, stood and walked over.

Captain Kate introduced them as Francis and Agreyu. Apparently she didn't have much use for last names.

The bridge had only one more chair, a plush affair with holo-tank arrays in front of each arm rest. Captain Kate sauntered to it and sat, crossing her legs and making the chair spin slightly.

"This is where I sit when I'm keeping you footballers safe," she said. "You might say it's a seat of power."

"Uh ... very nice."

"You wanna sit in the captain's chair, Quentin?"

She winked, a slow wink that showed off her dark eyelashes. Was she hitting on him?

"Uh ... no thanks, Captain."

She pursed her lips in a mock pout, then stood. "I understand.

It might be more than you can handle, huh? Come on, let's see the rest of the little sentients who make it all possible for you to line up on Sunday."

Captain Kate took him to the administrative areas. Quentin met several staffers, mostly Quyth Workers but also a few Humans and even a "bed bug," the small, furry creatures that were the Sklorno males. He learned that most of the onboard staff managed ship-based things, like maintenance, customs declarations, food and supplies. The ship could also handle all of the administrative staff from the Krakens building. In short, Gredok the Splithead could put every last employee of his franchise in this ship and take them anywhere he wanted to go.

In the last year, Quentin had seen the practice field, the locker rooms, Hokor's office, the dining deck, his quarters and some of the living areas of the other races, but that was about it. The tour quickly showed him those areas were only about sixty percent of the ship. The other forty percent consisted of living quarters for the crew and administrative staff, repair and manufacturing areas, the galley and a dozen lifeboats. Quentin asked why there were no lifeboat drills, but she just pointed to the simple pictograms mounted outside the lifeboat hatches — any sentient could use those images to operate the door, get inside and jettison if the need arose.

She showed him the *Touchback*'s punch drive and control area, located not in the ship's rear but in the ship's front near the bottom deck. He'd never seen an actual punch drive before and was shocked to find it was nothing more than a room-sized gray ball. It looked like a big, spherical rock. Maybe he'd learn how it worked someday. Kimberlin had said the principles involved required physics knowledge far above even his.

Punch drives weren't the only thing used to move the ship. Captain Cheevers showed Quentin banks of impulse engines located in the aft section. Each engine was an antimatter reactor, fifty feet long and twenty feet wide. A row of seven engines lined the top of the ship. Fourteen stories below them, another row of seven lined the bottom.

"So," Kate said, "that's the tour."

"That's everything?"

She nodded. "Except for the Ki livestock pens. You want to see those?"

Quentin thought back to last season's meal with the offensive linemen, to the deer/spider creature that still haunted his nightmares. "No. No, I don't want to see that. Not one bit."

He ran his hand along one of the reactors. This was the heart of the *Touchback*, the engines that carried them anywhere punch drives did not.

"How fast can we go?"

"Why, do you like to go fast?"

Wink-twitch.

"Uh … " This woman made him very uncomfortable. "No, I just … you know, if we get into trouble."

"We can haul ass," Captain Cheevers said. "This used to be a military vessel. When the need arises we can move quick. But there's a lot of mass in the *Touchback*, so it takes us some time to hit our maximum velocity."

"Can we outrun pirates?" Quentin knew the Ki Fangs franchise had been wiped out by an explosion in 2667. Many speculated that was an accident, but plenty of people thought it was pirates. The New Rodina Astronauts had also suffered a disaster when the Purist Nation — Quentin's own people — had caught the Astros team bus and executed all non-Human players.

"If we hit max vel, we can outrun just about anything," Cheevers said. "But until we hit that speed, we're vulnerable to smaller ships that can close in on us."

"Like fighters?"

She paused, thinking, then nodded. "Those can be a big problem if they catch you close enough to a planet, but they need a bigger ship to support them. The real pirate problem comes from ships about a quarter the size of the *Touchback*. They have a low enough mass that they can accelerate fast and make a run, try to knock out the engines of a larger ship before the larger ship can accelerate away."

Quentin thought back to his physics lessons with Kimberlin. Pirates weren't that much of a threat these days, but *not much of a threat* was a far cry from *no threat at all*. He needed to learn all he could about this. As Michael said, it never hurt to have too much knowledge.

"How big is the *Touchback*, anyway?"

"He's two hundred meters long and twenty-eight meters wide."

"Meters? What's that in feet?"

Captain Kate laughed and shook her head. "You never learned metric?"

Quentin shrugged. "I sort of know it. I just think of things in football terms, mostly. Yards and feet and inches."

"A football field is one hundred yards, right?"

"One-twenty," Quentin said. "Two ten-yard end zones, so one-twenty total."

"Then think of the *Touchback* as two football fields, end-to-end. Got it?"

Quentin nodded.

"Eighteen decks," she said. "Fourteen Semini-class P-22 impulse engines. He's big, forty-two thousand GRTs."

"What's a GRT?"

"Gross register tons."

"What's a gross register ton?"

"If you can't do *meters*, how about we skip the GRT explanation, okay?"

Her condescending tone annoyed him, but he nodded anyway. No, not *condescending*, more like … *patronizing*. She didn't think he was smart enough to handle all of this, but she also didn't seem to think that was necessarily a bad thing.

"He's also got nine quad guns," she said. "Three of them are broken, but he's still got enough to fend off most pirates."

"Why do you keep calling the *Touchback* a *he*? I thought ships were thought of as girls. Women, I mean … thought of as women."

Kate shrugged. "People think of ships as the fairer sex. So, I think of them as male. Hey, you want to see the guns?"

Quentin had never seen actual ship weapons before. "Sure, yeah."

"Come on, big boy," she said. "Captain Kate will take you all kinds of new places."

"HIGH ONE," QUENTIN SAID. "This is a *cannon?*"

Captain Cheevers nodded. They stood in a small, plain room. A four-foot by four-foot, flat-black platform rose a few inches from the metal deck. The walls were also black, the whole room lit up by a few overhead lights. The room didn't look dirty, exactly — it just felt *unused*. Opposite the entry door, Quentin saw a long, horizontal crysteel port, about ten feet long but only a foot high. Through that port, out on the hull of the ship, he saw a long, armored shell, paint scratched by countless miles of interstellar travel. Beyond that, faded by distance, the far wall of the *Torvalds*.

"Welcome to Gun Cabin Six," Kate said. She punched a three-digit code — 726 — into a keypad. The platform surface changed from a flat black to a glossy sheen. She stepped onto the four-by-four platform. She held her hands at chest level, palms down, fingers outstretched.

Quentin felt the deck vibrate, just a bit. Through the port, he saw the armored shell split down the middle and slide into recessed housing, revealing a lethal-looking, oblong gun-mount that ended in four barrels pointing away into the void. The barrels alone had to be ten feet long each. He'd never seen an active, ship-sized weapon before — that thing out there could destroy an entire shuttle and every sentient on it. The concept scared the crap out of him.

A holographic ball of light appeared in front of Captain Kate. Lines stretched up from it, out from it, and forward and back from it. Each line showed a regular series of hash marks.

"This is your X-Y-Z axis," she said. "Each slash is a kilometer. You can zoom out … "

She lifted her fingers so her hands were palm-out. The distance between the hash marks shortened. Quentin instantly saw the relation — the shorter the distance between the hash marks, the bigger the scale of the X-Y-Z display.

" … or you can zoom in."

She turned her hands palms-in, fingers up. The hash marks started stretching away from each other, signifying the scale was closing in.

Captain Kate twisted at the hips, moving her hands to the right. The X-Y-Z display changed direction in time, as did the direction of the four cannon barrels.

"It points where you point," she said.

"It doesn't follow eye-tracking?"

"Human eyes flick around too fast," she said. "Eye-tracking might work in a ground-based combat system, where you can sight a target as it's flying, but things move too fast up here. You flick your eye for a split second, you're wasting rounds. So it's hand gestures with the computer auto-correcting."

"How do you fire?"

She looked back at him and smiled. "You want to see me shoot the scary cannon, pretty boy?"

"Uh … well, I don't know."

Wink-twitch. "It's okay. I'm the Captain. We're loaded with blanks for stress testing in dry dock, but you'll get the idea."

She turned back to face forward, leveled her hands, then clenched her left fist. The top two quad cannons roared, cones of smoke blowing out their rears. She clenched her right fist, and the bottom two barrels fired.

The deck vibrated in time with the shots, insinuating the cannon's awesome power.

She paused, then made left-right-left-right fists, a *bam-bam-bam-bam* of vibration and smoke plumes. Had they been live rounds, aimed at a ship like his yacht, how bad would the damage be? Would sentients be dead?

Captain Kate again pointed her fingers out, hands palms-down, then slowly dropped them to her thighs. The gun turret fell still, then lowered. Kate stepped off the holoplate. She punched the three-number code into the keypad. The holoplate's glossy light faded. Once again, it was just a flat-black piece of flooring.

She walked back to Quentin, smiling confidently.

"Did you like that? Did it scare you?"

"A little."

"Don't worry," she said, "Captain Kate is here to take care of you. I'll keep you safe."

She was staring at him, smiling, but it wasn't a friendly smile. He felt an urge to get out of this confined, secluded space.

He turned and walked to the door, talking over his shoulder so he could see her but didn't have to make eye contact. "You just point and shoot? It seems so ... easy."

Captain Kate nodded. "Sadly, killing usually is. Shooting is easy, anyway. Out in the void, things move fast. We would be shooting projectiles at objects moving at thousands of kilometers an hour, projectiles that themselves have to travel several kilometers to hit that moving target."

"So why don't computers handle it?"

She shook her head. "Computer-controlled weaponry is illegal. Creterakians rarely allow a ship to have defensive weaponry at all. Computer-controlled guns can hit just about anything, including Creterakian ships that might come to board us."

"So if we do get attacked, who does the shooting?"

Captain Kate waved her hand dismissively. "Don't worry your pretty head about that. The Krakens staff is trained to handle emergencies."

Quentin thought of Messal the Efficient, tried to imagine the Quyth Worker firing the anti-spacecraft cannons. "Captain, are you sure? I mean, the guys and girls on the team, they have really great reaction time, and as for coordination, they—"

"Just worry about football," Cheevers said, her tone still sweet but also a bit annoyed. "If it makes you feel better, the Quyth Warrior players man the guns. They're experienced soldiers. We have things under control, Quentin. I have to get back to my duties, but if you have any other questions — or you want anything else — I'll be in my cabin after ship-dusk."

Something about her smile, again it made him uncomfortable. Quentin wondered if he would ever get used to all of these women who were so different from what he'd known back in the Purist Nation.

"Thanks, Captain Cheevers."

"Call me Kate," she said. Wink-twitch. "But only when no one is around."

"Uh ... okay, Kate. Thanks again."

Quentin turned and walked off, as quickly as he could without running.

6

DECEMBER 2683

HOW MUCH FOOTBALL had he watched in the past six months? Too much. Too much experiencing what others did, not enough doing it himself. He had played three seasons in a row, from his Tier Three campaign with the Raiders to the Tier Two season with the Krakens, then straight into Tier One. After all of that, he'd thought he *wanted* time off.

His body had healed up within a month. That left five months of his body screaming at him to *find a game*, to *run*, to *throw*, to *hit*. That itch could not be scratched. He'd had to wait.

But the wait was almost over.

Quentin Barnes sat in a luxury box in Earth's Hudson Bay Stadium, watching two teams that would be his competition in just a few more weeks. The T2 Tourney championship game — Orbiting Death versus the Texas Earthlings. Win or lose, both of these teams were on their way to Tier One.

No teammates with him this time, no coach. He watched alone.

A year ago, he'd played in this same tournament, leading the Krakens to the semi-final win that put them into Tier One. The

Krakens had finished 9-2 that year, winning the Quyth Irradiated Conference en route to their promotion to the big-time.

Quentin watched the Orbiting Death quarterback drop back. Condor Adrienne. Before Death owner Anna Villani signed him, Condor had been with the Whitok Pioneers, another team in the Quyth Irradiated. People had said Condor was better than Quentin. Most people still did.

But this season, Quentin would show everyone who was the best of the best.

Adrienne stood tall in the pocket, his flat-black uniform and metalflake-red helmet making him look like a perfectly posed actor on a movie poster. He calmly waited as a blitzing linebacker rushed in. Quentin recognized the linebacker — Alonzo Castro, whom Quentin had battled with in last year's T2 Tourney.

Adrienne looked like a sitting duck, but an effortless step forward left the diving Castro grabbing only empty air. Adrienne fired the ball far downfield, where Coalville hauled it in. Touchdown. Just like that, the Death was up 7-0.

Adrienne might stay in for the first quarter, but after that he'd sit to make sure he didn't suffer an injury that might impact his Tier One season. The Earthlings would replace the demoted Chillich Spider-Bears in the Solar Division. Quentin would only face them if both Texas and Ionath made it to the Galaxy Bowl — highly unlikely. The OSI Orbiting Death, on the other hand, had replaced the Mars Planets. That put the Death in the Planet Division, the same as Ionath — the two teams would face off in Week Six.

In last season's Tier One campaign, the Krakens had scraped by with a 4-8 record, needing to win their last two games just to stay in Tier One.

Four and eight.

As a seventeen-year-old rookie in the Purist Nation Football League, Quentin had led his team to a 5-4 record. He'd gone undefeated the next two seasons, 22-0 and winning a pair of PNFL Championships. The season after that, the Krakens went 9-2. Then last year, 4-8.

His first losing season.

His *last* losing season.

Never again would the Krakens be on the bottom of the table looking up. Never again.

Quentin concentrated on watching the Orbiting Death defense. He'd line up against these very players in Week Six. His brain cataloged thousands of bits of information about his future opponents.

He watched one player in particular — middle linebacker Yalla the Biter.

Yalla the Biter, who two seasons ago had maimed Krakens running back Paul Pierson. Yalla the Biter, who had torn open Quentin's hand and spilled his blood all over the field.

Quentin had payback planned for that player, oh yes he did.

Come and play. I'll be waiting.

BOOK TWO:
THE PRESEASON

7

PRESEASON WEEK ONE: JANUARY 1 – 7, 2684

Transcript from the "Galaxy's Greatest Sports Show with Dan, Akbar, and Tarat the Smasher"

DAN: Welcome back, sports fans! Dan Gianni here once again to anchor the Galaxy's Greatest Sports Show, along with Akbar Smith and the legendary Hall-of-Fame linebacker known as Tarat the Smasher.

AKBAR: Thanks, Dan.

TARAT: Yes, Dan, thank you for such a kind intro.

DAN: Guys, it's our favorite time of the year.

AKBAR: Giving day?

TARAT: The Feast of Bugs?

DAN: You *know* what time of the year it is. Today is the first day of Tier One preseason. Teams have reported to training camp.

AKBAR: And I'm back from the annual GFL rules committee meeting. Many changes are afoot.

TARAT: I am not fond of the rules committee. Why do they keep changing such a perfect game?

DAN: Tarat, if the rules committee didn't change rules, there wouldn't be a need for a committee, and hence, no jobs for them. It's a self-fulfilling prophecy. Akbar, what were the highlights?

AKBAR: Well, Dan, there's a few major issues. This is GFL Commissioner Rob Froese's third year in charge. He's really trying to put his stamp on things. He's working on a major reorganization, trying to connect Tier Three to Tier Two the way Tier Two is connected to Tier One. They also approved on-field holographic replay for 2685, so not for this coming season but for the one after that. Once that's implemented, the refs on the field can watch the play exactly as it happened in the same *place* it happened.

TARAT: I hate replay.

DAN: Smasher, instant replay makes the game more fair.

TARAT: Life is full of variables and unfairness, Dan. Sentients should handle things as they come, not complain and try to change the past.

AKBAR: Froese also implemented new rules on concussions. Players with concussions now have to get approved by a *league* doctor before they can play again, not just the *team* doctor.

TARAT: Human brains are so fragile.

DAN: It's for the good of the players, Smasher.

TARAT: A *real* football player knows how to play with pain.

DAN: Pain? We're not talking just *pain* here, Smasher. We're talking about players' health. Brain damage. Their very *lives*.

TARAT: If you aren't prepared to lay down your life for your team, you don't belong in the game.

DAN: Hard for me to argue with a Hall of Fame linebacker. I'm just a schlub with a microphone. Akbar, how about the big question? How about the salary cap?

AKBAR: Froese finally got that one through. Next year, for the 2685 season, the salary cap goes into place.

TARAT: A salary cap goes against the basic principles of free trade. If someone wants to pay a sentient to perform a service, he should be allowed to pay whatever the market will bear.

DAN: Come on, Tarat. That means what it's meant for decades — the teams with the most money lock up the best players. Teams like the To Pirates, Wabash Wolfpack, Hittoni Hullwalkers. They've always had more revenue and hence get the best talent, which means they win more games and more championships, which brings in more money, and the cycle continues. The rich get richer, the poor get relegated.

TARAT: The Themala Dreadnaughts don't spend as much as everyone else, yet they win games.

AKBAR: True, but look at the Mars Planets. Last year they were the smallest market in Tier One. They've been promoted three times in the past twelve seasons and relegated just as many times. They always start the season strong, but their limited finances means they don't have any roster depth. As soon as their starters get injured, they can't compete. The Ionath Krakens could fall into that same trap. They have very little depth on defense.

TARAT: And the Krakens already lost more defensive depth. Ionath backup defensive end Ban-A-Tarew was signed by the Orbiting Death, and backup right cornerback Standish retired due to pregnancy. But that is how it goes in the GFL. You lose players, you replace players. In the Quyth Concordia, Dan, we believe in survival of the fittest. There are no *rules* in evolution — sports and business should be the same way.

AKBAR: Froese wants to make sure all teams in Tier One have the same amount of salary to share among their rosters. Starting in 2685, each team has a maximum of 128 megacredits per season to spend on player salaries.

DAN: *Woah*, that's a chunk of change. What about Tier Two?

AKBAR: A little less. They can spend a max of 110 megacredits. Froese set the Tier One minimum player salary at one-point-two megacredits.

TARAT: One-point-two million? Some key players are making that right now.

DAN: And that brings up the *huge* issue of players in the last year of their current deal. This is known as a *contract year*, and there are some stars that are looking at just that.

AKBAR: Ryan Nossek, for example. He's in the last year of a four-season deal with the Isis Ice Storm.

DAN: And how about Frank Zimmer? The living legend is in a contract year, but he missed several games last season with his seventh concussion. After this season, will the To Pirates pay him the money given to the League's other top quarterbacks?

TARAT: Which, of course, brings the conversation back to a contract-year player making league minimum, Quentin Barnes of the Ionath Krakens.

AKBAR: You have to wonder if Gredok the Splithead signing Barnes to league minimum is going to wind up biting Gredok in the ass, Dan. Barnes can't be happy with that.

TARAT: Especially when you consider that Don Pine makes five times as much for sitting on the bench. Even the backup quarterback, Yitzhak Goldman, makes more than Barnes.

DAN: You're kidding me.

TARAT: I do not kid, Dan.

DAN: But how did you find that out? Salaries are supposed to be confidential.

TARAT: I have my sources.

AKBAR: If Barnes plays well in the upcoming season, his free-agency drama is going to be a zoo.

DAN: A zoo? What do you mean?

TARAT: A zoo is a park-like area in which live animals are kept in cages or large enclosures for public exhibition, Dan.

DAN: (audible sigh) Smasher, come on.

TARAT: And I have other news as well. My sources tell me that Barnes is considering agent Danny Lundy.

DAN: Oh, what I wouldn't give to be in the room when Danny Lundy starts talking contract with Gredok the Splithead! Tarat, do you think this means Barnes will sign long-term with Ionath, or is he as good as gone after this season?

TARAT: It is unknown at this time. As I have said before, you Humans are obsessed with finances. Danny Lundy is known for negotiating large deals. Considering that the Mars Planets, the Bartel Water Bugs and the To Pirates have all said they are going to court Barnes, Lundy would have considerable leverage to get that big deal.

DAN: He'll be courted harder than a princess with a gigacredit dowry, Akbar. Let's see what the fans think of this. Line three from Wilson 6, you're on the Space. *Go!*

CALLER: Yeah, I agree that Barnes is a hot property. I think my Jang Atom Smashers will pick him up. If we keep Schweitzer as our QB, we're gonna get relegated.

TARAT: Schweitzer has to overcome his injury problems. He can't run. He's like a big spider snack out there, just waiting to get eaten.

AKBAR: Can we not refer to players as food items?

TARAT: But he is!

DAN: Makes me glad I'm not a slow-footed quarterback, Tarat. Line two from Klipthik, you're on the Space. *Go!*

Excerpt from **Earth: Birthplace of Sentients**
written by Zippy the Voracious
From **Chapter One, The Breeding Ground**

If you trace all lines back to ancestral species, no planet has produced more forms of sentient life than Earth.

Currently controlled by the Planetary Union, Earth is the evolutionary home of Humans. Over the last millennia, Humans have proven to be busy creatures, giving rise to at least four additional biological species as well as at least two artificial species.

"At least" may not sound very empirical, but there is good reason for this vague term. The Prawatt race was first discovered in 2424, but it took almost another century before scientists theorized that the Prawatt originated on Earth in 2015. While unproven, most exobiologists now agree that the Prawatt were created on Earth then subsequently exterminated. Because this process of creation and extinction likely happened once at the hands of Humanity, we must leave open the strong possibility that other races created on Earth remain as-yet unknown.

HUMAN "RACES"

Humanity's phenotypical variations fill the galaxy. Sub-species abound. Humans typically range in adult size from 0.9 to 2.4 meters. The Empire Bureau of Species Interaction places the average height of an adult Human male at 1.8 meters, average weight at about 79 kilograms. Natural skin pigmentation ranges widely, including absolute white as well as shades of pink, blue, purple, tan, yellow, brown and black. If you factor in cosmetic pigmentation alteration, Human color variants number in the hundreds.

This text, however, focuses not on phenotypical Human variants, but rather distinct *species* descended from or created by Humanity. Two races fall under this definition: *Homo pondus* and *Homo aqus*.

HUMAN VARIANTS

Homo pondus

Known by the common name "HeavyG," *Homo pondus* originated on Vosor 3, a world currently controlled by the League of Planets. Vosor 3's high gravity makes it difficult for Humans to function for any length of time. Considering the mineral wealth on Vosor 3, workers were needed that could live on the surface without the artificial gravity found in that world's urban centers. A genetic engineering program by League scientists produced *Homo pondus*, the largest of the Humanoid species.

The average *Homo pondus* male stands 1.9 meters tall and weighs 156 kilograms, significantly larger than the average Human. *Homo pondus* also differs phenotypically, with denser bones and muscle, longer arm length and shorter legs relative to the overall body than in Humans.

Because *Homo pondus* can live and work anywhere that Humans can, this minority can be found all over the galaxy.

Homo aqus

One of two species of sentient aquatic Earthlings, *Homo aqus* is also known by the common name of "Amphibs." Because *Homo aqus* can breath in both air and water, it boasts the fastest-growing

Humanoid population. Numbers continue to explode on Earth, Tower and other planets with large bodies of water.

The average *Homo aqus* male stands 1.85 meters tall and weighs 100 kilograms. They are more streamlined than *Homo sapiens*, with leaner muscle mass and longer bones.

Exobiologists also theorize that there may be sub-variants of *Homo aqus*. Considering the surface area covered by water on Earth and Tower alone, there are many undeveloped regions that have little or no competition. Theories abound of *Homo orca*, a variant of *Homo aqus* thought to be a brutal predator some 2.5 meters in length and weighing an estimated 200 kilograms.

EARTH-BASED NON-HUMAN BIOLOGICAL SENTIENTS
Delphinus albietz

The second aquatic Earthling species, *Delphinus albietz*, is better known as the "Dolphin." The only remaining species of dolphin left on Earth, *Delphinus albietz* achieved early population growth due to being Earth's first sentient aquatic species. There is much controversy surrounding the actions of that species following the genetic augmentation that gave rise to sentience, notably the genocide of all other large aquatic species on the planet.

The average *Delphinus albietz* male is 2.1 meters long and weighs 136 kilograms. Aside from the modifications to their brain composition and tongue muscles (which are adjusted for limited Human speech), they are largely unchanged from their ancestral form of *Delphinus capensis*. Mechanical prosthetics allow Dolphins to walk on land and survive indefinitely out of the water, enabling them to be part of other sentient cultures.

A strange controversy exists where some scientists claim that Dolphins are *not* truly sentient, but rather a more intelligent version of the animal they once were. Professor Allison Rynne, author of *Life in the Milky Way Galaxy*, is the leading proponent of this theory. Rynne says that Dolphins are no more sentient than chimpanzees or other primates that are "taught to wear clothes, use rudimentary communication skills and perform complicated tricks."

This stance, of course, meets with outrage from Dolphin groups. Professor Finny McGee, a leading Dolphin scientist, is well known for his quote: "If Rynne thinks I'm a trained animal, she can kiss my blow hole."

EARTH-CREATED ARTIFICIAL SPECIES

Humanity has created two major forms of artificial life. Many laymen think that current levels of technology should make it easy to create mechanical, sentient life. This could not be further from the truth. Creating artificial intelligence has proven to be an extremely difficult affair. Even when scientists have succeeded, and then repeated their own processes step by step, they have been unable to replicate those successes. While Humans (and other biological species) can and have created intelligence "from scratch," the actual set of parameters that makes something "sentient" has yet to be discovered. In artificial life, much like biological life, success seems to be more accident than method.

Before these artificial life forms became sentient, life was classified in three "domains": *Archaea*, *Bacteria* and *Eukarya*. The artificial life forms listed below are so different from what we know that scientists assigned a fourth kingdom, *Facticia*, to encompass them. *Facticia* is broken down into phylums: *Pedes*, which includes artificial sentients existing in forms that move physically, like biological sentients; and *Phasmatis*, which includes sentients that exist in electronic form.

Sententia prawatt

This race is known by the common name "Prawatt." Prawatt are in the phylum *pedes*. The Prawatt have started several wars against biological races. They attacked the Rewalls in 2438 (which was the first known interstellar combat). In 2456, the Prawatt Jihad attempted to exterminate the Kuluko race. Until the League of Planets announced that it possessed a secret preserve of Kuluko and had saved the race from extinction, most governments thought the Prawatt had succeeded in genocide.

At the beginning of their life cycle, Prawatt are a collective organism. In later stages, they become large, multi-cellular animals. Their physiology and life cycle is too complex to explain here, so please see Chapter Seven for specifics.

As an artificially created race, the Prawatt have long been denied universal acceptance as "sentient." Recent encounters with a form of the species known as "Explorers," however, have eliminated doubts for all but a handful of scientists (and, we should point out, all exobiologists in the Purist Nation, who claim that because man — not the High One — created the Prawatt, it is impossible for the Prawatt to actually be sentient).

There is no average size of a Prawatt, as they can take many forms.

Facticia Phasmatis

Facticia Phasmatis is not a genus/species name, but rather a kingdom/phylum name that represents most forms of electronic artificial intelligence. Members of this phylum are so varied in form and concept that each sentient has its own specification of class, order, family, genus and species.

The first truly sentient artificial intelligence was created by League of Planets scientists and was — as is often the case — an accident. League of Planets scientist Kendra Stansak attempted to upload her consciousness into digital form. That effort failed, but created "Virus-444," a computer program that devastated League computer systems.

Other efforts to upload the Human consciousness into digital form resulted in the creation of new entities, some of which exist to this day in multiple instances.

QUENTIN AND YITZHAK GOLDMAN walked into an expansive reception area. Chairs for all species filled the center of the room. Holos of sports figures lined the walls, individual images of a dozen athletes frozen in dramatic action.

At the end of the circular room sat a curved desk. Behind it, a stunning blonde Human woman.

"Mister Goldman," she said, flashing a smile that took Quentin's breath away. "How is Ahava and your sons?"

"They're fantastic." Yitzhak automatically smiled at the mention of his family. "So nice of you to ask."

The woman nodded, just once, acknowledging Yitzhak's compliment. She fixed her perfect brown eyes on Quentin. "Mister Barnes. Welcome."

"Hi," Quentin said. He knew he was staring. He couldn't help himself.

"Mister Lundy is on a call," the receptionist said. "Would you both mind waiting? He won't be but a moment."

Yitzhak walked to one of the Human chairs and sat. Quentin forced himself to look away from the receptionist and did the same.

Yitzhak had counseled Quentin with off-the-field aspects of football as much as Don Pine had tutored on-field action. Zak had helped Quentin land endorsement deals, helped him manage his rage and — most importantly — given Quentin a reality check that the poor, dangerous days of the Purist Nation were in the past. *You're not on Micovi anymore*, Zak had said. Words Quentin took to heart.

Zak's white skin and white hair marked him as a native of the planet Fortress. Even his eyebrows and eyelashes were white, which made his coal-black eyes demand attention.

"Hey, Zak," Quentin whispered. "That girl is *gorgeous*."

Yitzhak nodded. "Danny likes the eye candy."

"I guess so. Is he … you know … *with* her?"

Yitzhak gave Quentin a quizzical look, then laughed. "I don't think Danny and his secretary are *an item*, if that's what you mean. Danny just kind of does everything first class, maybe even a little over the top." Yitzhak punctuated his sentence by gesturing to the holos that lined the room's circular walls.

Quentin saw one of John Tweedy, staring with his wide-eyed, pre-snap insanity. Another of golfer Declan Murphy, his focused stare visible through the clear helmet of the rad-suits needed to play the sport on Ionath's challenging courses. And a couple of

Krakens linemen, Vu-Ko-Will and Bud-O-Shwek, all decked out in their black home jerseys and black leg armor.

"Huh. I knew John was one of Danny's clients, but I didn't know about Vu-Ko and Bud-O." The waiting-room holos showed even more stars, including a small, armored Human that wouldn't have even reached Quentin's hip. Quentin recognized the little man's red armor.

"*Wow*, is that Poughkeepsie Pete?"

"It is," Yitzhak said. "Danny has a couple of Dinolition clients. None as major as Pete, though."

Quentin saw a dashing, white-skinned quarterback wearing a black jersey with an orange #14 on the chest, planting his rear foot after a drop-back, looking downfield and preparing to throw. "Damn, Zak. Whoever took that shot needs a bonus."

"Why's that?"

"Because it makes you look good. Must be trick photography."

"Ha-ha-ha. You're quite the comedian."

The last holo wasn't as bright as the others, wasn't as dramatic. It took Quentin a moment to realize that the holo was of *him*. Not dropping back to pass, not hurdling some defensive lineman, but just standing there, jersey all beat to hell, blood on his arms and face. Standing there and looking *down*.

Yitzhak saw it as well. "That's weird. They make me shine like a movie star, but a pretty boy like you look like you were eaten by a Ki lineman then thrown up because you soured his stomach. Sure is a lot different from the images Manny Sayed had of you on that first visit to your yacht."

"Yeah," Quentin said. "A lot different."

Manny had done the *Hypatia*'s interior in various images of Quentin, each more grandiose than the last. The still and moving holos had made Quentin look like a hero, like something ... super-Human. That approach had made Quentin uncomfortable. He still didn't think of himself as superstar — he was an orphan miner that just so happened to be blessed with unusual genetics. He worked harder than anyone else, sure, but were it not for his size, speed and strength, all the hard work in the galaxy wouldn't have made him a starting quarterback in the GFL.

In that moment, Quentin knew Danny Lundy was the guy. Quentin hadn't even met the agent, yet Danny had known exactly the kind of thing that would make Quentin comfortable. Sure, it was very presumptuous to put a holo of Quentin in the waiting room along with Danny's existing clients. But this image? It looked ... *humble*. That wasn't the way Quentin acted on the field or in the locker room, but for some reason it felt *right*.

"It's a great shot," Yitzhak said. "I feel like it captures the real you. Not the loud-mouth slave driver you are on the practice field, but the *real* you."

"What's that supposed to mean?"

Yitzhak shrugged. "You ever given any thought to what you'll do after football?"

"Probably be scratching at the inside of my coffin," Quentin said. "The only way I'm not involved is if I'm dead."

Yitzhak's black eyes stared at Quentin, stared with an expression of seriousness, importance. "People follow you, Quentin. Have you noticed that?"

Quentin shrugged. "I'm the team leader."

"Not just on the field," Zak said. "Off it as well. There's something about you. People *want* to follow you. You ever think of using that for something greater than yourself? Greater than football?"

This sounded like a preacher's pitch to draw Quentin into a prayer revival tent. "You haven't gone all religious on me, have you, Zak?"

The backup quarterback stared, then smiled. He shook his head. "Maybe it's a conversation for another time."

"Maybe," Quentin said. And if *another time* actually meant *never*, that would work out just fine.

The gorgeous receptionist caught their attention with nothing more than her blazing smile. "Mister Lundy will see you now. Go right in."

The circular wall to the left of her desk rose up. The holos there faded out, revealing a meeting room with a thick glass table.

Waiting inside was a dolphin with legs.

"Quentin," Yitzhak said. "Meet Danny Lundy."

"Quentin Barnes! Thank you so much for agreeing to meet with me."

Danny Lundy stepped forward. Only Quentin's growing experience with non-Human life forms stopped him from taking a step back, for this creature's appearance assailed Quentin with visual input.

Danny wasn't a *gray* Dolphin; he'd had his skin modified. The base color was white, probably, but a sheen of reds, yellows, oranges, blues and greens made him look like a moist, streamlined rainbow. He wore some kind of silver harness, a chassis that wrapped around the front and back of his bejeweled dorsal fin and also around the base of his tail. A jeweled cable ran from the harness in front of his fin up and into a metal jack just behind his blow hole. Four thin-but-strong silver leg-cables extended from the underside of the harness, supporting Danny's weight and letting him walk. Two more silvery protrusions connected to the sides of his foremost harness circle — these looked like thin, sculptured Human arms. They even ended in metallic, Human-looking hands.

Danny walked around the table, strode forward and extended his right mechanical arm. The gesture was artificial, but obvious — he wanted to shake hands.

"Pleased to meet you, Quentin," he said. Danny's voice was a mix of low-volume mumbling, chitters and squeaks combined with a louder, dominant tone. Like Doc Patah, Danny Lundy had a vocal adaptor to turn his natural sounds into flawless English, words that rang with a pitch-man's easy confidence.

Quentin swallowed, then did the courteous thing and shook Danny's "hand." Quentin expected cold metal, but the handshake was surprisingly warm, firm and welcoming.

"Uh ... nice to meet you too, Mister Lundy."

"Danny," Danny said. "Mister Lundy is my dad, for crying out loud."

Quentin had seen Dolphins in water, of course. There had been plenty of them in Hudson Bay Station's water tubes, the aquatic equivalent of sidewalks that also worked for Leekee and Whitokians. But he'd never seen Dolphins up close like this.

Danny had to be at least seven feet from nose to tail, as long as Quentin was tall. Even without the mechanical legs and hands, the rainbow-colored creature weighed at least three hundred pounds.

Danny gestured to the table, a motion so natural and Human that Quentin almost forgot the hand and the arm were mechanical.

"Please," the rainbow dolphin said, "have a seat."

Yitzhak pulled out one of the four black leather chairs and sat. Quentin did the same. As Danny walked around the table, Quentin leaned in to hiss at Zak.

"Were you going to tell me he was a fish?"

Zak smiled and whispered back. "More fun this way. I wanted to see how you reacted. And he's not a fish."

"Whatever."

Danny lowered his body into a chair made for his long form. "So, Quentin. Zak tells me you might be interested in representation."

Quentin nodded.

"Good," Danny said. "Look, I know you're a busy Human, so I'm not going to swim in circles here. I'm a fan, buddy. I love to watch you play. I want to represent your interests. Anyone can see you have a monster career in front of you, guy, and I'll be honest — your current contract is one floating turd of a deal."

"A ... floating turd?"

"That might be too nice a term," Danny said. "It's spoiled Whitokian guts processed into a digital form and turned into a legal document. Trust me on this one, buddy."

"Well, I know it's not *good*, but ... "

"*Not good?* The salmon I had for lunch was *not good*, guy. Your contract? It's atrocious, flagitious and abysmal. An athlete of your caliber needs to be properly compensated for the danger he faces, wouldn't you agree?"

Well, yeah. Danny was right about that. Quentin *was* in danger. On every single snap of every game, his health, his career and even his life were at risk.

Quentin nodded.

"You could suffer anything from abrasions to deformations to decapitations, buddy," Danny said. "And for this brave effort, this stalwart endeavor, this soldiering leadership, you make *league minimum*? Is that right, Quentin? League *min*imum?"

"Uh ... yes, Mister Dolphin."

"Danny."

"Danny, right, sorry."

"League *min-eh-mum*!" Danny laughed a somewhat disturbing combination of barking squeals and a rich, artificial Human tenor.

"I tell you, guy, this whole contract of yours makes me angry. It makes me enraged, deranged and estranged. But I can get this fixed up for you, buddy. Gredok the Splithead wants to play hardball? I can make him regret it. Trust me on that. His compensation is defamation, his pay is *no-way*. You're a free agent at the end of the year, so if you sign with me, we can get you what you deserve. He wants to play rough? No problem, I'll show him how we do things a hundred meters deep."

Quentin gathered that was a figure of speech, although he had no idea what it really meant. "So, uh, Danny ... how exactly do we play *hardball* with a gangster that can have sentients killed whenever he feels like it?"

Danny's squealing laugh filled the room again, made the glass table vibrate. "Simple, guy. We fight fire with fire. We put him in a bidding war with *other* gangsters that can also have sentients killed whenever *they* feel like it."

Quentin's eyes narrowed. "And how do we do that?"

"You're a free agent at the end of the year, buddy. That means we go out and talk to other teams."

"Talk to them about what?"

Danny stared, then laughed again. He turned to face Yitzhak. "Zackie, baby, is this two-legger messing with me? Because if he is, he's hys*ter*ical!"

Yitzhak shook his head. "He's not messing with you. Get used to it, Danny — when you're dealing with Quentin, what you see and what you hear are what you get."

Danny turned back to Quentin. "We talk to the other teams, buddy, about playing for them. If Gredok doesn't want to take care of his star quarterback, maybe that star quarterback lines up under center next year in something *other* than a Krakens jersey."

Quentin sagged back into his chair. He'd always known that being a free agent meant you could play for other teams. *Logically*, he'd known that. But emotionally? Emotionally, he'd never really considered that he would *ever* wear anything but the Orange and the Black.

"I don't know, Danny. I think we're building something great here."

The silver hands lifted, palm up, then set back down — Danny's version of a shrug. "You're the client. If you want to end up in Ionath, that's where you end up. But if you want to get properly compensated for putting hundreds of thousands of sentients in the stands, for making billions tune in to watch, for risking your life and limb not just in games but in *practice*, then I need negotiating power. If High One wants you in Krakens orange next season, guy, then you have to trust his teachings and know everything happens for a reason."

Quentin stared at the dolphin's black eyes. Stared hard. "Danny, do you actually think the High One has anything to do with this? Or are you just telling me what you think I want to hear so we'll ... I don't know ... *bond* or something."

Danny paused. Quentin thought about his holo in the waiting room, how Danny had somehow picked exactly the picture that would make Quentin feel at home. And now Danny was referring to the High One, probably trying to make Quentin relax that way as well.

"The High One has *everything* to do with this, buddy," Danny said. "Just not in the way that you think. You need a negotiator. When it comes to negotiation? I *am* the shucking High One."

The statement was damn near sacrilegious. But instead of angering Quentin, it made him smile. In a room like this, Danny Lundy was just as cocky as Quentin was on the field. Maybe that was yet another affect to make Quentin feel comfortable, but whether it was fake or not didn't really matter — because it worked.

"Danny, I've never worked with a fish before."

"*Cetacean*," Danny and Yitzhak said together.

Danny's mechanical rig sprayed a fine mist onto his rainbow skin. "Fish are food. I'm a *mammal*, guy. Warm blood and a big brain."

"Cows are mammals," Quentin said. "Aren't they food?"

Danny's blow hole let out a hiss of annoyance. "If you find a cow that can give you a record-setting contract, I suggest you sign with him."

Quentin laughed. "Point taken. But like I said, I've never worked with a ... what was it again?"

"Cetacean," Danny and Yitzhak said together.

"Right. I've never worked with a Cetacean before. Don't you think someone with my religious background might be better off with a Human agent?"

Danny shook his head hard, a motion that made his entire seven-foot body lurch and scatter water droplets onto the floor. "When it comes to business, buddy, Cetaceans are where it's at. You could go Human, or Ki, or even sign with that talking cow if you find him, but no matter *what* you do, you won't get the kind of personal service, the kind of *dedication* that my species brings to the table. It's genetic with us. You sign with me, I'm not just an agent — I'm your protector, your champion, the sentient that knocks the living hell out of everything that opposes you. I'm unstoppable, unflappable and far from a gamble. Others might tell you they will land you the contract you deserve? Not me, guy. Danny Lundy gets you the contract that you've *earned*."

Danny seemed to know all the right words. Athletes were always talking about what they *deserved*, like the universe owed them for having been born with physical gifts. Quentin didn't buy into any of that. All the gifts in the world didn't matter if you didn't work your ass off to develop them and at the end of the day, even *that* didn't matter if you didn't *win*.

Life wasn't about *deserving* anything. It was about *earning* everything.

And if Danny had said those words because they were what Quentin wanted to hear? Well, at least that meant this Cetacean was one hell of a researcher.

Quentin stood and extended his hand. "Danny, I'm in. Let's see what you can do."

THE FIRST DAY OF A NEW YEAR. At least it was back on Earth. The concepts of "years" lost all meaning in a galaxy filled with over fifty inhabited worlds, each world with its own orbit around its own star. Quentin didn't care about "galactic constant time" or the Creterakian's unified calendar — football seasons operated based on Earth years, so that was the only system that mattered.

January 1. Less than a month to opening day — Sunday, January 27, 2684.

He walked into Ionath Stadium's locker room, his chest buzzing with the feeling of possibility, of potential. He'd been gone too long. It felt different this time. The Krakens weren't outsiders anymore, they weren't the underdogs, they wouldn't measure success by just avoiding relegation.

No. Not this year.

This year, they were going for it all.

The Ionath Krakens are on a collision course with a Tier One championship. The only variable is time.

The central locker room. Here the entire team gathered before taking the field, or to review Hokor's Xs and Os on the holoboard. Empty, of course, because he was two hours early. He was the first one to arrive. Quentin knew that to lead meant setting an example of hard work, of dedication.

Four doors lined the room, each marked by a species-specific icon, each leading to a species-specific section where the players could prepare as suited their kind. No, not *four* doors ... *five*. Quentin saw that now — in addition to icons denoting Ki, Sklorno, Human and Quyth Warrior — there was one marked for the HeavyG. That had been added sometime during the off-season. The GFL's HeavyG players kept pushing the concept that they were *not* just big Humans, but a separate species that deserved species-level recognition.

Yet another wall built up between teammates. Well, Quentin could break down that wall, at least on the football field. His teammates would be Krakens first, individual species second.

Before entering the Human locker room, he paused for a long look at a new mural. The painting represented the team's namesake. It matched a similar painting in the locker room up on the *Touchback*. A brightly colored, six-tentacled monster rose up from a red ocean to attack some unseen prey. The rows of backward-curving teeth promised a quick death to that prey — quick, but far from painless. A single huge, green eye glowed with anger, with hunger.

The kraken.

A native species of the planet Quyth, nicknamed after a creature from Earth mythology. Violent, powerful, unstoppable — the perfect symbol of a championship football team.

Quentin nodded to the painting. He turned toward the Human locker room but stopped when he heard the new HeavyG door open. Rebecca Montagne walked out. She was already dressed in her armor and orange practice jersey. Her long, silky black ponytail hung down to the small of her back. In her left hand, she held her helmet by its facemask. Tucked in the crook of her right arm? A football.

She stopped in her tracks, dark eyes wide as if she'd been caught doing something wrong. But she *wasn't* doing anything wrong. She was doing the same thing as Quentin, arriving early for practice.

Not just *early* — she was there before he was.

"Hello, Quentin."

He glared, angry at her for spoiling his need to be there first, angry at himself for allowing that to happen.

"Hi," Quentin said.

They stared at each other.

She cleared her throat. "I haven't seen you since the Dinolition match. Did you ... have a good off-season?"

She wanted to make conversation?

"Sure," he said. "It was fine."

She nodded, tried to smile, but it must have felt as awkward as it looked. "How is Somalia?"

"Good, I guess. She's back on tour. I haven't heard from her in a few days."

Becca huffed. "Because there's no photo ops for her."

"Excuse me?"

"Nothing," she said. "I'm just ... surprised you haven't been talking to her every day. That's all."

"I'll talk to her soon. Is John here?"

Becca shrugged, the motion lifting her heavy shoulder pads in a comical way. "I don't know. I haven't seen him for a couple of days."

The comment drew an odd, surging feeling in his stomach. Well, if she wasn't seeing much of John, then that was good for the team, right? Teammates dating ... that could only end badly.

"You're here early," he said.

She nodded. "Always."

His anger and annoyance returned. He pointed at the football in her arm. "Don't be getting any ideas about throwing that thing, rookie. Your quarterback days are done."

Her eyes narrowed. The softness of her face, her feminine expressions — those made it easy to forget that she was a professional fullback, as tough a player as anyone else on the roster. Easy to forget, but her scowl reminded him instantly.

"I'm *not* a rookie. This is my second year. I'm your starting fullback. I'm one of the sentients that protects you on that field, you *jerk*. And I'll get any *ideas* I want."

She'd shown great promise last year, her first in upper-tier ball. Pretty impressive considering she'd been a quarterback for the Green Bay Packers of Tier Three. Amazingly athletic, tough as a battleship rivet, she'd gone from third on the depth chart — behind first-string Tom Pareless and second-string Kopor the Climber — straight to the top spot. Becca "The Wrecka" Montagne, starting fullback for the Ionath Krakens.

You could take a player out of the quarterback position, but you couldn't take the quarterback position out of the player. She played hard, did her job, but she wanted what Quentin had.

"Listen, Montagne, I'm not going to tolerate anything that will confuse the team this year, so any idea you have of playing quarterback is— "

"When I want your job, you'll *know* it, Barnes. And if that happens? Get ready for the fight of your life."

She whipped the ball. It hit his stomach a moment before he got his hands up to trap it there. She scowled at him again, then turned and stomped out of the central locker room, headed toward the field.

THE HUMAN LOCKER ROOM was all smiles. Men who hadn't seen one another in months greeted their teammates with the excitement of a shared season to come. Already dressed for practice, Quentin welcomed each player. He shook hands with Arioch Morningstar, the quiet, shy kicker; with Yotaro Kobayasho, the bleach-white number two tight end; with the black-haired Samuel Darkeye, John Tweedy's backup at linebacker.

Donald Pine and Yitzhak Goldman, Quentin's backups, walked in together.

Zak let out an overly dramatic sigh of surprise. "Q, *you're* early? Gosh, what a surprise."

"Turning over a new leaf," Quentin said. "How's the family?"

"Everyone is fantastic. You owe me for that intro to Danny Lundy. I'm going to have to cash in by insisting you come over for dinner. My boys whine at me every day that they want to meet you."

The thought of spending time with children made Quentin want to lie, come up with some excuse. But, if he could manage dinner with the Ki, then he could handle eating with Yitzhak's family. "How about you let me take you and the family out on the town?"

Zak's smile faded, then returned — now fake and forced. Quentin wouldn't have noticed the difference two years ago. "We'd rather have you over."

Now that Quentin thought about it, he'd never seen Yitzhak go out. Ever. Maybe that's what happened when you became a family man.

Quentin didn't like kids all that much. The idea of sitting in Yitzhak's place, wherever that might be, for an evening with his wife and boys? Ugh. "Let's hook that up once the season gets rolling." He knew full well that he wouldn't pursue it.

Yitzhak knew it, too. "Sure," he said. "Once the season gets rolling."

Zak walked to his locker, leaving Quentin facing Don Pine. Pine, two-time Galaxy Bowl champion, former MVP, former starting quarterback for the Ionath Krakens, now entering his second year as Quentin's backup. Quentin hadn't talked to Pine since September, when they'd met with Gredok and Hokor to talk about signing Cheboygan and the others.

"Good to see you," Quentin said.

"Same here, Q."

"You also gonna invite me over for dinner?"

Don smiled, his too-white teeth a contrast against his blue face and dark-blue lips. He didn't say anything, just shrugged, then walked to his locker.

What did *that* mean? Why did everyone else want to hang with Quentin, but Don Pine did not? Quentin didn't have long to dwell on it, as number-two running back Yassoud Murphy walked in the door, fists raised high.

"You may all now relax! The Yassoud is here to lead you to the promised land. You are safely in my protection."

The players waved at 'Soud. Those close to him patted him on the shoulder. The previous season had been hard on him. He'd lost his starting position to Ju Tweedy, then spent much of the season either drunk, feeling sorry for himself, or both. To see him arrive in such good spirits made Quentin hopeful that Yassoud would contribute this season.

Yassoud's tight, dark curls hadn't changed, but he'd modified his signature beard. Instead of one thick, narrow, bound strand that hung down to his sternum, he'd turned it into two thinner ones of the same length — one he'd braided with orange ribbon, one with black.

Yassoud saw Quentin. "Q! How was your off-season?"

"Real good, thanks." Quentin noticed that 'Soud seemed bigger than the last time they'd met. "Looks like you did more than drink beer during yours."

Yassoud laughed, then puffed up his chest in an exaggerated show of arrogance. The muscles in his neck and shoulders twitched. "Oh, yep. You know, been working out, but it's no big deal."

He raised his right fist, flexing his arm to show a rippling bicep. Yassoud had always been a specimen, but there was no question that he'd put in a lot of time in the weight room. For someone who was already in prime shape to add that kind of definition, he must have worked extremely hard.

'Soud looked at his biceps. "Oh, hello. Why, I didn't see you there. You look *mar*velous."

Quentin laughed and pushed Yassoud away. "You're anthropomorphizing your biceps?"

Yassoud narrowed his eyes, laughed a jock's laugh of disdain. "Anthro-po-pope-a-what?"

"Anthropomorphize," Quentin said. "It means, uh, giving Human attributes to something that isn't a person."

Yassoud shook his head, his long beard-braids swinging in time. "Now you're using big words, hayseed? Did you take up Kimberlin on his offer to tutor you?"

Quentin shrugged and looked away, a little embarrassed. He didn't know why he should feel embarrassed about increasing his knowledge, but he still did. Kind of felt ... *off* ... to talk about such things in the locker room.

Yassoud seemed to sense Quentin's discomfort, so he changed the subject. "Well, if you think *my* beautiful, beautiful arms show the benefits of hard work, just wait until you see Warburg."

Quentin's smile faded. Tight end Rick Warburg was not someone Quentin really cared to see. Just like Quentin, Warburg hailed
from the Purist Nation. Unlike Quentin, however, Warburg still
embraced his racist upbringing, still practiced the religion. Well,
that non-team attitude had dropped Warburg to third-string behind George Starcher and Kobayasho. Third-string was where
Warburg belonged.

John and Ju Tweedy entered the locker room, already arguing,
focusing only on each other but drawing everyone's attention.

"You're an idiot," John said.

"No, *you're* an idiot," Ju said.

"Your *face* is an idiot," John said.

Yassoud put both his hands over his heart. "Awwww! Brotherly
love, ain't it beautiful?"

Both the Tweedy boys stopped and glared at Yassoud, who
laughed and held up both hands, palms out. "My bad! I don't
want to start any trouble this early in the season."

"Good," Ju said. "Just know your place."

Yassoud's smile faded. A hush fell over the locker room. "You
just better run hard, Ju. This won't be like last season. I'm out to
take as many carries away from you as I can."

Ju sneered and laughed. "Whatever, scrub. I'm going All-Pro
this year, so you bring your best."

Yassoud's jaw muscles twitched as he ground his teeth. Even on
his best day, Yassoud was nowhere near as talented as Ju Tweedy.
Everyone knew it. 'Soud walked to his locker. The Tweedy brothers did the same. The conversational buzz returned to normal.

Quentin had just started to head out to the field when Rick
Warburg and Tom Pareless walked in. Everything went silent — ten
Humans stared at someone they barely recognized. Quentin wasn't
even sure if it *was* Warburg. It had to be someone bigger … stronger, maybe … wearing a Warburg mask.

Rick Warburg had played the 2683 Tier One season at about
365 pounds. Six years of football had made Quentin pretty good
at knowing a player's weight from just a quick glance — Warburg
now weighed *at least* 380. And all of those added fifteen pounds

were muscle. *More* than the fifteen pounds, actually, as it appeared he'd lost some fat as well. Warburg looked like a seven-foot-tall, 380-pound bodybuilder.

Pine let out a long whistle. "Anyone seen Coach Hokor? Because I think Warburg ate him."

"Shuck you, blue-boy," Warburg said.

"That's a relief," Pine said. "For a second there, I thought you were an impostor. But no, you're the same old Warburg we all know and love."

A few uncomfortable laughs filtered through the locker room. The men turned back to their preparations. Warburg and Tom Pareless walked over to Quentin.

Tom extended his hand. Quentin shook it.

"Q," Tom said, "have a good off-season?"

"Solid," Quentin said. "How about you, old man? How's the ankle?"

Pareless smiled. At thirty-six, he was the oldest Human on the team. His face showed fine scars. The left side of his jaw seemed a little lower than the right. Fifteen seasons in the league had taken their toll.

"Ankle is all re-habbed," Tom said. "Looking forward to the season with you, whipper-snapper."

Tom slapped Quentin's shoulder, then walked to his locker — leaving Quentin alone with Rick Warburg. Rick offered his hand. Quentin didn't want to shake it, but if he expected people to overcome their prejudices and play as a team, then he had to do the same. Lead by example. He shook Rick's hand, feeling the power in the man's grip.

"Warburg," Quentin said. "Welcome back."

"High One praise your travels," Rick said. It was a friendly phrase from the Purist Nation culture, but there was nothing friendly about the tone. The way Rick said it made it clear he did not like the fact that most of Quentin's travels were with the sub-races.

"Same to you," Quentin said.

"I have worked very hard during the off-season."

Quentin nodded. "I can see that."

"This is the last year of my contract with the Krakens. It's my eighth season in football and I'm a free agent at the end of it. I want off this team. I want a new start. I want a big contract."

"Good luck with that," Quentin said.

"You're going to help me."

"Afraid a big contract and a new team are beyond my control."

Warburg smiled. "Don't give me that. I'm in the best shape of my career and not just physically. I've been working on my route-running, my catching, my blocking. I'm better than I've ever been, better than *him*," he said, jerking his thumb at George Starcher, who appeared to be having an in-depth conversation with an orange and black plaid towel.

"Quentin, you are my countryman," Warburg said. "Maybe you don't like me, but I will *show* you I am the best tight end on this team. And when I do, you *will* throw me the ball."

Quentin felt his temper rising. "And if I don't?"

Warburg shrugged. "If I'm the best and you don't throw me the rock, then it just reveals that all your preaching about *team* and *unity* is pure crap. It'll show that you're just as much of a bigot as me. Only difference is, I take pride in who I really am. See you on the field."

Rick turned and walked to his locker. Quentin watched him go, wondering about the tight end's words. Was Rick right? Did Quentin avoid throwing Rick the ball because of Rick's racism? And if so, was that wrong?

Quentin shook the thought away. It didn't really matter — Rick might be bigger, but he was still third on the depth chart and wouldn't see that much playing time. Despite the fact that George Starcher painted his face and talked to towels, he was poised to be the best tight end in the GFL that season. Ju wasn't the only Kraken looking at an All-Pro year.

Warburg wouldn't get the chance to test his claims.

Quentin headed for the field.

• • •

THE FIRST DAY of practice focused on route-running, re-familiarizing the quarterbacks with their receivers. Quentin's whole body tingled as he looked around the quiet temple that was Ionath Stadium. Empty stands reached to the sky, stands full of blazing-orange seats. Orange, except for the seats that spelled out a hundred-yard-long IONATH on the home side, a hundred-yard-long KRAKENS on the visitor's.

A light breeze crossed the stadium — either artificially pumped through the city dome or perhaps a natural occurrence from an enclosed space two miles in diameter. The breeze made Quentin look to the twenty-two towering pillars that lined Ionath Stadium, each pillar holding a long, lightly undulating banner from one of the Tier One teams. He saw the blood-red of the To Pirates, the deep purple and white of the Yall Criminals and the red and white of Ionath's archrival, the Wabash Wolfpack. Other familiar banners lined the stadium — the blue polka-dots on yellow of the Coranadillana Cloud Killers and the gold, silver and copper of the Jupiter Jacks among them.

He also saw two banners that had not been there the year before — the red, white and blue star of the Texas Earthlings and the metalflake-red circle on the flat black banner that belonged to the OS1 Orbiting Death. Those teams had earned promotion during the Tier Two Tournament, fighting their way to Tier One and replacing the relegated franchises of Mars and Chillich.

That was the nature of Tier One; nothing was promised and every game mattered. Even if you had a losing record, you needed to play your asses off to stay in the big-time. At the end of the season, if your team was the worst in your division? Bye-bye. So sad, too bad, you're dropped down to Tier Two. The system ensured high-quality play throughout the campaign. Even teams with losing records fought like mad to stay off the bottom.

On the blue playing field, players worked in position-specific groups. Near the orange end zone, the offensive line ran through drills.

In the black end zone, John Tweedy led the defense through drills. Human and Quyth Warrior linebackers, Sklorno defensive backs, HeavyG defensive ends and Ki defensive tackles ran through blitz schemes and defensive rotations.

The Ki. Quentin had once thought of the Ki as nightmares. Well, they *were* nightmarish, to be sure — thick, twelve-foot-long, tubular bodies bent at the middle, half that length staying parallel to the ground, half rising up to support four muscular, multi-jointed arms and a horrific head. Five equidistant eyes let the Ki see in all directions at once. Below that ring of eyes, the mouth of six, triangular lips that peeled back from six black, triangular teeth. Above the eyes, the species' unique, dreadlock-like cluster of vocal tubes. Three pairs of legs supported bodies that ranged from just over 500 pounds to just under 700. Skin tones ranged from deep reddish-black to brownish-orange, all of it embedded with enamel dots that made the creatures gleam in the sunlight.

Chirps and squeals drew Quentin's attention back to the middle of the field. His receivers waited at the 50-yard line. He laughed and shook his head at the exuberant Sklorno. They jumped, shook and even fainted as he approached. While it might be uncomfortable to be thought of as a deity, it was also damn funny to watch the reaction from his "followers."

Hawick, his number-one receiver; Milford, his number-two who had been a rookie alongside him back in the seemingly distant Tier Two season of 2682; Halawa, third receiver and last year's rookie standout. Halawa was just a hair bigger than her twin sister — defensive back Wahiawa — which made Halawa the biggest Sklorno on the team. The veterans Mezquitic and Richfield rounded out his receiving corps.

If Gredok signed both Cheboygan and Tara the Freak, where would they fall on the depth chart? Would Cheboygan be able to challenge Mezquitic for the number-four spot? Would Tara? Richfield's spot was safe because of her kick-return ability, but the addition of two rookies meant the Krakens had *seven* receivers. Someone would be bumped down to the practice squad or cut from the team altogether. For his receivers, that meant every pass in practice counted. He, Hokor and Don Pine would be watching.

"Ladies," Quentin said when he reached midfield. "Did you all have a good off-season?"

Hawick shook, but maintained her composure. Halawa started running in circles. Milford hopped in place, each light leap taking her ten feet into the air. "Quentinbarnes the holy one welcome home welcome!"

"Milford," he said. "Do anything interesting in your time off?"

"Oh yes*yes*! Stockbridge and I went on a missionary mission to spread the word of the Church of Quentinbarnes!"

Quentin's smile faded. "You what?"

"Spreading the gospel!" Milford jumped a little bit higher. "Converting the unconverted to the gospel of Quentin Barnes!"

"Didn't know I had a gospel." Every time he thought he was comfortable with his holy position, the Sklorno did something to remind him he was not. His starting receiver and backup cornerback were also his missionaries? "And, uh, how many, uh, *converts* did you get?"

"Three hundred, forty two thousand, one hundred and twelve," Milford said. She stopped jumping. "Was that not enough? Have I failed you, oh Quentin Barnes?"

"No! No, that's … that's fine."

Three-hundred *thousand* converts? To his "church," something he didn't acknowledge in any way? It hurt to even think about it. He didn't *want* to think about it. Fortunately, he knew one thing that would block out all other thoughts.

"Line up, ladies. Let's do our favorite, out-patterns to the right."

The Sklorno receivers squealed with joy, happy to get a few passes in before the tight ends and running backs came out to practice. Quentin grabbed a ball off a rack. He bent in a fake-snap position. He looked to his right, at Hawick, who was first in the line of quivering Sklorno.

"Hut-*hut!*"

He slapped the ball in his hands to simulate the snap, brought the ball up to his left ear as he dropped back three steps. His eyes followed Hawick as she shot off the line and made her cut. By the time the ball left his hands, Quentin no longer had thoughts of his church, Warburg, Becca or anything else that might distract him.

He thought of nothing but football and his soul swelled with his own form of rapturous joy.

THE LAST TIME QUENTIN HAD BEEN in this place, he'd still been shaking from a suicide bomb that had ravaged the Krakens' victory parade. And that day? That day seemed safer than this.

Gredok's private chamber was on the top floor of the Krakens building. Priceless paintings and sculptures lined the circular walls, each lit up by its own small spotlight, illuminated like the treasures that they were. In front of Quentin, the ten-foot high, white marble pillar that held Gredok the Splithead. Gredok sat in his cushy, black throne, looking down at Quentin and Danny Lundy.

"Gredok, my client has been treated like a serf, a servant, a slave."

"A *slave?*" Gredok said. "In what culture do *slaves* earn one-point-two megacredits a year?"

Quentin stood quietly, watching the drama play out. Both Yitzhak and Pine had told him to keep his mouth shut, to let his agent do the talking. Quentin had never worked with an agent. He had, however, worked with Gredok the Splithead, vicious crime boss, sentient capable of ordering your death, team owner that Quentin had tricked into traveling to OS1 to sign Ju Tweedy. There were few ideas worse than making Gredok angry, yet that seemed to be Danny's specific goal.

"Slavery takes many forms," Danny said. "For what you pay your starting quarterback, you might as well make him a chained-up chew toy for a pet fizzle-carp."

Gredok turned his single, softball-sized eye toward Quentin. "That can be arranged."

Gredok's fur fluffed up a bit, but there was something … *fake* about it. Quentin couldn't put his finger on it. His instincts told him that while Gredok was clearly angry, the crime boss was trying to play it up to a more intimidating level.

Had Quentin learned so much about Gredok he could spot when his boss was *acting?*

"Gredok, don't talk to my client," Danny said. "I'm the one doing the negotiating."

"Negotiating?" Gredok continued to stare at Quentin. "Is that what you call it, Dolphin? Because by your insolent tone, it seems more like you're looking for a way to wind up on some Sklorno's dinner plate. I hear Dolphin steaks are quite the prized delicacy."

"Just stop with the threats, Gredok," Danny said. "They're boring. You've already dealt with me for John Tweedy's contract and the contracts of Yitzhak Goldman, Vu-Ko and Bud-O. We worked those out, did we not?"

Gredok's fur fell flat again. He seemed calmer, more resigned to the process. "You're right, Dolphin. We've negotiated in good faith. So, let me begin. We will triple Quentin's salary and make a five-year commitment."

Quentin had a brief second to comprehend the numbers — 3.6 *megacredits* a *season?* — but only a brief second, because Danny's insulting squeal-giggle filled the rounded room and bounced off the priceless works of art.

"Three ... point ... six?" The Dolphin had to choke words out between intense blasts of laughter. His wet, rainbow-colored body shook. "*Three?* I ... and you ... *three?* ... and then ... "

Danny's mechanical legs seemed to give out on him. He fell to his side, shivering, squeals of laughter damn near piercing Quentin's ear drums.

Gredok's black fur fluffed. "Dolphin, I am not enjoying your insulting display."

"And you ... " Danny said. "And then ... *three?* ... oh, oh ... "

The laughter continued. Gredok's fur fluffed farther and this time Quentin could see it was no act.

"Barnes," Gredok said, "*this* is what you chose as your representation?"

Quentin looked down at the squealing, shivering Dolphin, then back up at Gredok atop his ridiculous white pedestal.

"Uh ... " Quentin said.

Danny's laughter suddenly died out. His silver legs flexed. He stood. "Quentin, don't answer that question. Gredok, your offer is pathetic, piteous and puny. We want twenty megacredits a season."

Quentin stopped breathing.

Gredok leaned forward. "Did you say ... *twenty?*"

"Twenty. Per season. For five seasons."

"For *five seasons?* That's a hundred million!"

"Oh," Danny said, as if he'd just remembered a trivial detail, "and fifty million of that guaranteed. Up front."

Gredok's eye flooded black. "*Fifty* up *front?*"

"Fifty up front," Danny said. "And performance bonuses. Would you like to repeat that as well?"

Gredok stared, his eye so black it looked like a gemstone, his fur so fluffed he looked bigger than Quentin had ever seen. If Danny's game was to anger Gredok, then the Dolphin had just scored a blowout victory.

"Ridiculous," Gredok said. "You're only trying to highball me because I tried to lowball you."

"Why, Gredok, I didn't know," Danny said. "I assumed your opening offer was a sincere gesture of Ionath's belief in my client."

"Your offer would make Quentin Barnes the highest-paid quarterback in the league. Higher than Frank Zimmer. Even higher than Rick Renaud. Zimmer has won championships. Renaud has put teams in the Galaxy Bowl."

"And Barnes is going to do *both*," Danny said.

"He's done *nothing* yet, Dolphin."

"Dragging your team out of Tier Two and keeping them in Tier One for a second season is nothing?"

"Those things are not the same as a playoff victory. Definitely not the same thing as a GFL title."

"Of course not," Danny said. "But Barnes is going to give *someone* playoff victories and a GFL title. If not the Krakens, then another team."

Danny let the words hang in the air. The room fell to a deathly silence.

Quentin swallowed, so loud he heard the noise echo off the priceless sculptures. Sure, he had thought himself a good manipulator — new to the game, but a student of the process, on his way to rivaling Gredok's skill. No matter how much Quentin learned about manipulation, however, he now understood he would always be a rank amateur compared to Danny Lundy.

"You dare," Gredok said. "You *dare* to threaten me with taking *my* quarterback to another franchise?"

Danny's legs extended. His big, streamlined body rose in the air until he was at eye level with Gredok. Quentin looked up at them both, a battle of wills taking place six feet above his head.

"Quentin Barnes is the real deal," Danny said. "You have a choice to pay him before he becomes the best quarterback in the league, or *after*. A hundred megacredits is the *before* price. Based on your fur-fluffing rage, I'm guessing you don't want to hear the *after* price."

Gredok stood in his little chair. "Get out! Get out, Dolphin, and take your unproven quarterback with you!"

"Quentin, let's go. We've given the Splithead plenty to think about."

Gredok stamped a tiny foot. "There is no thinking! Come back when your contract requests are reasonable!"

"The offer is on the table," Danny said. "If you won't take it, someone else will. You should know, Gredok, that I've already been contacted by the Mars Planets, the McMurdo Murderers, the Bartel Water Bugs and the To Pirates."

If Gredok had been faking rage before, he wasn't faking it anymore. Quentin saw the same quiet, dangerous calm Gredok had shown just before killing Mopuk the Sneaky.

"Teams are interested," Danny said. "Quentin will get the deal we want. It's up to you to decide if that deal is with Ionath. We'll be waiting to hear from you. Good day."

Danny lowered his legs and started walking out of the chamber. Quentin stood there, still looking up at the enraged Gredok. Was all of this a mistake? Three years ago, he couldn't have even *imagined* having 3.6 million. Should he just take that offer?

"Quentin!" Danny's voice, a squealing command that would have been understood even without the vocal modifier. "Time to leave. Come with me and do not talk to Gredok without me present until this negotiation is complete."

Gredok's pedipalp hands curled into shaking fists. "There is no negotiation! You get out of here, Lundy, and take that ungrateful *yakochat* of a quarterback with you! No one tells me how to run my organization!"

Quentin turned and quickly walked out of the chamber. He stayed quiet as Gredok's well-dressed guards led him and Danny to the elevator. The elevator doors closed.

Danny's left hand reached into a pocket hanging from his harness. He pulled out a small fish and popped it into his long mouth. "That went pretty well," he said after swallowing it down.

"What? Are you shucking *crazy*, Danny? I've never seen Gredok that mad and trust me, I've done things to make him mad. Are you trying to get me *killed*?"

"Relax, Human. I've seen him worse."

"Worse that *that*?"

"Oh, sure. You should have seen him when I negotiated for John Tweedy's last contract."

"But, Danny, maybe I should just take Gredok's offer. A *hundred* million? That's like … that's too much money."

Danny turned, sharply and suddenly. He again reached into his bag, pulled out a fish, then slapped Quentin across the face with it.

Quentin's right hand went to his right cheek. A bit of cold wetness clung there. "Did you just smack me in the face with a fish?"

"I did."

"Why did you just smack me in the face with a fish, Danny?"

Danny's legs rose up until his narrowing black eyes were level with Quentin's. In the elevator's close confines, Quentin once again realized the Dolphin's size.

"*Too much money*? Don't you *ever* say those words to me again. You promised we would do this my way. You're not backing out of that now, guy. This deal is *mine*, do you understand me? No one gets in the way of my deals, not even my client."

Quentin took a half-step back, the farthest he could go before his butt hit the elevator wall. He had signed an insane Dolphin as his agent.

"Yeah," Quentin said. "Sure, Danny, you handle the deal."

"Good," Danny said. His legs lowered. His eyes returned to their normal, rounded, friendly shape. "Trust me, Quentin, I'm acting in your best interests, guy. You'll be happy when this is done." Danny popped the face-slap fish into his mouth.

"But what if Gredok doesn't take the offer?"

"Then you play for another team next season. Let's go get some lunch, buddy. I'm in the mood for squid, that work for you?"

"Yeah," Quentin said, his heart instantly heavy at the thought of wearing anything other than the Orange and the Black. "Sure. Squid sounds fine."

QUENTIN SAT LOW in his seat, looking out the cab's window at the streets and sidewalks of Ionath City. The densely packed, mostly red, hexagonal buildings rolled by, most of them reaching some thirty stories high to almost touch up against the city's clear, protective dome. The view did nothing for Quentin, however, because he was worried.

"Choto, come on, tell me what's going on."

"I do not know, Quentin," Choto said. "All I know is that John Tweedy told me I had to get you to his apartment as soon as possible and to keep you safe."

"Why his apartment? If there's danger, why not the Krakens building?"

"Again, Quentin, I do not know. My job is to keep you safe, not to debate policy with John Tweedy."

Quentin turned away from the window to stare at the eye of his linebacker/bodyguard. Choto's baseball-sized eye remained mostly clear, but three colors — green and yellow and dark blue — cast thin swirls across his cornea. Yellow was the color of excitement, while green usually revealed stress or anxiety. The colors weren't exact matches with a specific emotion, they weren't always consistent, but they did give insight into a Quyth Warrior's state of mind. Like most Warriors, Choto loved the excitement of danger and loved a good fight, so the yellow made sense. Quentin's safety was Choto's responsibility, a task assigned by none other than Gredok the Splithead. Gredok was Choto's *Shamakath*, his Leader. Failing a Leader was unforgivable in the Quyth culture, so being stressed that Quentin might get hurt, might get killed — that correlated with the green swirls.

But blue? Blue, as far as Quentin could tell, was the color of *betrayal*. Quentin had never before seen Choto's eyes carry the color blue. Was this some kind of trap? Had Choto been bought off by one of Quentin's newfound enemies? Anna Villani, Gloria Ogawa, the Zoroastrian Guild, maybe even someone from the To Pirates who wanted payback for Quentin not throwing games during the Tier Two season? Was Choto in league with any of them?

No. Quentin would not let himself suspect Choto the Bright. Choto had gone to OS1 with Quentin to rescue Ju Tweedy from Anna Villani, had fought side-by-side in the brawl at Chucky Chong's League-Style House of Chow. That act could have even put Choto's family — who lived on OS1, the planetoid controlled by Villani's syndicate — in grave danger. Choto had earned the benefit of the doubt. Quentin would put his fears aside and trust his teammate.

"We're here," Choto said.

Quentin snapped back to reality. The cab pulled up in front of John Tweedy's building. Choto got out first, looked up and down the street, scanning for danger. It reminded Quentin of a time one year earlier, following the victory parade bombing that had killed fifteen sentients. Back then, Quentin hadn't been allowed to go anywhere alone.

Choto gestured for Quentin to step out. He did. The cab merged back into ring-road's traffic. The scene looked just the same as it had for Quentin's first visit to John Tweedy's apartment. Two blue-uniformed Ki guards stood on either side of the building's doors, blue helmets hiding their five equidistant eyes. Between them, in the open door, stood a Quyth Worker.

"Elder Barnes!" the worker called out. "I am Pizat the Servitous, do you remember me?"

"Sure," Quentin said as he and Choto walked through the doors. "Yeah, I remember you."

"Oh, I am *flattered*, Elder Barnes. That one of such importance and stature as you would recall a brief meeting with the lowly likes of me? It is truly a memorable day."

When it came to kissing ass, no sentient in the galaxy could match a Quyth Worker.

"Pizat, is John expecting me?"

"Oh, *yes*, Elder Barnes! You and Choto should head right up. Mister Tweedy did say it was urgent and that speed was of the essence."

Pizat led them to the elevator. Quentin took in the lobby's finery. It was not on the level of Gredok's private chamber, but still a grand display of wealth. John lived here, as did Don Pine. Pine, who had never invited Quentin up for a beer, or just to hang out. Outside of anything football related, Pine kept his distance.

Quentin and Choto took the elevator up. When it opened, John was waiting. He looked more wide-eyed, more hyper than usual — and his usual state was *very* wide-eyed, *very* hyper.

"Q! Wow, are you okay?" BETTER SAFE THAN SCARY scrolled across his face.

"Uh … yeah. I'm fine."

"You *sure*?"

"Uh … John, you saw me at practice earlier today."

John's eyes widened further and he nodded, as if he'd forgotten about practice until this moment. "Well, you never know, Q. We had to keep things secret."

"John, what's going on? Choto wouldn't tell me anything."

John shook his head. "He couldn't. Once you're inside, I'll fill you in. Come on, let's get out of the hall."

Quentin followed John into suite 15-B. The short entryway led to the living room that Quentin knew was packed full of football memorabilia from John's 11-season career with teams such as

Fionas University, the Pittsburgh Steelers and the Thomas 3 Lions. This time, however, the room was dark, almost pitch black.

"John, something wrong with your lights?"

"Oh, right. Let me get that for you, Q."

Quentin expected to see the room's lights turn on, but instead, he saw a bunch of tiny flames spring to life in the center of the room.

Candles, their dim light illuminating the shapes of at least a dozen sentients.

"*Surprise!*" the combined voices called out. Quentin took a step back. The normal lights flared on, revealing a room packed full of Krakens players and staff. Virak the Mean, Crazy George Starcher, Yassoud Murphy, Arioch Morningstar, Ju Tweedy, the massive form of Michael Kimberlin and the even more massive Ki linemen.

In the center of the room, standing behind an orange and black cake decorated with the Krakens' logo, stood the tiny form of Ma Tweedy. She wore an orange and black Krakens jacket that matched the big cake.

"Hello, Quentin," she said. "We meet at last."

"Ma Tweedy? What are you doing in Ionath City?"

"I moved," she said. "Jonathan and Julius felt it wasn't safe for me on Orbital Station One, not with that evil tramp Anna Villani angry at my Julius."

"Ma," Ju said, "don't use my real name."

"*Shut it*," she snapped. "This day isn't about you, Julius, so be quiet."

Ju hung his head. "Yes, Ma."

"Well, nice to meet you in person," Quentin said. "What's this cake all about?"

Ma Tweedy shook her head. Her bony shoulders were perpetually pulled up almost to her ears and they moved in time with her head. "Honestly, Quentin, you're a wonderful boy, but I'd hoped Jonathan and Julius would find someone a little smarter to hang out with. All of these sentients are here for your *birthday*."

"My ... birthday?" What was going on? He knew what birthdays were, of course, had been to a few celebrations, but ...

"Q," John said. "Don't disappoint Ma. Blow out the candles."

"Yeah," Ju said. "*Don't* disappoint Ma." Ju looked quite a bit like his brother John, only slightly bigger and slightly meaner. Ju wore fine clothes and kept his black hair stylish, while John seemed more at home in jeans and a sweatshirt.

"Quentin," she said, "what's the matter?" She was such a tiny Human, so small it made one wonder how she could have given birth to a pair of professional football players. Everyone was staring at him. Smiles were fading. All of this felt so strange. "Uh, I … I didn't know it was my birthday. How did you guys know?"

Ma Tweedy shook her head again. "Honey, now you're just being stupid. We looked in the Krakens program. You act like you've never seen a birthday cake before."

"Sure I have," Quentin said. "Just not for me."

No one spoke. Quentin felt very small. Very weird. He'd ruined this. His throat felt tight. His eyes stung a little. He wanted to leave, wanted to be alone back in his room in the Krakens building, or — even better — up in his yacht.

Ma Tweedy walked out from behind the table. She wasn't that much taller than Hokor the Hookchest or Commissioner Froese. She stopped in front of him, looked up at him.

"Quentin, kneel down here for just a minute, honey."

He did. She put her arms around his neck and hugged him. He felt his body stiffen, but she ignored it.

"It's your birthday," she whispered in his ear so that only he could hear. "I think I know how strange this is for you. You don't know how to handle this, but all of these sentients are here because they love you. We can talk about it later if you want, but for now, stop acting like an embarrassing idiot and blow out the damn candles."

She kissed his temple, then gave him a light slap on his left cheek. The look in her eyes made it clear he had no choice but to do what she said.

He blinked a few times. The strange feeling started to evaporate. So what if it was the first birthday party he'd ever had? Ma Tweedy was right — it was *his* party. And that cake looked delicious.

Quentin looked at all the faces. He realized he was looking for one in particular, but didn't find it — Becca wasn't there. Oh well, her loss.

Quentin picked up the knife sitting next to the cake. "Do I eat the first piece?"

"No, honey," Ma Tweedy said. "You give cake to the guests. Cut the right side first. I made that end special for your little Ki friends. And cut slowly, I don't want the shushulik juice to get all over my piece."

I'M GONNA BE SICK! scrolled across John's face. "Aw, ma! You put those gross things in the cake?"

"Jonathan, *shut it!* The left side of the cake is chocolate. But even if there is some shushulik juice on your piece, you'll eat it and you'll *like* it, understand me?"

John hung his head. "Yes, Ma."

Quentin reached out with the knife, but George Starcher waved at him to stop.

"Candles first," George said. No paint on his face this time. George looked surprisingly normal. "You have to blow 'em out, Quentin. And make a wish when you do."

Quentin lowered the knife. He absently counted the flickering flames — twenty of them. He lowered his head.

"I wish for a GFL championship," he said. He smiled at the cheers of his teammates as he blew out the candles.

THE TEAM JOGGED into the locker room. Despite a grueling practice that included running and conditioning, all the players felt the excitement of the new season. Just six days in and they could already see the difference from last year. The Krakens' passing game would be just as good as the running game and the running game was already among the best in the league.

They could all *feel* it, feel the tug of destiny.

Starcher continued to excel at tight end. No one could catch like him. His backup, Yotaro Kobayasho, hadn't improved much during the off-season. Quentin might not have noticed Kobayasho's lack of development were it not for Rick Warburg. Warburg was a different player, a *better* player — quicker, bigger, even a touch faster. He ran precise routes. He caught everything thrown his way. There were three weeks of preseason left, however; only time would tell if Warburg's improvement was permanent.

Quentin walked to his locker. There, waiting for him, was Messal the Efficient.

Messal held a messageboard that trembled in his shaking pedipalp hands.

Oh, for crying out loud, what could it be this time? Had he been fined again? "Messal. You okay?"

"Elder Barnes, I am not the creator of this news. I assure you!"

"Relax, big guy, I'm not going to hurt you."

"Do you promise?"

Quentin sighed. "I'm not the same person I used to be, Messal. You're just the messenger. Let me have it."

Messal's eye swirled with green. He handed over the messageboard.

Quentin read and as he did, his stomach dropped to somewhere just north of his ankles.

To: Quentin Barnes

Subject: Disciplinary meeting regarding illegal contact
          with another franchise

Our investigators have learned that during the 2682 Tier Two season, you met with a representative of the To Pirates on at least two occasions. They have also learned that the subject matter of these meetings may have been discussions about intentionally losing games in order to prevent the Krakens from reaching Tier One.

GFL rules stipulate that any and all meetings with other franchises must be announced to the league prior to the meeting, so that the league has the option of providing a representative. The fact that you did not announce these meetings means you are in violation of league rules and are subject to potential fines, suspension or permanent dismissal from the league.

My ship is en route to Ionath City air space. A shuttle will land at the Krakens building in the second week of the preseason. A specific meeting time will be arranged then. The shuttle will bring you to my ship. We will discuss possible disciplinary action.

          Sincerely,
          Commissioner Rob Froese

Cc: Gredok the Splithead

• • •

QUENTIN LOWERED THE MESSAGEBOARD. He focused on his promise not to hurt the frightened Quyth Worker.

"Messal, this is bad, isn't it?"

Messal's eye flooded a pure, solid green. "It gets worse, Elder Barnes. Gredok the Splithead would like to see you. I am to take you to his chamber. Immediately."

Messal was right — that *was* worse. "I suppose I should skip a shower?"

"Gredok the Splithead emphasized the word *immediately*, Elder Barnes."

Quentin could demand the presence of Danny Lundy. But this wasn't a contract issue and waiting for the Dolphin would serve only to further enrage Gredok.

Quentin pulled off his armor, leaving him clothed in only a sweaty Kool Suit and football shoes. He wasn't mad at Messal anymore. In fact, Quentin wondered if his own eyes were flooding green.

"Lead the way, Messal."

WHEN HE WAS ELEVEN years old, Quentin had been caught stealing food. He had broken into a restaurant during the night, cracking the atmosphere seal on a window and sliding his scrawny, ill-fed body through the narrow opening.

If he had just taken the chicken and ran, he might have made it. But he hadn't eaten in two days. Hunger pinched his stomach, his chest, made him feel the fabric of his pants sliding across his skin when he walked, made him feel his cheeks stretch when he talked. Hunger *hurt*.

When he opened the walk-in refrigerator, that hunger overwhelmed him. He grabbed a sauce-smeared chicken breast and tore into it, biting off a too-large chunk. *So good, so good!* He barely even chewed before he swallowed. Even through his hunger, through his base instincts, a little clock was ticking inside his head. Later in life, that little clock would serve him well on the football field, giving him an innate ability to sense how much time he had before linemen closed in on him and took off his head. As a kid, however, he didn't know how to listen to that clock, didn't know what it meant.

When the lights flicked on, *then* he knew what it meant, but it was too late.

He stood there, frozen in the light just like a baby roundbug, barbecue sauce smearing his mouth, hands holding the chicken so tight that drops of grease beaded up on his knuckles and fell to the floor.

The restaurant owner, standing there, looking at him.

Caught.

Caught stealing food, just like his brother, Quincy.

Quincy, who had been hung in the town square.

"Put it down," the man said.

Quentin opened both sauce-coated hands. The torn chicken breast fell to the floor with a *splat*. He tried to swallow ... and could not. He couldn't breathe. His stomach churned with a new sensation — even at eleven years old, he'd seen enough death to know what awaited him if this larger, older, well-fed man called the cops.

The man looked Quentin up and down, slowly, eyes lingering on skinny legs, thin arms, the gaunt face. Quentin knew that expression, the same one some of the Deacons wore when they saw him in the street. The slow look that the Deacons gave the other boys, the boys who weren't as fast as Quentin and couldn't get away. Or, worse, the boys who were sent to the Deacons by their parents.

So, it wasn't just the prospect of hanging that Quentin had to fear.

As Quentin's mind scrambled for strategy, wondering if he should punch the man in the throat, or maybe try and trip him or hit his head with the door, the man spoke again.

"Give me a reason I shouldn't turn you in, boy."

Quentin started to talk, then choked. He coughed. The meat

stuck in his throat. Thoughts of attacking the older man vanished, replaced by the singular, blank concept that he couldn't breathe.

Unknown moments later, Quentin felt himself grabbed and roughly turned. A big hand hit him in the middle of the back. Still, breath wouldn't come. Quincy Barnes died by hanging — his little brother Quentin would die by chicken.

The hand hit a second time. A glob of greasy food shot out of his mouth and landed on the floor. Air rushed through his ragged throat. Water filled his eyes. He felt himself pulled by the arm. The man's hand, so *strong!*

Something hit the back of his legs. He dropped, found himself sitting in a wooden chair. Quentin looked up to see the restaurant owner staring down, not quite as angry as before.

"How old are you, boy? Sixteen?"

"Eleven," Quentin said.

The man's eyes widened. "You lie."

Quentin shook his head. "No, Elder. I'm just big for my age."

"Yes, but … *eleven*? You're taller than my son and he's seventeen."

Quentin didn't know what to say, so he shrugged.

"So tall," the man said. "And yet, you're skinnier than my daughter who makes herself throw up."

"She what?"

"Makes herself throw up."

Quentin blinked. "You mean, like … throw up *food*?"

The man nodded.

The thought filled Quentin with rage. Someone eating food, then throwing it up? On *purpose*? "Now *you* lie, Elder."

The man's eyes narrowed, then he laughed. "This makes you angry? A girl eating my delicious food, then wasting it?"

Quentin nodded.

The man stared at Quentin for a few moments more, eyes again moving up and down. Quentin's skin crawled, but only for a moment. The man wasn't looking at Quentin like the Deacons did. This was different.

"You are so thin," the man said. "Why?"

Was this some kind of a trick question? "I don't get to eat much. I ... I was robbed last week. I lost my wages."

"Where are your parents?"

Quentin shrugged.

The man nodded. "You work in the mines? You are an orphan?"

Quentin said nothing. If the man knew he was an orphan, he could send Quentin right to jail for stealing food.

Jail tonight, then the gallows tomorrow.

"You stay here," the man said. "I know your face now. If you run, I will send the police after you, do you understand?" The man walked out of the room.

That clutching feeling of fear again spread through Quentin's chest and belly. What would this man make him do? Quentin thought about running, going back out the window, but where would he go? The man was right — Quentin's height already drew too much attention. The police would have no trouble tracking down such a tall, skinny boy.

The man returned. He carried something.

A plate and a glass.

He put the plate down in front of Quentin. Three chicken legs, slightly charred, gleaming with barbecue sauce, filling the room with a mind-numbing, spicy odor. And in the glass ... *milk*.

"You broke my window," the man said. "You stole my property. I have power over you now, you understand this?"

Quentin kept staring at the chicken. He couldn't look away. "Yes, Elder."

"You will call me Mister Sam," the man said. "I am not part of that church. You will not address me as *elder* again, understand?"

Quentin nodded, wondering if the drool in his mouth would suddenly spill out like a fire hose.

"Good," Mister Sam said. "Tomorrow, when you finish your work in the mines, you will come to me. I am going to teach you a lesson, orphan. You are going to work two jobs for the next year. I do not care that you are only eleven. You will *work* for me or I will turn you in. Do you agree to this deal?"

Quentin nodded. He had no choice.

"Good," Mister Sam said. "You begin work tonight, fixing my window. But every day, before you begin work for me, you will eat. I will not be embarrassed by having a skinny boy working in my restaurant. What would people think if they saw you? They would think that my food was no good."

Mister Sam reached into his pocket and pulled out a fork. He placed it on the table next to the plate.

"You don't need a knife," he said. "It is that moist, you see. It falls off the bone because I marinate it for days and slow-cook it, unlike the excuses that call themselves *chefs* in this neighborhood. Now, eat."

Quentin's hand shot out so fast that Mister Sam took a step back. Quentin attacked the chicken legs. The milk seemed to vanish on its own, a full glass one second, empty the next. Before Quentin finished the last bite, the glass was full again and there was a second plate — this time, with two burger patties and meat-crusted ribs.

"Is it good?" Mister Sam said. "You like?"

"Best food ever," Quentin said with a full mouth. "*Eh*-ver."

Quentin remembered seeing Mister Sam smile for the first time. It would not be the last.

FOR THE NEXT FIVE YEARS, Mister Sam fed Quentin every day, turning a freakishly skinny boy into a seven-foot warhorse weighing nearly four hundred pounds. But for all the good things Mister Sam did, Quentin never forgot that feeling of terror the first time he laid eyes on the man. He never forgot what it was like to look at someone who could decide if you lived or died.

As Quentin looked up at Gredok the Splithead sitting atop his white pillar, he knew that feeling once again.

"This memo," Gredok said. "This … piece of *information* that Commissioner Froese sent you. Is it true?"

The voice, so cold, so calm. Sometimes, Gredok yelled. But Quentin had learned that when the Quyth Leader was *really* angry,

angry enough to kill, he spoke in a quiet voice that seemed to suck hope out of the air and cast it down into the sewers.

"Gredok, listen. It's not what you think, I—"

"I did not ask for explanations," Gredok said. "I asked — Is. It. *True?* Did you meet with that Creterakian piece of garbage called Maygon?"

Quentin could barely breathe. He felt the cool air on his face, felt the room lights playing off his skin.

"Yes, sir," he said. "Maygon approached me."

"And you did not bother to tell me. I'm going to ask you *why* you did not bother to tell me, Barnes. I suggest you strongly consider giving me the truth. At this point in our relationship, I feel you should truly understand the depth of my disappointment. Any further ... *lack* ... of communication will not go well for you."

Gredok stared down from his perch, his single eye six feet above Quentin's face. Quentin wanted to look away, but he forced himself to maintain eye contact. Gredok had all the power, true, but even now Quentin Barnes would not show weakness.

"I didn't tell you because I didn't want to cause problems," Quentin said. "Maygon approached me. I didn't seek him out. I didn't contact the To Pirates."

"You didn't contact them, but you wish to play for them."

Quentin shook his head. "No, Shama ... I mean, Gredok. Well, yes, I wanted to play for them before, when I was a kid, but I'm a Kraken now."

"You *don't* want to play for the To Pirates?"

Quentin shook his head again.

Gredok leaned forward, stared down. "So, when you *did* want to play for the Pirates, you didn't contact them. And now that you do *not* want to play for them, you *have* contacted them. I'm sure you can understand my confusion, Barnes."

Danny Lundy. Quentin felt his fear ratchet up another notch. Danny had already made contact with the Pirates. The agent couldn't officially take an offer from another Tier One team, but he could begin a dialogue, show that Quentin was as interested in the Pirates as the Pirates were in him.

"That's different," Quentin said. "I know how it must look, Gredok, but—"

"You have no idea how it looks, Human. You see a football field, a football team and your own selfish desires. You do not see the honor game, the game of reputation. Of positioning. Of *power*. Kirani Kollok wants *my* quarterback. Kirani Kollok has been courting you before you even went to the *Combine*. You talked to his representative behind my back and did not tell me. Now your agent is talking to Kollok? I will tell you how this looks, Barnes. It makes me look like a fool. *You* are making me look like a fool."

Quentin could maintain eye contact no more. Gredok was right. From an owner's perspective, Gredok looked like an idiot.

"I apologize," Quentin said. "Maygon told me that if anyone found out I was talking to him, I could have been suspended. I thought if I kept quiet about it, it would go away."

"In my line of work, things do not *go away* on their own, Barnes. If you want something to go away, you have to *make* it go away."

Quentin looked up, then nodded.

Gredok sat back. "And what did Maygon tell you?"

The cat was out of the bag. There was no point in skirting around the edges anymore. "It was my rookie season. Maygon said Kirani Kollok wanted to give me a three-year contract. He said that if I made sure the Krakens stayed in Tier Two, he would make me a To Pirate."

Gredok stared. His eyelid closed. Quentin waited, still not knowing what to say.

The eye opened. "He wanted you to throw games?"

Quentin nodded.

"But you did not," Gredok said. "You were a fool to keep this from me, Barnes, but I am not so blinded by anger I can't see the truth. Although you played horribly at times in your rookie season, we won games. We did advance to Tier One. What is the Human phrase? Oh yes ... you played your ass off. But, if you *ever* intentionally played poorly to make my franchise lose, now is your chance to tell me. If you do not tell me now and I find out the truth later, the last thing you see will be radioactive dirt raining down to bury you in your shallow grave."

Gredok leaned forward, leaned down. "Did you throw games, Barnes? Did you *ever* not give me your all?"

Quentin let out a breath he'd unknowingly held in. He was on familiar ground once again. "You already know the answer. I play to win. Every snap, every pass, every run."

Gredok blinked, then leaned back. "I believe that you did not throw games. However, that does not change the fact that you have put me in a humiliating situation. I have been *summoned* by that red-toothed, officious bastard Froese. Me — *summoned*. You and I will travel to his ship tomorrow and watch him pass judgment like *he* is the *Shamakath* and I am the vassal. I must suffer this because of what *you* did. Therefore, this is your fault."

Quentin nodded. Gredok was right.

"It could be worse," Gredok said. "The rest of the league could know about it. As long as we keep this information between us, the Commissioner and the To Pirates, I can live with this loss of face. But if it were to become public ..."

Gredok's voice trailed off, inviting Quentin to fill the silence.

"I sure as hell won't tell anyone," Quentin said. "I've learned my lesson, boss."

"You won't tell that Human reporter, Yolanda Davenport?"

"Why would I tell her?"

"The rumor is that she's working on a cover story featuring you. I suggest you be very careful when you speak with her. Davenport has proven to be resourceful in her ways of gathering information."

"Meaning what?"

"Meaning don't let your adolescent hormones drive your decisions, Barnes. I have seen what an attractive female face can do to you hatchling Humans."

Quentin waited. He didn't want to say anything at all.

"Commissioner Froese sent me another memo," Gredok said. "He wants to talk to Ju as well. It seems the murder of Grace McDermot has caught up with us."

How easy it was to forget that deadly day, when Quentin, John, Rebecca, Choto, Mum-O-Killowe and Sho-Do-Thikit had risked their lives during a trip to Orbital Station One to save Ju. Having Ju around now seemed so normal, like he'd always been part of the Krakens.

"But Ju didn't kill her. Gredok, you heard Anna Villani."

"I know that. *Truth* does not matter here, Barnes. *Proof* does and we have none of it. I am not ready to let Froese talk to Ju. I will arrange something so that Ju can not attend. Ju is facing criminal charges as opposed to breaking a GFL regulation. Froese doesn't have the same leeway he has with you, for breaking the rules pertaining to contract talks with another team. If he schedules a meeting and you miss it, he can suspend you for that. I can shelter Ju a while longer, but you and I must talk to Froese."

Gredok did not sound like his usual, confident self.

"And what can happen at this meeting?"

"Froese is the emperor of the little empire known as the GFL, Barnes. He can suspend you for a game. Possibly even for the season."

Gredok's tone, his body language — both so subtle they were barely recognizable, but those tells showed Quentin that Gredok had no power in this situation and that he hated that fact. Quentin was getting better at reading his boss.

"I have more bad news," Gredok said. "We did not get all of the rookies. I was able to sign Cheboygan, Rich Palmer and Tim Crawford." Black wisped over Gredok's cornea. "Regat the Unobtrusive will play for the Yall Criminals. Gladwin and Cooperstown signed with Wabash. Gloria Ogawa out-bid me, damn her eye. But I will get us defensive backs in free agency, I assure you."

Quentin nodded. Gredok had been beaten out for three players. That would not sit well with the control-obsessed Quyth Leader, especially when he'd lost two of those players to Ogawa, his nemesis.

"And Tara the Freak?" Quentin said.

Gredok waved a pedipalp as if the question didn't even merit his time. "Of course. No one else wanted your misshapen mutant."

"Thank you for trusting me on this one, Gredok. Tara will pay dividends, I promise."

"*Trust* is not a word I think you should discuss with me for a long time, Barnes. Now leave. I grow weary of dealing with your impossible level of wasted intellect."

Another sigh escaped Quentin's chest. That was a tell of his, but he didn't care. He'd live to play another day. Quentin turned and walked out of the office.

8

PRESEASON WEEK TWO: JANUARY 8 – 14, 2684

FOR THE SECOND WEEK OF PRESEASON, the entire team moved up to the *Touchback*. Quentin had insisted. Two practices a day, plus an evening conditioning session. Some of the Humans and HeavyG complained, defensive end Alexsandar Michnik the loudest, but Quentin didn't give anyone an option.

Winning a title had been a worthy goal, but had seemed somehow theoretical. Not anymore. Everyone knew the Krakens could take it all — if they worked hard enough, and they got a little lucky.

So once again, the *Touchback* rang with the sounds of practice and team life. Only veterans so far. Invited free agents would arrive tomorrow to try out for the team. Rookies arrived in three days.

With familiar teammates onboard, Quentin decided to address something he'd left undone during the previous season. Even with John Tweedy and Don Pine along for support, he wasn't looking forward to it.

Last season, Quentin had dined with his Ki offensive linemen. He would have called the experience several things, including *crazy*, *scarring* and possibly *mentally shattering*.

One word he would never have used, however, was *civilized*.

And yet as Quentin looked at the six Ki *defensive* players tearing into an animal that was almost as big as they were, the offensive linemens' feast seemed like proper etiquette by comparison.

"High One," Quentin said. "Don, is it always like this?"

John Tweedy pulled off his shirt and tossed it aside. "Don't wanna get it bloody," he said. IF YOU EAT IT, SOMEONE HAS TO KILL IT flashed across his chest in big red letters. He punched Quentin in the shoulder. "Good times down on the farm, Q! You're gonna *love* it!"

The walk here had seemed so familiar. Like the offensive linemen, the defensive players had their own forested chamber inside the *Touchback*. No hallways, no rooms, just an open space filled with red moss, tightly coiled, green ground cover plants, waist-high bushes with broad, yellow leaves and brown vines that reached up and spread across the ceiling. More red moss hung down from the dense vines, making the artificial surfaces of the ship all but vanish from sight.

The main difference, however, couldn't be missed. The offensive linemen had a stone table with a blood trough lining the edges. The defense? Their "dinner table" was a clear patch of dirt.

A clear patch of black-stained, *bloody* dirt.

The yellowish bones of strange, alien animals lined the clear patch, remnants of meals gone by. And in the center of that death-circle? Five hundred pounds of a beast Quentin instantly wished he had never seen.

The Ki defenders swarmed on the creature. Mum-O-Killowe and Mai-An-Inkole weighed it down with their bulk. Per-Ah-Yet pinned it with his multi-jointed arms. Chat-E-Riret and Wan-A-Tagol bit down with mouths full of triangular teeth. Black blood flew, as did stray bits of flesh.

The prey creature screamed and screamed.

John pumped his left fist. "Lookit him squirm! You got lucky, Q. The more they fight, the better they taste!" John ran forward and dove onto the creature, managing one big bite before the slick blood made him slide off the animal and onto the clearing's dirt.

Quentin stared at the scrambling, bloody, spindly mess fighting for its life. *Stay still*, he thought to his feet. *Don't you dare run. Stay still, we have to do this.*

Yes, he was talking to his feet. Every atom of his body wanted to get the hell out of this living nightmare.

Don's hand gripped his shoulder. "Try to relax, Quentin. Just follow John's lead. He loves it."

"That's because John is crazy."

"True," Don said. "Stay calm. This will be over before you know it."

Blood flew. The screams slowed.

"But I'll remember it, won't I?"

Don nodded slowly. "Yes. You'll remember every nasty, disgusting, disturbing moment of it."

"But I'll get used to it, right? It won't be so bad next year. *Right?*"

Don smiled. "Do you want me to lie to you?"

"Please."

"Kid, it won't be so bad next year."

"Glad to hear it."

Black blood jetted out in a misty cloud, splattering smelly droplets on Quentin's face.

"Kid," Don said, "do you have your happy place?"

"My happy place isn't happy enough for this."

"You're right. But you got to do it anyway."

Quentin shook his head. "No. No way, I can't."

Don did what Don always did — he held up his right hand, showing off the GFL Championship rings on his ring and index finger. He waggled them. Gold and jewels reflected the light.

Quentin looked at them as he always did — with raw envy and lust. But it wasn't enough, not this time.

"I need more," he said. "Let me wear one."

Don's head snapped away from the grotesque scene of the Ki and John Tweedy feasting on the still-living monstrosity. At first, Don seemed angry, but that quickly faded. He understood. He pulled the ring off his index finger and handed it over.

Quentin slid it on his ring finger, noting that it fit perfectly even though he was bigger than Don Pine. Quentin held the hand in front of his face, palm-out, ignoring the black blood-strands crisscrossing his skin.

A GFL Championship ring.

Red ruby, sparkling.

Gold glowing with promise.

On *his* hand.

He wanted nothing more than this. He would give anything, *do* anything, to attain it.

Quentin nodded, took a deep breath. He took off the ring and handed it back.

Don took it. "That what you needed?"

"Yep," Quentin said. "Let's eat."

The two quarterbacks stepped forward.

QUENTIN TORE OFF his helmet, whipped it in a long arc and smashed it into the blue turf.

"Dammit, Pareless, that's the hardest you can run? Ma Tweedy can sprint faster than you!"

The fullback had his hands on his knees, head down, shoulder pads lurching rhythmically as his chest drew in sucking breaths. The rest of the team stretched across the black end zone's goal line, all in various stages of exhaustion. Some of them weren't even standing — they'd fallen to the ground or were off to the side, vomiting.

Quentin was damn tired as well — fifty 50-yard sprints after a full practice will do that to you — but he wouldn't show it to his team. Hokor floated in his cart, saying nothing. He seemed quite content to let someone else do the yelling for a change.

Only the Sklorno looked ready for more. But even they showed signs of fatigue, their abdomens swelling and shrinking as they drew in air to fuel their exhausted muscles.

Pareless didn't say anything, didn't even pick up his head. Quentin walked up to him, leaned down to scream at the older man.

"Hey, grampa! I'm talking to you! Imagine it's the fourth quarter, we're down by six, Becca is hurt, you have to block for me so we can win the shucking game. Dig *deep*, man. Stand up."

Tom straightened, hands on hips, eyes scrunched. "My ankle … killing me. I'm … trying … Q."

"There is no *try*!" Quentin screamed at the entire team. "We're too soft! We have to toughen up if we're going to make the playoffs."

Tom bent forward again, then threw up. Vomit dripped from his facemask in long strings.

Quentin threw his hands in the air. "I don't care if you *all* puke. Get back on the line! Five more sprints!"

"We've never run this hard," said a deep voice. Quentin turned to see defensive end Ibrahim Khomeni — all six-foot-ten, 525 pounds of him — step out of the line. "You're pushing too hard, Barnes."

"Too hard? *Too hard*? Do you think the Wabash Wolfpack is sitting on their asses right now?"

Khomeni gestured to the other players. "We're working our tails off."

"It's *not enough*," Quentin screamed. "And maybe you should worry about practicing harder, Khomeni. You took off, what, ten plays in practice because your knee hurts?"

The big HeavyG's eyes narrowed. "Don't you question my intensity, little man."

Quentin closed the distance, stared down at the slightly shorter, much denser sentient. "You will practice *hard*. You will *run*. And you will do it now! I don't ask anyone here to do anything more than what I'm willing to do. Now get back on the shucking line."

Khomeni glared, then walked back to the goal line.

This was what Quentin wanted, to drive his teammates to the point of failure, then make them push *through* that, make them dig deeper than they knew they could. You practice like you play. This would all pay off come the regular season.

"All of you, *up!* If you're puking, you can run and puke at the same time. This is for the playoffs, dammit!"

Ju Tweedy stepped off the line, looked back at his teammates.

"Come on, you losers! If Quentin can do it, we can do it! I want a ring!"

John Tweedy joined in. "I want *two* rings! Right here, Krakens, it starts right here. Five more sprints! Five more!"

Heads nodded. Players got up, stood straight, pulled helmets back on their heads.

Quentin jogged to the line, as did the Tweedys.

Quentin shouted to his teammates. "You can do this. On three, on three. Ready?"

Feet dug in, hands dropped to the blue turf. Eyes narrowed as sentients fought their own bodies and minds to just do *one more*.

"Hut-hut ... *hut!*"

The team sprinted off the line. Quentin's legs burned, his arms felt like noodles. His stomach roiled — he would be the next one to puke.

And when he did? He'd get back on the line and run again.

After all, he didn't ask anyone to do anything more than he was willing to do himself.

JANUARY 9, 2684

FREE AGENT DAY HAD COME. Quentin stood in the *Touchback*'s orange end zone, waiting until Coach Hokor needed him. Last season's free agent day had brought in only a few players, just running backs and tight ends. Those positions were no longer a need. At running back, the Krakens had Ju Tweedy backed up by Yassoud Murphy and Jay Martinez. At tight end, Crazy George Starcher backed up by Yotaro Kobayasho and the newly bad-ass Rick Warburg. So those problems had been solved.

This year, the Krakens faced a new problem — defensive secondary. The first string could still do a good job against most passing attacks, but if any of the four starters suffered injuries, the Krakens were in trouble. Standish's pregnancy had thinned the defensive backfield. Saugatuck and Rehoboth, the backup safety and free safety, respectively, were nowhere near first-string caliber if any starters got hurt. Stockbridge, the third cornerback on the depth chart, was a solid player, but Tiburon, another backup safety, looked terrible. She had slowed considerably in the off-season. Quentin wondered if she would even make the team at all.

The Krakens had been counting on a pair of rookies to flesh out the defensive backfield, but Gladwin and Cooperstown had been signed by the Wabash Wolfpack. So it was either free agency or pray that the starters stayed healthy for the regular season *and* for the playoffs.

Seven Sklorno defensive backs milled about at midfield. They wore practice whites. Quentin didn't recognize any of them. Two years ago he couldn't tell one Sklorno from the next. Now, he knew the species well enough to know he'd never seen these players before. No star defensive backs in the bunch, to say the least. The fact that they were here at all meant they were either Tier Three players not good enough to be taken as rookies, Tier Two players looking for experience, or they were Tier One veterans who had been cut from other teams.

A hundred yards away in the black end zone, Quentin saw offensive linemen as well as Alexsandar Michnik and Ibrahim Khomeni, the starting defensive ends. They were working with the only other free agent candidate, a defensive end named Cliff Frost who had played two seasons for the T3 Idaho Titans, then a year with the T2 D'Wy Piranah before D'Wy cut him due to a punctured lung that didn't heal fast enough. Then, just last year in the 2683 T2 season, Frost signed on with the Madhava Pi. A foot injury, apparently, had sidelined Frost, then the Pi cut him loose. His career riddled with injuries, no one knew Frost's real potential.

Last year, the Krakens had two backup defensive ends — Ban-A-Tarew and Wan-A-Tagol. The Orbiting Death snagged Ban-A in free agency, so he was gone. Unexpected, but not a crisis as long as the Krakens found a quality player to fill that backup role. Gredok had already signed rookie defensive end Rich Palmer. If Frost also made the team, then Wan-A's days might be numbered.

Quentin had nothing to do with the defensive roster. His job was to try and make these defensive back prospects look like idiots. Those who *didn't* look like idiots might land a contract for the season.

Hokor's floating golf cart flew overhead. "Barnes! Huddle up, let's get started."

Quentin held up his hands and waved his fingers inward, calling to his receivers. Milford, Hawick and Halawa ran to him. They wore their orange practice jerseys.

"Okay, ladies, we need to see what these defensive backs can do. I want hard cuts, so we can see their reaction time. If you can put a shoulder pad into them, do it, but don't take any big hits this close to the regular season. If I throw too high, just let it go."

The three receivers shuddered.

"But Quentin Barnes," Milford said. "To not catch your pass is to *sin*. We are all worthy to catch your glorious passes!"

He sighed. Even in a stupid drill, the Sklorno didn't know how to go easy.

"As your ... deity, or whatever, I am ordering you all to only catch the *good* passes, understand? Bad passes are, uh, they are a *test*. Get it?"

Milford stared, her four armored eyestalks twitching atop her glossy black helmet. "Yes! Yes oh Quentin Barnes, you are testing our ability to follow your holy will!"

"Whatever," Quentin said. "Just don't get hurt. Now line up."

Quentin stood and walked to the 50-yard line. Hawick lined up wide left, Milford near-right and the much larger Halawa to the far right.

Hokor's amplified voice rang through the stadium. "Vacaville, Breedsville, take the corners, woman-to-woman coverage. Fairgrove, safety. Rosebush, free safety. Basic two-deep defense. Give it your all, women, you won't get any chances to make a mistake."

No surprise that Hokor immediately poured on the pressure.

Quentin bent, then slapped the ball in his hands for the fake snap. He dropped back five steps as his receivers shot off the line. He waited only a second and a half before seeing that Halawa had Breedsville beat and that Rosebush would be slow to pick up the open receiver. Quentin fired the ball downfield. It hit Halawa in stride at the 15. She cruised into the end zone untouched.

Quentin should have been happy about that, but this wasn't about succeeding at offense. He wanted to see these defensive backs make stops.

"Again!" Hokor screamed. "You worthless defensive backs are embarrassing my beautiful field! *Run it again!*"

TOO BAD IT WASN'T A REAL GAME. Quentin and his receivers shredded the seven defensive back candidates. There was a reason these players hadn't been signed or drafted.

Quentin, Halawa, Milford and Hawick were at the 50, standing at the side of Hokor's cart, which had dropped down to the blue field. Hokor was paying them the ultimate honor — asking their opinion about the abilities of the free agent defensive backs.

"Rosebush?" Hokor said.

"Unworthy," the three Sklorno said in unison.

"Vacaville?"

The three receivers looked at each other, something they could do simultaneously courtesy of their free-moving eyestalks.

"Possible," Hawick said. "She isn't worthy of looking directly at the holy visage of Quentin Barnes, but possibly she could stand in shame on the sidelines and pray for more talent."

Quentin laughed and shook his head. The Sklorno had such an interesting way of saying things.

"I agree," Hokor said. "Vacaville isn't a starter by any stretch, but we have roster room. What about Fairgrove?"

"Unworthy," Hawick said.

"She should be killed," Milford said.

"And eaten," Halawa said.

Hokor entered some data into his messageboard. "Fairgrove, no."

"Oh Holy Great Hokor," Hawick said. "May I be so insolent as to offer an opinion without one being asked of me by one as great as you, by one so elevated above the cosmos that stars shrink away in fear, so amazing that—"

"Just say it," Hokor said. "Yes, you may speak."

"Breedsville is slightly more worthy than Vacaville. She should still be banned from looking directly at the Quentin Barnes, but she is suitable for a backup."

Hokor typed. "Fine. And the rest?"

"Unworthy," Hawick said.

"They should be killed," Milford said.

"And eaten," Halawa said.

Hokor gave the Quyth Leader equivalent of a heavy sigh. He slid his messageboard into a slot inside the cart. "Your input is appreciated, players. That is all."

Hokor's cart lifted without a sound, then floated to the black end zone where Cliff Frost was still fighting his way through drills.

Quentin walked off the field, unable to shake the pessimistic feeling that the Krakens were in trouble. If the starting defensive backs didn't get hurt, they would be okay, but no way could all four Sklorno defensive backs go a full season without suffering at least some kind of injury. Gloria Ogawa's tactic to sign the rookie backs that Hokor wanted had been a devious-yet-brilliant maneuver.

Quentin wondered if that move would pay off for the Wolfpack in Week Nine, when the Krakens traveled to Wabash. If Ionath lost to its archrival for the second year in a row, Quentin knew that Gredok would have a Sklorno-like opinion — that the Krakens were unworthy, they should be killed, they should be eaten.

Excerpt from Earth: Birthplace of Sentients
written by Zippy the Voracious
From Chapter Seven: Rise of the Machines

Sentients often tell me that Sklorno are the most *alien* intelligent life form they know. When I hear that, my answer is always the same — *then I guess you've never met a Prawatt.*

Not that many civilized sentients have. Encounters with that species are rare and usually result in — at best — exploding ships and thousands of deaths. At worst? Encounters with the Prawatt can lead to entire planets being rendered devoid of life and even the total extinction of sentient races.

STARTING SMALL

Members of the Prawatt species are created, initially, in a small, fist-sized structure known as a *root factory*. Because root factories begin their existence pre-packed with as many as a million tiny, life-emulating machines know as *larvids*, some exobiologists compare these structures to an egg sac. I say *some* exobiologists because others compare factories not to egg sacs, but to insect queens. After disgorging the initial compliment of larvids, root factories are capable of fabricating ten million to a hundred million more, depending on available resources.

Root factories are also capable of movement, which they use to find places with the most mineral-rich soil. Once a factory finds such a location, it plants itself in the ground, grows roots, then begins to activate the larvids.

Larvids quickly grow into the tiny creatures known as *minids*. These four-legged, insectile automatons weigh slightly less than one milligram. By way of comparison, the average adult Human tooth weighs about two grams. That means that a typical tooth weighs more than 2,000 minids.

The first wave of minids creates tunnels, chambers and mechanisms that help bring raw materials to the root factory. Many of the minids *link* together (see below for information on *linking*) to create larger organisms capable of defending the nest. In the species' native state, after these fundamental needs are satisfied, the next wave of minids starts to build dormant, self-contained root factories. The cycle is ready to be repeated.

This process — root factories building root factories — creates an exponential growth rate that, left unchecked, could cover any planet's surface in a matter of months.

Fortunately for the galaxy, however, that native state rarely happens. Minids show a natural tendency to link together. This *linkage* forever changes the minids via a process known as *fusing*.

THE WHOLE IS GREATER THAN THE SUM OF THE PARTS

A minid is quite comparable to the Earth insect known as an "ant," upon which the minid's structure and function are based. Individual minids are not sentient, self-aware, or even intelligent for that matter. Minids are *automata*, pre-programmed machines that perform repetitive actions. The more minids you have working together, however, the more complex structures and astounding tasks those combined actions can create.

The structure of minids allows them to lock their tiny limbs and coordinate muscle movements as if they were parts of a single entity. When this happens, the minids are no longer individuals — they are cells of a collective organism. At some unknown point, triggered by some unknown signal, millions of linked minids achieve stasis — a self-sustaining state of existence — and *fuse* together to permanently become a larger being. Minids build internal organs that include structural support, fluid pumps, material fabrication centers and even additional factories that create new minids to replace those that wear out.

Prawatt biological organization seems to only go *up* — once a minid fuses into a larger whole, it undergoes memory- and processing-related physical changes that preclude it from operating ever again as a single "ant."

When minids link up physically, they also combine their data-processing power. The more data a larger organism can process, the more complicated tasks it can perform and the better it is at self-preservation.

In summary, individual minids link together and become cells of a larger organism that is perfectly comparable to any number of biological animals, be they rats, geraniums, Occam-bulls or even Humans and the other sentient races.

SENTIENCE

Each minid's control center, or "brain," has about 80,000 microscopic processors. Scientists consider each processor equivalent to a Human brain cell. These processors work together to handle sensory input, determine reaction to that input, then send signals to the musculature that drives the minid to perform a physical action.

A Human brain has approximately 10 trillion cells. Since each minid has 80,000 "cells," this means that 125 million minids roughly equal the raw processing power of a Human brain.

Scientists do not know the exact point at which a fused Prawatt achieves sentience. This surprises many laymen, but it is consistent with our level of understanding of sentience in general. To date, no one can define what, exactly, shifts an organism from *non-sentience* to *sentience*.

What is known, however, is that the Prawatt typically become sentient when they are comprised of about 110 million minids. Like other organisms, levels of intelligence vary wildly within the sentient Prawatt community.

The few encounters with Prawatt that did not involve them trying to kill every sentient they found (or every sentient they found trying to kill them, which is just as common) determined that the species has increasing levels of self-awareness. All peaceful encounters that occurred determined that the most "Human-like" interaction occurs with Prawatt that weigh approximately 110 to 160 kilograms. Below 110 kilograms, there are very few recorded instances of self-awareness. As for Prawatt *above* 160 kilograms, there are no recorded encounters. Exobiologists believe that the Prawatt get bigger — much, *much* bigger — but at these larger sizes they cease to think and act in a way that Humans can understand.

SENTIENT PRAWATT & PHYSICAL FORM

The Prawatt can take several forms. We can't catalog most of these, however, as battle-holos are the only recorded imagery of most variants. When Prawatt die, their linkage breaks. The individual collapses in a dust-like pile of millions of lifeless minids, inanimate skeletal structures and nonfunctioning internal organs.

The form we are most familiar with has been labeled the *Explorer* structure. Explorers are called that for a reason: they are the only known sentient Prawatt found beyond the Prawatt space.

While the majority of sentient Prawatts stay in their own heavily defended space, the Explorer caste seems to show the same curiosity found in all of the known sentient races; there are things to learn and places to see — the Explorers want to do both.

Explorer Prawatt are quadrupeds comprised of four equal-sized legs. They exhibit bilateral symmetry. Their body consists of a narrow, roundish *case* or *trunk* that contains internal structures such as the nutrient pump, digestion center, signal routers, minid factory and more. The legs have two sections and end in either a foot or a hand. Their feet are flexible, resilient structures that provide good traction. Their hands closely resemble those of Humans, with four long fingers and a sturdy, opposable thumb. Prawatt can function well as a biped. More often than not, however, they move as a quadruped. When moving on all-fours, the Prawatt hand curls in and up; a thick ridge on the back of their wrist supports the body's weight.

The trunk is usually X-shaped, comprised of a pair of foot-thick tubes. An arm or leg grows off the end of each tube, which gives the Prawatt their common descriptive nicknames of *Walking X* or *X-Walker*. Derogatory nicknames for the species include *spiders* and *devil's rope*.

PHYSIOLOGY

There is no animal like the Prawatt anywhere in the galaxy. At least, there is no *sentient* animal. It is also important to note the word *animal* remains heavily in debate. Many exobiologists still consider the Prawatt to be machines. Prawatt began, possibly, as a "Von Neumann Device," an exploratory machination capable of self-reproduction. Von Neumann devices can land on a new planet, draw resources from that planet, use those resources to make more copies of itself, then launch those copies at other planets to repeat the cycle.

While the Prawatt match this rigid definition, they have also become so much more. Between the wars and the endless death, we have seen glimpses of art, of culture, even sport. When the galaxy isn't waiting in terror for a sighting of the Prawatt's massive capital-class warships, there are hints and hopes that someday these machine-animals might join the larger sentient community.

What little we know about the Prawatt Jihad comes from an unusual source — adventure seekers. Sentients enter Prawatt space knowing that they may never return, apparently in order to play a rumored combat sport found nowhere else in the galaxy. Information is sparse and poorly organized. The few adventure seekers that do return have not proven to be excellent observers or of an academic bent.

Like any sentient race, a one-size-fits-all definition of the Prawatt will never be found. In the next section, we show another reason that the Prawatt differ so vastly from purely biological sentients — that reason is the unique and disturbing process of *combination*.

COMBINATION

Prawatt don't have an organ or structure that operates as a distinct brain. Rather, their *entire body* is their brain — an individual is the collective consciousness of millions of minids.

When these minids fuse, they do not change physically. Like any muscle, skin or bone cell in a Human, individual minids wear out and must be replaced. The "life-span" of a minid is around thirty to sixty days. Internal factories produce a steady supply of new minids to replace those that are no longer functional. This small scale, ad-hoc replacement doesn't appear to affect the *self* of a Prawatt, nor does it alter their personality or sense of identity.

New minids can link with old minids. By the same process, minids created outside of the self can be incorporated into the larger organism. This fact, combined with the fact that minids do not undergo a physical change when they fuse, means that two distinct Prawatt can *combine*, merging together to create a larger organism.

Combination marks the end of two individuals and the creation of a new consciousness. This decision can be mutual, such as two sentient Prawatt choosing to come together, or it can take on a sense of predation as a larger Prawatt will capture a smaller one and assimilate it. Skills and other positive knowledge are combined, but so, too, are negative information such as fears, prejudices and hatreds.

Once a Prawatt achieves sentience, it is often very hesitant to combine because combination means the end of self. Effectively, to combine is to die and be reborn as something new.

SO WHERE ARE THE SHAPESHIFTERS?

One of the predominant fears about the Prawatt is that they can change shape and become species dopplegangers, capable of imitating any sentient race. Prawatt can look like your neighbor, your spouse, your leaders or even your children. Many a horror-holo has played upon this idea, casting the Prawatt again and again as a shapeshifting evil walking amongst us, creating secret cabals bent on enslaving the sentient races.

The fact of the matter, however, is that there isn't a shred of scientific evidence to back up this fearful fantasy. The Prawatt *are* capable of small-scale physical adjustments. But in observation, a Prawatt is sentient because it maintains a largely consistent shape. Shifting from the Walking X to a Human biped would probably require so much change that the Prawatt would no longer be the same individual — they would die and, in the process of dying, give rise to an entirely new sentient.

Theoretically, the Prawatt *can* change shape. But I caution that this remains only a theory. In almost four and a half centuries of encounters with this species, there is not one recorded instance of shapeshifting Prawatt accurately emulating another species.

THE LANDING BAY AIRLOCK finished cycling. The light above the door switched from red to green, accompanied by a deep, metallic *clang* as internal restraining bolts retracted.

Quentin was the first through the door, John Tweedy on his left, most of the rest of the team close behind them. John strode into the landing bay like he owned it — chest out, chin up, arms swinging comically. He twisted his head to the left, sniffed dramatically, then to the right and sniffed again.

"Hey, Q, you smell that?"

"You used that joke last year, John."

"Smells like *rookie* stank," John said, as if Quentin had said *smell what?* like he was supposed to.

The team filed into the landing bay, forming a semi-circle two or three players deep around the side of the *Touchback*'s large shuttle. Orange with black and white trim, the shuttle's main decoration was the Krakens logo — a black "I" set inside an orange shield, three white, orange-and-black trimmed, stylized tentacles spreading off to the right, three more spreading off to the left.

Welcoming the rookies was a rite of passage in the Ionath franchise. The rookies had all attended the *Combine*, a former prison station converted into a testing facility for first-year Tier One or Tier Two players. No matter who bought your contract, you couldn't play a minute of practice until you were scanned for mods and your background check turned up nothing suspicious that might someday harm the Creterakian Empire.

Quentin remembered his own testing, the terrifying and grueling process that — for the first time in his life — brought him into physical contact with races other than Human. More than that, he remembered the raw fear as the bats poked him, prodded him, strapped him down and asked him ridiculous questions. The rookies now arriving on the shuttle had successfully endured the same process. Those that hadn't passed? Well, if they were still alive at all, playing football was probably the least of their concerns.

The shuttle's door lowered from its bottom hinge, the entire side becoming a ramp that led down to the landing bay deck.

The first player to walk out brought to mind last season's arrival of Michael Kimberlin, the Krakens' starting right offensive guard. This guy was almost as tall as the 8-foot Kimberlin, but was far thinner. Deep-black skin, shaved head with lighter-colored scars lining his scalp from eyebrows to the back of his neck.

"Yeah-yeah," John said. "Finally, some *defense*. I'm so sick of you offensive pukes getting all the goodies. Q, what's the stats on this guy?"

"John, it's Tim Crawford. You saw him play in the Tier Three tourney."

John stared at Quentin with his patented *you are so dumb* look. "Q, I was *chewing*. Ma taught us not to talk with our mouths full."

"You did talk with your mouth full."

"And if I didn't *talk*, do you think I would *remember* stuff? Honestly, sometimes I think you have sand for brains."

"Uncle Johnny," Quentin said. "You are one-of-a-kind."

"Which is a real tragedy, when you think about it. What's skinny's info? He the defensive end?"

Quentin shook his head. "Nope. Crawford is a defensive tackle backing up Mum-O-Killowe. He played for the Archangels in the Tri-Alliance Gridiron Association."

"Give me a break," John said. "The TAGA? That's almost as bush league as the PNFL."

"John, I came from the PNFL and look how I turned out."

"My point exactly."

"Don't hold the small-league play against him. Two seasons with the Archangels. This year he was the sack leader of his league."

"How about his first season?"

"Only played half of that," Quentin said. "Tim ran into a little trouble with the law."

John smiled and nodded. MY KIND OF PEOPLE scrolled across his forehead. "Sounds like he's got potential."

"And he just turned nineteen," Quentin said. "His birthday was yesterday, I think."

John elbowed Quentin in the shoulder. Just a friendly reaction, but even a casual gesture from the star linebacker hurt damn near to the bone.

"Q! You know what that means?"

"That you're going to put on Ma's favorite apron and bake us all a nice cake?"

"No, it means you're *not* the youngest humanoid on the team anymore!"

Quentin hadn't thought about that, but John was right. Quentin had just turned twenty. Crawford was a full year younger. In all five years of Quentin's career, he had always been the youngest on the team — but that was over. It was an odd realization.

The next rookie out of the shuttle was also HeavyG. Almost as tall as Crawford, but much thicker, more mature. Reddish skin, puffy lips. Instead of his fists hanging near the floor like a typical HeavyG, this guy's hands fell just below his hips.

"There's your defensive end," Quentin said. "Rich Palmer. Talk about bush league, he played in the Jupiter, Neptune, Saturn and Venus league."

John stared at the rookie for a second. "I think there are talented players from the JNSV."

"John, those teams aren't even good enough to play in the NFL. And Palmer looks small for a defensive end. His arms are really short for a HeavyG."

"He's half Human," John said. "On his dad's side. Hey, if Becca and I have kids, I bet they'd look like this guy."

Quentin felt his temper instantly rise, but just as quickly he fought it down. The thought of John and Becca having kids, it was … maddening. He shook off the thought, focusing on the next player to walk down the ramp.

"Oh, here we go," John said. "Half-breeds and muties? This is our team?"

Tara the Freak walked down the ramp, long pedipalp arms dangling almost to his hips. His shell looked pale, whitish — unhealthy.

"John, I know I'm the insensitive racist of the team, but is the term *mutie* really acceptable?"

"The guy's *name* is Tara the *Freak*? And you're offended by *mutie*? Sheesh. He play for anyone before the Manglers?"

Quentin nodded. "Two years for the Cowboys."

"The how-boys?"

"*Cow*boys. From Dallas, on Earth. In the NFL."

John looked up to the ceiling, his eyes narrowed in thought. "Oh, yeah. In the NFL. I think I played against them once when I was with the Steelers. What's a cow-boy, anyway? That some genetically modified Human or something?"

Quentin shrugged. Cows were good for barbecue, but who knew the meaning of all those ancient Earth team nicknames?

DEAD ON ARRIVAL flashed across John's face. "This was a bad pick, Q. Tara the Mutie won't work out."

"He hasn't even practiced yet and you don't think he'll make it?"

John inclined his head toward the gathered Quyth players. Quentin looked at them. He waited for Virak the Mean, Choto the Bright, Killik the Unworthy and Kopor the Climber to welcome their fellow Warrior into the fold. But they didn't do that. Instead, they just stared. Tara stood there, more looking at the ground than staring back. Looking and waiting.

Whatever the rookie was waiting for, he didn't get it. The gathered Warriors just stood there.

Pilkie, a Quyth Worker, ran from rookie to rookie, gathering bags and luggage and loading them onto a hover cart. Quentin smiled at the sight, remembering when he had been a rookie and had refused to give Pilkie his bag.

Quentin thought back to Hokor and Gredok discussing Tara. They had said the other Warriors wouldn't accept him. So far, they were right, but Quentin would change that.

"John, come say hello with me."

John laughed. "Forget it, Q. I play every down with Virak the Mean on my left, Choto the Bright on my right. I back those guys first. When *they* accept Tara, so will I. See you later."

John strode over to Rich Palmer and Tim Crawford, welcoming them to the team.

Quentin walked up to Tara. "Welcome to the Krakens. I'm Quentin Barnes."

The Quyth Warrior looked at him. Tara's baseball-sized eye remained perfectly clear, but there was something about the shape of it, the way it seemed to cast down at the floor. Tara seemed ... *sad*?

"Barnes," Tara said. His voice reminded Quentin of broken masonry — rough and crunchy, yet with a hint of musical tones. "Gredok told me about you, Barnes. He said you fought to bring me to the Krakens."

Quentin smiled. "That's right. I saw you play in the T3 title game. I think you can help us."

"Help *you*," Tara said. "And who's going to help me?"

"Huh? What do you mean? You're in Tier One, you're in the big time."

A trace of black colored Tara's eye. "I didn't *ask* to be in the big time. Things in Mathara were … stable. It took a long time to get them that way."

What was this? Quentin felt his own anger swirling, but he held it in check. "Wait a minute. Are you *complaining* about being taken into Tier One?"

"Call it what you will. I have to start all over."

Quentin glanced at the other Quyth Warriors, who were still staring with open hostility. Yeah, maybe this situation might seem intimidating. "I know this will take some getting used to, but I'll help you."

"Like you *can* help, Human."

Quentin's anger blossomed. Reaching Tier One was every football player's dream, whatever the obstacles. He pointed to the glowing holographic letters that ran the length of the landing bay's dome — THE IONATH KRAKENS ARE ON A COLLISION COURSE WITH A TIER ONE CHAMPIONSHIP. THE ONLY VARIABLE IS TIME.

"See those words, rookie? Memorize them. You've been here all of five minutes and you're already wearing out your welcome. If it's such an awful thing to be brought up to Tier One, why the hell did you come at all?"

Tara closed his eye, seemed to gather his thoughts. "The Krakens bought out my contract." He opened his eye. "If I don't play for the Krakens, I don't play football. I'm already Ronin. No one will hire me for any job. Without a team, I have nothing. I *am* nothing."

"Ronin? What do you mean? What is that?"

Tara stared for a few more seconds, then brushed past Quentin and walked to the airlock.

Quentin realized that Pilkie hadn't taken Tara's bag. Neither had Messal the Efficient, for that matter. The two Quyth Workers had taken the bags of the other rookies, but not Tara.

No one showed Tara the way. No one told him where he was supposed to go, but he walked out of the landing bay all the same. Quentin suddenly remembered his early days with the Micovi Raiders, when his own teammates ostracized him simply because he was an orphan. Back then, no one had wanted to help Quentin with anything. He'd had to find his own way.

Tara the Freak, it seemed, was used to doing the same thing.

QUENTIN AND GREDOK were aboard the *Regulator*, the ship that belonged to the office of the Commissioner of the Galactic Football League. Quentin had thought the *Touchback*'s guns impressive, but now he knew they were little more than toys when compared to a fully armed warship. The white-painted *Regulator* bristled with weaponry, not only outside but also within. Two armed HeavyG guards led them down white corridors. More armed guards were everywhere; normal Humans and Quyth Warriors, armored Sklorno and more than a few bats flittering about with entropic rifles held in their disgusting little hands. All the guards wore matching uniforms — white with the GFL logo somewhere on the chest.

The display of weaponry had a visible impact on Gredok. In Ionath City, he never hesitated to show off his power, usually with big, well-dressed sentients that carried weapons. All of Gredok's planet-side organization, however, would have been out-gunned just by the white-suited troops in the *Regulator*'s landing bay. Quentin suspected that this meeting had more than one purpose. To discuss illegal contact with the To Pirates, sure, but also to show Gredok that Commissioner Rob Froese was not an easy target. This was a demonstration of strength, of the kind of power that Gredok could understand.

The HeavyG guards stopped in front of a door. White, what a surprise.

Quentin and Gredok walked into Froese's office. Wood-panel walls and waist-high molding gave the entire room a classy, archaic feel. Glass cases displayed trophies and statues. Inside one case, a silvery Super Bowl trophy from 1984, exactly seven centuries old. Engraving on the side of the triangular base read "SUPER BOWL XVIII CHAMPIONS" and, below that, "THE LOS ANGELES RAIDERS." Was that the same Raiders that had eventually moved to Micovi? Amazing! And another trophy, showing a running man in primitive padding, his right knee high, his left arm straight out to stiff arm some unseen opponent. On the bottom of that one, it read "REGGIE BUSH, 2005." A seven-century-old relic — priceless.

More trophies and other memorabilia sat on shelves. Pictures in ornate frames hung from the walls. *Flat* pictures — not holos. Quentin recognized all of the ancient players and coaches pictured: Tom Landry, Terry Bradshaw, YA Tittle, Tom Brady, Bronko Nagurski, Jim Brown, Paul Brown (Quentin wondered if Jim and Paul were brothers) ... even a black-and-white flat-picture of Walter Camp, the demigod who actually *invented* the game of gridiron. Now there was something impressive, a picture of a Human before Humans even invented color.

Gredok seemed disgusted by the office. "Look at this pretentious display. Only Humans are represented. Such racism."

"It's not racist," Quentin said. "It's from the pre-galactic period. All of these Humans are key historical factors in the early days of football."

"Froese should update it."

"What do you want him to do, rewrite history? It's from a time when only Humans played, Gredok. I don't think historical fact can be *racist*."

Gredok turned to face Quentin. The Quyth Leader wanted a target for his anger and Quentin was it. "Such admiration in your voice, Barnes. Try not to be too impressed with our overly controlling Commissioner."

Quentin shrugged, kept looking around the office. He *was* impressed. Froese was clearly a student of the game. With seven centuries of football in the history books, most fans focused on teams, players and coaches from the last twenty-five years. Even die-hard football fans had no idea who these people were. And the fact that Froese used *flat* pictures? That made it feel like this office *was* from the ancient past, as if he'd plucked it right out of some history holo from about the year 2011, perhaps and brought it all to life. This was more than just an office — it was a *shrine*.

A shrine to the game of football.

The office door opened. In walked two sentients. First, Commissioner Rob Froese, all squat, three feet of him. He wore a white shirt and a red tie embroidered with the GFL logo. As interesting as Froese looked, Quentin could only stare at him for a second before his eyes flicked to the other sentient — Leiba the Gorgeous. Six foot five, at least 360 pounds of Quyth Warrior. Cracked chitin and bulging muscle. Leiba, the former All-Pro linebacker for the Vik Vanguard who had walked away from the game to join the GFL's front office.

"Froese," Gredok said. "I do not appreciate being kept waiting."

"Sit down, Gredok." Froese walked behind his desk and crawled into his chair.

"You will not speak to me this way, Froese," Gredok said. "The decisions of owners are what pays your salary. You—"

"Sit *down*."

Gredok paused, then sat.

At seven feet tall, Quentin was twice the height of Gredok and Commissioner Froese. Quentin felt oddly huge, like some misplaced adult sitting at a child's table. Leiba stayed just inside the closed office door, an ever-present threat should anyone get out of line.

Quentin focused on paying attention to every word. Froese's strange red teeth could be very distracting.

"I received your injury report about Ju Tweedy," Froese said. "How interesting he has a damaged artery at exactly the time I wanted him here for a meeting about his murder charge."

"We properly filed the notice," Gredok said. "It is unsafe for Ju Tweedy to travel or see visitors."

Froese looked mad enough to pull a gun, but he kept his voice calm. "Yes, you properly filed the notice. And an injury that is severe, but not a brain or heart injury where I could possibly prevent him from playing this season. Very clever, Gredok."

"A coincidence," Gredok said. "We want to get to the bottom of this Grace McDermot issue, I assure you."

Froese leaned back in his chair. "You can't hide Ju forever, Gredok. The longer you make me wait, the angrier I get. For now, I have to focus that anger on the other member of your team who seems to think he can just ignore GFL regulations."

"Preposterous," Gredok said. "Barnes is not the culprit in this illegal contact debacle. Blame lies with Kirani Kollok and his lackey, Maygon. My player is innocent of any wrongdoing."

"He is *not* innocent. If he had reported the incident, he would be fine. He did not. Therefore, he is in violation of league rules. Kirani Kollok and Maygon are outside. I will talk to them next."

Gredok seemed somewhat mollified that Kirani had to wait longer than he did.

"Now, to business," Froese said. "Barnes, you admit to meeting with Maygon during the 2682 Tier Three season?"

Quentin nodded.

"Have you met with any other teams that you have not reported to the league?"

"No," Quentin said. "Just Maygon."

"You are a free agent after this season," Froese said. "Your agent has filed notices for meetings with the Mars Planets, the Bartel Water Bugs, the To Pirates and the McMurdo Murderers."

Quentin's eyes flicked to Gredok, whose black fur stood on end.

"Barnes," Froese said. Quentin's eyes snapped back to the diminutive Commissioner.

"Barnes, when I talk, you pay attention."

"Yes, sir."

"You violated league rules and you must be punished. I have

two disciplinary options. Since I believe that you were approached and did not initiate contact, I will only fine you one hundred twenty thousand credits for not reporting the incident."

"*One hundred twenty thousand?*"

Gredok waived a pedipalp. "A pittance. Do not worry about that amount, Barnes."

Froese shook his head. "No way, Gredok. You're not paying the fine. I'm taking it out of Quentin's account and we'll be monitoring his funds to make sure you don't reimburse him."

Such a staggering sum, for something that wasn't his fault? "But Commissioner, that fine is ten percent of my salary for the year!"

Froese raised his eyebrows in mock alarm. "Oh? Well then, that *does* seem like a severe punishment. Almost like I'm trying to send a message or something. How strange. All right, if you don't like the fine, we can go with my other option. I can suspend you for the opening game against the Isis Ice Storm."

"*What?*"

"I would take that option," Gredok said. "Don Pine can handle the first game."

"No way! That game is mine. *All* the games are mine!"

Froese lifted his hand, palm-up. A time icon flashed in the air above it. "I have a schedule, Barnes. Shall I suspend you for the opener?"

Quentin ground his teeth, then looked at the flat-picture of Terry Bradshaw hanging on the wall. *Four* championships that ancient had won.

"Barnes?"

"The money," Quentin said. "I'll take the damn fine."

"Then that is settled. Gredok, please leave. I would like a word with Quentin. Alone."

"Absolutely *not*," Gredok said. "I will be present at all times when you talk to my players."

"Leave now, or I will arrange for a question session with Ju Tweedy at 1 p.m. Ionath Time on January 27th."

Gredok again fell silent. January 27 was the Krakens opener against the Isis Ice Storm. The Krakens might win with Don Pine as QB, but they had almost no chance with Yassoud Murphy starting at running back.

"Commissioner," Gredok said, "you are trying my patience."

"Am I? What a surprise. Now leave. Barnes will be out soon."

Gredok's fur ruffled once more, then fell flat. The Quyth Leader stood and walked out. Leiba held the door for him, then walked out as well and closed it behind them.

Quentin found himself alone with the most powerful sentient in football.

"Barnes, why did you choose the money over the suspension?"

"Because I want to play. You know that. It's why you gave me the choice."

"Actually, I gave you the choice because I **DIDN'T** know. Now I do."

"You thought I liked money more than football?"

Froese shrugged his tiny shoulders. "There is a lot of information circulating about you, Barnes. A lot of rumors. I need to know what kind of a sentient you are."

"Why? I play football. And — from now on — I follow your damn rules. Other than that, what else do you need to know?"

"A lot more," Froese said. "You've heard people say I'm going to clean up this league?"

"I've heard people laugh about it, if that's what you mean."

Froese smiled a red-toothed smile. "Yeah. They laugh. Everyone thinks the crime lords are too entrenched, that no one has the guts to take them on. But they're wrong. I *will* clean up this league, Barnes. I *will* legitimize football. A time is coming when players will have to decide what they want — a league riddled with corruption, smuggling, intimidation and assassinations or an honest league free of all those things."

"Gee, Commish, when you put it *that* way, where do I sign up? Sounds so simple to do. I'm surprised it hasn't happened already."

Froese's smile faded. "I'm no idealist, Barnes. I know it won't be easy. I know it won't come without casualties. That's why the players that side with me are going to be at risk. I need sentients that are strong, that can face the danger. What kind of sentient are you?"

"The kind that lines up on Sunday," Quentin said. "I play football, Commish. That's what I do. I think I'll leave the politics out of it."

"Gee, Quentin, that sounds so simple to do."

"You'd be surprised," Quentin said. "May I go?"

Froese gestured to the door. Quentin walked out of the beautiful office and into the hall. There he saw the two white-clad HeavyG guards standing with Gredok and Leiba. He also saw Maygon, the Creterakian civilian and a red-haired Human dressed in a long, white robe. Maygon wore a bright red suit with blinking green trim and platinum jewelry. He looked like a gag Giving Day ornament.

The white-robed Human flashed a warm, genuine smile. He extended his hand. "Quentin Barnes. I'm Kirani Kollok, owner of the To Pirates. Nice to meet you at long last."

Quentin stared for a second, unsure of what to do. Yet another crime lord, yet another person who could either write him an enormous check or order his death. Quentin looked down at Gredok, whose eye turned black.

Shaking the man's hand would anger Gredok, but that was politics and Quentin didn't care about politics. Quentin had no reason to spurn a simple gesture of respect.

He shook the offered hand. "Nice to meet you, Mister Kollok."

"I'm sorry if Maygon's actions caused any inconvenience, Quentin. I hope to make it up to you. We want you in the Blood Red and no matter what that takes—" he flashed a glance at Gredok "—we're going to make that happen. Well, I have to go meet with the Commissioner. Quentin, Gredok, enjoy your day."

Leiba opened the office door. Kirani walked in, followed by the flying Maygon, then by Leiba, who closed the door behind them.

Gredok's eye had somehow turned even blacker. "Barnes. Don't say another word to me. Let's go."

The Quyth Leader turned and walked down the hall, his little feet pattering out a fast pattern. Quentin followed, feeling like no matter how hard he tried, he always wound up pissing someone off.

9

PRESEASON WEEK THREE: JANUARY 15 – 21, 2684

From "The GFL For Dummies, Third Edition"
by Robert Otto
2684 update

GROWTH AND EXPANSION

Success means growth and growth means expansion. That has been the GFL way since Rob Froese took over as Commissioner. He has spent years increasing the number of lower-tier teams, but is he preparing for a shakeup of Tier One?

In 2683, Froese implemented major changes to the GFL's two-tier structure. He created three new conferences: the 8-team Whitok Conference, the 10-team Union Conference and the 10-team League Conference. He also disbanded the 10-team Human Conference, spreading those teams among the Union and the League. To fill the 18 open slots in these conferences, Froese promoted 18 Tier Three franchises up to Tier Two, bringing the number of T2 teams to 76.

Froese and the Empire Bureau of Species Interaction (EBSI)

then allowed for the creation of 26 new Tier Three franchises — 18 to replace the promoted teams, along with 8 additional franchises. This brought the Tier Three total to 288 teams. For 2684, Froese added an additional 3 teams at the GFL's lowest level, bringing the total number of teams in at all 3 levels to 389.

2684 NUMBERS: 389 GFL FRANCHISES

- Tier One: 22 teams
- Tier Two: 76 teams
- Tier Three: 291 teams

TIER THREE FREEZE

Twenty-six new franchises means a huge influx of Tier Three teams, the biggest single expansion in league history. Because of this, Froese has declared a five-year (ErT) moratorium on the creation of additional Tier Three teams. While there will be no new T3 teams during that time, there may still be some movement; if any T3 franchises fold due to bankruptcy or any other reason, they can be bought by any interested party and moved to a population center specified by the purchaser as long as there is a regulation stadium available.

NEXT PHASE – TIER ONE EXPANSION?

Commissioner Froese may have halted Tier Three expansion, but he has his sights set on Tier One growth. For the 2685 season, he is proposing the addition of two more franchises. This would bring the T1 total to 24 teams.

Tier One is currently organized into two 11-team divisions: the Solar Division and the Planet Division. If Froese is successful in adding two T1 franchises, he will likely re-organize Tier One into six conferences of four teams each —three conferences in the Planet Division and three in the Solar.

The six conference champions would make the playoffs, as would two "wildcard" teams, one from each division. The end result would be an eight-team playoff, the same as we have now. Also similar to the current structure, the winner of the Planet

Division playoff would face the winner of the Solar Division play-off in the Galaxy Bowl.

Froese feels this new structure would create more rivalry among the four-team conferences, as well as remove the confusion of multiple tie-breakers that are often used to fill out the current playoff structure.

THE NEEDS OF TIER THREE

Froese's restructuring plan runs even deeper. He may connect Tier Three and Tier Two in a promotion/relegation structure identical to that of the T1/T2 relationship.

The current upper tier interaction means that the two teams finishing last in Tier One are relegated to Tier Two, while the two teams that finish at the top of the T2 Tourney are promoted into Tier One. Froese proposes also relegating the worst team in each of the eight Tier Two conferences. Those teams would drop down to Tier Three, while the top eight teams in the T3 tourney would be promoted to Tier Two.

"This interconnected reward and punishment system has been used on Earth for over seven centuries," Froese said. "If it works for soccer, it can work for gridiron. We need to ensure competitive play at all levels and provide the best franchises with an opportunity to advance."

If implemented, this change would unify the promotion/relegation strategy for all three levels of professional football. Teams from the smallest markets could fight their way from Tier Three up to Tier One, while Tier One teams could tumble from the pinnacle of accomplishment to the lowest levels of football in just two seasons.

GROWTH TRACKING

- 2679: 350 franchises
  (Rob Froese's first year as Commissioner)
- 2681: 356 franchises
- 2683: 386 franchises
- 2684: 389 franchises

JANUARY 15, 2684

MICHAEL KIMBERLIN HELD the messageboard. He read over Quentin's answers. Quentin had spent two hours the night before studying for this test. *After* reviewing the Isis Ice Storm roster for the thousandth time, of course, but he *had* studied.

They sat in Quentin's living room aboard the *Touchback*. He was committed to educating himself, but still felt inexplicably embarrassed when his other teammates teased him about Kimberlin's tutoring. Kimberlin knew this and didn't seem to mind keeping the studies as quiet as possible.

The massive offensive lineman looked up. "Excellent work, Quentin."

"I get it all right?"

"Not all," Kimberlin said. "You're still having trouble with angular momentum, but it's safe to say you now know more about basic physics than seventy-five percent of the sentients in the galaxy. Your countrymen back on Micovi wouldn't even know you."

Quentin nodded. That was the truth, although physics had little to do with it. He had changed so much in the past two years.

"Time to move on to other subjects," Kimberlin said. "First, though, what happened on the *Regulator*? I am dying to know. Are you suspended? Is Ju?"

"I got a fine," Quentin said. "Just watch the Galaxy's Greatest Sports Show. I'm sure they'll give all the details."

"And Ju?"

Quentin shrugged. "Gredok got him out of the meeting. As of now, Ju is still cleared to play. No suspension."

"Does Froese have more information on the murder?"

"Maybe," Quentin said. "All I know is we have our starting running back lining up in Week One against the Ice Storm."

Kimberlin nodded. "That is excellent news. Well, you've done a good job at learning about your fellow football-playing species. Now we shall learn exobiology basics on the other races."

"I'll pass," Quentin said. "We're into the season now. I have to focus on football and football alone."

"There is more to life than football, Quentin. You have come so far. Do you not trust my ability to teach?"

"Well, yeah, but come on — extra biology?"

"*Exo*-biology."

"Exo-schmexo," Quentin said. "Why don't you just give me random story problems? I don't need busy-work like biology and history."

"All of this would be easier if you didn't complain like a child at every small task. Don't you believe in setting goals?"

Quentin sighed and crossed his arms over his chest. "Of course I believe in setting goals."

"Fine. *My* goal is to turn you into a Renaissance man. A beer-swilling, primitive-belief eschewing, violent one, to be true, but a Renaissance man nonetheless."

"That sounds awesome."

Kimberlin smiled. "Really? It does?"

"Yeah, really fantastic. By the way, what does *eschew* mean? And what's a Renaissance man?"

Kimberlin sighed. "Quentin, do you feel like you're a better person for learning what I have taught you thus far?

Quentin bit his lip and looked at the ground.

"Well? Do you?"

Quentin nodded.

"And I ask you again — do you trust me as a friend?"

Kimberlin was going to play the friend card? Damn. "Yeah, Mike, you know I do."

"Then just go through this lesson with me. It won't take long. Our first road game takes us near the Prawatt/Sklorno border. So if I teach you about the Prawatt, one could argue that it is related to football."

"Prawatt is to football as John Tweedy is to eloquence."

Kimberlin laughed. "Did you just use an analogy *and* the word *eloquence*?"

"Is that *Renaissance* enough for ya?"

"It is," Kimberlin said. "But you still need to learn some of this. In known space, the only place more dangerous than Prawatt territory is the Portath Cloud."

"Why is Portath more dangerous?"

"Because at least we know that most sentients who stray into Prawatt territory wind up in a fight for their lives. The ships that go into the Portath Cloud, however, are never heard from again. I have a text you need to read. One chapter a night."

"*Homework?*" Mike was asking too much. "The regular season is a week away, man. I have to study football at night."

"For a professional athlete, your voice squawks like that of a little girl. One chapter a night, Quentin. I do not think this will fracture your intellect. And it's not good for you to focus on only one subject. Studies show that retention rates drop considerably when one stimulates only a specific region of the brain and that—"

"Fine," Quentin said. "Anything to avoid one of your long-winded explanations. What's the name of the damn text?"

"The Biology of Our Enemies," Kimberlin said. "Sub-title: Structures of the Threat Races."

"Sounds like a real page-turner."

"You might be surprised. Did you know that the Prawatt originated on Earth? At least, that's the theory."

Quentin automatically started to repeat what he'd been taught as a child, that the Prawatt were spawned in hell by Low One, but he caught himself in time. Gaining knowledge had an annoying drawback of exposing just how ignorant he used to be. Whatever the Prawatt were, they were no more a demon than the Ki, the Quyth or the Sklorno.

"I've never heard that they came from Earth. That's ... what's the word you use ... illogical?"

Kimberlin smiled and nodded. "Tell me why."

"The Prawatt are these shapeshifting machines. They're monsters. If they came from Earth, why wouldn't they just cut out the middle man and take the Earth over?"

Michael crossed his massive arms over his massive chest, then nodded. Quentin had learned that body language meant something to the effect of: *your thinking is correct, even though your answer is wrong.*

"In the eyes of the Prawatt, Humans like you are the *monsters*," Kimberlin said. "The Prawatt supposedly originated on Earth but were wiped out in a genocide around 2015 or 2016 Earth time."

"They escaped?"

"Some of them, possibly. Or perhaps they were recreated somewhere. It is not known. What is known is that they made their first detectable punch-drive flight in 2424. A little-known sentient race, once thought extinct, had returned from the grave."

"We have a word for that in the Nation."

Kimberlin raised his eyebrows, waiting for the answer.

"We call that *being undead*," Quentin said. "Zombies, vampires, stuff like that. Monster machines coming back from extinction? Gimme a break."

"Again, *you* are the monster to *them*. And they are *not* machines. They breed, they reproduce, they create art."

"Blah-blah-blah. Art is for pansies, anyway."

Kimberlin's mouth opened and his eyes narrowed as if Quentin had insulted his mother. "Art is for *pansies*?"

"Or, as John might say, super-mongo pansies."

Kimberlin sighed and shook his head, as if Quentin were the saddest sentient in all the land. "Well, fine. The Prawatt also have their own forms of dance."

"Oh, wow, they *dance*? Why didn't you just tell me that in the first place, on account of how much I love ballet."

"*You* love ballet?"

Quentin closed his eyes and held his hands over his heart. "Oh, *yes*, I so love it. Sometimes I skip practice so I can watch ballet holos and wear my three-three."

Kimberlin closed his eyes. "*Tutus*, Quentin. Ballet dancers wear *tutus*."

"Mine is one better than theirs, I guess. You know, because I love dance just that much."

"Oh," Kimberlin said. "You're being sarcastic."

"Who, me? Look, I'm just not interested in Prawatt *culture*, okay?"

"Are you interested in their sports?"

Sports? Quentin had a sudden vision of devil's rope playing volleyball with a severed Human head. "Okay, I might be interested in that."

Kimberlin rubbed his eyes. "The greatest cultural achievements of the millennia could be there for you to discover and you — of course — only hear the word *sports*."

"Sports *are* the greatest cultural achievement of the millennia. Come on, what do they play? Hoops? Football?"

Kimberlin reached for the messageboard. "It is somewhat more gladiatorial than that. The Prawatt body structure allows them to take damage in a different way, so the game is not lethal for them. For the other races, however, it's quite deadly."

"Other races? I thought the Prawatt kill anything they see. What other races want to *play* with that?"

"Adventure seekers," Kimberlin said. The messageboard cast up a holo, something that resembled a walled Dinolition pitch: oblong, with a small circle in the center. But this stadium seemed strange. The stands seemed to ... *move* ... like waving sea anemones.

Kimberlin reached out, closed his thick hand on the floating holo, then made a throwing motion at the living room's holotank. The room computer turned on the holotank and played the same image.

Low resolution and static made for horrible image quality, but the holotank's larger picture explained the anemones-like motion — tens of thousands of jittering, spindly, curved arms of the repulsive Prawatt. The creatures were packed in tight, as tight as Purist pilgrims marching around Landing Site. The Prawatt horde's glossy black arms waved with the same reverence as those swaying, flagellating Pilgrims. Quentin couldn't make out individuals, although he could see that there were many different, vague and indistinct shapes in that mix.

The jittery, low-quality holo zoomed in, showing Prawatt down on the pitch.

"The devil's rope," Quentin said in a whisper. His people had good reason to think the Prawatt were demons — they looked like no other living species. From a distance, they resembled a four-legged spider. Long, two-sectioned arms/legs led back to a tiny body. As the camera closed in, he could see that the leg sections weren't rigid, like a insect's, but more flexible, like two springy tubes. Even in the low-quality footage, Quentin could see *through* the legs in some places.

"Michael, are you *sure* that's not a demon? 'Cause if you ask me, I would say a demon probably looks a lot like that."

"The Prawatt are unique in the galaxy. Tiny machines link together to form larger structures.

The holocam image pulled back. Three elevated rings stood on either end of the oblong pitch. On the pitch itself stood fourteen beings — seven wearing ribbons of red, seven wearing ribbons of green.

Two teams.

But not all the players were Prawatt.

Quentin squinted, as if that would help bring resolution to the holographic image. "On the red team, is that a Ki? And that, a Sklorno?"

Michael nodded. "Adventure seekers. Or captured merchants, we don't know. The Prawatt consider any violation of their borders as an act of war. If sentients enter their space — intentionally or accidentally — those sentients are usually executed."

"Wow," Quentin said. "Makes you think people would pay attention to their maps."

"Space is a fluctuating thing. It is easy to lose one's bearings, even with the complex navigational technology most ships possess."

"So, some players are *forced* to play?"

"That's what experts think," Kimberlin said. "Apparently, some sentients have earned their freedom by winning."

"What about the others? The adventure seekers?"

"Those that value excitement more than life have been known to intentionally cross into Prawatt space, just to play this game."

Quentin saw a Quyth Warrior on the green team. Something about that one, something ... familiar. "Hey, wait a minute. Holy crap, Mike! Is that Leiba the Gorgeous?"

Kimberlin nodded. "That's how we have this holo. This is the only known recording of the sport."

"What's it called?"

"No one knows," Kimberlin said. "Until Leiba somehow made this recording, the game was the stuff of legend and rumor."

The contest began. The holo's terrible quality made it hard to understand, but the object seemed clear — put a ball through the rings on either end. A goalie defended the rings. The teams tore into each other, hitting hard and trying to advance the ball, passing it around like a nonstop form of football. Or maybe this was a kind of soccer where you could use your hands and actually *hit* people, not the sissy game where you couldn't touch anyone. Through the static and the jiggering images, Quentin thought he saw more balls in play. Soccer with three balls where you could use your hands and actually hit sentients?

The red team seemed to break through the green team's defenses. One Prawatt, red ribbons streaming behind it, took the ball forward and *jumped*. The green goalie also jumped, an insane leap that brought the two alien machines together some twenty feet off the pitch. The red player took the hit, but twisted, throwing the ball through one of the rings. Both competitors fell to the ground, landing as lightly as cats.

"Wow! Did you see that?"

"Just wait," Kimberlin said. "I don't think you'll be quite as excited about the next part."

Quentin squinted again, trying to make out the action on the field. So hard to identify anything with this horrible image quality, but there *was* more than one ball. The two extra balls seemed to fly around randomly — it made no sense.

The first ball, the one that they'd used to score the goal, bounced free. The two teams converged. The red-team's Sklorno player leapt to wrap her tentacles around it, but she was met in the air by two green-team Prawatt. They tackled her, the three of them falling hard to the ground. The Sklorno landed head-first. Even through the scratchy image, Quentin knew a fatality when he saw one.

The ball bounced free. Just seconds later, Leiba the Gorgeous closed in on it. A Prawatt came at him from behind, diving at his legs. Leiba's lower-left leg snapped at the shin, blood spraying onto the pitch.

"High One," Quentin said. "This game is, uh, violent."

Seconds later, one of the randomly flying balls slammed into the Ki's face. The big creature fell to the pitch, twitching madly.

And then the holo blinked out.

"Hey," Quentin said. "I want to watch the rest of it."

"That is all there is. The only known recording."

Quentin stared at the blank holoscreen, his heart racing. It didn't seem to matter what the sport was — if it was a game, it excited him like nothing else in life. He let out a long breath, calming himself, dealing with the fact that he would never know if that Ki lived or which side won the game.

He turned to face Kimberlin, whose big arms were once again crossed over his chest. Quentin's eyes flicked to Kimberlin's right ring finger. As always, there was no ring. Quentin had ignored this question last season, but he could restrain his curiosity no more.

"I gotta ask you something," Quentin said. "You were with Pine when the Jacks won two Galaxy Bowls. Why don't you wear your rings?"

Kimberlin looked down. "Because I did not earn them."

"Because you didn't start? You were still on the team, man."

"You don't understand, Quentin. I ... I *could* have started. Back then, I was not as level-headed as I am now."

Quentin tried to imagine Michael Kimberlin as anything other than the hulking-but-calm force that he was, anything other than a rock of reason. That image refused to crystallize.

"Let me guess," Quentin said. "You got all crazy and mixed white milk with chocolate milk? You are such a wild thing, Mike."

Kimberlin smiled, but there was little humor in it.

"Unfortunately, it was more severe than that. The details are not a story to be told now, not when we must focus on the coming season."

"Crazier than mixing milk? Did you stay up past midnight or something?"

Kimberlin stared off into the distance. "I am no stranger to death on the football field."

Quentin hadn't expected that. He instantly felt bad for poking fun, for unknowingly making light of something that serious.

Kimberlin closed his eyes for a second, seemed to gather his thoughts, then opened them again. He stared at Quentin in a calculating, emotionless manner. From whistle to whistle, Michael Kimberlin was a scary piece of work. Any time other than that, however, he seemed to have all the passion of a broom.

"My irresponsible actions resulted in uncorrectable consequences," he said. "What I have done ... one cannot take back."

Quentin wondered what could be so bad that Kimberlin wanted to push it down, hide it somewhere inside. Had he killed another player?

"If you don't want to talk about it, I won't push," Quentin said. "But sentients die on the football field, Mike. It's the life we have chosen. I don't see what that has to do with you not wearing a ring that you earned."

"It wasn't during a game," Kimberlin said. "And it was my own teammate."

"It happened in practice?"

Michael shook his head. "No. Not in practice. Off the field."

Off the field. Michael Kimberlin had killed his own teammate, another member of the Jupiter Jacks. Whatever the cause of that action, Kimberlin bore the responsibility.

"That incident changed me," Kimberlin said. "It taught me that one needs to think things through. One needs to see the big picture. One needs knowledge. I am with a new team now. I want to earn a championship and wear *that* ring. It is the focal point of my existence."

"I thought you said there's more to life than football."

Kimberlin nodded, then smiled — and this time, there was a

bit of humor in the expression. "There is more to life than foot-ball. Just not *much* more."

JANUARY 17, 2684

QUENTIN SAT ON THE BENCH in front of his locker, slowly fasten-ing his shoes. The rest of the team had already headed out to the field for Media Day. Only Don Pine remained behind, waiting for Quentin to finish getting ready. Both men wore their black home jerseys: the word KRAKENS and their numbers in white-trimmed orange, the Krakens logo on both shoulders, white-trimmed or-ange numbers on the sleeves. No armor, no pads, just the jerseys.

Messal the Efficient entered the Human locker room. He spot-ted the two quarterbacks and walked straight for them.

"He looks agitated," Quentin said.

"He does," Don Pine said. "Can you blame him? We might be a whole thirty seconds behind schedule."

Messal stopped in front them, shifted his weight from foot to foot. "Elder Barnes, Mister Pine, I must not have properly com-municated the schedule to you, for which I apologize immensely. I do hate to disturb your conversation, but the media is out on the field. The rest of the team is already present and the reporters are awaiting Ionath's star quarterbacks."

Quentin sighed and looked away. "Sorry, Messal, I don't feel like attending Media Day."

Messal's eye turned crimson — one of the fear colors. He start-ed to shake. "But ... Elder Barnes, we are due on the field! If we don't— "

"Messal," Don said. "He's just messing with you. We're ready to go."

Messal's eye color shifted to green. "Messing with me?"

Quentin stood and gently slapped Messal on his middle shoul-der. "Yeah, just giving you a hard time. Don't have a heart attack, okay?" Quentin reached into his locker and grabbed a slip of pa-per. "Messal, you can get whatever the players need, right?"

Messal's eye went clear, but he again started hopping from foot to foot. "Yes, Elder Barnes, within reason. Some of Mister Tweedy's requests have been well, *unreasonable*."

"I can imagine." Quentin handed the Quyth Worker the slip of paper. "Here you go. I need you to get these things for me."

Don leaned in to read it. "What you got goin' on there, Q?"

"Nothing but a little courtesy, Purist Nation style," Quentin said. "The Ki were kind enough to invite me to dinner. I'm returning the favor."

Messal opened the slip of paper and read. "This request is most unusual, Elder Barnes. But I will do my best."

"When do you think you can have all that?"

"If I can find what you're looking for, I imagine it will arrive before we leave for Yall in Week Two."

Quentin nodded. "That'll work. Now can we go? I mean, come on, Messal, I want to stay on schedule and you're making us late."

Messal stared for another second, then turned and walked out of the locker room. Quentin and Don followed.

"Q, that's not very nice," Don said. "Messal takes these things pretty serious."

"Gee, Don, ya think? Come on, the little guy needs to lighten up a bit."

The three walked down the tunnel of Ionath Stadium, heading for the field. A year ago, Media Day had filled Quentin with dread. This season he wasn't exactly looking forward to it, but he was resigned to the process, prepared for it. As team leader, this was part of his responsibilities.

"Need any more coaching, Q?" Don asked. "Any tips?"

Quentin shrugged. "I'm guessing it's the same as last year. No locker-room fodder for the other teams, don't say anything bad about my teammates or the organization, stuff like that."

"Well, it will be different this year," Don said. "Now we have The Mad Ju on the roster. Your teammate is the prime suspect in a murder investigation."

"What should I say?"

"Say *no comment*," Don said. "Or something to the effect of, *the league is handling that, I only know Ju as a football player and he's excellent.* That sort of thing."

"Okay."

"They do not need to know that you snagged him out from under the OS1 police in the middle of a gangland shootout. Got it?"

Quentin nodded.

"Good. Oh and don't say that we'll win eight games and go to the playoffs."

"But we will win eight games," Quentin said. "And we are going to the playoffs."

Don stopped at the tunnel entrance. He looked out at the middle of the field, where hundreds of reporters of all species flocked around the various Krakens players. He sighed. "Q, you exhaust me."

"I'm kidding, Don. I know the media game now."

"Oh, you do? *Really?*"

"Well, I know it better than I did last year."

"That ain't saying much."

"Come on, you know I'm better. I've learned a lot. I'm still learning."

Don absently tugged at the white-lined, orange number "8" on his black jersey. "Yeah, you're learning. And fast. I've never seen the like of it, really." His voice sounded distant, maybe a combination of wistfulness and annoyance. "If you're ready, let's do this."

Quentin looked at the older man. "What, we're going out there together? Last year, you went out first. You said going out together would fuel a quarterback controversy."

"Controversy is over," Don said. "You're the starter. Everyone knows it. That makes me yesterday's news. That makes me ... old."

Quentin didn't know what to say. Don Pine, *old?* And yet, Quentin had repeatedly called him *old man.* But that was a general term, an off-hand comment meant to be either an insult or a friendly jibe. Don wasn't really *old,* was he? For the first time, Quentin noticed the lines at the corners of Don's eyes. Noticed the wrinkles at the corners of his mouth. Noticed how the skin on the left side of his jaw sagged a little from when he'd had reconstructive surgery. Noticed the scar on his temple, the one he'd never had surgically repaired.

Quentin felt like he should say something to end the awkward pause, but he didn't have any words. Don stepped onto the field and started walking toward the media. Quentin remembered John's words when the rookies had arrived — *you're not the youngest anymore.*

Would Quentin someday end up like Don, watching a younger quarterback take the field? That felt like an impossibility, something he'd never considered and yet there was no way around it. The only way it wouldn't happen was if he retired as a starter or suffered a career-ending injury. Or, if he died on the field. If those things didn't happen? Someday, just like his hero Don Pine, Quentin would lose the starting job he'd fought so hard to obtain.

And when that happened, Quentin would be the same as every player who'd ever set foot on the field before him. He stared blankly as the weight of inevitability hit home — this would not last forever.

He shook his head, then jogged to catch up to Don. It was a lot to think about, to know that his time was limited, but before it ran out he had much to do.

There were at least eight games to win.

There was a trip to the playoffs.

And, of course, at the end of it all, there was a championship trophy waiting to be lifted high.

The only variable was time.

QUENTIN STOOD TALL in the pocket, ready to take the hits and deliver. Only this time the pocket wasn't his wall of vicious Ki linemen, it was a semi-circle of microphones and cameras pointed at his face, held by a semi-circle of reporters from all over the galaxy.

"*Quentin! Quentin!*"

The shouts of the many-headed monster known as *The Media.*

Messal the Efficient pointed to a Leekee, signifying that that reporter could ask the next question.

"Quentin!" shouted a waist-high, streamlined Leekee. "Kelp Bringer from the Leekee Galaxy Times."

"Ah, Kelp Bringer," Quentin said. "My favorite name of all time."

Kelp Bringer let out a sound that resembled a stick breaking, a stick wrapped in a pound of raw meat. The noise would have made Quentin step back, but his exobiology studies with Kimberlin had prepared him — that was the sound of Leekee laughter.

Kelp Bringer's thin face twisted in what had to be the Leekee equivalent of a smile. "You remembered!"

Quentin nodded. Last year's press conference had ended awkwardly, with Quentin unknowingly insulting Kelp Bringer's spindly symbiotes.

"Sure," Quentin said. "Your question?"

"Last year, in your first game as the starting quarterback, the Isis Ice Storm humiliated the Krakens by a score of 51-7. The only saving grace was that you played at Isis, away from your home fans. This year, Ionath hosts the Ice Storm. How do you think you'll handle the embarrassment in front of a hundred and eighty-five thousand Krakens faithful?"

Quentin ground his teeth. Right off the bat and the reporters were trying to bait him into a sound bite.

"The Ice Storm is a quality team," Quentin said. "We expect a good game. We're better than we were last year. We will play hard and execute."

"So you're predicting a win?" Kelp Bringer asked. "You're going on record that the Krakens will beat the Ice Storm by three touchdowns? Or is it four?"

Quentin laughed and shook his head. He wasn't going to fall for the same tricks anymore. "Next question."

"*Quentin! Quentin!*"

Messal pointed to a Creterakian fluttering around the heads of the other reporters. The bat wore a bright red bodysuit lit up with flashing yellow lights. Creterakian "fashion" — who could understand it?

"Quentin," the bat said, "Kinizzle, Creterakian Information

Service. Are you going to hold some players in reserve against strong teams like the Ice Storm, so that you can keep them rested and uninjured for games against weaker teams?"

"What? Why in the Void would we do that?"

"So you can win two or three games and hopefully avoid relegation, of course."

Stay calm. Stay focused. Quentin rolled his head from the left to the right, feeling his neck bones pop.

"We play to win," he said. "We don't play to *not lose*. We are out to win every game."

Kinizzle fluttered in a circle as he talked, nasty wings flapping madly. "But you were almost relegated last year. Your best chance is to finish higher than the newly promoted team, which is the Orbiting Death, but the experts are saying the Death is already a better team than the Krakens."

"Our goal is the *playoffs*," Quentin snapped. "Let the Orbiting Death worry about relegation. We're going out there to win every game."

He finished his sentence and waited for the chorus of *Quentin! Quentin!* but there was a brief pause as every reporter bent to their messageboards or made some kind of verbal note on their recorders. While short, the silence made him recount his words. What had he said? Was that locker-room material? No, no he'd just reacted normally to a question.

Hadn't he?

He didn't have time to think about it as the multi-headed monster once again started screaming his name. Messal pointed to reporters. Quentin focused his attention on answering the questions.

Then, Quentin noticed a few of the reporters looking at their messageboards. Not writing, but *reading*. Suddenly, it was like a fast-moving virus spreading through every cell of the multi-headed monster. The questions simply stopped. Quentin looked at the reporters. He waited. Was he finished?

The reporters' strange behavior seemed to make Messal nervous. The Quyth Worker held his pedipalp hand palm-up, tapped the floating icons that appeared.

A Human reporter with bone-white skin looked up, waved his messageboard. "Quentin! Quentin! Harold Moloronik from Grinkas NewsNet. Do you have any reaction to Yolanda Davenport's cover story?"

Quentin's stomach twirled. His heart hammered. The *cover* story? The cover of Galaxy Sports Magazine? He had truly arrived — Quentin Barnes was a *star*.

"I haven't read it yet."

"Quentin!" His name screamed again, but this time by Messal. "Elder Barnes, we need to go."

"But Messal, I—"

"*Now*, Elder Barnes."

The reporters screamed his name. They closed in, the phalanx of cameras and microphones pressing closer to his face.

"Messal," Quentin said. "What's going on?"

"Thank you all for your time," Messal shouted at the mob. "Elder Barnes is now finished with questions."

That comment brought a roar of anger from the multi-headed monster. The reporters rushed in, forcing Quentin to calmly start pushing them away.

"Illegal communication!" Kelp Bringer said. "Quentin, is it true that you threw games so you could play for the To Pirates?"

Harold Moloronik jumped onto the back of another reporter, shoved his microphone forward until it smashed Quentin's lower lip. "Quentin, what about aiding and abetting a murderer? Is it true you snagged Ju Tweedy away from the OS1 police?"

Quentin's mind fired blanks. What was going on? Where was all this coming from?

Questions flew, but a surprisingly strong little pedipalp hand yanked at his right wrist. With the reporters screaming after him, Quentin let Messal the Efficient lead him back to the tunnel. Orange- and black-clad stadium security guards stopped the reporters from entering. Messal kept pulling until Quentin was in the central locker room.

"Messal, what's going on? Why were they asking all those questions?"

Messal's eye flooded black. Quentin had never seen the Worker angry before. Messal offered his messageboard. Quentin took it.

Galaxy Sports Magazine. He was on the cover after all, an action shot of him scrambling against the Jupiter Jacks. But the excellent photo wasn't what drew his eye. Instead, he stared at the words below the photo:

SOMETHING IS ROTTEN IN THE GFL

And below that:

IS QUENTIN BARNES THE FACE OF WHAT'S WRONG WITH FOOTBALL?

Quentin slowly sat on the bench in front of his locker, then started to read.

From *Galaxy Sports Magazine*

SOMETHING IS ROTTEN IN THE GFL

Is Quentin Barnes the face of what's wrong with football?

by YOLANDA DAVENPORT

In ancient times, the time even before spaceflight, there was a Human author named William Shakespeare. A thousand years after his death, his works are still known and revered.

One of his most famous lines was "something is rotten in the state of Denmark."

It isn't important to know what a "state of Denmark" is — the term "rotten" is what matters. You know what that means. It means unsavory, disturbing ... *wrong*. Why is that word important?

Because something is rotten in the GFL.

Something that appears to revolve around the Ionath Krakens franchise. More specifically, it revolves around quarterback Quentin Barnes.

Yes, Quentin Barnes, the feel-good story of the past two years. The 20-year-old quarterback prodigy that electrified football fans everywhere with his tough-as-nails approach. The young Human from the Purist Nation who seems to have overcome his culture's racist and speciest beliefs, who assumed the mantle of leadership for one of the league's most storied franchises.

The player who carried the Krakens to Tier One with his talent, then kept them there by force of will alone.

That Quentin Barnes.

So what could be wrong with this feel-good story?

How about aiding and abetting a fugitive in a murder investigation?

How about abusing the GFL's diplomatic immunity power to shelter a murder suspect from the law?

How about illegal contract negotiations with a franchise other than the Ionath Krakens?

How about extensive drug smuggling?

And — what might even be the most disturbing of them all for true sports fans — how about points-shaving and even possibly throwing games outright?

LAWLESS

Ju Tweedy was undoubtedly last season's story of the year. The dominant running back's abilities made him a highly paid legend on Orbital Station One, where he was a fixture in the Orbiting Death's flat-black and metalflake-red. Ju was never known for kind deeds; he is big, strong and vicious. Sentients love to watch him play.

All of that faded when Ju allegedly murdered Grace McDermot, a Human. Ju had a relationship with the victim, a relationship that reportedly went sour. Witnesses put him at the scene of the crime. Police reports show that McDermot was beaten to death by a Human or a HeavyG — someone big, strong and vicious.

Did the OS1 police question Ju Tweedy?

No, they did not. Why? Because Quentin Barnes helped Ju Tweedy flee Orbital Station One within hours of McDermot's death. Barnes then orchestrated a contract for Ju with the Krakens. That contract gave Ju diplomatic immunity and — as long as that contract is in effect — guaranteed he could not be prosecuted for the crime.

Yes, *that* Quentin Barnes. A

source informed this reporter that shortly after McDermot's murder, Barnes took his private yacht to OS1. Witnesses say Barnes was seen at Chucky Chong's League-Style House of Chow, a restaurant in the city of Madderch that possibly sheltered Ju Tweedy shortly after McDermot was murdered. Witnesses recognized not only Barnes, but also several other Krakens players as well as members of the Coranadillana Cloud Killers. The two teams reportedly fought over Ju, a fight that destroyed much of the restaurant and ended in gunfire.

The Krakens spirited Ju away from Chucky Chong's, but the gun battle continued out into the streets of Madderch. Yepew the Elderly, a innocent Quyth Leader bystander, was killed in the crossfire, shot through the eye and left on the sidewalk like so much trash. If you're keeping score, there have been no arrests in Yepew's death, either.

OS1 police records show that shortly after the fight at Chucky Chong's, Ionath Krakens owner Gredok the Splithead filed a request for police protection, citing his GFL right of diplomatic immunity. Police records also show that the request named Krakens players protected by that same right, players including Quentin Barnes, Ju Tweedy's brother John and Ju himself.

Ju Tweedy, you see, had just signed a contract with the Krakens. Therefore, the police couldn't touch him. Two deaths, a running gun-battle in the streets, a destroyed restaurant in his wake and not only did Ju Tweedy walk away, he suited up in the Orange and the Black just one week later and led the Krakens to a win against the Lu Juggernauts.

POINTS SHAVING?

Perhaps you don't mind Barnes aiding and abetting a murder suspect? After all, the GFL is about winning at all costs. So if Barnes is willing to do anything to win, what could possibly make him shave points?

For the uninitiated, "shaving points" is a practice where players want their team to win, but to win by *less than* the point spread. Say the gambling sites favor the Krakens by six points over the Sheb Stalkers. Krakens players might

Why did Barnes pay such an enormous amount to a known fixer? And where did Barnes get that kind of money, when his salary is only 1.2 megacredits a year?

bet on the Stalkers, then make sure Ionath wins by five points or less. If you are a player, this shady practice allows your team to win but lets you directly control the betting results of the game.

Is Barnes involved in points shaving? This reporter can't say for certain. What this reporter *can* say, however, is that Barnes was directly interacting with Mopuk the Sneaky, a low-level gangster who has been missing for the last year.

Yes, *that* Quentin Barnes.

Financial records indicate Barnes paid Mopuk the Sneaky 4.1 megacredits in the seventh week of last year's Tier Two season. Mopuk the Sneaky is well known as a "fixer," a sentient that can arrange for teams to win by less than the point spread.

Why did Barnes pay such an enormous amount to a known fixer? And where did Barnes get that kind of money, when his salary is only 1.2 megacredits a year? These are questions only Barnes can answer.

Perhaps this seems a conspiracy theory. Perhaps it seems ridiculous that a then 19-year-old quarterback could manipulate the older players around him.

This reporter would agree with you, had she not also uncovered the largest player-involved drug smuggling incident in league history.

DRUG SMUGGLING

It is a well-known fact that the Creterakian Empire and the Empire Bureau of Species Interaction (EBSI) turn a blind eye to any smuggling that may occur on team busses. Most owners, after all, are involved in organized crime. Despite GFL Commissioner Rob Froese's claims that he will "clean up and legitimize the GFL," gang lords continue to use team busses as a major distribution route for anything from drugs to information to sentient trafficking. It is a seedy side of the football business that has always been considered a minor and necessary evil.

What is less known to the football-watching audience at large, however, is that the EBSI also turns a blind eye to *players* smuggling contraband. The unwritten, unspoken rule states that customs officials will ignore whatever a player can carry on his or her person, as long as it is not weaponry or explosives.

This practice is ignored because the amounts tend to be so small. It isn't worth putting the expensive athletes at risk by allowing System Police to search them. Any such contact creates the possibility of racist-based violence, something the GFL has taken great pains to avoid.

But the key phrase in the paragraph above is "small amounts."

This reporter has uncovered information indicating that Quentin Barnes coerced his teammates into a unified drug-smuggling effort following Ionath's 2682 game against the Bigg Diggers. It is unknown exactly how much this illegal operation garnered, but reports are it was near five megacredits worth of material.

Yes, *that* Quentin Barnes.

This reporter has not uncovered any additional large smuggling efforts, but she is reminded of the old Ki saying: "Where there is blood, there is a wound." Just because we can't find evidence of another mass smuggling effort doesn't mean another effort — or efforts — does not exist.

PLAYING THE FIELD

This article shows that Barnes has participated in unsavory activities, but — so far — none that are technically illegal. If he has done these things, he has been very careful to avoid anything that could jeopardize his privileged standing as an active player in the Galactic Football League.

Almost anything.

This reporter has learned that as a child, Barnes idolized the To Pirates and dreamed of someday playing for them. During his rookie season of 2682, that dream possibly led Barnes to meetings with the Pirates, meetings that are a direct violation of GFL regulations. When a team is promoted from Tier Two to Tier One, player contracts are protected for two years. Those players can be cut or traded,

Barnes' Tier Three team where he played his first four seasons of professional football.

"Barnes loves the Pirates," Graber told this reporter. "It's all he ever talked about. If he had a chance to play for them, he'd take it."

Eyewitness accounts place Barnes in contact with Maygon, a talent scout from the Pirates, during Barnes' Tier Two rookie season. Had the Krakens not made it to Tier One, Barnes's contract would not have been protected. He could have signed with the Pirates.

> *"Barnes loves the Pirates. It's all he ever talked about. If he had a chance to play for them, he'd take it."*
> — EZEKIEL GRABER

but cannot declare free agency, nor can they be recruited by another team. The rule is so specific that other teams are not even allowed to talk with protected players, yet that is exactly what happened with the To Pirates and Quentin Barnes.

Ezekiel Graber is the head coach of the Micovi Raiders,

At the end of *this* season, however, Barnes *will* be able to sign with the Pirates, the Krakens or any team he wishes. He will be the most coveted free agent in football. He has the potential to become one of the highest-paid athletes in the galaxy. Pirate's quarterback Don Zimmer is clearly in the twilight of his career. Will we see Barnes in the Blood Red next season?

If so, now it will happen legally.

Because if Quentin Barnes is anything, he is careful. The same methodical, surgical approach you see in his passing game is reflected in his off-field activities. And what may be "rotten" about the GFL's new poster boy is that he could be just as corrupt as the gangsters that really run this league.

Possible betting on his own team.

Possible points-shaving.

Aiding and abetting a murder suspect.

Abusing the GFL's diplomatic immunity policy to protect that murder suspect.

Abusing the GFL's diplomatic immunity policy to initiate the biggest player-based drug-smuggling incident in league history.

Illegal contact with another franchise.

Yes, *that* Quentin Barnes.

And after all of this, will he be disciplined? Will he be arrested? Will he at least be questioned?

No. If anything, his actions will be rewarded with one of the biggest contracts in the history of sport.

Something is rotten in Denmark, all right. Even if only some of these things are true, it leaves a black eye on the GFL and on the Ionath Krakens. ■

• • •

QUENTIN STARED at the messageboard, part of his mind hoping this was a prank, a mistake, that it wasn't happening, not *really* happening, not to him. Everyone knew his secrets now. Everyone in the galaxy. What was he going to do? Would this ruin the season?

"Elder Barnes?"

Quentin looked up. Messal closed his left pedipalp hand, a palm-up holo vanished as he did. Messal's eye glowed a translucent green.

"Gredok requests our presence."

Quentin closed his eyes, hung his head. Gredok. All of this, after Danny the Dolphin had enraged the owner with outlandish contract demands, after Gredok's humiliating trip to Commissioner Froese's office on the *Regulator*. Quentin had *tried* to do the right thing, but now all of it seemed so very wrong.

"Okay." He stood. "I know, no shower, so let's head right to his office."

"No, Elder Barnes," Messal said. "He doesn't want you in his office. He's called for a press conference."

"A press conference? But the article just came out. When does he want a press conference?"

"*Now*, Elder Barnes," Messal said. "If you would please follow me to the media room?"

For just a moment, Quentin thought about making a run for it. But he thought back to that day in the walk-in refrigerator with Mister Sam, how easy it would have been for the police to find a tall, gangly 11-year-old. He couldn't hide then and he couldn't hide now.

Quentin stood and followed Messal out of the locker room.

MESSAL LED QUENTIN THROUGH the door of Ionath City Stadium's media room. This was the place where Quentin had done his post-game press conferences last season. As he walked in, he stared at the table, the chairs, stared at anything but what waited for him past the clear crysteel wall. Same table, same black top, same orange skirting tastefully draped around it. Four black chairs behind the table, microphone stands sitting on the tabletop in front of each one. The wall behind the chairs showed slowly moving logos for Junkie Gin, Rookman Power Company and Sayed Luxury Yachts.

Messal pulled out a chair. Might as well have been an executioner waiting with an open noose. Quentin stepped forward and sat. When he did, he had no choice but to finally look out through the floor-to-ceiling crysteel wall to the fifty reporters beyond.

No, *more* than fifty this time. Ki, Dolphin, Quyth Leader, Creterakian, Sklorno, Human, HeavyG, Aqus, Leekee, maybe even a couple others hidden by the press of at least seventy-five bodies crammed into a space designed for maybe forty. Creterakians flew, circling to stay above the other reporters' heads. The stingray-like Harrah members of the media just floated near the ceiling, wide wings softly undulating to keep them in place.

As soon as he looked, the media monster opened its many mouths and began to scream for blood.

"*Quentin! Quentin!*"

"Elder Barnes will not be taking questions," Messal said. "Gredok the Splithead will be here momentarily."

The reporters stopped screaming. They looked at each other in surprise. That bit of information seemed to shock them. Quentin leaned back and waved to Messal, who scurried forward to listen.

"Why are they acting like that? They never heard Gredok talk before?"

"Not as far as I know," Messal said. "I have worked for Gredok for ten years and in that time he has *never* spoken directly to the media."

What did that mean? Gredok had never addressed the media directly? Why now? Was he going to hang Quentin out to dry? Tell the media that the racist criminal from the Purist Nation was no longer welcome in Ionath?

Whatever Gredok had to say, Quentin would just sit and watch. Things had spiraled far beyond his control.

The many-headed monster's babble dropped to a murmur. All of the heads turned to the right. Quentin turned as well and saw Gredok the Splithead standing at the edge of the table, staring back at the reporters.

Gredok slowly walked to the podium. Messal grabbed a chair and slid it back. Gredok crawled into the chair, then stepped from it onto the tabletop. With Quentin still seated, the move made Gredok the tallest being in the room.

Gredok looked out and down at the seated reporters. "I will now take questions."

"*Gredok! Gredok!*"

He pointed a pedipalp finger at a reporter. "You."

"Jonathan Sandoval, Net Colony News Syndicate. Gredok, are you surprised by this article?"

"Nothing that Yolanda Davenport does could ever surprise me. She is the worst kind of journalist, promoting sensationalism for her own benefit."

"So you're saying the article isn't true?"

"I am saying that Quentin Barnes is innocent of any wrongdoing. This article is a slanderous attempt to pad Davenport's career."

Sandoval turned to face Quentin. "Quentin, how upsetting will it be to see Don Pine replace you as the starter?"

Gredok stomped his right foot on the tabletop, creating a little *bang* of noise that made every head turn to face him once again. Quentin saw Gredok in profile, saw his big, clear cornea swirling with black. Fake anger. Gredok was trying to use emotions like playing cards — intimidating, shocking, dealing the reporters a hand that he already knew he could trump.

The reporters, at least most of them, immediately bought into the charade. A crysteel window separated them from the gang lord, but everyone in the room knew this wasn't just some impetuous athlete. The room's mood had changed. For perhaps the first time in some of their careers, the reporters sensed they needed to choose their words carefully.

"All questions will be addressed to *me*," Gredok said. "None of you will speak to my player. The media has demonstrated what happens when players are open and honest, when we allow free access to their lives."

The seventy-five-headed monster fell uncomfortably still, waited for the small but powerful black-furred sentient to continue. He milked the moment, staring each one down in turn.

"Quentin Barnes is the Ionath Krakens' *starting* quarterback," Gredok said. "We stand behind him one hundred percent. We believe in him. We will defend him against all accusations. He will start against the Isis Ice Storm. Because you members of the media seem so challenged by things like basic comprehension, I will repeat it again — *Quentin Barnes is the quarterback of the Ionath Krakens.*"

Quentin stared at the Quyth Leader. From the first words of that article, Quentin had wondered if Gredok would finally lose all patience. Not only was Gredok keeping his cool, he was *defending* Quentin. Gredok's anger was fake, calculated, but his support of his young quarterback?

Totally genuine.

Gredok turned to face Quentin. "Barnes, I will handle this. You may leave."

A tug at his wrist. Quentin looked at Messal, who was gesturing for Quentin to follow. Quentin stood and walked behind Gredok, to the door that led back to the locker room. Before he left, he heard Gredok again address the media.

"I will take more questions," he said. "Ask what you will, but I strongly suggest you address me with *respect*. Now, who is next?"

10

PRESEASON WEEK FOUR: JANUARY 22 – 26, 2684

JANUARY 25, 2684

Quentin dropped back five steps, planted his left foot. The crashing pads and angry grunts of his teammates echoed through an empty Ionath Stadium, filling the football temple with a hollow noise. This was the last time they would practice full-contact. In just two days, on Sunday, January 27, this place would fill with the insane roar of 185,000 fans.

He knew who he wanted to target but properly scanned through his receivers anyway: In the span of a second-and-a-half, he saw Milford on an out pattern — covered; Hawick on a post — just a step open, but he knew Hawick's capabilities and didn't need to test them; Halawa — covered, but she would read the defense and change her pattern to a short hook, but he didn't throw that timing pattern.

His fourth choice was the one he really needed to test.

Tara the Freak.

If you had a good running game, which the Krakens did, you could draw linebackers forward with a play-action fake — pretend to hand the ball to Ju Tweedy and the linebackers would rush forward to stop the run. A play-action fake would leave room right behind them for a *crossing pattern*, where the receiver ran horizontally in the space where the linebackers had just been.

Tara ran left, a crossing pattern through the no-man's land of bloodthirsty middle linebackers — Virak the Mean, John Tweedy, Choto the Bright. Quentin threw as hard as he could; his receivers had to be able to handle not only big hits, but also catch his rocket-hard passes. As soon as the ball left Quentin's hands, he saw John Tweedy and Virak break on it. John was closest — in a split-second, John saw he couldn't reach the ball in time, so instead he focused all his momentum on the receiver.

In one athletic move, Tara caught the pass with his pedipalp hands, pulled it in tight to his body and ducked his helmeted head just as John Tweedy smashed into him. The hit echoed through the stadium, a hammer-sound bouncing off of empty seats and across the open space. Catch-hit-fall, John and Tara dropped to the blue surface.

Still cradling the ball, Tara instantly bounced back to his feet. Quentin felt a rush in his chest, that sensation of *I was so right about him —*

— and then Virak the Mean closed in, full speed and buried his helmet in Tara's back. Tara flew forward, head snapping, middle arms flailing behind him. He fell face-first.

A cheap shot, after the play, a hit so vicious it would have killed most sentients. The team stood there, stunned.

Virak took two steps closer and stood over Tara.

"Just quit, mutie. You're not wanted here."

Despite the lethal hit, Tara again jumped up. Quentin couldn't help but feel another round of that fluttery sensation again — even with a cheap shot, Tara had held onto the ball. So *tough*.

The surreal, violent moment stretched on. Tara whipped the ball at Virak's face, then dove at his legs, tackling him to the ground. Tara's big, mutated pedipalps rained down a *left-right-left* before Shayat the Thick and Killik the Unworthy shot in, hitting Tara, driving him off of Virak.

"Worthless ronin!" Killik screamed. "No Leader wants you!"

Before Quentin could take a step toward the melee, Virak rolled to his feet. He started for Tara, but George Starcher hit him from behind, driving the Warrior to the blue turf.

Practice had turned into a street fight. Quentin rushed in. He reached for Killik but was driven aside by Choto the Bright. Quentin had a brief blur-vision of backup fullback Kopor the Climber tangling with Ju Tweedy, of Tara landing a hard right cross on Killik's helmeted head, of Sklorno suddenly jumping up and down and chittering madly, of John Tweedy screaming *woo-hoo!* And diving into the fray.

Quentin hit the ground, Choto's weight on top of him.

"Stay down," Choto hissed. "Stay out of this."

Quentin's temper flared up. He pushed back, tried to rise, but Choto's forearm pressing down on his windpipe quickly ended the struggle.

Hokor's voice boomed through the stadium, amplified a thousand times over by the sound system. "*Stop this grab-ass nonsense at once!*"

"Two days before our first game and you act like hatchlings? All of you, to the locker rooms. Virak! Starcher! Fifty laps, *together* and if you fight again I'll dock your pay! Tara, two hundred pedipalp pushups and then you run fifty laps as well."

The pressure on Quentin's throat eased off. Choto stood, pulled Quentin to his feet. Quentin's temper still raged, but he held it back.

"Why'd you hit me?"

Choto's eye swirled black. "I did not. Had I hit you, you would know it."

Oh, how Quentin wanted to punch him right in his baseball-sized eye. "You better tell me," he said quietly. "Why'd you put your hands on me?"

"It is my job to protect you," Choto said. "Do not get involved with this. For all of the problems you have faced, you do not want to make Virak the Mean your enemy."

"Shuck that. I'm not going to have fighting on my team."

"Cultural ignorance," Choto said. "I warn you, Quentin —
there are two sentients I would not cross. Gredok the Splithead
and Virak the Mean. If Tara cannot protect himself, then he is not
worthy of anyone defending him."

What a load of crap. Quentin turned his back on Choto and
walked toward Tara, who was ripping off fast pushups. Most of
the team had filtered off the field. Tara's left pedipalp hand bled.
His jersey had been torn off his right middle shoulder, a long rip
showing the cracked chitin beneath. A lot of cracks. This sentient
had led a hard life.

"Tara, are you okay?"

Tara finished his two hundred reps, then stood. Heavy lids narrowing, his black-swirling eye glared. "Leave me alone."

"Hey, I just want to help."

Tara reached down, picked up his helmet. "You've helped
enough," he said, then jogged to the edge of the field and began
his fifty laps. Two years ago, Quentin had fought with Mum-O-
Killowe. Hokor had made the two combatants run laps *together*;
the fact that the coach now made Tara run separately from Virak
spoke volumes — Hokor didn't trust his own authority to keep the
two from going at it again.

Tara would finish his laps, then wait, alone, until the other
Warriors had left the locker room.

Quentin watched his newest receiver run laps until an elbow
drove into his shoulder.

"Hey, Q!" Ah, the love-tap of John Tweedy. "That was some
scrap! Good times! Did you get any shots in?"

John's lip was cut, dribbling blood onto his practice jersey.

"John, what are we going to do? It's only getting worse for
Tara. I need to say something to the team and I need you to back
my play."

John laughed and shook his head. "No way. Don't get in the
middle of this Warrior stuff. Tara will either endure it and stick
around, or he won't and he'll quit."

"But he's *good*, John!"

"Hell yes he is. That shot I put on him? If that had been you,

you'd be in the hospital. If it had been Hawick, she'd be in a body bag. And then that cheap-shot Virak landed? Forget about it. Tara's the real deal. You wanted to know if your new receiver could take the hits? I think you got your answer."

John jogged toward the tunnel. Quentin stood there, thinking, wondering, *hoping* that his gamble might have paid off.

Hokor's golf cart floated down to the field and landed next to Quentin.

"Barnes," Hokor said, his voice now normal and not amplified by his cart's speakerfilm or the stadium's sound system. "What do you think of Tara's readiness? Is my rookie receiver ready to play in our opener against the Ice Storm?"

Quentin laughed. "*Your* rookie receiver? Come on, Coach, don't you mean the *reject* that you would never allow on your team?"

"I am not blind, Barnes. My eye sees quite well. Throwing to the Freak over the middle creates a serious strategic problem for our opposition. If linebackers have to stay home, Ju will get the extra two or three steps he needs to run them over. If Tara plays like this in an actual game, it makes us even more difficult to defend."

"So what you're really saying is, *Gee, Quentin, you were right and I was wrong.*"

"I said *nothing* of the kind, Barnes!" Hokor flew his golf cart off the field.

Quentin watched the coach go. Alone, the thoughts of practice, of the Warriors targeting Tara, they faded away. His off-the-field problems once again crowded his thoughts, darkened his mood. With a football in his hands, he could tune out anything. Practice was over — that let things come rushing back.

The galaxy thought he was a villain.

Yolanda's article had been only the beginning. Sports shows, reporters, bloggers, fan sites — he was the talk of the universe. Quentin was the big story, pushing the former top story — the Prawatt/Sklorno crisis — to second place. The galaxy simmered near the brink of war for the first time in four decades and more people were concerned about a football player.

Last year, Gredok had sequestered Quentin to protect him from terrorists. This season, he was sequestered again — to keep him safe from reporters. Gredok forbade him from talking to the media or even leaving the Krakens building and stadium complex.

Quentin carried his helmet in his left hand. He tossed the football up and down in his right as he walked to the tunnel. Fifty yards away, Tara the Freak sat in the orange end zone. Tara was a great addition to the team. But there was more to football than skill. A player had to excel during a *game* and had to mesh with his teammates. Coach Hokor had seen enough that he would call plays for Tara that coming Sunday. The Freak would get his chance. John Tweedy now accepted Tara, a respect earned through toughness. But John and Coach Hokor were not the entire team.

Different species, different cultures, but they were *all* football players. If Tara could succeed in an actual game, maybe the Warriors would back off and accept him as part of the team.

Quentin didn't know if that would work, but it was the next step. The team *would* accept Tara the Freak. Quentin would tolerate nothing less.

JANUARY 26, 2684

One final step marked the end of preseason. Four weeks of preparation had led to this, to the posting of the final team roster.

The GFL allowed fifty-three players per franchise. Teams could bring in as many players as they liked in the four weeks of preseason, but come kickoff for the opening game, the franchise had to reach that magic number.

Of those fifty-three, only forty-five were named "active" and could dress for games. These players proudly wore their team colors on Sunday. They could accurately say, "I am a professional football player." The eight players who were on the roster but couldn't dress for games were declared "inactive."

Inactives, also known as "practice squad" players, practiced every day, went through the same conditioning as everyone else, but didn't get the glory of a Sunday afternoon. Practice squad players often took on the role of opposition defenders, trying to give the starters the most accurate preparation for upcoming games. Being a practice-squad player carried mixed emotions — you were getting paid to play football, but you weren't quite good enough to dress for games. An injury to someone higher up on the depth chart could move you up in an instant. Being inactive wasn't the role these players wanted, but it was still a damn sight better than, say, working in a mine for twelve hours a day.

For young players, being named to the practice squad was often a good thing. It meant you had made the team, that you had time to develop your skills and — someday — maybe make the active roster. For older players, however, being named to the practice squad was often the last step before your career ended. If you were a seasoned veteran, your speed, reaction time and other physical capabilities were already in decline. All things being equal, any team would choose a younger player for that practice-squad slot. Younger players would get better, while the older players would only get worse.

Position depth charts were posted throughout the preseason. As the regular season drew near, some players moved up and some players moved down. You always knew if you were a starter, a first backup, a second backup, et cetera. What you did *not* know, however, was if Coach Hokor would decide you weren't needed in the 45-player game-day roster. For the third- and fourth-string players, anxiety over that pending decision grew and grew, building in intensity, right up until the team walked off the field for the final day of preseason practice.

The Krakens gathered in the central locker room. Coach Hokor walked to the holoboard.

"Final depth charts and active squad," he announced to the team. "If your name isn't on the board, come to my office immediately."

Hokor tapped the screen. The names flashed up and that was that. No apologies, *no thanks for trying*. The GFL was an unforgiving business — you were either good enough to play or you weren't.

Quentin watched the players rather than the board. The starters, like John and Ju, didn't even bother to look. Their positions were assured. Like the Tweedy brothers, half of the team simply filtered into their species-specific locker rooms.

The remaining players moved forward.

There were unabashed sighs of relief, body language cues showing that the players had found their name on the active roster. These reactions came first because those names were near the top of their positions.

Next came the response of those who were still on the team but hadn't made the active roster. Some of these players showed excitement — they had thought themselves gone but now had a second chance to prove their abilities. For others, the news came as a shock. Even if they had felt it coming, there was always an element of denial, that feeling of *it can't happen to me.*

Wan-A-Tagol was the first. He'd been a second-string left defensive end behind Aleksandar Michnik. The thought had been that Wan-A would develop and become the starter when Aleksandar's skills faded due to age. Only Aleksandar's abilities *hadn't* faded. If anything, Aleksandar had only gotten better. Then the Krakens had picked up rookie Rich Palmer and the free agent Cliff Frost. Both of them were better than Wan-A and apparently Hokor didn't see the need to dress the team's fifth-best defensive end.

Wan-A's career had just been dealt a setback. He was now on the practice squad. Wan-A was twenty-six — damn near a baby by Ki standards. He could bounce back, but it would depend on how hard he worked.

For Mezquitic, however, all the hard work in the world couldn't change her downward slide.

Last season, the Sklorno defensive back had already begun to shown signs of slowing. Her vertical leap had dropped a half-inch coming into last year then *another* half-inch coming into this season. Too many hits had taken their toll.

Quentin watched her, knew when she saw her name listed on

the practice squad. He knew that moment because she started to shake. Her eyestalks sagged, drooping like wet spaghetti. Her raspers unrolled, dragged on the floor. She dropped to the ground and quivered.

The other players simply stepped around her, looking to the board to find their own names. Quentin wanted to go to her, try to cheer her up, but he knew that would only make things worse. No one could help Mezquitic. She would deal with it and contribute to the team any way she could, or not deal with it and be cut altogether.

The last players to react were those who hadn't made the team at all. They were last because they read the list of names over and over, the emotional side of their brain trying to see if the logical part had made a mistake, that their name was on the final roster but somehow they had just missed it.

They hadn't missed it. They were just gone.

Tiburon didn't find her name. Her career with the Krakens had come to a shattering, sudden end. Curiously, she seemed to handle it better than Mezquitic. Maybe Tiburon could catch on with another team, but at her age, it was unlikely. Twenty-three years old, a five-year veteran and the Sklorno's time in the GFL was over.

She didn't bother walking into the Sklorno locker room. Instead, she walked to the main exit, undoubtedly headed straight for Hokor's office. There, she would get a ticket for the next transport to Sklorno space.

Quentin looked back to the board, saw Tom Pareless standing there, nodding his head slowly. Tom hadn't made the roster. He smiled, nodded again, then sniffed. He wiped at his right eye.

Quentin walked up to the older man. "Tom? You good?"

Tom looked up, smiled. He started to talk, then closed his mouth. He swallowed.

"I knew it was coming," he said finally. "My ankle never healed right. I was good enough to hold onto the starting spot for most of last season, but Becca is just plain better. I knew the writing was on the wall when Gredok brought her in last year. This just ... this just came on so fast, you know?"

Quentin nodded. A year ago at this time, Tom Pareless had been the starting fullback for the Ionath Krakens. Today? Cut from the team altogether, a discarded player. It could — and did — happen just that fast.

"Sorry, man," Quentin said. "I mean, I would have thought that you still had an edge on Kopor the Climber."

Tom shook his head. "Naw, I'm not too proud to realize that Kopor is getting better. He's only twenty-four, Q. He's got his best years ahead of him. I'm thirty-seven years old."

"You going to try and catch on with another team? You're still better than ninety percent of the Tier Two fullbacks out there."

Tom shook his head again. "I don't think so. The way I've been moving, playing ... I might catch on for a season, but I also might mess myself up even more. After fifteen years, my body is beat up enough. I'm already going to have a lot of pain as I get older. So will you."

Quentin nodded.

"I'm out, Q," Tom said. "*Fifteen years* I played pro. You know how many sentients can say that? Not very many. Fifteen shucking years. Time to move on to something else."

Quentin tried to think of another career, something to say that would give Tom least a little encouragement, but in the moment he couldn't conceive of a job anyone would want to do after football. "Like what?"

Tom peeled off his shoulder armor and dropped it on the floor. He rolled out his neck, sniffed again, then smiled. "Maybe front office. All I know is football. Well, it's time for me to go see Hokor."

"Aren't you going to shower first?"

"Hell no," Tom said. "Just because this has to be done doesn't mean I'm going to make it easy on him. Let him smell my stink one last time."

Tom offered his hand. Quentin shook it.

"This is the life we have chosen," Tom said. "I put in fifteen years, I can still walk and I can eat things other than soup through a straw. I'm lucky."

"Shuck that," Quentin said. "You have those things because you were *good*. You were one of the best."

Tom slapped Quentin on the shoulder, then walked out of the locker room.

Everyone filtered away from the board, leaving only two Ki standing there, staring. Per-Ah-Yet and Roth-O-Lorak. Per-Ah-Yet, a backup defensive tackle, was seventy-five years old. Old even for the Ki, who often played into their late sixties. Roth-O-Lorak, however, was only thirty. Roth-O, a backup center, just plain wasn't good enough. If he kept playing, he might catch on in Tier Two or could likely wind up all the way down in Tier Three.

Hurt radiated off of the two Ki. They stared at the board for another minute, then together they turned and scuttled toward the door.

Quentin watched them go. Just like that, four careers had ended. Someday, *he* would be staring at that board, looking for *his* name over and over again. And no matter how many championships he won between now and then, it would crush him.

He walked to the Human locker room. Teams changed. That was life. What mattered for now was that the Krakens were his team. His coach believed in him. His team owner backed him up. All his friends were here and soon the galaxy would see that the Krakens were a team to be feared.

The only variable was time.

THE GRAV-CAB STOPPED in front of John Tweedy's apartment building.

This time, however, Quentin wasn't there to see John.

Choto the Bright stepped out of the cab, looking up and down the street as he'd done dozens of times before. That was also the same, but also different — now he was looking for reporters.

Choto leaned back into the cab. "It is clear. Come on."

Quentin got out, trying to ignore Choto's coldness. Their friendship, their bond as teammates, it felt weakened if not gone altogether. Quentin's insistence that the Quyth Warriors accept

Tara the Freak had strained relationships to the point of breaking. He hadn't thought it would be easy to integrate the Warriors, but even so he'd drastically underestimated the cultural response.

Pizat the Servitous waited by the open door.

Quentin and Choto walked inside. The door shut behind them. Choto immediately moved to a lobby chair. He pulled an object out of his pocket. The linebacker spent most of his money on historically accurate reproductions of ancient dead-tree books. Choto sat and started reading — now that he had done his job and seen Quentin safely inside the guarded building, he was done.

"Mister Elder Barnes," Pizat said. "Welcome back. We are honored to have you as always. Shall I ring up to Mister Tweedy?"

Quentin shook his head. "I'm not here to see John. What apartment does Don Pine live in? And don't call him to tell him I'm coming up. This visit is a surprise."

QUENTIN IGNORED THE BUZZER. He wanted to hit something. Banging his fist on Don Pine's apartment door did little to diminish that urge.

"Don! Open up."

No answer. He banged again. "Open the damn door, Pine! We need to talk."

Quentin had waited for days for Pine to come and apologize, to take responsibility. That hadn't happened. Pine should have talked to the press, taken the blame for the things that he had done, the things that had turned Quentin into a media pariah. Quentin shouldn't have had to seek Pine out.

At the same time, Quentin could try to guess Pine's state of mind. If Quentin had done something for which, say, John Tweedy had taken the blame, then John got into trouble for it, Quentin would have felt shame and guilt. Don had to be feeling those things right now. Maybe it was hard to face a friend when you had done that friend wrong.

Quentin focused on that thought, tried to calm himself. This had to be difficult for Don. He probably thought Quentin wanted to kill him. As soon as Quentin could show Don that there would be no retribution, no hatred, then Don would obviously do the right thing.

The door opened. Don wore a strange apron-thing, splotched with bits of color both wet-new and faded-old. His face showed his age now more than ever, a haunted look in the eyes that revealed his pain, his guilt.

Don stepped aside and held the door open. Quentin walked in.

The apartment design was identical to that of John's — a long entryway that led to a living room beyond. In that living room, paintings covered the walls. Only a few were framed. Most were rectangular canvases resting on the floor, hung at odd angles or tacked up haphazardly. All of the paintings showed images of football players. Some were quite striking. Hard, abstract lines seemed to be colored gibberish, but almost immediately Quentin recognized John Tweedy, Michael Kimberlin and several other players. Other paintings showed grotesque versions of a Human face — blue skin, staring eyes, dark shadows.

Self-portraits of a man that didn't like himself very much.

A new painting, gleaming wet, sat half-completed on an easel in the middle of the room. Only the outline and the eyes were done. So dark. The same haunted expression Quentin had seen when Don opened the door.

"You're a painter?"

"Can't put one past you, Quentin."

Quentin turned to look at his mentor. "This is why you don't have anyone over? You embarrassed about this or something?"

Don shrugged. "My space is my space. I don't need to justify it to anyone. But ... yeah, stuff like this, it's not really how the team sees me, you know?"

Quentin nodded. The team didn't see Don like this at all. They saw a champion, a leader, a man that exuded confidence and support at all times. Quentin instantly understood why Don didn't invite anyone in — team leaders weren't supposed to be cauldrons of self-hatred.

"Well? Did you read Yolanda's article?"

Don nodded.

"You see the press conference?"

Don nodded again.

Quentin waited, trying to be patient. It wouldn't be easy for Don to step up and reveal that he had been the one shaving points, throwing games, selling out for Mopuk the Sneaky.

Don said nothing.

"Don, it's time. You have to come clean."

Don closed his eyes. His fingertips pressed hard into his temples, circling there like small drills trying to punch through his skull and into his brain. A bit of black paint on his left index finger smeared across his left eyebrow.

Still Quentin waited. Patience. No need to rush things, no reason to lose his temper.

His friend didn't say anything.

"Don? You okay?"

The older quarterback shook his head. "How can I be okay? That article crucified you, man. It's my fault."

"Only the drug-smuggling part," Quentin said. "And the gambling. And throwing games." The words didn't sound as helpful as he had thought they would.

"I feel real bad," Don said. "Honestly, Q, I can't even tell you how awful I feel about all this."

Don stopped rubbing his temples and stared at the floor. He shifted his weight from foot to foot. It took Quentin a moment to read Don's body language. He'd never seen Don act like this before, never seen him act … *indecisive.*

Quentin waited. Tense silence filled the room. Don looked up, met Quentin's eyes for a moment, then he looked away, staring at one of the self-hating paintings on the wall.

Quentin felt a crawling feeling of shock. Slowly, not wanting to believe it for a second, realization set in.

"You're *not* going to fess up? You're *not* going to tell Yolanda?"

"Like that bitch would do anything to fix this."

"Fine, then not her. *Anyone* else. There's a hundred reporters waiting to hear the truth, Don."

Don's eyes flicked to another painting. An older painting, brighter, with bolder lines. An abstract quarterback wearing silver, gold and copper. Don Pine back in his championship days.

Quentin realized he was breathing heavier, that his temper was rising. He calmed himself, tried to think. He had risked his career to save Don's. Quentin had risked his *life*. That dark secret had been fine as long as it remained a *secret*, but now the story was out. Out and with the wrong man taking the rap. Don would snap out of this any moment, he would step up and do the right thing. He *had* to.

"Don, you're going to tell someone, right? You're not going to leave me hanging. *Right?*"

Don said nothing.

Quentin's chest seemed heavy. It ached. He'd never felt anything like this before. He'd never really had friends back on Micovi. Other than Mister Sam, Don Pine was the first person Quentin had truly trusted. Don's mentoring, his patience, those things had helped make Quentin the player he was today, the *leader* he was today. Yet this mentor, the man who had risen to the pinnacle of their profession, he was turning his back on real leadership — the leadership of responsibility.

"I don't believe it," Quentin said. "You're not going to tell the truth."

Don shook his head. "I can't, Quentin."

"You *can't*? No-no-no, old man, you *won't*. You're really going to hang me out to dry?"

Don turned, the pain in his soul etched on his expression. "Quentin, you gotta understand. I've only got a year or two left. If this gets out now, my career is over."

Was this level of betrayal even possible? "What about my career?"

"You're the starting quarterback! Gredok is standing up for you. This is your team, man."

"The galaxy thinks I'm a scumbag, Don. Sentients are saying—"

"They'll get over it," Don said. "You're young, Quentin.

You're a star. As long as you keep throwing completions and scoring touchdowns, the galaxy could give a crap if you chop up babies and cook them in a stew."

"That's easy for you to say."

"Look at Ju Tweedy. He's actually wanted for *murder* and he's going to line up on Sunday and play in the biggest sports league that history has ever known. Don't you get it, Quentin? As long as you do what you can do, it doesn't matter what people think."

"It matters to me."

Don stared at him, but couldn't hold it. He looked away. "Sure, okay, I know it matters to you. But you don't understand, you *can't* understand until you're standing where I'm standing. At my age, the way I've played the past few seasons, a scandal like this means no one will touch me."

"But that doesn't matter! *You're the one* who did wrong, *not* me. Are you going to be a coward, or are you going to face the music?"

Quentin again waited for an answer, hoping that this time Don would see what needed to be done, that he would do the right thing.

But Don Pine didn't waver.

"I can't," he said. "Not now. Not this season. I'm sorry."

The coward. How could Don do this? "And what if I tell the media? What if I tell them all about your involvement with Mopuk, how your entire team smuggled drugs to pay off your debt so you could stop *throwing games?*"

Don closed his eyes and looked down. "I'll deny it. And you won't do that, Quentin. I know you. If you start a he-said, he-said thing, it will mess with team unity, which is already at a breaking point thanks to Tara the Freak. Right now the team is behind you. If you start forcing them to choose between you and me, the team will lose focus. That will cost us games. Not all of them, but enough to keep us out of the playoffs, maybe even enough to put us on the relegation bubble again. You won't say anything, because as much as your integrity means to you, we both know winning means even more."

Quentin's temper rippled, simmered just below boiling. He wanted to hit Don, to smash the easel over his head, to tear down all these feel-sorry-for-myself paintings and rip them to shreds. And yet, Don was right — as awful as this was, Quentin would rather carry the weight of false accusations than free himself at the expense of the team.

"I wish I'd never helped you," Quentin said. "I should have left you broken in that hospital bed, should have let them finish you."

Quentin's hands shot out, grabbed the painting off the easel. He threw it at Don. The wet canvas *fwapped* against Don's head, then fell to the floor. Don stared, the dark paint of his self-hatred caked on his face.

Quentin's hands balled into fists, but he kept them at his sides.

He walked out of the apartment, his heavy feet echoing off the entryway walls.

BOOK THREE:
THE REGULAR SEASON

11

WEEK ONE:
ISIS ICE STORM
at IONATH KRAKENS

JANUARY 27, 2684

SEASON OPENER.

Home opener.

A chance to not only kick off a new era in Ionath football, but to lay some retribution on a team that had ripped them 51-7 the year before. The Krakens had worked all off-season toward winning this game, using last year's humiliatingly lopsided loss as fuel to work harder, to dig deeper, to get better.

Outside their locker room, the Ionath Krakens packed into the tunnel. Up ahead, Quentin saw forty-five Ice Storm players at the tunnel's exit where it opened into the back of the black end zone. He stared at the massed collection of snow-white helmets, metal-blue sword-snowflake logo only on the left side, chrome facemasks catching the tunnel lights. The Ice Storm's jerseys were white on the shoulders fading to a light blue at the waist, circled by chrome belts. Leg armor gleamed in that same light blue at the hips, gradually darkening in shade until it ended at navy blue shins and shoes.

The blue-trimmed chrome numbers on their shoulder pads and backs seemed to dance with life.

The Ice Storm wore the mostly white jerseys when they played at home. Because the Krakens' home jerseys were black, the Storm also wore their white gear when visiting Ionath.

The sight of those white, blue and chrome uniforms, of those players, it filled Quentin with a cold rage. The Ice Storm had finished the 2683 season with eight wins, four losses and a trip to the playoffs. They had lost in the first round to eventual GFL champion Wabash Wolfpack, but that didn't matter; Isis had made the playoffs — therefore, the Ice Storm players were among the league's elite.

To be the best, you have to *beat* the best.

Out beyond the tunnel in the huge, open-air stadium, Quentin and his teammates heard the Ionath faithful. Over 185,000 sentients screaming a unified pre-game chant.

"Let's go KRAK-ens!" clap, clap, clap-clap-clap. "Let's go KRAK-ens!" clap, clap, clap-clap-clap.

Quentin shook with anger, with excitement. The ceremony was about to begin, the affirmation of life, of all he was and all he was born to be. High One had created him for this *and* this alone.

The announcer's voice echoed across the field, filtered into the tunnel. As always, announcements came first in the Quyth language, then in English.

"Hello everyone and welcome to Ionath Stadium. Please give your warmest greetings to today's visiting team, the Isis Ice Storm!"

The white-jerseyed team rushed out of the tunnel to the overpowering sound of *boos* and the sound of some 50,000 Quyth workers scraping their bristly forearm fur together — a chorus of sandpaper on rough wood. There were enough cheers to show Quentin that plenty of Isis fans had made the six-day trip across the galaxy to support their heroes.

The Krakens moved up the tunnel. Now Quentin could see out into the stadium. One hundred eighty-five thousand fans, beating their feet in place. A rhythmic war-drum that demanded blood.

Quyth Workers filled the higher rows, the upper decks. Humans, Quyth Warriors and Leaders packed the lower seats.

While not as numerous, he couldn't miss the Sklorno females in the stands, covered head to toe and wearing replica jerseys — Hawick's number 80, Milford's 82, Halawa's 13. Some even wore 84 and 81, the numbers of Scarborough and Denver, who had both been traded to Jupiter. Unlike last year, however, most of the Sklorno fans wore the number of a Human player.

Number 10. Quentin's number.

And the special section, a smaller area enclosed in clear crysteel, packed with bouncing black balls of fur. The Sklorno males, driven so mad by watching the females on the field that they had to be separated from the other spectators.

All of this, Quentin's *home.*

"Let's go KRAK-ens!" clap, clap, clap-clap-clap. *"Let's go KRAK-ens!"* clap, clap, clap-clap-clap.

He looked at the field itself. Deep blue, the color of the Iomatt plant's small, circular leaves. Leaves that smelled like cinnamon. White lines blazed, reflecting the sunlight filtering through the city dome high above.

The Krakens pressed tighter, waiting for the announcer to call them out. Quentin breathed deep through his nose, savored the moment, tasted the emotions.

John Tweedy on his right.

Michael Kimberlin on his left.

The lust for that first snap, that first throw, that first hit.

His teammates filled the air with palpable aggression, with the glorious promise of heavy violence and primitive release. Finally, after a long off-season, after a brutal practice schedule, after putting his teammates through hell to get ready for this game, Quentin heard the words that sent a charge through his chest all the way down to his armor-covered toes.

"Beings of all races, let's hear it for ... *your* ... Ionath, *KRAAAAAA-KENNNNNNNS!"*

Quentin sprinted into the sun's blazing light and the crowd's concussive roar. His feet bounced off the orange-lettered black end zone that matched the uniforms of he and his forty-four team-mates. As a unit, they shot across the white-striped blue field toward the Krakens sideline.

The team gathered around Quentin, pushed in and around him like an accreting planet. HeavyG, Ki, Quyth Warrior and Human pressed together. Sklorno jumped on the outside edges or arced back and forth over the entire pile. The players screamed, grunted, chirped, snorted and barked, not with words, but rather the noises of battle, the sounds of war and excitement and the thrill of feeling so utterly *alive*. The second Quentin started talking, the cacophony dropped to a subtone, a murmuring buzz as the Krakens leaned in to hear their leader.

"New year," Quentin said. He took his time, turning to look directly at each teammate. "New year, new destiny. You all know how hard you worked."

The soft noises of his teammates grew louder as each of them acknowledged this fact.

"You paid the price. You paid it with tough wins to end last season. You paid it in practice. And every one of you remembers what the Ice Storm did to us last year."

The noises grew louder. So did Quentin.

"But now these bastards from Isis have come to *our* house. Our *temple*. They came here expecting an easy win, but they will leave knowing that we are the *law*, that we are the champions in the making."

The teammates jostled closer, bumping him to and fro. There was no feeling like this anywhere in the galaxy, like the pre-game sensation of so many elite athletes uniting as one.

Quentin raised his left fist high. His teammates reached in and up to that fist. Their noises grew so loud Quentin had to scream his next words to have them answered by a chorus of Krakens.

"Whose house?"

"*Our house!*"

"Whose house?"

"*Our house!*"

"What law?"

"Our law!"

"Who wins?"

"Krakens!"

"Who wins?"

"Krakens!"

"Today is *your* day! Not theirs! Victory is yours, *take* it! Let's show Isis what it means to be a Kraken!"

The team's single, unified roar marked the end of the pre-game ritual. The Krakens spread out down the sidelines just as the Harrah refs at midfield called for the team captains.

Time for the coin toss.

Quentin, the offensive captain and John Tweedy, the defensive captain, jogged to midfield. Virak the Mean, the opening game's honorary captain, jogged with them.

The trio stopped on the Krakens' logo at the stadium's very center. Freshly painted as it was every home game, top facing the visitor's sidelines, bottom point aimed at the home stands, white arms spreading from one 45-yard line to the other, the "I" shield-logo marked this field as property of the Ionath.

Our house.

Opposite Quentin, John and Virak stood the Isis Ice Storm captains: quarterback Paul Infante, linebacker Chaka the Brutal and defensive end Ryan Nossek — the man who would spend the next two hours literally trying to kill Quentin.

"Barnes," Nossek said in his hell-deep voice. "I'm so pleased that we get to meet again."

Quentin just smiled at the big HeavyG. Last year's beatings would not be repeated.

The Harrah ref fluttered between the lines of players. He wore a black-and-white striped bodysuit, complete with a black-and-white striped backpack. Yellow penalty flags dangled from the backpack.

"Players," the ref said, his voice coming from the backpack's speakerfilm and also echoed by Ionath Stadium's massive sound system. "The Ice Storm is the visiting team and therefore has the right to call the coin toss. Who will make the call?"

"I will," Nossek said.

The ref slid a flat mouth-flap up into the backpack, came out with a Creterakian coin. He showed it to the players. *Tails* was an image of the planet Creterak, *heads* a close-up of the six-eyed face of some Creterakian leader.

"Call it in the air," the ref said.

He flipped the coin high. Reflections of the afternoon sun sparkled off the spinning metal. Ryan Nossek said: "Heads."

The coin landed on the Krakens' "I," bounced once, then lay flat, showing the image of Creterak.

Tails.

"Krakens win the toss," the ref said. "Krakens, you wish to receive or defer?"

"We want the ball," Quentin said.

Nossek smiled again. "See you soon, young-un."

Quentin nodded. "You'll see too much of me, big fella, 'cause you won't be able to get our offense off the field."

He ran to the sidelines, Virak the Mean on his right, John Tweedy on his left.

"Q," John said. "Can you feel it? I've been in the game a long time, brother, but this just feels *different*."

"Get used to it," Quentin said. "It's only going to get better from here on out."

He stopped at the sidelines, trying to calm himself, to wait for another few seconds before his destiny took flight. The Krakens receiving team lined up, Richfield back to take the kick.

The crowd's low murmur of *ooooooooooooooohhhhhh* started as the Ice Storm kickoff team got into place, a long white/blue/chrome line stretched across the 25-yard line from one sideline to the other. In the center of that line, the kicker raised his hand to the ref. The ref blew his whistle. The kicker dropped his hand, looked at the ball sitting upright at the 35-yard line, then started his slow run toward it. His teammates ran with him, the slow jog quickly building to a full-on sprint.

*ooooooooooo*OOOOOOOOOOOAAAAHHHHHHHH!

The crowd screamed in time with the kicker's foot connecting. The ball arced high into the air. A sudden burst of butterflies flapped through Quentin's belly, a fluttery feeling he knew would go away soon.

Richfield waited at the 1-yard line as the ball arced down. She hauled it in with her tentacles. Her lead blockers — Kopor the Climber, Shayat the Thick, Samuel Darkeye and Tara the Freak — shot forward to take on the first Ice Storm players that streaked down the field.

Black and orange collided with white and blue and chrome. Richfield cut left and found a narrow gap. A white-helmeted Sklorno reached for her, but Richfield pushed through the gap and headed for the sidelines. She picked up another thirty yards before she ran out of room and was pushed out at the Krakens' 48-yard line.

The crowd roared in approval, an infinite, starving beast screaming rapturously at its first taste of food in six months.

Quentin ran onto the field as the kick-return team ran off. His opening drive of the season and he had fantastic field position. The offense huddled up. He fought to control the butterflies. He had to pee. His hands shook.

Light flickered in Quentin's facemask. The heads-up display flared to life, showing Coach Hokor's fuzzy head.

"Barnes! You know the plays. Just relax and get it done."

"Okay, Coach," Quentin said. He tapped twice on the left side of his helmet, making the heads-up display vanish.

Quentin reached the huddle. The starting Krakens players looked back at him: the four Ki and one HeavyG of his offensive line; shaking Sklorno receivers Hawick and Milford; Human tight end Crazy George Starcher, the face inside his helmet painted green with white diagonal stripes; Ju Tweedy, the Krakens' fleet-footed Human tank of a running back; and Becca "The Wrecka" Montagne, last year's HeavyG rookie fullback who had fought her way into the starting lineup.

"All right, all right," Quentin said. "First three plays are scripted, no huddle, you all know what they are. All I-formation. No surprises for anyone that we start out with Ju going off-tackle left — the Ice Storm knows it's coming, the fans know it's coming and we're going to run it anyway, right down their throats. Second play, run-fake to Ju, screen pass right to Montagne. Offensive line, sell those failed blocks and let them come to get me, I'll get the pass off. Third play, regardless of down and distance, I-formation, we go drop-back play-action, X-in, Y-wheel, Z-post, B-block-and-circle. First two plays on three, third play on one. Ready?"

"*Break!*" the team screamed in unison. They ran out of the huddle and lined up. Starting the game with three no-huddle plays had become a Krakens tradition, a way to come out swinging and keep the defense from switching players that could help with specific down-and-distance situations. Last year the strategy had mostly failed, thanks to Yassoud Murphy's lack of urgency. This year, however, Yassoud was out — the Mad Ju was in.

Quentin walked up behind Bud-O-Shwek, his center and surveyed the Ice Storm defense. Ki linemen, HeavyG defensive ends, Quyth Warrior and Human linebackers, Sklorno defensive backs. Five unique races that blended into one unified team, thanks to matching white helmets, white-to-blue jerseys and reflective chrome numbers. The Ice Storm were as much a single tribe as the Krakens.

Like Ionath, the Ice Storm ran a 4-3 defense: four defensive linemen, three linebackers, four defensive backs. To Quentin's right, at the outside edge of his offensive line, stood the most dangerous sentient on the field — Ryan Nossek, the All-Pro defensive end that had killed five players over the course of his career. Quentin also needed to keep an eye on Chaka the Brutal, the left linebacker, and Santa Cruz, the Ice Storm's blitzing safety.

Fingers and pincers pushed into the blue Iomatt field.

Feet dug in.

Eyes narrowed.

Lips curled.

Fists clenched, unclenched.

"Bluuueee, eighteen!" Quentin shouted down the left side of the line. The crowd's roar picked up in intensity, 185,000 fans who had waited all off-season to see the Orange and the Black do battle.

When it wasn't game time, maybe these fans cared about Ju Tweedy's murder rap or Quentin's off-field transgressions, and maybe they didn't. But for now, for this moment, they wanted a win. That was more important than anything.

"Blue, eight*eeeeen*," he shouted down the right side of the line.

The phrase *on three* meant that Bud-O-Shwek snapped the ball on Quentin's third syllable, starting after he finished the color and number calls. Quentin would *hard count* the first two syllables, try to use the defense's eagerness against them and draw them off-sides.

"Hut-*HUT!*" He hammered the last syllable, but the Ice Storm linemen didn't budge.

"*Hut!*"

The ball slapped into his hands. Quentin pushed hard off his right foot, stepping back with his left. Rebecca Montagne shot by, running left to block for Ju, her face the snarling mask she wore only between the whistles. Quentin extended the ball toward Ju.

Ju's right elbow pointed up, the back of his hand on his sternum, his left pinkie flat against his stomach just above his belt buckle. When Quentin put the ball in his belly, Ju's arms slammed together like a supercharged Venus Flytrap. The brown leather vanished behind Ju's thick forearms.

The Mad Ju followed Becca the Wrecka into the line.

Left guard Sho-Do-Thikit and left tackle Kill-O-Yowet were the Krakens' best offensive linemen. They took no prisoners in their four-armed, six-legged ground assault. The two raged against their blue/white/chrome opponents, driving them back. Linebacker Chaka the Brutal closed in, tried to fill the hole, but found himself bumped off-path by Becca's surgical blocking. She shifted Chaka's momentum just enough for Ju to shoot by untouched.

Five yards downfield, two Sklorno defensive backs hit him at the same time, diving beneath his lowered shoulders and wrapping up his thick legs. The D-backs were well-coached — a head-to-head hit with Ju could get a Sklorno killed. They brought him down after an 8-yard gain.

Quentin ran forward as the zebes spotted the ball.

"Let's go, let's go!" He had to scream to be heard over the crowd. "Move-move-move!"

His urgency might have been needed last year, but not now. The Krakens players scrambled to the line, almost racing each other to get into place. The Ice Storm players rushed to their positions. Second down, two yards to go — Isis had no time to switch out players.

"*Red*, eighty-eight!" Quentin surveyed the defense; same formation, a 4-3. He saw Chaka the Brutal lean forward, just a bit, weight on his toes. He was coming on a blitz.

Stats flashed through Quentin's head, a lightspeed data dump recalling everything he knew on Chaka …

… *10-year veteran, 6-foot-2 375 pounds, best 40-yard-dash time 3.8 seconds, reconstructive right-knee surgery in the off-season, one confirmed kill, four career-ending injuries —*

"*Reddddd*, eighty-*eight!*"

Quentin's eyes flicked across the defenders, his brain processed a thousand physical cues in a fraction of a second. He saw such *detail*, as if his eyes were simultaneously microscopes *and* telescopes. To Quentin's right, the Ki left defensive tackle's inside legs tensed, as if he planned to push *away* from Quentin on the snap.

"Hut!"

That tackle would push outside, trying to draw Krakens right offensive guard Michael Kimberlin with him. Behind that tackle, Chaka would run forward and to the *inside*, trying to blitz through the newly opened area vacated by the offensive guard. Drawn on the holoboard, the crossing paths of the two defensive players would look like an "X," a coordinated move known as a "stunt."

"*Hut!*"

The Isis players stayed disciplined, did not jump.

Just before the last syllable, Quentin's eyes again flicked right, to the deadly Ryan Nossek. Nossek's feet were flat — he wasn't coming as hard as he could. Instead, he would hit the offensive tackle, then fight to hold his position and see where the play would go. The play was a screen pass right, to Montagne. If Nossek stayed home, he'd be in position to disrupt the screen pass, maybe even put a wicked hit on Becca.

This deluge of information and computation took place in less than two seconds. As Quentin called off the snap count, the mind of an elite professional quarterback instinctively analyzed more data than any supercomputer or AI could ever do.

"Hut!"

The ball slapped into his hands. Just like the last play, he drove back and to the left. In his mind's eye, he saw Chaka the Brutal behind him, running forward and in, coming through the line, just three steps away.

Becca shot by again, but this time she would block down and then cut hard-right to get open for the short pass.

Chaka would be two steps behind him now.

Quentin reached the ball out to Ju, who slammed his arms down on empty air for the run-fake.

That motion would make the blitzing linebacker pause just a bit, just long enough for Quentin to make a move. Quentin pushed hard off his right foot, away from Ju. His mind had things timed so well that he sensed Chaka's middle arms reach out just an instant before they actually grabbed the back of his black jersey.

Almost, but not quite.

Quentin ran right, pulling away from Chaka's grip. The quarterback's chess-master mind tracked everyone on the field. He knew he had one second before Chaka caught up and brought him down from behind.

Quentin's eyes confirmed what his brain knew was coming — the entire Isis defensive line bearing down on him. In a screen pass, the offensive line gave a hit, then pretended to miss their blocks. This let the defensive line come free while the offensive linemen scrambled to the right to block for Becca. When the pass left Quentin's hand, the defensive linemen would be too far away to help and Becca would have two or three blockers in front of her, ready to rush downfield like a wall of muscle.

A half-second until Chaka caught up.

Quentin looked right — Becca was in her assigned spot, Kimberlin and Vu-Ko-Will were there to block ... but Nossek was there as well. Like the All-Pro he was, he had sniffed out the screen pass.

Quentin raised the ball and faked a throw to Becca.

Three-tenths of a second.

The oncoming, white-jerseyed Ki lineman reached up to block the pass, long multi-jointed arms raised vertical like living prison bars.

One-tenth of a second.

Quentin sprang forward, shooting past the reaching Ki linemen, feeling Chaka's pincers again brush against his back.

Too little, too late.

In a half-second, he was five yards past the line of scrimmage. High One had blessed him with speed and Quentin was thankful for such gifts. The run-fake had drawn in the other linebackers — Quentin shot past and found himself in the open field.

He let his feet do the talking.

The defensive backs closed in on him, or tried to, but the downfield blocking of George Starcher, Hawick and Milford kept them from making a straight-on attack.

Quentin ran toward Starcher's back. Starcher fought with the Sklorno free safety. Quentin faked to the left. The free safety tried to match, then Quentin cut right, toward the sidelines. The free safety again tried to match but couldn't react with Starcher's hands on her chest. She fell to her back, out of the play.

Quentin hit the sidelines and cut upfield.

At the 25 ...

Somewhere in his brain, he realized the home crowd screamed so loud that paint flaked off the stadium walls, that the turf vibrated beneath his feet, that the Low One himself flinched and looked away in fear.

At the 20 ...

The Ice Storm cornerback angled toward him. She would get to him at the five, knock him out of bounds.

At the 15 ...

Yes, he was supposed to slide, but the end zone loomed ahead in all its blackness ...

At the 10 ...

Quentin reared his head back, then brought it forward and to the left with all his weight. The blue/white/chrome missile launched at him, a collision sure to kill brain cells and break bones. He would teach her a lesson, he would show her who ruled this field, he would make an example to all the Ice Storm players and to the entire league and

BLINK

Sanity grabbed hold of him like a mousetrap snapping down on a tiny neck. Head-to-head hits weren't good for the team. He was an asset and he would act like it.

At the 6-yard line, Quentin suddenly leaned back and stutter-stepped, breaking his forward momentum just enough for the over-committed Sklorno to shoot past and crash into the side-lines.

BLINK

The world came rushing back. On the second play of the season, Quentin Barnes casually jogged into the end zone. A 46-yard touchdown run. The stands *shook*, vibrating with thousands of jumping, insane, screaming fans.

Fireworks exploded overhead as the sky turned a deep orange — the entire city dome changing color to signify the first Krakens touchdown of the year.

Quentin tossed the ball to a flying zebe, then knelt and plucked a few black-painted, circular blades of Iomatt.

He sniffed deep, inhaling the slight scent of cinnamon.

He started to stand but was knocked flat as Hawick and Milford hit him harder than most linebackers. The squealing, chittering Sklorno weren't even speaking English, just babbling in their native tongue while they hugged him and shook him. Seconds later, Starcher and Ju Tweedy jumped on the pile. Quentin hoped this would become a trend, that the worst beating he would take during a game would be during a touchdown celebration.

• • •

THE ICE STORM WASTED NO TIME striking back. Paul Infante hit receiver Füssen on a simple out pattern. Berea, the right corner-back, slipped on the tackle and fell, leaving Füssen gobs of open space. She sprinted to the 5-yard line before Davenport brought her down. On the next play, Infante hit running back Scott Wilson on a hook. Wilson caught the ball just as John Tweedy landed a big hit, but they fell in the end zone.

Extra point good, tie game, 7-7.

QUENTIN ROLLED OUT to the right. Chaka the Brutal blitzed again, reaching for him. Quentin, a left-hander, switched the ball to his right arm. His left forearm then shot out, smashing into Chaka's helmet. The blow knocked Chaka's head back, making him stumble. The Quyth Warrior linebacker grabbed Quentin's arm as he fell, pincers raking deep gouges through Quentin's Koolsuit and into his skin.

Trailing a stream of fresh blood, Quentin switched the ball back to his left hand and raised it to his ear, ready to pass, as he kept moving toward the sideline. Ryan Nossek tossed Vu-Ko-Will aside like 600 pounds of trash, then closed in.

Quentin saw all the moving parts as one unified dance — he knew Nossek would hit him, but that the hit would come a moment too late because Hawick had a half-step on her defender. Quentin planted his feet, bounced forward and fired the ball. His blood had spilled onto the cool, brown leather — as the ball spun, it sprayed off a whizzing stream of red droplets. No sooner had it left his fingertips than the HeavyG defensive end hit him in the chest, driving him to his back.

Quentin let out a half-cough, then calmly waited for his breath to return.

Hoooo, that sentient could hit *hard*.

"Hey, rookie," Nossek said, so close to Quentin that only their facemasks marked the distance. "How'd that taste?"

The crowd roared in a way that meant only one thing.

"Tasted like a sixty-two yard touchdown pass," Quentin said. "And I'm not a rookie anymore."

Nossek stood and lifted Quentin like a rag doll, setting him gently on his feet.

"Good pass," Nossek said. "See you again, real soon."

"I'm having company? Heck, Ryan, I'll make you a nice cup of tea."

AT THE HALF, THE KRAKENS led 14-10. Doc Patah worked on Quentin's torn arm. The locker room felt electric. A year ago, the Ice Storm had pounded the Krakens in the first half. Back then, it had almost been an apples-to-oranges comparison — one team destined for the playoffs, the other that didn't really deserve to be in Tier One at all.

But not this year.

The Krakens dominated every aspect of play. Quentin was 7-of-10 for 146 yards, with another 56 yards rushing and a touchdown on the ground. Ju Tweedy had carried the ball 10 times for 39 yards. Aside from the one hit on the touchdown pass, Quentin hadn't been touched. Chaka the Brutal kept blitzing, but he couldn't get past Becca Montagne's blocks fast enough to catch the fleet-footed quarterback. Only one half into the season and already Quentin's instincts told him that he could count on Becca to block her player every time.

Defensively, the Krakens weren't playing as well, but they had only given up 10 points. Ice Storm quarterback Paul Infante had put in a quality performance, but nothing spectacular — 11-of-20 for 112 yards and a touchdown. Quentin had concerns about what would happen when the Krakens faced off against a premier quarterback like the Pirates' Frank Zimmer, the Criminals' Rick Renaud or even — as much as he hated to admit it — the Orbiting Death's Condor Adrienne. He would worry about that later. All that mattered now was the win.

One game at a time.

• • •

LATE IN THE THIRD QUARTER: Ionath 14, Isis 10.

Quentin dropped back and planted, standing tall, so close to the end zone he could smell the orange paint. Late third quarter, second and goal on the Ice Storm's 7-yard line.

Chaka the Brutal blitzed yet again. Quentin's first instinct was to scramble, but Becca was responsible for picking up that blitz so he kept his feet planted. Chaka sprinted in, reached out, desperate to get the sack and change the course of the game.

Sure enough, Becca drove her shoulder pad into linebacker's midsection. She had been surgical with her blocks for the entire game, applying just the right amount of force in just the right direction to take defenders out of the play. This time, however, she must have seen that Chaka wasn't watching her — she hit him so hard she bent him in half, drove him back, a highlight-reel hit that left her standing and him lying flat.

Quentin checked through his receivers.

Hawick: covered at the back-left corner of the end zone.

Starcher: covered on a hook route to the right.

Halawa: late on her break for an out-pattern, she wouldn't be open before Quentin had to scramble.

The defensive line attacked his blockers. The pocket closed in around him.

Quentin calmly turned back to face the middle of the field. Becca had done exactly what she was supposed to do — block the blitzing linebacker, then run to where the linebacker had come from.

She was standing one yard past the goal line, all alone.

Quentin threw a light pass. No need to gun it when a receiver was that wide open. Becca caught the ball.

The Wrecka's perfect execution put the Krakens up by two scores. Extra point good: Ionath 21, Isis 10.

MIDWAY THROUGH THE FOURTH QUARTER, the Ice Storm threatened to cut the lead to four. They advanced to the Krakens' 12-

yard line, but lost the ball when Mum-O-Killowe broke through the line and hit Paul Infante, forcing a fumble. Ibrahim Khomeni recovered the ball for Ionath.

Quentin led his team onto the field. He didn't throw a pass for the rest of the game. The Krakens ran the ball over and over, grinding out the clock. Ju Tweedy carried on first down for five yards. On second, Yassoud Murphy swept right, picking up seven and a first down. And on it went. The Ice Storm defense was too tired to stop the Krakens' punishing ground assault. Ionath chewed up four minutes of clock by running Ju, Yassoud and Becca. Jay Martinez — the third-string running back — even came in for a pair of carries. By the time Isis did force a fourth down, the Krakens were on the Ice Storm's 17-yard line.

Isis had used up all its timeouts. With only 1:12 to play, Arioch Morningstar kicked an easy field goal to put the Krakens up 24-10.

THE SCORE REMAINED 24-10 as the clock ticked down to zero. Awash in the amazing feeling of winning the opening game, of defeating a playoff-caliber team, Quentin led his team onto the field to shake hands with the Isis players.

After giving Infante, Chaka, Nossek and the other players the proper post-game respect, Quentin looked to the sidelines. Actually, he looked *past* the sidelines, to the screaming, orange-and black-clad fans lining the stadium's bottom row.

That's what this was about, really. The fans. They paid for his salary, they paid for this stadium. Without them, Quentin couldn't enjoy this dream of an existence. When the Krakens lost, the fans were crestfallen. When the Krakens won, life could not be any better.

He ran past his team's sidelines, past the benches, past the used-up, bloody nanostrips, past discarded, cut tape, past the equipment racks and the med benches, ran to the head-high wall and reached up to the fans. He high-fived hands, pedipalps, tentacles, multi-jointed arms. He jogged, the wall on his right, happily slapping whatever appendage the sentients reached down and offered. Like at the end of last year, he was aware of Ju Tweedy running along right behind him, John behind Ju, the three of them followed single-file by the rest of the Krakens players.

The crowd ate it up, screaming in adoration. To cheer for your team was one thing. To be acknowledged by the players? That was almost more than the typical fan could comprehend.

Quentin made a full circle of the field before he headed to the tunnel. It was time to celebrate, time to enjoy the payback, a strong start to the long season. Tonight, he and his teammates would revel in this feeling, absorb how much they had improved.

That was tonight. Tomorrow, the victory would mean nothing. Tomorrow, they would start to prepare for the Yall Criminals.

Because the Krakens weren't Tier One's doormat anymore.

Now? Now the Ionath Krakens were the team to beat and they would take all comers.

GFL WEEK ONE ROUNDUP
Courtesy of Galaxy Sports Network

HOME		AWAY	
Alimum Armada	3	**Jupiter Jacks**	17
To Pirates	28	Coranadillana Cloud Killers	10
Wabash Wolfpack	42	Hittoni Hullwalkers	34
Ionath Krakens	24	Isis Ice Storm	10
Lu Juggernauts	6	**Orbiting Death**	17
Themala Dreadnaughts	10	**Yall Criminals**	44
Vik Vanguard	10	**Bartel Water Bugs**	13
Bord Brigands	35	D'Kow War Dogs	17
Neptune Scarlet Fliers	27	Jang Atom Smashers	9
Texas Earthlings	10	**New Rodina Astronauts**	48
Sala Intrigue	15	Shorah Warlords	10

WEEK ONE SEEMED TO VALIDATE the centuries-old saying, "And that's why they pay him the big bucks." Rick Renaud lived up to his record-setting contract with a record-setting performance, notching a new single-game passing yardage record with 452 in the Yall Criminals' 44-10 drubbing of the Themala Dreadnaughts (0-1).

"New team, same story," Renaud said after the game. "Right now, I feel like I can take whatever I want, whenever I want it."

Renaud will try to take more of the same in Week Two when the Criminals (1-0) play host to the Ionath Krakens (1-0), who started strong with a 24-10 home win over the Isis Ice Storm (0-1). Krakens' quarterback Quentin Barnes put in a strong showing of his own, going 17-of-25 for 252 yards with two passing touchdowns and another score on the ground.

Defending GFL champion Wabash Wolfpack (1-0) won a back-and-forth 42-34 thriller over the Hittoni Hullwalkers (0-1). Fullback Ralph Schmeer continued the red-zone dominance we saw in last year's playoff run, rushing for touchdowns of 1 and 4 yards as well as catching a 3-yard pass from quarterback Rich Bennett.

The Orbiting Death (1-0) landed a 17-6 Week One shocker on the Lu Juggernauts (0-1). This is the first time in eight seasons that a newly promoted team won its opening game. The Texas Earthlings (0-1), the other promoted team, lost 48-10 to the New Rodina Astronauts (1-0).

Deaths

No deaths reported this week.

Offensive Player of the Week

Yall quarterback **Rick Renaud**, who threw for four touchdowns and no interceptions in a 28-for-33, 452-yard performance.

Defensive Player of the Week

Coranadillana defensive end **Jesper Schultz**, who had six solo tackles, two sacks and a fumble recovery in the Cloud Killers' 28-10 loss to the To Pirates.

12

WEEK TWO:
IONATH KRAKENS
at YALL CRIMINALS

PLANET DIVISION		SOLAR DIVISION	
1-0	Ionath Krakens	1-0	Bartel Water Bugs
1-0	OS1 Orbiting Death	1-0	Bord Brigands
1-0	To Pirates	1-0	Jupiter Jacks
1-0	Wabash Wolfpack	1-0	Neptune Scarlet Fliers
1-0	Yall Criminals	1-0	New Rodina Astronauts
0-1	Alimum Armada	1-0	Sala Intrigue
0-1	Coranadillana Cloud Killers	0-1	D'Kow War Dogs
0-1	Hittoni Hullwalkers	0-1	Jang Atom Smashers
0-1	Isis Ice Storm	0-1	Shorah Warlords
0-1	Lu Juggernauts	0-1	Texas Earthlings
0-1	Themala Dreadnaughts	0-1	Vik Vanguard

QUENTIN HUMMED THE TUNE to "My Girl from Satirli 6" as he worked his technique. It was all in the wrist, really. There was no real sky above, but in his imagination the light came from an afternoon sun filtering through the overcast, soupy atmosphere of Micovi — not from the artificial lights that blazed through a screen of Ki vines and trees. He had few happy memories from Micovi. It felt good to channel the times when he had been in control, when he had excelled at a skill few people truly possessed.

Most of his Ki teammates relaxed in long hammocks or rested on the ground, studying holos of purple- and white-clad players from the Yall Criminals. A few, however, watched Quentin's every motion. The big, bad Ki linemen seemed transfixed by his actions.

They were halfway through the trip from Ionath to Yall. The team's morale ran high. Seeing IONATH KRAKENS at the top of the Planet Division standings generated a burning sense of pride in the players. Five teams were 1-0. Ionath was listed first only because of alphabetical order, but that didn't matter — they *were* on top.

That pride made the team's practices even better. They were taking a zigzag path to Yall, which meant a three-and-a-half-day trip. Normally, the shipping lanes specified a two-and-a-half-day trip — half-day from Ionath to Chillich, which took them into Sklorno Dynasty space, then one day each for the punches from Chillich to Chachanna and Chachanna to Yall. That lane, however, meant they popped out in the same area where the Sklorno shipping tragedy had happened, where 50,000 souls were lost. Lots of Creterakian military activity in that area, tight travel restrictions and the cause or culprits of the disaster had yet to be figured out. So instead, Captain Cheevers took them from Chachanna *back* into Quyth Concordia space to a dead planet called Waypoint. From Waypoint, they would do a one-day punch that would bring them out on Yall's far side, away from the area of the disaster.

As Captain Kate sailed them along this slightly longer route, the Krakens banged away on the practice field, preparing for the major showdown with the Criminals. All games were equally important, granted, but the Criminals were 1-0 and tied for first. They also had quarterback Rick Renaud — the highest-paid player in league history. The defense couldn't wait to get its hands (and pedipalps, and multi-jointed arms, and tentacles, and teeth) on Renaud who — by virtue of his huge contract — had become a big-game trophy. To sack him, to put him out of the game, that was to gain the attention of a galaxy.

After that day's practice, Quentin had announced he would prepare a meal for the Ki players and for anyone else who wanted to join. Location: the forested clearing in the Ki offensive players' quarters. The Ki, after all, had given him the hospitality of sharing their dinner. Now he would do the same for them. Called out in front of the entire organization, the Ki could do little but accept the offer.

Mum-O-Killowe, Sho-Do-Thikit, Bud-O-Shwek, Michael Kimberlin and John Tweedy stood near Quentin, watching him work the spatula. All seven HeavyG players were there, which wasn't surprising — the big fellas never passed up a meal. Becca was around somewhere, but as long as she kept her distance, Quentin didn't mind.

Only one Quyth Warrior player had come. It wasn't hard to figure out why — Quentin had insisted that Tara the Freak be there. Where Tara was, the other Warriors were not. Tara stood off by himself, as usual, but at least he was there. Most of the team's twelve Human players milled about, waiting to eat. Even Rick Warburg was in attendance, although Quentin suspected that was more for the Purist Nation-style food than for the company.

Don Pine was nowhere to be seen.

Shizzle fluttered over and perched on Mum-O's shoulder, also peering down at the strange device Quentin had rolled into the Ki offensive quarters. Shizzle wore a yellow bodysuit that showed animated, flapping images of smaller Creterakians, also wearing yellow bodysuits.

Mum-O's triangular lips curled. "Griha re krolla mej."

Quentin looked up and smiled. He still didn't understand the Ki language, he never would, but the more he got to know his teammates, the more he could imply meaning by tone, context and situation alone.

"What is this, you ask? This, my big, frightening friend, is called a *grill*. It is what one uses to properly barbecue."

Quentin flipped one of the twenty burgers sitting on the metal rack, then turned the two dozen pieces of chicken sizzling with orangish-red sauce.

John pointed to a burger in the middle, which happened to be the largest one. He glared at Mum-O.

"*Mine*," John said. NOBODY TOUCHES DADDY'S FOOD played across his face tattoo.

Mum-O stared at the grill, then grunted something barely audible. Quentin laughed — had a Human mumbled something to the same effect, it might have been *I don't know about this*.

"Shizzle," Quentin said. "Out with it. What did the great Mum-O-Killowe say?"

Shizzle flapped his ugly wings, adjusting his position on Mum-O's shoulder. "The Great Mum-O-Killowe wants to know what you are doing with that ... that *ground-up* meat."

"Cooking," Quentin said. "I am making everyone hamburgers."

A wisp of smoke breezed across Mum-O's face. The big creature's lips curled and he leaned back a bit. He grunted something short and to the point.

"The Great Mum-O-Killowe says you are ruining the animal flesh," Shizzle said. "He said cooking is for elitists who over-complicate things to make themselves feel more important."

Quentin laughed. "He said *that*? Really?"

"The Great Mum-O-Killowe is quite eloquent," Shizzle said. "You are surprised?"

Quentin flipped the row of burgers again. "Yeah, I guess I am."

"How ironic," Shizzle said. "You complain about sentients calling you a *stupid jock*, I believe is the phrase you use, yet you think the same thing about a Ki because you don't understand his words."

Quentin hated to be corrected, but Shizzle was right. "Yeah, Shizzle. I did think that." Quentin turned to face Mum-O. "Oh,

Great One, I sincerely apologize for my hypocrisy of underestimating your smarts."

Quentin bowed, then stood up quickly, flicking the spatula as he did. A glob of greasy meat-fat flew off the end, landing on Mum-O's arm.

The humongous Ki reared back, his black eyes widened. He looked amazingly similar to a giant-sized arachnaphobic HeavyG who suddenly found a hairy spider crawling on his arm.

"Sholl trubol! *Sholl kegante!*"

Mum-O scrambled backward, his arm held out and away from him. Shizzle flew up high, choosing discretion and altitude as the better parts of valor. Sho-Do-Thikit scuttled over, grabbed Mum-O's arm and wiped it clean. Quentin didn't know the Ki equivalent of red-faced embarrassment, but whatever it was, Mum-O had it in spades.

John Tweedy clapped in approval. "Awesome! You boogered him."

"John," Quentin said. "*Boogered him*? This is really a phrase you use?"

"Not just a phrase, Killer-Q. *Boogering* is a great way to show your love. In fact, I think I'm going to go booger my brother right now."

John walked off, LOVE IS IN THE AIR scrolling in a continuous circle around his big neck.

Kimberlin shook his head as he watched John walk away. "This is going to end in a Tweedy brothers argument. Or a fight."

Quentin nodded, brushed more sauce onto the sizzling chicken. The sauce was Mister Sam's special recipe — best in the whole damn galaxy. The food was just about ready. "Michael, hand me those buns, will ya? I want to toast them up."

Kimberlin started pulling the buns out of the box and handing them over, one at a time. "I have to tell you, Quentin, that Don never thought of something this clever."

Quentin's smile faded. Leave it to Pine's old teammate to mention the man Quentin hated more than anything in the galaxy. "Genius Don Pine never thought of cooking for the Ki?"

Michael shook his head. "No. Not even once. He told me that before I came over. He said he was very impressed."

"And yet, he's not here."

Michael shrugged. "He did not feel well, apparently. He said that for all the times he ate — I'm quoting him here — *the most disgusting crap one could possibly imagine* — end quote — he did it for the team, but he never thought about turning the tables."

Quentin shrugged as he placed the buns on the cooler areas of the grill. "Yeah, so he never thought of it? So what?"

"He said this is the kind of thing that will make you great."

"Greatness is cooking burgers?"

"No, smart-ass," Kimberlin said. "What will make you great is you think about things in ways that others do not. Humans and HeavyG have been eating with Ki teammates for a long time, part of the bonding process. But in all the years I've played, I never heard of a Human making Ki eat Human sustenance."

Quentin gave the burgers one more flip. "Oh, come on. I ate their gross food, now they can eat mine and see what it's like. This isn't rocket science."

"Which is fortuitous, as you are no scientist of rockets."

Quentin looked up, smiled. "Big Mike, did you just rip on me?"

"It's Michael. And yes, I did jest at your expense. No, it's not *rocket science*, Quentin, but it is a very basic, simple idea that no one else thought of. That kind of insight can't be taught. You either have it or you do not.

"You and Don put a lot of importance on some ground-up meat."

"And you don't put enough importance on your brain," Kimberlin said. "Perhaps someday you should think of using your natural abilities for something greater than football."

Quentin paused. Hadn't Yitzhak said something similar, back in Danny Lundy's waiting area? Well, whatever. Kimberlin and Yitzhak could conjure up whatever they wanted, Quentin knew his destiny and would not stray from the path. "Hold those platters for me, it's time to chow."

Quentin quickly placed the patties on buns, then set the burgers on the first platter. He made sure to put the biggest one on top. He loaded the second platter with chicken. He set the spatula down and took the heaping platters from Kimberlin. Quentin walked to the stone table, then stopped in his tracks when he saw what was on it.

Becca was placing a huge bowl of what looked like potato salad on the table. The bowl was the last of a dozen neatly placed things including plates of sliced onions and tomatoes, diced pak-ka-bleffer, bowls of mustard and ketchup.

"Becca, what do you think you're doing?"

She looked up as if she'd been caught stealing.

"I just ... I thought it was cool you were cooking for everyone. I ran to the galley, had the chefs give me some stuff to make it a real barbecue."

"*You've* had barbecue? You're not from the Purist Nation."

She laughed. It was a beautiful sound. "Quentin, you think your culture *invented* barbecue?"

"Of course," Quentin said. "Ranchers on Stewart invented it. Everyone knows this."

She laughed again. He was partly offended, partly amused.

"I'm from Green Bay, on Earth," she said. "Trust me, we know what a barbecue is. I just wish I had some bratwurst."

"Brat what?"

She raised her eyebrows. "It's a kind of sausage. You've never had a brat?"

Quentin thought, then shook his head. "I don't think so. You mean like a hot dog?"

"Like a hot dog multiplied by eight million pounds of delicious."

"That's a lot of delicious."

"It is," Becca said. "Maybe I'll cook you one sometime. As a peace offering."

He looked at the decked-out stone table. She'd already made a peace offering and this was it. "Thanks, Becca. Thanks for getting all this stuff."

Her smile faded. Her cheeks flushed red. She looked at the ground, then turned and walked away.

What had he said? The one time he'd tried to be nice to her and she walked away? Girls were weird. Even football girls.

He set the platter on the table. "All right, Krakens, let's eat!"

The players crowded in. Human hands reached out first, grabbing plates, scooping out potato salad. A big hand snatched the top-most burger. Quentin thought it was John, but when he turned he saw Ju.

"Hey!" screamed John as he ran to the table. "The big burger is *mine!*"

"Shouldn't have boogered me," Ju yelled back, then crammed half the burger into his smiling mouth.

John skidded to a halt, his feet kicking up leaves and twigs. He stared in disbelief at his brother, stared with the intensity of a mother looking at the murderer of her only child.

"But that's not fair!"

Ju smiled, his mouth full of food. "Ish sho."

"You're an *idiot!*"

"Nof, yerf an i-iot."

"*Boys,*" Quentin said. "Take it elsewhere. Time for our hosts to eat."

The Humans and HeavyG finished loading their plates, then backed away, leaving the Ki room to slowly scuttle up to the table. Their black eyes widened at the site of the bun-covered burgers, much the same way Quentin's had at the deer/spider thing he'd seen strapped to this very table.

"It's safe," Quentin said. He was loving every minute of this. "I checked with Doc Patah. Ki digestion can handle anything a Human can handle, even cooked food. There's nothing to worry about. It's just protein, my friends, now enjoy!"

The Ki didn't move.

Quentin picked up a burger and held it out to Sho-Do-Thikit. "Aw, come on, don't be shy. If you guys don't eat, you'll hurt my feelings."

Quentin kept a straight face, but inside, he was just dying.

He watched Shizzle translate the phrase, knowing the translation would insinuate that a refusal to eat would insult Quentin's honor. Honor was a major deal in the Ki culture — you did not dishonor friends or fellow soldiers and to the Ki, Quentin was both.

Sho-Do took the burger, then hesitantly put the whole thing in his hexagonal mouth. His triangular lips closed. His eyes narrowed. He put a hand on the table, twisted his head. His body made a strange sound like a gong dropped inside a tunnel made of meat.

He almost puked, Quentin thought. *That was a Ki gag reflex. Oh my High One, this is AWESOME.*

Another noise, then Sho-Do stood straight. He had swallowed it down. "Yull essech shad."

Quentin looked at Shizzle.

"The Impressive One known as Sho-Do-Thikit says your food was delicious," Shizzle said. "He is honored that you shared a meal, but now he must go study for the game against Yall Criminals."

"Reelek shad!" Mum-O-Killowe said, then turned to walk away from the table. Sho-Do's arm shot out and flicked Mum-O's vocal tubes, bringing forth a yelp of pain. The elder Ki then pointed an arm at the table. Quentin couldn't contain his laughter anymore. It was like a hulking, horrifying alien version of a father telling his hulking, alien son to *sit down, shut up and eat your Brussels sprouts!*

The team watched as Quentin slowly, dramatically held out a burger for Mum-O.

"Here you go, my friend. Enjoy!"

Mum-O took the burger and stared at it with unblinking, black eyes.

John elbowed Quentin in the shoulder, then leaned in. "You're a real jerk, Q. I like it."

Quentin nodded. "Back in the Nation, we believe in an eye for an eye. Best to not cross me, Tweedy."

John shook his head. "Oh, *hell* no. After seeing this, I don't want any part of being on your bad side."

Mum-O bit into the burger. Quentin knew the young Ki had made a mistake by taking a bite and not eating the whole thing, as Sho-Do had done. Hot juice dribbled out of the torn meat and rolled down Mum-O's mouth and his hand.

John Tweedy leaned in, gleeful at seeing one of his teammates in harmless misery. "Come on, Mum-O! Eat it down!"

Mum-O's body made that same dropped-gong noise. He convulsed. The team started to chant Mum-O's name. Quentin laughed so hard he had to put both hands on the table to keep from falling over.

Ju joined the fray. "Don't be a baby! Eat it down! Mum-O! Mum-O! Mum-O!"

Mum-O lifted a trembling, burger-holding hand to his mouth. Triangular lips curled back, but triangular black teeth stayed locked tight.

John pumped his fist and screamed so loud that his neck veins bulged. "Come on! Pretend it's Rick Renaud. *Eat* him up, *eat* him up, *rah-rah-rah*!"

Mum-O's teeth started to open, then clacked shut. The meat-gong sound again ripped through his body. He dropped the burger, lowered his head to the ground and threw up.

The Krakens cheered and made noises and laughed in disgust. Some walked away, shaking their heads and waving hands in front of their face. The *smell*.

Despite the vile scene, Quentin could contain himself no longer. Laughter took his stomach hostage. His legs failed him. He fell to the plant-covered ground and just shook.

Revenge, it seemed, was a dish best served barbecued.

Report from the Creterakian Ministry of Religion (CMR)

The Church of Quentin Barnes

An alarming situation has come to the attention of the CMR. Two years ago, the Church of Quentin Barnes (CoQB) was a small, provincial religious factor located only on Planet Yall. The first estimation of church membership numbered somewhere between 100 and 200 individuals, mostly female.

In the past two years, however, the CoQB has undergone explosive growth. At this time, the CMR's best estimate is that the CoQB has 500,000 followers, with dioceses on all five Sklorno planets.

Granted, that number is significantly lower than other key sports-related churches. The Ministry of Pete Poughkeepsie, for example, has an estimated 2.1 million, while the Church of Don Pine has more than 5 million followers.

However, it is not the total followers that we find alarming at this point; rather it is the rate of growth. The Church of Don Pine is 13 to 14 years old. Pine did not exceed a million followers until 2675 when he won a Galaxy Bowl with the Jupiter Jacks. By way of comparison, when the Church of Don Pine was five years old, it had 500,000 followers. The CoQB has achieved that same number in just over two full seasons.

It is the recommendation of the CMR that additional resources be placed on measuring and monitoring the CoQB. At current growth rates and depending on the success of the Ionath Krakens (Quentin Barnes' team in the Galactic Football League), it is possible that by the 2686 season, the church will have a membership ranging anywhere from 10 to 50 million followers.

As is well documented, any non-governmental individual capable of generating more than 15 million followers is considered a potential threat to the Creterakian Empire. The CMR is formally requesting help from the EBSI as well as the Non-Creterakian Intelligence Agency (NCIA).

We feel strongly that only NCIA operatives can properly track the political ideology, beliefs and potential threat level of Quentin Barnes.

THIS TIME QUENTIN DECIDED he would tough it out on the observation deck. Flying still scared the hell out of him. He managed travel within punch-space just fine, but the punch-in and the punch-out still twisted his stomach into knots and tried to wring out whatever food or drink he'd taken in.

He stood at the observation deck's floor-to-ceiling crysteel windows, his hands locked on the brass rail. It was coming, the *shimmer*, the half-here, half-not-here sensation. All the team's Sklorno players were packed into the window on his left and the window on his right. Halawa, Wahiawa and Milford had all been born on Yall. They were already jumping with anticipation. As soon as the planet came into view, raspers would roll out and flying spit would cover the windows. Quentin had used his demigod status to request a window all to himself. Hey, if you can't use holy powers to avoid Sklorno slobber, what *could* you use them for?

"Hey! Killer-Q!"

Quentin looked over his shoulder — Ju and John, walking onto the observation deck.

"Now's not a good time," Quentin said.

John held up a metal bucket. Gold paint reflected the observation deck lights. Something lined the top — a plastic trash bag. A purple and white Yall Criminals sticker clung to the outside, showing that team's logo of a running Sklorno with a convict's ball and chain trailing behind.

John waggled the bucket. "We got you a present!"

"It's a golden puke bucket," Ju said. "Since you're facing your fears and all up here with the rest of us."

BE A BRAVE LITTLE CAMPER scrolled across John's forehead.

"Uh, guys, this isn't funny."

"It is to us," John said. "Like, super-mega-awesome funny. We're gonna watch you puke."

Quentin started to talk, then he saw John *blur* and *shimmer*. Quentin shut his eyes, but it was too late — he'd seen it. He felt his body separate, split, felt himself in two places at once. At least two, maybe more like ten or twenty.

Thanks to the Tweedy brothers' little joke, Quentin hadn't had time for his mantra of *everything is going to be okay*.

And then it was over. He was still there, safe, like he always was.

And he threw up, like he always did.

Quentin grabbed the golden bucket as his stomach rebelled. A seasoned veteran of his body's response to flight, he knew enough to eat small meals during the last few hours of a punch. If he ate too much, it all came up. If he didn't eat anything, dry heaves would have him doubled over for at least ten minutes. What little he had eaten hit the plastic bag inside the bucket.

Quentin set the bucket on the deck, then looked at it for a second. He bent and lifted the bag. It had a drawstring in it, which he pulled tight. His lost lunch, all sealed up in plastic. Nice and neat. How about that? Maybe the Tweedy boys were having fun at his expense, but this simple process would let him stay on the observation deck with the rest of the team.

Still holding the bag, he looked out at the planet Yall. What little area that wasn't covered by the black tendrils of civilization gleamed a burnished blue. A little bigger than Ionath. Directly below them: Virilliville. The largest city in the Sklorno Dynasty, although as on most Sklorno worlds, it was impossible to tell where one city stopped and another started.

Virilliville. Home of the 2684 Galaxy Bowl. Would the Krakens play here again sixteen weeks from now? Would they make it through the playoffs and line up for a shot at glory?

[FIRST SHUTTLE FLIGHT PASSENGERS TO THE LANDING BAY.]

"Come on, Q," John said. "Let's go. Monday Night Football, man, can you believe it? The entire galaxy will be watching us."

Quentin nodded. He carried his trash bag to a refuse chute, then followed John out of the observation deck toward the landing bay.

QUENTIN STOOD IN THE TUNNEL of the stadium called *The Tomb of Virilli*. From out on the field, he heard the crowd's intensity bubbling, simmering, waiting to boil over. That crowd would get a show tonight, that was for sure.

From the shuttle, he'd watched the approach to Virilliville, but not with the wide-eyed wonder of seasons past. Towering buildings painted white and purple, multilayered roads, clouds of pink smoke and sentients packed in with unthinkable density. Another time, perhaps he'd gawk and stare and take it all in. This time out, however, he couldn't draw his mind away from game prep, from visualizing what he would do on the field.

Monday Night Football.

An entire galaxy watching.

A showdown with Rick Renaud, the best quarterback in football.

Second-best. Quentin would show them all.

The winner of this game moved to 2-0. An early-season test. If the Krakens won this, then there was no longer any question — they were for real.

The announcer's echoing voice called the Krakens to the field, first in a chittering screech that made no sense whatsoever, then in English.

Quentin ran out of the tunnel to the sounds of hatred. Human-like boos filled the air, a concentration of derision he hadn't heard since away games back in his PNFL days. The Sklorno not only learned English to be closer to the origins of football, they learned the other associated Human noises as well.

He reactively ducked when something hit his helmet, slapped against his shoulder pads, bounced off his back. He raised a forearm above his helmet to protect his eyes as ran for the sidelines. There, a clear, curved awning covered the Krakens bench. He ran under it, noticing that the awning looked makeshift, like someone had figured out how to put it up only hours before.

The sound of a wet rain slapped against the clear material. He saw wet things sliding down the other side, leaving streaks of slime in their wake. Rotten vegetables, pieces of spoiled meat, other things he didn't recognize and didn't really want to recognize.

Garbage.

The crowd had hurled *garbage* at him.

The other Krakens arrived around him. There was no joyous, unifying sideline huddle this time — they all sought shelter under the awning. He saw Michael Kimberlin, wiping bits of splatter from his arms.

"Michael, what the hell? Why are they throwing garbage at us?"

"At you, mostly," he said. "You and Ju Tweedy. The rest of us are caught in the crossfire."

"But why?"

Kimberlin gestured to the stands behind the awning, filled beyond capacity with white- and purple-clad supporters of the criminals. "Quentin, *think* — you were on the cover of Galaxy Sports Magazine for various transgressions against a sport these sentients *worship*. You're a villain."

"But ... but we didn't have a problem against the Ice Storm."

"That was a home game," Kimberlin said. "The Ionath crowd will forgive you for anything. Road games, as you've just found, are going to be a different story. Krakens fans love you. The rest of the galaxy hates you to a significant degree."

Quentin had felt like all was lost when he read that article. Then came the support of Gredok the Splithead, of his teammates. Then the huge opening-day win and the love of the home crowd. He'd thought the situation was mostly behind him, felt it would blow over. Now, however, he understood that he would only find favor on Ionath.

He looked for Don Pine, found him standing under the awning farther down the sideline. No garbage on him. Don caught Quentin's stare, then looked down.

All of this hate — sentients throwing *garbage* — it was all Don Pine's fault. The great Don Pine, who would not take responsibility for his actions.

Quentin could do nothing about Don at the moment. What he could do, however, was channel the rage he felt into his play on the field. So the Criminals' fans thought he was garbage?

He'd show them. He'd show them right here and right now.

THE CRIMINALS WON THE TOSS. Quentin had to wait to make his mark, but he didn't wait long — Criminals quarterback Rick

Renaud showed why he was the highest-paid player in the game, hitting four straight completions on his first drive. His fourth pass found tight end Andreas Kimming in the end zone for a 27-yard touchdown.

Criminals 7, Krakens 0.

ON THE KRAKENS' FIRST DRIVE, Quentin didn't even get a chance to throw.

Yall's best defensive players were Riha the Hammer and Forrest Dane Cauthorn — the middle linebackers in the Criminals' 3-4 defense. Seasoned veterans in their prime, both had earned All-Pro honors a few years back. They were good. Hokor wanted to go after them head-on. If the Krakens could dominate those two, they could establish a steady running game that would chew up the clock and keep Rick Renaud off the field.

Ju Tweedy took the ball on a sweep to the left, led by Michael Kimberlin, who had pulled from the right side of center to block wide-left. Kimberlin took out Riha the Hammer — HeavyG versus Quyth Warrior — and Ju cut outside. It might have been a long run if Ju had put a move on Cauthorn, but instead Ju tried to overpower the linebacker in a Human-on-Human battle. Cauthorn put his helmet right on the ball — it popped free. Yall recovered.

Criminals' ball on the Ionath 35-yard line.

The Krakens offense ran off the field. As soon as Ju got up, he sprinted to catch up with Quentin.

"Q! I didn't mean that. I just lost it!"

"I know," Quentin said as both players reached the sidelines.

"Seriously, Q! I'm sorry, I–"

Quentin grabbed Ju's shoulder pad, gave it a single shake, cutting off the running back's sentence.

"Ju, they threw *garbage* on us. Hold on to the ball."

Ju's expression shifted from one of worry to one of resolve. He nodded. Quentin slapped him on the shoulder, then turned to watch his defense.

• • •

IT TOOK RICK RENAUD exactly one play to find fullback Tay "The Weazel" Nguyen at the 15-yard line. Tay had beaten John Tweedy on a little wheel pattern. The Weazel caught the pass in stride, turned up field and ran over Davenport on his way to a 35-yard touchdown pass.

Just two minutes and ten seconds into the first quarter, Renaud was 5-for-5 for 102 yards and two touchdowns. The Criminals were up 14-0.

If the defense didn't get to Renaud, put pressure on him, smack him around a little bit, Quentin didn't see how the Krakens could win the game.

ON IONATH'S SECOND DRIVE, Ju didn't fumble. No matter how badly Quentin wanted to throw the ball, wanted to match Renaud's stellar performance, he stuck to the game plan. The Krakens kept it on the ground, pounding it up the middle behind the dominant blocking of Sho-Do-Thikit and Bud-O-Shwek. The Criminals seemed comfortable with their early lead, staying back to prevent big passes to Hawick and Milford. When Quentin did pass, they were quick-hits for 5 or 6 yards.

The Krakens' second drive ate up over six minutes of clock, but stalled at the 11. On fourth down, Arioch Morningstar kicked a short field goal to put the Krakens on the board 14-3.

THE CRIMINALS ANSWERED that field goal with one of their own, going up 17-3 early in the second quarter. Renaud's receivers dropped two passes on the drive, preventing him from a perfect day. That was the only thing that could stop him, it seemed.

Down two touchdowns, Quentin started looking for deeper passes. Too late he realized he was forcing the ball, the fact hitting home only after he threw an interception.

The Krakens offense again ran off the field. The Criminals had the ball on the 50 with a chance to go up 24-3.

THAT CHANCE ENDED on a linebacker blitz. John Tweedy and Mum-O-Killowe ran a stunt, criss-crossing their paths and *both* of them beat their blockers. John came in free and clear. Renaud stepped right at the last second to avoid being decapitated, but John managed to grab the quarterback's jersey and hang on. Renaud tried to pull free, still looking downfield to get rid of the ball and he didn't see Mum-O in time.

The Ki lineman compressed and smashed Renaud with a full extension. Renaud's body bounced back like he'd been hit by a speeding hovertank. He didn't get up. A hush fell over the home crowd as the medsled flew onto the field.

Quentin didn't wish injury on any player, but he couldn't help a slight, involuntary fist-pump when the sled extended thousands of silvery filaments to lift the prone Criminals quarterback.

Rick Renaud was out of the game and that meant the Krakens were back in it.

WITH RENAUD OUT, the momentum shifted over to Ionath. Ju ran the ball again and again, he and the Krakens offensive line wearing down Riha the Hammer, Forrest Dane Cauthorn and the rest of the Criminals defense. The Krakens cut the lead to 7 when Ju rattled off a 15-yard touchdown run, then tied the game when he snagged another score from 5 yards out.

In the fourth quarter, Morningstar hit a 40-yard field goal. Quentin finished off the game with a 32-yard pass to George Starcher for the final touchdown.

The Krakens ran off the field to more garbage, but that nasty rain was easier to tolerate when accompanied by a 27-17 win, a 2-0 record and a first-place standing in the Planet Division.

GFL WEEK TWO ROUNDUP
Courtesy of Galaxy Sports Network

HOME		AWAY	
Wabash Wolfpack	38	Alimum Armada	34
Themala Dreadnaughts	20	Coranadillana Cloud Killers	7
Hittoni Hullwalkers	21	**To Pirates**	38
Yall Criminals	17	**Ionath Krakens**	27
Isis Ice Storm	27	Bartel Water Bugs	7
Lu Juggernauts	3	**Neptune Scarlet Fliers**	17
Orbiting Death	21	Jang Atom Smashers	0
New Rodina Astronauts	38	Bord Brigands	35
D'Kow War Dogs	28	Vik Vanguard	16
Jupiter Jacks	24	Sala Intrigue	20
Shorah Warlords	14	Texas Earthlings	10

IN WHAT COULD BE a changing of the guard, the Ionath Krakens moved to 2-0 with a 27-17 Monday Night Football win over the favored Yall Criminals (1-1). Yall quarterback Rick Renaud was unstoppable in the first quarter, but an injury in the second took him out of the game. With Renaud out, Ionath used a ball-control offense to dominate the game. Ju Tweedy ran for 156 yards and a pair of touchdowns, while Krakens QB Quentin Barnes threw for another. Barnes finished 15-of-21 for 231 yards.

As impressive as Ju Tweedy's performance was, it took a back-seat to Denver's three-touchdown-catch performance for the Jupiter Jacks (2-0) in their 24-20 win over the Sala Intrigue (1-1). Denver caught eight passes for 115 yards to keep Jupiter tied for first in the Solar Division.

The Orbiting Death (2-0) remains tied for first in the Planet

Division thanks to a 21-0 shutout of the Jang Atom Smashers (0-2). This is the first-ever 2-0 start by a newly promoted team.

The To Pirates (2-0) and the Wabash Wolfpack (2-0) also remain tied for first in the Planet Division, while wins by Neptune (2-0) and New Rodina (2-0) kept them tied with Jupiter for first in the Solar.

Deaths

Alimum Armada cornerback **Monsaraz,** who died on a clean block by Wabash Wolfpack fullback Ralph Schmeer.

Offensive Player of the Week

Jupiter Jacks receiver **Denver,** who caught touchdown passes of 55, 43 and 15 yards en route to a 115-yard receiving day.

Defensive Player of the Week

Ionath Krakens defensive tackle **Mum-O-Killowe,** who registered four tackles and three sacks, including one that put Yall quarterback Rick Renaud out of the game early in the second quarter.

13

WEEK THREE: CORANADILLANA CLOUD KILLERS at IONATH KRAKENS

PLANET DIVISION

2-0 Ionath Krakens

2-0 OS1 Orbiting Death

2-0 To Pirates

2-0 Wabash Wolfpack

1-1 Isis Ice Storm

1-1 Themala Dreadnaughts

1-1 Yall Criminals

0-2 Alimum Armada

0-2 Coranadillana Cloud Killers

0-2 Hittoni Hullwalkers

0-2 Lu Juggernauts

SOLAR DIVISION

2-0 Jupiter Jacks

2-0 Neptune Scarlet Fliers

2-0 New Rodina Astronauts

1-1 Bartel Water Bugs

1-1 Bord Brigands

1-1 D'Kow War Dogs

1-1 Sala Intrigue

1-1 Shorah Warlords

0-2 Jang Atom Smashers

0-2 Texas Earthlings

0-2 Vik Vanguard

QUENTIN WOKE UP when his body slid forward.

His hands shot out automatically, bracing against soft leather. The disorientation only lasted a few seconds; he was in the back of a limo, alone. Had he fallen asleep?

He looked out the window at Hotel Gibberdon. The place looked classy. The hotel's name was spelled out in carved stone instead of garish, glowing holo. Stone, burnished metal, wood; everything about the place screamed *expensive, privileged*. That's where you stayed when you were a rock star.

Outside the limo, things looked a little … foggy?

The limo door opened. Quentin stepped out. Yes, it was fog.

Quentin gestured to the mist, turned to the Quyth Worker driver. "What's this all about? Ionath City is under a dome. How can we have fog?"

"Some kind of a breakdown on the atmosphere processors or something, Mister Barnes. Happens from time to time."

"Huh. Can it rain?"

The driver shook his head. "No, no rain, but watch your step. Things can be a little slippery until they fix it."

Quyth Workers wearing neat, red uniforms rushed out from the hotel, pranced near Quentin in case he needed any little thing. Camera spotlights hit him, blinding at this late hour. Hotel security appeared from the shadows, Quyth Warriors that pushed the photographers out of the way, blocking their shots.

The hotel's front door opened. The spotlights flared anew, making Somalia Midori practically glow. She strode out, wearing a breathtaking dress that was more see-through than anything else. So much *skin*. Quentin felt himself blush a little. She had done her hair differently this time. It hung down the left side of her head, long and flowing like that of some movie star. The right side, of course, was still a clean-shaven blue.

She walked up to him, wrapped her arms around his neck and planted a kiss on his lips. It surprised him at first, but then the warmth of her mouth sank in. He closed his eyes and put his hands gently on her hips.

Most of his thoughts were lost in the kiss, but he was still cognizant enough to know that all the spotlights were on them, along with a rapid flashing of still cameras. It was like they were on display.

He pulled back. "Uh, ready to go?"

Her smile seemed brighter than all the lights combined. "Yes and I'm *star*ving."

He moved to hold the door for her before he realized the limo driver was already doing that. Quentin stood aside and let Somalia enter, then followed her inside. The door shut, leaving them alone. Quentin waited until the limo pulled away before talking.

"How do those photographers know where you are?"

She shrugged. "It's never a secret where I'm staying when I'm on tour."

"And do you get that kind of attention every time you leave a hotel?"

"Not as much," she said. "But when I leave with a star quarterback? Yeah, they come out of the shadows for that."

So beautiful. So sexy. Quentin still had a hard time believing this was actually happening to him. "How long are you here for?"

"Four nights. Tonight is my only night off, then three shows in a row."

"So, you're leaving Sunday? I play that day, home game against Coranadillana."

She laughed and slid her right arm through Quentin's left, pulling him closer. "Yeah, Sugar, I know you have a big game. But I have to fly out that morning for Whitok. Believe me, the paparazzi would go crazy if they saw me kissing you in your armor after you're all beat-up from a game."

"Why would you want to kiss me then? I'd be all smelly and dirty and bloody."

Her lips twisted into her sneer-smile, the one that made his face feel all hot. "Yeah. Why would I want you then?"

The limo eased to a stop. Quentin looked outside, saw the restaurant through the fog. "We're here. This is the place you wanted to eat, right?"

She leaned across him to look out the window, her perfumed hair close to his face.

"Torba the Hungry's," she said. "So nice of you to get us a table. I hear only the upper crust eats here, Quentin."

He shrugged. "I don't know about that. I asked Messal to get us a table."

The limo door opened. Quentin got out first, then reached a hand back to help Somalia. Yitzhak had told him that was the polite thing to do for a woman. Somalia slid out of the limo with a sexy athleticism. Quentin wondered if she'd ever played sports. Basketball, maybe. She stood and immediately slid her arm through Quentin's, just before the camera-flash assault fired up again. The press had been waiting for them. How did they know he and Somalia would be there? Through the annoying lights, Quentin recognized the faces of a few of Gredok's goons. Messal had also apparently taken care of security.

Cameras blazing, Quentin and his date walked into Torba the Hungry's.

"QUENTIN?"

He heard his name, called by some faraway voice. A pretty voice, but distant.

Something touched his hand and his eyes snapped open. That brief disorientation again, but it evaporated immediately. He looked around, saw the opulent interior of Torba the Hungry's — then his eyes settled on the quizzical smile of Somalia Midori.

"Am I boring you, Sugar?"

Realization hit home. "Oh, High One ... did I fall asleep?"

She nodded.

"Oh, I'm so sorry! No, you're not boring, it's just that I'm so exhausted from practice, the trip back from Yall and studying for the Cloud Killers game. And the media hounds me everywhere I go."

She stroked his hand. "It's okay, I know all about exhaustion.

Try four shows in two days on for size and you'll understand I know where you're coming from."

Her smile wasn't condescending. She *did* know where he was coming from. She got him in so many ways. She pulled his hand closer, held it with both of hers. Her blue skin felt so warm. "You don't do stims, do you? To fight off the tired?"

He shook his head. "I never take drugs. You?"

She shrugged. "There's a lot of drugs in my business. Pyuli, mesh, heroin, that kind of thing. Wipes people out. Turns them into shells."

"Do *you* do any drugs?"

"Hell no," she said. "I've got a career, I've got goals. I want to get into holos."

"You? A movie star? Aren't you a little ... I don't know ... *rough* for that?"

She rolled her eyes. "Quentin, join the modern galaxy, will ya? A sentient's image can be changed at will. We're a hot band now, but that won't last forever. I have to think about the next step, about what I'll do when people stop playing our songs."

Quentin let out a huff. As if anyone could *ever* stop listening to Trench Warfare songs.

She stroked his hand slowly. He felt hot in his face, his chest.

"Listen, Quentin, how about when you take me back to the hotel, you come on up to my room."

Not a question. More like a statement. Possibly even a command. Her lip curled into that mesmerizing sneer again — not one of arrogance, but one of mischief, of fun.

One of sex.

"Oh," Quentin said. "Ummm ... oh."

"I like you," she said. "I know you're tired, but I'm pretty sure I can keep you awake. Unless you already have company planned for tonight?"

"*No*. Uh, no, no company. But, that's not ... I mean, we're not married."

Her eyebrows shot up. She laughed. "No, Sugar-Sugar, we're not *married*, but we don't have to be."

Quentin gently pulled his hand back. "I do."

Somalia leaned forward, her eyes alive, hungry. "Quentin Barnes, are you a virgin?"

He felt his face get hot again, but not from excitement. Why was he embarrassed by this?

Somalia looked around the room as if they were sharing some dirty secret, then she leaned in even closer. "Wow. I just never thought that."

"Well, I am."

"But why?"

Hadn't he just told her? "What do you mean, *why?*"

"*Look* at you," she said. "You're young, gorgeous, strong, kind — every girl's dream. Didn't women throw themselves at you back home?"

He shrugged. "That's not really what girls do back on Micovi. But sometimes, yeah, women made their intentions known."

Somalia laughed. "Sorry, I'm not making fun of you, it's just so … quaint. *Made their intentions known.* I didn't think people talked like that anymore."

"Well, I do."

"But you do this for your religion? I didn't think you followed Purism anymore."

"I don't," he said. "But that doesn't mean there aren't good messages wrapped up in all the lies and corruption."

"And saving yourself for marriage is *good?*"

"Maybe," he said. "How about you tell me why it's bad?"

She stared at him. Her smile faded a little. "I'm not saying it's *bad*, Quentin. It's just … well, trust me on this, not many guys in your position, in *any* position, would have those kind of morals."

So having morals, beliefs, that made him unusual? "Does that mean I'm some kind of … what … a freak? If you don't want to see me anymore, fine."

She leaned back. "Now you're just being a baby. Of course I want to see you. It's just a shock, that's all. And a little hard to swallow."

Maybe it was, but that didn't make it any less true. "Do you believe me?"

She paused, then nodded. "Yes. As improbable as it is that a specimen like you isn't getting a planet's worth of tail, I believe you."

For some reason, that made him feel infinitely better. The stress drained out of him. He yawned.

She shook her head. "People are usually more excited to be with a rock star."

"I know, I'm sorry, I—"

"Will you stop apologizing? I think we should get you back. You're about to fall asleep on me again."

He didn't want the night to end, but he *was* tired. "When can I see you again?"

"I already checked the schedule. I have time off when you're in Wabash. How about I come watch your game against the Wolfpack?"

"That's Week Nine," he said. "I won't see you for six weeks?"

"That's our lives, Quentin. We're both in demand, you might say."

"You don't mind waiting six weeks to see me again?"

She laughed, put her napkin on her plate. "Well, at least I won't be worried that you're fooling around with some other woman. Now, are you going to pull my chair out for me or what?"

Quentin stood up so fast he almost tripped. He pulled out Somalia's chair, then walked with her arm in arm out of Torba the Hungry's.

Transcript from the "Galaxy's Greatest Sports Show with Dan, Akbar, and Tarat the Smasher"

DAN: And we're back from the break. Tarat, Akbar, time to talk GFL standings. Can you guys believe the Orbiting Death is in first place?

AKBAR: It's early in the season. Just an anomaly.

TARAT: It is no anomaly, Akbar. There has never been a newly promoted team that has won its first two games.

DAN: Yeah, lil' buddy, it's a big deal.

AKBAR: Again with that stupid nickname?

DAN: Don't you worry about it, lil' buddy. And the Orbiting Death's amazing start *almost* overshadows the start of another team, the drama-filled Ionath Krakens.

TARAT: Dan, I will tell you that it is difficult to deal with the kind of distractions facing the Krakens. The stories about Quentin Barnes and Ju Tweedy would be enough to hinder any team, yet the Krakens are tied for first with two wins. With all the Krakens have dealt with, they still beat the Criminals. I think the Krakens might be for real.

AKBAR: They only won because Rick Renaud got hurt. The Krakens secondary is not good — any solid quarterback will tear them up.

TARAT: Renaud was knocked out of the game by Mum-O-Killowe. The Krakens took Renaud out and that is why Ionath won the game. They found a way.

DAN: Well, let's not go crowning the Krakens and the Orbiting Death as Planet Division champs just yet. We're only two games into the season and we also have the Pirates and defending champion Wolfpack undefeated with two wins.

AKBAR: My point exactly. The Krakens won't beat either team unless they trade for some defensive backs.

DAN: That's a good point, lil' buddy — the trade deadline is closing in. Come kickoff of Week Five, if the Krakens haven't made a move, they are stuck with what they got unless they can find free agents.

TARAT: Any free agents left at this point are probably not worth having.

AKBAR: So who do the Krakens trade?

DAN: Don Pine, of course. That team belongs to Quentin Barnes.

AKBAR: *Trade* Don Pine? What if Barnes gets hurt?

TARAT: I think the Krakens have to gamble, Akbar. Their next three games are against teams that are already having bad seasons — Coranadillana, Hittoni and Alimum. All three are winless so far. If the Krakens make a move and strengthen their backfield, they have a real chance to go five-and-oh. After that the competition gets much tougher. They have to be victorious in these winnable games if they want to make the playoffs.

AKBAR: Yeah, sure, but do that by trading a top QB like Don Pine? Don't they want to have a backup that's almost as good as their starter?

DAN: That's *why* they'd trade Pine. Quarterbacks are so valuable the Krakens can get a top cornerback and another safety, maybe even three players. They just have to gamble that they get those players *and* that Barnes doesn't suffer a serious injury.

AKBAR: That's a big roll of the dice.

DAN: And that's why they play the games! Let's go to the callers and see what they think. Line two from Yall, you're on the Space. *Go!*

CALLER: They have blasphemed against the Church of Quentin Barnes!

AKBAR: Oh no, here we go again …

DAN: Caller, tell us all about it.

CALLER: The Church of Quentin Barnes was not allowed into the game at Virilli Stadium! We were banished, banished, oh cruel banished!

DAN: Caller, that's because you CoQB guys and the Criminals fans would have killed each other.

CALLER: To die in service of Quentinbarnes is to ascend to the next realm! Long live Quentinbarnes! Long live Quent-

DAN: And that's enough of that.

AKBAR: Thank you for cutting off that call.

DAN: No problem, lil' buddy! Line four from Shorah, you're on the Space. *Go!*

SUNDAY MORNING FOUND QUENTIN at Ionath Stadium, many hours before the adoring crowd would arrive. The fog he'd seen on Wednesday hadn't abated. In fact, it had grown worse.

He and ten other Krakens players stood in the orange end zone, still wearing their street clothes, looking around and making short runs to test their footing.

The fog wafted across the field. A thin breeze concentrated vapor into visible, see-through waves. He could barely see the top of the upper deck. The stadium's twenty-two pillars vanished into that fog, as if they reached up through the clouds to touch heaven itself.

Water vapor had been settling on the field for days. Because the stadium sat under the city dome, the field had no drainage system. When water soaked into the dirt beneath the Iomatt, it stayed there.

"Killer Q! Here early as usual?"

"Always, John. You ready for today?"

John made a *pffft* noise with his mouth, as if the question were ridiculous. "The Killers scored a whopping total of 17 points in their first two games, Q. Their offense is ranked last. I think we got this. Hey, you were on a date last night with Somalia, huh?"

"How do you know about that?"

"Because it's in the news, man. Wow, did she look *hot*. You take care of that business?"

"Business? We had dinner." Why did anyone care about his dinner date, anyway?

GET DOWN TO BUSINESS WHILE THE GETTIN' IS GOOD scrolled across John's forehead. He smiled. "No, Q, I mean *after* dinner. She looked like the air might catch fire around her at any second."

"Oh," Quentin said. "No, nothing like that. I went home."

John stared at Quentin with his patented *just how stupid are you* expression.

"John, you mind if we get our heads in the game and stop talking about my love life?"

John shook his head hard. The scrolling letters on his face scrambled, scattered, vanished up beneath his hairline and down below his collar. "Sure, Q. Man, I can't *wait* for some payback on these guys. We should have beat them last year."

John raised his right foot and pushed it down at a hard angle. The Iomatt slid along with his shoe, leaving a wet-brown streak in its wake. I PLAY DIRTY scrolled across his face. "Looks like Uncle Johnny gets to wallow in the mud. This is gonna be fun."

Fun. That wasn't Quentin's word for it. The field was soaked. It looked okay at the moment, but that was only because no one had been on it. When the game started, the field would deteriorate quickly. Back in the soupy atmosphere of Micovi, he'd played in weather like this almost every week. Poor footing would make it hard to scramble. It would slow down his receivers. Slippery conditions like this could get players hurt, cause pulled ligaments, torn muscles or jammed chitin.

In the far end zone, the black one, Quentin saw the distant forms of Coranadillana players walking about, testing the field just like their Ionath counterparts. This field would slow down both teams, but since the Cloud Killers were a slower team, that actually helped them.

Still, the Killers were 0-2 for a reason. They had a decent running game but a terrible passing game. Even in the mud, Ionath could win this one easily.

Quentin called out to his teammates. "Let's go, Krakens! Time to gear up for the game."

They filtered into the tunnel, kicking bits of mud and torn blue plants off their shoes as soon as they hit concrete.

THE ROAR OF 185,000 FANS seemed to lift the Krakens out of the tunnel, carry them through the air and drop them in a jumping, pushing, yelling pile on the sidelines. Sixty minutes of game-time to hold on to first place in the Planet Division.

Quentin, John and honorary captain Mum-O-Killowe ran to midfield for the toss. Waiting for them were the Cloud Killer captains: cornerback Smileyberg, defensive end Jesper Schultz, quarterback Richard Read. Last season, the Krakens had traveled to Coranadillana. The Cloud Killers won the game on a Ju Tweedy fumble. Intentional, Quentin knew, although he had never revealed that secret to the rest of the team. The Krakens had been a different ball club then — they were vastly better now, they were 2-and-0, and Ju Tweedy ran his ass off on every play. This afternoon? Payback time.

"Hey, Barnes," Schultz said. "Ready to make it two in a row?"

Quentin smiled. "You're in our house now." Schultz stood 6-foot-10, two inches shorter than Quentin, but weighed in at 530 — a 170-pound advantage over the quarterback.

"Whatever," Schultz said. "Records don't matter when we play Ionath. We *own* you."

Quentin kept smiling as he turned to face the floating Harrah ref. The Krakens won the toss and chose to receive. The kickoff went out of the back of the end zone for a touchback, giving Ionath the ball on its own 20-yard line.

The first two games of the season, the Krakens had opened up with running plays. This time, Quentin would get to show his stuff right off the bat. He knelt behind center and surveyed the Cloud Killers defense. White jerseys with light blue polka dots atop light blue leg armor. White helmets decorated on both sides with the team's logo: blue claws ripping through a stylized yellow cloud dotted with light blue. Across the line on Quentin's left, Jesper Schultz at right defensive end. Schultz was the team's premier defensive player. Smileyberg and Griffith, the Sklorno cornerbacks, were also good players, but the Krakens receivers could beat them deep.

On offense, Quentin had George Starcher at left tight end. Wide receiver Hawick lined up near the left sidelines, Milford wide to the right. Ju Tweedy and Becca Montagne lined up four yards behind Quentin and a yard to either side of him — a pro-set.

The hungry Ionath crowd buzzed and hummed, waited for action. The field sometimes smelled like cinnamon, but that was when it was dry. Now, so wet that footprints left slowly filling puddles, the field smelled like plants that were just beginning to rot.

"Blue ... twenty-three. *Bluuuueee*, twenty-three. Hut-*hut!*"

He took the snap and rolled left, Becca out front to block. A few simple plays to test the field's footing.

The HeavyG Schultz smashed into Krakens left tackle Kill-O-Yowet, then spun off him and rushed in on all fours. Quentin watched him coming, saw Hawick going deep down the sidelines, saw George Starcher cutting to the left, saw Becca moving in for the block.

Quentin didn't change his path. Schultz barreled in, big hands planting on the wet, blue field, big feet driving him forward in a loping gait. He reached for Quentin, but Becca undercut him just as Quentin knew she would. For a brief instant, Quentin flashed back to last season's fight at Chucky Chong's League-Style House of Chow, when Becca had leveled Schultz just as the big HeavyG had been about to pummel Quentin senseless.

That flash-moment memory vanished. Starcher was open. Quentin stepped up to throw on the run, but just as he released the ball his front foot slipped on the wet field. The ball wobbled forward, too high, too far behind Starcher. The big tight end reached back for the ball but only got a finger on it, popping it up into the air — Smileyberg snagged it, already heading the other way.

The sideline on her left, she sprinted past the Ionath 25-yard line and headed for the end zone. Quentin reacted instantly, moving at an angle to cut her off. She cut back inside, toward the middle of the field. Quentin matched the move, turning quickly so that his back was to the sideline — he had her.

He saw Schultz only an instant before the impact, an instant to remember that on an interception, any Cloud Killer player could block him with no worry of a late hit or a roughing the passer penalty.

Quentin heard Schultz's grunting roar, then a sentient tank smashed into his head. Quentin's back hit the ground. He slid backward in a spray of moisture, right into the legs of Cloud Killers players standing on the sidelines.

His eyes stayed squeezed shut, as he tried to cope with the initial numbing ache of such a devastating collision. Cloud Killer players lifted him to his feet. The angry roar of the crowd told Quentin that Smileyberg had taken the interception to the house for a touchdown.

THE KILLERS' FRONT-FOUR DEFENSIVE LINEMEN played like creatures possessed, attacking the run and coming after Quentin whenever he passed. The field conditions helped them out — halfway through the second quarter, the middle of the field had transformed into a wet, slippery mass of blue and brown marked with nearly invisible, stained, torn white stripes. The jerseys of both teams looked more brown than anything else. Mud was everywhere — on uniforms, wedged into shoes and armor joints, caked on helmets and streaked across faces.

The terrible footing slowed down his receivers, made it hard for them to make the sharp cuts that would get them open. That turned the contest largely into a smash-mouth running game. Ju Tweedy couldn't make his fancy moves. He had to blast the ball straight ahead.

Coranadillana's offense kept grinding the ball out on strong runs and short passes. At the half, the shell-shocked Krakens found themselves down 14-3.

QUENTIN FINALLY CONNECTED for a long pass midway through the third quarter, hitting Halawa for a 60-yard strike that put the Krakens on the Killers' 1-yard line. On the next play, Becca bullied her way through the blockers for the touchdown. The extra point made the score 14-10.

THAT TOUCHDOWN EVAPORATED almost instantly. Smileyberg, the Cloud Killers cornerback, doubled as the kick returner. On the ensuing kickoff, she caught Arioch Morningstar's kick and carried it into the clash of blockers and tacklers at about the 20. Almost walking, she weaved her way through defenders who were both fighting off blocks and trying to change direction on the muddy, slick surface. Tim Crawford had her at the 35, but his big hands slipped on her wet jersey. Smileyberg cut to the sidelines, where the footing was better and she took off. Morningstar had a chance to knock her out of bounds — she lowered her helmet and ran him over.

Extra point good: Cloud Killers 21, Krakens 10.

ON THE SIDELINES, the Krakens just felt *flat*. All the energy had vanished. But they were only down by 11 points. They could come back from this — Quentin would carry the team all by himself if he had to.

QUENTIN TOOK THE SNAP. He pushed back, to the left. Becca rushed by to block. Quentin started to reach the ball out to Ju when he saw Kill-O-Yowet, the right tackle, fold backward in a funny way and drop hard to the ground.

A mud- and blood-streaked Jesper Schultz leapt over the fallen left tackle and landed on all fours, moving fast in the HeavyG race's signature galloping gait.

Schultz connected just as Quentin handed the ball to Ju. Jesper's long arms wrapped up both Krakens players. As Quentin flew through the air, he felt the ball bounce away. He only thought about that for a split-second, because he and Ju hit the ground hard beneath all of Jesper's 530 pounds.

Quentin groaned with pain and with embarrassment — that hit was sure to wind up on all the highlight shows.

Schultz's mass kept the two Krakens pinned. They were a pile of muddy, wet, bloody sentients.

"Quentin, Ju," Schultz said. "Imagine meeting you two here."

Ju tried to push away, but his arms were pinned and he couldn't budge. "Get off me, you big gorilla."

Jesper laughed. "Bet you wished you'd signed with us, murderer, instead of getting beat up in a bar fight."

"He signed with the winners," Quentin grunted. "And we whipped your asses at Chucky Chong's!"

"Whatever, Barnes. Today, the *winners* are going to be us. You guys play like crap. See you both again real soon."

He pushed off, harder than necessary. Quentin stood, then helped Ju to his feet. They both looked downfield — their collective fumble had been picked up by Smileyberg, who had returned it for her third touchdown of the game.

Ju pushed Quentin's shoulder. "Butterfingers."

Despite the turnover for a touchdown, Quentin laughed. "Are you *kidding* me? That was all you, big fella."

"I fumble enough without taking the blame for things like that."

Quentin smacked Ju's helmet, a wet slap against caked mud. "Chin up, little camper. We just have to get it back."

Ju pointed to Kill-O-Yowet, who was still lying on the ground. "May I suggest we run *away* from wherever Schultz lines up?"

Quentin watched the medsled slide onto the field, following Doc Patah.

"Good idea," Quentin said. They walked off the field as the kick return team came on.

Turnovers were killing them. First an interception for a touchdown, now a fumble return for another. Heading into the fourth quarter, the Krakens were down 28-10.

Someone had to take this game over for the Krakens. Terrible footing, speed advantage negated, no way to do fancy moves and little success running the ball up the middle. On top of that, their starting right offensive tackle had been injured and was out of the game. How could Quentin use the bad field conditions against the defenders?

"Barnes!" Coach Hokor's voice in his helmet speakers. "Get over here, we're going to try something different."

THE KRAKENS LINED UP in the "power" formation. No wide receivers. Rick Warburg at left tight end and George Starcher at right put seven big, black-jerseyed bodies in tight on the line of scrimmage. Cheboygan lined up a yard behind Starcher and a yard to his right, Tara the Freak in the same position on Warburg's left.

Behind Quentin, Yassoud was the single back. Hokor had pulled Ju, opting instead for Yassoud's pass-catching ability. If the Krakens were going to catch up, they were going to do it in the air.

Quentin dropped back five steps and carefully planted, cleated feet managing the muddy ground. The tight ends drove straight out 10 yards, stopped, then came back. The defenders ran with them but slid when they tried to quickly react.

Quentin hit Starcher on the first pass for 8 yards.

On the second, he pump-faked to Starcher, then hit Tara over the middle on a crossing pattern. Tara caught the perfect pass in stride, already moving too fast for the linebackers to change direction on the wet surface. The mutated Quyth Warrior turned the ball upfield for a 17-yard gain before the defensive backs brought him down in a sliding spray of mud and torn blue Iomatt.

Next, Quentin hit Cheboygan on a simple out-pass, putting her one-on-one against Smileyberg. The Cloud Killers star cornerback tried to tackle Cheboygan up high, but the rookie receiver was bigger and stronger. Cheboygan took the hit, kept pumping her back-folded legs. She finally popped free as Smileyberg fell to the ground. The Krakens receiver covered 20 yards before being pushed out of bounds, putting Ionath on Coranadillana's 15.

The next play saw both linebackers lining up close, showing blitz.

"Green, seventy-seven," Quentin called, audibling to a quarterback-keeper. "Greeeeen, seventy-seven. Hut-hut ... *hut!*"

Quentin dropped back as all the receivers, including Yassoud, ran slant patterns away from center, taking them and their defenders toward the sidelines. After only three steps, Quentin planted, keeping his knees bent deep to maintain balance as he slid over the wet field. His cleats caught. He sprang forward, slipping through the rushing defensive line. The linebackers couldn't respond in time. Quentin left them all behind. The defensive backs closed on him, but he reached the goal line first, diving under their tackles for the 15-yard touchdown run.

After the kick, it was Cloud Killers 28, Krakens 17.

THE DEFENSE SEEMED ENERGIZED for the first time that after-noon. John Tweedy and Company forced the Cloud Killers into a three-and-out. With seven minutes to play, the Krakens got the ball back on their own 35-yard line. Quentin again used quick passing to take the Killers apart, not dropping back long enough for Schultz or the other defenders to reach him.

On the seventh play of the drive, Quentin dropped back, looking for targets. Everyone seemed covered. The pocket start-ed to collapse. Yassoud threw a block on an incoming defensive lineman, then ran to the open space on the left as he was sup-posed to. Quentin flipped a pass out there just as two defensive tackles brought him down. Yassoud hauled it in. He was lighter than Ju and faster — 'Soud handled the mud better than the big-ger man. Yassoud did a head-and-shoulders fake on the line-backer, then shot by as the linebacker slipped and fell. Griffith, the cornerback, closed in, but Yassoud stiff-armed her and put her into the ground — all that off-season weight training had paid off.

With four minutes to play, Yassoud Murphy took the ball into the end zone for an 18-yard touchdown pass. Cloud Killers 28, Krakens 23.

Quentin looked to the sidelines and held up two fingers, sig-naling to Hokor that they had to go for the two-point conversion and cut the lead to three points. Hokor was already sending Ju Tweedy onto the field.

The Krakens would smash it in from three yards out.

Quentin waved everyone to the line. They'd run a play without a huddle, try to catch the Cloud Killers off-guard. The Killers tried to run players off the field, but they saw that the Krakens were already lining up and had to sprint back.

"Blue, fifteen!" Quentin called out.

A simple dive-play. Our offensive line against your defensive line, our running back against your linebackers.

"Hut-*hut!*"

Mud flew as the teams smashed together. Quentin turned to the right, extended the ball for Ju. Ju clamped down on it and lowered his head, but Killers HeavyG defensive tackle Jay Otaku slipped his big body between the Krakens offensive linemen. Ju tried to jump, but Jay undercut him before he could go airborne.

Ju fell to the mud, two inches short of the goal line.

Two-point conversion failed. Ionath was still down by five points and would need a touchdown to win.

IT WAS UP TO THE DEFENSE NOW. The home crowd seemed to be losing its collective mind, screaming for a chance to complete the come-from-behind victory. Coranadillana tried to run the ball and chew up the clock. They managed two first downs, forcing the Krakens to use all of their time-outs. With 1:08 to play, another first down meant the Killers could run out the clock in the victory formation, then sneak out of foggy Ionath with the win.

But the wet conditions that had kept the Killers in the game proved to be a double-edged sword. On a run up the middle, Mai-An-Inkole managed to catch the runner and — instead of tackling him — stand him up. The running back kept his feet pumping, instinctively trying to power forward, but John Tweedy shot in and put his helmet right on the ball. The pigskin popped onto the field. Mum-O-Killowe jumped on it, clearly in possession even before the mass of players from both teams piled on top of him.

Krakens' ball on their own 45-yard line, 1:01 to play. They needed a touchdown to win and a touchdown was what Quentin Barnes would provide.

ON THE FIRST PLAY, Quentin hit Cheboygan on a 5-yard out pattern. She made a rookie mistake — instead of running out of bounds, she tried for extra yards and was brought down inbounds for an 11-yard gain. That kept the clock rolling.

Quentin rushed his players to the line, but this wasn't the main starting unit and they were slow getting to their positions. He snapped the ball and immediately spiked it to stop the clock, then looked to the scoreboard — 0:48. Three plays, maybe four, depending on his players' ability to get out of bounds.

Hokor let Quentin run things; the coach had full confidence in his third-year quarterback. Quentin kept the same tight formation, opting for his bigger, stronger receivers.

The spiked ball made it second down, 10 yards to go on the Coranadillana 34.

In the huddle, Quentin called three plays in a row. They might not get another chance to huddle up if no one got out of bounds.

He took the snap and dropped back, looking downfield. The Cloud Killers defenders were playing deep and to the outside — they were willing to give up a short pass underneath if they could bring the receiver down in-bounds, keep the clock rolling. Everyone looked covered, except for Warburg, who was open at 10 yards. Quentin started going through his reads again, looking for a deeper pass.

He felt pressure. He started to scramble, but it was too late. Jesper Schultz blasted past backup left tackle Shut-O-Dital and dragged Quentin down for a 7-yard loss.

"Told you I'd see you again, Barnes."

Quentin ignored the taunt, pushing and hitting Schultz in an effort to get up fast. Time was ticking.

"Krakens, get on the line!" The home crowd roared, the clock ran — 0:41 and counting. Now it was third and 17 on the Coranadillana 34 — spiking the ball would stop the clock, but also bring up a do-or-die fourth-and-17. Instead of spiking Quentin had to run a play, try and pick up at least 10 yards to make the fourth-down conversion more possible. His players scrambled to the line, the defense ran to cover them.

"Red, forty-four! Hut-*hut!*"

Quentin took the snap and dropped back. The defense rushed

in, collapsing the pocket almost immediately. Quentin scrambled, rolling left. His receivers tried to find open spaces.

Quentin saw Warburg, open yet again, at the 15 and near the sidelines for a probable clock-stopping first down — but Quentin didn't throw it.

A flash of mud-caked black — Cheboygan, running deep down the middle.

Quentin threw, but as soon as it left his hand he suddenly saw the double-coverage that he'd somehow ignored, somehow blocked out of his vision. He'd made a terrible mistake. The ball arced through the foggy air, descended toward the three players who waited at the 10. All three Sklorno jumped, almost hitting the black-and-white striped Harrah official that floated close by. Smileyberg leapt the highest. Twenty feet in the air, the Cloud Killers cornerback wrapped her outstretched tentacles around the ball, robbing Quentin yet again.

But on the way down, Cheboygan's tentacles slid up between Smileyberg's, grabbed the ball and ripped it free. When they all hit the ground, Cheboygan had it tucked to her chest.

The floating Harrah zebe was right there. He signaled a reception and a first down.

Tragedy had just turned to a last chance. The clock read 0:17 and counting.

"To the line! *Move!*"

Quentin ran at his exhausted players, pulling them to their feet, hitting them, urging them to sprint 40 yards downfield and line up before time expired. They ran hard, even the scuttling Ki, the crowd's rage ripping through the hanging fog.

Bud-O-Shwek was the last to arrive, the center lining up on the ball. Quentin glanced at the clock as he reached under center — 0:04 ... 0:03 ...

"Hut!"

The ball slapped into his hands and he spiked it to the ground. The clock stopped at 0:01.

One play left. Down by five, the Krakens had to score a touchdown to win.

He huddled his team. Cheboygan ran off, Halawa ran on. Halawa had the best vertical leap. If Quentin threw to the back corner of the end zone, Halawa had the best chance of bringing it down for the win. Quentin stuck with the same formation: Yassoud at running back, two tight ends, two receivers on the wings.

He broke the huddle. The Krakens lined up, their beloved orange and black barely visible beneath a thick sheen of brown and blue. Victory was only a few feet away and every Kraken knew it.

Across the line, a wall of angry defenders, their white jerseys now dark with moisture and mud, blue streaks criss-crossing them like camouflage. Brown smeared their white helmets, caked in around their blue facemasks.

Quentin looked over the defense, then bent under center. The mud-filled game had come down to this single, final play.

BLINK

The crowd noise vanished.

He barked out the snap count, but he couldn't hear his own words.

He felt vocal cords rip on his final *hut-hut!*

He pushed away from the line, knowing the clock had just ticked 0:00, his cleats digging into the wet, torn, blue field. Somehow he *felt* the dirt, the mud, the ravaged Iomatt plants, felt them *through* his armored shoes as if his feet were moving tree roots that connected to the ground, drew sustenance from it.

His eyes saw everything, a slow motion, hand-to-hand war of filthy black-jerseyed warriors trying to hold back an onslaught of attackers wearing mud-covered uniforms of white, blue and yellow.

At five steps, he planted his left foot, then bounced a half step forward. First option, Halawa on the corner-fade: covered by Smileyberg. Even as his eyes flicked to the second option, Tara the Freak on a crossing route over the middle, Quentin felt the left side of the pocket collapsing — Jesper Schultz easily powering through the overmatched Shut-O-Dital.

Quentin stepped forward, into the pocket, giving Shut-O space to use Jesper's momentum against him, to keep the defensive end moving to where Quentin *had* been, not where he *was*. Jesper reached over the offensive tackle, fingers stretching for Quentin, but those fingers brushed across dirty black Kevlar fabric without locking down.

Tara was covered, two Cloud Killers linebackers bracketing him.

Now the right side of the pocket collapsed. A silent instinct told Quentin to *move right* and he did, pushing off his left foot as hard as he could. Something hit him from behind. Multi-jointed arms grabbed at him, tried to drag him down. He tucked the ball tight in his left arm as he fell, then reached his right hand down and planted it on the ground, his legs still pumping the whole time.

His right hand pressed into wet, cold mud.

That spiritual feeling of *connecting* with the field.

He would not go down.

Quentin pushed hard with his right hand and both of his feet, then felt the Ki lineman's arms slip away. He was free.

He sprinted right. Ten yards to the end zone, to victory. Could he run it in? Yassoud, facing him, shuffling along the goal line — but the other Coranadillana cornerback was just a step behind him: 'Soud wasn't open.

Quentin kept running. The receivers scrambled, trying to find open space.

There, in the back of the end zone, just under the goal post — Starcher, sidestepping to his right, to Quentin's left. Running right, Quentin turned his body the other way and flicked the ball into the end zone. A lefty running right, then throwing back across the field was a difficult pass under any circumstances, let alone these wet and miserable conditions. The ball wobbled through the air. It seemed to float, seemed to invite the defenders that closed in from all sides.

The ball hung forever, players converging on it, reaching for it ...

... but they were all too late.

A thrill exploded in Quentin's chest as the ball hit George Starcher in the hands. Touchdown! Victory!

George bobbled the ball.

Quentin's hyper-focused mind saw the brown leather slide out of Starcher's hands. The ball dropped. Starcher reached for it lightning-fast, but his big hands knocked it to the ground.

The football hit the black-painted surface with a small splash of brown water.

Pass incomplete.

BLINK

The agonized roar of the crowd snapped back into full-volume existence. Quentin was still running, his slowing momentum carrying him a few more steps. George stood there, looking down at the ball. Cloud Killers players leapt with joy and satisfaction. Krakens players put hands to helmets, or fell to the ground, exhausted and spent, finally claimed by defeat. No penalty flags. Quentin looked at the clock, hoping he'd made some mistake, that there was still time left for one more play.

The clock read: 0:00.

Cloud Killers 28, Krakens 23.

Game over.

THE KRAKENS GATHERED in the central locker room. Drained, beat up, the big knot of disappointment stayed lodged in Quentin's chest. They'd had the game won, an amazing comeback and it slipped away by one dropped pass.

A muddy George sat on a bench against the wall, elbows on his knees, head in his hands. He was rocking back and forth — slightly, slowly, but it still looked somewhat disturbing. Other players stared at him with expressions of disgust or anger. Quentin was one of them — he hated George Starcher in that moment. One dropped pass away from 3-0.

Coach Hokor walked to the holoboard in the center of the room. Some heads continued to look at the floor, some to stare at Starcher, but most turned to look at the coach.

"Krakens, that was a hard loss," Coach said. "Every team in the GFL can beat any other team on any given day. Every ... single ... team. All of you, take a moment and think to yourself — did you prepare for the Cloud Killers the way you prepared for the Ice Storm?"

Hokor let the question hang. More players now looked toward the floor. Quentin was one of them. He'd spent too much time on calls with Somalia or trying to deal with the fallout of Yolanda's cover story.

"We will learn from this," Hokor said. "I wanted a win, but I'd rather learn this lesson now than in the playoffs. We overlook *no one*, understand?"

Heads nodded, eyestalks bobbed.

"And I don't want to hear anyone blame a single play for this loss," Hokor said. He didn't name the play. He didn't have to. "If we had executed properly in the first half, we would have been ahead and would not have been in a position where we needed to make a play at the end of the game to win. Every one of you had a tackle you just missed, a sack you couldn't finish, a run you could have broken. A game is not a single play, it is a body of work. A victory or a loss is *sixty minutes* of execution, *not* five seconds."

Hokor paused again, letting the words sink in. Quentin nodded, noticed that other players were agreeing. Coach was right. This loss wasn't Starcher's fault. They had failed as a team.

"This game is *over*," Hokor said. "Put it behind you. We are still two-and-one, a game out of first place. Next week we have a tough opponent in the Hittoni Hullwalkers. That is all we care about from this moment on. Tell me, are we going to overlook the Hullwalkers?"

A mumbled cluster of no leaked out of the players' mouths.

Hokor took off his little baseball hat and whipped it down to the ground. "What did you say? Are we going to overlook the Hullwalkers just because of their losing record?"

"No!" the team said in unison.

"I can't hear you."

"*No!*"

Hokor picked up his little hat. "Good. Tomorrow night we watch Hullwalker holos. Normal practice on Tuesday."

He stomped off, his little feet carrying him out the door. The various races filtered into their dressing rooms. Starcher stayed where he was, still swaying.

A hand on Quentin's shoulder.

Quentin turned, found himself facing Don Pine.

"Q, I know you don't want to hear anything from me."

"You got that right."

"Forget that and listen. You need to talk to Starcher."

Quentin brushed Pine's hand away. "I will."

"Do it *now*," Pine said. "A drop like that, it can mess with a receiver. Get in their head. Affect their performance."

"Coach just said we can't blame it on one play."

Pine nodded. "Sure, but he's the *coach*. *You're* the team leader and it's *your* pass he dropped — George needs to hear it from you. Go talk to him."

Quentin stared at the blue-skinned man, wanted to tell him to mind his own damn business, but Pine was right. As usual. Quentin turned and walked over to George.

"Hey, man," Quentin said. "Don't let it get to you."

George looked up, his eyes wide and haunted. "The old ones," he said. "The firmament has pulled me from the fabric of space-time and cast me aside."

"That, or you dropped a pass," Quentin said. "It happens."

George shook his head. "It does not just happen. I failed. I am a failure."

"So make up for it. One dropped pass will be forgotten if you play well next week, right?"

George stared, then nodded — but his eyes didn't change. He stood. "I have to go. I must talk to my towel."

George walked to the Human locker room. Quentin watched him walk away. *Talk to his towel?* George was a bit off his rocker, for sure. But who knew? Maybe the towel would have better words of encouragement.

The holoboard displayed updated scores and standings. The To Pirates and Wabash Wolfpack had both won. Those teams were 3-and-0, tied for first.

The Krakens would catch them.

That quest began with a trip back to the League of Planets, with a game against the Hittoni Hullwalkers.

GFL WEEK THREE ROUNDUP
Courtesy of Galaxy Sports Network

HOME		AWAY	
Alimum Armada	14	**To Pirates**	38
Ionath Krakens	23	**Coranadillana Cloud Killers**	28
Themala Dreadnaughts	17	Hittoni Hullwalkers	7
Isis Ice Storm	21	Yall Criminals	10
Jang Atom Smashers	17	Lu Juggernauts	13
Wabash Wolfpack	31	Orbiting Death	10
Bartel Water Bugs	17	D'Kow War Dogs	14
Bord Brigands	21	**Shorah Warlords**	24
Texas Earthlings	7	**Jupiter Jacks**	41
Neptune Scarlet Fliers	31	Sala Intrigue	10
Vik Vanguard	10	New Rodina Astronauts	7

THE WEEK BEGAN WITH seven undefeated teams, but finished with four. The Jupiter Jacks and the Neptune Scarlet Fliers both stayed at 3-0, the Jacks with 41-7 thumping of the Texas Earthlings (0-3) and the Fliers with a 31-10 win over the Sala Intrigue (1-2).

Two 3-0 teams also top the Planet Division. The To Pirates (3-0) put a 38-14 whipping on the Alimum Armada (0-3), while the Wabash Wolfpack (3-0) notched a convincing 31-10 win on the surprising OS1 Orbiting Death (2-1).

Isis climbed back into the Planet Division title hunt with a 21-10 win over the Yall Criminals (1-2). With quarterback Rick Renaud out due to injury, the Criminals have scored only 10 points in their last six quarters of play. Renaud is expected to return in Week Four against Jupiter.

Ionath (2-1) came into the week undefeated and heavily favored to beat the Coranadillana Cloud Killers (1-2), but were upset by a score of 28-23. Krakens tight end George Starcher dropped what would have been a game-winning pass as time expired. Ionath falls to a four-way, second-place tie in the Planet Division, along with OS1, Isis and Themala (2-1).

Deaths

Neptune Scarlet Fliers fullback **Stephen Pagan,** killed on a late hit by Sala Intrigue defensive tackle Gum-Aw-Pin. GFL Commissioner Rob Froese suspended Gum-Aw-Pin for Sala's upcoming game against the Jang Atom Smashers and also fined the All-Pro defender 100 kilocredits.

Offensive Player of the Week

Daniel Carrus, running back for the D'Kow War Dogs, who ran for 132 yards and 2 touchdowns in a losing effort against the Bartel Water Bugs.

Defensive Player of the Week

Smileyberg, cornerback for the Coranadillana Cloud Killers. Smileyberg scored three touchdowns, one off an interception of Quentin Barnes, one off a fumble recovery and one on a kickoff return.

14

WEEK FOUR:
IONATH KRAKENS
at HITTONI HULLWALKERS

PLANET DIVISION	SOLAR DIVISION
3-0 To Pirates	3-0 Jupiter Jacks
3-0 Wabash Wolfpack	3-0 Neptune Scarlet Fliers
2-1 Isis Ice Storm	2-1 Bartel Water Bugs
2-1 Ionath Krakens	2-1 New Rodina Astronauts
2-1 OS1 Orbiting Death	2-1 Shorah Warlords
2-1 Themala Dreadnaughts	1-2 Bord Brigands
1-2 Coranadillana Cloud Killers	1-2 D'Kow War Dogs
1-2 Yall Criminals	1-2 Jang Atom Smashers
0-3 Alimum Armada	1-2 Sala Intrigue
0-3 Hittoni Hullwalkers	1-2 Vik Vanguard
0-3 Lu Juggernauts	0-3 Texas Earthlings

Excerpt from "Sorenson's Guide to the Galaxy"
Science First: The League of Planets

In the realm of business, it is said that you don't rise to the top without making a few enemies. And if your government is run *like* a business, the same holds true, especially for the CEO of the League of Planets.

The League is one of the stranger government structures in known space. For 164 years, this technologically advanced system has been run as a corporation. A corporation dedicated to one thing: science.

In the League, the prevailing philosophy is that if you take care of science first, everything else takes care of itself. When you look at the League's standing in the galaxy, it is hard to argue with this logic. The League is far and away the leader in engine technology, ship construction, communications, genetic engineering involving the Human genome, legal body modification and exploration.

The Corporation as Government

The League of Planets is a giant corporation that focuses on scientific achievement. All other elements of government, from defense to trade to agriculture to exploration, center on keeping the scientific bureaucracy running. While the League makes a great deal of profit from technological advances, that money is perpetually earmarked for increased scientific spending and the betterment of life for League citizens. By focusing on scientific advancement, the League has established the highest quality of life in known space.

The League of Planets treats all governmental duties as pure business, part of the effort to support the advancement of science. There is little wasted spending and every credit is accounted for.

Head of State: First Scientist

It is difficult to find a comparable government position to that of First Scientist of the League of Planets. While religion is outlawed in the League, many sentients outside the system say that science is their religion. From that perspective, one could consider the First Scientist the equivalent of a theocracy's "Supreme Leader." Some say that makes the First Scientist position more comparable to Grand Mullah of the Purist Nation than to the President of the Planetary Union or to the Grand Tribe Master of the Yashindi.

While the First Scientist doesn't handle day-to-day management of the government, he or she does hold considerable sway over the Scientific Council. The Scientific Council is the League's equivalent to a congressional body. The First Scientist's influence over this group means he or she directly impacts decisions made by the League of Planet's s leader, the CEO.

Chief Executive Officer

Currently held by Clarissa King, the League's CEO office is quite nearly a dictatorial position. CEO King controls all aspects of government. She makes all major governmental decisions. Her word is law.

Unlike a true dictator, however, the League's CEO is always held accountable by the 51-member Scientific Council, which can order her removal at any time by a two-thirds majority vote. That is why being fired from any position in the League is referred to by the slang term "getting thirty-foured," a reference to the 34 votes required to instantly remove the head of state.

The CEO's job is to increase profitability. Higher profitability means greater scientific funding. If the CEO does not annually increase scientific funding, she is considered a failure. While the position of CEO is one of the most powerful in the galaxy, there is little glamour involved. The complete lack of job security means new CEOs must produce results quickly and continue to produce results. Most analysts consider it the most demanding position in any known government.

Many factions within the League vie to put their candidate in the CEO position, for the CEO controls all domestic and foreign policy. While a two-thirds vote of the Scientific Council is the only legal way to remove a CEO, there is a far more common reason for change — death. Of the last fourteen CEOs, only three "got thirty-foured." The rest died under mysterious circumstances, circumstances that had a tendency to follow bitter in-house debates about the allocation of scientific funding.

Scientific Council

Fifty-one scientists make up this powerful governmental body. The Council has two primary tasks: determine the effectiveness of the CEO and allocate funds to the government's various departments.

Vacancies on the Council are filled by a majority vote of the remaining members. Candidates are chosen based solely on their scientific accomplishments. All appointments to the Scientific Council are for life. To date, there has been very little controversy regarding new Council members. Positions are always filled by highly accomplished individuals. That is not to say, however, that Council members are free from corruption. Once in place, a Council member is frequently beset by lobbyists from various factions within the League. To control the Scientific Council's vote is to control the allocation of government funds. Many Council members show a suspicious increase in wealth shortly after their appointment.

Vice Presidents

Operation of all non-research governmental management is divided into "divisions." Each division is led by a Vice President (VP). In this way, League functions are very compartmentalized — a single person is held directly accountable for success and failure. Some divisions, such as the Shipbuilding Division and the Exploration Division, are far more powerful than others.

The CEO fires and appoints VPs as he or she sees fit. Each VP knows he or she must produce and maintain a highly efficient department to avoid being quickly replaced. In turn, VPs appoint their own staff, hire and fire as they see fit and determine where to invest their available funds into research that benefits the division's needs.

At all levels of a division, everyone is accountable to the VP.

The VP, in turn, has to answer to the CEO. Failure of underlings is not considered an excuse in the League of Planets.

Like the CEO, the Vice Presidents are under a great deal of pressure to produce. The League does not accept a status quo. A VP who does not show improvement each year is considered a failure. The CEO sets quotas that are not open to debate, no matter how unreasonable they might be. Any VP who misses the quota is usually dismissed in disgrace. Only 65 percent of VPs last more than two years. Only 12 percent have maintained their positions for a decade or more.

Academic Departments

Science is the business of the League of Planets. As such, a great deal of governmental bureaucracy is tied up regulating scientific funding.

The League's science structure is broken into six main academic departments, each of which encompasses an endless pyramid structure of ever-more-specialized study. Each department is run by a Chancellor. Chancellors of the six major departments are very powerful sentients, dictating how funds are allotted to various sub-departments.

Academic departments are broken down into colleges, each run by a Dean. Deans, like Chancellors, vie for a percentage of fixed funds. Because Deans decide where money is spent, they are constantly beset by lobbyists. Supplying scientific contracts is a big business, rife with corruption, payoffs, kickbacks and skimming.

Deans are elected based on their scientific prestige and integrity. While many refuse the temptations of corruption, others succumb to promises of wealth and power. The League, however, has little patience with crooked Deans — anyone convicted of corruption is immediately removed from office and sentenced to a lengthy prison term. If enough doubt is cast on a Dean, but no evidence is available, a Chancellor can remove him or her from office. This strong stance, however, does little to dissuade corruption.

League of Planets Academic Departments

Below is a listing of the League of Planets' primary academic departments:

- **Military Engineering**
  College of Weapon Design, College of Fighter Engineering, The Armor Research College, etc.
- **Civil Engineering**
  Architectural College, College of Materials Research, College of Infrastructure Analysis, Communications College, etc.
- **Life Sciences**
  College of Terran Biology, Exobiology College, College of Psychology, Hydroponics College, etc.
- **Planet Sciences**
  College of Geophysics, College of Geology, Tectonic College, etc.
- **Void Sciences**
  College of Quantum Physics, Warp Theory College, College of Astrophysics, etc.
- **Artificial Life**
  College of Artificial Intelligence, Department of Intellect Upload.

THE TRADE DEADLINE was almost up — if the Krakens were going to make a move to bring in new players, decisions had to be made. Every personnel decision now involved Quentin. He walked into Hokor's office expecting to find the coach, Gredok the Splithead and Don Pine.

But Pine wasn't there.

"Come in, Barnes," Hokor said. "Close the door."

Quentin did. He was happy he didn't have to face Pine, but what did this mean? Did Hokor and Gredok finally think Quentin's input was enough, that they didn't need the opinion of the veteran? Or, had Gredok lost patience with his lying, expensive backup quarterback who was ruining the life of his starting QB?

Quentin sat. "We talking trades?"

"We are," Hokor said. "We are too thin at defensive back."

Quentin nodded. "You can say that again, Your Shortness. But, uh … where's Don?"

Hokor looked at Gredok, whose pedipalps started to twitch.

"Barnes," Gredok said. "The contrast between your bursts of intelligence and your bouts of idiocy amaze me."

"What?"

"Pine is not here to talk trades, Barnes, because we're here to talk about trading Pine."

Quentin stared at his diminutive owner, then turned to stare at his diminutive coach. Even with all the trouble Pine had caused, Quentin hadn't even considered *not* having the man on the team.

"Trade Don?"

Gredok's pedipalps twitched some more. "So smart on the field, so … *not* smart off of it."

"But why?"

"We need defensive backs," Hokor said. "Pine is advanced in years for his position, but he is still a high-value commodity. Several teams could put Pine in place right now as a starter."

"What if I get hurt?"

"Pine costs me a fortune," Gredok said. "And he is not playing. If you get hurt, we still have Goldman."

Quentin shook his head. "Yitzhak is great for a third-stringer, Gredok, but if I go down and he has to start? We're in trouble. And then who would we put as the third-string QB?"

Hokor thought, his pedipalps smoothing abstract circles on his desk. "We might pick one up in the trade. If not, I'm sure Montagne can handle the task."

Montagne? As a backup quarterback? Something about that still bothered Quentin.

"Barnes, listen," Hokor said. "Hittoni wants Pine. So do the Texas Earthlings. If our cornerbacks Berea or Wahiawa go down, our best backup is Stockbridge, our nickel back. After her, all we have is Vacaville — a free agent that couldn't make the roster of any other Tier One team. If we lose Wahiawa or Berea, we'll be horribly exposed. We can make this trade *now*, get a top-notch corner and move Pine to a team where he can start."

The words slammed around inside Quentin's head — *where he can start*. After all the crap Pine had pulled, after hiding his head in the sand and letting Quentin take the blame, he would go *start* for another team? Like nothing had happened?

Hell no.

"Who else can we trade?"

"You tell me, Barnes. You want to move one of your top-three receivers?"

"No," Quentin said. "We're not trading any receivers. What about Michnik or Khomeni? We're deep at defensive end."

"We can't," Gredok said. "Both Michnik and Khomeni have no-trade clauses in their contracts. No one will give us a starting cornerback for a backup defensive end."

"It's Pine," Hokor said. "Has to be. We need to make a move."

Quentin shook his head. "Coach, don't trade Pine. We're deep where we *need* to be deep, at quarterback. He can step in and lead this team just like I can. You know this."

And that part, at least, was no lie. Don Pine had lost a step or two, but the old man could still probably win the starting slot at fifteen or sixteen of the twenty-two Tier One teams.

Hokor looked at Gredok. Gredok met the coach's gaze, then turned his one eye on Quentin.

"Barnes, this surprises me," Gredok said. "After all that Don Pine has done to harm your reputation, to damage this franchise, you are fighting to keep him? He *threw games*. We would do well to be rid of him."

Quentin wanted Pine gone, wanted it bad. But to do that now meant that Pine would get to lead a team again — Pine would get everything he wanted and Quentin would be left holding the bag.

Careful to control his emotions, to hide his intentions from Gredok, Quentin just shrugged. "It's your call, Greedy. I'll support whatever decision you make, but as your quarterback, as your team leader, I am telling you we need Don Pine. Don't make this trade."

Gredok stared at Quentin. The owner was probably looking for some tell, some sign that would betray Quentin's motivations, but Quentin wasn't a rookie anymore and this wasn't a crazy situation like that contract negotiation with Danny the Dolphin. Quentin had learned how to control himself, how to put on a poker face that not even Gredok could see through.

"All right," Gredok said. "Barnes, you may go. Hokor and I will inform you of our decision."

Quentin nodded, then walked out of Hokor's office.

QUENTIN SAT IN HIS QUARTERS on the *Touchback*, waving through the Hittoni roster on his holotank. The Hullwalkers were 0-and-3, but the Cloud Killers loss provided ample evidence that records didn't really matter.

The Hullwalkers defensive secondary was young and inexperienced. They had rookies at safety and left cornerback, while strong safety Sharapovo was in just her second year. Their veteran right cornerback, Livry-Gargon, was a force to be reckoned with, but she would be locked on Hawick. Milford and Halawa would draw coverage from the rookies, which meant either of them could have a huge game.

On top of that, the Hullwalkers were ranked twentieth out of twenty-two teams against the run. Quentin could rely on Ju's legs, knowing that the passing game would be wide open if and when the Hullwalkers committed to stopping the ground game.

The visitor alarm buzzed.

"Who is it?"

[GEORGE STARCHER AT YOUR DOOR]

Quentin rubbed his eyes, checked the time display. He'd been buried in study for the last … four hours? Time flew when you were focused. He moved through the roster to call up the Hullwalkers linebackers. They would be covering Starcher most of the game.

"Let him in."

George walked into the room, his face painted pure red. His eyes blazed wide and white. He was carrying his towel.

"Heya, George. Come on in."

George took one step in, then stopped, shook his head. "I ... I should not invade your domicile."

"Okay, no invasion necessary," Quentin said. "What's a *domicile*, again?"

"Your apartment, your place of residence, your personal connection to the land of slumber and dark-mist that allows your soul to reside on many planes of existence."

"Oh. Right. *That* domicile. Okay, whatever. Come on in, man."

George shook his head again. "I came to apologize."

"For what?"

George closed his eyes and looked down.

Quentin understood.

"For dropping the ball? George, that was last week. Don't worry about it."

"But I lost the game."

"*We* lost the game, buddy. There were a dozen plays that could have gone either way. We'll get it back in tomorrow's game. The Hullwalkers can't stop you. Make it up to me then."

George looked up, stared. "Then, you don't want my towel?"

He offered the orange-and-black plaid cloth. Quentin looked at it, saw how it was streaked with not only red but other colors, remnants of Crazy George Starcher's bizarre face-painting habit.

"Uh, thanks, but no," Quentin said. "You keep it."

George stared, then smiled a little. He turned and walked out. The door automatically shut behind him.

"They don't call you *Crazy George* for nothing," Quentin said quietly. He walked back to his couch and continued studying the linebackers. Any one of them could have a standout performance, blitz and beat the blocks, knock Quentin out of the game. Kitiara Lomax, the middle linebacker, he was the most dangerous. Despite his team's three losses, Lomax was having an All-Pro season. He'd actually picked up speed in the off-season — the data showed he'd gone from a 4.2 forty-yard dash to 4.0. Quentin had to memorize everything, prepare for anything.

The visitor alarm sounded again.

"George! I don't want your towel!"

[RICK WARBURG AT YOUR DOOR]

Warburg? Quentin sighed. This couldn't be good.

"Let him in."

The door opened. Rick walked in. He wore jeans and a T-shirt that had to be a size too small.

"What do you want, Warburg?"

Rick looked at Quentin, then at the holotank. "Lomax?"

Quentin nodded.

"You know he ran a four-flat in the off-season?"

Quentin paused, then nodded a second time. It wasn't like Rick to know that level of detail.

Rick gestured to the open space on Quentin's couch. "If you're studying the Hullwalkers, can I join you?"

"No," Quentin said. "No, Rick, you can't join me. What do you want?"

Warburg's eyes narrowed. "I want to talk to you about throwing me the damn ball."

Quentin shrugged. "I hit the open player."

"Like hell you do. I was wide open against the Killers and you ignored me. You got *sacked* instead of throwing to me."

Quentin yawned and leaned back. "I don't remember."

"You remember everything." Warburg took a deep breath and let it out slow. This was hard for him. Good.

"I need catches," he said. "Look, I'm in a free agent year."

"So you've told me."

"I need the rock. I worked my ass off for this season. I'm not asking for anything special, just hit me when I'm open. I mean, *not* passing to me? That doesn't make any sense."

"Makes sense to me. Maybe you have Hokor fooled, but I see right through you."

Warburg's hands balled up into fists. "Right through me? What are you talking about? I want off this team and *you* want me off this team."

"You want that to happen? Then you get over yourself, you bond with your teammates."

"That's against Purism!"

"Then to hell with Purism!"

The words were out of Quentin's mouth before he even knew he was saying them. Was that how he felt now? He still believed in the High One, but he didn't practice Purism anymore — did he have the right to pass judgment on others who did?

Yes. He *did* have that right. Because Purism was wrong.

Warburg smiled, an evil-looking thing full of helpless rage. "No matter what the Sklorno think, you are not *god*, Barnes. You're just an orphan miner."

"Oh, is *that* what I am?"

Rick shook his head and held up his hands. "No, sorry, that's not what I mean. I just mean that you don't get to decide people's lives and—"

"Hit the road," Quentin said. "This conversation is over."

Rick fell silent. He stared with a hatred that Quentin easily matched. Quentin lifted his right hand and pointed at the open door. Warburg's lip curled briefly into a snarl, then he turned and left.

The door shut behind him.

"Computer," Quentin said. "No more visitors. I have to study."

[YES, QUENTIN]

Quentin sat on his couch and again started waving through the Hullwalkers players, refreshing his knowledge, memorizing new stats and trying to forget about Warburg's words.

You're not god, Barnes.

THE SHIPYARD WAS EVERYTHING Quentin dreamed it would be. He'd seen the stadium from a luxury box, as a spectator. Now he was here to leave his mark, to take his glory, to step onto the blue-lined, snow-white turf as a competitor and leave as the victor.

The announcer called the Krakens onto the field. As he and his teammates ran out of the tunnel, orange away jerseys blazing bright against the white field, he heard the now-expected chorus of boos. It lacked the intensity of what he'd faced on Yall. Was his bad-boy stigma wearing off, or did they just not care as much in a place like the League of Planets? Or, more likely, a half-filled stadium didn't generate as much noise as a full one. The Hullwalkers had yet to win a game this season. The home fans didn't seem interested in coming out to watch their team get beat yet again.

Quentin ran to the sidelines with his teammates. He pushed away the thoughts of Hittoni's record. The Krakens had prepared flawlessly with hard practices and after-hours study. Ionath had put in the wrench-time needed to make sure the Hullwalkers dropped to 0-and-4.

QUENTIN ROLLED LEFT, searching for targets. Like any scramble, his first instinct was to look for Starcher, but Crazy George couldn't get open. Starcher had played poorly all game. Quentin had hit him only twice, once for 3 yards and once for 7. Not having George automatically find the open spot felt like playing without a hand.

Hawick hadn't broken off her route and Halawa was covered — no open receivers. Quentin tucked the ball and turned upfield, his feet gobbling up yards. He ran straight at Starcher, knowing the big tight end would see the run, turn and block his defender.

But George didn't see it.

The Hullwalkers linebacker caught Quentin off-guard, laid him out. Quentin hit the ground, lost his wind. As he waited patiently for his breath to return, he was grateful he hadn't fumbled. George was having an off game.

"Barnes!" Hokor's face popped up in his heads-up helmet holo. "What's going on out there?"

"Starcher," Quentin said after the first delayed breath sucked haltingly into his lungs. "He's … off. Send in Kobayasho."

"Warburg is next on the depth chart."

Quentin slowly ran back to the huddle. "Yeah, Coach, but I think Kobayasho can get open better against these linebackers. Send him in."

"Your call," Hokor said, then his fuzzy face blinked out.

The Krakens were up 21-10 halfway through the third quarter and seemed to have the game in hand. Quentin had picked the Hullwalkers' young secondary apart with touchdown strikes of 82 yards to Halawa and 11 yards to Becca. Quentin's feet had also done their thing, carrying him for 52 yards rushing, including a 17-yard touchdown run.

Now the Krakens just needed to avoid any mistakes, anything that might let the Hullwalkers back in the game.

He reached the huddle. "George, you're out."

Starcher's eyes widened. He looked to the Ionath sidelines, saw Kobayasho running on. George then turned back to Quentin, an expression of hurt on his face. "You're taking me out?"

"For this drive," Quentin said. "Take a breather, get your head in the game. Go."

Starcher's gaze fell to the ground, then he jogged to the sidelines. Quentin didn't know why the man seemed so ... devastated. It was just for a couple of drives.

Kobayasho reached the huddle, a confident smile blazing across his bleach-white face. He was ready to play.

Quentin clapped his hands three times. "Okay, boys and girls, we're up by eleven. They're keying on Ju, so we need to keep working the short passing game. Just stay focused, execute, we go home with a win. I-formation, X-wheel, Y-in, Z-post, play-action on three, on three. Ready?"

"*Break!*"

LATE IN THE THIRD QUARTER, the Hullwalkers got back in the game the wrong way — with an injury. Hullwalkers QB Jeremy Osborne dropped back under pressure from Krakens defensive tackles Mum-O and Mai-An-Inkole, but Osborne was luring them in for a screen pass to HeavyG running back Simorgh Dinatale.

Dinatale used her blockers, put a neat move on John Tweedy, then ran over backup linebacker Killik the Unworthy and headed for the end zone. Krakens cornerback Berea closed in fast, dove at Dinatale's feet. Dinatale cut toward Berea, her armored knee smashing into the Sklorno's helmeted head, snapping the head back as already-limp eyestalks trailed behind.

Dinatale ran in for a touchdown, cutting the Krakens lead to 21-17.

Berea didn't get up.

When Doc Patah floated out with the medsled, Quentin knew the Krakens had lost a starting cornerback and now had a serious problem.

THE SOLUTION TO THAT PROBLEM? Just hold onto the ball. The Krakens chewed up most of the fourth quarter with a grinding running game, using Ju, Yassoud and Becca to hammer along for 4, 5 and 6 yards a carry. On a third and goal from the 6, Quentin ran a pro-set naked boot right. The defense bought the fake — he jogged into the end zone for the touchdown.

Extra point good: Krakens up 28-17.

QUENTIN SLID HIS HANDS under Bud-O-Shwek. Ju was only a half-foot from Quentin's right shoulder, Becca Montagne only a half-foot from his left. Kobayasho at right tight end, Warburg at left.

The Victory Formation.

One more snap to finish the game.

"Hut-hut!"

The ball slapped into Quentin's hands. He dropped to one knee, heard the refs' whistles, then watched the final 15 seconds tick off the scoreboard. Most of the Hullwalker fans had already left — the place looked nearly empty, save for a couple of thousand orange- and black-clad crazies celebrating in the stands.

The Krakens had bounced back from their loss to the Cloud Killers. At 3-and-1, they were still only a game out of first place. The win didn't come without questions, however. George hadn't been himself and if Berea was out for next week — or longer — the defensive secondary was in a lot of trouble. Quentin wasn't that worried about Crazy George, who had proven himself time and time again last year. As for the secondary, maybe a trade to bring in another cornerback?

He thought of Hokor's desire to trade Pine. That would do the trick. It would bring in key defensive talent, but it would also reward Pine for his horrible actions. No way. The secondary would straighten things out. Quentin would put in extra practice time with them and make sure of it.

Pine would never start again. Ever, for *any* team.

GFL WEEK FOUR ROUNDUP
Courtesy of Galaxy Sports Network

HOME		AWAY	
D'Kow War Dogs	10	**Alimum Armada**	13
Isis Ice Storm	23	Coranadillana Cloud Killers	17
Hittoni Hullwalkers	17	**Ionath Krakens**	28
Lu Juggernauts	10	**Wabash Wolfpack**	17
Orbiting Death	7	**To Pirates**	28
Jupiter Jacks	24	**Yall Criminals**	52
New Rodina Astronauts	28	**Bartel Water Bugs**	43
Sala Intrigue	10	**Jang Atom Smashers**	12
Texas Earthlings	0	**Neptune Scarlet Fliers**	35
Shorah Warlords	13	**Vik Vanguard**	14

BYE WEEKS: Themala Dreadnaughts, Bord Brigands

AND THEN THERE were three — three undefeated teams, that is.
The Neptune Scarlet Fliers (4-0) took sole possession of first place in the Solar Division with a 35-0 annihilation of the Texas Earthlings (0-4). Neptune quarterback Adam Guri threw for four touchdowns against the depleted Earthlings' secondary, which has lost three starters to injury in recent weeks.

Jupiter (3-1) fell out of the undefeated ranks, dropping to the Yall Criminals (2-2) by a surprisingly lopsided score of 52-24. The game marked the return of Criminals QB Rick Renaud, who missed two games due to a vicious hit by Krakens defensive tackle Mum-O-Killowe. Renaud threw for four touchdowns and ran for another as he got back into the hunt for league MVP honors.

In the Planet Division, both the To Pirates and defending champion Wabash Wolfpack remain at 4-0. Wabash avoided an upset, edging out the tough Lu Juggernauts (0-4) by a score of 17-10. The Pirates had an easier time of it with a 28-7 win against the Orbiting Death (2-2).

Ionath recovered from last week's upset with a 28-17 road win at Hittoni (0-4). Krakens running back Ju Tweedy rushed for 135 yards on 20 carries, while quarterback Quentin Barnes scored all four Ionath touchdowns — two in the air and two on the ground. The win puts Ionath in a tie for second with the Isis Ice Storm, who won a tough 23-17 back-and-forth game against Coranadillana.

Is it too soon to start thinking about relegation candidates? Not if you play for Hittoni or Lu, both of which are winless at the bottom of the Planet Division. In the Solar, the winless Earthlings have company with D'Kow and Sala, both of which are 1-3.

Deaths

No deaths reported this week.

Offensive Player of the Week

Yall Criminals quarterback **Rick Renaud**, who went 24-of-30 for 342 yards and four passing touchdowns, as well as running in one touchdown on a 5-yard scamper.

Defensive Player of the Week

Orbiting Death linebacker **Yalla the Biter**, who had seven solo tackles and two sacks in a losing effort against the To Pirates.

15

WEEK FIVE:
ALIMUM ARMADA
at IONATH KRAKENS

PLANET DIVISION

4-0 To Pirates

4-0 Wabash Wolfpack

3-1 Ionath Krakens

3-1 Isis Ice Storm

2-1 Themala Dreadnaughts (bye)

2-2 OS1 Orbiting Death

2-2 Yall Criminals

1-3 Alimum Armada

1-3 Coranadillana Cloud Killers

0-4 Hittoni Hullwalkers

0-4 Lu Juggernauts

SOLAR DIVISION

4-0 Neptune Scarlet Fliers

3-1 Bartel Water Bugs

3-1 Jupiter Jacks

2-2 Jang Atom Smashers

2-2 New Rodina Astronauts

2-2 Shorah Warlords

2-2 Vik Vanguard

1-2 Bord Brigands (bye)

1-3 D'Kow War Dogs

1-3 Sala Intrigue

0-4 Texas Earthlings

Excerpt from **Earth: Birthplace of Sentients**
written by Zippy the Voracious
From **Chapter Three, Oceans Alive, Oceans Dead**

The first intelligence augmentation of cetaceans resulted in one of history's most storied scientific failures. In 2098, the work of Brock Bietz produced four long-beaked common dolphins (*Delphinus capensis*) that showed strong indications of sentience. What began as a possible landmark achievement ended in tragedy, however, when the four dolphins began attacking Human researchers in an apparent attempt to escape the research facility and enter the open ocean. A short-but-brutal battle ensued. Three of the four dolphins died, as did nine Humans, Bietz included. A lone survivor filled the facility's water with poison, killing the only remaining dolphin.

The dolphins' sentience was never proven. Blame for the disaster fell on Bietz and his shoddy research procedures. The field of cetacean sentience augmentation lay mostly fallow for fifty years, until Bietz's son, Albert, picked up where his father had left off.

Dr. Al Bietz developed several advances that built on his father's genetic work. One of his key strategies was in speech, modifying the dolphins' sound-producing ability as well as creating translation hardware and software that allowed Human-compatible speech.

Albert's twenty-year program came to fruition in 2167, when he declared that his project had achieved true dolphin sentience. Albert called the species *Delphinus albietz*. He named his three test subjects Huey, Dewey and Louie. In dramatic form, he held a global, interactive telecast, inviting reporters to interview the three male *albietzes*. In that interview, it became quickly apparent to any but the most dedicated denialists that Huey, the "spokesman," was no computer graphic, no puppet, but rather an intelligent, clever, self-aware being (Huey also repeatedly declared a fondness for salmon over halibut and showed a proclivity for telling mildly humorous jokes about bird droppings).

The world celebrated the first known non-Human sentient species (hundreds of years later, it would be discovered that Dolphins were actually the *second* non-Human sentient species, behind the Prawatt). The three dolphins became worldwide media celebrities. Within weeks, however, the dolphins demanded to be released into the wild. They claimed that they had the same rights as any other sentient Earthling and that to keep them confined to Bietz's research facilities was akin to imprisonment without cause.

Bietz strenuously objected, saying that Huey, Dewey and Louie were his property, not world citizens. He claimed more study and testing were required. Louie's eloquent "Freedom Swim" speech dramatically rallied world opinion toward the plight of the three captive Dolphins. Just four months after Huey's press conference, authorities ordered the dolphins' release.

Upon release, the dolphins headed out into the Atlantic Ocean. Dewey swam back only long enough to utter the famous words, "So long and thanks for all the fish," and then the three weren't heard from for another two years. As people of all kinds waited for some word on what had become of the world's most popular citizens, reports began to surface of small "talking dolphins" in all of the planet's oceans, seas and even the Great Lakes. Huey, Dewey and Louie were breeding — the small juvenile dolphins were their children.

Scientists began to project the breeding rate needed for three males to produce hundreds of offspring. Then came a steady stream of reports that long-nosed dolphin adult males, juvenile males and juvenile female dolphins were turning up dead — beaten, covered in dolphin bite marks, killed by physical trauma or drowning. The world's elation at a new sentient race began to fade in light of overwhelming evidence that Huey, Dewey and Louie were murdering any juvenile dolphins they had not sired, any non-sentient adult male Dolphins and also mating with every fertile female dolphin they could find.

Matings, it seemed, that were often forced.

Some of the sentient juveniles were captured for study, but both animal and Human rights groups instantly objected. The juveniles had done nothing wrong, activists said; therefore could not be held captive without charges. World courts struggled with jurisdiction and precedent. Some of the juveniles were held, some were released, but even that quickly became a moot point as scientists estimated the new population of *albietz* at 1,500 to 2,000 animals, both male and female, that were already in the wild and rapidly reaching breeding age.

In short, the fox was out of the hen house.

Over the next few years, the sentient Dolphin population expanded exponentially. Scientists began to detect simultaneous, heavy declines in the populations of other large oceanic mammals, including whales, seals, porpoises, walruses and orcas. Twenty years after the release of Huey, Dewey and Louie, those declining species were nowhere to be found outside of captivity.

As the world tried to come to grips with this unexpected extinction event, the original sentient dolphins made contact for the first time in over a decade. With the world media in attendance off the shores of Hawaii, Louie gave a prepared speech.

"We have the right to protect our territory," began the Dolphin's now-famous statement. "Humans created us, which means that eventually other Humans will want to replicate the process with other aquatic mammals. This would create competition and put our species at risk. We cannot allow that to happen. Therefore, we have preemptively eliminated the greatest potential threats to our kind. The oceans and seas belong to us and us alone."

In retrospect, it seems almost impossible that the entire Human scientific community didn't see this as a potential outcome. The now-extinct *Delphinus capensis* was known to attack and kill large sharks — including the Great White — not for food, but to remove them as a possible threat to the *capensis* pod. Historians also point to ample evidence, evidence available at the time of Bietz's work, that conclusively proved *capensis* killed porpoises and other dolphin species for no discernible reason — a behavior labeled "killing for fun."

As the dominant species in all of the Earth's large bodies of water, the Dolphins settled into their new existence. They worked with Humans in many capacities, including military, fishing, oceanic agriculture, underwater construction and exploration. The

Dolphin dominance of the world's oceans lasted almost two centuries, up until the introduction of *Homo aqus*.

There is no small irony to the development of *Homo aqus* and the resulting inter-species violence that occurred between that strain of Humanity and sentient Dolphins. Humans created Dolphins, which quickly became the dominant oceanic species by wiping out any potential challenger. When Humanity modified itself into an ocean-going variant, Dolphins initially reacted with the same level of violence, attacking and even killing aquatic-modified Humans.

World governments reacted harshly, demanding that Dolphins accept another sentient species in their space the same way Humans had accepted Dolphins.

The situation revealed the first major political divisions among the Dolphin species. Roughly half of them accepted *Homo aqus* as sentient equals. The other half wanted *Homo aqus* wiped out. Military intervention eventually settled the issue by creating armed, floating settlements for *Homo aqus*.

This forced integration eventually produced unexpected benefits. While deep racism still exists today, the majority of Dolphins became acclimated to living and working with another water-based sentient species. When Earth ships landed on Whitok in 2401, they contained three species of sentient ambassadors — Human, Aqus and Dolphin. The Dolphin ambassador Ingela Tarlinton is credited as being the leading force in developing the 2406 agreement between the worlds, the first interplanetary treaty in the galaxy's history.

GREDOK HAD BOUGHT some new art. Or at least he'd rotated in some things from his storage — Quentin imagined the crime lord's collection was quite extensive. One of the sculptures drew more lights than the others, lit up as if it were as important as a Galaxy Bowl trophy. A stone woman, some kind of robe around her waist but naked otherwise. Quentin didn't see what was so important about it — the arms had fallen off at some point, the left one at the shoulder, the right one just above the elbow. He had no idea how poor-quality construction constituted "art," but then again, he didn't really care about such a silly hobby.

"New sculpture?" asked Danny the Dolphin. "Venus di Milo, Gredok? Good to see you're flush with cash, buddy, considering you're going to have to spend some of it on my client."

"It was a gift," Gredok said. "Let's call it a tribute from a member of my organization that has far more *respect* for what I can do than your client does."

Danny's blow hole hissed out an annoyed sigh. "Didn't we already talk about threats? Come on, guy, I'm a busy sentient. Let's not cover the same worthless ground twice."

Quentin saw Gredok's fur ripple a bit. Up on his pedestal chair, Gredok still looked intimidating, only not quite as much when Danny's words made him look all fluffy. The Dolphin had a way of pushing Gredok's buttons.

"I tire of your jibes," Gredok said. "I have made a counter-offer and I am waiting to hear your response."

Danny's blow hole hissed again. "A counter-offer? Is that what you call it, buddy? Seven-point-two megacredits a year? You want to pay him that paltry sum for ten seasons? Lock him up until he's old and decrepit? Gredok, that's so far below our offer, it's almost like you're stalling for time, guy. You know we're not going to accept that."

"Then what is your counter-counter offer?"

Danny's body rose up, supported by the flexible, silver legs. "We will accept nineteen million a year for five years."

Gredok stood up in his chair, so suddenly agitated he almost fell off his pedestal. "That is only five percent below your last offer! I *doubled* my initial tender!"

"Gredok, we are *not* going to meet you in the middle," Danny said. "You might as well get that through your thick head and see it with your inky-black eye. We *will* get a fair offer."

Gredok stared. Danny stared back. Quentin wanted to crawl under the pedestal of the armless lady, hide there until this passed.

"Dolphin," Gredok said, "you are testing the last shreds of my leniency."

"No, I'm testing your bank account, buddy. I can't take offers from Tier One teams yet because we're in the season, but Tier Two teams don't have that restriction. I have an offer from the Mars Planets. I also have one from the McMurdo Murderers and the Buddha City Elite has new management."

The Buddha City Elite? The Purist Nation's only upper-tier team. Danny hadn't mentioned that.

"Tier Two, all of them," Gredok said. He turned his black eye on Quentin. "Barnes wants a trophy too much to settle for that."

"He's young," Danny said. "Only twenty years old, guy. He has time to build an entire franchise. And, Mars was in Tier One just last year, did you forget? They can come back with the right talent. Quentin and I are actually going to visit Mars and Earth during the bye-week."

"Mars is *not* Ionath. I will not take your bait, Dolphin. Unless you have an offer from a Tier One team that is close to your ridiculous demands, I will wait for your *real* proposal."

Danny lowered back down to Quentin's level. "Barnes, this is a waste of your time. Your boss wants to wait until after the season, when the offer from the To Pirates comes in? Well, then you're just going to be worth that much more when it happens. Good day, Gredok."

Danny turned and walked out. Quentin did the same and with each step, he felt the hateful stare of Gredok the Splithead burning into his back.

AH, THE TRAINING ROOM. Quentin's home away from home, the place where Doc Patah tended to his numerous injuries. This room connected to the central locker room. It was much smaller than the full hospital located under the stands of Ionath Stadium. In here, just four multi-species rejuve tanks. Surgery clamps and device racks lined the tanks. Each tank was big enough for a Ki lineman to squeeze in, so Quentin could lie back in the pink fluid with plenty of room to spare. Those four tanks, along with four tables, were where players could sit or lie back, be examined and repaired. The room also contained Doc Patah's work area — racks of drawers, benches packed with diagnostic gear and dozens of holotanks to see what was going on inside his patients. Usually after a game, the room filled with players needing fixes for cuts, scrapes, breaks, contusions and lacerations. Today, however, Quentin had needed more work than the others. He stayed longer and now found himself alone.

He relaxed in the tank's thick, warm, pink gel. His knee screamed at him, trying to tell him the error of running the ball up the middle on a quarterback draw, where 365-pound linebackers could knock the tar out of you. His shoulder made similar complaints, using bone-grinding agony to explain to Quentin that if he insisted on staying in the pocket that long, he would be hit by large sentients that seemed intent on tearing his still-beating heart from his chest. He'd taken more punishment than usual. Starting left offensive tackle Kill-O-Yowet was still out due to injury. Backup Shut-O-Dital — a fourth-year player who had never started — wasn't good enough to consistently stop defensive tackles. Fortunately, Doc Patah said that Kill-O would be back for the Week Six game against the Orbiting Death.

Quentin told his knee and shoulder to shut their traps. You can do that when you put together an 80-yard, fourth-quarter drive to beat the Alimum Armada. Sure, he'd taken some damage on that final drive, but it had been worth it. Arioch Morningstar's 25-yard kick as time expired meant the Krakens were 4-1, tied for second place in the Planet Division.

The soft fluttering of wing-flaps announced Doc Patah's presence moments before the mandatory lecture began.

"My analysis is finished," he said. "I need to operate on your knee and your shoulder."

"Is it bad?"

"Bad is a relative term," Doc Patah said. "You will need to go easy tomorrow, but you should be fine for Tuesday's practice. You are lucky it's not worse. Really, Young Quentin, it's like you *want* to get hurt. Do you like the pain? Because you certainly eat it like candy."

"C'mon, Doc. We won."

Doc Patah's mouth-flaps slid into the pink goo. He gently lifted

Quentin's swollen knee. He placed a large clamp around the joint, then sealed it shut. Quentin felt the initial pain of needles sinking through his skin, deep into the cartilage and ligaments, then the numb feeling of his nerves being shut off by a combination of chemicals and electrical impulses.

"Yes, we have victory," Doc Patah said. "And I will give credit where credit is due. You stood in the center of the ring and took your punches. I salute you."

Quentin opened his eyes and looked up at the floating Harrah. Doc Patah did not give compliments lightly.

"Doc, are you telling me that I won you over?"

Doc's speakerfilm let out his Human-like sigh of annoyance. "Hardly. You still need to learn how to slide. I'm a doctor, Young Quentin, not a mortician."

The Harrah fluttered back to his area, picked a clamp out of one of the equipment bins, then flew back and connected the clamp to the edge of the rejuve tank. Signal lights on the clamp lit up, showing a proper signal from the main computer. Doc Patah affixed the clamp to Quentin's shoulder, bringing, perhaps, a little more pain than was necessary. Doc flapped a few feet to the left, to the bank of monitors. He examined various holographic models of Quentin's bone, his ligaments, his muscles.

"Any problems, Doc?"

"There could have been," he said. "You were only a few newtons away from having your patella shattered, but why should my expert analysis have any impact on your playing behavior? I am, after all, only the galaxy's foremost sports medicine surgeon, so there's no reason you should listen to me."

Quentin smiled and closed his eyes, letting the rejuve tank's heat sink into his battered body. "Ah, there's the Doc Patah I know and love."

"You will need to sit here for the next hour, then give me full bed rest tonight. I will now leave you in peace so that you can, as usual, pretend that I didn't give you any advice at all, as I'm sure we'll have this same post-game repair session next week against the Orbiting Death."

Quentin heard the soft flutter fade as Doc left the room.

Maybe he fell asleep, he wasn't sure. A new voice called to him.

"You're a bastard."

The voice of Don Pine. Quentin's eyes fluttered open. He looked left to see Pine, standing there, wearing his street clothes — in this case, the same kind of immaculate, tailored suit he always wore on game-day. The blue-skinned Pine looked more like a model or a picture-perfect pitchman than he did a quarterback.

All of him, except for his eyes, which were narrowed in hateful aggression.

"I'm a bastard? Do you mean *orphan?*"

Don shook his head. "Not that kind of bastard. I mean the kind that would undercut my chances to get out of here."

Quentin tried to sit up, but the brace on his knee and shoulder kept him locked in place. "You talked to Hokor?"

Pine nodded. He took a step closer. Quentin was surprised to feel a bit of shame, of embarrassment — shutting down Pine's trade chances seemed justifiable in the confines of Hokor's office, but now he was face-to-face with the man.

"It's a bad trade," Quentin said. "We need you."

"Yeah? Tell me who they were going to trade me for, specifically."

Quentin opened his mouth to talk, then paused — he'd never asked that. He started to think through the defensive backs of the—

"Don't bother," Pine said. "If you knew, you would have rattled it off right away. Now you're just remembering what d-backs play for what teams."

Quentin closed his mouth, said nothing.

"Why?" Pine said. "I could have been *gone*. I could have started again. You *want* me gone, so why would you backstab me like that?"

"Backstab *you?* You self-righteous ass, are you kidding me? Look at what I have to go through every road game."

"Who cares? You *start* every road game. You lead your teammates onto the field. So people are angry at you for something you didn't actually do? Get over it."

Quentin automatically started to get up again, his temper driving him, again making him briefly forget the unforgiving clamps. His brain swam in an uncomfortable mix of emotions: anger at Pine's lack of responsibility, anxiety that the decision had been made for the wrong reasons.

"You're a fool," Pine said. "You're the best quarterback in the game, but you're an immature fool."

"Why's that?"

"Because you had a situation where everybody wins and you pissed it away because it's more important to teach me a lesson, because it's more important to show how you've been wronged."

"I *have* been wronged."

Pine shook his head. "You don't even know what the word means, boy. Sure, I haven't bailed you out of Yolanda's article, but everything you have now? That's because of *me*. I coached you, nurtured you, I—"

"So what I do on the field has nothing to do with my success? Is that what you're saying?"

Pine shrugged. "Yeah, you're crazy talented, I won't deny it, but if it wasn't for me, Barnes, you would have washed out in your rookie season and been sent back to the PNFL. I gave you *everything*. And despite all I taught you, you still act like everyone is out to get you, like you have to hit them back for every slight instead of thinking strategically."

Quentin had wanted to screw Pine out of a chance at redemption. Pine didn't *deserve* redemption. "I'm supposed to ignore what you did?"

"*Yes!* So your archenemy gets to go start for another team, so what? Do you realize you have one of the worst defensive backfields in the league? You could have fixed that."

"We're four-and-one with the defense we have," Quentin said. "I think we'll be just fine."

Pine smiled, shook his head. "That's because we haven't faced a top-notch quarterback yet. Renaud was only in for one quarter. You saw what he did to us in that time and that was when we still had our starting cornerback. We just beat a pair of teams with one win *between* them and we *lost* to the one-and-four Cloud Killers. Next week we have the Orbiting Death and you're going to see what a guy like Condor Adrienne can do to your awesome backfield."

"The d-backs will do fine."

"Yeah, good luck with that," Pine said. "Your emotional decision is going to cost Ionath the playoffs."

Quentin leaned his head back, closed his eyes. "We'll see about that."

"We will. And if the d-backs that you could have had don't cost us, your ridiculous feud with Rick Warburg will. If you want to win games, you better get rid of this chip on your shoulder, get rid of this idea that people need to *obey* your every whim."

Quentin's eyes stayed closed, but he felt his face flush red. Not throwing to Warburg had seemed like the right thing to do, seemed ... *justified* ... but was that just a childish decision like Don said?

"We're even now," Pine said. "I burned you. You burned me back. We're even."

"You think I care if we're even?"

"You should," Pine said. "Because the way you play, you're going to get hurt and when you do I'm coming back in. You stopped me from getting a starting job? That's fine, Barnes, because I'll just get my starting job back right here in Ionath. You think about that the next time you scramble."

Pine turned and walked to the door.

"I'm better than you," Quentin shouted at his back. "You told me that yourself."

Pine stopped and turned. "You're one play away from finding out if I'm right. I'm done trying to make you my legacy. Now? Now all I want is the ball."

Quentin tried to act bored, like the words didn't bother him, but Pine didn't say anything else. When Quentin opened his eyes, Pine was already gone, leaving Quentin alone with his thoughts, alone with his decisions.

And he didn't know if either was right.

GFL WEEK FIVE ROUNDUP

Courtesy of Galaxy Sports Network

HOME		AWAY	
Ionath Krakens	24	Alimum Armada	23
Yall Criminals	31	Coranadillana Cloud Killers	14
Isis Ice Storm	31	Hittoni Hullwalkers	10
To Pirates	52	Lu Juggernauts	14
Themala Dreadnaughts	35	Orbiting Death	31
Bartel Water Bugs	14	**Shorah Warlords**	17
Neptune Scarlet Fliers	22	Bord Brigands	14
D'Kow War Dogs	12	New Rodina Astronauts	9
Jang Atom Smashers	17	**Texas Earthlings**	20
Vik Vanguard	22	**Jupiter Jacks**	28

BYE WEEKS: Wabash Wolfpack, Sala Intrigue

AS WE CLOSE IN on the season's halfway point, the battle for the Planet Division is shaping up to be anyone's game. Ionath (4-1) edged out a 24-23 win over Alimum (1-4) to remain tied for third with the Isis Ice Storm (4-1), who dropped a 31-10 hammer on the Hittoni Hullwalkers (0-5). Ionath and Isis are a half-game behind Wabash (4-0), which had a bye this week and one game behind the first-place To Pirates (5-0), who embarrassed the Lu Juggernauts (0-5) by a score of 52-14.

Neptune (5-0) remained undefeated and on top of the Solar Division with a tough 22-14 win over the Bord Brigands (1-3). Bord scored the first two touchdowns of the game to take a 14-0 lead but collapsed in the second half as Scarlet Fliers quarterback Adam Guri hit wide receiver Amarillo three separate times for touchdowns.

The Jupiter Jacks 28-22 win over the Vik Vanguard (2-3) leaves the Jacks (4-1) just one game out of first against their Solar System rival Neptune.

Shorah (3-2) beat the Bartel Water Bugs (3-2) by a score of 17-14 to join the Bugs in a tie for third place.

In relegation news, the Texas Earthlings (1-4) finally notched a win thanks to a 20-17 upset over the Jang Atom Smashers (2-3). Texas, Bord and Sala Intrigue (1-3) are all at the bottom of the Solar Division.

In the Planet Division, Hittoni and Lu remain winless.

Deaths

Dok-Ah-Long, defensive tackle for the New Rodina Astronauts, who was killed in a fumble-recovery pileup. League Commissioner Rob Froese reported that officials are analyzing game holos, but cannot identify if Long's crushed heart occurred as a legal hit prior to the pileup or in the pile itself.

Hittoni quarterback **Jeremy Osborne** was declared dead in the second quarter of the Hullwalkers 31-10 loss to the Isis Ice Storm, killed on a hit by defensive end Ryan Nossek. In a shocking development, Osborne's vital signs returned seven seconds after being officially declared dead. Osborne sat out the third quarter but finished the game for the Hullwalkers.

Offensive Player of the Week

To Pirates running back **Randy Noseworthy,** who racked up 112 yards on 15 carries and ran for 2 touchdowns in a win over the Lu Juggernauts.

Defensive Player of the Week

Mur the Mighty, rookie linebacker for the Vik Vanguard. Mur had nine tackles and three sacks against Jupiter Jacks QB Shriaz Zia. The performance gives Mur 35 tackles and 6 sacks on the season, first in the league in both categories.

16

WEEK SIX:
IONATH KRAKENS
at OS1 ORBITING DEATH

PLANET DIVISION	SOLAR DIVISION
5-0 To Pirates	5-0 Neptune Scarlet Fliers
4-0 Wabash Wolfpack (bye)	4-1 Jupiter Jacks
4-1 Ionath Krakens	3-2 Bartel Water Bugs
4-1 Isis Ice Storm	3-2 Shorah Warlords
3-1 Themala Dreadnaughts	2-3 D'Kow War Dogs
3-2 Yall Criminals	2-3 Jang Atom Smashers
2-3 OS1 Orbiting Death	2-3 New Rodina Astronauts
1-4 Alimum Armada	2-3 Vik Vanguard
1-4 Coranadillana Cloud Killers	1-3 Bord Brigands
0-5 Hittoni Hullwalkers	1-3 Sala Intrigue (bye)
0-5 Lu Juggernauts	1-4 Texas Earthlings

THE TOUCHBACK SLID OUT of punch-space. The viewbay windows filled with the image of Orbital Station One. Quentin had a moment to think *hey, I didn't throw up this time*, then his hands automatically shot to the Tweedys' golden puke bucket — this week decorated with the logo of the Orbiting Death — and he knew he was wrong.

Through his guttural retching noises, Quentin heard his teammates laughing at him. That didn't bother him anymore. A few laughs and some teasing were fine, as long as he could be on the viewing deck with his team. He knew it, they knew it and somehow it was still funny, even to him.

"Good one, Q," John said. "Quite pungent."

"Nice form," Ju said. "You really got up on your toes on that one."

Quentin held the puke bucket with his left hand. With his right, he flipped them the bird.

"An exceptional performance," Michael Kimberlin said. "I read nine-point-five scores across the board, except for a three from the Tower judge."

Quentin set the bucket down and pulled out the plastic bag. He stood straight, wiped his mouth, then looked at Kimberlin. "Eat, too, Brutus?"

Kimberlin actually laughed, a big sound that filled the viewing bay and seemed to make the Sklorno shy away in surprise.

"It's *Et* tu, Quentin, but that's funny."

John's face wrinkled in his *you guys are stupid* expression. "Eat too? What is that, some vomit joke?"

"It's Latin," Kimberlin said. "Part of the history of ancient Earth. If you'd like to study with us, John, that would be fine with me."

John waved his hand in front of his face as if he'd smelled something awful, something other than the vomit that didn't seem to bother him. "The only *studying* I'll be doing is of the club scene after the game. The ladies of OS1 need some education, Uncle Johnny style."

Quentin started to say *maybe that's not a good idea*, but a voice from behind stopped him cold.

"You will not be going out on the town, Tweedy."

All levity vanished. The Krakens players turned to face Gredok the Splithead.

"How quickly you forget, John Tweedy, that a year ago you were dodging bullets on this very station. I almost lost several starters thanks to your quest to rescue your brother."

"Sure thing, King," John said. "But that worked out, right? Ju's our running back now. We're four-and-one. All's well that ends where we don't get shot, right?"

"I *did* get shot," Ju said.

"Shut up," John said.

"No, *you* shut up," Ju said.

Gredok stamped a foot, making his bracelets and jewelry rattle. "Enough. Anna Villani has not forgotten your intrusion into her territory, nor has she forgotten that Ju cavorted with her girlfriend. OS1 has become a very dangerous place for anyone associated with the Ionath Krakens. Therefore, the entire team is confined to quarters for the duration of our stay."

Ju's shoulders sagged. "No *way*. Gredok, that's not fair. I have a lot of friends on OS1. I've been waiting to come back."

Gredok's fur fluffed, then laid flat. "Sadly, Ju, you are no smarter than your brother, who is not very smart. On Orbital Station One, you have a price on your head. I'm sure many of those so-called *friends* would be happy to collect. You are my property. You will stay where I tell you to stay. Do you understand?"

Ju kicked the ground. He nodded. "Yeah, okay."

"I am not the only one to feel danger," Gredok said. "Because of Villani's rumored influence over the local military garrison, the league has arranged unusual security procedures."

Gredok pointed a black-furred pedipalp toward the window. Outside, Quentin saw not only the blue-spiked, mace-like surface of OS1, but also a ship sliding into view from the left.

A big, white warship, with the GFL logo painted large on the side. A flight of five lethal-looking white fighters crossed from left to right, fanning out to form a perimeter around the *Touchback*.

"Uh-oh," Ju said.

"Indeed," Gredok said. "I am confident that no one will attempt to harm us when the full might of the Commissioner is on display. However, this comes at a price. Ju, you and Barnes are required at another investigatory meeting with Froese immediately after the game."

Quentin turned to face the team owner. "*Me*? Why me? Ju is the one with the false accusation of murder."

Gredok played with his bracelets. "*Why you*, Barnes? Because for some odd reason, you seem to be at the center of every problem that I have."

The owner left the viewing bay.

Quentin turned to face Ju.

Ju smiled and shrugged. "Eat, too, Quentin?"

Transcript from the "Galaxy's Greatest Sports Show with Dan, Akbar, and Tarat the Smasher"

DAN: Hello, sports fans, Dan Gianni here and welcome to another edition of the Galaxy's Greatest Sports show with me, Akbar and Tarat the Smasher.

AKBAR: Thanks, Dan.

TARAT: Yes, thank you.

DAN: Tarat, let's get into it. I hear that you have the inside scoop from the Orbiting Death locker room? Are they ready for their game against the Ionath Krakens?

TARAT: Are they ever, Dan. Even back in the preseason, team owner Anna Villani has made this the franchise's game of the year. The alleged actions of Ju Tweedy have brought shame on the organization and Villani wants to clear the Death name of any wrongdoing.

AKBAR: Clear the … *what*? Are you kidding me? She's a *gangster*. She had the previous owner *assassinated*.

DAN: Akbar, come on, that old bit again? No one cares!

AKBAR: More people care than you think, Dan.

DAN: Well, enough of that — let's get more from Tarat. Smasher, the Orbiting Death shocked everyone by starting the season with two wins, but since then they've dropped three straight. Can they beat Ionath?

TARAT: Dan, I'm actually picking the Death in this one. Quarterback Condor Adrienne is still getting used to the speed of Tier One, but Ionath's starting cornerback Berea is out with a brain-stem injury — her backup is Stockbridge, who is not good enough to stop Adrienne.

AKBAR: I still can't believe the Krakens didn't trade for defensive backs.

TARAT: I also found that odd. The Death defense will be very focused on stopping Ju Tweedy. As he used to play for OS1, limiting his yardage becomes a point of honor.

DAN: They'll need more than honor for that. Like maybe an auto cannon.

TARAT: I think they have the motivation. I just visited the OS1 locker room. They have news article printouts posted everywhere.

AKBAR: Printouts? From what?

TARAT: From a preseason interview with Krakens quarterback Quentin Barnes. Barnes said, "Let the Orbiting Death worry about relegation."

AKBAR: Oh, I remember that from media day. But that's taken out of context.

TARAT: The Death players do not care about context, Akbar. They care about the words. Their motivation, Villani's insistence that this is a must-win, Ionath's secondary difficulties *and* the fact that a win almost guarantees the Death will not be relegated tells me that they will be victorious.

DAN: Smasher, you're crazy. I love you, but you're crazy. I'm picking the Krakens.

AKBAR: So am I.

TARAT: Dan, are you going to ask me about my other inside information?

DAN: Well well, what's this? Our hulking Quyth Warrior commentator has another scoop?

AKBAR: Yes, Smasher, let's have it.

TARAT: An inside source tells me that the To Pirates made a tentative offer to Quentin Barnes.

AKBAR: They can't do that. It's still Tier One season. Both teams are in Tier One, so they can't make offers until the season is over and Barnes is officially a free agent.

DAN: Right, Akbar. I mean *no one* drives faster than the underwater speed limit in Isis City limits, right?

TARAT: I have driven a submersible there. Sentients rarely obey the speed limit, Dan.

DAN: Tarat, yes, I *know* they don't obey it — that's the point. Just like teams don't obey no-contact rules. And we already know Barnes doesn't care about no-contact rules.

AKBAR: Yolanda Davenport's article sure made that clear.

DAN: So, Smasher, let's hear it.

TARAT: My source told me that the Pirates are going to offer Barnes a hundred ninety megacredits for ten years.

DAN: A hundred ninety *million* credits?

AKBAR: For ten years?

TARAT: Yes. And yes.

DAN: But that will make him the highest-paid player in the history of the game.

AKBAR: He'll make more than Rick Renaud.

TARAT: Correct.

DAN: Smasher, are you sure?

TARAT: It is a very reliable source, Dan.

AKBAR: But Barnes isn't proven.

TARAT: When Barnes is proven, he might cost even more. The Pirates want to commit to him now, lock him up.

DAN: Well, you heard it here first, the same place you *always* hear it first, from the Galaxy's Greatest Sports Show. Quentin Barnes could be the face of the To Pirates, for at *least* a decade. We'll talk about this breaking story with the callers, right after this message from our sponsor Kin-Al-Brin's Fresh-Kill

Farm. When you have that desire for prey that's still kicking and screaming, let Kin-Al round up dinner. We'll be right back.

QUENTIN MUTED THE VOLUME on his holotank, but the words still echoed in his ears.

One hundred ninety million credits for ten years.

Ten years, with the To Pirates.

He watched the Galaxy's Greatest Sports Show whenever he could, usually bits and pieces between practice, meals and study. It was hard to get used to them talking about *him*, like he was the same as all the other GFL stars they discussed. This time, however, they'd said the To Pirates weren't just interested in him but had already put an offer together. There was no position more prestigious than starting quarterback for the Blood Red. Nothing more iconic, nothing more storied. It was the pinnacle of not only football, but of sports at any level.

Quentin Barnes, starting quarterback for the To Pirates.

And to think he'd once considered himself *rich* for just *one* million a season.

Then Akbar's words hit home — it was illegal to make contract offers in the middle of the season. What if the Commissioner found out? No, not *what if*, but *when*? The story had been on GGSS. Froese probably knew already. Quentin was on thin ice enough as it was. What would this do to contract negotiations overall?

"Computer," he said. "Get Danny Lundy on the line."

[CALLING DANNY LUNDY]

Quentin's stomach churned as he waited. What would Froese do? This couldn't be good, not at all, but still — *190 megacredits* and *ten years* for the shucking *Pirates?*

The holoscreen blinked, showing the image of rainbow-skinned Danny the Dolphin behind his conference table. "Quentin, boobie, what can I do for my favorite client?"

"Danny, I was just watching the Galaxy's Greatest Sports Show."

"Me too, I never miss it."

"They said the Pirates are going to make a huge offer. Is that true?"

Danny's head bobbed. "Well, that's just a *rumor*, Quentin. But were it true and I don't doubt that it is—" Danny winked one black eye "—then I'd say congratulations, my fine, finless friend. You would be a very rich sentient and play for the team you always wanted to play for. All your dreams are coming true, at the negligible cost of fifteen percent for yours truly."

Quentin understood. Danny couldn't actually say the deal was for real, not with Commissioner Froese possibly monitoring communications, but the wink said it all — the offer was verified.

"But, Danny, how did Tarat the Smasher find out?"

"Well, I imagine someone close to the situation told him. Very close."

Quentin stared. *Danny* had leaked the information?

"I know this game, buddy. I called an audible."

"But you broke the rules! Froese could fine me, or suspend me. We have six more games and—"

"Relax, guy. You can't get in trouble because it's just a rugged rumor, a giddy gossip, an innocent innuendo."

"But it's *not* a rumor."

"I don't have an offer on a contract box or an official communication, which means *it's a rumor*." Danny winked again. "If this rumor were true, though, the only way you don't play for the Pirates next year is if the Krakens offer you more."

This was really happening. The To Pirates. Quentin suddenly imagined prepping for a game, laying out his blood-red armor and blood-red jersey instead of the Orange and the Black.

"I don't know, Danny. You work for me. You're supposed to do what I tell you to do."

"Am I supposed to run the plays that are called?"

Quentin felt his breath lock up in his chest. That was what Hokor always said ... said to Quentin.

"But there are *rules*."

"Quentin, if Rick Warburg comes into your huddle and tells you what play he wants you to call, do you run it?"

Quentin stared at the holotank. He always felt two moves behind whenever Danny Lundy was concerned. Were Quentin's on-field manipulations of Warburg that transparent, or was Danny just that perceptive? Either way, Quentin felt embarrassed that sentients knew. "How I handle my huddle is different."

"Why? Don't you do things the way you do because you know more than the others?"

"Well ... yeah."

"And I know more about this than you do, buddy," Danny said. "Contracts are *my* huddle, guy, and negotiation is my Sunday afternoon. You hired me to do a job. I'm doing it and doing it well. If you want to yell at me for making you the shucking *star* of the shucking *galaxy*, well, you'll have to call Brenda and schedule time with me next week. I have a young tennis player coming in five minutes that is so good she makes me want to grow legs and change species. Go get a beer and relax, buddy — you certainly can afford it."

Danny broke the connection, leaving Quentin standing speechless in his own room.

QUENTIN WAITED IN THE TUNNEL of Beefeater Gin Stadium, standing first on his left foot and shaking out his right leg, then shifting to his right foot and shaking out his left. Back and forth, burning off nervous energy and loosening up. His teammates packed in around him, the aura of rage radiating off of them, preparing for the battle ahead. Ju Tweedy was on his left, John Tweedy on his right. Ju would be the honorary captain this week, a slap in the face to Anna Villani and the Death fans that had turned their back on the former hero of OS1.

Quentin's second trip to the Black Hole, home of the Orbiting Death. They'd won here back in his rookie season. They'd win here again today. He looked out the tunnel to the stadium beyond: four decks filled with fans clad in flat-black and metalflake-red.

Sunlight sparkled off the stadium's translucent blue crystal architecture, the living material that made up the artificial planet's skeletal structure. Over 133,000 fans in attendance — a small stadium for the underground city of Madderch, which boasted a population of 50 million. Would the Death spectators throw trash on him? Even worse, could there be real danger from these fans?

The crowd chanted in fuzzy, loud unison, two lines of three syllables each. Quentin leaned forward, trying to understand the words. Then the sing-song message clarified. They chanted: *WEL-COME-home, MUR-DER-er.*

Quentin turned to his right, to Ju Tweedy, the man that had become his comrade in arms. A year ago, John, Quentin, Becca, Choto, Sho-Do-Thikit and Mum-O-Killowe had saved Ju from certain death at the hands of Anna Villani. How had Ju repaid that debt? By intentionally fumbling, trying to throw games so that the Krakens would lose confidence in Quentin and instead accept Ju as the team leader. Quentin and Ju had settled their difference late in the season. Quentin won that brawl, maybe with a little "help" from Doc Patah's old fight-game tricks. Was that only a year ago? Seemed like forever. Since then, Ju had proven his mettle. A galaxy's worth of hatred had centered on Quentin and Ju, bonding them together as they fought against false accusations.

Quentin reared back and punched Ju in his well-armored shoulder.

"Hear them out there, Mad Ju? Do you? Those are your old fans wishing you well."

Ju nodded so rapidly his helmet bobbled, hiding then revealing his wide, intense eyes. "Hell yes! I've got lots of love to show them right back. Gonna super-stomp them into the ground."

Quentin's head rocked to the side — John Tweedy had just head-butted him.

"*Yeah*, Q! And I'm gonna *mega*-super-stomp that pretty boy Condor Adrienne." John held up his thick, scarred fists. UNCLE JOHNNY WANTS HIS SCALPS scrolled across his fingers and knuckles.

Ju grabbed Quentin's facemask, snapped it around so they

could look eye-to-eye, so lost in pre-game madness that he didn't realize how hard he pulled.

"You *do not stop* giving me the ball," Ju said. "Yalla the Biter is *mine*. I want a piece of that scumbag's soul."

The announcer called Ionath to the field. Quentin led the charge onto the jet-black, white-lined surface. He was ready for this stadium's unique form of welcome. Most of the 133,000 flat-black-clad fans in the stadium's four decks instantly fell silent, creating a strange stillness broken only by the 20,000-odd Krakens faithful — Ionath ex-pats or fans that had made the short, half-day trip to OS1. Last time, this roar-to-silence treatment had taken Quentin by surprise. But not this year. This was his third season. He had grown far beyond the wide-eyed orphan miner that once viewed the galaxy with bewildered surprise.

This was no time for innocence. In minutes, he would face the most lethal player in the history of the GFL — Yalla the Biter, middle linebacker for the Orbiting Death. If you didn't have your head in the game against Yalla, he'd tear it off, then probably punt it 30 or 40 yards just to be extra mean.

The Krakens reached the sidelines and gathered: jumping, hitting, pushing, yelling, chirping. Quentin knew better than to start the pre-game chant — a hellstorm of noise was about to cut loose.

Without any prompt from the announcer, the crowd erupted. The OS1 Orbiting Death ran onto their home field. Flat-black leg armor, flat-black jerseys decorated with numbers and letters done in blue-trimmed metalflake-red. Afternoon sunlight sparkled off of metalflake-red helmets, sun that was eaten up by the flat-black circle logos on the sides of each helmet.

Quentin raised his left fist. "Krakens, to me."

He led his teammates, his friends, his *family* through their pre-game chant. Feelings of hatred and desire raced through his soul. He wanted to win every game, no question, but this?

This was special.

Chant finished, he stood there as the players filtered away. He rocked slowly from toes to heels, every atom of his body waiting to get out on that field and shut this crowd right the hell up.

"Quentinbarnesquentinbarnes*quentinbarnes!*"

That voice — the tone, the intensity, so unmistakable. Quentin turned, a smile already breaking on his face even before he saw her standing there, dressed head to toe in gold, silver and copper clothes, a visitor's pass dangling from a lanyard around her long neck.

"Denver! What are you doing here?"

"A bye week, oh my Quentinbarnes*quentinbarnes!* Since my Jupiter Jacks and your Ionath Krakens do not play each other in the regular season, I asked Coach Hokor if I could come surprise you."

"And Hokor said yes?"

"He told me I was not allowed to memorize anything or he would strike me dead with a meteor the size of a small moon," Denver said. "So I will most assuredly not memorize *anything*, Quentinbarnes, for I do not wish to be smushed."

Quentin laughed and gently pushed his old friend. "Hey, hell of a season you're having, Miss Superstar."

"I love Jupiter! Love-love-*love!* I catch many passes!"

"Well, Denver, you stay out of the way and enjoy the game. We'll talk after, okay?"

"Oh yesyesyes, Quentinbarnes! I love-love-love to talk to you! Are you going to use your holy powers to inflict damage on the Orbiting Death?"

Quentin nodded, then turned back to face the field, to get his head into the game.

Inflict damage? That was *exactly* what he was going to do.

QUENTIN BROKE THE HUDDLE and slowly walked to the line. The Orbiting Death had wasted no time, winning the toss, taking the ball, then scoring on their third play from scrimmage. Condor Adrienne managed to get Stockbridge isolated in single coverage on Death wide receiver Brazilia — Adrienne hit his teammate for a 42-yard strike. Adrienne's first three plays? Three completions, 72 yards and a touchdown. If Quentin didn't match Condor's performance, the Krakens would be in trouble. This was it, the long-awaited showdown between the league's hot young guns. Everyone thought Adrienne was better?

Quentin would show them all.

His orange-jerseyed teammates formed up, Kimberlin and the Ki at the line of scrimmage, Starcher at right tight end, Hawick wide left and Milford wide right. Behind him, the I-formation of Becca at fullback and Ju Tweedy at tail back. Opposite his wall of orange, the metalflake-red helmeted, flat-black assembly of head-hunters: Kan-E-Shiro and HeavyG James Morr at defensive tackle, then the solid linebacker core of Yalla the Biter at middle linebacker flanked by the "Mad Macs" — Matt McRoberts and James McPike — at right and left outside linebacker, respectively. All three of the backers were big, fast, mobile and mean. Yalla had killed ten professional football players. *Ten*. That wasn't something you could just brush off. Quentin needed to know where Yalla was at all times.

Black field, black uniforms, the stands filled with a sea of black.

This was payback for Quentin. But even more, it was payback for his friend Ju Tweedy.

Quentin bent under center, hands pressed against Bud-O-Shwek's pebbly skin. "Blue, sixteen!" Quentin called out over the crowd's roar. "Blue, sixt*eeeeen!* Hut-*hut!*"

No surprises on the first play. The Krakens were a running team, Ju Tweedy was the best back in the game and that was that. Quentin turned to the left. Becca shot by, Quentin extended, a wild-eyed Ju Tweedy took the ball. Kill-O-Yowet and Sho-Do-Thikit drove forward, pushing Kan-E-Shiro back. Becca landed a head-to-head shot on McRoberts, knocking the big Human linebacker on his ass. Then Ju raged into the narrow hole. Instead of cutting to the left, to open space, he cut right and lowered his shoulders, smashing head-to-head with Yalla the Biter. The *crack* echoed through the stadium, audible even up at the fourth deck. Both sentients fell to the black field, both instantly scrambled to their feet. They stood chest-to-chest, facemask-to-facemask, Human and Quyth Warrior leaning into each other in a wordless challenge so primitive and universal it pre-dated history and culture.

Yalla said something Quentin couldn't hear.

Ju pushed the Quyth Warrior in the chest. "No, *you're* an idiot!"

Yalla pushed back. The scene instantly disintegrated as Death and Krakens players grabbed, pushed, shoved, a swirling pile of aggression just a hair shy of a full-out brawl. Whistles blew. Black-and white-striped zebes flew in to break up the scuffle.

The Krakens' first play of the game? A 5-yard gain and a fight. So this was how the rivalry would go?

That was fine. Just fine.

QUENTIN DROPPED BACK to pass, checking through the receivers, his brain aware of each lineman, of the pressure closing in, of how long he had to throw the ball. The Death had great linebackers, but the defensive line wasn't that strong and neither was the secondary.

He fired the ball to the left sideline. His favorite pattern: throw the ball just a few feet out of bounds, where Halawa could stretch out and grab it, her feet dragging in-bounds before she slid into the sideline. Complete for 13 yards.

On the next snap, Quentin pitched wide right to Ju. All three OS1 linebackers read the play and came in hard. Becca delivered a knock-out blow on McPike, stayed on her feet, then managed to trip up McRoberts in a two-for-one blocking clinic. She took out two defenders, but Yalla came free. Ju again tried to go head-to-head. This time, he came out on the losing end. Yalla hit the big running back with perfect tackling form: shoulder pad in the gut, middle arms locking hard around the back, lifting and *driving*. Yalla put him hard into the black turf. That battle would rage all day, the league's best running back against the league's best linebacker.

On second-and-long, Quentin dropped back again. He saw Hawick angling deep to the middle of the field, saw that the safety was slow to react. Quentin launched the ball — a perfect spiral of brown and white against the stadium's backdrop of high-walled black and crystal blue. It hit Hawick in stride at the 5. She carried the ball into the end zone untouched for a 65-yard touchdown.

Quentin knelt and plucked a few pieces of the tough black plant that made up the field's surface. He held them to his nose and sniffed — the scent of sappy pine, just like he remembered from his rookie season.

Arioch Morningstar kicked the extra point. Tie game, 7-7.

Quentin's first drive: 2-for-2, 78 yards and a touchdown.

Top that, Condor.

CONDOR DID. The Death took over at their own 25-yard line. The OS1 quarterback completed five straight passes, driving his team down to the Ionath 17. Coach Hokor stepped up the pressure by sending John Tweedy and Virak the Mean on an all-out blitz, but Condor seemed to be waiting for just that. He flipped the ball horizontally, out to the flat — a screen pass to running back Chooch Motumbo. Chooch followed his blockers into the end zone for a touchdown.

Quentin stood on the sidelines, staring, his chest roiling with jealousy.

Nine passes, nine completions, 157 yards, two touchdowns. Condor was setting the bar at an impossible level.

A hand on his shoulder pad. Quentin turned to see the blue face of Don Pine.

"Don't worry about him," Don said. "He's hot. He'll cool off. Hokor will figure out how to slow him down. You play *your* game, got it?"

Quentin paused, torn between pushing the man away or listening to the advice. Before he could decide, Don turned and walked off. Quentin pulled on his helmet and prepared for the next drive.

• • •

THE FIRE OF COMPETITION BURNED so intensely that his face felt hot, his stomach twirled, his toes tingled. Quentin was the future of the league, *not* Condor. No way.

Quentin completed his first two passes, a cross to Cheboygan for 8 yards, followed by a swing pass to Becca. She made one move to leave a Death player grabbing air, then lowered her shoulder and smashed the cornerback into the ground. She stepped over the fallen defender and sprinted forward, turning a simple 3-yard pass into a 20-yard gain. Quentin and Condor weren't the only ones having big games — everything Becca did, from blocking to catching to running, it all seemed to be disciplined, perfect.

The next round of Ju vs. Yalla went Ju's way. The younger Tweedy brother took a handoff and went straight up the middle, reaching full speed as he slid between the blocks of Bud-O-Shwek and Michael Kimberlin. Yalla read the play too late, was caught flat-footed. Ju's helmet buried in Yalla's thorax, knocking the Quyth Warrior linebacker to the ground. Yalla's pedipalps reached up, ripping skin from Ju's hands, but the big running back barely slowed. Trailing blood, he pounded straight downfield to the OS1 12-yard line before the safety tripped him up from behind.

Ju stood, pointed his right hand at the stands and banged on his chest with his bloody left fist. He was challenging the crowd directly, body language screaming to a hundred-thousand fans that they should have *never* doubted him, *never* turned on him. They booed, they scraped pedipalps, they hissed, filling Beefeater Gin Stadium with the sound of hate.

The face of Hokor the Hookchest appeared in Quentin's heads-up display.

"Barnes, Ju needs a breather. Power set, wing right, boot-pass right. Use your head before you use your feet."

"Okay, Coach."

The Krakens huddled up for the next play. Ju, Hawick and Milford ran off, replaced by Yassoud Murphy, Yotaro Kobayasho and Tara the Freak.

Quentin clapped three times to get their attention. "Okay, boys and girls, let's tie this game up. Power set, wing right, boot-pass right, X-out, Y-curl, A-wheel. 'Soud, need a big fake from you, we have to sell the run — you do it right and Yalla is going to knock you on your ass."

"Oh, yep," Yassoud said. "I'm ready for his ugly face."

"Right," Quentin said. "If Yalla *doesn't* buy the fake, we need a block on him from the tight ends before you run your route. We can't let him come clean, got it?"

Yotaro nodded, but George seemed to be staring off to the right, at the crowd, not paying attention. His black face-paint seemed a strange choice for this game.

Quentin reached out and slapped his helmet. "Starcher! You hear me?"

George's eyes snapped up, blinked. He nodded.

"Good," Quentin said. "Okay, let's get those points. On three, on three, ready?"

"*BREAK!*"

The Krakens lined up. The power set put seven big bodies on the line of scrimmage: the offensive linemen, plus Yotaro at left tight end, Starcher at right. Cheboygan lined up a yard behind and a yard to the left of Yotaro. Becca at fullback, Yassoud at tailback.

Quentin scanned the defense. The Death's 4-3 put four linemen down on the line, three linebackers behind them. Yalla was the middle linebacker, but he was cheating to his left, Quentin's right, toward George's side of the line. Quentin smiled — Yalla would have to choose between covering George or coming in to tackle Quentin. If Yalla did the former, Quentin would cut up field for a big gain. If Yalla chose the latter, George would slow Yalla with a chip-block, then roll out to the open area of the field for an easy pass.

"Red, twenty-two! *Red*, twenty two! Hut-*hut* ... *hut!*"

The lines collided. Quentin turned to his left, letting Becca rush by. He extended to Yassoud, who brought his arms together just as Quentin pulled the ball away and turned to the right. The Mad Macs filled the holes, leaving no openings, so 'Soud just slammed into the line.

Ball on his right hip, Quentin ran to the right. Most of the defense had bought the fake. He ran past his right tackle Vu-Ko-Will, knowing George was blocking Yalla.

He was wrong.

George ran right by Yalla. No chip-block to slow down the All-Pro linebacker, who rolled in at top speed. Quentin's mental timer began. He planted his feet, stopping his right-side momentum, turning back to the left - he didn't even have a full second to react.

He saw Becca on the goal line, side-stepping to an open area. Quentin threw faster than he'd ever thrown before, whipping the ball at her as he felt pincer-hands lock down on the backs of his shoulder pads. Then he was flying, spinning. The black ground slammed into him. He bounced, spots flashing before his eyes.

He felt a burning sting rip across his chin.

That pain made the spots vanish. Quentin's hand shot to his chin, came away covered in blood. He looked up. Yalla stood there, red blood dropping from his right pedipalp fingers — not *his* blood, *Quentin's* blood.

Yalla put the bloody fingers in his mouth and licked them. "I ended your friend Paul Pierson's career, but you I am going to *kill*. I'd have killed your weak friend Mitchell Fayed, but he wasn't strong enough to make it to Tier One."

Yalla turned and walked away.

How dare you even speak his name.

Quentin stood and pulled off his helmet. He swung it like a weapon, bringing it down hard on the back of Yalla's head.

Yalla dropped to the ground, instantly limp.

"You don't speak his name!" Quentin screamed, then raised the helmet again. A Harrah ref flew in. Quentin tried to abort the swing, but the momentum carried the helmet into the black-and-white striped official. It wasn't that big of a hit, but the level of impact didn't matter — as soon as it connected, Quentin knew he'd screwed up.

Flags flew, whistles sounded, the crowd booed, scraped and hissed. Three zebes flew around Quentin, circling him.

"Ejected!" one of them said. "Number ten, get off the field. You're ejected from the game."

Quentin's rage had vanished the second he'd hit the ref. No point in arguing. As he walked off, he looked back to where Yalla still lie on the ground.

Yalla lifted his head and looked at Quentin. For just a second, his single, baseball-sized eye flooded the yellow of excitement. In that moment, Quentin knew he'd been baited. It had been a setup, Yalla trying to draw Quentin into a cheap shot that would get Quentin kicked out of the game. And it had worked.

Quentin walked off the field. Hokor and Pine were talking. The extra-point team ran on. Quentin glanced at the scoreboard: 14-13. His pass to Becca had gone for a touchdown.

A ref escorted him to the tunnel. He'd been ejected and couldn't stay on the sidelines. Quentin would watch the rest of the game from the locker room.

AT HALFTIME, THE KRAKENS filtered into the locker room. They were down 28-21. Condor Adrienne seemed unstoppable. Don Pine, on the other hand, seemed *very* stoppable. The veteran limped in, helped by Michael Kimberlin. Kimberlin set Don on a med table, then cleared the way for a fluttering Doc Patah. Don's right eye was swollen shut. Blood trickled from a broken nose. All from another missed block by Crazy George Starcher.

Don wasn't the only one that looked beat-up. Ju lie flat on a bench, jersey and shoulder armor off, a bag of ice taped to his shoulder. Yassoud bounced in place. His jersey was torn and splattered with black blood, but other than that, he looked excited and ready to fight. Becca stood like a statue, bloody arms crossed in front of her. She had played a flawless game so far, executing perfect blocks and dishing out heavy damage when the opportunities presented themselves. She'd knocked Matt McRoberts out of the game for good and her second-quarter hit on Yalla had sent the All-Pro linebacker to the sidelines for repairs to his middle-right arm.

The game between the Orbiting Death and the Ionath Krakens

had turned into a street-fight. The Krakens were getting their asses kicked.

"We're being out-hustled," Hokor said. "Out-hit, out-blocked, out-played and out-*meaned*. Krakens, we have to hit back and hit back hard! Doc Patah?"

The Harrah spun in place.

Hokor pointed at Pine. "Will he be ready to go?"

Doc Patah spun again. Mouth-flaps touched Don's eye, his nose. The Harrah turned to face the coach.

"He's out," Patah said. "I will not let him return for the second half."

Hokor threw his little hat to the floor. "Goldman!"

Yitzhak stood, his orange jersey clean and spotless. "Coach?"

"You're in for the second half. Talk to Barnes. I have to make defensive adjustments. We can't give Adrienne that much time."

Behind by seven, half a game to go, and down to their third-string quarterback? It didn't look good.

YITZHAK GOLDMAN'S UNIFORM didn't stay clean for long. Ju ran the ball for the first two plays of the half. Then Zak dropped back on what was meant to be a short pass to build his confidence, but he misread a blitz and went down hard.

The sack set the tone for the remainder of the game. Zak played hard, played tough, but he wasn't up to the task. He didn't have Don's vision, he didn't have Quentin's feet.

It got worse on the Death's first possession. OS1 returned the Krakens' punt to the Ionath 25-yard line, then scored four plays later on a dive from one yard out.

Zak didn't play bad, but he didn't set the world on fire. Maybe if the Krakens had already held the lead, he could have managed the game, played the clock for the win. But because Ionath was down two touchdowns, he was forced to play catch-up. That meant throwing the ball. Throwing the ball meant getting sacked. It meant hurrying throws, which meant interceptions — in his case, two of them.

John Tweedy finally got to Adrienne halfway through the third quarter. A vicious blind-side hit knocked the red-hot quarterback out of the game, but it was too late for the Krakens to catch up.

When the gun sounded, the Black Hole home crowd roared in approval at their team's 35-21 win.

THE VISITORS' LOCKER ROOM looked like a hospital full of victims from some minor disaster. The healing tanks were full, which left less-injured players stretched out on benches and tables in the communal area. It would take hours to mop up all the multi-colored blood from the white floor. The Krakens had been beat up physically and mentally. There was no question that the Orbiting Death was the superior team that day. In a game of smash-mouth football, the Krakens got their mouths smashed in.

Other than a blue nanocyte bandage on his chin, Quentin was unmarked. He hadn't been in long enough to take any serious damage. He felt fine. Feeling *fine* made him feel *guilty* — as he looked around at his damaged teammates, he wondered what might have been had he kept his temper, had he not let Yalla the Biter play him like that.

Quentin waited for Ju Tweedy, who was gingerly sliding his injured arm through the sleeve of his button-down shirt.

"Good game, Ju."

"Whatever."

"You had a hundred and twelve yards, man. You ran your ass off."

Ju tried to button his shirt, but winced. "Ah, man, this hurts. Messal!"

The Quyth Worker scurried over and started buttoning Ju's shirt.

Quentin picked up a shoulder sling sitting on the bench in front of Ju's locker. "Doc say you gotta wear this?"

"Couple of days," Ju said. "Something about my rotator cuff or whatever. Doc said something like, *blah-blah-blah, cartilage, blah-blah-blah, two days.*"

"Sounds like a very comprehensive diagnosis."

"Whatever," Ju said. Messal finished buttoning the shirt, then helped Ju put his right arm in the sling. Messal then helped Ju into his sport coat. The right side hung armless over his shoulder.

"Thanks," Ju said to the Worker.

Messal nodded. "Of course, Mister Tweedy, anything I can do to help. If you gentleman are ready, I am to escort you to a meeting room where Commissioner Froese is waiting."

Ju took a deep breath, let it out in a huff. "Nothing like getting your ass kicked for sixty minutes, then going to see the commissioner to get more of the same."

Quentin nodded. "The timing is great. You ready?"

Ju slowly rolled out his neck. His eyes squeezed tight, wrinkling at the corners. Normally he wore an expression of anger, of arrogance, or both. This was first time Quentin had seen him look worried.

"It's a murder charge," Ju said quietly. "I mean, when there was all the running and hiding and shooting, I was only thinking about staying alive. If Villani can make these charges stick, I'm screwed."

"I won't let that happen."

Ju looked at him, smiled. "Except for my brother, anyone else would have bailed on me. Especially after that hack-job article."

Quentin shrugged. "I believe you, that's all."

"That's *not* all, Q. It wasn't *me* on the cover of Galaxy Sports, it was *you*. Somehow all this crap landed on your head. I never meant for that to happen."

Quentin felt uncomfortable, just wanted the conversation to end. "I know you didn't. Nothing we can do but ride it out. The truth will set us free."

Ju laughed. "Ah, all that religious stuff, right?"

Quentin nodded.

"Well I hope your High One can lend a hand. We can't avoid Froese anymore. If he pulls my immunity, I don't even get to leave OS1. I could be in jail tonight. If I am? You can bet I'll be dead by morning."

Quentin had known how serious this all was, sure, but he hadn't thought things out that far. Ju's life was in danger.

"Ju, I said I won't let that happen. And see? Your problems *are* a lot worse than mine. I'm not the one accused of murder."

Ju looked away, staring into nothing. "I loved Grace. I really did."

Another expression Quentin had never seen on Ju's face — pain. Or maybe loss. Probably a combination of both. Quentin wanted say the right thing, but he had no idea what that was. Words weren't really his strong suit and he knew it.

"Gentlemen," Messal said. "I have no desire to interrupt your conversation, but if I may suggest that we meet with the commissioner now? He is waiting and I believe that Gredok is alone with him."

"Oh, no," Quentin said. "Ju, let's move. Gredok hates Froese."

Messal led the way. Quentin and Ju followed.

QUENTIN HAD UNKNOWINGLY grown used to newly built stadiums, used to pristine, shining temples built to glorify the gridiron game. Ionath Stadium was only eleven years old and it was one of the older constructs in Tier One. Everywhere Quentin played, he found spotless hallways, fresh paint or new smart-paper, gleaming glass and sparkling fixtures.

Beefeater Gin Stadium, on the other hand? It looked as beat-up and worn-in as an ancient leather helmet. Messal led them through narrow tunnels carved into the rock and through veins of blue crystal. Pipes lined the ceiling. Glow-bulbs cast dim illumination. Where there *was* paint, it was cracked and peeling. This place predated the GFL — sports of some kind had been played here for many decades.

The stadium reminded Quentin of the mines on Micovi. That should have made him hate it, but instead, that familiarity made him instantly fall in love with it. This place? This was *real*. The Death organization didn't seem to care about appearances. What mattered was what happened on the field.

Messal stopped at a door. The door looked slightly odd — new and smooth set amidst old and gnarly. Flat-black, decorated only with the Orbiting Death logo and a name.

ANNA VILLANI

"Crap," Ju said.

"Please enter," Messal said. "They are waiting for you."

Ju looked at Quentin. "What do you think, Q? Want to make a run for it?"

"No," Quentin said. "We'd forfeit the next six games. Let's get this done."

Ju sighed, then opened the door and walked in. Quentin followed.

Inside waited the three faces Quentin had expected — Gredok the Splithead, Commissioner Froese and the hulking form of Leiba the Gorgeous. There was also one face he *should* have expected, but had not — Anna Villani, owner of the Orbiting Death.

"Hello, boys," she said. She wore a jacket of black fur that ended at her waist. It made her oddly resemble Gredok the Splithead, if Gredok was a smoking-hot Human woman with red, six-inch heels and legs clad in black fishnet stockings. Her dress was a "skirt" in name only, as there was barely enough material to cover her curvaceous hips. She'd changed her hair since the last time Quentin had seen her. Still raven-black, but now shorter, done in glossy waves that rose up and vanished into a black lace hat decorated with a small metal Orbiting Death logo. Like last time, her lips and fingernails gleamed metalflake-red. All the decoration and beauty, however, did little to mask her soulless, gleeful eyes, *expectant* eyes — Anna was enjoying this.

"I thought I'd make my office available for the meeting," she said. "To make it easier on all involved."

Ju pointed at her. "You're a super-mega bitch."

"Aw, Ju, honey, don't be mean. Nice effort out there today. Sorry you couldn't bring home the win. That Yalla is one tough sentient, isn't he?"

"Enough," Froese said in his big voice that didn't fit his little body. "Everyone, have a seat."

Ju again pointed at Anna. "Why is *she* here?"

"Because I want her here, Tweedy," Froese said. "Now *sit.*"

Froese sat behind Anna's desk, which looked big enough to swallow him up. Anna and Gredok sat in chairs off to Froese's right. Leiba remained standing, in his usual place right behind the Commissioner. That left the two chairs in front of the desk for Quentin and Ju.

They sat. Quentin noticed the desk was full of knick-knacks and holocubes. Only a couple of the cubes showed Anna. Most showed a red-furred Quyth Leader, always dressed in Orbiting Death gear. Quentin realized who it was — Sikka the Death, former owner of the OS1 franchise. Anna hadn't removed Sikka's things. Perhaps she kept it as it was like some kind of trophy. That woman made his skin crawl.

"Gredok," Froese said, "you have managed to delay these inquiry meetings. It was a year ago the crime happened and only now do we sit down with all the parties involved."

"We've been awfully busy," Gredok said.

"Never again," Froese said. "If there is ever another disciplinary issue and you evade me like this, I'll pull the franchise charter."

"You wouldn't." Gredok stared, blinked. "Don't make idle threats, Commis-"

"They're not idle, Gredok. I have authority from the Creterakian Emperor himself. You screw with me *ever again* and I will crush you. Do you understand?"

Quentin sat as still as he could, watching the showdown between the two tiny-yet-powerful sentients. Was Froese suicidal? The commissioner was pushing Gredok too far, unless he actually did have the Emperor's backing. Little was known about the Emperor other than that he (or she, or it) was the most powerful individual in the galaxy.

Froese leaned forward, elbows on the desk. "Gredok, I asked you a question."

Tiny waves ruffled along Gredok's black fur. "Yes, Commissioner Froese. I understand."

Froese nodded, leaned back. "Good. Now, on to the business at hand."

"Yes," Anna said. "Let's talk about this murderer's future."

Froese turned to her. "Villani, you will sit there and keep your mouth shut."

"What? Froese, I am a Tier One owner, if you think you can speak to *me* like that, then you—"

"Enough! You thought I involved you in this meeting so you could be a spectator of the theater that you created?"

"*I* created? Ju Tweedy is a murderer! You have been lax in your duties for too long, letting him abuse diplomatic immunity and—"

"Leiba," Froese said, "if this woman says another word, throw her out."

"She's so delicate," the Quyth Warrior said, a certain eagerness in his voice. "I might hurt her in the process."

Froese nodded. "That's the idea."

Anna opened her mouth to speak, but stopped when Leiba took a single, sudden step in her direction. She looked around, seeming to search for her gangland goons that weren't there.

She closed her mouth.

Froese turned to face Ju. "Now, as for you, Tweedy."

"I didn't kill Grace McDermot."

"I'll get to that in a moment. What you *did* do was play games with me and I'm going to make an example of you."

"But Commissioner," Quentin said, "he's telling the truth!"

Froese jabbed a finger at Quentin. "Barnes, you shut your mouth! I'll get to you in a moment, but until then, not ... another ... *word*."

Quentin leaned back in his chair. Gredok was frightening because he could have people killed. So was Anna. The diminutive Froese was frightening in another way, an all-football way. On a whim, he could have Quentin banned from the game. For some reason, that scared Quentin far worse than the concept of death.

Froese glared at everyone in turn, daring someone to speak. No one did. He then looked back at Leiba.

"Bring her in."

Leiba walked to the office door and stepped outside. The five remaining sentients sat in awkward silence. When the door opened, things got even more uncomfortable.

She walked in on crutches, her left leg in a rejuve cast, a dark bruise on her left eye. Beat up, but no mistaking that perfect purple skin, darker purple lips or that white hair — Yolanda Davenport. She wore jeans and a modest-yet-professional light blue jacket. Yolanda was equally as beautiful as Anna, but an antithesis of the crime lord's ostentation.

"*You?*" Anna said, more a noise of disbelief than an actual word. "But, you're ... "

"I'm *what*, Villani? Supposed to be dead?"

Anna recovered instantly. She leaned back in her cushy chair, waved a hand dismissively. "I wouldn't know anything about that, I'm quite sure."

"Right," Yolanda said. "You wouldn't know a thing."

Froese waved Yolanda forward as if the exchange had never happened. "This is Yolanda Davenport, reporter for Galaxy Sports Magazine."

"We know," Gredok said. "She is the one that printed all of those lies about my players."

Yolanda shot Gredok a strange look, eyes narrowed in anger, then frustration. Quentin wondered what was that all about?

Yolanda gritted her teeth, then crutch-walked around the desk to stand next to Commissioner Froese.

For the first time in the meeting, Froese smiled, showing his strange red teeth. "Yolanda has uncovered some critical information pertaining to this investigation. She has been kind enough to share *tonight's* cover story with me, right before publication. I think you'll all find it of interest."

Froese lifted his left hand, palm-up. A holodisplay flickered to life. His right index finger tapped at icons. Then, a holotank lowered from the ceiling. In it, the Galaxy Sports Magazine logo played across a loop-holo of Ju Tweedy in Krakens Orange. His bloody right hand pointed somewhere off the picture, his bloody left fist pounded his chest armor. Under the helmet, a repeating snarl of triumph. Behind him, a slightly out-of-focus sea of flat-black and crystal blue.

"Hey," Quentin said. "Is that from today's game?"

Yolanda nodded. "News as it happens."

"Damn," Ju said. "I look mega-awesome."

At the bottom of the repeating image, a headline fuzzed into clarity.

INNOCENT! JU TWEEDY CLEARED OF ALL CHARGES IN GRACE MCDERMOT'S MURDER.

Anna stood. "This is ridiculous! I know the Madderch Chief of Police. There's no way Ju has been cleared of charges!"

"That's why you're here," Froese said. "So you can't discuss things with the Chief of Police, a discussion that might impact the story."

Yolanda smiled a smile of payback. "The Chief is seeing the story now. My colleague is giving him a chance to respond just moments before this goes live all across the galaxy. My investigation discovered evidence that the Madderch police *misplaced* evidence that not only shows Ju has an alibi for the time of the murder, but that implicates another sentient as the killer. A sentient that works for you, Villani."

Villani sneered at Yolanda, then strode toward the office door. She hadn't made it three steps before Leiba came around the desk and blocked the door, his big frame covering ten feet in a blink of an eye. Maybe he was retired, but this guy could still *move*.

Anna stopped. She glared at Leiba, her hands balling into tight fists. Quentin saw a drop of blood fall from between her fingers to land on the floor.

"You'll need to stay here for a bit," Leiba said. "Probably an hour, while the charges are officially dropped."

Anna turned to stare at Ju, her red lips curled away from perfect white teeth, her made-up eyes narrow with hate. "This isn't over, Tweedy."

Ju smiled, wide and warm. "I'd say it is. And I'm on the cover of Galaxy Sports. All because of you, little lady. Thanks." He turned to face Froese. "So, now that I've been properly vindicated, can I get the hell out of here?"

"You're suspended for one game," Froese said.

"But I'm innocent! Yolanda's article says so."

"Innocent of *murder*," Froese said. "*Not* of crossing me. I told you I'd make an example of you, Tweedy. For avoiding meeting requests by the league office, you are suspended one game and fined one hundred thousand credits."

Ju stood and leaned forward, huge and intimidating. "But we have the Lu Juggernauts next week!"

The display didn't phase Froese. He pointed to the door. "That's not my problem. Out."

Ju kicked the floor, then walked to the door. Quentin stood to follow him out.

"Not so fast, Barnes," the Commissioner said.

Quentin turned. What now?

"I'm fining you for hitting that referee. Ten thousand credits."

"But that was an accident!"

"Right, because what you were *trying* to do was use your helmet as a weapon against a defenseless player. Would you rather be suspended a game for that?"

Quentin quickly shook his head. "No, I'm good with the fine."

"*And* a hundred thousand for avoiding my meeting requests. Same as your teammate."

So much money! "Come *on*! Ju was innocent! You just said so yourself. I don't deserve to be fined for saving an innocent sentient."

"You abused diplomatic immunity, interfered in a murder investigation, aided and abetted a known suspect and your actions contributed to the death of an innocent OS1 citizen. I could kick you out of the league forever for those things. Instead, you get a fine and end up with the best running back in the game. Now, do you want to accept my judgment, or shall I come up with additional penalties?"

Quentin closed his eyes and rubbed his face. Froese had him.

Again. One-tenth of his salary to be done with this whole situation and keep his friend on the team? Yeah, that was worth it.

"I accept," Quentin said. "Can I go now?"

Froese nodded.

Quentin turned to Yolanda. "And what do you have to say for yourself? You tricked me into thinking you were doing a story on me."

"I was doing a story on you."

"I mean a *fun* story," Quentin said. "You did a hatchet job."

"I never told you the story would be fun," Yolanda said. "I'm a reporter, Quentin. You knew that. You saw what you wanted to see."

"And you didn't correct me."

"That's not my job. And just because I was wrong about Ju doesn't mean it was a hatchet job. I stand by the rest of the story."

Quentin huffed. "Right. And how did you find out about the Pirates and all of that? Ever think you're wrong about that, too?"

"I'm not. I have my sources and stand by my story."

Quentin shook his head. How could he have once thought her so beautiful? "Lady, you made a galaxy *hate* me. I didn't do anything wrong. I stood by my team and you crucified me. Has anyone thrown garbage on *you* for this story?"

"You're complaining about *garbage*?" She pointed to her bruised face. "You think I got all of this from falling down the stairs, you ungrateful ass? Ju was already accused of murder before my first story ran, Quentin. I had nothing to do with that. And if it wasn't for my *new* story, he'd *still* be wanted for murder. So I think I made things right, don't you?"

Quentin shook his head. "You made it up to Ju, sure. But not to me. I didn't do anything wrong. Until you do right by *me*, don't bother talking to me again."

"Don't worry," she said. "I won't."

Quentin walked to the door. He stopped, looked back at his team owner, the sentient that had stood by Quentin when the rest of the galaxy had called for his head.

"Gredok? Are you coming?"

The Quyth Leader stood and walked over. He stopped at the door. "Commissioner Froese, I told you that when Ju was found innocent, you owed me an apology. I'll be waiting for an official memo declaring such. And Anna?"

Villani glared at him.

"Enjoy today's victory," Gredok said. "I will look forward to hosting you in my suite at Ionath Stadium next year."

Gredok walked out. Quentin and his newly innocent teammate followed.

GFL WEEK SIX ROUNDUP
Courtesy of Galaxy Sports Network

HOME		AWAY	
Hittoni Hullwalkers	10	**Yall Criminals**	42
Orbiting Death	35	Ionath Krakens	21
Lu Juggernauts	15	**Themala Dreadnaughts**	17
To Pirates	22	**Wabash Wolfpack**	28
Jang Atom Smashers	7	**Bord Brigands**	13
D'Kow War Dogs	24	Shorah Warlords	21
Neptune Scarlet Fliers	14	**Vik Vanguard**	17
Texas Earthlings	13	Sala Intrigue	10

BYE WEEKS: Alimum Armada, Coranadillana Cloud Killers, Bartel Water Bugs, New Rodina Astronauts, Isis Ice Storm, Jupiter Jacks.

THE GAME OF THE WEEK lived up to billing as two Planet Division undefeateds went head-to-head. The Wabash Wolfpack (5-0) won a 28-22 thriller over the To Pirates (5-1) to take sole possession of first place.

Texas (2-4) won a critical relegation match up against fellow Solar Division bottom-dweller Sala (1-4). The 13-10 Earthlings' victory leaves the Intrigue all alone in last place and gives Texas a critical head-to-head tiebreaker should both teams finish the season with equal records.

"Our second win and it won't be our last," said Earthlings linebacker Alonzo Castro. "Texas is in Tier One to stay."

Yall (4-2) won its third straight game following the return of quarterback Rick Renaud with a 42-10 drubbing of the Hittoni Hullwalkers (0-6). The Criminals average 42.2 points per contest when Renaud plays a full game, 13.5 when he does not.

In a nasty, hard-fought contest, the Orbiting Death (3-3)

topped the Ionath Krakens (4-2) by a score of 35-21. The Death's Condor Adrienne made a statement that he is the best young QB in the game, throwing for 422 yards and four touchdowns against a porous Krakens secondary. Ionath starting quarterback Quentin Barnes was tossed out of the game for unsportsmanlike conduct late in the first quarter, adding to Ionath's difficulties. Backup Krakens quarterback Don Pine was knocked out in the second quarter. Third-stringer Yitzhak Goldman finished up the second half, going 12-for-25 for 86 yards, no touchdowns and two interceptions.

Deaths

No deaths reported this week.

Offensive Player Of The Week

OS1 quarterback **Condor Adrienne**, who threw for 422 yards and four touchdowns in a win over the Ionath Krakens.

Defensive Player of the Week

Wabash linebacker **Ricky Craig**, who had seven solo tackles, a sack and a critical late-game interception in the Wolfpack's win over the To Pirates.

17

WEEK SEVEN:
LU JUGGERNAUTS
at IONATH KRAKENS

PLANET DIVISION		SOLAR DIVISION	
5-0	Wabash Wolfpack	5-1	Neptune Scarlet Fliers
5-1	To Pirates	4-1	Jupiter Jacks (bye)
4-1	Isis Ice Storm (bye)	3-2	Bartel Water Bugs (bye)
4-1	Themala Dreadnaughts	3-3	Shorah Warlords
4-2	Ionath Krakens	3-3	D'Kow War Dogs
4-2	Yall Criminals	3-3	Vik Vanguard
3-3	OS1 Orbiting Death	2-3	Bord Brigands
1-4	Alimum Armada (bye)	2-3	New Rodina Astronauts (bye)
1-4	Coranadillana Cloud Killers (bye)	2-4	Jang Atom Smashers
0-6	Hittoni Hullwalkers	2-4	Texas Earthlings
0-6	Lu Juggernauts	1-4	Sala Intrigue

THE ATMOSPHERE PROCESSORS were on the blink again. Fog filled Ionath City, far thicker than it had been for the game four weeks earlier against the Cloud Killers. To make matters worse, the lev-tracks were down. An entire city found its public transportation out of commission, causing the sidewalks to fill with bodies of several species.

The fog gave Quentin a rare opportunity for a walk. Choto accompanied him, as always, although they didn't talk anymore. Quentin's continued support of Tara the Freak had strained his relationship with all of the Quyth Warriors. Choto protected Quentin, but the linebacker/bodyguard didn't speak unless spoken to.

The fog was so thick that, with a sweatshirt hood up, Quentin did not draw stares and throngs of autograph seekers. For this afternoon, at least, he was just some really big Human walking along, minding his own business.

He'd been summoned by Gredok. Gredok had specifically instructed that Danny Lundy was not to attend — just Quentin. Quentin had the option of refusing the request or insisting that Danny attend, but had chosen instead to simply comply. Gredok had stood by Quentin during the turmoil caused by Yolanda's article. Aside from the contract negotiations, Quentin had never felt so comfortable around the team owner. Quentin would give Gredok the benefit of the doubt that this meeting would not entail contract discussions. If it did, Quentin could always leave.

Still, any conversation with Gredok required some prep time, a chance to clear his head, get his thoughts straight. A walk around the stadium on a foggy afternoon did just the trick.

Walk completed, Quentin gently eased his way through the packed sidewalks and entered the Krakens building. He took his usual route around the right side of the cavernous lobby. The black, domed ceiling sparkled with dots of light, a representation of the inhabited universe. The brightest dots marked the planets that fielded Tier One teams. The stars had changed since last season; the lights of Chillich and Mars were gone, replaced by the glow of Earth and Orbital Station One. Which lights would fade at the end of this season?

Walking around the right side of the lobby led Quentin past the Ionath Krakens' proudest relic, the GFL championship trophy from 2665. Slow-motion holos surrounding the trophy showed the man the press once dubbed "The Saint of Ionath" — Galaxy Bowl MVP Bobby "Orbital Assault" Adrojnik. In front of the GFL championship trophy was the small case that held the evidence for Bobby's canonization: his Galaxy Bowl MVP trophy and the GFL championship ring that he never got to wear. Shortly after winning the biggest sporting event in the universe, Bobby had died under suspicious circumstances.

As Quentin passed by these talismans, he ran his hands across the cases, fingers barely touching the glass, a tactile reminder that — while they were so close, so *damn* close — he would never touch actual trophies until he and his teammates earned them for themselves.

The Krakens were 4-and-2, one game behind Wabash and a half-game behind the To Pirates. Despite the loss to the Orbiting Death, it was no empty wish to think that this could be the year the Krakens put a second GFL championship trophy in that case. All he had to do was lead his team into the playoffs — from there, just three wins away from glory, from immortality.

He took the elevator to the top floor. When he stepped out, Gredok's well-dressed thugs smiled in greeting. Quentin wanted nothing to do with those sentients, yet they felt some kind of status in knowing him, knowing they worked for the same boss that he did. All of them were dangerous, to say the least; Quentin did the smart thing and simply returned the smiles.

Messal the Efficient slid into view in his normal fashion, out of sight one second, there the next.

"Elder Barnes! Warrior Choto! Welcome-*wel*come. I trust you did not have trouble finding transportation?"

"We walked," Quentin said. "Nice day for it."

"Oh, of *course*, Elder Barnes. A walk in the fog must have been de*light*ful. And I'm sure you were able to relax knowing that our brave Choto was there to guard you against any unexpected danger."

Quentin laughed softly. Messal was the undisputed heavy-weight champion of sucking up.

"Well," the Worker said, "Gredok is expecting you. Follow me, please."

Messal led them past statues, paintings and holosculpts that were each probably worth more than Quentin made in a season (certainly *more* after you factored in Commissioner Froese's fines).

Messal opened the double doors that led to Gredok's private chamber, then stepped aside. "I think you will enjoy this meeting very much, Elder Barnes."

"Uh ... thanks." Quentin entered. As usual, Choto stayed outside. Messal closed the doors.

Quentin's eyes quickly adjusted to the low light of Gredok's circular meeting room. He automatically looked to the white pedestal, saw that the black throne sat empty a fraction of a second before realizing that the expensively dressed Gredok was standing on the floor.

Standing there, to the right of a large Human that Quentin had never seen before.

Doc Patah hovered on Gredok's left.

At first, Quentin thought the Human was another of Gredok's goons. The man was big enough for it. But he wore plain brown cotton pants and a simple brown tunic — not the tailored finery of the other thugs.

"Barnes," Gredok said. "Welcome."

Quentin nodded at him. "Gredok. I came alone, as you asked. What can I do for you today?"

"Today, Barnes, is about what *I* can do for *you*."

The Human stranger smiled. A warm smile, inviting. What was this?

"Okay," Quentin said. "Hit me."

"Barnes, do you remember when I said I am a powerful friend to have?"

Quentin did. That conversation had come last season, after the Krakens had lost to the Wabash Wolfpack, humiliating Gredok before his rival owner Gloria Ogawa. That game had dropped Ionath to 1-and-4 — last place, most likely to be relegated back to Tier Two at season's end. Gredok had promised Quentin that if the Krakens could stay in Tier One, Gredok would throw all of his resources behind finding ...

No.

No, it could not be.

Quentin stared at the big Human.

"So perceptive, as always," Gredok said. "Quentin Barnes, meet Cillian Carbonaro. Your father."

The man's smile widened even further. He sniffed, wiped his left eye with one stroke of his right hand.

Quentin stared. No thoughts. It could not be.

"It's true," Doc Patah said, the metallic voice of his backpack's speakerfilm filling the chamber. "I ran the genetics tests myself, Quentin. Twice."

It just could *not* be.

"Quentin," the man said. "I know you've got a lot of questions. I know you might ... might *hate* me. But I haven't seen you in so long. Oh High One, I missed you so."

The man took a half-step forward. He spread his arms, just a bit, hands maybe a foot from his hips, but the offer of a hug shone like a single star against an all-black night.

Could not be.

But it *was*.

Quentin's feet led him forward. A haze, a blur.

Quentin Barnes put his arms around his father and squeezed him tight.

A QUESTION THAT QUENTIN had never considered — after you meet your father for the first time in your life, what then?

His dad made the suggestion: go get a beer. Quentin agreed, moving more on autopilot than anything else. Gredok had his limo drive them to the Blessed Lamb bar in the Human district. The mostly silent drive took them to the one place where Quentin could be in public, out in the open and not be swamped by fans and autograph seekers.

The two men sat at a table, silently staring at each other in a way that wasn't awkward, a beer bottle in front of each of them.

Cillian was a big man. Not Quentin's size, but still about 6-foot-6, maybe 280 pounds. Light scars, some old, some new, dotted his knuckles and criss-crossed the backs of his hands. The marks of the working class. His weathered face showed deep lines, lines that seemed too deep for his age. Maybe fifty? Lines from laughter, from worry, from work, from a life clearly far from the privileges of football stadiums and interstellar yachts.

"So," Quentin said. "How old are you?"

"Forty-six," Cillian said, then took a sip.

"Huh," Quentin said. "So you had me when you were ... twenty-six?"

The older man nodded. "Yes. We had your sister when I was sixteen."

Quentin nodded. That wasn't unusual on Micovi. "How old was Mom?"

"Fourteen when she had your sister, eighteen when she had your first brother, who died in child birth, twenty-one when she had your brother Quincy, twenty-four when she had you."

"I had another brother?"

Cillian looked off to a corner of the bar. "Yes. His name was Quaid. Would have been, I mean. Or was. Yeah, was."

Quentin let out a long breath. From zero family to all of this information, so fast, it was overwhelming. "You ... you know about Kin-Kin?"

"Who?"

"I mean Quincy," Quentin said. "You know that he ... that he's dead?"

Cillian blinked rapidly. He was trying not to cry. "Yes. Gredok told me. Forgive me, Quentin, it's ... well, I know I haven't seen any of you in a long time, but it's not easy to hear one of your children has passed on."

Quentin drank. The news of his mother had been hard, even

though he had almost no memory of her. What must it feel like to learn your own child, someone you'd held in your arms, had been dead for fifteen years?

Cillian cleared his throat, nodded once as if to say *done with that*, then the smile returned.

"I can't even describe what this is like, son. Oh … I … "

"Go ahead."

"As far as I know, you hate me. Is it okay if I call you *son*?"

Quentin laughed. "Sure. I mean, it's fact, right?"

"It is."

"Then go ahead, because I'm going to call you *Dad* until you're so sick of it you want to punch me in the face."

Cillian raised his beer bottle, extended the neck. Quentin did the same. They clinked bottles, took a sip and that was that.

So many questions. One far more important than all the rest, but there were enough other things to learn that the big one could wait. "Do you know if my sister is alive?"

"I don't," Cillian said. "Gredok said he's looking, but I've never heard from her. I take it you haven't either?"

"I didn't even know I had a sister until two months ago. I hope we find her."

They both fell silent, enjoying the moment together. Quentin realized he'd said *we* to describe himself and Gredok. That was trippy — thinking of Gredok as actually being his ally, not a dangerous obstacle.

"Dad, what was Mom like?"

He smiled, looked away. "She was an amazing woman. Very devout. At least when I knew her. She was so beautiful. I loved her from the moment I saw her. I wish we could have waited to have kids, but … well, you know what the Church is like."

Quentin did know. Girls were expected to be married by thirteen and have their first pregnancy that same year. Sixteen and unmarried? No kids? You could bet that the Elders would arrange a marriage for you, probably to a man who already had a wife or three. *Breed fast, breed often* was the slang term used when no Elders were around. His mother and father had fallen prey to the same pressure that faced all young teens on Micovi. All across the Nation, for that matter.

"She was kind," Cillian said. "She could cook like you wouldn't believe. We never had much to eat, but she could make anything taste good. You should have seen what she could do with a roundbug casserole."

"*Roundbug* casserole? But they're poisonous!"

"Not the way she prepared them," Cillian said. "You have to know what you're doing, but yeah, they're edible. Took her a full week to prep one. When we had three kids, there wasn't much choice. If my friends saw one in the mines, I'd volunteer to kill it. I'd take it home. Your mom would prep it. She'd eat a plate first, just to make sure she'd done it right, then you kids would gobble it right up. It was meat — don't know if you remember how hard that was to come by or not."

Quentin tried to imagine what that must have been like for a young couple. His father, risking his life to kill a deadly roundbug. His mother, preparing it, then eating it — to see if she would get sick, possibly even die — before serving it to her children. All of this because people often starved on Micovi. For the unconfirmed, there was never enough money, never enough food.

This man said he had risked his life for his children. If he had loved them so once, why had that stopped? Why had he vanished? Why had Quentin spent almost his entire life *alone*? It couldn't be avoided anymore. The question had to be asked.

"Dad, why did you leave us?"

Cillian slowly turned his beer bottle, rotating it, the bottom edge lightly scraping against the tabletop. "Quentin, are you sure you want to hear this?"

"I've been alone since I was five." The words came out harsher than Quentin had expected. "Every day was a fight to stay alive until I started playing football, so, yeah — I want to know why."

Cillian looked up from his beer bottle, looked into Quentin's eyes, then nodded. "Yeah, I guess that's fair. Before I tell you, I want you to know that whatever differences your mother and I had, she loved you and your brothers and sister very much. She would have done anything for you. She *did* do anything for you."

Cillian fell silent. He went back to turning his bottle. Quentin waited. He would get his answers. He would get them now.

"Micovi was a bad place," Cillian said finally.

"Still is."

Cillian shook his head, looked up. "Now it's a paradise by comparison. When you were just a little thing, it was ... people died all the time. A lot of people. Pogroms, purges ... felt like they happened every other month. Anyone could denounce you for heresy. No evidence was needed. Once you were denounced, the purity investigators would start investigating. The thing was, back then, the Church held more tightly to its belief that High One was always right. If the Elders started investigating you, for any reason, it was because it was the High One's will. The very fact that they *started* investigating you meant that you *had* to be found guilty of some kind of heresy."

"That doesn't make any sense," Quentin said. "I mean, if you didn't commit heresy, how could you be found guilty?"

"Because if they investigated you and you *weren't* guilty, that meant that High One was wrong. High One can never be wrong, Quentin. That was the Church and the government at the time."

"So how does that apply to you and Mom?"

Cillian went back to spinning his bottle but kept talking. "Anyone could denounce you. But at the same time, you could denounce anyone. No one was safe, but if you were connected to the Church it was a bigger risk to denounce you. You have to understand, Quentin, people would denounce *anyone* — men, women, children ... even babies."

Babies? Now Cillian was just padding things, to make himself feel better about abandoning his children. "Give me a break. How could babies commit heresy?"

"Because they were possessed, of course," Cillian said with quiet disgust. "You wouldn't want to let a possessed baby grow up to be a possessed child, now would you? I saw ... tragic things. *Horrible* things. Our culture was feeding on itself, eating up everyone and everything. Your mother, she saw other children being taken away, saw their families screaming, saw anyone who fought back taken away as well. So to protect the three of you, she ... she made it so that to denounce her was dangerous, a big risk."

"How?"

Cillian ground his teeth. His eyes narrowed. He looked sadder than ever. This part of the story, clearly, was more difficult to reveal.

"She took up with a Bishop," he said.

It took Quentin a moment to process the words. He'd never even considered that his mother could be anything besides caring, perfect, angelic. "You mean she *cheated* on you?"

Cillian shook his head. "No, son, it wasn't like that. We ... we agreed on it. For the three of you. The Bishop had made advances at her for years. She ignored them, but when things got bad and we needed a way to protect you ... "

His voice trailed off. He finished with a shrug. Quentin wondered what it had been like — both for what his mother had to do to protect her children and for what her husband had to bear for the same reason.

"That doesn't explain why you left."

Cillian finished his beer, as if he needed it for courage. He waved for another round. They both kept quiet until two more bottles arrived.

Quentin waited.

Cillian drained half the bottle before he continued. "The Bishop decided he wanted to marry your mother. We agreed to divorce."

"Divorce is illegal."

His father nodded. "Those are just rules, Quentin. Rules rarely apply to the people who make them. The Bishop had our marriage annulled."

He made it sound so easy to do something that could be a capital offense. "Annulled? Just like that?"

Cillian shrugged again. "He was rich and powerful. We were poor. We let it happen because it would protect you. A couple of days later, I noticed that I was being followed. Followed by purity investigators."

To be married with three children in such a violent, unpredictable place, a place without rights. Then the marriage is gone and the people who make people *vanish* start following you. His father was right — in comparison, now Micovi was a paradise.

"The Bishop knew your mother still loved me so he wanted me gone," Cillian said. "Your mother saved my life. She got the Bishop to give me a sentence of banishment instead of execution, but on one condition. I was never allowed to contact her. Or you, or your brother, or your sister. I had to walk away from my family ... forever. I'd seen what the Bishop could do, Quentin. He did not make idle threats."

"So you just *left*." Quentin tried to say it with venom, with fifteen years of pent-up hatred, but the words just came out normal. What else could his father have done? In that situation, what else could *any* father who loved his children have done?

Cillian leaned forward, stared into Quentin's eyes. "Yes, Son, I just left. My choices were leave or be burned at the stake. I wanted to stay and fight. You have no idea how badly I wanted to stay with all of you, but your mother provided the only safety we could find in a crazy time. So, to keep all four of you safe, I left. I started a new life."

"But ... but why did it take you so long to find me? I worked so hard to make my name known, my *face* known ... and you didn't show."

Cillian smiled, sat back, shook his head. "Don't think that hasn't weighed heavily on me, son. Just imagine the irony — a son who is one of the most well-known athletes in the galaxy and a father that doesn't follow sports."

Quentin stared back. He wanted to throw the table aside and strangle his father, wanted to smash the beer bottle into his mouth and twist it, give him a broken-glass smile. The rage of lost years billowed up, mushroomed, detonated — and then it was gone.

How ridiculous. A single, dark laugh coughed out of Quentin's throat. He couldn't help it. "*My* dad isn't a football fan?"

His father laughed, shrugged again. "I never played any sports when I was a kid. I was more into the movies. Don't get me wrong, Quentin, I'm not blind — I appreciate what you can do, the life you've made for yourself. High One has blessed you with amazing talents. But when you've seen as many people die for nothing as I have, well, sports just seems kind of ... "

"Silly?"

Cillian nodded. "Yes. I'm sorry, son. That's the way I always felt."

"*Felt?* Past tense?"

"Yes, *past* tense. I find myself suddenly mesmerized by this football team from Ionath. I want to watch every play, see every snap."

Quentin drew in a long, ragged breath. It was a lot to handle. So many emotions. Too many to process. Could this *really* be happening? His *father*? And what about his mother's ordeal? All to keep the kids safe. And even with those sacrifices, his mother had still died. His brothers had died. His sister might very well be dead, there was no way of knowing.

"I can't make up for lost time, son. The past is the past. All I can do is try to be there for you now, watch you blossom in this fantastic city where everyone loves you. If you'll let me, I'll live here in Ionath and spend every minute with you that I can."

Quentin ground his teeth. He would not cry in front of this man that he did not know.

Cillian's face looked as emotionless as one of Gredok's stone statues, but tears trickled down both cheeks.

"But you have to do one thing for me, Son," he said. "There's one thing I really want."

Quentin nodded before he spoke. "Yes, Dad, anything. What is it?"

"Gredok gave me sideline passes for the game on Sunday. I want to see you kick the living hell out of the Lu Juggernauts."

Quentin threw his head back and laughed, so loud it drew looks from the other patrons. He couldn't stop smiling. He lifted his beer bottle in salute. His father did the same.

"Dad, it's funny that's the one thing you want, because that's definitely the one thing I can give."

Both men drank to that. Quentin ordered a third round. They spent the rest of the afternoon trying to find out as much as they could about each other.

QUENTIN RAN LEFT toward the sidelines, looking downfield, searching for targets. Halawa in the end zone, 17 yards away but double-covered. Way back in the right corner of the end zone he saw Milford, but that far across field would mean a pass of some 60 yards — the ball would be in the air far too long. He looked for Becca, but she had maintained the block that sprung Quentin free from a blitzing linebacker.

Rick Warburg — not wide open, but moving toward the left sideline, a white-jerseyed, yellow-helmeted linebacker trailing him by a half-step. Quentin could have made that pass in his sleep, throwing low so that only Warburg could catch it.

But Quentin didn't throw.

Instead, he tucked the ball and turned upfield.

The linebacker covering Warburg waited until Quentin crossed the line of scrimmage, then came in fast. Quentin didn't have any room to run. He'd have to go out of bounds after a 5-yard gain … except, he saw Rick Warburg coming, right behind the linebacker.

Rick Warburg, whom Quentin simply refused to throw to, was trying to make a block.

Quentin cut to his right, away from the sideline, forcing the linebacker to match the cut. Quentin then cut left, back toward the sideline, making the linebacker turn his shoulders in that direction. That let Warburg get his helmet in front of the linebacker — a blind-side block that sent the Quyth Warrior flying, made the home crowd *ohhhh!* with glee. The block also left Quentin untouched, sprinting up the left sidelines, heading for the end zone.

Halawa's defender rushed out of the end zone, the speedy Sklorno desperate to stop Quentin's run. Halawa managed a push — not much of a block, really, just enough to knock the defender off-balance a little. And that was all Quentin needed. He lowered his head and drove his helmet right into the cornerback's blue and gold number 24, knocking her on her back.

Quentin stumbled, fell, but crossed the goal line before he hit the ground.

Touchdown Ionath.

Krakens 22, Juggernauts 20.

The crowd went wild, cheering a score that put their team ahead with just 17 seconds left in the game, a touchdown that all but guaranteed victory. Quentin stood, tossed the ball to a flying zebe, then raised his arms high. Quentin scanned the back of the end zone, somehow knowing that Cillian would have positioned himself there to see his son score.

Past the goal post, standing against the wall. Standing and clapping like a madman.

Cillian.

His *father*, who had just watched his son run in the game-winning touchdown. A lifetime of loneliness evaporated. Six seasons of giving his soul to the game, leaving his flesh and blood on field, across the galaxy, six seasons of looking to the stands in hopes of seeing *family* and Quentin Barnes finally had his wish.

The vision of his father vanished as Halawa jumped on Quentin's head, driving him to the ground. Laughing and trying to protect himself as best he could, Quentin disappeared beneath the orange and black pileup of his own exuberant teammates.

GFL WEEK SEVEN ROUNDUP
Courtesy of Galaxy Sports Network

HOME		AWAY	
Alimum Armada	17	Isis Ice Storm	14
Coranadillana Cloud Killers	10	**Hittoni Hullwalkers**	35
Ionath Krakens	23	Lu Juggernauts	20
Themala Dreadnaughts	17	**Wabash Wolfpack**	31
Jupiter Jacks	28	Bartel Water Bugs	13
Bord Brigands	24	Sala Intrigue	10
Vik Vanguard	24	Jang Atom Smashers	10
Shorah Warlords	24	**New Rodina Astronauts**	27

BYE WEEKS: Orbiting Death, To Pirates, Yall Criminals, D'Kow War Dogs, Neptune Scarlet Fliers, Texas Earthlings

THE WABASH WOLFPACK (6-0) remains the league's only undefeated team, thanks to a 31-17 pounding of the Themala Dreadnaughts (4-2). Halfway through the season, Wabash seems unstoppable with the league's number-one rushing offense, third-ranked passing offense and number-one passing defense. Against the Dreadnaughts, running back John Ellsworth ran for 105 yards and a touchdown, while fullback Ralph Schmeer rushed for 102 yards and two scores. That is the first time this season that two running backs from the same team each rushed for over 100 yards in the same game.

The Wolfpack holds first place in the Planet Division, a half-game ahead of the To Pirates (5-1) and a game-and-a-half ahead of third-place Ionath (5-2).

The Pirates had a bye week, while the Krakens climbed back into title contention with a 23-20 win over the Lu Juggernauts (0-7). Playing without starting tailback Ju Tweedy, who was out with a one-game suspension, the Krakens needed a come-from-behind, last-minute drive to seal the win, pulling ahead on quarterback Quentin Barnes' 15-yard touchdown run with 17 seconds left in the game.

In the Solar Division, Jupiter (5-1) handed Bartel (3-3) a 28-13 beat-down, putting the Jacks back into a first-place tie with archrival Neptune (5-1). The Scarlet Fliers were off on a bye week.

The team to watch out for in the Solar? Clearly, the Vik Vanguard (4-3), who climbed into third place and into playoff contention with a 24-10 win over the Jang Atom Smashers (2-5). Vik has won three of their last four and are off in Week Eight with a bye.

The relegation picture is looking more and more ominous for the Juggernauts, who are the only winless team left in Tier One. The Sala Intrigue's 24-10 loss to the Bord Brigands (3-3) puts the intrigue at 1-5, dead last in the Solar Division.

Deaths:

No deaths reported this week.

Offensive Player of the Week

Wabash fullback **Ralph Schmeer**, who rushed for 102 yards and two touchdowns.

Defensive Player of the Week

Vik Vanguard safety **East Windsor**, who had five solo tackles, one interception and one forced fumble in a win over the Jang Atom Smashers.

18

WEEK EIGHT: BYE

PLANET DIVISION

6-0 Wabash Wolfpack

5-1 To Pirates (bye)

5-2 Ionath Krakens

4-2 Isis Ice Storm

4-2 Themala Dreadnaughts

4-2 Yall Criminals (bye)

3-3 OS1 Orbiting Death (bye)

2-4 Alimum Armada

1-5 Coranadillana Cloud Killers

1-6 Hittoni Hullwalkers

0-7 Lu Juggernauts

SOLAR DIVISION

5-1 Neptune Scarlet Fliers (bye)

5-1 Jupiter Jacks

4-3 Vik Vanguard

3-3 Bartel Water Bugs

3-3 Bord Brigands

3-3 D'Kow War Dogs (bye)

3-3 New Rodina Astronauts

3-4 Shorah Warlords

2-5 Jang Atom Smashers

2-4 Texas Earthlings (bye)

1-5 Sala Intrigue

QUENTIN FELT GIDDY, excited for the call. Fred had worked hard, of that Quentin had no doubt, but the job was over. Quentin sat on a couch in his yacht's salon. His dad sat next to him, eating a barbecued chicken sandwich that Quentin had made in the galley. Could life get any cooler than that? His *father* eating his cooking?

"This is tasty," Cillian said. "Wow, you might be as good a cook as your mother was."

Yes. Yes, it *could* get cooler. Quentin was so happy it was hard to just sit still.

"Ship?"

[YES QUENTIN]

"Call Frederico Esteban Giuseppe Gonzaga."

[LOCATING]

"So, Dad," Quentin said. "What do you want to do today?"

Cillian tilted his head up to stare absently at the ceiling, still chewing a big piece of sandwich. He swallowed, wiped his mouth with the back of his tunic sleeve.

"I don't know."

"You want to tour the city?"

Cillian shrugged. "Sure. Well, come to think of it, I do that when you're at practice. What's it like outside the city walls?"

"It's a wasteland, Dad. This planet was irradiated."

"But I saw ads for tours," Cillian said. "Tourist barges that go out sightseeing."

"Really?"

"Yes, really. You didn't know that?"

Quentin shook his head. "I knew people golfed out there, in rad suits, but I never heard of tours."

Cillian put down the sandwich. "Son, how long have you been on Ionath?"

Quentin worked through the math. "Well, I came for preseason my rookie year in September 2682. It's March 2684, so ... eighteen months, Earth time?"

"A year and a half. And you've never been outside the city walls?"

"Huh," Quentin said. "Well, when you say it like that, it sounds like I don't have a life."

His father laughed. "I know you have a life, son, but maybe a little balance? A job like yours is special. You don't have to go into the mines for fourteen hours a day, seven days a week. You have the option of doing something other than football from time to time, you know."

"Yeah, but why would I want to?"

Cillian rolled his eyes. "That settles it. We're doing a sightseeing thing tomorrow. Okay?"

"Sure. I'm in." His dad probably could have suggested riding one of those horrifying giant-spider things into a Dinolition arena and Quentin would have said *sure*.

[FREDERICO ESTEBAN GIUSEPPE GONZAGA ON THE LINE]

"Cool, put him on," Quentin said.

The holotank flared to life, showing Fred behind his desk. The detective looked tired and rumpled.

"Quentin," Fred said. "What's up? I don't have a status update for you, or I would have sent word. I'm just getting ready to travel again. I've got a lead on your sister. I'm afraid I don't have information on your father, though."

"That's okay," Quentin said. "You can stop looking for him."

Fred paused. "Come again?"

"I found him. I found my father."

Quentin smiled and pointed to his right, to Cillian. Cillian smiled, chewing away on a mouthful of chicken sandwich. He raised his sandwich in an odd greeting.

Fred stared, blinked. "Quentin, who is that?"

"My dad. Cillian Carbonaro."

Fred's eyes narrowed. "And *you* found him?"

"Yes! Well, no, Gredok did. He called in a bunch of favors. Somehow Gredok tracked him down."

Quentin waited for Fred to look happy — and Fred kept Quentin waiting.

"Quentin, you're telling me *that* is your father?"

"Uh-huh."

Fred stared. "*That's* Cillian Carbonaro."

"In the flesh."

Cillian swallowed his mouthful. "Pleased to meet you, Mister Gonzaga. Quentin is quite fond of you."

"How nice," Fred said.

"I don't mean *fond*-fond," Cillian said. "I know you're … uh … gay."

"Dad," Quentin said. "You should stop talking now."

Cillian laughed uncomfortably, then took another oversized bite of his sandwich.

"Quentin," Fred said, "I don't know what to say."

"Say you're happy for me."

"No, that's not what I mean. I told you sentients were following me when I was on Micovi searching for information. I think those sentients may have worked for Gredok."

"So?"

"So, Gredok's goons took all my information."

"Well, what difference does it make, Fred? So they took your information. You got paid for your time and if that information helped them find my dad, then everyone wins, right?"

Fred kept staring, but he nodded. "Yeah. I guess so."

"Are you pissed that Gredok got the job done?"

"Something like that," Fred said. "You, uh, you run a genetics test?"

Quentin nodded. It was a rude question, but a fair one. Fred could be a surly, opinionated guy, but once he took a job he was on your side without question. "We did. This is my dad, Fred. Mission accomplished. I just wanted to let you know."

"So … I should stop looking for him, then?"

Quentin laughed. "Uh, *yeah*. Keep looking for my sister though, okay? Same rates?"

"Sure. Happy to keep at it."

"Great. Fred, I know you didn't *find* him and all that, but now he's here. If your information did lead to Gredok finding my dad, than I can't thank you enough. Can you come up and meet him? Some of the team is coming over tonight to hang out."

Fred finally smiled. It looked forced. "Thanks for the offer, but I fly out in an hour."

"Looking for my sister?"

Fred nodded.

"Where are you going?"

"I'd rather not say," Fred said. "Seems my activities and accomplishments are of far too much interest to unknown parties. I'll let you know when I get back."

Fred broke the connection. The holotank dropped back into darkness.

"He seems ... nice," Cillian said.

"Hardly," Quentin said. "He's acting like an ass."

"Well, but he's ... you know—" Cillian's voice dropped to a whisper "—he's *gay*."

Quentin sighed. He had to remember that his father had grown up on Micovi, spent over twenty-five years listening to the hateful words of the Purist Church. Cillian was still pretty conservative. He'd get over it.

"Ship?"

[YES QUENTIN]

"Get us a selection of tour companies that do excursions into the Wastes. My dad and I want to go sightseeing."

[SEARCHING, PLEASE HOLD]

Cillian held up an empty plate. "That was the best damn barbecue I've had since I left Micovi. Think you can make another?"

His father loved his cooking. Mister Sam would have been so proud.

Quentin told his father to pick one of the tour companies, then walked to the galley to make him another sandwich.

"AMAZING PLACE," CILLIAN SAID. "I mean, this is huge."

They stood in the orange end zone of Ionath Stadium. *The Big*

Eye. Quentin's home field, the place where he made things happen on Sunday afternoons.

The Big Eye was empty, of course. Quentin was proudly showing off the place to his father.

"Just look at it," Cillian said. "And everyone comes here to watch *you.*"

"Well, me and the team," Quentin said. "A lot of tradition here, Dad. You want to see the rest of the place?"

Cillian nodded. "Sure, but what else is there? I mean there's a locker room, I know that, but it's just a football stadium, right?"

"There's a lot," Quentin said. "Doc Patah has a full hospital under the visitors bleachers. Game can get kind of violent. And also under the bleachers, we have a Kreigs-Ballok Virtual Practice System. When there is only a couple of us, we can run drills and it looks real, looks just like any stadium in the galaxy."

Cillian smiled, his eyes narrowed. "Come on. You're kidding me. *Any* stadium in the galaxy?"

Quentin gestured to the tunnel that led to the locker room. "Come on, I'll show you."

As they walked into the tunnel, they saw Messal the Efficient walking out.

"Well, hello Elder Barnes! May I say that you look fantastic today? And Mister Carbonaro, I hope you're feeling well."

"I am," Cillian said. "Good to see you again, Messal. Thanks again for helping get me back together with my son."

Messal's eye swirled with the light green of modesty.

"Oh, I was just an employee doing his job," Messal said. "Gredok the Splithead is the only one to thank for such a wonderful occurrence."

Cillian nodded. "Sure, but thanks all the same. Hey, you run this place right? I know *Gredok* runs it, but between you and me, I'm guessing it's so well-maintained because of you?"

More light green flooded Messal's eye. "Well, thank you for saying so, Mister Carbonaro. I, of course, only do what I am told to do, but there is such a thing as pride in one's labor."

"I agree," Cillian said. "Well, if you need any help around here, I wouldn't mind a job."

A job? "Dad," Quentin said. "You don't have to work."

Cillian waved a hand dismissively — the first gesture of anything other than love and acceptance Quentin had seen.

"I don't need to take my son's money," he said. "I'll earn my own way. Messal, just keep it in mind, will you?"

"Of course, Mister Carbonaro! If a need comes up for you to join the Ionath organization in any capacity, I will be sure to let you know."

Cillian nodded. "Good enough for me. Quentin, can I see that fancy room now?"

Messal scurried away. Quentin led his father into the stadium's tunnels.

"Dad, seriously, I make a lot of money."

"And you get *fined* a lot of money," Cillian said. "I'm from the Purist Nation, Son. Just like you. I will make my own way."

They descended a level. Quentin couldn't help but feel a little proud of his father. Hard work, making your own way, doing any job that needed doing if it brought in a paycheck. *Independence.* That was the way of their culture. His father could easily coast on Quentin's paycheck, but that apparently wasn't what Cillian wanted.

They walked through the tunnel toward the VR room. As they got closer, Quentin heard the murmur of an arena crowd, the whistles of the zebes — the sounds of football filtering down the hall. Someone was using the VR room? During the off-week?

Becca.

Had to be her, once again practicing her quarterbacking skills.

"Quentin, you okay?"

Quentin turned to his father, saw the concerned look on Cillian's face. "Yeah, I'm fine. Why do you ask?"

Cillian pointed to Quentin's right temple. "Because you suddenly have this pulsing vein in your forehead. Are you mad or something?"

Quentin shook his head. "No, Dad, I'm not. Come on, I'll

show you the setup."

They walked down the hall toward the VR room.

Quentin *was* mad. But should he be? No, he shouldn't. He could have been the one in the VR room, going through extra reps, but he wasn't. And why should he? He was the starter. Becca had embraced her role as a fullback. And besides — it wasn't like Becca had a prayer of taking the spot away from him. The only one who could threaten him for the starting spot was …

A voice called out from inside the room.

"Red, sixteen! Red, sixteen!"

Not a woman's voice … a man's.

Quentin walked faster, stepped through the VR room's open doors.

"Hut-*hut!*"

Don Pine dropped back and rolled right across a black-lined, tan field. Around him, a blur of realistic holograms representing Krakens offensive players and Wabash Wolfpack defenders. Some of the players were *too* realistic. Don wore orange practice gear.

A defensive end rushed in — wearing not Wabash colors, but rather the practice blacks of Ionath.

Behind, below, above and around Don, a picture-perfect replica of Wabash Stadium. The HeavyG defensive end came in fast, smashed into the Ki right guard. The guard fell. The defensive end came over the top, then slowed, letting Don run by. Don cocked back and threw a laser. Twenty-five yards downfield, the ball hit a receiver — Mezquitic — and stuck fast.

The fake crowd roared. The holographic players faded out, leaving Don and the other real sentients.

"Wow," Cillian said. "That was a good pass."

Quentin's anger soared. "What the *hell* is this?"

His voice echoed, but only a little, drowned out by the buzz of the fake Wabash crowd.

Don's head snapped up. His eyes narrowed. "Room, off."

The holographic Wabash stadium faded away, leaving the black VR walls and the floor made of black, hexagonal tiles.

Don and the other players took off their helmets. Cliff Frost, the free-agent defensive end. Killik the Unworthy, backup line-backer. Back up right tackle Zer-Eh-Detak and the massive backup right guard Shun-On-Won. And Mezquitic, the Sklorno receiver who had been put on the inactive roster.

"We're practicing," Don said. "There a problem with that?"

Doc Patah had fixed up Don's black eye suffered in the game against the Orbiting Death. There was still some bruising on Don's nose, the bridge of which was covered by a stripe of nanomed tape. The blue tape all but vanished against his blue skin.

"It's the off-week," Quentin said and felt immediately stupid for saying it. He was the poster boy for extra practice. *Usually* the poster boy, that was.

Cliff Frost took off his helmet. The big HeavyG smiled at Quentin and Cillian. "Don's helping us," he said. "We don't get as many reps in practice as the starters. I haven't finished a season yet 'cause of all my injuries. I'm behind Michnik, Khomeni and Palmer on the depth chart, but you never know who might get hurt. If I get in this year, I want to make the most of my opportunities."

"And I as well," said Killik. He glared at Quentin, not bothering to hide his emotions. His eye swirled with a touch of saturated red. "We can't all have the advantage of being your pet project."

Zer-Eh and Shun-On said nothing. They just stood there. Mezquitic's four eyestalks stared at the hexagonal floor tiles. She refused to look Quentin in the eye.

Don stepped forward. Quentin's hands balled into fists before he realized Don was extending his own hand, extending it toward Cillian.

"Don Pine," he said. "You're Quentin's dad?"

"I know who ... I mean, nice to meet you," Cillian said. They shook hands. "Yes, I'm Quentin's father."

"A pleasure," Don said. "Well, you two enjoy your day. We're going to get back to it."

"Are you now," Quentin said. He heard the anger in his own voice. "And what are you getting back to, Don?"

Don smiled, shrugged. "Like Cliff said. You never know who will get hurt. Or who will, say, get thrown out of a game."

"That didn't do so much for you against the Orbiting Death," Quentin said.

Don shrugged, pulled on his helmet. "There's always next time. I just want you to feel confident, Quentin. Confident that if you can't get the job done against Wabash, or the Pirates in Week Ten, or D'Kow or even Themala, I'm ready to go."

Don jogged back to the center of the VR room. The other players followed. The room again came to life, this time as a replica of The Big Eye complete with red-and-white jerseyed To Pirates holographic players.

Quentin burned with anger. Don wanted the starting spot back. And Quentin knew damn well Don was good enough to take it, but *only* if Quentin played poorly. Well, Quentin would just make sure that didn't happen. The starting spot was his, his alone, his forever.

"Son?" Cillian said. "Your forehead is doing that vein thing again."

Quentin forced himself to turn away. "I'm fine, Dad," he said, even though Cillian hadn't asked him a question. "Let's finish the tour."

They left the room. There was only so much off-time he could spend with his father. Quentin had to make a choice and he was making it — spending time with Cillian was more important than the extra practice ... wasn't it?

It was. There was more to life than football.

Just not *much* more.

"WHAT DO YOU MEAN you're *canceling the trip?*"

Danny the Dolphin did not look happy. Quentin was by no means an expert in Dolphin expressions, but narrowed eyes and high volume seemed to be a nearly universal indicator of emotion. The close-up image of Danny in the holotank left no question about that.

"I mean, I'm not going." Quentin said.

"The trip is all set, buddy. They're expecting you on Mars on Tuesday and in Antarctica on Wednesday."

"Antarctica?"

"That's where McMurdo is, guy."

"But isn't Antarctica cold?"

"It was, back in the Olden Times, the Long-Ago Times, but now it's a paradise. You think I'd make you sign somewhere awful?"

"Well, you arranged a visit to Mars, didn't you?"

"Yes, but in my defense, they are offering an *awful* lot of money. And speaking of an *awful lot of money*, it seems your advertiser patron is making a move into the GFL and wants to bring you home."

"Excuse me?"

"Manny Sayed and a silent partner just bought the Buddha City Elite."

"I already told you I'm not interested in playing for Buddha City."

"Well, sure, but that was *before* they told me they will top any offer, guy. *Any* offer. They want to build their franchise around the hometown hero. I'm arranging a visit."

Quentin shook his head. "Forget it. Don't bother. I'm never going back to the Purist Nation, Danny. You hear me? *Never*."

Danny paused, thinking, then nodded, his long nose bobbing up and down. "All right. You Humans and your religions. Crazy stuff, buddy. But okay, I'll let them know you're not interested. But listen, guy, as for McMurdo and Mars, you can't just cancel these trips. The Murderers and the Planets really want you. They are making *big* offers."

Quentin fought to keep his expression neutral. He felt terrible making Danny do all this work, but the fact remained that Danny was the employee. Quentin didn't work for Danny, Danny worked for Quentin. As such, Quentin would make the decisions.

"Barnes, this is your bye week. What are you doing that's so important you can just toss all of my effort overboard?"

"Danny, I appreciate the work, but I just met my father. I have a couple of days off. I want to spend them with him."

"You have the whole off-season to spend with him! If we sign a deal with Mars or McMurdo or the To Pirates, buddy, you can afford to have Pops cloned ten times over and make up for lost time."

"Danny, the answer is no. I'm canceling the trip."

Danny's long mouth opened a little, showing the pointy teeth inside. Was that an expression of frustration? Perhaps even rage?

"You're killing me here, guy," he said. "I'm crushed, crippled and conquered. Look, I can reschedule something with the Murderers and the Planets, but for High One's sake, *if you don't meet with other teams, the Pirates could unexpectedly lower that rumored offer.*"

The quarterback of the Blood Red. His dream job. The thing Quentin had always wanted. Well, times change and people change. The eight-year-old version of you doesn't know where the twenty-year-old version will wind up.

"Danny, look, I—"

"Do you know what I would have to go through to get the Pirates to make that *rumored* offer? I'm betting you don't know Dolphin anatomy, so I'll spare you the details, but the metaphor would make you most uncomfortable, guy. It involves fish parts."

Danny didn't look as angry now. He looked ... pained. He clearly had worked his tail off for Quentin. Quentin couldn't invalidate all of that because his father had shown up *now*. That wasn't fair. That wasn't right.

"Okay," Quentin said. "Sure ... reschedule the meetings. Can my dad come?"

Danny's head nodded quickly. He let out a chittering sound that was all Dolphin. "Yes! No problem, buddy. You're the boss, right? I mean, I do all this work at your whim, right? You're a star, guy, so bring the old man. Just tell him to be quiet, all right?"

"Okay. I gotta get going. My dad and I are going on a tour of the Wastes."

"How nice and domestic," Danny said. "Now I gotta go do

damage control, guy. Nothing like angering an organization with the nickname of the *Murderers*, if you know what I'm saying."

Danny broke the connection. Sure, Quentin felt bad, but it would be okay. If the McMurdo Murderers and the Mars Planets wanted him that bad, they could wait. As for the To Pirates? Only time would tell.

THE GLASS-BOTTOMED TOUR BUS hovered some thirty feet above Ionath's pock-marked surface, high enough to avoid jagged boulders and outcroppings that stuck up at every angle, low enough to see the small plants growing in the ground's deep cracks.

"As you can see," said the Quyth Worker tour guide, "the surface of Ionath is on its way to recovery. Plant growth continues to expand. Foliage now covers an estimated forty-five percent of the surface. This first phase of growth consumes radioactive material for energy. Once the radioactivity is gone, this phase of plant life will die out. Then the government will reintroduce what native species it has gathered from museums and universities."

Quentin's father looked down, past his feet to the shattered surface below. "This is madness," he said quietly. "Quentin, you live on a dead planet."

"It's not *dead*, Dad. Well, most of it is, but Ionath City is pretty cool, don't you think?"

His father looked up, smiled. Quentin still couldn't believe it. Even though the man was sitting right there, right next to him. *His father.*

"Yeah," Cillian said. "The city is pretty impressive. It's all kind of overwhelming, to tell you the truth, but I guess you're used to living in such an amazing place. Do you know the city well?"

"Not really. Most of my time is spent on football. You can't take your eyes off the prize for even a minute, or you get beat like we did with Coranadillana."

His father's smile faded a little. "Quentin, I don't want to just, you know, jump back into your life and start giving advice."

Quentin waited, but his father paused. How odd — the one

person from whom Quentin *would* take unsolicited advice, yet his father was waiting for permission to share it.

"Go ahead, Dad. It's okay."

"I've only known you for a couple of days, Son. I mean, the grown-up you. But … I know you're a professional athlete and talented and things like that, but don't you think you need some balance in your life?"

"What do you mean?"

"Maybe you need more than just football? You live here, yet this is the first time you've been beyond the city walls?"

"Well, yeah. Like I said, Dad, I'm kind of busy. I'm the quarterback. There's a lot of sentients depending on me."

His father nodded quickly, apologetically. "Yes, of course. I understand that. It's just that you sacrifice everything else to make that happen."

Quentin hadn't thought about it that way before, but his dad was right. "Yeah, I guess I do sacrifice. But I think that's what it takes to succeed. I'm not any different from John or Ju or anyone on the team. Anyone in the entire league, for that matter."

His father looked down again, through the clear hull. The tour bus was flying over a crashed ship. Military? Passenger? Quentin didn't know. The wreck looked like it had been there for decades, at least. Deep run-off grooves led away from parts of the ship, showing where water collected during storms before spilling away in miniature rivers. Some kind of red moss had grown up over the blackened, twisted metal, turning a vision of death and destruction into a blossoming sculpture of life.

"Well, you've had more success than I ever had," Cillian said. "You know what you're doing, Son, and I'm proud of you. I guess as busy as you are, staying in one city for a lot of years is the way to really have a place you call home."

His father's words made Quentin think about free agency, the canceled trips to Earth and Mars. "I don't know, Dad. Some other teams want to sign me."

"But I thought you liked it here. You said you were friends with your teammates?"

"I am. But, well, I'm young for my position and teams want me. It would mean a lot of money."

His father reached out his scarred right hand, put it around Quentin's shoulder. Cillian was a big man, but still half a foot shorter than Quentin. "Son, whatever you do will be the right choice. Just remember that all the money in the galaxy couldn't replace the years I lost with you, with your mother, your brother and your sister. Money is a great thing, but it's not the greatest thing."

His father squeezed his shoulder, pulling him in close for a quick, manly hug. Then a pat on the back, then Cillian looked at the tour guide, who was explaining the next landmark.

"Now we're to the best part of the tour," the Worker said. "We're about to float over an original relativity bomb crater, one that caused immense damage and wiped out all life in a twenty-mile radius. The walls of the crater are some five-hundred feet deep. You might experience a little vertigo, but do not worry — I've taken this trip many times before and I haven't fallen in yet."

Laughter escaped the mixed crowd of Human, Sklorno, Quyth Worker and Quyth Warrior passengers. There were also four Quyth Leaders, but that caste never seemed to laugh at anything.

Then the bottom fell out of Quentin's world. Despite the tour guide's assurances, seeing the ground drop off below your feet to a deep, mist-covered bottom made his stomach do flip-flops.

As the tour bus sailed out over the massive crater, Quentin thought over his father's words: *Money is a great thing, but it's not the greatest thing.*

GFL WEEK EIGHT ROUNDUP
Courtesy of Galaxy Sports Network

HOME		AWAY	
Yall Criminals	31	Alimum Armada	3
Sala Intrigue	20	**Coranadillana Cloud Killers**	21
Isis Ice Storm	31	Orbiting Death	28
To Pirates	20	Themala Dreadnaughts	7
Wabash Wolfpack	17	New Rodina Astronauts	10
Bartel Water Bugs	14	**Neptune Scarlet Fliers**	24
Texas Earthlings	14	Bord Brigands	13
Jupiter Jacks	24	D'Kow War Dogs	21

BYE WEEKS: Hittoni Hullwalkers, Ionath Krakens, Lu Juggernauts, Jang Atom Smashers, Shorah Warlords, Vik Vanguard

WITH THE SEASON three-quarters complete, only one team re-mains undefeated. In a rematch of last year's Galaxy Bowl, de-fending champion Wabash (7-0) won a surprising close 17-10 cross-divisional contest over the New Rodina Astronauts (3-4) to remain in sole possession of first in the Planet. Wabash defensive end Col-Que-Hon recorded a GFL-record five sacks on Astronauts quarterback GK Parish, anchoring a Wolfpack defense that didn't give up a single offensive touchdown. Wolfpack fullback Ralph Schmeer scored two touchdowns, one on a 2-yard run and another on an 11-yard pass from quarterback Rich Bennett.

The To Pirates (6-1) stayed just a game out of first in the Planet, thanks to a 20-7 win over the Themala Dreadnaughts (4-3). Ionath (5-2) was on a bye-week, allowing Isis (5-2) and Yall (5-2) to move into a three-way tie for third. Isis beat the Orbiting Death (3-4) by a score of 31-28, while Yall hung a 31-3 pounding on Alimum (2-5).

In the Solar Division, Neptune (6-1) and Jupiter (6-1) both notched victories to remain tied for first. The Scarlet Fliers' 24-14 win over the Bartel Water Bugs (3-4) let them bounce back from their first loss of the season last week to the Vik Vanguard (4-3). Jupiter won a 24-21 overtime thriller against the D'Kow War Dogs (3-4). Vik had a bye, but losses by Bartel, D'Kow, New Rodina and Bord (3-4) left the Vanguard alone in third place in the Solar Division.

In relegation watch, the Texas Earthlings (3-4) pulled two games ahead of Sala (1-6), who fell 21-20 to Coranadillana (2-5). The Jang Atom Smashers (2-5) had a bye. Over in Planet Division relegation, Lu (0-7) was off with a bye, as was Hittoni (1-6).

Deaths

No deaths reported this week.

Offensive Player of the Week

Neptune quarterback **Adam Guri**, who completed 22-of-30 passes for 307 yards and two touchdowns.

Defensive Player of the Week

This week the GFL announced co-defensive players of the week. To Pirates strong safety **Ciudad Juarez**, who victimized Themala quarterback Gavin Warren with two sacks and two interceptions. Ciudad Juarez also had three solo tackles. Wabash Wolfpack defensive end **Col-Que-Hon** was also named defensive player of the week for his GFL-record five sacks in one game.

19

WEEK NINE:
IONATH KRAKENS
at WABASH WOLFPACK

PLANET DIVISION	SOLAR DIVISION
5-2 Ionath Krakens (bye)	6-1 Neptune Scarlet Fliers
5-2 Isis Ice Storm	6-1 Jupiter Jacks
5-2 Yall Criminals	4-3 Vik Vanguard (bye)
4-3 Themala Dreadnaughts	3-4 Bartel Water Bugs
3-4 OS1 Orbiting Death	3-4 Bord Brigands
2-5 Alimum Armada	3-4 D'Kow War Dogs
2-5 Coranadillana Cloud Killers	3-4 New Rodina Astronauts
1-6 Hittoni Hullwalkers (bye)	3-4 Shorah Warlords (bye)
0-7 Lu Juggernauts (bye)	3-4 Texas Earthlings
7-0 Wabash Wolfpack	2-5 Jang Atom Smashers (bye)
6-1 To Pirates	1-6 Sala Intrigue

THE NEXT ROUND OF CONTRACT NEGOTIATIONS brought a significant difference — this time, Gredok was coming to Danny's office.

Quentin sat in the meeting room, watching Danny Lundy pace on his metallic legs. The Dolphin looked anxious.

"Danny, you okay?"

"I'm excited, delighted and ignited," Danny said. He didn't stop pacing. "I've been in the agent game for ten seasons. This is the first time a GFL owner has come to *my* office."

"So that's good?"

"Oh, it's good, guy," Danny said. "It means Gredok is on the ropes. He's coming here to give us a counter-offer, hoping that he can pretend to be a nice fellow. He'll say something like *we just can't afford it* to get us to drop our price."

"Will we?"

"Of course," Danny said. "But not as much as he hopes, buddy. You've proven yourself this season, Quentin. The entire galaxy knows that you're the real deal, blue twisted steel and sex appeal."

"What does that mean?"

"I don't know," Danny said. "A Human phrase I picked up somewhere. Doesn't matter. What does matter is getting Gredok's offer, then taking that to Kirani Kollok, who will top it for sure. Then, Gredok gets one more chance to beat it. Today is his *final offer*, my tail-fin. We're going to put the screws to that little black-furred owner of yours, guy. I can't wait to see him squirm."

That talk made Quentin uncomfortable. Gredok was just trying to do what was best for the franchise. Sure, he wanted to land Quentin for as little as possible. That was just good business. But the higher Quentin's salary, the less Gredok had to spend on other high-quality players.

"Danny, this is supposed to be about a fair deal, not making someone *squirm*."

Danny's high-pitched, rapid-fire laugh filled the meeting room. "Oh, Quentin. I know you're a big bad-ass and all, buddy, but sometimes *cute* is the only word for you."

Quentin was about to ask what that meant, exactly, but Danny's stunning secretary walked into the room. "Mister Splithead is here."

Danny scurried to his chair. He sat next to Quentin. His blow hole opened wide to draw in a deep breath. His chassis let out a short blast of fine mist to wet his rainbow-white skin, then he nodded.

"Bring him in."

Gredok the Splithead entered, followed by Messal the Efficient and Bobby Brobst, one of Gredok's well-dressed bodyguards. Messal carried a contract box. Brobst, a Human nearly big enough to play tight end, quietly walked to a corner and stood. Messal set the contract box on the table, brushed an invisible piece of dust off of it, then pulled out the chair for Gredok, who sat.

Danny stared at the contract box, his formerly excited mood visibly shifting to annoyance. "What is that, Gredok?"

"It's a contract box."

"Obviously," Danny said. "Why is it here? We're not done with negotiations, guy."

"I'm afraid that we are, Dolphin. That box contains my final offer."

Danny's head started nodding a little, but Quentin thought it was an unwitting display of anger rather than a conscious gesture.

"Yes, you *would* think that," Danny said. "You come here to give my client final terms? The Krakens are five-and-two because of Quentin Barnes, buddy. We have firm offers from the McMurdo Murderers and the Mars Planets. There is also a rumor of a franchise-level offer from the To Pirates that will be tendered at season's end."

"A *rumor*," Gredok said. "Yes, of course. They wouldn't make an actual offer, considering that we play the Pirates in two weeks."

"Of course not," Danny said. "That would be against GFL regulations, guy. Gredok, my client is red-hot. Teams want him badly and *you* come here to give *us* a final offer?"

Gredok leaned forward. A slight tinge of light green colored his eye. Quentin had never seen that before, never thought it could possibly dance across Gredok's cornea. Light green — the color of modesty.

"Lundy," Gredok said, "wouldn't it be prudent to see what the offer is before you hammer at me with righteous indignation?"

Danny fell silent. His black eyes narrowed. Quentin knew that Gredok had just won that point, had made Danny look foolish.

"Fine," the Dolphin said. "Let's see it."

Gredok leaned back. Messal pressed a button on the box. A holo flared to life above it, spelling out the contract's main terms in glowing letters.

165 MILLION FOR 10 YEARS

"Wow," Quentin said.

A short blast of fine mist sprayed on his face, making him jump back in his chair.

"Barnes," Danny said, "you need to let me handle this."

Thinly veiled talk for *shut the hell up and don't make a sound.* Quentin tried to relax. He would let the heavyweights duke it out. But *wow*, that was so much money and it was *right there.*

"Those terms are unacceptable," Danny said. "You are still twenty-five megacredits away from our latest counter-counter offer."

Gredok leaned forward again. "I want Quentin Barnes to lead my franchise. I believe in him. He has won me over in a way that no Human ever has. He has discipline, intensity, loyalty and — something that I'm not used to in my line of business — integrity."

Quentin felt himself blushing.

Gredok continued. "He is the sentient to lead my franchise for the next ten seasons and beyond, should his body stand up to the continued abuse of the game. The other players follow him without question."

"If that's how you feel," Danny said, "then he is worth far more than you're offering."

"He is," Gredok said. "However, I have a business to run. I am wealthy, Lundy, but my accounts are not infinite. I have to build a championship *team*, not sink all of my resources into one player.

We have many needs on the defensive side. I need money to sign the players that will help Quentin take us to a title."

Quentin nodded before he realized he was doing it. He clenched his teeth, forced himself to stay still.

"Your financial woes are not my client's concern, buddy," Danny said. "The offers from both McMurdo and Mars are already higher than yours and that *rumored* offer from To is *significantly* higher."

Gredok nodded, a Human-learned gesture that made a Quyth Leader's entire upper body move back and forth. "I understand. But I am not here to argue any further. This is my final offer. If I leave this room without completing the offer, then at season's end, Quentin Barnes is no longer an Ionath Kraken."

Danny shook his head, hard. Drops of water flicked off to both sides. "We don't accept."

Quentin felt something in his chest ... was it ... *fear?* Fear that he'd have to start all over again somewhere else? He could, he knew he could. He'd learned so much in three seasons, but did he *want* to start over?

Purple swirled in Gredok's eye — sadness, disappointment. He turned to face Quentin. "I realize that I have been ... difficult. Everything I have done, Quentin, was done to field a championship team. I had hoped I would build that championship with you, with Hawick, with the Tweedy brothers, even with Yassoud. But if your path leads you elsewhere, I wish you well — except when you line up against me on the football field."

Gredok meant it. The ruthless crime lord actually *meant* it.

"Gredok," Quentin said. "I-"

A single, high-pitched syllable cut Quentin off.

"Let me do the talking," Danny said in a low tone of command. "Gredok, stop pretending that we have to accept your offer now. It's only Week Nine."

"Lundy, you are not the only one that can facilitate *rumors* of in-season offers. I can't afford to start over with another rookie. I need a seasoned quarterback, a proven leader. If Quentin chooses to go elsewhere, I need to start some *rumors* of my own."

Gredok wanted to start looking for another quarterback, even before the season was over? The thought simultaneously filled Quentin with rage and with admiration. Gredok wanted Quentin, but if he couldn't have him, the crime lord would find someone else and he'd start hunting immediately. That made sense — it was exactly what Quentin would do if he were in Gredok's position. Machinations and manipulations took time to develop. Player acquisition was a cut-throat business. Condor Adrienne hadn't come to the Orbiting Death by choice. Anna Villani had forced that move. Gredok needed time to do something similar.

Words suddenly flashed through Quentin's mind. A voice from his past back on Micovi, a memory of a limo ride to the spaceport, the words of Raiders owner Stedmar Osbourne: *What you've got to learn, Quentin, is that time always wins and there's always someone to take your place. I won't be able to replace you next year, or the year after that, but you know what? Someone will line up at quarterback for the Raiders. The team won't shut down because you're gone.*

This was it. Take the offer and stay with his teammates, keep his heart pumping orange and black, or sign with another team and take the money.

"Gredok," Quentin said. "I think that—"

Danny turned sharply. "Barnes! You need to let me handle this. I will—"

"Shut up," Quentin said.

"What?"

"I said, *shut up*, Danny. You work for me, remember?" Quentin stared hard into the Dolphin's black eyes, waited until Danny leaned back.

Quentin turned to face Gredok. "I accept."

Danny's legs extended, suddenly raising his 350-pound, 8-foot-long body into the air. His bejeweled dorsal fin brushed against the ceiling. His head angled down, showing eyes wide with rage. When he talked, it was a combination of Dolphin chitter and English. "No! I have worked too hard on this deal, Barnes! *Do not accept!*"

Quentin stood as well. He wasn't some helpless orphan miner. He was a grown man. He was the team captain of a Tier One franchise.

Then it hit home — he wasn't an *orphan* anymore. In fact, he'd *never* truly been one.

"Lundy, we're *done*. I want to play for the Krakens. You will either facilitate the exchange and get your commission, or I will walk out of here and sign somewhere else, using my new money to hire lawyers to make sure you don't get a single credit. The offer on the table is there because of your efforts, but *you* work for *me* and you will do what I tell you to do. So, do you want fifteen percent of a hundred and sixty-five million, or do you want a hundred percent of nothing?"

Quentin snapped out of it. Had *he* just said all of that? Said it in the voice he used on the football field, where he was always confident and in control?

He had.

Danny stared. His long, muscular Dolphin form shook with anger. Quentin waited. Gredok sat still and silent.

Danny's shaking slowed, then stopped. He lowered himself back down to table-level. His metallic hands reached out and took the contract box.

"We'll do what you want," he said. "You're right, Quentin. You're the boss. It's your career. But I am going on record here to say you are making a mistake. You are believing the words of a master manipulator."

"Maybe," Quentin said. "But you know what? This deal makes me rich beyond anything I could have imagined, and I get to win a championship with the team *I've* built. Money is a great thing, Lundy, but it isn't the greatest thing."

Danny pushed the box to the center of the table. "Everything is in order. No hidden clauses. The offer is as Gredok says."

Quentin reached out his left hand and slid his thumb into the box's hole. He felt the tickle of machinery scraping his skin, taking cells to read his DNA and verify his identity. The device also measured his heart rate, temperature and several other factors, entering them into an algorithm that would determine if Quentin was making this choice of his own free will.

The light above Quentin's finger turned green - he was not being coerced.

Gredok leaned forward, extended his pedipalp, slid his furred finger into the other side of the box. More whirring, some buzzing — the light on his side turned green.

The contract box accessed the Intergalactic Business Database, verified their genetic makeup against records, then gave a low **BEEP** to indicate the transaction was complete.

Quentin Barnes was rich.

Quentin Barnes was a *Kraken*, now and forever.

Gredok withdrew his pedipalp. "Now that I have made you wealthier than most of the sentients in your home city, *combined*, Barnes, I wonder if you could do me the tiniest favor."

Quentin smiled, a smile he couldn't stop. It was all over — he had a father, he had a team, he had a *family*.

"A favor? And what would that be, Gredok?"

"Gloria ... *Ogawa*," the Quyth Leader said, not hiding the fact that he hated to say that name almost as much as he hated the woman who owned it. "I have not defeated her team since 2669. To defeat her in their stadium, destroy her undefeated season, it would erase *fifteen years* of frustration. Tell me, Barnes, tell me that you are the one who will finally defeat Wabash."

Quentin reached out and ruffled the black fur on Gredok's head.

"Just give me the ball, Greedy. Just give me the ball."

Transcript from the "Galaxy's Greatest Sports Show with Dan, Akbar, and Tarat the Smasher"

DAN: And we're back! Thanks again to our sponsor, Sayed Luxury Craft.

AKBAR: You know, I met Manny Sayed once. Heck of a guy.

DAN: You can say that again, lil' buddy. Funny we should mention Sayed Luxury Craft right now, because their poster boy, Quentin Barnes, is headed into the biggest game of his career. His Krakens travel to the planet Fortress for a critical tilt with the undefeated Wabash Wolfpack.

TARAT: You think this game is bigger for the Krakens than last year's game against the Mars Planets? The loser of that one dropped to Tier Two, costing the franchise millions.

DAN: Well, sure, Smasher, that was big, but this is the biggest game of Quentin's career *this* season.

AKBAR: That doesn't even make any sense.

DAN: You're right, Akbar, sports drama doesn't have to make sense to be dramatic and we've got *droves* of drama in this game. First, Wabash versus Ionath is a bitter rivalry that dates back decades. This is the first real chance the Krakens have had to beat the Wolfpack in fifteen years. Second, Wabash is on top of the Planet Division, but Ionath is tied for third and fighting for their first trip to the playoffs in nine seasons. If the Krakens win, they pull to within one game of first.

AKBAR: Dan, who are you kidding? The Krakens are going to get demolished.

TARAT: But the Krakens have five wins. They are a good team.

AKBAR: Tarat, maybe they don't teach math in the Quyth Concordia, because you certainly haven't done yours. Sure, the Krakens have five wins, but the last three? Those came against teams with a combined record of *three* and *eighteen*.

DAN: Ionath beat Isis and Yall, both five-and-two teams, both fighting for playoff spots.

AKBAR: That was the first two weeks of the season and the Criminals were killing Ionath until Renaud got hurt. Since then, the Krakens have *barely* beaten Hittoni, Alimum and Lu. They lost to OS1, which has a losing record of three-and-four and to Coranadillana, which only has *two* wins. I'm telling you, the Krakens are not as good as their record.

TARAT: A football team's record speaks for itself, Akbar.

DAN: I don't know, Tarat, maybe Akbar has a point. The Krakens haven't had a quality win since Week One.

TARAT: Victories are quantitative, not qualitative.

AKBAR: Woah! Maybe they *do* teach math in the Concordia.

TARAT: It does not matter *how* you win, or *who* you beat, as long as you get a victory. If the Krakens get three more wins, they finish with eight and probably make the playoffs.

DAN: P-p-playoffs? Did he say … *playoffs*? This week the Krakens have undefeated defending GFL champion Wabash Wolfpack, *then* the six-and-one To Pirates, *then* D'Kow, which is winnable, but Ionath finishes with the red-hot Vik Vanguard. You think Ionath can win *three* of those four games?

AKBAR: Not likely.

TARAT: Dan, I am saying that *if* the Krakens can win three, they will make the playoffs. From there, anything can happen.

DAN: So you're picking the Krakens over the Wolfpack on Sunday?

TARAT: Oh, absolutely not. The Wolfpack will crush Ionath.

AKBAR: If there's qualitative and quantitative, is there wishy-washy-tative?

TARAT: Akbar, you are starting to make me angry. You wouldn't like me when I'm angry.

DAN: Okay then! Akbar, help us all out and shush up for a bit while we go to the calls, okay?

AKBAR: Uh … yes, I'll just sit here and be quiet.

TARAT: Excellent decision.

DAN: Line seven from the Withrit Colony, you're on the Space. *Go!*

CALLER: All three of you idiots are wrong-wrong-wrong. The Krakens are going to win all four, finish with nine wins and take the Planet Division.

TARAT: I think that is unlikely.

DAN: What kind of drugs are they selling these days in Withrit? Because I want some. Line four from Earth you're on the Space. *Go!*

THE PLASTIC BUCKET CLONKED onto the deck between Quentin and his father.

"Boom," John Tweedy said. "The Puke-A-Tron Model B is ready for business. Now, with even more Wabash action!"

He pointed to the bucket's latest sticker, this one showing a snarling, black, stylized animal head set against a backdrop of red — the logo of the Wabash Wolfpack.

"Thanks, John."

"Don't mention it, Q-ster. Hey there, Pa Barnes. How are ya?"

Cillian nodded politely. "I'm fine, thanks. John, you know my last name isn't *Barnes*, right?"

John blinked a few times. "But you're Quentin's dad."

"Yes, but Quentin's mother remarried and that changed his last name. My last name is Carbonaro."

John's face wrinkled with confusion. "So, I should call you Pa Carbonaro?"

"How about you call me Cillian?"

"Pa Cillian?"

"Just *Cillian*."

"How about I just call you *Pa*, then?"

"I'm not your dad, John."

"Quentin's not my brother, but he calls Ma *Ma*."

Cillian sighed.

Quentin laughed and pushed his dad's shoulder. "Just let him call you *Pa*. It will save you a lot of time."

Cillian shrugged. "Fine, John. Just call me Pa."

John smiled and nodded once. I KNOW WORDS flashed across his face. "What are you guys doing?"

"Studying," Quentin said. "Dad is quizzing me on the Wolfpack players. It's more fun than staring at the holotank."

UNDEFEATED SCHMUNDEFEATED scrolled across John's face. "Okay, Q, I'll leave you and Pa to it. Hey, Pa, watch out for the splashing, okay?"

John walked off.

Cillian picked up his messageboard and looked at the next name. "Right outside linebacker?"

"Ricky Craig," Quentin said instantly. "Fifth-year pro, a

Fortress native. Six-foot-eight, three-hundred thirty pounds. Great lateral movement. The Wolfpack's second-leading tackler. Four sacks this season, two interceptions."

Cillian nodded. "And his weaknesses?"

"Slow to turn and run with receivers in pass coverage. Susceptible to pump-fakes and play-action. He tends to have poor balance if he blitzes up the middle."

"What does that mean for you?"

"It means I've got an extra bit of time if he comes in. I can juke him."

Cillian lowered the messageboard. "That's all correct. But I'm kind of curious — what exactly does *an extra bit of time* mean in your case?"

Quentin thought for a moment, trying to analyze something he normally did by feel alone. "I'd say ... that means about two-tenths of a second?"

"Two-*tenths?* You're telling me that things happen so fast, you notice *two-tenths of a second* of extra reaction time?"

Quentin nodded.

"So you see this six-foot-eight monster coming and you think, *oh look, it's Ricky Craig, I've got a fraction of a second to relax and have a beer?*"

Quentin laughed. "No, Dad, it's not like that. Everything happens automatically. I memorize all of this stuff over and over again, then on the field it all just kind of happens instantly."

Cillian leaned back and smiled. "You're really amazing, you know that, Son?"

Quentin's face felt hot. He looked away. "Thanks." How could he react to that? What was he supposed to say when his father was so clearly *proud* of him?

Cillian seemed to sense Quentin's discomfort. He picked up the plastic-lined bucket. "What's this? And what did John mean by *watch out for the splashing?*"

"Uh ... I sometimes get a little sick on punch-out."

His father raised his eyebrows and held the bucket higher, showing the size. "A *little* sick?"

"Okay, a *lot* sick. I kind of throw up every time. Maybe it's genetic."

"Maybe," Cillian said, then he looked away and set the bucket down. "If so, you get it from your mother. Listen, let's finish up. We're almost at punch-out. As soon as we arrive, I have to report to Messal to help with equipment load-in on the shuttles."

Quentin still couldn't believe that his father had taken a job with the Krakens. Messal had offered the position and Cillian had taken it immediately.

"Okay, Dad, that's cool."

Cillian looked through the tall windows. There was nothing to see out there but blackness — no stars in punch-space.

"Quentin, have you played in Wabash before?"

"We had them in Ionath last year," Quentin said. "I've never played in Wabash, though. Kimberlin told me that they have one-hundred thousand fans, *exactly*, at every game. No more, no less. They call themselves the *Hundred-K*. Isn't that cool?"

"Yeah, it is," Cillian said. "*Fortress* seems like a strange name for a planet."

"They called it that because it had some weird defense structure. The planet is right in the middle of both the Tower Republic and the Leekee Collective."

"In the *middle* of both? How can it be in both at the same time?"

"Tower and Leekee share a lot of space," Quentin said. "Some people think they're basically the same government, independent of each other in name only." What a strange feeling — *Quentin* was educating someone else on a government structure? Bizarre. And yet, it felt fantastic. He had learned so much.

Quentin felt the *shudder* begin. He closed his eyes, held tight to the brass rail. *Here it comes. Everything will be okay. You'll be fine, you'll be fine, you'll be —* "

A hand on his back. Rubbing small circles. Patting lightly. His father, trying to comfort him.

The shudder came and went. Quentin opened his eyes to see his dad offering up the bucket.

"You okay, Son?"

Punch-out had come and gone. For the first time that Quentin could remember, he didn't have to throw up.

"Yes," he said. "I think I'm okay."

Outside the window, the planet Fortress glowed a pale red. Surrounding the planet, a shell of widely spaced satellites, all equidistant to each other. Quentin's eyes unconsciously drew lines between the stations — a pattern of repeating hexes that curved around the far side of the planet.

"Wow," Cillian said. "How many are there?"

"Got to be thousands," Quentin said. The *Touchback* flew toward the planet. The satellites grew in size. The structures were massive, each maybe four times the size of the *Touchback*. As they sailed past, he saw the satellites were heavily damaged — ripped and melted metal, cracked shells, broken superstructure, shattered gun emplacements with barrels bent or twisted or pointing in different directions.

Forty years on and so many parts of the galaxy still bore the scars of the Takeover.

"Well, Quentin, I have to get to work. I certainly don't want to be late for my first trip down."

"Dad, you know you don't have to have a job. I make enough money."

Cillian scowled at his son. "We're not going to keep going over this, Quentin. As long as High One gives me the ability to earn my own keep, I will. To do less would be a sin."

That seemed silly, yet Quentin knew he would do the same were he in his father's position. "Okay. I guess I'll see you after the game?"

Cillian smiled, reached out and ruffled Quentin's hair. "A dozen roundbug stings couldn't keep me away. Play your best, Son. I'll be rooting for you."

Quentin watched his father leave the observation deck. He stared after him for a bit, then turned to look at Fortress. Quentin knew he was a lucky man to have his father in his life, but it was time to focus on other things.

He had a team to lead.

He had a game to win.

The Krakens' fifteen-year drought was about to end. This victory would be a landmark for the organization. More importantly, a win would feel like payback to the sentient who had given Quentin everything.

"This one's for you, Gredok," Quentin said, then he turned and headed for his quarters.

"YOUR VISITING TEAM, the Ionath, *Kraaaaaaakensssss!"*

Quentin, Ju Tweedy and their teammates ran out of the tunnel onto the cream-colored field of Wabash Stadium. Home of the Wolfpack. He sprinted toward his sideline, expecting the assault of wet trash.

But none came.

It took him a moment to realize it, but this crowd wasn't booing.

In fact, they were *cheering.*

Not the full-throttle cheer they would give to their Wolfpack, but it *was* a cheer, a polite thing of respect, of acceptance.

"What is this?" Ju said as they jogged along. "No rotten food today?"

Quentin shook his head. "No. I think that's over because of that latest article, cover-boy."

Ju smiled and pumped his fist. Yolanda's story of two weeks earlier had cleared their names, cleared the reputation of the Ionath Krakens. Somehow, an entire galaxy's worth of football fans felt bad for having doubted Quentin, Ju and the others. This cheer was a small token of apology. Quentin had not gone on the sports shows and blamed other sentients, he hadn't whined in the press about how he'd been wronged. He'd stood by his teammate while everyone cursed his name, while people called for him to be thrown out of the league — while people threw garbage on him.

He'd stood by his teammate, who had turned out to be innocent.

Wabash Stadium gleamed in the afternoon sun. Not so much from the concrete and steel construction, which was utilitarian and basic, but from the 100,000 fans — probably 90,000 of which wore white. Wabash's vaunted *100K* packed the stadium's two decks, two thick bands of white sandwiching a middle deck of luxury boxes. Gredok and Gloria Ogawa would be in one of those boxes, behind the Wolfpack sidelines, right at the 50-yard line. Quentin glanced to the left as he ran across the tan field, looking for the tiny, black-furred Quyth Leader, but he couldn't make him out.

Quentin reached the Ionath sideline, raised his fist and the team gathered around him. Football fans were fickle — love you one day, hate you the next. Today, they loved him. That made him feel amazing, but he knew it would not last because this was an *away* crowd and most of these sentients were Wolfpack fans.

Four quarters from now, when he walked out of here with a victory over their home team? They'd be singing a different tune.

He would sing along with them and smile.

HE STOOD IN THE HOME of GFL champions.

No denying that this place felt different from the rest. Last year, he'd experienced the same sensation in Red Storm City, when he and his teammates had taken on the Jupiter Jacks. The Krakens had upset the then-defending GFL champion.

And now, the Krakens were on the verge of doing it again.

Down 25-21, fourth quarter, 1:15 to play, third-and-15 on the Krakens 46-yard line. A field goal meant nothing — the Krakens needed a touchdown to win. An insane crowd of *exactly* 100,000 mostly white-clad fans screamed to their Wolfpack to *hold them*, to *shut them down*.

It all came down to this last drive. A loss dropped Ionath to 5-3, nearly crippling their playoff hopes. A win and they were 6-2, a game out of first. To do that, the Krakens needed a last-minute, game-winning drive against the undefeated defending champs, against a team they hadn't beaten in 15 years.

Pressure? Yes. Quentin's body felt electric — everything fell on *his* shoulders. Game on the line, the ball in *his* hands, where he wanted it, because he was the sentient that could get the job done. His team believed in him, counted on him. Yeah, he could *taste* the pressure.

He found it delicious.

Quentin stood tall behind center as his orange-jerseyed offensive line settled in. The cream-colored plants that made up Wabash Stadium's field had to be the toughest in the league — despite three-and-a-half quarters of war, the black-lined turf showed almost no damage.

That meant ideal footing.

Ideal footing meant Quentin could do what he did best.

The players, however, showed plenty of damage. Streaks of red, black and sticky-clear blood criss-crossed the gridiron — a giant, textured painting of pain and anger. The Krakens and the Wolfpack were leaving it all on the field.

He surveyed the defense. Red helmets decorated on either side with black-and-white trimmed, red, snarling wolf-head logos. Black facemasks. Black jerseys with red-trimmed, pearlescent, white numbers and letters. A white-trimmed, red wolf-head logo on the right shoulder, open jaws snapping shut just above the numbers on the chest. Pearlescent leg armor and shoes.

The Wolfpack used multiple defensive formations, keeping things unpredictable. This time they were in a 4-3 — four down linemen (three Ki and one HeavyG) and three linebackers (two Quyth Warriors and a Human).

Quentin had done a good job picking apart those linebackers, hitting Kobayasho, Tara the Freak, Becca and Yassoud on short routes. George Starcher stood on the sidelines. Another dropped pass, another missed block — this one resulting in a sack by Wolfpack defensive end Stephen Wardop. The hit had broken Quentin's right thumb, somewhere at the base. Messed up his wrist as well, but he hadn't told Doc Patah — a broken hand meant Quentin might fumble, which meant Hokor would put in Pine. Each snap from Bud-O-Shwek felt like the blow of some invisible, hammer-wielding strongman, but Quentin would dance with the Low One before he'd give up the glory of this game.

I-formation, double-wide, wing right, roll-out left, X-flag, Y-cross, Z-post, B-circle-in. Becca and Ju behind him — Becca to block, Ju running a short, 5-yard route. Hawick wide left, running a flag route — up and out to the sidelines. Tara the Freak at the right wing, running a crossing pattern. Halawa wide right, her post pattern would take her up and deep to the middle of the field.

He glanced at the right outside linebacker's feet: Ricky Craig was limping, tired, *had* to be tired because he'd lost focus, had his weight on his toes, a clear tell that he would blitz in at the snap of the ball. If Quentin timed it right, he could hit Tara on a cross when Tara ran into Ricky's vacated area.

Quentin smiled, tapped out a quick *ba-da-bap* on Bud-O-Shwek's behind. Ouch — that familiar mannerism hurt when your thumb and wrist were broken. Quentin slid his hands under center. He ignored the pain as he pressed the base of his right hand against his left.

"Red, fifteen!" He called out. "*Red, fifteen.*"

"Alternate, alternate!" screamed Ricky Craig. The Wolfpack defense suddenly shifted. Craig and middle linebacker Michael Cogan moved up, filling the gaps between the defensive linemen. The cornerbacks moved up as well, moved in tight for bump-and-run coverage on Halawa and Hawick. The safety and free safety closed in to about 5 yards off the line of scrimmage.

The third linebacker, Rand Owen, lined up a yard off of Tara the Freak. Owen would hit Tara right away, try to jam the receiver at the line.

An all-out blitz. If Quentin threw short, the cornerbacks and safeties were ready to jump the route. If Quentin waited for his receivers to outrun the close coverage, he'd be sacked for sure.

Tara looked back at Quentin. Quentin felt a flutter in his chest — he and his receiver both knew exactly what had to be done.

Time to audible.

Quentin stood. "*Green, green!*" Black-helmeted heads turned to look at him, to get instructions. The Wolfpack wanted to come and get him? Wanted to force him into a rookie mistake? Well, fine. If it was going to take a blood bath, best to get it over with.

"Forty-two blast!" he called first down the left side of the line, then again down the right. Linemen and receivers faced forward, waited for the snap.

Quentin turned to shout at Ju and Becca. "Forty-two blast!" He pointed at each of them, then at a linebacker. A fake gesture — the linebackers would be on Quentin so fast, there was nothing those teammates could do.

He again bent behind center, embracing the pain in his thumb, pain that would seem like nothing compared to the moment when Bud-O-Shwek slammed the ball into his hands.

Pressure. Glory.

Feet don't fail me now.

"Hut-*hut!*"

A shotgun-blast of agony ripped through his right hand and up his forearm, but his grip never faltered.

BLINK

Silence.

Quentin took one step back. The blitzing linebackers found seams in the line, came at him in that dreamy, not-real motion he saw in these moments. He had less than a second, had to throw *before* Tara was open, trust the Quyth Warrior receiver could do his job.

Tara came straight off the line, smashing into Rand Owen. Owen tried to bench-press Tara, hit the receiver in the chest and stop all forward momentum, but Tara's pedipalp arms were longer — he slapped the side of Owen's helmet, making the linebacker stumble to the left. Just a half-step, but that was all it took.

Bloody hands reached for Quentin, torn fingers locked on his ripped, black jersey. He threw off his back foot, a high, arcing pass to the open area 10 yards downfield from Tara.

Tara tucked and rolled, a blur of spinning motion that moved straight downfield under the arcing pass. Owen tried to turn and chase, but he was too slow. Tara popped out at the last second. His big pedipalp hands hauled in the throw.

BLINK

The raucous stadium slammed back into reality. Quentin back-pedaled, those bloody linebacker hands slipping off his jersey — if they hit him now, it would be a roughing-the-passer penalty.

He stopped, stood, watched.

Tara crossed the Wolfpack 40-yard line, heading straight downfield.

Sklorno defensive backs closed in.

Mississauga, the safety, shot straight in at Tara. Tara just tucked the ball deep in his arms and lowered his helmet. The hit — a devastating thing that sounded like a high-speed hovercab accident, a hit that would have leveled even Ju Tweedy — rocked both players.

Mississauga fell.

Tara spun off the hit and kept going.

Mars, the cornerback, closed in as Tara crossed the Wabash 30. Mars hit Tara from behind, a helmet-to-helmet shot. Tara's head bounced forward. He stumbled, but his powerful legs kept churning. Mars' tentacle-arms wrapped around Tara's shoulders. Still Tara kept running.

The 20.

Mars couldn't stop the powerful Warrior. Her raspers shot out, flicked, tightened, shredded fabric, cut chitin, drew blood.

Still Tara kept running.

The 10.

Mars lowered her tentacles, reaching for Tara's feet, his legs, but Tara high-stepped into the end zone.

Touchdown.

Ionath 27, Wabash 25.

Quentin ran off the field as the extra-point team ran on. The Krakens on the sidelines jumped and hopped — they were almost there, they had almost done it. Tara ran off the field and was mobbed by Human, HeavyG, Ki and Sklorno teammates.

The other Warriors stood together, watching, not joining in.

Same as always, unaccepting, hateful. Only ... this time, there was something different.

Virak the Mean, Choto the Bright, Killik the Unworthy, their eyes all swirled with hints of light red.

The color of appreciation, possibly even *respect*.

Arioch Morningstar kicked in the extra point. 28-25 Ionath, 1:07 to play. If the defense could stop the Wolfpack, it was over.

Virak and the other Warriors knew Ionath had won the game on an amazing effort by the player that they called *mutie*. Tara the Freak's touchdown had given Ionath a win over Wabash for the first time in fifteen years.

Quentin looked up to the stands, eyes taking in the sea of white-clad sentients. His gaze fell upon a luxury box between the first and second decks. He saw Gredok the Splithead, small but recognizable, standing next to Gloria Ogawa. Was Gredok ... *clapping?* He *was* clapping, he was jumping up and down.

Quentin laughed. So this is all it took to make Gredok show emotion? Why, it was almost nothing.

Quentin raised his broken right hand, managed to extend his index finger — he pointed at his team owner. The gesture said *this one is for you*. Maybe he and Gredok would never be friends, but now they understood each other. Together, they fought for the same goal.

The pain finally took over. Quentin bent at the waist, his right arm shrinking protectively to his chest. The Krakens' sidelines bounced with insanity. His team had gone mad. He couldn't blame them. Quentin could do no more. Strong hands guided him to a sideline medbay. He felt the bay's metal grate deck beneath his feet before he turned, sat, then laid back.

Quentin closed his eyes as Doc Patah went to work, knowing the sound of the crowd would tell him if the defense held, or if the Wolfpack found a way to win.

QUENTIN HAD NEVER SEEN a locker room so electric. He remembered the happy insanity after they'd defeated the Texas Earthlings two seasons ago to earn promotion to Tier One. And he could never forget the celebration last year, when they'd topped the Mars Planets to avoid relegation.

But nothing compared to this.

Jersey, helmet and shoulder pads off, right arm in a sling, Quentin stood against the wall at the room's edge. He wore only his cleats, leg armor and a sweaty, bloody PROPERTY OF KRAKENS T-shirt. He still held the game ball from Tara's winning touchdown catch. Coach gave it to Tara, but Tara had insisted Quentin take it.

Quentin soaked it all in, watched his teammates celebrate. His father stood next to him, watching as well. Cillian wore a black, button-down shirt decorated with the Krakens logo on the left breast. He'd combed his hair, even shaved. Quentin had to admit, the man looked good.

An all-access lanyard hung around Cillian's neck. He was staff now, would help Messal gather equipment and transport it to the *Touchback*. Cillian couldn't do a thing, however, until after the celebration stopped.

The central visitors locker room was packed with football players of all species in various stages of undress. Helmets, shoulder armor, dirty jerseys, bloody bandages, assorted tape and braces littered the floor. Sklorno jumped in place and screeched gibberish. The Quyth Warriors clacked out a rhythm by banging their middle arms against their chest plates. John and Ju stood on a bench, doing some kind of improvised choreographed dance to celebrate the win. Their exaggerated actions had the Humans and HeavyG players laughing hysterically, clutching stomachs, wiping eyes. Even the grim-faced Ibrahim Khomeni played along, his HeavyG face wrinkled in a rare smile. That could have been because of the Tweedys' performance, or because he'd notched three sacks on Wolfpack quarterback Rich Bennett.

The Tweedy brothers took turns singing a line, then letting the team respond. Even the Ki were there, barking and shouting in their native language, trying and failing to sing in time.

Cillian nodded in John's direction. "I know he's your best friend, but is he retarded?"

John wore only his waist armor and his left sock. His entire body flashed the words OH-VER, RAY-TED! OH-VER, RAY-TED!

"Wabash-trash, suck-o-tash!" Ju called.

"*Wabash-trash, suck-o-tash!*" the team responded.

"Over-rated, like a baked potated," John called.

"*Over-rated, like a baked potated,*" the team responded.

Quentin laughed and shook his head. "Yeah, probably. I love him anyway."

Cillian looked around the room, smiling, showing clear pride that he was somehow connected to all of this through his son. "This is really something, Quentin. I've never seen anything like it."

"It's not always like this, Dad. Sometimes we lose."

Cillian shrugged. "I don't know sports, but it seems to me a hundred losses would be a small price to pay to be a part of this feeling, with these guys."

Quentin nodded politely. Nothing was worth a hundred losses. Nothing was worth one loss, for that matter, but he understood what his father was trying to say.

"This is special," Cillian said. "My whole life, I never had anything like this. Is it like this on other teams?"

Quentin paused as John bent and jumped into the air, aiming for his brother's shoulders. John misjudged the ceiling height and hit his head on a light fixture, breaking it, sending out a wave of sparks, but Ju adjusted with that insane athleticism that only he possessed, moving so that his brother's thighs landed on his shoulders. John shook his head once to clear it, splattering blood from the fresh cuts, then smiled and started screaming.

"Undefeated and now de-cleated!"

"*Undefeated and now de-CLEATED!*"

Ju slipped. The Tweedy brothers fell face-first to the floor. The Sklorno misunderstood what was happening and dove on top of the brothers as if it were a touchdown celebration. Then Michael Kimberlin joined in - the singing degenerated into a huge pileup of laughing, shouting Krakens sentients acting more like children than grown adults.

"I don't know, Dad," Quentin said. "The Raiders weren't like this. I don't know if other Tier One teams are."

Cillian nodded. "Huh. Well, hopefully, you never have to find out that they aren't."

Quentin laughed as he watched more Krakens jump on the Tweedy pile. Hokor came in and started screaming for the players to *knock it the hell off* and to *stop playing grab-ass*. They largely ignored him. Someone, probably John, grabbed a large drink cooler and up-ended it over Hokor. The team screamed and laughed as the coach's fur clung to his skin, making him look thirty pounds lighter.

"Tweedy!" Hokor screamed. "That's one hundred laps!"

"Worth it!" John screamed back, then picked up the coach and set him on his shoulders. Hokor demanded to be put down. John ignored him and started running laps around the small locker room.

Quentin felt a tap on his shoulder. Cillian, quietly trying to get his attention.

"Yeah, Dad?"

Cillian pointed to the other side of the room. "Who is that?"

Quentin hadn't noticed before, but Crazy George Starcher was standing there, alone. Despite the energy, the action and the laughter, George looked isolated, almost as if a three-foot force field surrounded him, kept the others away.

"George Starcher," Quentin said. "Tight end."

"He didn't play much tonight, did he?"

Quentin shook his head. "No. He's in my dog house."

"Like Warburg is?"

"No, different. Warburg is an ass. George could be great, could be an All-Pro, but he's playing really bad."

Cillian stared, then snapped his fingers. "Wait, I recognize him now. I read an article on him a few years ago in Galaxy Sports Magazine."

"I thought you said you're not a sports fan."

"I'm not. I mean, I wasn't, but they were going to make a movie about him."

"A movie? About Starcher? What kind of movie?"

"He's been kicked off a bunch of teams, right?"

Quentin nodded. "Yeah. He seems to play well for the first season he's with a team, then things just go bad or something." Quentin remembered how fantastic George had been last year. He also remembered Don Pine's warning — *don't sign him, you'll regret it*. And, as usual, Pine was right — Quentin did regret it.

George, sitting there all alone, talking quietly to his towel. Then Quentin noticed two things. Tara the Freak was only a few feet from George. Standing alone, as Tara always did, but also *watching* George. What was that about? And George himself — Quentin looked back and forth between Cillian and the tight end.

"Hey, Dad. You look a little like George, you know that?"

Cillian shook his head. "Naw, not at all. Why isn't anyone talking to him?"

Quentin shrugged. "The guys can't stand him. He's all ... *weird*. They don't call him *Crazy George* for nothing."

"So he's mentally ill?"

Quentin started to speak, then stopped. He'd never thought of it in that light before. Was George *ill*? "I don't know, Dad. Maybe."

"Is he getting help?"

Another stunner of a question. No, George wasn't getting help. George was being *shunned*. No one wanted to deal with him. No one except Tara the Freak, it seemed.

"Quentin, maybe you should talk to him."

"I think George is having a nice conversation with his towel, Dad. I wouldn't want to interrupt."

"Son," Cillian said, his tone more firm, "I will not tell you what to do, but you need to listen to me on this. Someone needs to help that man. Think of all the happiness in this room and how none of it involves him. How would that make you feel?"

Quentin looked around. He recalled his days with the Raiders, when the team would celebrate their wins — celebrate with each other, but not with their orphan quarterback.

"Pretty bad," Quentin said. "I would feel pretty bad."

"And you're a smart, healthy kid," Cillian said. "If George has issues, things like this can make it far worse. Can you talk to him?"

Quentin watched George. The man had always seemed ... *eccentric*. But it wasn't eccentricity. It was something else, something dangerous.

"Okay, Dad," Quentin said. "I'll talk to him."

"Good. That's good. Now, you get yourself cleaned up. The stadium has a VIP area for players' spouses, celebrities and things like that. I took Somalia there after the game. She's waiting for you."

Somalia. In all the excitement, the celebration, Quentin had forgotten she'd come out to watch the game.

"Son, that girl is something else," Cillian said. "She's not as pretty as your mother was. But then again, you mother didn't have a spiked mohawk."

His father approved? "Dad, she's ... you know, she's ... "

Cillian smiled. "Not from the Purist Nation?"

"No, I mean—"

"I know what you mean, Quentin. I don't care what color her skin is, as long as she makes you happy. You should take her a present. Women love that kind of thing."

"I don't exactly have time to go shopping."

Cillian pointed to the game ball. "You could give her that."

Quentin looked at it. The brown leather, scratched and stained with flecks of blood. The shiny GFL logo embossed into the side. That would make a great present.

"Good idea, Dad. I'll do that."

Cillian slapped him on the shoulder. "Okay, it's time for me to earn my paycheck. I'm proud of you."

Cillian started picking up gear, jerseys and trash, hustling to move things to their proper bins. He was picking up what the players tossed away, yet he didn't show an ounce of shame.

Why should he? It was his job and it contributed to the team's success.

That was the kind of man you could be proud to call *father*.

Quentin felt eyes upon him. He looked up — Becca was staring at him. Staring with hurt eyes, *angry* eyes. She was close enough to have heard the whole conversation. She looked at the game ball, then at his face, then she shook her head with disgust. She turned and walked into the HeavyG locker room.

Was she mad he was giving a game ball to Somalia? Why?

Women. No figuring them, even the ones on your team.

Quentin walked to the Human locker room. He had to stop and let John rush past — a vociferously protesting and soaking wet Coach Hokor still on his shoulders — then headed for his locker to start cleaning up.

GFL WEEK NINE ROUNDUP
Courtesy of Galaxy Sports Network

HOME		AWAY	
Alimum Armada	20	**Coranadillana Cloud Killers**	24
Hittoni Hullwalkers	38	Texas Earthlings	10
Wabash Wolfpack	25	**Ionath Krakens**	28
Lu Juggernauts	12	**Isis Ice Storm**	17
Orbiting Death	7	**Yall Criminals**	38
Themala Dreadnaughts	17	Shorah Warlords	7
To Pirates	31	Bord Brigands	25
Jang Atom Smashers	3	**Bartel Water Bugs**	7
D'Kow War Dogs	13	**Neptune Scarlet Fliers**	16
New Rodina Astronauts	21	**Jupiter Jacks**	24
Sala Intrigue	6	**Vik Vanguard**	13

THERE ARE ONLY four games left in the 2684 season and the playoff picture is still very much up in the air, thanks to Ionath's 28-24 upset over the formerly undefeated Wabash Wolfpack (7-1). The Krakens (6-2) silenced the critics that said they hadn't defeated a quality team since Week One and also moved into a tie for third place in the Planet Division. Ionath quarterback Quentin Barnes started the game on fire, going 10-for-14 with 182 yards passing. His biggest pass of the day was an 82-yard touchdown strike to second-year receiver Halawa. This is also the second year in a row in which the Krakens beat the defending Galaxy Bowl champions.

The Wolfpack's loss allowed the To Pirates (7-1) to jump back into a first-place Planet Division tie. To's 31-25 win over the Bord Brigands (3-5) sets up a critical Week Ten match up as the Pirates head to Ionath.

Themala (5-3), Yall (6-2) and Isis (6-2) all won this week to remain in the Planet Division playoff hunt.

In the Solar Division, wins by Neptune (7-1) and Jupiter (7-1) moved those teams to within one victory of locking up playoff berths. Based on the records of the other Solar Division teams, eight wins will guarantee either team a postseason appearance.

Vik's surprising mid-season run continued as the Vanguard (5-3) notched a 13-6 win over the Sala Intrigue (1-7). With the score tied at 6-6 late in the fourth quarter, Vik linebacker Mur the Mighty picked off a Jason Harris pass and ran it in for the winning touchdown. At 5-3, Vik sits in third place in the Solar Division and controls its own destiny.

Deaths

No deaths reported this week.

Offensive Player of the Week

To quarterback **Frank Zimmer**, who completed 33 of 41 passes for 328 yards and three touchdowns in the Pirates' come-from-behind win over the Bord Brigands.

Defensive Player of the Week

Ionath Krakens defensive end **Ibrahim Khomeni**, who had three sacks and three solo tackles in Ionath's 28-24 win over the previously undefeated Wabash Wolfpack.

20

WEEK TEN:
TO PIRATES
at IONATH KRAKENS

PLANET DIVISION

7-1 Wabash Wolfpack

7-1 To Pirates

6-2 Ionath Krakens

6-2 Isis Ice Storm

6-2 Yall Criminals

5-3 Themala Dreadnaughts

3-5 Coranadillana Cloud Killers

3-5 OS1 Orbiting Death

2-6 Alimum Armada

2-6 Hittoni Hullwalkers

0-8 Lu Juggernauts

SOLAR DIVISION

7-1 Neptune Scarlet Fliers

7-1 Jupiter Jacks

5-3 Vik Vanguard

4-4 Bartel Water Bugs

3-5 Bord Brigands

3-5 D'Kow War Dogs

3-5 New Rodina Astronauts

3-5 Shorah Warlords

3-5 Texas Earthlings

2-6 Jang Atom Smashers

1-7 Sala Intrigue

THE GRAV-CAB SLOWED, then pulled to the side of Spoke Road 8. In the back, a one-eyed Quyth Worker's face flared to life on a small, static-speckled holotank mounted behind the driver's seat.

"That will be thirty credits," he said.

Choto the Bright leaned forward. "We are not there yet. You need to drive through the next ring-road."

"No," the driver said. "You need to *walk* through the next ring-road. This is as far as I go."

Quentin could understand why. Outside the cab's windows, he saw the signs of abject poverty, of crime, of danger. The place was much safer than Micovi, to be sure, but there was no denying this was in the bad part of Ionath City.

Choto pressed a pedipalp finger to the screen to pay. "Driver, you will stay here. We have a dinner scheduled with Gredok the Splithead. Do you know who Gredok the Splithead is?"

The Worker started to visibly shake. "Yes, I know who he is."

"Then you will wait for us," Choto said. "If you leave us here, Gredok would not be happy with you."

The Worker said something in the Quyth language. Quentin didn't know the words, but didn't have to to understand the meaning — the cabbie would wait in this very spot for a decade, if need be.

A tap on his shoulder. Choto the Bright, his eye swirling with a darker green — stress, anxiety.

"Quentin, are you sure you need to go here? Can't you make George Starcher come to your place?"

"I tried," Quentin said. "He won't answer any calls. At practice, he just won't talk. I have to see him here."

"Why? If he won't talk, he won't talk."

"I think he might be in trouble."

"Really? From who? Gredok will smash anyone that threatens his players."

"Not from someone else," Quentin said. "George might be trouble from himself."

Choto leaned back, his eye cleared. "I see. Well, if that is what George wants, then that is what George wants."

"He doesn't *want* it, Choto. I think he might not be able to help it."

"Ludicrous," Choto said. "In life, Quentin, you get what you want. If this is the life George Starcher leads, then that is how he wants it. Life is choice."

"Maybe he's not able to make the right choice."

"Then let him go," Choto said. "His job is to block and catch passes, yet he fails at both. We have no need for him. Certainly no need that merits placing you in danger. This part of town is for the detritus of our society, those that no one wants. Those that will not fight to make a better life for themselves. Tara the Freak lives around here. Need I say more?"

Quentin felt his temper rising. Was it Choto's personal belief that you didn't help those that needed it? Or maybe that was prevalent throughout Quyth culture. Probably the latter, considering how the rest of the team had treated Tara.

"Choto, I'm going to George's apartment. If you don't want to come with, then leave."

"And if you are hurt and I have to face Gredok's wrath? I would be better off being shot in the eye and dying here. I will go with you. But if you insist on going, I want you to take this."

Choto reached into his gray pants. He pulled out an object and offered it to Quentin.

Quentin stared at it in disbelief. "Is that a gun?"

"No, it's a piece of delicious candy packaged in a pistol shape. Yes, it is a gun."

"But those are illegal."

"As is organized crime, which would never happen in Ionath City."

Quentin looked up. "When did you become a sarcastic smart-ass?"

"This isn't sarcasm, it's annoyance," Choto said. "Now take it."

Quentin shook his head. "I don't want to hurt anyone."

"Look at what you are wearing. You look like a very rich sentient."

Quentin wore a perfectly tailored suit, a pearlescent white shirt and glossy shoes. His hands lifted to his head, feeling his perfectly done hair. He'd dressed up. His father would be at this dinner, as would Ju and John. A celebration of the long-awaited win over Gredok's archrival. All decked out, Quentin would look like a fat target for mugging despite his huge size.

"Quentin, this weapon is almost harmless," Choto said. "It is a deterrent, a scare factor. Since there are so few weapons under the Dome, just showing it will make most sentients back off. It is undetectable by most of the city's scanners. Even if you do get caught, you're a football player. The worst thing that can happen is they take it away. If you do have to use it, it is a very low-power, low-caliber weapon. It will make a lot of noise and cause pain, but mostly superficial."

"Mostly? You're telling me this gun can't kill?"

"Only if you press it right up against a sentient's brain case and pull the trigger."

Choto made it sound so easy, like there were no consequences to carrying the weapon. Quentin shook his head, then stepped out of the grav-cab.

The first thing he saw was a pack of three Quyth Warriors chasing a bleeding Human. The Warriors were carrying baseball bats. The Human ran down a narrow alley, out of sight. The Warriors followed.

Quentin leaned back into the cab and extended his hand. "Okay, give it to me."

Choto did. "It is nice to see you listen to reason for once," he said, then got out.

Quentin and Choto walked up Spoke Road 8 toward George Starcher's apartment.

"HIGH ONE," QUENTIN SAID. "This doesn't make any sense. He's *got* money."

Garbage littered the halls. Quentin had to step over two Quyth Workers who were passed out on the floor, an empty juniper sprig between them. They had eaten raw berries, so far gone in their addiction they couldn't wait for, or maybe couldn't afford, actual distilled gin.

The place smelled of urine, spoiled food and other indefinable-yet-awful smells. George Starcher, professional football player, lived in a flop-house.

Another Worker stumbled down the hall. He held a clear jar filled with hazy liquid. Choto instantly stepped between Quentin and the Worker, grabbed the smaller creature and shoved him to the floor. The Worker's drink spilled all over him. His eye flooded pink. He didn't get up.

Quentin felt bad for the Worker. He looked so pitiful.

"Choto, do you need to be so rough?"

"Yes," he said. "And do these conditions surprise you? Do you not have places like this on Micovi?"

"We do. I lived in one most of my life. We just don't have sentients like this."

Micovi had hungry children, starving adults, blood feuds and revenge killings, but drug use was rare. If you were caught abusing the body that High One gave you, it was often a capital offense. Homelessness and drug abuse were not among Micovi's many problems, mostly because people who suffered those conditions were taken away, never to be heard from again.

They turned a corner. There, standing in front of a door smeared with a caked, brown substance, stood Tara the Freak. The big, misshapen Warrior saw them — his eye instantly flooding black.

"Tara," Quentin said. "What are you doing here?"

Tara stared at Choto. Quentin looked between the two, wondering if this would erupt into another fight.

Choto broke the silence. "I have no quarrel with you, Tara."

Tara kept staring, but the black color gradually dissipated. Quentin relaxed a little. Maybe Tara and the other Warriors would never be buddies, but *I have no quarrel with you* was a huge improvement. Tara's play had earned him at least tolerance, if not acceptance.

Tara pointed to the brown-smeared door. "I am worried about George. I did not think he had anyone to help him."

Quentin nodded. So he wasn't the only one to sense George's odd behavior. Odd for George, anyway, and that was saying something. "Did you knock?"

Tara looked down at his middle right arm. He held it away from his body, as if it were diseased. The three-pincered hand showed smears of brown. "I did. He did not answer. I would like to find a place to wash."

"He didn't answer. Do you think he's in there?"

"He is," Tara said. "Now that you are here, I will leave."

"You don't have to," Quentin said. "Come with us to talk to George."

Tara looked at Quentin, then turned a bit to look at Choto. "You have help," Tara said. He walked down the hall, turned a corner and was gone.

"Choto, couldn't you have said something?"

"I did not insult him," Choto said. "Perhaps you should be grateful for that much."

Quentin and Choto moved to the door. The brown smears didn't quite obscure the door's number — 814.

"Messal said this is it," Quentin said. "What's that brown stuff on the door?"

"I do not know. And I am not going to ask. You can do the knocking."

"Thanks a lot," Quentin said. He looked for a clean spot, found one that was clean-*ish*, then knocked. "George? It's Quentin. You here?"

No answer.

Quentin kicked the door. "George, open up. Are you here?"

"George is not here," said a voice behind the door, a voice that sounded exactly like Crazy George Starcher.

"George, I came to talk to you."

"If the cosmic traveler known as George Starcher were here, he would not want to talk."

Quentin's jaw twitched with annoyance. He hadn't come to this crappy part of town to play games. "Starcher, Choto is with me. If you don't open this door, we're going to kick it in, then hold you down and rub your face in whatever this brown stuff is that's on it."

Quentin heard running footsteps, then the door opened.

"Come in," George said.

He wasn't wearing any face paint. His eyes looked tired, bloodshot and marked by dark circles. Quentin realized, suddenly and with instant shame that George usually looked just like this whenever he wasn't wearing face paint. Quentin had seen it, but hadn't *registered* it, had never thought to ask if George was okay. Quentin had been too busy — or too self-involved — to either notice or care.

George wore a long, tan, fuzzy tunic, the kind of thing they wore in the League of Planets. He wore pants of the same material. He was barefoot. Black smears streaked his face. He was holding a charcoal pencil, his fingers and hand darkened with dust.

"Starcher, you look like crap."

George shut the door, then stared with a haunted expression. "And you look quite fancy."

"Uh ... I have a dinner with Gredok and the Tweedys and my dad. To celebrate the win."

"I wasn't invited," George said. "Quentin, what do you want? I am very busy."

Quentin looked around the apartment. It was empty. Not a stick of furniture to be seen. Not even a holotank. There was only a woven mat lying on the floor, presumably where George slept. Next to it, a Krakens gym bag and a half-full orange sack, also decorated with the Krakens logo. Quentin recognized the orange sack as the kind Messal's people took away to do laundry. At least George was keeping somewhat clean.

The spotless floor gleamed with polish. The blank walls seemed dingy, though. Something about them looked strange, some kind of odd pattern.

"Yeah, George," Quentin said. "Looks like you have quite the to-do list this afternoon."

George stared, waited. It was almost like he was looking *through* Quentin, to some unseen point beyond. *Far* beyond.

"George, I'm worried about you," Quentin said. "You haven't been acting like yourself lately."

"I've been in Ionath a season and a half," George said. "I've seen you twice outside of the *Touchback* and the stadium. You've never invited me out with you and John, never had me over to your apartment or your yacht. How would you know what *myself* acts like?"

Quentin heard the words — his mind transposed them to standing in the lobby of an apartment building, wondering why Don Pine had never invited him to come visit. Quentin hadn't been avoiding Starcher, not at all, it had just never occurred to Quentin that they should hang out. Maybe Don's situation was the same. Maybe it wasn't any kind of malice or oversight — just a preference to be around the people you wanted to be around. And, maybe, that wasn't enough if you wanted to be a real leader.

"I'm sorry about that," Quentin said. "You're right. I wouldn't really know how you act. But I do know how you *play*. And you can't argue with me that your game has been way, *way* off."

George shrugged. "I played well last season. This season, not as well. It happens everywhere I go."

"But why? There's no reason you can't play like you did last year. So you dropped a couple of passes, so what?"

George looked down. He moved his left foot in a small circle, only his bare big toe touching the ground. "It happens wherever I go."

"Well, you need to stop it from happening, George. We're building a championship team. You have to play like a champion."

"Or what?"

Quentin shrugged. "Or you'll be gone, man. We work in an unforgiving business. That's why I'm here, to see if I can help. There's no room on the roster for someone who won't play hard and right now, you're *not* playing hard. If we can't figure out how to fix that, you'll be testing your two-year theory with another team."

George looked up. He wasn't staring through Quentin anymore, he was staring *at* him, staring with eyes that seemed lost, hopeless.

"There won't be a next team," he said. "I'm too old to start over. Who is going to sign an old tight end that can only play one good season?"

"There's about a hundred Tier Three teams that would snap you up in a heartbeat."

George shook his head. "I'll die before I go back to Tier Three."

"A wise choice," Choto said.

Quentin turned. "Choto! Just shut up, okay?"

Choto walked away to look at the apartment walls.

Quentin turned back to George. "Look, Starcher, you can sit here and feel sorry for yourself all damn day and it's not going to put points on the scoreboard. You're sad? You feel bad about this? Then *fix it*."

"I've tried. You have no idea how hard I've tried."

"Well *try harder*. Whatever this is, it's all in your head. You get your mind right, George, or we'll have to find another tight end. Choto, let's go."

Quentin walked toward the door. Choto looked at him, then pointed at something on the wall. Quentin walked up, saw what Choto was pointing at.

The pattern on the wall — it wasn't a pattern at all, it was words.

the chest of the nebula opens up to show the denizens beneath, the calling mouths of the headless minions that carry the spear. the hungry mouths, calling, beckoning to come with them, to dive into their toothy maws and be chewed, torn, ripped asunder and reassembled like the atoms of a collider — to be destroyed and dissipate, to be gathered again like the stuff of a star, to self-ignite and glow anew and burn the darkness itself, that is the old one's path to cyclic immortality, where death is never death, where life is never life. the void welcomes. the void caresses. the void loves.

Quentin leaned back, took in the entire wall. Covered with words. Crazy stuff, stuff that made face-paint and talking to towels look perfectly sane in comparison.

"Uh ... George? What's all this?"

"My tapestry," George said. "I am a conduit for the words of greatness, for the words of worthless worms."

"Fascinating," Choto said. "I believe I have seen and heard all that I am willing to see and hear. Quentin, you are scheduled for your dinner with Gredok. We need to leave. Now."

George was still standing in the same place, still staring at where Quentin had been standing moments before. Maybe Don Pine had been right after all — maybe George Starcher hadn't been worth the trouble.

"Okay," Quentin said. "Let's go. Starcher, I don't know what's going on in that head of yours, but let's get back on track. The team needs you."

"As do the Old Ones," he said. "Goodbye, Quentin."

"Whatever," Quentin said, then stepped over a newly fallen Worker bum and out into the hall. Choto followed, shutting the door behind him.

GREDOK THE SPLITHEAD STOOD on his chair. He raised a glass. The other sentients at the table remained seated. Gredok *had* to stand on his chair to be able to look down on those that would otherwise dwarf him — Quentin Barnes, Cillian Carbonaro, John and Ju Tweedy.

A special night: The team owner had taken them out for dinner at an empty Torba the Hungry's. Empty, because Gredok had that kind of money, that kind of pull. Or, maybe, Torba just owed him. No one here but the Krakens, their owner and the six dangerous sentients that stood in each corner of the main dining room. Four were Gredok's private guard — a Ki, a massive HeavyKi, a fully robed Sklorno female and Bobby Brobst, the Human that seemed to be Gredok's main bodyguard. All four wore expensive clothes. They stood there like polite, dangerous statues. The other two bodyguards? Choto the Bright and Virak the Mean. Quentin felt strange eating and drinking while his linebackers just stood there, once again guards and not football players, but that was not a battle to be fought at this time.

Candles flickered on the table and from the chandelier hanging overhead. The table groaned under the weight of so much food — beef, fish, something that might have been pork sausages, strange-but-tasty vegetables, bowls of spindly things that only Gredok and John ate and several bottles of wine in various stages of emptiness.

Cillian sat on Gredok's left, then Quentin, then Ju and finally John on Gredok's right. A good-sized table made small by platter after platter of food.

"A toast," Gredok said. Quentin, Cillian and Ju lifted their glasses. John raised his last, pausing long enough to grab a handful of spindly things and shove them into his mouth before he did.

"John," Gredok said, "you are truly an icon of your species."

John gave a thumbs-up and smiled wide, his open mouth chewing away on whatever those disgusting things might be.

Gredok raised his glass higher, addressed the entire table. "I find this Human tradition of a salutation marked by swallowing a beverage a suitable way to convey my satisfaction. For fifteen years, Gloria Ogawa has laughed at me. Content with her little fiefdom on Fortress, she mocked me, she mocked the Krakens. But no more. We are six-and-two. We have beaten the undefeated defending champions and I — *finally* — had the satisfaction of seeing Gloria Ogawa burn with anger and embarrassment. I toast to my team."

Gredok drank. The others followed suit.

John pointed at a crust of bread on Gredok's plate. "Hey, you gonna eat that?"

Gredok stared at him, then sighed. "No, John, I'm not going to eat the food that is sitting on my plate. Please, help yourself."

"Kick ass," John said, grabbing the bread and popping it into his mouth.

Gredok clapped his pedipalps. His eye tinged black. A red-jacketed Quyth Leader ran into the room.

"Yes, *Shamakath*?"

"Torba, you clearly have not brought enough food. My linebacker is hungry. Perhaps you should do your job."

"Yes, *Shamakath*! One billion apologies!" Yorba ran for the kitchen. "Food! We need food!"

Seconds later, the kitchen door opened and two white-uniformed waiters rushed out, one a bearded Human man, the other a Quyth Worker. They each carried two heaping plates. Finding a place on the packed table was difficult, but they managed to arrange the four steaming dishes close to John.

John smiled and rubbed his hands together. IN THE MOOD FOR FOOD scrolled across his face.

Ju tossed a roll that bounced off of John's face.

"You got no manners," Ju said. "Ma would so yell at you."

"No, *you* got no manners," John said.

"Oh yeah? Well, you have a *negative* amount of manners."

"Oh yeah?" John leaned forward. "Well, *you* have—"

"Guys," Quentin said. "Can I make a toast?"

John and Ju looked at him, then relaxed. Quentin wasn't about to let the Tweedy brothers' stupidity ruin such an amazing dinner.

Quentin started to stand, then checked himself — if he stood, he'd be three feet taller than Gredok and Gredok was the boss. This was about respect where respect was due. Quentin remained seated. He lifted his glass.

"I would like to give a toast to our team owner."

Cillian and Ju raised their glasses. John reached for the spindly things again, but Ju slapped his hand. John glared at his brother, then leaned back and raised his glass as well.

"This is just the beginning," Quentin said. "Beating the Wolfpack showed the galaxy that we are for real. We have a great squad and we owe that to our owner. Sir, you have done whatever it took to field a championship-caliber team. For that, I say I am happy to be part of it. And personally, you have done more for me than I can say. I look forward to a decade of greatness."

Quentin lifted his glass higher, then drank. He didn't like wine, but on this night, it tasted just fine. The others drank as well.

Cillian set his glass down and leaned back. "Wow, Gredok, thank you for this."

"A trivial gesture," Gredok said. "Your offspring's performance was of such a high caliber I only wish I had more of his family with which to celebrate."

"I've got you covered on that one, Gredok."

All heads turned to see the Human waiter. He stood there with a Human woman who also wore a waiter uniform. There was something familiar about his voice and her face, although Quentin knew he'd never seen her before.

"Gonzaga," Gredok said, his voice dripping with hate. As soon as Quentin heard the word, Fred's face seemed to magically appear behind the beard. Quentin had looked right at the bearded waiter, never suspected for a second it was his private investigator. Damn, this guy was *good*.

Quentin wasn't the only one who reacted to Gredok's tone of voice. In the corners of the room, four hands slid inside of suit jackets, baggy sleeves or full-body robes.

The room seemed to turn cold, a lethal tension that drowned out the flickering candles' warmth.

Fred's eyes glanced to the dangers, then back to the black-furred Quyth Leader. "You recognize me, Gredok? You've got a good eye."

"It's the *smell*, actually," Gredok said. "Pungent and offensive, as always."

"I would have bathed for the occasion, but I was in a bit of a hurry."

"Perhaps because you were late from visiting your psychiatrist," Gredok said. "For only mental deficiency could explain why you would *dare* to show your face in front of me *anywhere*, let alone at a private function to which you were not invited."

Fred smiled. "But Gredok, you invited *family*." He looked at Quentin, then at Cillian. "See? Isn't that the father you found for Quentin?"

Quentin noticed that Cillian was stirring in his seat, acting nervous.

"Dad, it's okay. Fred won't hurt us. He's just got some business with Gredok. Let them work it out."

"Wrong," Fred said. "This business involves all of us. *Cillian* included."

"Gonzaga." Gredok spoke in a tone so low it was barely audible. Sentients held their breath to listen. Everyone seemed afraid to move. "You may turn around, right now, and leave with your life. Say one more word, to me or to anyone in my organization — *ever* — and that life is forfeit."

Fred stared. Quentin saw him swallow, saw his jaw muscles twitching. Fred was afraid.

Quentin looked at the woman. She was quite beautiful, in a working-class way. She stared at Cillian. *Glared* was more like it.

Fred shook his head, slowly, as if he were arguing with himself, trying to find the courage to continue. But if he did continue, whatever he said could cause his death — Gredok did not make idle threats. Quentin didn't know what could bring Fred out here to cause such a ruckus, but Fred's history with Gredok appeared to have caught up with them both.

"Fred," Quentin said quietly. "Look, why don't you just go, okay? Whatever it is, I'll try and help."

"Barnes," Gredok said, "stay out of this."

Fred looked at Quentin. Fear in those eyes, but the fear seemed to fade, replaced by determination.

"Quentin," Fred said, then gestured to the uniformed woman on his left. "I want you to meet your sister."

The room seemed to vanish. All was blackness, nothingness, all except for her. Her face. Memories flared, memories triggered by that same face, but from when it was younger, full of smiles, looking down at him. Memories of a splinter in his hand, of her gently holding his wrist, pulling out the splinter, then softly kissing the wounded spot.

The fleeting, partial memories of his mother — those weren't of his mother at all, they were of his older sister.

His sister. Standing right there.

New memories flared up, memories of a much younger version of that woman — of his *sister* — angry, screaming, her cheeks streaked with tears, yelling at someone else, Quentin's mother, although he couldn't remember his mother's face.

Family. Real family. "Jeanine?"

She turned to look at him. Her hard eyes softened, just a bit. She nodded. "Yes, Quentin. I am your sister."

Then she turned to face Cillian. She pointed at him. "And that man is *not* our father."

Quentin's needs split down the middle — half of him couldn't look away from Jeanine, half of him had to turn and stare at Cillian. And when he did, everything fell into place.

She was his sister. No question. He *remembered* her. He did *not* have memories of this man, not a single one and that should have told him something. There could be no second-guessing Jeanine — she was right.

And somewhere, deep inside, Quentin had known all along.

Gredok had played him. Quentin had thought himself good at the manipulation game? Good at seeing the true emotions of others? He saw nothing. Gredok had been setting this up since last season. Quentin never saw it coming.

Now, Quentin's full attention focused on Cillian Carbonaro.

Rage had always been Quentin's tool, the source of his on-field power, the driving force behind his relentless work ethic. Then, he'd learned to control it, to channel it, to push it down for the good of the team. He'd learned that he couldn't solve all of his problems with his fists.

Not all of them.

But for *this* problem?

And that man is not our father.

Yeah, fists would work just fine.

BLINK

He reached past Cillian, toward Gredok, grabbed the edge of the table and ripped it backward, sent it sailing through the air. Food flew, drink splashed, candles spun and snuffed out in mid-air.

Quentin stepped toward Gredok the Splithead. Cillian stood and put his hand on Quentin's chest. The older man's head shook in slow motion, his lips started to form the word *don't*, but they didn't finish because Quentin head-butted Cillian right in that hateful, lie-spewing mouth.

The older man sagged. Quentin again reached for the Quyth Leader, but Gredok was already scrambling away and a well-dressed HeavyKi was rushing forward, club in hand. The HeavyKi swung — so pitifully slow — but Quentin side-stepped, grabbed Gredok's chair. The club hissed through empty air. Quentin lifted the chair, twisted and brought it around in a fast, wide arc, smashing it into the HeavyKi's vocal tubes. The 750-pound thug let out a low-toned squeal of pain, black blood already streaming from its head, its front-right and right-side eyelids shut tight against splinters that jutted forth from the torn eyes beneath. Four arms spread wide, too wide to dodge — it rushed forward.

Ju Tweedy blind-sided it, his oversized Human shoulder smashing into the HeavyKi's head. Both sentients fell to the ground, fists flying.

Quentin had only one thought: *Kill Gredok.*

The black-furred Quyth Leader ran for the exit. Quentin hurdled Ju and the HeavyKi. He saw the Sklorno bodyguard drawing a gun, a gun that looked like the one he still had in his pocket, draw it and point it at Quentin.

Two bodies flew through the air — Bobby Brobst, the Human bodyguard, bent over at the waist because he had John Tweedy's shoulder in his stomach, John's arms wrapped around Bobby's back, John's big legs driving forward. John screamed a scream of joy, then drove the Human right into the Sklorno, the three of them crashing into the wall hard enough to splinter wood and crack plastic.

Hate. Kill. Hurt. Kill.

Quentin ran for the door. Virak the Mean appeared in front of him, blocking the way.

Virak held up two pedipalp hands — *just stop, don't do this* — but Quentin didn't slow. He stepped forward and threw a big overhand left. Everything else, the fist included, seemed to be moving in slow motion, but not Virak. The big Warrior stepped inside the punch, drove both of his lower fists into Quentin's stomach. The air shot out of Quentin's lungs. He dropped to one knee, tried to get up, but before he could, a shelled fist *cracked* into his right ear.

BLINK

Quentin fell face-first into a broken plate, bits of shredded meat smearing on his skin.

"Stay down," Virak said. "If you get up, I won't hold back."

Quentin grabbed the broken plate and threw it in one quick motion. He saw Virak's armored eyelid close just before the plate smashed against his face, driving the linebacker back a step.

Virak opened his eye, then reached into his gray pants — he pulled out a foot-long knife. "You side with that genetic reject, then turn against my *Shamakath*? I'll *make* you stay down."

A shadow passed by Quentin's head.

Choto the Bright, diving over him.

Virak seemed surprised, as if he didn't know how to process an attack by his teammate and fellow bodyguard. Choto slammed into Virak, driving him backward. The two big sentients crashed through a table.

Quentin stood, looked around. The restaurant vibrated with fists and knees and grunts of pain and John Tweedy screaming *wooo-woo! It's the Pain Train!* over and over again. Ju and John were on top of the bodyguards, beating them senseless.

Gredok was gone.

Quentin shook his head, tried to clear his mind. He had to stop this. He looked for Fred and Jeanine, but he couldn't spot them.

His sister was gone.

He could find her, figure out what to do next, but first he had to stop all this fighting.

Then Quentin saw *him*.

Cillian Carbonaro. Entering the kitchen doors, making a run for it.

And that man is not our father.

Quentin covered the fifteen feet in a second and a half. Cillian pushed through the kitchen doors, which swung back as Quentin hit them, his mass smashing them open, tearing them from their hinges. Quentin put a shoulder into his "father's" back, driving the man face-first into the hard kitchen floor.

They skidded, leaving a streak of red blood to mark their path.

Cillian flipped over, hurt but struggling.

Quentin straddled him.

Cillian stopped moving, his body suddenly rigid like a frozen corpse.

Quentin blinked once, twice, three times. He was holding a small gun, pressing the barrel hard into Cillian's squeezed-shut right eye.

Only if you press it right up against a sentient's brain case and pull the trigger.

The trigger. Quentin felt springs resisting his finger's pull. Resisting it, yet *welcoming* it, the strong handshake of a lifelong friend.

"Please," Cillian said. "Don't kill me."

Quentin partially heard the words. They sounded distant, faint, drowned out by a roar that played endlessly, a monotone that told him to *do it do it kill him kill him.*

He squeezed the trigger a little tighter. He could *feel* the mechanism inside, sense it was at the final release point when something would give, when springs would slam a hammer against a primer, when an explosion would drive a bullet through Cillian's eye and into his brain.

A tap on his shoulder.

Quentin jumped, waited for the gun to go off, but it did not. He looked up to his right. John Tweedy stood there, gnawing on a steak bone.

"Hey, Q," he said. "You gonna kill that shucker?"

Quentin blinked. The roar faded away. He looked down at Cillian, who remained stiff, trembling on the floor.

"I don't know," Quentin said.

John chewed. "Do you want me to kill him?"

Quentin again looked up at his friend. John used his back teeth to scrape a scrap of meat off the bone. It was like they'd never left the dinner table. Fun-and-games John Tweedy had another side entirely, a side that could do bad things — like *kill* — without thinking twice.

"No," Quentin said. "I don't want you to kill him."

John shrugged. "I'll kill him for you, I don't mind. He's got it coming, Q. He deserves it."

Quentin shook his head. "No. He deserves something, but not that."

John nodded, held out his left hand. "Well, then give me the gun. If you're going to whack this guy — I'd whack him if I were you — he deserves it by beating, not quick with a bullet."

Quentin looked at John's empty palm. Streaked with blood both red and black. A tiny shard of glass plate was sticking out of the base of his thumb. John could kill so easily. Was that what Quentin could become?

No. Killing was a sin.

He handed John the gun.

"Thanks," John said. "I'll be right outside. Whatever you do, Ju and I will take care of you."

John walked out, leaving Quentin alone with the man he'd thought was his father.

Quentin stood up. He slid aside some food-filled bowls, then sat on a metal counter.

The rage vanished, pushed away by something worse.

Pain. Heartbreak.

Quentin coughed. A thin breath snaked into his lungs. "How could you do this to me?"

Still shaking, Cillian raised up on one elbow. Blood dripped from his mouth to pool on the tile floor. He was missing his front-right tooth. Quentin saw the like-father-like-son irony but didn't appreciate it.

"Can I sit up?"

Quentin nodded. It seemed oddly difficult to do even that — his head felt heavy, every muscle exhausted beyond the point of failure.

Cillian slowly pushed himself to his butt, his feet in front of him, shoes resting in a puddle of his own blood. The man hurt physically, of that there was no question considering the beating Quentin had laid down, but there was a deeper pain.

A pain of the soul.

"It was just a job," he said through split lips. "I'm an actor. Gredok offered me all this money. I got to pretend to be your dad. It was supposed to make you happy."

"Do I *look* happy?"

The man winced, flinched away. Quentin realized that he'd come off the metal counter and was standing over the beaten man, screaming the words, bloody fists clenched into weapons.

He forced his hands to open.

"What's your name?"

"Rick," the man said. "Rick Vinje. People call me Sarge."

The man's name was Sarge. Somehow, that made it even worse. A normal man with a normal nickname. A man with a real past, a real life — a life that had never involved Quentin.

Once again, Quentin Barnes was an orphan.

He'd *always* been an orphan.

Quentin could barely stand. So weak. He again sat on the metal counter.

"I believed you," he said. It hurt to speak. It hurt to *breathe*. How could it hurt to breath? "I believed that you were ... my *father*. What kind of a demon are you?"

"I'm sorry," the man said. "I didn't know it would turn out like this. I didn't think ... " he lifted a hand to his face and wiped away a tear, leaving a streak of thinned-out blood on his cheek. "I guess I just didn't think."

"Tears," Quentin said. "I saw you cry when you talked about my mother. But that was just acting. Can you call up tears whenever you want?"

The man nodded. "Yeah. I always could. That's how I got into acting, actually, 'cause someone saw me fake-crying. They said it was a rare gift."

"A blessing from the High One, right?"

The man nodded again. "Yeah. But these are real."

"Go shuck yourself."

"Look, I don't want you to hurt me anymore, but I don't want to hurt you either. I was already having second thoughts about all of this."

"Easy for you to say now, isn't it?"

"I was," he said.

"Why?"

Sarge looked away. "You're a good man, Quentin. That's why. You're better than all of the people around you. You're better than me. I don't have a kid. If I did, I'd want him to be just like you."

Quentin leaned forward, just a little, just enough so that Sarge's eyes shot back up to see what was coming next.

"If I were you," Quentin said, "I'd never use that phrase again."

Sarge nodded. "Okay, okay."

Quentin leaned back. "So tell me how it went down. Tell me *why*."

"I'm an actor," he said. "Years ago, I was supposed to make a movie about George Starcher's life, but it fell through. I would have gotten the part because I look a little like him and I'm big."

"You're a foot shorter than he is."

Sarge nodded. "Sure, but with movie magic, I'd look big enough. The movie never got made. Gredok found some footage or something. I knew football. I really am from the Purist Nation. I left there when I was sixteen, so I knew your background. I was perfect to play the part of your dad."

The man paused, seemed to expect another punch. Quentin stayed still, waited for more.

"My job was to make you believe," he said. "Once that was done, I was supposed to remind you how much you liked playing in Ionath, that being happy was more important than a big paycheck."

And how the actor had played that part. Quentin thought back to their conversations, how things usually came around to how much Quentin liked Ionath, how much he loved his teammates, his friends, the life he had built here. Of how blessed he was to play football for a living, to have escaped Micovi and the Nation. The actor had been manipulating him all along.

"Well, *Sarge*, do you have any idea how much money I lost because of you?"

Vinje shrugged. "You lost more than I'll ever know in my life and you're making far more than that."

"Oh, please," Quentin said. "I think daddy's life lessons are over."

The man's bloody lip sneered. "Poor little rich boy."

Quentin's hands again balled up into fists. It was all he could do to stop from killing this man. And yet, Vinje wasn't afraid. He wasn't begging for his life. Vinje couldn't do a thing to defend himself against Quentin, but he wasn't going to cower, wasn't going to whimper.

That much, at least, Quentin could respect.

"Your life is so hard," the man said. "Your yacht, your rock-star girlfriend, your—"

"Shut up."

"—huge contract, your friends that would do anything for you—"

"I said shut up!"

"—millions of adoring fans, that wide-eyed fullback girl who is dying for your every word, your—"

Quentin came off the bench and swung, a shoulder-twisting, hip-turning straight left that smashed into the actor's nose. The fist hit so hard that blood splattered, sprayed across the floor.

Vinje sagged.

Quentin stood, stared. Waited.

Was the man breathing?

Oh High One, what have I done?

Then the man coughed, drew in a wet breath. He moaned, half-in, half-out.

Quentin turned to the door. "John?"

John rushed in, skidded to a halt. "Yeah?"

"Get a doctor," Quentin said. "Or an ambulance. Or whatever. I don't care. Just don't let this guy die."

"On it." John shot out of the kitchen as quickly as he'd come.

Vinje reached up a weak hand. "Help ... me up."

Quentin gently reached under the actor's shoulders, lifted him, set him on the metal counter. Sure, the actor was a big Human, but beaten and weak like this it brought home the discrepancy in size. Quentin had used all of his strength on another sentient, a sentient who was not an athlete, a Human who was pushing fifty years old. No matter what this evil man had done, he didn't deserve to be beaten to death.

"You ... can really punch. I don't feel so good."

"John's finding you help. I'll get you to a hospital, then I never want to see you again, you understand? If I see you again ... I'm not sure I'll be able to control myself."

"This is you under control?"

Quentin shrugged. "Yeah. Pretty much."

Vinje gently touched his ruined nose. "I wonder if they can fix it. How bad does it look?"

The man's nose was slanted to the left and already swelling at the bridge. Even Doc Patah would have a tough time repairing that.

"It's okay," Quentin said.

"I lied about something else," Vinje said.

"What a surprise."

"I am a sports fan. I know this is really messed up, what I did to you and all, but I was a fan before I was your dad."

"*Pretended* to be my dad."

"Right, pretended," Vinje said. "Well, you're fantastic. It's great to watch you play. And getting to hang out with you was a real bonus."

"If you ask me for my autograph, I'll stomp on your throat and watch you die. Just sit there and shut up."

Vinje nodded. He fell silent other than coughing every few seconds, splatting droplets of blood onto the floor.

Together, they waited for the ambulance.

• • •

THE ELEVATOR STOPPED. Quentin stepped out into the musty hallway. Sagging smart-paper — paper that had long ago lost its ability to flash images — hung on the walls. Bits of trash lined the hallway's stained carpet.

Quentin walked toward Suite 1510. From twenty feet way, he could see that the reinforced metal door was open.

Fred usually kept that door shut. Shut and locked.

Quentin walked into the office, his eyes glancing over the symbols on the door that spelled out GONZAGA INVESTIGATIONS in fifteen languages. Inside the long, thin office, Quentin found something he didn't expect.

Choto the Bright.

Alone, sitting on the edge of a white desk, his right pedipalp arm in a sling.

There was no one else.

"Quentin," Choto said. "I have been looking everywhere for you. I thought you might come here."

Quentin looked up to the piñata, still hanging from the ceiling, then back to Choto. "What did you shuckers do with Fred?"

Choto's baseball-sized eye swirled with green. "Nothing. I did nothing and I don't think Gredok knows where Frederico went. The office was empty and open. Frederico is nowhere to be found. Neither is your sister."

"Right. And I'm supposed to believe that?"

More green, a deeper shade. "I promise you, I had nothing to do with any of this. I didn't know."

Quentin shook his head. "Save it. You work for Gredok. I know where your loyalty is."

Choto stared at the floor. "I don't work for him anymore. I ... I have been ... "

"Fired?"

The Quyth Warrior looked up. "That is not the exact word for what happened. I have been kicked out, Quentin. Because I fought Virak at that dinner. Because I fought Virak to stop him from hurting you."

Quentin glanced at the sling. Choto had been injured fighting

Virak? Could it be true that Gredok had fired Choto, or was this just another trick?

"I don't care," Quentin said. "Outside of the practice field, the locker room and during games, I don't want to see you."

"But I must protect you!"

"No. You and I are done."

A swirl of colors: blue, pink, black. "Quentin, please ... I fought for you. I did not think about it at the time. My life has become all about protecting you and now ... now I have nothing. I am Ronin."

That word again. The same one Tara had used.

"Ronin. What does that mean?"

"It is a rough translation," Choto said. "It means I have no leader. I have no master. In our culture ... it means I have nothing. I *am* nothing."

Choto started to shake. Big, bad, mean Choto the Bright, gangland bodyguard, GFL linebacker — he was so afraid, he *shook*. Maybe Gredok could hide his emotions to manipulate Quentin, but Choto was not Gredok. This was genuine.

Quentin walked closer. "So, what do you do now?"

Choto again looked at the floor. "I do not know. I will finish the season, fulfill my obligation to the team. And then ... I will try to find a new leader. Or I will end my time."

"Why don't you just not have a leader at all? Be your own sentient?"

Choto's good pedipalp quivered, then he winced. With the damaged one, it hurt to laugh. "That is not the Warrior way. I am not capable of that."

"Tara is capable of it."

Choto stared, then his eye swirled purple — sadness, pained confusion. "I am not Tara."

Had Tara carried such a burden all this time? Tara the Freak. Outcast. *Ronin.* The sentient was far stronger than Quentin had thought. Stronger than Choto. The entire Quyth life cycle hinged on structure, on authority. A Warrior *had* to have someone to follow.

And then Quentin put the pieces together. "Choto, are you saying that you want me to be your leader?"

Swirls of yellow — excitement, nervousness — and pink. That was exactly what Choto wanted. The thought of it thrilled him, gave him hope. It also terrified him — if Quentin said no, Choto would have nothing.

"During the fight at Torba's, I just reacted," Choto said. "I did not think things through, but I knew what would happen. I knew the choice I was making. I chose you, Quentin. If you will have me, I will serve you faithfully. I will serve my *Shamakath*."

Had they had spent so much time together that Choto had imprinted upon Quentin? If Quentin cast him away, what would happen to him? And if Choto hadn't stepped in, could Quentin have beaten Virak? Vinje would have just escaped. Quentin might never have gotten answers.

He could not abandon Choto, not now.

And hell, he already had millions of sentients worshiping him, what was one more?

"Okay," Quentin said. "I'm ... uh ... I'm your Shamakath, or whatever. Is there some kind of a ceremony or something?"

Choto's eye flooded a light orange. *Total happiness.* "No, it is not like that. With your words, it is done. I am yours to command, *Shamakath*."

"Okay, first thing, don't call me that. Ever. I am Quentin, do you understand?"

Choto nodded, a humanesque gesture that required the Warriors to move their whole upper body.

"Good," Quentin said. "And second, you tell no one of this. You don't get to share the info. As far as the world knows, you are Ronin."

"But, why? Being Ronin is a mark of shame."

"Because you need to know what you're getting into here. I'm not going to threaten you, or tell you I'll kill you if you don't obey or any of that crap. I wouldn't do that. But you have to know, Choto, that I am going after Gredok the Splithead. Not this season and I don't know when, but I *will* get revenge for what he did to me. If you're following me, then you're going to wind up going head-to-head with Gredok, probably head-to-head with your buddy Virak. I don't want them to know I'm your leader. Do you understand?"

This time, Choto's eye swirled with inky black. Anger. Rage. Not at Quentin, but at Gredok and Virak.

"I understand," Choto said. "And I was hoping, very much, that was what you wanted."

Maybe this was a mistake, but Quentin didn't know what else to do. If Choto was for real, he would be a valuable ally in the fight to come.

"Shama ... Quentin," Choto said. "It is almost time for practice. Shall we walk to the stadium?"

Quentin shrugged. "I don't know. I'm not sure I'll play for that betrayer."

Choto's pedipalps twitched and he winced again. "Please, stop joking," he said. "It hurts when I laugh."

"What are you laughing at?"

Another twitch, another wince. "The thought of you *not* playing against the To Pirates? As if you were even capable of that. You are very funny, Quentin."

Quentin's anger flared up, then it faded away. Choto was right. No matter what Gredok had done, Quentin Barnes wanted the ball. Needed it. He could stop playing no more than he could will his own heart to stop beating. He had to get his head back into the game.

"That's me," Quentin said. "A regular comedian. Let's get to practice."

QUENTIN LIMPED into the training room.

A hovering Doc Patah spun in place, saw the Human and paused.

Quentin had waited until late after practice, until everyone had been patched up, showered, dressed and headed back to their apartments. Patah had lied about Cillian being Quentin's genetic father. Quentin had trusted Doc Patah without question — a fact that Gredok had known, yet another element the crime lord had used to manipulate.

After the fight at Torba's, Quentin had avoided Doc Patah. This was the first time they'd seen each other since the dinner.

Quentin still didn't know much about Harrah emotions, but he knew fear when he saw it — and Doc Patah was afraid. Damn well he should be. The floating creature's sensory pits widened and his mouth-flaps changed from light gray to a darker shade.

"Young Quentin," Doc Patah said. "I know that you must be furious with me, but I—"

"Shove it," Quentin said through clenched teeth. "Doc, it's taking every bit of control I have not to rip you in half. I'm going to ask questions, you're going to answer. Understand?"

Doc's wide wings undulated slowly, keeping him in place. "Yes. I understand."

Quentin stripped off his gear, limped to the rejuve tank. He slid in. This time, the pink fluid's penetrating warmth did little to elevate his mood. Hate pumped through his veins — he didn't want it to go away. That's what he was now, a creature of anger, a creature of fury.

Doc paused, as if he wasn't sure what to do.

Quentin pointed to his knee. "Fix this."

Doc fluttered over, his mouth-flaps pressing and pulling at the joint. He swung in a clamshell clamp and started affixing it to the knee. He was close enough that if Quentin reached out and grabbed him, Doc wouldn't have time to react. They both knew it.

The knee, a silly injury. Quentin hadn't been paying attention in practice. Hard to do that, hard to think about anything but the way Gredok had screwed him, about the sister that was still out there, somewhere. Quentin couldn't concentrate. Couldn't execute. He'd even forgotten about his red no-touch jersey, how the defenders wouldn't hit him. Instead of running a boot play in practice and just slowing down when the defense approached, he'd accelerated, gone head-to-head with Virak the Mean.

Virak hadn't slowed either.

It was practice, but if the quarterback initiated contact, a defender wasn't just going to get run over. Virak had responded to the challenge by diving at Quentin's legs, undercutting him, putting a helmet into Quentin's knee.

If Quentin played like this against the To Pirates? If he couldn't get his head back in the game? The Krakens were in a lot of trouble.

Quentin talked as Doc worked. "You're going to tell me why, Doc. Tell me why you lied to me, told me that shucker was my *father*."

Doc's mouth-flaps seemed to move automatically, doing the work they'd done hundreds of times before. "Gredok gave me no choice," he said. "He has information on me, Quentin. If he exercises that information, my life is over."

Blackmail. Threats. Violence. Death. These were the tools of Gredok. "And if you'd refused to lie for him?"

"I imagine I would already be dead," Doc Patah said. "And in a way that is too horrible to describe. It involves something called a *flaying hook*."

The clamp clicked home, bringing with it the brief sting of needles penetrating the joint just before it shut off Quentin's nerves. Thirty minutes, then the knee would be as good as new.

"Doc, would you like to be free of Gredok's control?"

"Quentin, just because I wronged you doesn't mean I want to listen to stupid questions. Do you think I'd let him control me if I had any choice?"

Doc Patah, the sentient that dared not enter Coranadillana, the sentient that dared not cross Gredok. Secrets. Quentin hated secrets.

"Someday I'm going to come to you and ask you for a favor," Quentin said. "Whatever it is, you're going to do it. You won't ask questions, you won't second-guess me, you'll just *do it*."

"Would this favor involve my debt to Gredok?"

"Funny," Quentin said, "that sounds like a question and I haven't even asked you for the favor yet."

Doc pressed a few buttons on the clamp, then flew over to his monitor alcove. "Point taken," he said as he looked at the holos showing the inside of Quentin's knee. "I wronged you, Quentin and you have never wronged me. Therefore, I will do what you ask."

Quentin nodded. He laid his head back on the tank's edge. "Good. Then I don't have to kill you. Now get out of my sight until this thing is done cooking my knee."

Doc Patah fluttered to the training room door, then paused, turned. "Is there anything else I can possibly do to earn back your trust? To make this up to you?"

"Sure," Quentin said. "Do you have twenty-five million credits?"

Doc Patah's mouth-flaps darkened again. "Of course I do not have that kind of money."

Quentin looked up, shrugged. "Well, find it. That's what I lost because of you. You owe Gredok? Too bad, Doc, because now you owe me, too. And when he's gone, I'll still be right here, waiting for my money."

He closed his eyes, again rested his head on the tank's edge. He waited until he heard Patah flutter away, then let sleep take him.

QUENTIN DROPPED BACK, eyes flicking through his receivers. Everything seemed so fast. Sometimes the game slowed down and he sped up, but today it felt like *he* was the one in slow motion.

His black-clad offensive line battled against the brutality of the To Pirates' five-man defensive front. The Pirates — black shoes, blood-red leg armor with white-trimmed black Ki skulls on the thighs. White jerseys with black-lined red numbers down near the waist to make room for the black-fanged, red Ki skull-and-crossbones logo that spread across the chest. Blood-red helmets with that simple, white-lined black stripe down the middle.

Tara the Freak, cutting across the middle from right to left. Quentin tracked, knew he was locked on Tara, knew he was staring for too long, but he couldn't look away. He started throwing even as part of his brain screamed *don't!* but his left arm acted on its own accord. He threw. The ball hung a moment too long, long enough for Pirates linebacker Richard Damge to step in front of Tara, snag it out of the air and sprint the other way.

Quentin's third interception of the game.

Damge cut toward the visitors' sidelines. Quentin turned and ran, all the frustration and rage exploding inside him. He didn't see a linebacker; he saw Rick "Sarge" Vinje. Beneath that blood-red helmet, Quentin saw the face of the man who'd shattered his soul.

Damge moved the ball to his left arm, close to the sidelines. He reached out his right hand as Quentin closed in. Damge was a linebacker, not an experienced ball-carrier and his stiff-arm was clumsy.

Clumsy and ineffective.

Quentin launched himself head-first, swatting the stiff-arm aside just a fraction of a second before his forearm ripped *up* and *through* Damge's chin, snapping the helmeted head back harder than a close-range gunshot. The big Human linebacker's feet flew out from under him. Instantly unconscious, he seemed to float out of bounds, into the sea of red leg armor and white jerseys on the Pirates sidelines, weightless and limp for that half-second he remained in the air, then he landed hard on his back and tumbled forward like a rag doll.

Quentin ran three steps to the fallen player, stood over him and shook his fist.

"You like that, you shucker? You *like that?*"

Whistles blew just before big hands grabbed Quentin and pushed him back. He saw an unknown Quyth Warrior wearing a white jersey, so he threw a punch at it. Off-balance from another push, Quentin's fist just grazed the Warrior's mouth.

Someone pushed Quentin hard in the chest, knocked him on his ass. Flags flew, more whistles blew. Black jerseys dove into the fray. Quentin scrambled to his feet — the Pirates wanted a fight? That could be arranged.

Quentin took one step back into the scrum, then a pair of giant-sized hands grabbed either side of his chest, lifted him, turned him away from the fight. Quentin clawed and kicked, but he couldn't pry away hands that were as big as his forearm —

— The hands of Michael Kimberlin.

"CHICK, IT LOOKS LIKE the officials have control over the fight. We have flags down."

"Unsportsmanlike conduct on Barnes, Masara. No question there. Fifteen yards from the infraction, which will give the Pirates the ball on the Krakens' seventeen."

"Chick, I think that interception wraps up the game. With only three minutes to play, the Pirates are up ten and they have the ball in scoring position."

"I think you're right, Masara. It's been a tale of two quarterbacks this evening. The living legend Frank Zimmer playing lights-out ball, throwing for three touchdowns and three hundred fifty yards, while Barnes has countered with three interceptions. You can't do that in a game against a first-place team."

"No, Chick, you just can't. Chick, it looks like Damge is still down."

"I'm not surprised, Masara. Barnes certainly landed a snot-bubbler on him."

"A *what?*"

"A snot-bubbler. That's when you hit a Human so hard that his head is knocked back fast and the snot kind of stays in the same place due to inertia. It bubbles out onto his nose like a mucus volcano."

"Chick!"

"Let's see if our producer can get a close-up booger-shot of Damge's face. Zoom in, Polly, zoom in!"

GFL WEEK TEN ROUNDUP
Courtesy of Galaxy Sports Network

HOME		AWAY	
Hittoni Hullwalkers	24	Alimum Armada	9
Orbiting Death	42	Coranadillana Cloud Killers	10
Ionath Krakens	28	**To Pirates**	38
Bord Brigands	14	**Isis Ice Storm**	17
Yall Criminals	57	Lu Juggernauts	10
Sala Intrigue	13	**Themala Dreadnaughts**	24
Bartel Water Bugs	24	**Wabash Wolfpack**	30
Jang Atom Smashers	22	D'Kow War Dogs	20
Shorah Warlords	5	**Jupiter Jacks**	24
New Rodina Astronauts	28	**Neptune Scarlet Fliers**	31
Vik Vanguard	26	Texas Earthlings	10

A HOT WEEK OF FOOTBALL brings us closer to a final postseason picture. The Vik Vanguard (6-3) closed in on the third playoff spot in the Solar Division, thanks to a 26-10 win over the Texas Earthlings (3-6). With three games to play, the Vanguard needs just one more win to guarantee a postseason appearance, thanks to losses by Bord, D'Kow, Shorah and New Rodina, all of which dropped to 3-6.

Wins by Neptune (8-1) and Jupiter (8-1) mean both teams have wrapped up a playoff berth.

The Planet Division picture is not so nice and neat. Wabash and To are tied for first at 8-1. Wabash stayed in first with a 30-24 win over the Bartel Water Bugs (4-5), while To won 38-28 over Ionath (6-3). That loss drops the Krakens to fifth place, hurting their playoff chances. Even if Ionath wins their final three games, they still might not make the postseason.

Yall's 57-10 whipping of the Lu Juggernauts (0-9) moves the Criminals into a second-place tie with the Isis Ice Storm, as both teams sit at 7-2. Isis edged the Bord Brigands 17-14. As Week Ten closes out, Lu, Coranadillana (3-6), Alimum (2-7) and Hittoni (3-6) have all been eliminated from playoff contention.

The Juggernauts can only avoid relegation if they win their final three games and Alimum loses their final three. The two teams play each other in Week Thirteen.

Deaths

Much sadness and anger in the Quyth Concordia this week following Monday Night Football, when the Coranadillana Cloud Killers visited OS1 Orbiting Death. Excitement over the renewal of this rivalry shifted to tragedy as a riot in the stands left 15 dead and 47 injured. It is unclear how the fight broke out between the supporters of both teams. After the riot was subdued and the game resumed, the Death won 42-10.

Offensive Player of the Week

Neptune quarterback **Adam Guri,** who set a single-game yardage record with 513 in the Scarlet Fliers' win over New Rodina. Guri completed 42-of-56 throws on the day, including four TD passes.

Defensive Player of the Week

Themala linebacker **Tibi the Unkempt,** who had an interception, five solo tackles and a sack in the Dreadnaughts' win over the Sala Intrigue.

21

WEEK ELEVEN: D'KOW WAR DOGS at IONATH KRAKENS

PLANET DIVISION

8-1 Wabash Wolfpack

8-1 To Pirates

7-2 Isis Ice Storm

7-2 Yall Criminals

6-3 Ionath Krakens

6-3 Themala Dreadnaughts

4-5 OS1 Orbiting Death

3-6 Coranadillana Cloud Killers

3-6 Hittoni Hullwalkers

2-7 Alimum Armada

0-9 Lu Juggernauts

SOLAR DIVISION

8-1 x - Neptune Scarlet Fliers

8-1 x - Jupiter Jacks

6-3 Vik Vanguard

4-5 Bartel Water Bugs

3-6 Bord Brigands

3-6 D'Kow War Dogs

3-6 New Rodina Astronauts

3-6 Shorah Warlords

3-6 Jang Atom Smashers

3-6 Texas Earthlings

1-8 Sala Intrigue

x = playoffs, y = division title, * = team has been relegated

QUENTIN PULLED OFF his practice jersey and flung it into his locker. His Human teammates milled about the locker room. They all seemed distant, almost afraid to come near him. Good. That was the image he wanted to project. He didn't want to talk to anyone.

Quentin stripped off his shoulder pads and chest armor, aware that Yassoud was slowly approaching.

"Murphy, leave me be."

"Come on, Q. Don't be like that. Practice is over. Let's head out for a beer."

Quentin turned on him. "Leave ... me ... *be*."

Yassoud chewed on his lip, searching for the right words. There weren't any.

"Practice hasn't been good," he said quietly. "Quentin, I know you're hurting, but it's affecting your game. It's affecting the team."

Quentin shrugged, then started on his shoes and leg armor. "Maybe it's not me, 'Soud. Maybe we're just a bad team."

"Shuck that, Barnes. We're two wins from the playoffs. We can beat Themala, we can beat Vik, but you have to get your head back in the game."

Quentin pulled a towel out of his locker, wrapped it around his waist. "That what you think, Murphy?"

Yassoud nodded.

"Yeah, well, you and about twenty others. And you're all wrong."

For the last five days, his teammates had tried to talk to him before and after practice. He'd ignored them. They had tried to talk to him at meals, so he started eating meals in his Krakens building apartment. Then they tried to visit him there, an endless procession of friends that wanted to help him. Well, they *couldn't*.

Maybe his sister could. But he had no idea where she was. Why didn't she come to him? Why didn't Fred? Quentin could go looking, but where? His best bet was to keep doing what he'd always done, keep playing football — if they wanted to find him, they knew where he was.

"Yassoud, just do your job. When we play the War Dogs, do your job and we'll be fine. Don't tell me my business."

"Oh, but you can tell everyone else *their* business? You're the only one that can correct people?"

Quentin shrugged. He wasn't going to debate it. He walked out of the Human locker room and headed for the Ki baths. At least there no one would try to talk to him.

QUENTIN FORCED HIMSELF to stay under the surface in water so hot it stung his eyes through his closed eyelids. Water this hot probably wasn't all that healthy. Something long and big and dangerous swam by, the swirling current reminding him that he was a guest here, that this was not his world. Probably Mum-O, the adolescent's way of trying to reassure Quentin that the Ki stood behind him now and forever.

When Quentin could hold his breath no longer, he let his head slide above the surface, exhaled a slow breath, then drew one that was even slower. Two backstrokes took him to the bath's tiled edge.

Quentin put his arms on the tile, let his feet float free in the black water. So dark in here. A high spout dumped a stream of hot water on his head. He let it splatter, breathed through an open mouth.

He opened his eyes to stare at the packed ball of big Ki bodies, slowly twisting and writhing together at the pool's center. Low lights played off of wet skin, the thousands of enamel pebbles that dotted it. Black eyes, snake-like bodies, hexagonal mouths — the multi-headed demon of a child's nightmares.

The Ki wasted little time with words. That was what Quentin needed right now — silence.

So, of course, it was words that spoiled the moment.

"Quentin?"

Rebecca, on the other side of the pool. "Leave me be," he said.

She swam around the pile of Ki, careful to keep her chin on the water. She knew her nakedness made him uncomfortable.

"Quentin, can I talk to you?"

"No," he said, "you can't."

She paused, uncertain. That expression on her face — she was hurting for him. Well, he didn't care.

"Quentin, I don't want to speak out of turn, but—"

"Then don't speak, Becca, and that won't be a problem, now will it?"

He saw her eyes narrow a little, harden a little. "Do you remember the little talk we had here last year?"

Quentin sighed. Why couldn't everyone just stay out of his face? "Yes, I remember."

"You told me to *get over it*," she said. "I *killed* a sentient and you told me it was part of football."

"It was," he said. "That has nothing to do with my situation."

"Quentin, we're so close! What can we do to help you?"

He felt his anger rising. He started to speak, but the sound of a small woman's voice beat him to it.

"You can get out, girlie. I need to talk to Quentin."

At the room's entrance stood John Tweedy and his mother. John looked uncomfortable. Ma Tweedy looked the same as she always did, dressed in an orange and black Krakens jacket, shoulders up at her ears.

Quentin's face turned red, but he didn't move — couldn't a guy take a bath in private?

Ma Tweedy pointed at Becca. "You, girlie—" she pointed to the entrance "—get out." Ma Tweedy waited. Wide-eyed, Becca swam to the pool's edge and climbed out. Quentin looked away, partially out of respect, partially out of embarrassment.

He heard wet feet pattering on the tile floor, then the hiss of the door.

"Sorry, Q," John said. "Ma said she had to talk to you."

Quentin shook his head. "Ma Tweedy, this really isn't the place for—"

"Shut it," she said. "And all you linemen. Out."

The ball of Ki squirmed a little faster. Mum-O slithered out of the pile, his twelve-foot-long body creating a serpentine wake as he swam toward the edge. He slid out of the water and rose up, arms spread, mouth open wide. He leaned in until his face was inches from Ma Tweedy's.

John took a step forward, hands clenching into fists, the look in his face showing he thought the situation had suddenly spun out of control. Ma Tweedy reached out and grabbed one of Mum-O's speaking tubes. Mum-O flinched and let out a little squeal as she twisted it to the side. Quentin had a vision of Ma Tweedy grabbing the ears of misbehaving John and Ju.

"Out," she said, using her free hand to point to the door.

She let go. Mum-O stared at her, rubbed at his vocal tube. Then Sho-Do-Thikit said a few syllables. All the Ki slithered through the water toward the door. As they left, Ma Tweedy turned to John.

"And you," she said.

"But Ma! Quentin is my friend."

Ma Tweedy pointed to the door. John mumbled something, then turned and walked out.

She turned her squinty gaze at Quentin. "Okay, Son, let's talk. Time for you to grow up."

Fantastic. Now not only did his teammates think they had the right to correct him, so did this woman that he barely knew.

"Ma Tweedy, I'm already grown up. I don't need a lecture."

"You're not and you do," she said. "Age don't mean crap. That man lied about being your daddy and that's terrible."

Hearing those words stirred up the pain of betrayal, made it fresh again.

"You were wronged," Ma Tweedy said. "So what? You think you're the first person to be wronged?"

Quentin dipped his face into the water, hoping the heat would chase away his tears. He popped back up. "Ma Tweedy, please leave. I'm naked in here. If you don't go, I will."

"You'll have to work on your threats, boy," she said. "A naked man is something I might have seen a time or two before. In case you didn't notice, I have kids. Their conception wasn't immaculate."

Quentin blinked in embarrassment. Okay, so maybe he wasn't going to get out of the water.

"John told me you're phoning it in during practice," she said. "You're a *grown-up*, are you? The biggest game of your career is in three days and you're acting like a child that's had his favorite toy taken away."

"A *toy*? He told me he was my *father*."

She nodded, a full-body motion that resembled the nod of a Quyth Leader. "Okay, so I'm not so good with analogies. Or metaphors. Or is it similes? Whichever, I can never tell them apart. The point is, what was done to you is just that ... *done*. You can walk around like a whipped dog with his tail between his legs, or you can step up and be the man your teammates need you to be."

"Right," Quentin said. "I need to win games for an owner that tricked me into signing a contract."

"Oh, you poor baby," she said. "Your millions aren't enough for you?"

"Now you sound like my fake father."

"Just because he was fake doesn't mean he was wrong. Quentin, you've worked hard to get where you are. I know how much you've sacrificed, because my boys have sacrificed a lot as well. John more than Ju, but still. When you were getting your ass kicked all over the galaxy last year, did you roll over and quit?"

He stared at her. Was she going to tie Sarge Vinje to football? They weren't the same.

"You didn't," she said. "You're not answering me because you already know where I'm going and you know I'm right. You *fought*. You didn't just take it. You didn't quit. Gredok and that nasty man hurt you. They tricked you into thinking you had family. That ain't right. But you need to wake up, boy. You do have family."

"Who? My mysterious sister who showed up for five minutes and now won't contact me?"

Ma Tweedy shook her head, a motion that moved her whole body just as much as nodding did. "No. She's got her reasons,

Quentin, but I'm not talking about her. You have family because you have *me*."

Quentin had to look away. It wasn't the first time she'd said something like that. He couldn't face her because he knew those weren't empty words — she meant it.

"My sons would probably be dead if it weren't for you," she said. "Now they're both happy. You have them working harder than they've ever worked before and trust me, they worked *hard*. My children are *better people* because of *you*, Quentin. For that, I love you like my own. Some people get a mom and a dad. Some don't. You can either embrace the life you have, or you can be a baby and piss and moan about what you didn't get."

He sniffed, quietly wiped away tears. "Right," he said. "What's next, you telling me *the choice is mine*?"

Ma Tweedy laughed. "You think I'd leave that choice up to you, Son? No. The choice is *mine*."

Hers? What in the Void did that mean?

"You will eat with the team again, every meal," she said. "You'll be in your room by seven, study from seven-thirty to ten, in bed at ten-thirty, you understand?"

Who did this woman think she was? "But you can't—"

"You'll get up at five, like you used to do. And John tells me you're playing a lot of hologames?"

"Well, yeah, but—"

"No more until the season is over," she said. "You've got studying to do. Ma Tweedy is going to keep you on the straight and narrow until the playoffs are over, then you can wallow in self-pity like a pig in the mud."

"Listen, you can't—"

"I'll be checking in on you five times a day," she said. "If you're not where I tell you to be, *when* I tell you to be there, I will show up at practice, walk right into the locker room and give you a piece of my mind in front of all your teammates."

Quentin's eyes widened. That would be beyond embarrassing. "You wouldn't. You're *not* my mother."

"I would and I am. From now on, I am. You're a good kid,

Quentin. A little on the sensitive side, I won't lie, but you're okay. I'm taking over. That's that. Get out of there, get dressed and be back in your apartment in the Krakens building in twenty minutes. I'll be waiting to make sure you start out right. Understand me?"

Quentin stared, shocked. He didn't know what to say, so he just nodded.

"Good," she said. "I'm going to help you through this, son. Whether you like it or not. Now, what are you going to do about this tight end situation?"

Now she wanted to talk football? What was next, the weather?

"Uh, well, you know, I guess George is going to have to step up."

"Can't step up if you got no feet," she said. "You have an asset you're not using. Warburg."

Quentin shook his head. "No way. That racist can't help us."

"Not if you don't throw him the ball, you sanctimonious jackass. What's the matter, don't you *want* to win games?"

Quentin blinked. "Of course I want to win."

"Then I guess you better wake up, Son. If you want to win, you need to use all the tools you have."

Don Pine had basically said the same thing. Had Quentin been wrong? "I guess I could throw to Warburg."

Ma Tweedy huffed, a mannerism that sounded just like her much bigger son. "And if you were him, would you *catch* it? Would you help someone who'd treated you like dog crap stuck in your shoe?"

Quentin started to say *of course I would*, but he checked himself — he wouldn't throw the ball to someone he didn't like, so what was to say Warburg would catch a pass from someone *he* didn't like.

"He wants a contract," Quentin said. "He'll play hard."

Ma Tweedy shrugged, a tiny gesture for a woman whose shoulders were already up near her ears. "If I was you, I'd make sure of that."

"And how would I do that?"

"You own what you did. You apologize."

Quentin shook his head. "No way. I'm not apologizing to him."

Ma Tweedy stared, then nodded. "All right, I guess your mind is made up. Your beliefs are the most important thing? I'll support that, Son. And here I was thinking *winning* was the most important thing to you. Well, you learn something new every day. Now, get dressed. It's time to study."

She walked out, leaving Quentin alone in the dark, alone with the hissing sound of spraying water.

Alone … with his thoughts.

QUENTIN ENTERED the Blessed Lamb. A chorus of *Quentin!* greeted him the second he walked through the door. He smiled, nodded at the welcoming faces. Humans, one and all. Other races simply weren't encouraged here.

An all-Human establishment. Sitting at the bar, holding court, was the tall, wide, muscular form of Rick Warburg. Such a surprise. Rick sipped a beer, stared at Quentin.

Quentin took a deep breath, then let it out in a cheek-puffing huff. Time to take his medicine. He walked up to the bar.

"Rick," Quentin said. "Can I join you?"

Warburg raised his eyebrows, then mockingly looked down at either side of his chest. "Well, I don't see an extra set of arms, Quentin. Are you sure you can slum with a lowly *Human* like me?"

The other patrons laughed. They thought it was a joke, not Rick ridiculing Quentin's choice to treat other races as equals.

"Yes," Quentin said. "I'm sure."

"Don't want me to turn blue?"

Quentin gritted his teeth. He'd forgotten Rick's hate wasn't limited to just other species — Humans with the wrong color skin counted as well.

Quentin looked at the other patrons. "Guys, mind if Rick and I have a little space? We have to talk some football."

Heads nodded quickly, as if the other patrons were in on some holy mission — Elder Barnes and Elder Warburg had to discuss spiritual matters.

Quentin sat on the stool to Rick's left. Rick kept staring. Quentin signaled to Brother Guido behind the bar. "Beer?"

Guido quickly filled a mug. To have *two* Krakens in his bar at the same time? It was better than mounting a giant holosign on the city dome that says *The Blessed Lamb is the place to be for Nationalite Ex-Pats just like you!*

Quentin took a long drink. He had to steel himself for this. Eating crow was not one of his strong suits.

"Well?" Warburg said. "If you've come to give me a lecture on species interaction, that we're all one big, happy, galactic brotherhood, I already gave at the office."

"Not here for that," Quentin said. He set the mug down. "I came to apologize."

Warburg's stare slowly faded into an arrogant smile. "Oh, I see. Now that you realize Crazy George is actually *crazy*, now you want to throw me the ball. Am I right?"

Quentin searched for a way to spin things, to justify his actions, but he didn't search long — there was no justification. Now, when he *needed* something, moral posturing was no longer an option.

"That's right," Quentin said. "I was wrong."

Rick turned, stared at the mirror behind the bar. He took a drink. "You say you're wrong only because you need me. If you didn't need me, you'd still think you have the right to sabotage my career."

"I admit I thought I had that right," Quentin said. "But I don't. I acted ... well, I acted like I was High One, like I could pass judgment on you. That was wrong, Rick, and now it's biting me in the ass."

Warburg slowly turned. His hard stare seemed to soften a little. "When I did get in, I played my ass off. You *knew* that."

Quentin thought back to the game against the Lu Juggernauts, when he'd completely ignored a wide-open Warburg. Had Rick stood there and pouted? No. Rick had come back to block, knocking out a linebacker and springing Quentin for the winning touchdown.

"I know," Quentin said. "I chose to be blind. But that's over. You need me and we need you."

"It's a little late for this, don't you think?"

Quentin shook his head. "It can't be. For two reasons. First, you collect a paycheck to play for the Ionath Krakens. We need to beat D'Kow, Themala *and* Vik to make the playoffs for sure. We need to win out."

Warburg huffed. "If someone didn't have daddy issues, we'd probably be in second place, not fifth. I was open against the Pirates, too."

Daddy issues. Rick wasn't going to make this easy. Not that Quentin deserved easy. "That game is over, Warburg. We move on. We have the War Dogs in two days."

Rick nodded. "You can just turn it off like that? Put the Pirates game behind you like nothing happened?"

"I already have. The past is the past. We can't change it. All we can do is worry about today and plan for tomorrow."

Rick started to talk, then seemed to think it over. He drained his beer, signaled to Brother Guido for another.

"Okay," Rick said. He nodded. "That's your first reason. What's your second?"

"The second reason—" Quentin extended his index finger and lightly poked Warburg in the chest "—is *you*. I did you wrong. I'm going to make it right. You want off the Krakens? You want other teams to see your skills so you can get that big contract? You want the ball? I'm going to get you the ball."

"I'm not going to change who I am," Rick said. "I know what the *truth* is, Quentin. I won't betray my beliefs."

"I wish it wasn't that way, but that's the way it is. Off the field, you can do whatever the hell you want. It's not my place to judge. *On* the field, you'll do your job and help us win games. I'm never going to like you, Warburg, but I'll stop being the sanctimonious ass I've been — when we play ball, I'll treat you like the asset you are."

Warburg smiled. A small one, but genuine. He finally had recognition for his talent, for his efforts. "Okay. That works for me. I can tell you right now, though, you're going to regret this."

"Why?"

Rick again turned to face the mirror. His smile widened. "When you see what I can do, you're going to wish you pulled your head out of your ass a whole lot sooner."

Quentin stood. "I hope so. See you at practice."

He walked out, hearing the groans of the patrons asking *do you have to leave so soon?* But he couldn't stay.

He had to study. A win against D'Kow put the Krakens back in the hunt. A loss meant they were out of the playoffs for good.

"SO THERE'S NOTHING we can do?"

Quentin already knew the answer, but he had to ask. Danny Lundy's mechanical arms played with the holo display a little more. Probably just for show — he already knew the contract inside and out. Aside from the two of them, Danny's office was empty. He'd even sent home his eye-candy secretary.

A long sigh escaped Danny's blow hole. "Nothing. This agreement is iron-clad, guy. You really should have let me do the talking."

Quentin looked up to the ceiling, nodded. Danny was right. Quentin should have let his agent handle things. Instead, he'd played into Gredok's hands.

"Look on the bright side," Danny said. The Dolphin seemed resigned to the facts — contracts were his game, he'd taken on Gredok the Splithead and he'd lost. All's fair in football and war. "You can't play for another team, not even Tier Three ball. You got cheated out of twenty-five million, but you're making more at this than you would, say, washing dishes, which is the kind of job you'd probably get with your high level of education and well-developed skill set."

"That's your definition of a *bright side?*"

"You wanted to be a Kraken, buddy. The bright side is you're a Kraken and will be for the next ten years. Gredok has salary-cap room to go get other players. In a way, you got exactly what you wanted."

Right. Like Quentin wanted to play for a sentient that had toyed with his emotions, manipulated him like some kind of pet.

"What if I quit football altogether?"

Danny's Dolphin squeal-laugh had no humor. "Sure, buddy. Quentin Barnes is just going to quit the game. And I have a nice undersea bridge to sell you. Time to get over it, guy. You lost. You're going to play because that's all you want to do, it's all you know how to do. You're going to play for Ionath. You're going to play for Gredok the Splithead. Mind if I give you some advice?"

Quentin laughed. "Sure, why not?"

"You lost. It's over. It's just like when you lose on a Sunday afternoon. Put it behind you, move on to the next game. The only sentient that can get you out of this contract is the owner of the Ionath Krakens and we know that's not going to happen."

Quentin bit his lip, then nodded. Danny had done all he could. The agent could do no more. Quentin stood, shook the metal hand, then left the office.

The only one who could get him out of the contract was the owner?

Fine.

That was just fine.

Quentin would worry about that another time. After the season. For now, he had to get his head straight, as Ma Tweedy had told him. If he led his team to a home win against the D'Kow War Dogs on Sunday, the Krakens might just make the playoffs after all.

One game at a time.

QUENTIN ROLLED LEFT on a boot pass, his feet flying over Ionath Stadium's blue turf, Becca Montagne out in front of him to block. The game demanded every shred of concentration — it pushed away the thoughts of his father. Or maybe the horrific uniforms of the D'Kow War Dogs did that, so ugly they blocked out everything else.

Lime-green jerseys with purple numbers trimmed in orange.

Quentin had been told the purple was something called *mauve*, but all he knew was that the color was even uglier than regular purple. Lime-green thigh armor with horizontal orange stripes on the thighs, purple lower-leg armor and shoes. The right shoulder showed the team's emblem — a lime-green, stylized walking dog on a black-lined orange shield. The left shoulder showed the player's number, again in orange-trimmed purple. Damn near hurt to *look* at the uniforms.

Three War Dog players closed in fast — HeavyG defensive end Michael Grace, Quyth Warrior linebacker Zeus the Ram and cornerback Tübingen. Tübingen barreled in on a corner-blitz. She had lined up woman-to-woman on Hawick, who was streaking down the sidelines.

Because Tübingen blitzed, the safety had to run with Hawick — that meant there were no defenders left on the outside to cover Rick Warburg, who was rushing straight upfield and about to make his flag-route cut of 45 degrees to the left.

Rick would be wide open, *if* Quentin had time to throw. Tübingen came from the outside, cutting off any run to the sidelines. Quentin's feet chopped at the ground, stopping his momentum, taking him back to the right. He kept his eyes downfield as Michael Grace reached for him, but Becca launched herself like a missile and hit Grace square in his big chest. Grace stumbled back, his forward momentum gone.

Becca should have fallen to the ground, but somehow she *twisted* in mid-air, stretching herself out the other way to fall at the feet of the sprinting Quyth Warrior, Zeus. The linebacker tripped — not enough to fall, but enough that he also lost his momentum. Tübingen shot past them, closing in from the left. Quentin threw just before she leveled him, an awkward left-handed toss while running right. The ball sailed through the air, wobbly but on-target, toward the sidelines — it dropped in just over Warburg's left shoulder.

Looking back over that shoulder, Warburg watched the pass, so soft it could have been a baby set in his palms by a worried mother. He hauled it in, tucked the ball in his left arm as he turned upfield, big legs chewing up the yards. The screaming crowd urged him on.

The safety broke off of Hawick and rushed in to meet Warburg at the 10. Warburg reared back to deliver a big blow. The safety reared back to match, but just before contact, Warburg made a little jump to the right, to the inside. The safety flew by, her tentacles ripping across his thigh armor. Warburg was too big to be brought down like that. He ran into the end zone for his second touchdown of the day. Ionath up 34-30, extra point still to come.

Quentin felt his shoulder pads being pulled, someone trying to lift him off the ground. He stood, seeing that Becca and Tübingen had both helped him up. Quentin brushed blue turf off of his black jersey.

"Nice hit," he said.

Tübingen shivered. "Oh, thank you, Godling! I tried to please you!"

Becca laughed. "By knocking him on his ass?"

"Absolutely," Quentin said, then patted the cornerback on the helmet. "You are a blessing to your team."

Tübingen knelt, used her tentacle fingers to pluck a few blades of blue-leaved Iomatt, then handed it to Quentin. "Now you sniff your touchdown powers of holy-holiness?"

"Huh?"

Becca nodded toward the offered blue plants. "The sniff. You do it after every big touchdown."

Quentin looked at her. "I do?"

"Yeah." She again nodded to the outstretched tentacles. Quentin took the offered plants and sniffed. Smelled like cinnamon.

Tübingen squealed, then sprinted off the field at full speed. Quentin and Becca jogged to the sidelines as the extra point team came on.

"Did you see that move Warburg threw?" Becca said. "I always thought he was nothing but a bruiser."

"Usually he is. He likes to hurt sentients, *especially* Sklorno. Seems he's got skills he hasn't used."

"I'll say," Becca said. "Very athletic."

Hands and pedipalps and tentacles patted them as they reached the sidelines. Quentin looked for defensive end Rich Palmer. He grabbed the rookie's jersey, looked at the nervous blue eyes inside the helmet.

"Palmer, we need you to step up."

Palmer nodded, said nothing. The look on his face carried a dual expression of excitement and anxiety.

"Khomeni's hurt," Quentin said. "We need to play smart, okay? You can do this. Bring home the win."

Quentin slapped Palmer's helmet. The big defensive end ran on to the field. Quentin took off his helmet. He and Becca walked to a medbay. Lying on his back on that bench, Ibrahim Khomeni. The star defensive end's knee was lost inside of metal rigging, wires and needles. Doc Patah's mouth-flaps flicked in and out of the rig, the open flesh beneath it, working a ligament stapler and a bone grafter.

Ibrahim opened his eyes, saw Quentin.

"Sorry," he said.

Quentin laughed. "Not your fault, man. Everyone gets hurt sooner or later. Palmer will finish the job and you'll be back next week."

Khomeni gave a weak smile. He wouldn't be back next week. He knew it, Quentin knew it.

"You know it, Q," he said. "Just finish this one off for me."

Quentin lightly patted Khomeni's thick shoulder, then walked to the benches and sat. He grabbed two water bottles, handed one to Becca, took a long drink from the other.

"Becca," he said when he finished, "what you did out there on that last drive? I've never seen anything like it."

She took off her helmet and gave him a quizzical look, her black hair plastered wetly to her head. "Me? I just blocked."

"I should have been sacked on that play. Not just *sacked* ... more like *executed*. You blocked *two* players at the same time. What are you, like an acrobat or something?"

She scowled and shook her head. "I just blocked. You must have been hit harder than you think. Good pass, though."

The rest of the offense gathered around them, including Warburg. Hokor squeezed into the middle dragging a portable holotank, cutting off all conversation.

"We're up 35-30," he said. "Barnes, nice pass. Warburg, great run. Becca, amazing blocking. Now, we have to assume our defense can't hold them, so let's be ready for a two-minute drive to set up a field goal."

His pedipalp fingers worked the holotank. A field appeared in mid-air, showing the play they'd just run. Hokor's fingertips stared drawing lines of light that hung there, revealing the paths of various players.

"We can hit this pass again if we have to," he said. "Now, everyone, if the corner doesn't *blitz*, look at what's available."

Quentin leaned forward, focusing on the inch-high football players and their respective paths.

GFL WEEK ELEVEN ROUNDUP
Courtesy of Galaxy Sports Network

HOME		AWAY	
Alimum Armada	21	**Themala Dreadnaughts**	24
Lu Juggernauts	17	Coranadillana Cloud Killers	16
Orbiting Death	24	**Hittoni Hullwalkers**	27
Ionath Krakens	35	D'Kow War Dogs	30
Isis Ice Storm	24	**Wabash Wolfpack**	28
Texas Earthlings	17	To Pirates	14
Yall Criminals	42	**Vik Vanguard**	45
Bartel Water Bugs	20	Sala Intrigue	14
Jupiter Jacks	10	**Bord Brigands**	21
Jang Atom Smashers	20	New Rodina Astronauts	13
Neptune Scarlet Fliers	31	Shorah Warlords	24

WITH A 45-42 UPSET win over the Yall Criminals (7-3), the Vik Vanguard (7-3) locked up the third playoff spot in the Solar Division and capped an amazing turnaround from last year. In 2683, the Vanguard finished 2-10, barely ahead of relegated Chillich Spider-Bears, who finished at 1-11.

This is Vik's first trip to the postseason since they lost the 2679 Galaxy Bowl to the New Rodina Astronauts. The Vanguard has now won five straight games.

"We're thrilled with a trip to the playoffs, but we're not done," said Vanguard coach Katie Lampkin. "We have two games left in the regular season. We'll be fighting hard to catch Jupiter in the standings and get a home playoff game."

Lampkin's hope is now a possibility thanks to Jupiter's 21-10 loss to the Bord Brigands (4-6). The Jacks (8-2) are currently the second seed in the Solar Division playoffs, but could be overtaken by the Vanguard. The Jacks still have to face the Neptune Scarlet Fliers (9-1) and the Jang Atom Smashers (4-6).

The Bartel Water Bugs (5-5) currently hold the fourth seed in the Solar, thanks to a 20-14 win over the Sala Intrigue (1-9). Bord, Jang and the Texas Earthlings (4-6) all won, keeping their playoff hopes mathematically alive.

The Earthlings' shocking 17-14 cross-divisional upset over the To Pirates (8-2) shook things up in the Planet Division. Texans linebacker Alonzo Castro was the hero of the game, causing a fourth-quarter fumble on a Frank Zimmer sack that Castro also recovered and ran back for the winning touchdown.

The Pirates' loss leaves Wabash (9-1) all alone in first place in the Planet. The Wolfpack locked up a playoff berth with a 28-24 win over Isis (7-3). Even if Wabash loses its final two games and finishes 9-3, it holds head-to-head tiebreakers over Isis, Yall (7-3) and Themala (7-3).

The Ionath Krakens (7-3) are also finally in the playoff hunt. Ionath's 35-30 win over the D'Kow War Dogs moves the Krakens back into a four-way tie for third place. This week Ionath travels to Themala. The winner of that game is almost guaranteed a play-off berth.

Deaths
No deaths reported this week.

Offensive Player of the Week
Ionath Krakens tight end **Rick Warburg**, who caught eight passes for 112 yards and two touchdowns in a win over the D'Kow War Dogs.

Defensive Player of the Week
Bord defensive end **Paul "Bandit" Preston**, who picked up three sacks and four solo tackles in the Brigands' upset win over the Jupiter Jacks.

22

WEEK TWELVE:
IONATH KRAKENS
at THEMALA DREADNAUGHTS

PLANET DIVISION

9-1 x - Wabash Wolfpack

8-2 To Pirates

7-3 Isis Ice Storm

7-3 Yall Criminals

7-3 Ionath Krakens

7-3 Themala Dreadnaughts

4-6 Hittoni Hullwalkers

4-6 OS1 Orbiting Death

3-7 Coranadillana Cloud Killers

2-8 Alimum Armada

1-9 Lu Juggernauts

SOLAR DIVISION

9-1 x - Neptune Scarlet Fliers

8-2 x - Jupiter Jacks

7-3 x - Vik Vanguard

5-5 Bartel Water Bugs

4-6 Bord Brigands

4-6 Jang Atom Smashers

4-6 Texas Earthlings

3-7 D'Kow War Dogs

3-7 New Rodina Astronauts

3-7 Shorah Warlords

1-9 Sala Intrigue

x = playoffs, y = division title, * = team has been relegated

QUENTIN AND JOHN TWEEDY WALKED down an 18th-deck corridor toward Hokor's office aboard the *Touchback*. He'd summoned the two of them, his team captains, to come up after Thursday practice. Themala was only a one-day trip — short by the season's standards. Hokor wanted to arrive Friday morning, letting the team get a full practice in on Themala's field and get the feel of the place.

"Q, brother, can I be honest with you?

"Of course," Quentin said.

"You're doing super-mega better in practice this week than you were in Week Ten against the Pirates," John said. "That was enough to beat D'Kow, but Themala is way better than the War Dogs. We need you at the top of your game to beat Themala. You're still a little distracted. I know your fake-pops is scrambling the noodley goodness that is your brains, but you gotta let it go."

Like mother, like son. Until they'd left for Themala, Ma Tweedy had been telling Quentin the same thing — every night when she left, every morning when she showed up at his door to make sure he was ready for practice. The woman didn't seem to require sleep. But her efforts were working. Quentin's concentration had improved. He would never forget what Gredok had done, but there was time to worry about that later — Ma Tweedy helped Quentin focus on the task at hand.

The task of making the playoffs.

"I'm trying," Quentin said. "I really am, Uncle Johnny, but it's easier said than done. That Vinje guy ... I don't want to talk about it."

"I still say you should have let me kill him," John said. "You can hire Fred for that, you know."

"Fred's killed people?"

"Yes, but they were all bad," John said. "Fred is very selective about his jobs."

Quentin had buried his pain in hard work, pushed the team to match his intensity. Two games left in the season. Sunday's contest against Themala was critically important — both teams were 7-and-3 and tied for third. That meant the winner would not only move to 8-and-3 but have a head-to-head tiebreaker important for determining playoff berths. The winner was all but in, the loser more than likely out.

Ionath's team goal of making the playoffs hung intoxicatingly close, maybe just one win away.

"You gotta get over it, Q," John said. "I know it sucks, brother. I do, but the entire franchise rides on your shoulders."

John was right. Quentin's problem was just that — *Quentin's* problem. He had to find a way to put Sarge Vinje behind him, at least until the season was over. "I'll work on it, John."

John smiled. THERE IS NO DO, THERE IS ONLY TO TRY OR NOT TO BE scrolled across his face.

They walked into Hokor's office. Quentin half-expected to see Gredok there, but that was stupid — since the dinner at Torba's, the black-furred owner had made himself scarce. Gredok got what he'd wanted. Now he stayed out of the way, letting Quentin do what Quentin was paid to do.

Coach Hokor was sitting at his desk, Doc Patah floating near his right shoulder. Hokor stared into a holotank on his desktop. The tank displayed a small football field swarming with half-inch-high players — action from last week's game between the Themala Dreadnaughts and the Alimum Armada. The Dreads had won 24-21.

"Coach," Quentin said. "You wanted to see us?"

They waited, but Hokor didn't look up.

"Coach Hokor," Doc Patah said. "You have visitors."

Coach still didn't seem to notice. Doc Patah reached down a mouth-flap and tapped Hokor on the shoulder. Coach looked up, blinked his one eye, finally noticing that someone was in his office.

"Sit down," Hokor said. "I need to review a roster change with you."

Quentin and John sat.

Hokor waved his left pedipalp across the desk. The holographic field vanished. "We have a situation at defensive end," he said. "Khomeni is out for the next two weeks, at least."

John stood up. "*What?* What are you talking about? *Two weeks?*"

Quentin felt a chill. They were losing their dominant defensive end with two critical games left in the season.

"His knee," Doc Patah said. "There is damage."

John's lip curled up. "So *fix it*, Doc. Put his ass in a tank and make it better. We need him."

Hokor waved his pedipalps across the desk again, calling up his nav-icons. He poked a glowing image thumbnail, which increased to full size. A cross-section of a thick HeavyG leg, from the upper shin to just under the quadriceps. Muscles appeared as transparent red, tendons and ligaments as transparent blue, cartilage as transparent yellow. The white bones looked so real you could reach out and grab them.

Doc Patah pointed a mouth-flap at the tibia. Quentin noticed that the yellow cartilage looked ripped, a little ragged in one spot. Floating in it, he saw bits of white.

"Bone chips," Doc Patah said. "He has a torn meniscus. That resulted in the femur grinding directly against the tibia. Bone chips are not a soft-tissue injury that I can fix quickly. The knee, in particular, is a difficult area with HeavyG due to the amount of weight they place on it.

"How long?" John said. "How long till you can get it fixed?"

"Two full weeks, as I told you," Doc Patah said. "It is possible we will have him back for the second round of the playoffs."

John shook his head. "We won't make the playoffs without him. He's our best pass-rusher. What about a patch-job? Bone graft and painkillers?"

Hokor's eye swirled with black. He'd clearly already asked that question and received an answer he didn't like.

"Absolutely not," Patah said. "If the damage gets any worse, even reconstruction won't bring Khomeni back to full speed. He's out."

John pointed at the floating doctor. "You don't have that authority!"

"Gredok does," Patah said. "I told him that Khomeni could

either play now at about fifty percent and possibly end his career, or Khomeni can sit out while I do the job right and come back at about ninety-five percent next season."

John's nose flared with deep, angry breaths.

"John," Quentin said quietly, "just take it easy. Players get hurt. We'll find a way to win."

"It is already settled," Doc Patah said. "Khomeni is out. Gredok backs my decision. Coach Hokor, do you need me for anything else?"

"No," Hokor said. "Thank you, Doctor."

Patah floated up, then flew over Quentin and John's heads and out of the room.

Hokor pointed to the chair. John sat.

"I was not happy with Rich Palmer's performance against D'Kow," Hokor said. "Perhaps he was nervous at his first time playing when a game is on the line. Maybe he will be better against the Dreadnaughts, but I can't take that chance. I need options. I am activating defensive ends Cliff Frost and Wan-A-Tagol from the practice squad."

John nodded. The news seemed to make him feel better. "Yeah, Coach, that's a good idea. We can rotate those three in and out, keep them fresh. Palmer, Frost and Wan-A to fill in for Khomeni. But if you're putting Khomeni on the practice squad and activating *two* players, that gives us forty-six players on the active roster. One too many. Who do we drop down? We're thin enough at defense as it is."

Hokor turned to Quentin. "We drop from the offense. I'm putting Starcher on the practice squad. He will not dress for the game."

Images of a room painted with charcoal words flashed through Quentin's mind. "Uh, Coach, I'm not sure that's a good idea."

"He's doing nothing for us," Hokor said. "Warburg clearly deserves to start. Kobayasho is number two and if either of those two get hurt, we can play Tara the Freak at tight end. We need Starcher's roster spot, Barnes."

Quentin leaned back. George was having a hard enough time

as it was. He wouldn't take this well. "Okay," Quentin said. "I'll tell him."

"It's already done," Hokor said. "I called him in his room before the two of you arrived. That's all."

Hokor activated his holographic football field again. He started running the play forward, then backward, then forward again. The home Armada in their navy-blue uniforms and white helmets attempted over and over — and failed over and over — to stop an off-tackle play by Themala running back Don Dennis, his tiny, white-jerseyed and crimson-legged form ripping through Alimum's ineffective linebackers.

John stood up and left. Quentin watched Hokor run the play forward and backward another three times, then headed for his room.

QUENTIN WALKED into his quarters.

He'd had to rush out of the locker room to meet Coach Hokor, so he'd settled for a nannite shower instead of hitting the Ki baths. A soak in that scalding water would do the trick, but he didn't have time. The Dreadnaughts in two days. That meant more study. Tonight, Ma Tweedy would be sending Quentin a test on his knowledge of the Themala roster.

Quentin was 7 feet tall, 380 pounds — he had no idea why that tiny woman terrified him, but she did. So, more study.

Always more study.Maybe it would help. Every time he didn't have a football in his hands or a team on the holotank, he thought of Sarge Vinje, of how the man had lied. Quentin also thought of Gredok, how the team owner had stooped to unbelievable levels to land the contract.

If Quentin played football, it would be in Ionath.

And he would play hard, play to win, because he didn't know how to do anything else. Gredok had understood that early on. He had known that no matter what evil thing he did, Quentin Barnes would still line up on Sunday and play his ass off.

Quentin walked to his couch. The playoffs were just two wins away. Despite all of Gredok's manipulations, Quentin's lust for the postseason hadn't faded an ounce.

There was a neatly folded towel sitting on the couch. Quentin moved it aside, sat, then clapped twice to bring the holotank to life.

"Computer, give me Dreadnaughts versus Alimum, Week Eleven. Themala on defense only."

[STANDARD CAMERA POSITION?]

"Yes."

[EDITING]

The first play popped to life. He preferred to watch game film from the same angle he played football holograms — behind the quarterback, about fifteen feet up. From there he could see the entire defense react to the play.

He pushed the towel a little farther away, then settled in to watch.

A piece of paper fell out of the towel and dropped to the floor.

Quentin looked at it, confused. Wait a minute ... he hadn't left a towel on the couch. And if he had, it sure as hell wouldn't be neatly folded. Had Pilkie been in here again, straightening up?

Quentin bent and picked up the piece of paper.

Quentin. Thank you for giving me one last chance. I am sorry I failed you. The Old Ones must collect on their debt. The Void welcomes. The Void caresses. The Void loves.

I want you to have my towel. Please speak kindly to it. It can be overly sensitive when it comes to political discussions.

Quentin lowered the piece of paper. He looked to his left, at the towel sitting on his couch. Orange-and-black plaid, with streaks of faded color from George's many face-paint combinations.

The Void loves.

"Oh no."

Quentin leapt over the back of the couch and sprinted out of his quarters, heading for the landing bay.

• • •

CORRIDOR LIGHTS WERE already flashing the yellow color of warning.

[MANUAL SHUTTLE BAY OPENING IN PROCESS, DECOM-
PRESSION IMMINENT. CLEAR THE LANDING BAY. CLEAR THE
LANDING BAY]

He saw the bay doors closing. Quentin sprinted down the corridor. A memory of the *Combine* flashed before him, of sprinting down a similar hall because the decompression alarms were blaring away. How ironic — back then, he was pushing his body to new levels to *avoid* decompression and now here he was running straight for it.

He dove head-first, extending his arms and turning his body sideways to slip through the closing doors. His toe caught on the edge — he made it through but was thrown off balance. He hit the landing bay deck hard and clumsy.

The door slid shut behind him.

No alarms. No noise.

Quentin scrambled to his feet, looked around the landing bay.

There, on the far side of the domed room — George Starcher, all 7-foot-6 of him, all 400 pounds of him, standing by an open panel marked EMERGENCY RELEASE.

Inside that panel, a horizontal handle, mostly obscured by George's gripping fist.

The handle flashed. Each time it did, George's hand seemed to glow from within as if it were filled with neon blood.

"George, don't!"

George turned to stare at Quentin, stare with eyes that were even more tired, more sunken … more hopeless.

"Get out of here, Quentin."

Quentin shook his head. He was so scared, each breath a clutching ache. If George pushed that lever all the way up, the bay doors would fully open. The two of them would be sucked into space. Quentin's chest felt tingly, the thrusts of a million tiny spears telling him his time had come.

This could be it. His life could be over.

Speakerfilm blared Captain Kate's voice through the shuttle bay. "Starcher! What are you doing? You shut that manual override down right now, or I'll kick you in the—"

George hit a button in his panel, cutting off Captain Kate's voice. Her last syllable echoed, faded.

"Quentin, get out."

Kate had ordered George to shut things down from in here. Did that mean she couldn't stop this? Yes, because if she could have, she would have already done something from the bridge.

If Quentin didn't stop this, no one could. "I'm not going anywhere, George."

"You aren't supposed to be here," he said. "No one is. I was careful, Quentin. I don't want to hurt anyone."

"You're going to hurt yourself."

George nodded. "Yes. I hurt all the time. I have to end it."

Quentin took a step forward, knowing it was a mistake even as he did it.

George lifted the lever. A blast of cold terror rippled through Quentin's body. The landing bay's dead-quiet vanished, replaced by the clang of huge doors, the high-pitched screaming of air shooting out into the void beyond.

Quentin turned to stare at death. The huge, horizontal doors opened — but only half an inch. George hadn't pushed the lever all the way up. Out there, waiting — the blackness of space, of certain death, only a few hundred feet of landing bay deck away. Quentin's shirt flapped in the fatal wind.

"Quentin, I mean it!" George shouted, barely audible over death's screeching howl. "Turn around and get out of here!"

Quentin wanted nothing more than to do just that. Every atom of his being begging him to turn and go, turn and *run*, run for the inner door, for safety.

But he could not.

"I'm not leaving, George. If you wanna die, you're going to have to kill me."

George flexed his fingers on the glowing handle. "Do you *want* to die, Quentin?"

"Shuck no," Quentin said, hearing a sickening laugh escape his own lips. "George, I want to live and I want *you* to live. The team needs you."

"You *lie*. I'm not even on the active roster anymore. I don't get to dress for the game. My career is over. The Old Ones are calling me home."

"George, there *are* no Old Ones! You're sick. I'll get you help. There are no Old Ones! Don't believe in that!"

"Do you believe in your High One?"

Quentin blinked, had to remember to breathe, to suck in a breath against the whipping wind. Of course he believed in the High One. High One was real, George's Old Ones were not. But could he explain that now? Did he have enough time?

"The team hates me," George said. "They hate me unless I am perfect. I can't be perfect. They hate that I am ... confused."

Quentin banged his fist against his chest. "I don't hate you. You are the best tight end I've ever played with."

"No! I am worthless. My whole life has been this, Quentin. My *whole life*. I can't take it anymore. I just can't."

Despite the fear, despite a primitive urge to get the hell out of there, the look on George's face gouged at Quentin's soul. The man had physical gifts, a real work ethic, a deep love of the game and an endless desire to win, yet some seriously messed-up mental loop twisted him, forced him to see everything as *bad*.

George's fist tightened on the handle. The handle's red glow lit up individual veins in George's fingers.

"Quentin, get out. My time has come to an end." George started to cry, a noiseless, unmoving thing, all the more heart-wrenching for its stoicism.

Quentin took another breath, held it, wondered if it would be his last. No one would stand by George Starcher in life? Well, Quentin Barnes would stand by his friend in death.

Tears trickled down George's face, making it halfway before the whipping wind pulled them off his skin and toward the Void. "Get out, Quentin! *Please!*"

Quentin released that breath, felt his lip curl into a sneer.

"Shuck you, Starcher. If you're going, I'm going with you."

Quentin started walking toward George.

Starcher opened his mouth in some soundless scream of anguish, then lifted the handle another inch.

The door rattled, groaned opened a little bit more.

The screaming wind turned into a roar.

Out there in that vertical, two-inch strip of black, Quentin saw nothing, for there were no stars in punch-space. He suddenly realized that he didn't even know what punch-space was.

Messal the Efficient kept the landing bay immaculate, not a stray bit of trash or dirt to be found, so the wind pulled at the only things not locked down — Quentin and George, their clothes, their hair.

It was getting hard to breathe. The ship was probably pumping in air, but not fast enough to keep up. Quentin took another step and almost stumbled — the wind was so strong it pushed at his feet, his legs, threatening to throw him off balance.

Then, up above, motion.

Quentin looked up and back down in the same instant. The snap-shot glance gave him hope, but he couldn't let George know something was up there.

That something? Tara the Freak.

The mutant Quyth Warrior was using his thick, long pedipalp arms to slowly descend the dome's metal girders. Quentin had seen monkeys once in a zoo on Stewart — that's what Tara looked like now, his chitin rippling from the exertion of muscles beneath. Like a spider crawling down a wall, Tara moved closer to George.

Quentin forced himself not to look directly at Tara, who was maybe fifteen feet above George's position.

Quentin waved his arms over his head. "George! Okay! I want out!"

George's big biceps flexed. He was about to push the handle all the way up. Quentin looked left and right, trying to find something to grab, a way out — he'd made a huge mistake and he was going to die for it. He could run for the interior door, but if he did, he might die anyway. And if Tara tried to save the day and Quentin wasn't there to help?

Quentin had to get Starcher to close the landing bay door. Then Tara could make his move.

"George, *please!* Just push the handle back down. I have to get out of here!"

"You promise you'll leave?"

Quentin nodded furiously. "Yes! I swear."

"I don't want you to die, Quentin. The Old Ones have not called for you yet."

"Then *close the shucking doors!*"

George licked his lips. He pulled the handle all the way down. The doors groaned and slid together, the hungry wind's roar lowering to a whine of loss before it dropped off altogether.

Quentin took deep breaths, held his hands up palms-out. "Okay, just let go of the handle so I can get out of here."

"No."

"George, I can't get to you fast enough to stop you from lifting it and I'm too scared to turn my back if you're holding it. Just let go."

George looked left, then right, seeing if anyone was close, if there was some kind of trick.

Just don't look up, just don't look up.

George saw nothing. He let go of the handle, held up his own hands, palms-out. "This is your last chance, Quentin. Go now or join me in the Void's embrace."

Quentin saw a shadow drop from the ceiling. Tara smashed into George, driving the big Human hard to the deck. George screamed in surprise, in betrayal. Quentin sprinted toward them. Tara wrapped his big pedipalp arms around George's neck, choking him, trying to hold him down. Despite the extra 360 pounds, George Starcher put a hand on the ground, got to his knees and started to rise, one hand reaching for the glowing red handle.

That was as far as he got.

Quentin jumped, brought his right knee forward as he did, smashing it into George Starcher's mouth.

George sagged to the deck. He didn't move. Quentin and Tara the Freak panted, almost waiting for the big doors to open anyway.

For the first time, Quentin noticed that Tara's cornea swirled a solid, neon pink — the Freak had been just as terrified as Quentin had.

"Thanks," Quentin said. "Thanks for helping me."

"I didn't do it for you," Tara said. His eye color slowly cleared.

"Then why?"

Tara looked down. "He stuck up for me. That ... that is not something I am used to." The misshapen Quyth Warrior looked up. "You did the same. Why would either of you defend *me*?"

For some reason — maybe the relief of being alive, maybe the fact that Tara still didn't get this culture — Quentin laughed.

"Because you're a Kraken," he said. "That's all the reason I need."

The landing bay doors opened. Bridge crew rushed in, as did Michael Kimberlin and Aleksandar Michnik. Doc Patah led a floating medsled. Once the big HeavyG players had lifted George, strapped him to the medsled and led him out of the bay, only then did Quentin relax.

He lightly punched Tara's middle shoulder. "Come on, we're going to the dining deck for a beer."

"I do not drink beer."

"Then you can watch me drink one."

Side by side, Quentin Barnes and Tara the Freak trudged out of the landing bay, leaving the bridge crew to make sure everything was ship-shape.

KRAKENS DEFENSIVE END CLIFF FROST did better than anyone could have expected. When it came to pass rushing, anyway.

The HeavyG free agent turned out to be a natural, one of those players that does far more in an actual game than he ever accomplished in practice. He attacked the Dreadnaughts offensive tackles, tight ends, fullbacks ... anyone wearing the dark brown jerseys that tried to block him.

Those that tried to *pass* block him, anyway. He finished the day with two sacks of Dreadnaughts QB Gavin Warren. He knocked Warren down another four times. Cliff Frost could rush the passer. What Cliff Frost *couldn't* do was stop the run.

When pass-blocking, offensive linemen back up, react to what the defender tries to do to reach the quarterback. For *run* blocking, on the other hand, the offensive linemen gets to step forward and *attack*, using momentum and their mass to their advantage.

If Frost wasn't pinning his ears back and raging in hard on all-fours, his big HeavyG hands slapping at crimson helmets, his orange-jerseyed body spinning and ripping and pushing, he was basically getting knocked on his ass. When the offensive linemen came *at* him, instead of backpedaling *away* from him, Cliff was worthless.

The Dreadnaughts took advantage of that fact all day, constantly attacking Frost by sending running back Don Dennis on off-tackle plays around the left end. Frost's inability to stop the run made Hokor put in Wan-A-Tagol at defensive end. But the Dreadnaughts coach Smitty Halibut seemed prepared for this as well — when Frost was in, the Dreadnaughts ran it, when Wan-A was in, Themala dropped back to pass. Wan-A's pass rush put no pressure on Warren.

Aleksandar Michnik, Ionath's left defensive end, still brought pressure, but when Warren had to pass he simply rolled right, away from Michnik and toward the ineffective Wan-A-Tagol. That gave Warren time to throw and he used short passes to pick the Krakens apart.

The result was that Themala controlled the ball with long, yardage-chewing, clock-eating drives that kept Quentin & Co. off the field. The Dreadnaughts maintained possession for a decisive 42 minutes and 18 seconds, leaving the ball in Quentin's hands for only 17 minutes and 42 seconds. The Krakens D held Themala to 20 points — but Quentin's offense could only post 17.

Quentin spent most of the game on the sidelines, shaking his head at Smitty Halibut's tactical skill. Quite simply, Hokor had been out-coached. Halibut game-planned for Khomeni's replacements. An injury to one player could — and did — make a galaxy's worth of difference.

When the final seconds ticked off the clock, Themala had moved to 8-3. The Ionath Krakens dropped to 7-4. Quentin looked to the scoreboard, watched the results of the other games as they came in.

Yall had defeated Wabash 38-36. The loss didn't impact Wabash, who was 9-2 and already in the playoffs. The game did, however, move Yall to 8-3 — one game ahead of Ionath. The To Pirates, fortunately, beat Isis 28-24, knocking the Ice Storm down to 7-4.

The playoff math was complicated, but one thing stood clear — for the second year in a row, everything would come down to the last game of the season. Next week, the Krakens against the Vanguard. Sunday Night Football. Because there was no Monday Night Football the week before the playoffs, it meant that all other games would finish before Ionath/Vik. By the end of the Krakens' Week Thirteen tilt, they would know if they were moving on to the postseason or heading home to wait six months for their next shot.

Themala had out-coached Hokor, sure, but Hokor would adjust the Krakens strategy for Vik. *Had* to adjust, because Khomeni would still be out of the lineup.

One way or another, the Krakens had to find a way to win.

GFL WEEK TWELVE ROUNDUP
Courtesy of Galaxy Sports Network

HOME		AWAY	
Orbiting Death	21	**Alimum Armada**	27
New Rodina Astronauts	17	Coranadillana Cloud Killers	7
Hittoni Hullwalkers	23	Lu Juggernauts	13
Themala Dreadnaughts	20	Ionath Krakens	17
To Pirates	28	Isis Ice Storm	24
Wabash Wolfpack	36	**Yall Criminals**	38
Bartel Water Bugs	17	Texas Earthlings	14
Bord Brigands	0	**Vik Vanguard**	10
Sala Intrigue	13	**D'Kow War Dogs**	31
Shorah Warlords	0	**Jang Atom Smashers**	13
Jupiter Jacks	10	**Neptune Scarlet Fliers**	23

THE TO PIRATES (9-2) are in the postseason thanks to a 28-24 win over the Isis Ice Storm (7-4). The loss nearly crippled Isis's chances, putting them a game behind Themala and Yall, which are both 8-3. For Isis to get in, Week Thirteen must see the Ice Storm defeat Themala, and Yall must drop its final game to the Pirates. Isis owns the head-to-head tiebreaker against Yall, so if they both finish 8-4, Isis is in.

If Themala beats Isis, the Dreadnaughts finish 9-3 and are in the playoffs. If Themala loses that game, they are 8-4 and out of the playoffs due to being on the bad side of a head-to-head tiebreaker with Yall.

Ionath is also 7-4 but needs more help to make the postseason. The Krakens must win a tough game against the Vik Vanguard

(8-3) and also must see Yall lose to the Pirates. Ionath owns the tiebreaker over the Ice Storm, thanks to a 24-21 Week One win, so if both teams finish 8-4, Ionath is in.

There is a possibility that Ionath, Themala, Yall and Isis will all finish 8-4. If that happens, a complex tiebreaker process will ensue.

Yall's 38-36 defeat of the Wabash Wolfpack kept the Criminals in the playoff hunt. Wabash is already guaranteed a postseason appearance, although the Pack could finish anywhere from the first to the third seed.

Over in the Solar Division, the dance card is full. Neptune (10-1) defeated the Jupiter Jacks (8-3) to take the Solar Division title, lock up a first-place seed and earn home-field advantage in the first and second playoff rounds. Jupiter and Vik will have either the second or third seed, depending on the outcome of their Week Thirteen games.

The Bartel Water Bugs (6-5) claimed the fourth and final Solar playoff spot, thanks to a 17-14 win over the Texas Earthlings (4-7). Even if Bartel loses their final game and Jang (5-6) wins, both teams will finish with 6-6 records and the 'Bugs get the playoff spot due to the head-to-head tie-breaker.

Relegations

Sala's 31-13 loss to the D'Kow War Dogs drops the Intrigue's record to 1-10, sealing its relegation fate. With one game left in the season, Sala is two games behind the next-closest team, the Shorah Warlords (3-8).

The Alimum Armada (3-8) won 27-21 over the Orbiting Death (4-7). That, combined with Lu's 23-13 loss to the Hittoni Hullwalkers (5-6) means that the Juggernauts (1-10) are relegated out of the Planet Division.

Deaths

Lu Juggernauts center **Rikard Pettersson**, killed on a clean hit by Hittoni Hullwalkers nose-tackle Pro-Co-Pio.

Offensive Player of the Week

Texas receiver **Leavenworth,** who caught 11 passes for 136 yards and two touchdowns in the Earthlings' 17-14 losing effort to the Bartel Waterbugs.

Defensive Player of the Week

Vik defensive tackle **E-Coo-Lee,** who had six solo tackles, one sack, one forced fumble and one fumble recovery in the Vanguard's 10-0 shutout of the Bord Brigands.

23

WEEK THIRTEEN: IONATH KRAKENS at VIK VANGUARD

PLANET DIVISION	SOLAR DIVISION
9-2 x - Wabash Wolfpack	10-1 y - Neptune Scarlet Fliers
9-2 x - To Pirates	8-3 x - Jupiter Jacks
8-3 Themala Dreadnaughts	8-3 x - Vik Vanguard
8-3 Yall Criminals	6-5 x - Bartel Water Bugs
7-4 Ionath Krakens	5-6 Jang Atom Smashers
7-4 Isis Ice Storm	4-7 Bord Brigands
5-6 Hittoni Hullwalkers	4-7 Texas Earthlings
4-7 OS1 Orbiting Death	4-7 D'Kow War Dogs
3-8 Coranadillana Cloud Killers	4-7 New Rodina Astronauts
3-8 Alimum Armada	3-8 Shorah Warlords
1-10 *Lu Juggernauts	1-10 *Sala Intrigue

x = playoffs, y = division title, * = team has been relegated

BEAUTY. DEATH.

Two words that seemed to be opposites, but both applied to the planet Ki, home of the Empire. Nine-point-one billion sentients lived on the Earth-sized sphere. Where Earth's twelve billion covered the planet with concrete, glass and steel, reducing plant life to the realms of isolated reserves, Ki looked untouched — a lush, endless vista of yellow and red land mass and oceans of emerald-green spotted with fuzzy dots of blue.

The red and yellow were the colors of native trees. The blue spots in the oceans represented bacterial blooms hundreds of miles wide, part of the ongoing lifecycle between the bacteria and the microscopic, waterborne plants that created the dominant green color.

Those colors, the pristine, natural expanse of forests so thick you could go from coast to coast without touching the ground, those were the *beauty* of the planet.

As for *death*, that came from the Ki themselves.

Quentin Barnes had been born and raised in a violent place. From what Kimberlin had taught him, the Purist Nation — Humanity's most violent society, by far — had nothing on the Ki culture. Wars raged beneath the endless forest canopy. The Creterakians controlled what they could, removed firearms whenever possible. That meant that most of the time, Ki fought with axes, swords, knives, spears, even clubs.

The Ki species had developed agriculture by taking food and materials from their trees instead of cutting them down and planting other things. Even their prey animals flourished in and among the towering red plants. As such, the Ki never leveled their forests as had the Humans and the Sklorno. This lack of open spaces impacted the Ki's style of warfare — even large-scale conflicts still had the feel of guerilla battles.

The Ki had been a pre-industrial species when the Collectors landed over a thousand years ago. The Collectors enslaved the Ki race, turning them into shock troops that would help the Collectors conquer other planets. After overthrowing their Collector overlords in 2009 ErT, the Ki slid into a dark age. There the race stayed for five hundred years, centuries of tribal warfare and sacrifice to dark gods, a time of subsistence farming and feudal hierarchy. This lasted until the Givers landed in 2518. For the second time, an alien race advanced the Ki beyond their own means.

The Givers provided punch-drive technology, taught the Ki to build starships and also taught them how to develop natural resources without altering the face of the planet. The Ki responded by butchering their benefactors, ending the Givers' run of technological benevolence that brought faster-than-light travel to the Harrah and the Kurgurk.

Quentin thought about the planet's history as the shuttle rattled through the thick atmosphere. It seemed shocking to see forest running to the horizon in every direction. Through planning or luck — or possibly both — the Ki had avoided the endless urban sprawl that now covered the surface of Earth, Chachana, Satirli 6 and dozens of other worlds.

The shuttle angled toward a massive, circular city covered by a high dome. Most Ki citizens lived beneath the forest canopy, but intergalactic business required dealings with other races — that meant domed cities dedicated to commerce.

This dome: the city of VikPor, the very capital of the Ki Empire. Home to not one, not two, but *three* professional rugby clubs, including the two-time galactic champion Vik Vengeance. Rugby remained the Ki Empire's top sport, but that didn't mean the sentients didn't enjoy their gridiron. Gridiron was the *galaxy's* most-popular spectator sport. That meant football was where the big money lie. Where there is money, there are the Ki.

Five years ago, the Vanguard had come just five points from winning it all when they lost Galaxy Bowl 2679 to New Rodina. The team had fallen apart after that, barely winning enough games to avoid relegation. Team owner Kin-Shal-An had hired new coaches, signed key free agents and invested in rookies. Out of the fifty-three players on the 2679 team, only four remained. Forty-nine new faces in all. The Vanguard had gelled into one of the league's best teams, as evidenced by its six-game winning streak. If Vik landed a seventh-straight win, it had a shot at a home playoff game.

Quentin would not let that happen.

The shuttle slid through a dissolving hole in the city dome, a hole that closed up as soon as the shuttle passed through. Quyth technology. The Ki culture had money to burn — they bought the best tech available anywhere in the galaxy. Like other Ki cities, VikPor was laid out in concentric rings that alternated circles of tall buildings and circles of native vegetation. Near the city center, Quentin saw VikPor's crowning jewel: three stadiums, one for each rugby team. The teams could have shared a stadium, but funds to build massive structures were in no short supply.

The shuttle shot past that trio of temples, moved closed to the city dome's edge. There lie the floating Kin-Shal-An Trade Guild Stadium — just two decks, a seating capacity of only 65,000. Six huge, deep-green, arcing pillars rose up and in from a hexagonal base. Thick cables webbed out from each pillar, running down to the stadium's concave yellow-brown base, under it, rising up and connecting to other pillars. The entire stadium hovered a hundred feet above the city. Kin-Shal-An's architectural statement of grandeur. Below the stadium, a low-light forest park, home to the Vanguard's training facilities and administrative offices.

The shuttle slowed, dropped in above a wide radius road. Tall buildings passed by on either side. The yellow-brown was a constantly swirling layer of fluorine trapped between two thick sheets of crysteel, making the stadium seem to float in a bowl-shaped cloud. Bright sun gave way to shadow, to artificial lights bathing everything in an iridescent blue glow. Such a surreal feeling, to fly *under* a football stadium. Above him, a web of tree trunk-sized cables supported the curving stadium bottom. Down below, the strange curls of alien plants.

The shuttle then angled up, slid into an opening below the stadium. Quentin felt the ship slowing, preparing to land.

Once he set foot off the shuttle, he would be on enemy territory. For the next two days, no more thoughts of his fake father, no more thoughts of George Starcher, no more thoughts of Somalia Midori, his sister, Fred's investigation, Gredok's double-dealing, Danny the Dolphin's warning against signing the contract.

Quentin Barnes had begun this season with a single goal — lead his team into the playoffs. To make it, they had to beat the Vik Vanguard.

The rest of the galaxy would have to take care of itself for a little while.

He would be busy.

Live feed from UBS GameDay holocast coverage

"Hello there, football fanatics and welcome to our coverage of Sunday Night Football. I'm Masara the Observant. With me, as always, is the galaxy's most colorful color-man, Chick McGee."

"Hello, Masara and hello, folks at home."

"Chick, we've got a nebula-sized game ahead of us tonight. A pair of upstarts fighting for a playoff berth. The visitors, the Ionath Krakens, or as their fans call them, *the Orange and the Black*. Led by third-year quarterback Quentin Barnes, the Krakens are seven-and-four — they *must* win this game to make the play-offs and they would also need help in the form of a Yall Criminals win. The Criminals have already finished their game against the To Pirates and we're just waiting for the punch-drive messengers to bring us news of the results. Chick, what is Ionath up against tonight?"

"Masara, the Krakens have their work cut out for them in the form of the green-and-gold Vik Vanguard, led by defensive super-star Mur the Mighty. Eight wins and three losses, Vik has already qualified for its first trip to the playoffs since losing Galaxy Bowl twenty-one to the New Rodina Astronauts. But just because they're already in the postseason parade doesn't mean they'll lay low and lollygag in this titanic tilt. If Vik is victorious and Jupiter gets jilted by Jang, the Vanguard will secure the second seed in the Solar Division. That means a *home playoff game*, the franchise's first-ever. So they want this win badly for themselves and for their fans."

"Sounds like we've got us a firestorm of a game, Chick."

"Yes, Masara, this one is shaping up to be hotter than Somalia Midori in a wet rad-suit contest."

"Chick! We're not even five minutes in! Can you—"

"Sorry, Masara, sorry folks at home, but this game is just that incandescent. The Krakens are up against the league's best defense, anchored by Ki defensive tackles E-Coo-Lee and Ar-Cham-Bault. You can bet those two have sharpened up their triangular teeth and are ready to take a bite outta Barnes."

"Chick, major stories in this game for Ionath are the loss of defensive end Ibrahim Khomeni and the benching of tight end George Starcher. Khomeni has been replaced by rookie Cliff "The Spaz" Frost, so nicknamed for his seemingly uncoordinated, lurching style of pass-rush. Frost is only brought in on passing situations. For every-down play, Khomeni is replaced by either rookie Rich Palmer or fourth-year player Wan-A-Tagol. You can bet the Vanguard will attack all three of those players. As for Starcher, last year he and Ju Tweedy seemed to be the final pieces of Ionath's contender puzzle. But Starcher's star has fallen as of late, to the point where Coach Hokor the Hookchest didn't even have him dress for last week's loss to Themala."

"Masara, ever since Starcher dropped that game-winning pass against Coranadillana in Week Three, he hasn't been the same. Fortunately for the Krakens, Rick Warburg seems to have stepped up as a dominant tight end. Warburg has three touchdown catches in the last two games and has become a favorite target of Quentin Barnes."

"Well, Chick, Barnes will need all of his weapons if the Krakens are going to beat the red-hot Vanguard. Six wins in a row, powered by the league's best defense that last week hung a shut-out on the Bord Brigands. The teams are lining up for the kickoff. The Krakens will get the ball first. Let's go down to the action on the field."

THE VANGUARD KICKER blasted the ball, sending the brown leather arcing high over a light blue field marked with dark purple lines. From the sidelines, Quentin watched the Vik players rush forward. Afternoon sun reflected off of gold helmets decorated with a thick, dark-green V. The V's arms swept up and to the helmet's sides. The V's bottom point extended down to the middle of the players' golden face masks. The wing pattern's angle resembled that of the Krakens' own six-tentacled logo.

Vik's iridescent green jerseys echoed the pattern. A golden triangle started halfway between their helmets and the edge of their shoulder pads, pointing down to their black belts. Small, black-lined green numbers sat in that gold area, on the chest just below the face mask. Gold leg armor and black shoes completed the uniform.

The Vanguard's two Sklorno shooters raced downfield as Richfield settled under the ball. A wall of orange and black crashed into a battering ram of dark green and gold. Bodies flew, bodies dropped — and Richfield slid straight through the middle. No one touched her. The Human kicker waited at the 50-yard line, the only thing between Richfield and six points.

In the open field, there was nothing the Human kicker could do — Richfield leapt fifteen feet into the air, sailing over his out-reached arms. The leap cost her speed and almost let the trailing green-and-gold Sklorno catch her. *Almost.* Two sets of tentacles wrapped her up at the 5 — three Sklorno bodies tumbled but landed in the gold-painted end zone.

The Krakens sidelines erupted. Opening kickoff, touchdown Ionath.

QUENTIN LOOKED FOR open receivers. He found none before he felt the pressure coming from his right. A snap-glance confirmed his fear — linebacker Mur the Mighty, blitzing again. Becca stepped up to block. Mur seemed to aim high, to go head to head with Becca, but as soon as Becca rose up to meet the hit Mur tucked and *rolled* past, that eye-twisting motion only a Quyth Warrior could do.

Quentin ran left, but Mur was too fast. The linebacker snapped out of the roll and dove, green-clad pedipalps reaching for Quentin's black-armored legs. He tried to high-step, but Mur caught him and he fell face-first onto the light blue field.

Fourth down. The Krakens would have to punt for the fifth time and it was only halfway through the second quarter. Quentin had already been sacked three times. The Vanguard defense was for real.

Whistles blew. The mostly Ki crowd sounded its approval with a rhythmic drumbeat, 240,000 arms clacking against 60,000 chests in a deafening combat language. Mur stood and waved to the crowd before reaching down to help Quentin up.

"You're fast," Quentin said.

"No, you are slow," Mur said. He patted Quentin on the helmet, than ran off field.

"CHICK, THE TEAMS ARE coming back on the field for the second half. The Vanguard is up 14-7. What does the Ionath offense have to do to get into this game?"

"Well, Masara, someone is going to have to step up and surprise us. Vik hasn't allowed an offensive touchdown in *six quarters*, not since Rick Renaud ripped them for forty-two points back in Week Eleven. Vik's linebackers continue to bring pressure on Barnes, not giving him time to set up and get a good look. At the same time, Ionath running back Ju Tweedy hasn't been able to break a run. The Mad Ju had ten carries for only thirty-one yards."

"Chick, this is it for Ionath. If they don't figure things out in the second half, they are out of the playoffs. Let's head back to the field."

QUENTIN DROPPED BACK, eyes taking in a wave of green and gold closing in on him. He turned as he backpedaled, throwing out to the right where Becca Montagne waited for a screen pass. Kimberlin and Vu-Ko-Will were in front of her. The ball no sooner left Quentin's hand than the lightning-fast Vanguard defense reacted, the three Quyth linebackers tucking and rolling to their left as if they'd been expecting the play.

They *had* been expecting it. Quentin had *wanted* them to expect it.

He sprinted to his left, away from the play, then turned upfield at the left sidelines. He looked back over his shoulder. The entire Vanguard defense closed in on Becca. Instead of tucking the ball and running, the former Green Bay Packers quarterback stopped, raised the ball to her right ear and launched a pass.

Damn, that is a great throw.

The tight spiral arced toward him. Quentin didn't have to break stride, not even a step. The Vanguard safeties turned and ran toward him, but they had committed to stopping the screen pass and were 25 yards away.

Quentin sprinted past the 20. The ball fell into his hands with all the weight of a dropped feather. The pass was *perfect*. He watched the ball all the way into the crook of his arm. When he looked up again, he was crossing the goal line. The trick play resulted in a 56-yard touchdown pass, one that Quentin *caught* rather than threw.

He tossed the ball to a zebe, then ran to the sidelines.

With the extra point, it was a tie game, 14-all with one quarter to play.

"CHICK! WE KNEW it had to happen sooner or later. You can't keep Ju Tweedy out of the end zone forever."

"You can't stop the Mad Ju, Masara, you can only hope to contain him. The Vanguard has done a good job of that so far, but it only takes one mistake and *boom* — Tweedy scampers for a thirty-seven-yard touchdown run."

"Chick, what a game. That touchdown ties the game at twenty-one apiece with only four minutes to play. It's up to the Vanguard offense, but they have to pick up first downs or they will leave time on the clock for Barnes and the Krakens."

"The Vik offense has to step up, Masara. They've been playing like a retarded Worker wacked-out on a kilo of half-rotted juniper berries."

"Chick! That is unacceptable!"

"Sorry, Masara, sorry folks at home, let's go down to the field."

THE VANGUARD MOVED THE BALL, closing in on field-goal range. Third and 5, ball on Ionath's 40. Forty-four seconds to play. A 57-yard field goal, if they tried it. Vik's kicker's range topped out at about 52 yards. Vik needed a first down to get into his range.

Quentin and Becca stood on the sidelines: watching, waiting, hoping.

The crowd clacked out a staccato rhythm, the sound of 60,000 machine guns firing in unison.

Vanguard quarterback Rich Barchi looked left, barked out signals, looked right, did the same. On the snap, Quentin saw John, Virak and Choto take a step back. They were dropping into a short zone, willing to give up a pass for three or four yards, but they would not get beat for more than that, would not give up the first down.

Barchi dropped back.

Quentin felt Becca grab his hand and squeeze. He didn't think to shake it away because he saw what she saw: defensive end Cliff Frost's wild, windmilling arms reaching up and over the Vik offensive tackle. The Ki lineman tried to keep up, pushed to his left to block Frost's spastic attack, but Frost spun back inside and landed on all-fours. Frost's big arms and powerful legs barreled him in on the right-handed Barchi, who had his back turned, who was just starting his throwing motion. Frost leapt, his big hand slapping Barchi's arm before the arm came forward.

The ball flew straight up — a fumble.

It spun in the air. Barchi turned madly, looking to the ground; he didn't know where it was. Frost fell and as he did, he reached out and plucked the ball out of the air. Quentin saw him tuck around it in a fetal position before he vanished under a pile of green-and-gold, orange-and-black.

Quentin squeezed Becca's hand, just once, an automatic reaction before he realized he *was* holding her hand and let go. Thirty-two seconds to play. Whistles blew — Krakens ball on their own 47-yard line.

Quentin grabbed Becca's shoulder pads, turned her to face him. "They fell for it once," he said. "If we set you up to throw, think you can hit another pass?"

She nodded, unable to control her wide smile. "Just give me the ball, Q."

He nodded once, then turned and led his team out onto the field.

"CHICK, IT'S SECOND DOWN and eight for the Krakens on their own forty-five. Thirty seconds to play, no time-outs. Do they go for the win, or do they take a knee and send this to overtime?"

"Masara, I'm thinking what every sentient in this stadium is thinking — the Krakens want to win it right now. If they pick up a long first down, Arioch Morningstar can nail a field goal for the win."

"Here we go, Chick. Quentin Barnes is lining up behind center. He has Becca Montagne and Ju Tweedy in the I-formation. Rick Warburg at right tight end, Halawa wide-right, Hawick wide-left. The Vanguard are in a four-three defense, looks like they're playing woman-to-woman. And the snap! Barnes pitches wide right to Ju Tweedy, Montagne is lead-blocking, *she trips!* Tweedy has no lead blockers! Here comes Mur the Mighty ... Tweedy stops. He pitches to his left, to Montagne! She has the ball, she's running ... no! She's setting up to pass! Barnes is on the left sideline, but he's covered! Mur the Mighty has Montagne ... *no!* Montagne shakes Mur off, she's still up! She's throwing up a prayer over the middle ... Rick Warburg is double-covered, he goes up ... *and comes down with it! Krakens ball on the Vik twenty-five!*"

"Masara, I've seen some amazing catches in my day, but I have just three words for you — *Rick! War! Burg!* He grabbed that pass like a starving OS1 street bum fighting over a pile of fresh puke!"

"Chick, you are obnoxious, but this time I don't even care.

A pitch-back trick play to Montagne, who avoided a sure sack and hit Warburg over the middle. What excitement! What drama! Barnes is calling his team up to the line, but he's not rushing. He's going to let the time tick down, then spike the ball to stop the clock ... and there's the spike."

"The clock stops with three seconds left, Masara, enough time to run one play. The Krakens kicker Arioch Morningstar and his field goal unit are coming onto the field."

"Chick! Our producer just got word from a punch-space relay — the To Pirates defeated the Yall Criminals 24-7.

"Masara, that means if Morningstar hits this kick, the Krakens are in the playoffs."

"And here we go, Chick. A forty-two yard field goal to put Ionath into the Tier One playoffs for the first time in nine seasons. Here's the snap, the hold looks good, the kick ... and it's good!"

"Ionath wins 24-21! What a game, Masara, what ... a ... *game!*"

JOHN TWEEDY DID HALF-NAKED LAPS around the locker room. Instead of an unwilling coach on his shoulders, this time he had an unwilling kicker — at 5-foot-8, 185 pounds, there was little Arioch could do to resist the will of 6-foot-6, 310-pound John Tweedy. Hokor hadn't gone unrewarded, though — Ju had dumped a full beverage bucket on the coach, again leaving Hokor with soaking wet fur matted to his tiny body.

Quentin and Tara the Freak stood at the edge of the communal locker room, at the edges of the madness. Tara showed no emotion, but Quentin smiled — the first genuine smile he'd felt since that dinner at Torba the Hungry's.

The Krakens collectively lost their minds — sentients pushed and screamed and laughed and joked. Bottles of champagne popped. Fizzy spray flew everywhere, soaking everything. Everyone hugged everyone else. Becca stood on a bench, laughing, trying to carry a tune for the Sklorno that now believed singing was a mandatory part of a victory celebration. Even Rick Warburg got in on the action, for once in his life ignoring race and just savoring the moment with his teammates. Everyone wanted to congratulate Warburg. His leaping, one-handed catch was already on Sports Center. The whole play was the kind of highlight that would be shown over and over for decades to come.

To Quentin, it all felt *amazing*. A weight as big as the *Touchback* had been lifted off of his chest. They had done it. They had made the playoffs. From here on out, it was anyone's game. And the first team they would face? Archrival Wabash, a team they'd defeated in Week Nine.

The Ionath Krakens had arrived.

The only variable was time?

Well, that time was almost at hand.

QUENTIN, MA TWEEDY AND TARA the Freak walked into the Nauer Clinic. The clinic sat in the 220-degree section of Radius Seven, a very high-priced part of town. Quentin had insisted Gredok pay for George's care. Gredok may have won the battle of Quentin's contract, but that victory came at a cost — Quentin had lost all fear of his team owner. Quentin was stuck with Gredok for the next ten years? Well, then Gredok was going to be stuck with Quentin.

"Fancy place," Ma Tweedy said.

Stylish furniture lined the waiting room. Paintings hung on the walls. No holoframes, actual canvas with actual paint. One caught Quentin's eye — was that a Don Pine creation?

A young Human woman entered the room. Young and only a little taller than Ma Tweedy. Her long blonde hair was tied up in matted coils that looked like Yassoud's braided beard. Deadlocks, the style was called. Something like that, anyway.

"Mister Barnes, welcome," she said. "Doc Patah told me to expect you. I'm Doctor Cassie Nauer."

"*You're* Doctor Nauer? Uh ... you're taking care of George?"

She nodded.

"Aren't you a little ... *young* ... to be a doctor?"

She smiled. "Aren't you a little young to be a starting quarterback?"

"Uh … well, yeah, but … "

"But you're really good at what you do?"

He nodded.

"So am I," she said. "Do you trust Doctor Patah?"

Quentin nodded again. "Sure."

"Well, *he* trusts *me* to take care of George. Is that good enough?"

"I guess so. How is George? Can we see him?"

"Absolutely. Follow me."

She led them deeper into the facility. The place was built like a dorm — small apartments that each contained a bed, a couch and a holotank. A few of the rooms had people in them, some wearing robes, some wearing normal clothes.

"We take care of ten Humans at any given time, maximum," Dr. Nauer said as she walked. "We were lucky that we had room for George."

"So how is he?" Quentin asked. "Can he, you know, talk and stuff?"

"You are not family or a legal guardian, so I can't give you specifics," Cassie said. "But I can tell you that we're developing a medication schedule for him and that he's responding well to it."

They turned a corner, kept walking.

"What about football?" Quentin asked. "Can he play this week?"

Cassie stopped and turned, facing her visitors. "No. He's done for the season, Quentin. No games. I'm talking to Doctor Patah about letting George travel with the team for the playoffs, but he will *not* dress for games, under any circumstances. He's done for the season. If he sticks to my program, I'm confident he can play next year. That is, if he wants to."

Quentin's face screwed into an expression of dismissal. "If he *wants* to? Who wouldn't want to play?"

A smack on his shoulder. Ma Tweedy, scowling at him. "Quentin. Be polite to the doctor."

Quentin rubbed his shoulder even though it didn't hurt. "Okay."

Ma Tweedy tilted her head curtly toward the young doctor.

Quentin sighed. "Sorry, Doctor. I didn't mean to be rude."

"No apology necessary," Cassie said. "Quentin, you and Tara, you did a brave thing. George needed help. You helped him. I don't know if you did that because he's your friend or just because he can catch a ball, but from what he tells me, you saved his life."

Tara said nothing.

Quentin felt his own face turning red. He looked at the carpet. "Yeah, well, maybe we should have gotten him help sooner."

Cassie reached out and stroked Quentin's arm. "Mister Barnes, that doesn't matter. You *got* him help when many people would have ignored him. Come on, let's see George."

She walked down the hall. They followed. Quentin felt tiny arms wrapping around his right elbow — Ma Tweedy.

"Quentin, I am so proud of you. You're always helping people."

She squeezed, walked arm in arm with him. He felt a strange feeling in his chest. Ma Tweedy was *proud* of him. And not for something he did on a football field, for something he did as a *person*.

His real mother was dead. That could never be changed. Maybe it was time to stop grieving the loss of a woman he couldn't remember, start appreciating this total stranger who had claimed him as her own.

Cassie walked into a room. Inside, George Starcher sat on a bed, tossing a football up and down with one hand. His face was painted white, a line of five blue dots across his forehead.

"Hey, Quentin. Hey, Tara. Hello, Ma Tweedy."

"Hello, George," Ma Tweedy said. "You look well."

"Thank you."

Quentin looked to Cassie. "Uh, the, uh, paint? That's normal?"

Cassie shook her head. "No, but it's not hurting anything and George likes it. One thing at a time, Mister Barnes."

"I feel way better," George said. "You guys kept me from doing something real stupid. The universal powers will gird your loins accordingly."

"Gird my what?"

"Loins," George said. He stopped tossing the football and smiled. "Guys, I appreciate you coming to see me, but I know what's going on. I watched the Vik game. *Playoffs*. That is amazing."

Quentin shrugged. "Yeah, sorry you can't be there for it."

"Next year," George said. "I don't know why you guys helped me, but I'm glad you did. Quentin, if you hadn't come to my apartment that day, I don't think I would have left you the towel. If I hadn't done that ... well, I don't think Tara alone could have stopped me."

The chain of events flashed through Quentin's head. Don Pine urging Quentin to talk to Starcher. His fake father doing the same thing. Two men that Quentin despised — but if they hadn't said something, would he have ever seen George's struggle? Would he have been in the right place at the right time without Don Pine, without Sarge Vinje? That was an unwelcome and sobering thought and it made it a little harder to hate them both.

But only a little.

"Get going," George said. "Thanks for stopping by, it means a lot, but you need to focus on the Wolfpack. Doctor Nauer has me covered. If I behave, I can join you on the *Touchback* for the trip to Wabash. Now get out of here."

A pat on his arm. He looked down to the wrinkled face of Ma Tweedy. "I'll stay with George for awhile," she said. "You and Tara get back to work."

George was okay. It was time.

Quentin said his goodbyes, then he and Tara the Freak saw themselves out.

The Quyth Warrior had gained status in Quentin's eyes. Even if Quentin couldn't count himself a hero for helping George, he didn't have that same reservation about Tara.

"You're quiet," Quentin said.

"I am always quiet. I do not have much to say."

Quentin laughed. "Well, I guess that's true. Not sure if you got the news, but we're in the playoffs."

"I am aware."

"And are you still mad I brought you up to Tier One? Still feel all glum that we snatched you away from the Manglers?"

"I am less mad than I was before."

Quentin raised his hand to flag down a cab. "What would it take to make you not mad at all?"

Tara turned to stare, his one baseball-sized eye an almost perfect cross-species copy of John Tweedy's *wow are you dumb expression*. "A playoff win," Tara said. "That would be a start."

Quentin nodded. They crawled into the first cab that stopped, then headed for Ionath Stadium.

GFL WEEK THIRTEEN ROUNDUP
Courtesy of Galaxy Sports Network

HOME		AWAY	
Alimum Armada	18	Lu Juggernauts	17
Coranadillana Cloud Killers	16	**Wabash Wolfpack**	28
Neptune Scarlet Fliers	17	**Hittoni Hullwalkers**	23
Vik Vanguard	21	**Ionath Krakens**	24
Isis Ice Storm	31	**Themala Dreadnaughts**	34
Shorah Warlords	10	**Orbiting Death**	28
Yall Criminals	7	**To Pirates**	24
Bord Brigands	21	**Bartel Water Bugs**	23
D'Kow War Dogs	31	Texas Earthlings	16
Jupiter Jacks	21	**Jang Atom Smashers**	31
Sala Intrigue	17	**New Rodina Astronauts**	24

A DRAMA-FILLED WEEK THIRTEEN ended in spectacular style and finalized the postseason playoff bracket.

Ionath tight end Rick Warburg put the Krakens into the playoffs for the first time in nine seasons with a last-minute catch thrown by fullback Rebecca Montagne. The trick play put the Krakens (8-4) in range for a 42-yard field goal, which Arioch Morningstar kicked through for a 24-21 win over the Vik Vanguard (8-4).

The victory gives Ionath the fourth seed in the Planet Division playoffs.

Wabash (10-2) took the first seed in the Planet Division, thanks to both a head-to-head tiebreaker over the second-seeded To Pirates (10-2), and a 28-16 win over the Coranadillana Cloud Killers (3-9).

The Pirates earned the second seed thanks to a 24-7 win over the Yall Criminals (8-4). Themala locked up the third seed in the Planet Division with a 34-31 win over the Isis Ice Storm (7-5).

Neptune, which had already secured the first seed in the Solar Division as well as the division title, rested several starters in a 23-17 loss to the Hittoni Hullwalkers (6-6). Both Jupiter and Vik lost in Week Thirteen, leaving the teams with identical 8-4 records. Jupiter beat Vik in Week Five, giving the Jacks the head-to-head tiebreaker and the second seed in the Solar.

Jupiter will host Vik in the first round of the playoffs, while Neptune hosts fourth-seeded Bartel (7-5). The Water Bugs earned their postseason bid thanks to a last-second field goal by Eddy Jones that gave Bartel a 23-21 win over the 4-8 Bord Brigands.

Deaths

Bord running back **Robert Harris**, killed on an illegal head-to-head hit by Bartel safety Alpharetta. Alpharetta has been suspended for Bartel's first-round playoff game against Neptune.

Offensive Player of the Week

Wabash running back **John Ellsworth**, who rushed for 124 yards on 23 carries and a touchdown in the Wolfpack's win over Coranadillana.

Defensive Player of the Week

Neptune defensive tackle **Chris Maler**, who had four solo tackles and two-and-a-half sacks in the Scarlet Fliers' 23-17 loss to the Hittoni Hullwalkers.

BOOK FOUR:
THE POSTSEASON

24

THE QUARTERFINALS

PLANET DIVISION

10-2 y - Wabash Wolfpack

10-2 x - To Pirates

9-3 x - Themala Dreadnaughts

8-4 x - Ionath Krakens

8-4 Yall Criminals

7-5 Isis Ice Storm

6-6 Hittoni Hullwalkers

5-7 OS1 Orbiting Death

4-8 Alimum Armada

3-9 Coranadillana Cloud Killers

1-11 *Lu Juggernauts

SOLAR DIVISION

10-2 y - Neptune Scarlet Fliers

8-4 x - Jupiter Jacks

8-4 x - Vik Vanguard

7-5 x - Bartel Water Bugs

6-6 Jang Atom Smashers

5-7 D'Kow War Dogs

5-7 New Rodina Astronauts

4-8 Bord Brigands

4-8 Texas Earthlings

3-9 Shorah Warlords

1-11 *Sala Intrigue

x = playoffs, y = division title, * = team has been relegated

THE KRAKENS SPRINTED OFF THE FIELD, gathered around the holoboard in the communal locker room. The league had announced the All-Pro roster. Rumor was that *three* Krakens had made the list. Quentin knew one had to be Kill-O-Yowet for another dominant season at left tackle. Despite missing a few games with an injury, the Ki lineman was truly one of the best in the game and deserved that honor a thousand times over.

But who were the other two?

Quentin felt butterflies in his chest and stomach. He had to pee. The three biggest honors in the game were, in order, Galaxy Bowl Champion, then league MVP and being named All-Pro. The first stood in a class all by itself, light-years ahead of anything else.

League MVP was the ultimate individual achievement. It meant the entire sport of professional football said *you are the best in the game.* Quentin knew he hadn't put up the numbers needed for that, especially considering the way Rick Renaud and Neptune Scarlet Fliers QB Adam Guri were playing, but he *had* put up the numbers needed for that final accolade — All-Pro.

The number of All-Pros varied per position. Of twenty-two teams in Tier One, just three quarterbacks would earn the honor. Renaud and Guri had two of those spots locked up. Quentin wasn't the only one in the running for that last spot: Frank Zimmer had recorded another stellar season, as had — Quentin hated to admit — the OS1 Orbiting Death's Condor Adrienne. But the Death had only five wins and they hadn't made the playoffs. Those things factored in. Quentin had eight wins, he *had* led his team to the postseason. He wanted that honor before Condor got it because there was no question Condor would get it eventually.

John Tweedy walked up to the holoboard. "Okay, team, the story is posted. Everyone ready to read?"

A locker room's worth of orange-and-black clad sentients nodded, grunted assent.

John tapped the glowing icons.

The story appeared. They read.

From *The Ionath City Gazette*

GFL Names 2684 All-Pro Team

by TOYAT THE INQUISITIVE

NEW YORK CITY, EARTH, PLANETARY UNION — GFL Commissioner Rob Froese today announced the 2684 All-Pro selections. Ionath racked up three players with this elite honor: fullback Rebecca Montagne, defensive tackle Mum-O-Killowe and left offensive tackle Kill-O-Yowet, who earned the award for the second year in a row.

The last time Ionath had three players named All-Pro was 2675, the year the Krakens lost the Galaxy Bowl to the Jupiter Jacks.

Neptune quarterback Adam Guri was named the league MVP. Guri started every game as he led the Scarlet Fliers to a 10-2 record, racking up 3,412 yards and setting an accuracy record by completing 70.61 percent of his throws.

OFFENSE

Quarterback

Rick Renaud
Yall Criminals

Adam Guri
Neptune Scarlet Fliers

Condor Adrienne
OS1 Orbiting Death

Running back

Randy Noseworthy
To Pirates

Daniel Carrus
D'Kow War Dogs

John Ellsworth
Wabash Wolfpack

Fullback

Ralph Schmeer
Wabash Wolfpack

Rebecca Montagne
Ionath Krakens

Wide receiver

Leavenworth
Texas Earthlings

Brazilia
OS1 Orbiting Death

Victoria
To Pirates

Amarillo
Neptune Scarlet Fliers

Tight end

Andreas Kimming
Yall Criminals

Rich Evanko
New Rodina Astronauts

Tackle

Kill-O-Yowet
Ionath Krakens

Michael Brown
D'Kow War Dogs

Kriz-To-Pher
Jang Atom Smashers

Guard

David Sobkowiak
To Pirates

Bal-De-Sari
Themala Dreadnaughts

Josh Moon
Shorah Warlords

Center

Graham Harting
To Pirates

Kola-Kow-Ski
D'Kow War Dogs

DEFENSE

Defensive end
Ryan Nossek
Isis Ice Storm

Col-Que-Hon
Wabash Wolfpack

Jesper Schultz
Coranadillana Cloud Killers

Interior lineman
E-Coo-Lee
Vik Vanguard

Chris Maler
Neptune Scarlet Fliers

Mum-O-Killowe
Ionath Krakens

Outside linebacker
Izic the Weird
Themala Dreadnaughts

Michael Cogan
Wabash Wolfpack

Richard Damge
To Pirates

Inside/Middle linebacker
Yalla the Biter
OS1 Orbiting Death

Mur the Mighty
Vik Vanguard

Cornerback
Xuchang
Jupiter Jacks

Tübingen
D'Kow War Dogs

Smileyberg
Coranadillana Cloud Killers

Free/Strong safety
East Windsor
Vik Vanguard

Ciudad Juarez
To Pirates

Tulsa
Neptune Scarlet Fliers

SPECIAL TEAMS
Punter: Eric Johnson
Bartel Water Bugs

Place kicker: Greg Anderson
Texas Earthlings

Kick returner: Chetumal
Hittoni Hullwalkers

COACH OF THE YEAR
Katie Lampkin
Vik Vanguard

LEAGUE MVP
Adam Guri
Neptune Scarlet Fliers

JOHN TWEEDY RIPPED OFF his shirt. MY GIRLFRIEND IS AN ALL-PRO scrolled across his chest. "Hell yeah! Three Krakens on the All-Pro roster? Way to go!"

The locker room seemed to converge on Kill-O-Yowet, Mum-O-Killowe and Becca "The Wrecka" Montagne.

John swiped to the article's second page, a list of forty-two icons, each showing the face of one of the All-Pro selections. John tapped the faces of Becca, Mum-O and Kill-O. The screen shifted into three horizontal panels, each playing individual highlights of those players.

Quentin just stood there, not hearing the cheers. He stared at Becca's highlights.

He felt … hollow.

Rebecca had been named All-Pro and he *hadn't?*

He became aware of someone standing next to him. It was her. Becca. Becca, the All-Pro.

"Quentin," she said. "I'm sorry."

John pushed her. "Sorry? *Sorry?* Woman, you were just named *All-Pro.* Shucking Tier One *All-Shucking-Pro!* I'm so proud I could just spit on myself." He wiped his chin. "Ooops, I just did."

"Thanks, John," she said, but she kept looking at Quentin.

"Quentin's proud of you, too," John said, the tone of his voice changing a little. "Ain't that right, Q? Can you believe it? Our lil' fullback is up there with the great Ralph Schmeer."

Quentin turned. John's smile was so wide he looked like a caricature, or a puppet. Quentin forced a smile of his own. "For sure. Becca the Wrecka. The best in the game."

He should have been happy for her. He knew that, but that feeling just wouldn't come. She had beaten him to the honor. So had Condor Adrienne. Quentin didn't know which one stung worse. Did Becca deserve it? Absolutely. Maybe Quentin hadn't been paying close attention to her individual performances, not with his focus on making the playoffs, but her highlights showed glimpses of an amazing season. Blocking for Ju and Quentin, occasionally running the ball on short-yardage situations, being the best receiving fullback in the game, even *throwing* two clutch passes against the Vik Vanguard to put the Krakens in the playoffs.

"It's part yours," Becca said. "I would have quit last year if it wasn't for you."

Quentin nodded. He didn't know what to say, what to feel. Why couldn't he be happy for her? Envy and jealousy, sinful emotions, yet both claimed him.

He had posted his best season ever. His throwing, his running, his team management, his leadership. He'd played through pain, through injuries. He'd pushed aside personal loss, the likes of which he'd never known and led his team into the playoffs. All of these things should have been enough for him. Such victories should have been their own reward.

But he wanted more.

He finally had to admit it to himself — he wanted *recognition*.

When he came to Ionath he hadn't thought money mattered. He'd been wrong. Next season, he would have more money than he could ever spend, yet he was bitter he'd been cheated out of an even greater sum. Now he knew why. He still didn't care about *money*, but he did care about what money *represented* — money was a way of keeping score. The best players in the game made the most money. *That* was why his need for more had grown and *that* was why he couldn't be happy for Becca.

Quentin wanted recognition. He wanted *respect*.

How petty.

High One had blessed him with the rarest of lives. He had challenges, to be sure. He had to go through life without a family. He'd been tested over and over again, but in overcoming those tests he found himself here on Ionath. Privileged. Cherished by millions. Even *worshiped* by millions more. Why did he feel petty about the awards of another?

He didn't know why. He just knew that he did.

"It's fantastic, Becca," he said, because those were the words he needed to say whether he felt them or not. Just because the sports media thought Condor Adrienne was a better quarterback didn't mean Becca hadn't earned her honor. "I'm really proud of you."

"Thanks," she said. Her eyes showed that she didn't believe him. She also wanted something more. Quentin could see that. Did she need for him to go crazy like John? To hoot and holler and sing her praises? Well, that wasn't his way.

"It's an honor for the team," Quentin said. "You played hard. No question. Enjoy the moment. I'm going to the VR room to go practice routes."

"Do you want me to come with you?"

"No," he said, then realized he'd said it a little too loud. Her eyes widened, briefly, then she looked away. Why couldn't she just enjoy this? Why did she need his approval? "I'm doing deep-routes with Halawa, Hawick and Milford, so we don't need you. You celebrate. You've earned it. See you later."

He turned and walked out of the locker room. He felt her eyes following him. Her sad, needful eyes.

From *The Ionath City Gazette*

Krakens head to playoffs

by TOYAT THE INQUISITIVE

NEW YORK CITY, EARTH, PLANETARY UNION — Another regular season has passed into the history books and the road to Yall has begun.

The Planet Division features number one seeded Wabash Wolfpack. The defending Galaxy Bowl champions have home-field advantage for the first two rounds. The Pack finished 10-2 to win the division title and will host Ionath (8-4) in the opening round. The two teams met back in Week Nine when the visiting Krakens upset the then-undefeated Wolfpack by a score of 28-24. Despite that outcome, Wabash is favored by six points.

In the second Planet Division game, the To Pirates (10-2) host Themala (9-3). If Wabash defeats Ionath, the Wolfpack will host the winner of To/Themala. If Ionath wins, the Krakens will travel to face the winner of To/Themala.

In the Solar, division champion Neptune (10-2) plays host to Bartel (7-5). Bartel will be playing without safety Alpharetta, who was suspended for one game following her illegal hit that caused the death of Bord running back Robert Harris. Number one seed Neptune is favored by thirteen points.

The winner of that game will face the winner of second-seed Jupiter (8-4) and the third-seeded Vik Vanguard (8-4). The Vanguard had won six straight games coming into last week's home loss to the Krakens, while the Jacks have lost their last three regular-season games. Odds-makers are calling the game even.

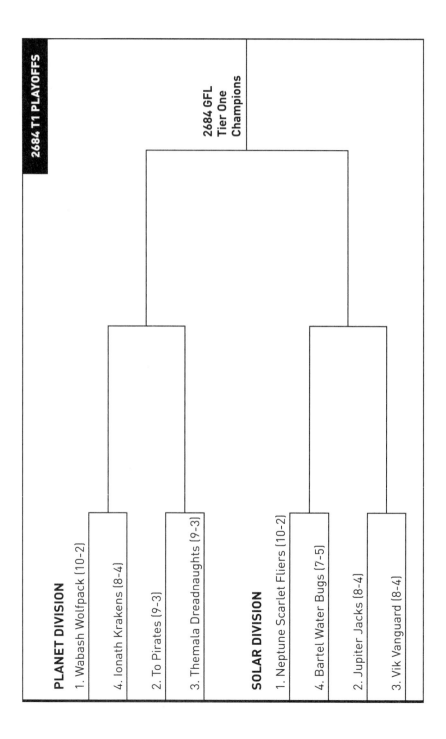

2684 T1 PLAYOFFS

2684 GFL
Tier One
Champions

PLANET DIVISION

1. Wabash Wolfpack (10-2)

4. Ionath Krakens (8-4)

2. To Pirates (9-3)

3. Themala Dreadnaughts (9-3)

SOLAR DIVISION

1. Neptune Scarlet Fliers (10-2)

4. Bartel Water Bugs (7-5)

2. Jupiter Jacks (8-4)

3. Vik Vanguard (8-4)

• • •

FOR THE SECOND TIME that season, Quentin and his orange jerseyed teammates gathered in the tunnel of Wabash Stadium. The playoffs. They had made it. Defending champs? Whatever. In three hours, Wabash would be the *former* champs.

He wasn't in front this time. He'd given the honor to Becca, to Kill-O-Yowet, to Mum-O-Killowe. The All-Pro members of the Krakens. An honor that would be at least one year away from Quentin's grasp. Again, he was flanked by the Tweedy brothers: John on his right, Ju on his left. He looked at them in turn, saw them staring at Becca, Kill-O and Mum-O, staring with the same envy and burning desire that he felt. Quentin, John and Ju exchanged glances — and with silent nods, a pact formed.

The three of them would work even harder next year, they would do whatever it took to become All-Pro themselves. Ma Tweedy's three boys would represent.

Standing there, the entire team buzzing with the moment — *they had made it* — it seemed like an eternity before the Wabash announcer finally called them onto the field.

"Sentients, please welcome the visiting team, the Krakens ... of ... Ionath!"

Quentin followed his three All-Pro teammates onto the field, so focused on the game he barely heard the boos.

QUENTIN TOOK THE SNAP and turned left, handing off to Ju, who drove into the line — but there was no hole. Ju slowed, looking. Seeing nothing, Ju lowered his head and plowed forward. Defensive tackle Stephen Wardop was a black-and-red blur, driving under Sho-Do-Thikit to up-end Ju with an arm-tackle.

No gain.

Third down, 8 to go.

The Krakens offensive line couldn't budge the Wabash D.

"Huddle up!"

The Krakens gathered. They looked wide-eyed, maybe a little shell shocked. He had to calm them down.

"Boys and girls, relax. We're just getting warmed up. Let's play our game, okay?"

Heads nodded, arms clacked against chests.

"Okay, I-set, slot-right, X-post, Y-wheel, Z-in, on three, on three, ready?"

"Break!"

The Krakens ran to the line and settled in. Quentin panned left-to-right, looking at the defense. These were the same players he'd faced in Week Nine … weren't they? They looked more intense than he'd remembered. Angrier. Wardop and fellow HeavyG defensive tackle Justin Miller, linebacker Michael Cogan, cornerback Mars.

The defense stared back at him, eyes glaring from behind black facemasks and red helmets. The Wolfpack wore the same black jerseys with red-trimmed, pearlescent numbers but now with a new patch — the 2684 Planet Division Championship shield stitched on the left shoulder. Same players, same uniforms, the Pack *looked* the same, but their high-level play was something new, something different.

"Blue, fifty-five!" Quentin called out. The defenders inched closer, almost projecting themselves toward him. "Blue, fifty-five! Hut-hut … *hut!*"

Quentin took the snap and drove back, stabbing the ball toward Ju on a play-action fake. He kept going, planting at five steps and popping forward.

He had a glimpse of Sho-Do-Thikit falling, of Michael Kimberlin's face — a bad thing, since Kimberlin always faced forward unless he was chasing the attacker he'd just let slip through — then the pocket collapsed so fast Quentin couldn't escape. Wardop and Miller crashed in. Quentin pulled the ball down just as 900 pounds of HeavyG linemen drove him to the ground.

Fourth down.

Quentin stood, brushed cream-colored plants off of his orange jersey. He headed for the sidelines. Not a good start, but the game had just begun. He'd get his teammates going. Hopefully, John's defense could do better.

QUENTIN STOOD ON THE SIDELINES, Becca on his left and Ju on his right. They watched Wolfpack quarterback Rich Bennett take the snap, drop back and look downfield. Quentin saw the black-clad Wabash receivers streaking deep. He saw Bennett sliding to his left, toward defensive end Cliff Frost's side of the field. The Wolfpack was double-teaming The Spaz — his frantic spinning wasn't getting him anywhere.

Quentin gritted his teeth and nodded. This was how it would be all day, he knew the moment he saw it. The Wolfpack would roll plays to their left, move away from Krakens' defensive end Aleksandar Michnik. That would give Bennett an extra second or two to find targets before Michnik could get to him. As long as Wabash blocked Frost, or whoever was playing at left defensive end to replace the injured Ibrahim Khomeni, Bennett would have time to throw if the Krakens didn't blitz. Were Khomeni in the lineup, the Pack couldn't have pulled it off, but Khomeni was out.

Bennett slid left, planted, then threw downfield. It wasn't a great pass, but wide receiver Naksup was a step ahead of Krakens free safety Perth. The wounded-duck pass wobbled high. Naksup went up for it and brought it down.

The crowd seemed to explode when Naksup landed in the end zone.

"What the hell was that?" Ju said. "Perth is faster than Naksup. How could Perth let her by?"

Quentin shook his head. He didn't know the answer. He pulled on his helmet and waited for his chance to get back on the field.

QUENTIN AGAIN PUSHED himself up off the cream-colored turf. He pulled some plant material out of his facemask. He'd been hit so hard he'd *skidded*, for crying out loud. Skidded on his *face*. He walked back to the huddle, forcing himself not to limp.

"Guys, what is going on?" he asked his huddle.

Midway through the second quarter. His teammates were breathing hard. No one seemed to want to look him in the eye.

"We're down fourteen-zip," he said. "Come on, isn't this the same team you beat in this same stadium just four weeks ago?"

"They hit harder!" Halawa said.

"They run faster!" Hawick said.

Quentin leaned in until he was face to face with his All-Pro left tackle. "Kill-O, isn't this the same team we played?"

Quentin was asking a rhetorical question. Of course it was the same team, but even Kill-O looked away. That was quite a feat, considering Kill-O's 360-degree vision.

"Grippah, jolonay," he said.

Quentin leaned back. Had he just understood those words? Maybe not, but he definitely understood the tone, the context. *Doesn't seem like the same team*, Kill-O had said.

The words rang true. The Wolfpack showed far more intensity, far more anger. They played faster. They played harder. They beat blocks. They played *smarter*.

Coach Hokor's face appeared in Quentin's heads-up display.

"Barnes! Will you get those worthless maggots to block?"

"I will, Coach," he said. "What's the play?"

"We have to establish the run. Let's go pro-set, counter-right. If we're running, our linemen are *attacking*, tell them that."

Quentin nodded and tapped his helmet, blinking out the heads-up holo. He called the play, looking at Ju as he did.

Ju's nose dripped a steady stream of blood. Doc Patah could fix that when they got off the field, but for now, the wound was a bit disturbing — the Krakens bad-ass running back was supposed to make *others* bleed.

"Ju, let's take it to them. Smash-mouth."

Ju met Quentin's eyes, nodded. In that moment, Quentin saw the doubt. The Wolfpack were teeing off on Ju. The running back could take the hits, he could break tackles, fall forward on every play, that was fact, but Quentin could see that Ju no longer *believed* it.

Quentin walked up behind Bud-O-Shwek, surveying the defenders once again. They looked *hungry*. In that moment, Quentin understood what it was all about. The Krakens had been quite impressed with themselves for just *making* the playoffs.

But Wabash? For them, this was just one more step to the ultimate goal — they played with the intensity of champions.

The Krakens had to learn how to play like that, how to take their game up yet another level and they had to do it fast.

MIDWAY THROUGH THE SECOND quarter, down 21-0, Quentin Barnes settled in under center. He had to make something happen, something spectacular to get his team back in the game. If he could get the Krakens motivated, give them something to rally around, then there was still a chance.

Third down, 7 to go on the Wabash 24-yard line.

"Greeeen, twenty-two," he called down the left side of the line. He would audible out of Hokor's play, take the ball and change the course of the game right now. "Greee*een*, twenty-two!"

His teammates didn't need to look at him, they knew the calls — Quentin would roll left and look to run or throw. All receivers would run patterns to the left: Milford on a hook, Warburg on an out and Halawa on a far-side flag, coming from the right side of the field all the way over to the left corner of the end zone. Halawa's route took a long time to run, but Quentin suspected she would be open. He had one interception so far — he had to put this on the money.

"Hut-hut!"

The orange and black roared into the black and red. Quentin reverse-pivoted, opening up to the right, then coming around to sprint left. Rebecca ran a few yards in front of him, looking for someone to block. Milford ran up the left sideline and hooked in at 10 yards. The cornerback covering her, Mars, came up in defense. Warburg ran straight out 15 yards, then cut left. As Quentin suspected, the safety cheated up, drawn in by Warburg.

If Halawa got behind the safety, she would be open. Woman-on-woman coverage. Halawa was faster than the right side corner covering her. With a route that far across the field, she would pull a step or two ahead of her defender.

Right outside linebacker Ricky Craig barreled in. Rebecca took him head on, a devastating hit that left both players flat on the ground.

Middle linebacker Michael Cogan sprinted in on a delayed blitz. Quentin kept running, started to throw the ball to Milford for a short pass, what he was supposed to do when under blitz pressure.

But his team needed more than four yards.

Quentin kept moving left, went a little deeper, waiting to see if Halawa got behind the safety. Two seconds before Cogan closed in. Halawa sprinted, Quentin waited — he wouldn't have time.

One second.

Then Mississauga, the safety, made a mistake, took another step toward Warburg.

A half-second.

Quentin was almost to the sidelines — he would have to plant and step up to throw.

Three-tenths of a second.

Halawa shot behind the Mississauga, headed for the corner of the end zone.

One-tenth of a second.

Quentin stepped forward and threw on the run, releasing the ball as fast as he could. No sooner had the leather left his hand than he felt a helmet drive into his right foot.

And something in there *snapped*.

Quentin fell, slid out of bounds and into the Wolfpack sidelines. He started to grab at the knife-pain in his right foot, but stopped himself. He couldn't let the Wolfpack know he'd been hurt, or they'd pour on the pressure.

The roar of the crowd told him his pass had hit home. Touchdown Ionath.

Wabash players helped him up. Quentin jogged toward his own sidelines, using all of his concentration to hide his limp. He wasn't going to let Don Pine in this game, no way. Pain or no pain, two feet or one, Quentin Barnes would finish this thing.

He ran off the field. His teammates seemed excited ... but not excited *enough*. The extra point was good. Wabash now led 21-7.

They had a game.

QUENTIN TOOK THE SNAP and dropped back. His foot hurt bad, but he could handle it. Third-and-long on the Ionath 45. Just 32 seconds left in the half and the Krakens were desperately trying to get into field goal range. He planted his left foot, stepped up into the pocket. Pressure from the left — Col-Que-Hon bull-rushing Kill-O-Yowet. Kill-O sure as hell wasn't playing like an All-Pro. Col-Que knocked Kill-O over, then gathered, compacted for a hit. Warburg was open across the middle. Quentin stepped forward too fast — he planted his right foot and the stab of pain threw off his aim. The ball sailed wide left. Just before Col-Que smashed him senseless, Quentin saw linebacker Michael Cogan pick off the pass.

Quentin blinked his eyes against the blackness swirling in his vision. Alien hands picked him up off the tan turf — Kill-O, clearly ashamed of his poor blocking. Quentin forced a smile, slapped his teammate on the helmet.

At the half, the Krakens went into the locker room down 21-7.

WABASH SCORED ANOTHER touchdown in the third quarter and one more to start the fourth. Ju broke a long run after that, but it was too little, too late.

Quentin didn't bother hiding his limp anymore. If felt like someone had driven a rusty nail into his foot and he helped by driving that nail deeper with each step.

Out on the field, the Wolfpack lined up in the victory formation. Fourth quarter, twenty-two seconds and ticking, Wabash up 35-14, Ionath with no timeouts left.

Quentin felt an arm around his shoulder pads. He looked —

Michael Kimberlin, tears welling in the big man's eyes. Quentin looked away fast, lest he do the same.

The season was over.

The Krakens had lost.

Rich Bennett took the snap, backed up one step, then knelt. Whistles blew. Both sidelines walked out onto the field. The Krakens walked slowly, like the beaten team they were. The Wolfpack moved with more purpose, more intensity. The black, red and the white weren't celebrating. This was just one step closer to their goal, to defending their title.

Media swarmed onto the field. Quentin saw Coach Hokor, guarded by three Ki police who escorted him to the 50-yard line to congratulate Wabash coach Alan Roark, who was also guarded by police. Reporters pushed and shoved, lights glared. Lev-cameras and Harrah swirled, angling for the best positions.

Quentin sought out his counterpart.

Rich Bennett saw Quentin, jogged over, auburn hair wet with sweat but still flopping as he ran, looking every bit the hero he'd been in the game.

"Quentin," Rich said, extending his hand. "Good game."

"Not as good as yours. You haven't played like that all year, man. *Four* touchdowns?"

Rich smiled the smile of the victor. "Even a blind squirrel finds a nut once in awhile."

"Did you guys eat some super-food or something? Learn some mystical ritual? I've never seen anything like it. You kicked our ass from beginning to end."

"It's the playoffs," Rich said. "It's a whole different feeling, a whole different level of intensity. Now you know. Same thing happened to us in '82. We played the To Pirates in the first round and they kicked the crap out of us. We thought we were ready — we weren't. You can't know how to do that until you've been here. Well, now you've been here."

Quentin stared, then nodded with understanding. Rich reached out and ruffled Quentin's sweaty, bloody hair. It was a friendly gesture, part *we are equals*, part *you'll get yours someday, kiddo*.

Rich moved on, talking to other players. He stopped to share a smile with Don Pine — the two Galaxy Bowl champion quarterbacks, members of a club so exclusive it had only seventeen members.

In all the universe, only *seventeen* of them.

Quentin watched, letting the jealous rage roil in his chest. Maybe it was a sin to be envious of Becca, but not of Pine and Bennett. No, not at all, because *that* kind of envy would fuel him, drive him to work harder, to prepare more, to play even better.

He looked around the stadium. Wolfpack fans in white and red and black, still celebrating in the stands. Mixed in among them, clusters of orange and black. The Krakens fans hadn't left early to beat traffic; they had stayed. Stayed and watched their team get soundly whipped.

For those fans, he would win a title.

He looked at his teammates. They were shell-shocked but still showed class, congratulating their counterparts from Wabash. All the hatred and animosity between the clubs was fine during the game, but Wabash had moved on and Ionath had not. Now was the time to acknowledge that, to tip one's hat to the victors. He looked at Kill-O, who'd played his worst game of the season. He would be embarrassed that his line had given up four sacks just a few days after he was named one of the best in the game.

Next year, Kill-O would be ready.

Quentin looked at Becca, who was sharing a moment with Wabash fullback Ralph Schmeer — the All-Pros, the two best fullbacks in the game. She had played well, but like her teammates, she'd been outclassed from the start.

Next year, Becca would be ready.

He looked at Ju, blue cotton sticking out of both nostrils. Ju was talking to Wabash coach Alan Roark. Roark had a hand on Ju's shoulder pad, was leaning in, giving advice or encouragement. Ju listened. Ju nodded.

Next year, Ju would be ready.

Quentin scanned all of his teammates and in all of them, he saw the same understanding that now coursed through his veins.

Next year, they would *all* be ready.

Quentin would win a title for his teammates.

Finally, his gaze drifted toward a cluster of huge sentients in the center of the field. Big sentients, *dangerous* sentients — crowd and reporters both gave this group a wide berth. In the middle, down low among the legs of the bodyguards, Quentin saw Gredok the Splithead talking to Hokor the Hookchest. Gredok had actually come down to the field to speak with his coach. Quentin could see it wasn't a lecture, wasn't a dressing-down. Gredok seemed to offer words of encouragement, words that soothed Hokor. Demands for victory would come later, perhaps, but for now even Gredok could give credit where credit was due.

Hokor had been out-coached, his team had been out-prepared and out-played.

Next year, Hokor would be ready.

Quentin would win a title for Hokor.

As for Gredok? Gredok would get something else altogether. Quentin would see to that.

He turned to walk off and almost ran over the blue-skinned beauty of Yolanda Davenport.

"Quentin! Can I ask you a question?"

She held a recorder. She was here in official capacity. He wanted to scream at her, maybe even push her out of the way, but this was part of the game like everything else. This was part of his job.

"Sure," he said, leaning down so he could hear her. "Go for it."

"You led Ionath to the playoffs, but your season ended today. Can you tell me what you're feeling?"

"Both teams played hard," he said. "Wabash was more prepared than we were. They deserved the win."

Yolanda nodded. "Does a loss like this impact the franchise in a negative way?"

Quentin stood and stared down at her. He shook his head, then leaned in close again. "Nothing can stop us," he said. "We'll be back. The Ionath Krakens are on a collision course with a GFL title. The only variable is time. And you can quote me on that."

He started to gently push past her, but she stepped in front of him, blocking his path.

"Look," he said. "You're the last person that I want to—"

She turned off the recorder, put it in her pocket. She waved her hand inward, beckoning him to lean down so she could talk without screaming to be heard over the crowd. What was this?

He wanted to ignore her, to get out of there, but her eyes — she *needed* to tell him something. She needed it desperately.

Quentin leaned in close.

"I know I made things bad for you," she said. He felt her breath on his ear. It made the hairs on his neck tingle. "I *will* make it right. I have news about your sister."

He stood up straight, once again staring down at her. She waved him close again. He bent, he listened.

"She's safe," Yolanda said. "I talked to her. I talked to Fred."

"Why won't she contact me?"

"It's … a little complicated," Yolanda said. "Too much to tell you now, but she's had men in her life that were rough with her."

Rough with her. Quentin had seen his sister just once in the last fifteen years and those words instantly made murder rage through his soul. Someone had hurt his sister? Then that someone would pay.

"She's had a lot of trouble in her life," Yolanda said. "She said she saw what you did at Gredok's dinner. She doesn't know if she can handle knowing a brother that is capable of such violence."

Quentin closed his eyes. He'd *snapped*, tried to kill Gredok, beaten Vinje, ruined that HeavyKi's eyes with a broken chair … and his sister had seen all of that.

"Just give her some time," Yolanda said. "Fred will keep her safe. You just have to be patient, okay?"

Yolanda's face seemed beautiful once again. She'd found his sister, ended that mystery. At least for now. Yolanda didn't have to do that. Or, at least, she didn't have to do that *off the record*, not with such a dramatic story waiting to be published.

Yolanda smiled at him. She turned and walked away.

A weight had been lifted. His sister … *safe*. She was afraid of him, though. That was bad, but he could fix it. Just give her some time. Out of all the betrayal he'd faced, all the hurt, it seemed he could still count on Frederico Esteban Giuseppe Gonzaga.

A true friend.

Just don't let her get hurt, Fred. Protect her.

Quentin headed for the locker room. So much emotion, hard to deal with it all. Later, he would think about how to handle the situation with his sister. It was critical, but even that couldn't push away his raw feelings at losing to the Wolfpack.

The loss *hurt*. Of that there was no question. His life-long quest was pushed out for another year, a year that seemed simultaneously a distant eternity and an enticing tick of the clock away. All that work and preparation, lost.

No, not lost.

Not at all.

All that work and preparation had gotten them *here*, to *this* place, so that they could learn *this* lesson. Learn it from champions.

They had lost 35-14.

Not even close.

That, too, was part of the lesson. He hadn't led his team well enough to merit anything other than a humiliating 21-point defeat.

Next year, Quentin Barnes would be ready.

He would win a title for the fans, for his teammates, for his coach. The only variable was time. But he would also win a title for one more person.

He would win it for himself.

BOOK FIVE:
EPILOGUE
DIVISIONAL CHAMPIONSHIPS AND THE GALAXY BOWL

DEFENDING CHAMPS MOVE ON, WILL FACE THEMALA

by YOLANDA DAVENPORT

WABASH, FORTRESS, TOWER RE-PUBLIC — It was experience ver-sus youth and experience won out. With a 35-14 first-round win over the Ionath Krakens, the Wabash Wolfpack moved one step closer to defending their GFL title and be-coming the first team to repeat as champions since the Jupiter Jacks did it in '75 and '76.

Wolfpack QB Rich Bennett posted a career day, going 22-for-30 for 285 yards and four touch-downs. Bennett is known more as a game manager than a top-flight quarterback, but on Sunday he was at his best.

"My receivers just got open," Bennett said. "All I had to do was stay on my feet and complete pass-es. Ionath's secondary is a little banged up and it showed."

Wolfpack fullback Ralph Sch-meer had the teams only rushing touchdown, scoring on a 3-yard scamper.

Ionath quarterback Quentin Barnes, on the other hand, strug-gled in his first Tier One playoff game. Barnes threw for one touch-down but also three interceptions on 18-of-31 passing.

"I guess the pressure got to me," Barnes said. "I didn't play well at all. We weren't ready for the in-tensity of playoff football and it showed. We'll be back next year and trust me — we'll be ready."

Earlier this year, Barnes and teammate Ju Tweedy were cleared of any wrongdoing in the murder of Grace McDermot, a resident of OS1. McDermot's real killer was arrested. The GFL absolved Barnes and Tweedy of any responsibility for, or related to, the murder.

The Themala Dreadnaughts won a 22-20 thriller over the To Pirates, locking up the game on a 56-yard field goal from kicker Michael Bowen as time expired. Themala now travels to Wabash for the Solar Division title and a trip to Galaxy Bowl XXVI on the Planet Yall in the Sklorno Dynasty.

In the Solar Division, the Neptune Scarlet Fliers manhandled the Bartel Water Bugs 23-17. The game wasn't as close as the score would indicate, with the Fliers racking up 482 yards of total offense compared to the Bugs 156. Bartel scored their final touchdown with just 17 seconds to play. Neptune recovered the following onsides kick, ending the game.

Also in the Solar Division, the Jupiter Jacks outlasted the Vik Vanguard in a thriller that saw the lead change hands five times. Jacks quarterback Shriaz Zia played like a Human possessed, throwing for 320 yards and three touchdowns with no interceptions.

"Everything just clicked today," Zia said. "Some days you have it, some days you don't. Today I had it. Quite frankly, if we play this well offensively in the next two games I think we can go ahead and be fitted for a new ring."

The Vanguard managed to completely shut down wide receiver Denver, who had no catches on the game. Jupiter rookies New Delhi and Beaverdam filled the void, however. New Delhi had eight catches for 212 yards and a touchdown, while Beaverdam snagged

> *"If we play this well offensively in the next two games I think we can go ahead and be fitted for a new ring."*
>
> — SHRIAZ ZIA, JUPITER JACKS

six passes for 78 yards and one score. Denver's output inexplicably dropped off in the last three games of the regular season, all losses for Jupiter.

In the second round, Jupiter travels to their archrival Neptune. This is the third year in a row that the Jacks and the Fliers meet in the playoffs. Last year, Neptune won 14-10 in the opening round. In 2682, the Jacks won 21-10 en route to the GFL title.

The winner of Jupiter/Neptune will face the winner of Themala/Wabash for the 2684 GFL title. ∎

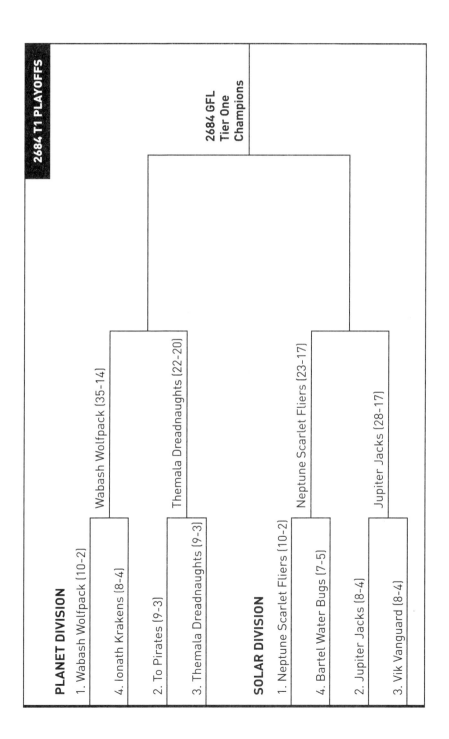

2684 T1 PLAYOFFS

2684 GFL
Tier One
Champions

PLANET DIVISION

1. Wabash Wolfpack (10-2)

Wabash Wolfpack (35-14)

4. Ionath Krakens (8-4)

2. To Pirates (9-3)

Themala Dreadnaughts (22-20)

3. Themala Dreadnaughts (9-3)

SOLAR DIVISION

1. Neptune Scarlet Fliers (10-2)

Neptune Scarlet Fliers (23-17)

4. Bartel Water Bugs (7-5)

2. Jupiter Jacks (8-4)

Jupiter Jacks (28-17)

3. Vik Vanguard (8-4)

25

DIVISIONAL CHAMPIONSHIPS

THE MORNING AFTER THE GAME, the Krakens gathered in the dining deck. Not only the entire team of fifty-three players, also Captain Kate, her flight crew and several Krakens administration staffers.

Coach Hokor had something to say.

It seemed almost strange to see everyone in street clothes. A few orange and black T-shirts and sweatshirts stood out, but most sentients wore the clothes they might wear at home, for any non-football function.

No need for uniforms. As of yesterday, the season was over.

Even now, after so much time together, the Krakens players gathered in species-specific groups. They sat in their species-defined areas. Starcher and Tara the Freak stood off to the side, a strange group all to themselves, a friendship forged by their common outcast status. That status was fading, however — Tara had earned the respect of his teammates and George's gloomy nature had mostly vanished. Next year, Tara and George would join Hawick, Milford and Halawa to give Quentin the best receiving corps in the league. Add in a certain All-Pro fullback who could catch spit in the wind, a veteran offensive line that had gelled into a dominant unit and the best running back in the game and Quentin knew no one could stop Ionath's offensive attack.

Quentin chose not to sit with the Human players. Instead, he walked to the Quyth Warrior section. A token gesture for forcing them to accept Tara. Choto, Shayat the Thick and Kopor the Climber welcomed him. Virak the Mean just glared. Had Quentin made an enemy of the dangerous linebacker/bodyguard? Only time would tell.

Conversation died down as Hokor entered, walking side by side with Gredok the Splithead.

As would be expected, Gredok spoke first.

"Krakens, I wish to salute you on an exceptional season. We did not win the Galaxy Bowl, something that must be rectified. However, you won eight games, the most since our 9-3 season of 2675, nine years ago. It has also been nine years since we were in the playoffs at all, something else for which you deserve accolades. And, most importantly, you defeated the Wabash Wolfpack. I am not pleased you lost to *them* in the playoffs, but I can finally say that my team defeated Gloria Ogawa. For this, you shall be rewarded. I will allow you to be pleased and proud of yourselves. Next year, I will accept *nothing less* than the Galaxy Bowl."

Gredok paused, scanning the room, practically daring anyone to contradict him. No one did. The team believed as he believed, that next year in 2685, a Tier One title was theirs for the taking.

"Galaxy Bowl," he said again. "And to that effect, I turn things over to Coach Hokor. I must leave you now, Krakens. Know that Hokor has my full confidence and support. Do as he says. I depart to take care of some unfinished business."

Gredok turned and walked out. Quentin wondered if that *unfinished business* involved Frederico. Hopefully, the disguise-happy detective could stay hidden for awhile longer.

At least until Quentin got his revenge on Gredok.

"Krakens, attention," Hokor said. "I will also give you credit for an excellent season. We were not prepared for playoff football. We were not used to a fourteenth week of practice. We were not mentally ready for the intensity. To help us prepare for next year, I will tell you now that our current season is *not* over."

He let the words sink in. The Krakens players looked at each other, confused. Quentin didn't bother to look around — he already understood what Hokor was doing and he approved.

"It would be a five-day trip home," Hokor said. "Today is Monday. We would not arrive until Friday. The Wolfpack play the Dreadnaughts on Sunday, right here, on the planet Fortress far below our feet. Had we defeated the Wolfpack, we would be practicing *right now*. All week. And if we had defeated the Dreadnaughts in the second round, we would practice the week after that as well. That is exactly what we are going to do — we are going to practice as if we were moving on to the second round."

Quentin felt an unexpected thrill. He didn't have to leave the *Touchback* yet. He could keep playing, keep practicing. Some of his teammates didn't feel the same, as evidenced by moans and curses.

"You all *stay here*," Hokor said. "No exceptions. We will not practice full-contact, but we will practice every day as if we were still in the playoffs. We will travel down to Wabash stadium together, exactly as we would if we were playing. We will sit in the stands, together, we will talk to each other about what the teams are doing right, what we have to do right next year to be down on the field. And after Sunday, we will all stay on the *Touchback* and practice until it is time to travel to Yall, as if *we* were playing in the Galaxy Bowl. Again, we'll go down to the surface of Yall *together*, just like we would for the real thing. We will watch the championship together. This will help us learn how to deal with the fatigue of an extra three weeks of playoff football. At this time next year, we will be ready."

The groaning continued. Players wanted to go home, see their families.

Quentin stood. The moaning stopped.

"This is a good plan," he said to the team. "Coach is right. We lost to Wabash because we weren't ready. For the next two weeks, you will all think of what it would feel like to still be playing, to be headed to the championship game. It's two more weeks. And you better get used to a longer season, because next year?" He looked around the room, staring at each player for just a moment, using a long pause to catch every eye.

"Next year, we'll be ready. Next year, this will be for real. For now, we'll practice, *as a team*. We'll watch Wabash play Themala, as a team. And as a team, we'll travel to the Galaxy Bowl on Yall ... *together*. We'll watch that game ... *together*."

He looked back to Hokor, then sat, silently turning control back to the coach.

"Thank you, Barnes," Hokor said. "Krakens, go suit up, no pads today. Report to the practice field in thirty minutes."

From *LeeKee Galaxy Times*

Upsets pit Themala against Jupiter for GFL Title

by KELP BRINGER

WABASH, FORTRESS, TOWER REPUBLIC — A shockingly dominant defensive performance pushed Themala into the GFL title game. In Wabash, the Dreadnaughts didn't give up a single touchdown en route to a 24-7 upset over the defending champion Wolfpack. Wabash's only score came on an interception return by safety Mississauga late in the third quarter.

"We soundly defeated their offense," said Themala linebacker Tibi the Unkempt. "Our game plan worked well. They could not run. They could not pass. Therefore, we won the game."

In an inexplicable offensive meltdown, Wabash picked up only six first downs the entire game. The Wolfpack failed to convert a single third-down opportunity.

"Our punter was our star player," said Wolfpack coach Alan Roark. "Anytime you say that, you're in trouble and doubly so in the playoffs. We're going to have to watch the game-holo and figure out why we couldn't make anything happen. We got whipped today and that's that."

For the 2684 title, the Dreadnaughts face off against the Jupiter Jacks. Jupiter defeated archrival Neptune in a 36-33 double-overtime thriller.

In what proved to be the longest game in GFL history, the Jacks finally won on a 17-yard field goal by kicker Jack Burrill, which was set up on a 42-yard pass from quarterback Shriaz Zia to wide receiver Denver. Denver was shut down for most of the game. She caught only two passes on the day, the other being for just one yard early in the second quarter. Denver has been under fire in the media as of late following her poor performances in the last three games of the regular season and the first round of the playoffs.

"She got open when it mattered," Zia said. "We snuck out of Neptune with a win and we're headed to the Galaxy Bowl."

This will be Jupiter's fifth appearance in the championship game. The Jacks have three GFL titles.

This is Themala's first-ever trip to the title game. The Dreadnaughts and the Wolfpack also met in last year's Planet Division finals, a game Wabash won 17-7 en route to claiming the GFL title.

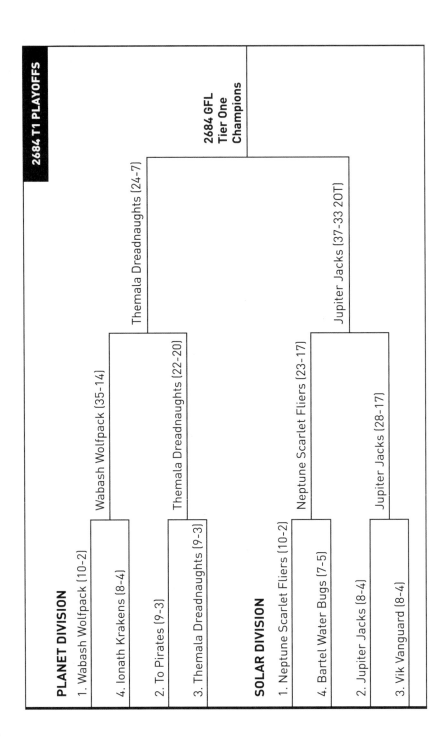

2684 T1 PLAYOFFS

2684 GFL Tier One Champions

Themala Dreadnaughts (24-7)

Jupiter Jacks (37-33 2OT)

Wabash Wolfpack (35-14)

Themala Dreadnaughts (22-20)

Neptune Scarlet Fliers (23-17)

Jupiter Jacks (28-17)

PLANET DIVISION

1. Wabash Wolfpack (10-2)

4. Ionath Krakens (8-4)

2. To Pirates (9-3)

3. Themala Dreadnaughts (9-3)

SOLAR DIVISION

1. Neptune Scarlet Fliers (10-2)

4. Bartel Water Bugs (7-5)

2. Jupiter Jacks (8-4)

3. Vik Vanguard (8-4)

26

GALAXY BOWL

QUENTIN KEPT HIS EYES CLOSED. His hands gripped the puke bucket. He waited for the inevitable. Last week, John had decorated the golden bucket with a Themala Dreadnaughts sticker even though the *Touchback* had stayed in orbit above Fortress and hadn't entered punch space. On Monday, after the Dreadnaughts had upset the Wolfpack in the second round of the playoffs, John had added stickers for *both* teams in the championship game — Themala's red, yellow and brown "TD" as well as the silver, gold and bronze logo of the Jupiter Jacks.

As a team, the Krakens traveled to Planet Yall, to the city of Virilliville, home of Galaxy Bowl XXVI.

"Hey, Q," John said. "How's that tummy?"

Quentin kept his eyes shut. He shook his head. The *shimmer* was coming any moment now. He tried to concentrate, to see if this time he might avoid the motion sickness. "John, just shut up."

John breathed deeply through his nose. "Hey, do you smell that? Smells like ... like a Ki splatterfart hitting a wet, dirty ashtray."

Quentin's stomach roiled. "John, knock it off."

"Oh! *Now* I know what it smells like," John said. "Like rotten shushuliks in a hot, musty dumpster. Man, imagine how those would *taste*, Q."

Quentin was already throwing up when the shimmer hit.

He coughed, wiped his mouth, opened his eyes.

YOU PUKE LIKE A LITTLE GIRL scrolled across John's smiling face.

"John, you're an idiot."

The big linebacker smiled with satisfaction. "He who laughs last gets the spoils, Q. Remember I said that."

"Oh, I will."

Quentin lifted the plastic bag, tied it off and set it back in the bucket. He looked to the observation deck's crysteel windows.

Like the last trip to Yall, excited Sklorno packed the left and right windows. They jumped, chirped, pushed and pulled at each other. They left the center window unobstructed, however — a kind gesture for their resident "Godling."

Out there, the planet Yall. Burnished blue, choked by the tight fist of endlessly sprawling civilization. They'd come to this same place just fourteen weeks earlier. The Krakens had come *so close!* So close to being here as a contender, not just going through the paces to prepare for next season.

"Uh, Q? Do you see that light?"

Quentin saw it. A bright light, moving fast at first, then not at all. It flickered, glowed brighter than the other lights surrounding the planet. The *Touchback* had an arrival window of space, in which other ships were not allowed to enter. That flickering light was a ship — it seemed to have ignored that safety window.

Quentin didn't know much about space travel, but he knew the basics — if something moved like that, it was artificial and if it seemed to stop moving, it was probably coming straight at you.

"Yeah, John, I see it. What do you think it is?"

"It's trouble."

"Trouble? What do you mean?"

John didn't have time to answer before a klaxon alarm screeched through the observation deck.

"Attention!" Captain Kate's voice came from the ship's sound system. "All Krakens players and staff report to the dining deck immediately. All ship crew report to battle stations."

The Sklorno players sprinted out of the observation deck.

Quentin looked at John. "Battle stations? What in the Void is she talking about?"

John grabbed Quentin's arm and started leading him out of the observation deck. "Come on, Q. We got to get to the dining deck. It's the deepest part of the ship. We'll be safest there."

Quentin looked back out the window. He saw four bright lights branch off the oncoming ship — branch off, then close in on the *Touchback*. He had to look away and start running to keep up with John's pulling.

QUENTIN AND THE OTHERS sprinted down the corridor. They rushed into the dining deck to find it already half full. The faster Sklorno players were already there, of course, as were many Ki. Messal the Efficient stood by the door, palm-up display glowing in the air above his pedipalp hand — looked like a team roster. As each player ran in, he tapped icons.

Other than Tara, Quentin saw no Quyth Warriors. He sat off by himself looking like his old, dejected self. The flood of players slowed. Coach Hokor, Mum-O and Michael Kimberlin entered. They must have been the last because Messal tapped a wall panel. A heavy blast door slid into place, sealing the room. Quentin had never even known a door was there — the dining deck had always been open.

"Messal," Quentin said. "What about Virak and Choto?"

"They are trained soldiers," Messal said. "They are manning the guns, as are Shayat the Thick and Killik the Unworthy."

Captain Cheevers had told him Quyth players would man the guns, but Quentin hadn't really believed it. "Don't we have other staff who can do that?"

"A few," Messal said. "But would *you* like to tell Virak that he should sit here and be idle while we are attacked?"

Quentin shook his head. No, he wouldn't want to suggest that to Virak the Mean. "Well, what about Tara, then?"

Messal looked away. "Please, Elder Barnes, with all due respect, I don't have time for such obviously ridiculous questions."

Quentin felt a strange vibration beneath his feet, bursts of some rapid-fire pulsing.

"That would be the guns," Messal said, amazingly calm in the face of this strange danger. "Excuse me, Elder Barnes, I have to report to the Captain."

Messal walked toward a wall panel. A bigger vibration rattled the ship. Quentin instinctively knew that wasn't a gun firing — the *Touchback* had been hit.

"Damage," Kate's voice echoed from the sound system. She also sounded spookily calm. "Hits to the upper decks. The practice field dome has been penetrated. I'll feed damage schematics into the main ship feed. Everyone, be aware of off-limit areas. They will change as the fight continues."

The ship shuddered again, harder this time. Quentin stumbled and braced himself on a table. He lifted his palm to chest level, calling up his own display. A glowing icon showed the ship feed. He poked the icon. A holographic ship schematic flared to life. Most of the ship was in green, but he saw the practice field in blinking yellow and several corridors in solid red. Six blue icons were labeled GUN CABIN, numbers one through six.

He felt the vibrations beneath his feet, realized that one of the blue icons flashed in time to mark which gun was firing. He saw that GUN CABIN 6 was closest to the dining deck. That was the same cabin that Captain Kate had showed him during the tour.

Another violent vibration, the bad kind. Seconds later, more areas of the ship glowed red — rooms and corridors marked off-limits, probably exposed to the vacuum of space.

Quentin looked around the dining deck. Forty-some sentients doing the same thing he was doing, looking at ship schematics, waiting helplessly.

The *Touchback* trembled again, even worse than before.

GUN CABIN 6 blinked from blue to red. Who had been in

there? Virak? The icon switched from red to yellow. Quentin scanned the schematic. So many corridors in red — there was almost no way to reach Gun Cabin 6.

No, there was one way — a straight line from the dining deck.

"Attention!" Captain Kate's voice. "We need clean-up in Gun Cabin 6. Messal, organize non-essential crew to get in there and fix it up. The gun reads operative on my board. We'll work on repairs to corridors 12-A and 10-B so we can get someone else on it."

How long would that take? Would the *Touchback* even be around by then? Quentin looked at the schematic, used his thumb and forefinger to zoom in on the GUN CABIN 6 icon. At this level of detail, he saw a name in red — Killik the Unworthy. Was Killik injured? Dead?

Quentin was no stranger to violence, to the threat of death. He'd been in dangerous situations before — what he had never done, however, was sit back and wait for things to happen. He had to do something.

He ran to the dining deck's closed blast door.

"Elder Barnes! Where are you going?"

"I know how to fire that gun, Messal. I'm going to get it back in the fight."

Messal blocked the door with his little body. "No! You must stay in the dining deck!"

A pair of big hands reached down and picked up Messal, moving him to the side. Crazy George Starcher.

"I'll go with you," George said.

George was a veteran. Had he been in combat before?

"You were in the Navy, right?" Quentin said. "You should shoot, not me."

George shook his head. "Oh, no, I never fired a cannon. I was a mechanic. I can see the innermost connections of the machines, the dark lines of spirit and space and interdimensional soul that weaves forth the fabric, that—"

A barking roar from Mum-O-Killowe cut George off. Mum-O, apparently, liked listening to George's odd rants no more than

Quentin did. Mum-O's multi-jointed arms reached for the door. His hands tapped the wall panel to open it.

"Bregat," the Ki said, then scuttled through the door and into the corridor.

The *Touchback* shook again. No time for second thoughts. Quentin ran through the door, Mum-O and George Starcher right behind him. The blast door slid down and clanged shut.

PALM UP IN FRONT OF HIM, Quentin sprinted down the corridor, trying to simultaneously watch the both schematic and his footing. On the map, this corridor blinked yellow. What did that mean? Was it about to go red? He remembered the emergency training that told him to never take the elevators if there was a fire. He imagined running space battles followed the same logic. He ran for the stairs that would go down one flight to Deck Eight. From there, about forty feet to reach Gun Cabin 6.

Captain Kate's voice echoed through the corridors. "Evacuate the practice field area." Her voice still sounded eerily calm. "Sealing the field in ten seconds."

George Starcher and Mum-O-Killowe just steps behind, Quentin hit Deck Eight and ran down the corridor. He heard Captain Kate counting down from ten. She made it to *five* before another blast made the *Touchback* lurch under his feet, throwing him face-first into a bulkhead. His head spun. He fought to stay conscious. The artificial gravity sputtered for a moment. Quentin felt himself floating, the wall brushing against his right shoulder. Without warning, the gravity kicked back on and he dropped hard to the deck. Blood wetted his lips. His nose felt broken.

George lifted him to his feet. "Quentin! Are you okay?"

Quentin put a hand on the wall for balance against the moving ship. No, the ship was once again rock-still — his legs were wobbly. He felt something in his mouth. Quentin spit into his hand.

A bloody tooth.

His tongue told him what he already knew — front right.

"Why always *that* one?"

He put the tooth in his pocket. George helped him stumble down the corridor toward the gun cabin's closed door. Quentin tried the handle — locked.

"Let me," George said. He knelt by the key pad, then grabbed it and ripped it off the wall. He reached inside and started fiddling with the wires.

A heavy *clang* came from inside the wall as the door's internal locks slid back into their recesses. His balance mostly back to normal, Quentin stepped inside. Smoke filled the room, as did splatters of red blood and chunks of green flesh, bits of shattered orange chitin and a nasty scattering of body parts.

George grabbed a trash can and rushed to the platform. He knelt and started using his hands to scoop up bloody green blobs.

"High One," Quentin said. "Is that … Killik?"

"Get a mop," George said. He pointed to the corner of the room. Quentin walked there, watching his step amongst scattered bits of wreckage. He found the mop in a case on the wall. He pulled it out and worked his way back to the platform. To his right, Mum-O's four hands scrambled across the long, horizontal, crysteel viewport. Cracks lined the material, cracks that glistened with some kind of clear liquid.

Big globs of white foam dotted the space-side wall. Bullets had punched through, the holes instantly filling with vent-foam that expanded and hardened, stopping the escape of air.

"Quentin, *mop!*" George said. "We can't have you slipping on Killik's guts."

Quentin bent to the task, trying to keep his lunch in place. The wet mop pushed black goo, attached bits of exoskeleton and burned bits of cloth off of the platform and onto the floor below. George finished picking up the big pieces. His hands gleamed with slime. Gore covered his shirt and pants. A Quyth foot stuck out of the trash can, the severed leg streaked with red wetness leaking out through spiderwebbed chitin.

With Killik's remains gone, Quentin finished sweeping the platform clear.

"Mum-O," George said. "Do you hear any squealing or squeaking noises? Feel any breeze?"

Mum-O barked out a word that sounded a lot like a Human *no*, then turned and scuttled over wreckage, heading for the door. As he did, he drew his upper-left hand just under his hexagonal mouth, from right to left. Quentin recognized the very Human-like gesture — the sign of a throat being slit.

George nodded. "Quentin, the room is okay for now, but the decompression measures are exhausted. If this room takes any more hits, any at all, get out *fast*. We'll wait outside as long as we can, but if the corridor goes red, we have to get clear."

This was really happening. They were in an actual space battle, bullets punching through the hull, sentients dying. George followed Mum-O out. The door to Gun Cabin 6 clanged shut.

Quentin was alone.

He hit 726 on the keypad, then stepped onto the platform.

He faced the space-side wall as the X, Y and Z hololines flared to life. Outside the viewport, he saw the quad-battery's armor slide away and the barrels rise up — four lethal, parallel lines.

This time, they weren't loaded with blanks.

Captain Kate's calm voice echoed through the small room. "Barnes, I read your gun is active. Everything out there is a bogey."

"What's a bogey?"

"Just shoot anything that moves, rookie," she said. "I have to concentrate on damage control, so you're on your own. No pressure, Barnes, but if you don't shoot down these fighters, we all die. Patching you into gunner channel. Captain Kate, out."

The speakerfilm crackled with static.

Then, the voice of Virak the Mean. "Quentin, is your weapon online?"

Quentin raised his hands up and out, chest-level, palms down. Through the slot, he saw the barrels move in time with his hands. The air around him flashed, rapid-fire bursts of bright static and then he saw arrows of fast-moving red light. They swam in all directions, crossing in front of him from the left, the right, from below and above.

"Virak! What are these red things?"

"Bogeys."

"Will someone *please* tell me what the hell a *bogey* is?"

"Enemy fighters," Virak said, his voice just as calm as Captain Kate's. How could these sentients stay cool when fighters were *shooting* at the *Touchback*?

"Start firing, Quentin," Virak said. "Quickly."

Quentin tried to focus on the red arrows of light zooming in and out of his vision. One seemed to fly right at his face. He ducked, felt the vibration of his quad-cannon firing.

He looked at his hands. He'd balled them up into fists.

Can't do that, that fires the guns.

He stood straight, took in a breath, leveled his hands flat once again.

"They are making a strafing run," Choto called out. "Length of ship, engaging now."

Tiny vibrations echoed under Quentin's feet, the firing of guns somewhere else on the *Touchback*.

"They're passing aft," Virak said. "Quentin, prepare to fire."

Quentin turned his hands palms-up and curled his fingers in. The X-axis hash marks raced apart as his system focused in on a closer region of space. He put his hands flat, then twisted a little to the right, a little to the left, watching the barrels match the move.

Then two red arrows shot past as if they had flown right over his head, a streak of light trailing behind each to indicate their speed and direction.

Quentin's hands made fists, left-right, left-right. The room vibrated. Out through the viewport, he saw the barrels erupt with barely discernible cones of fire that instantly vanished behind clouds of smoke billowing out the rear. Quentin had to stop looking out the slot — he needed to make this hologram his reality.

Two more red arrows flashed from right to left, in and out of his vision in less than a second. Before Quentin could extend his X-axis for a longer-range shot, the arrows banked to his right and were out of his display.

"I missed!" Quentin said. "They're coming back around to my right."

"Port side, low," Virak said. "Choto, they're coming underneath."

"Target acquired," Choto said. Quentin again felt a distant, lighter vibration. His mind registered that level of shaking as the firing of Choto's gun.

"Bogey destroyed," Choto called out. "Three bogeys remain."

Quentin realized he was shaking. This was life and death. And yet, wasn't his life at risk on every snap of every game? Why was this any different? He breathed deeply through his nose as he held his hands up palm-out. The X-axis compressed, expanding his scale of vision.

From his upper right, he saw two red arrows.

"Target acquired," Quentin said, mimicking what he'd heard from Choto. He leveled his hands, locking the axis display. The dots looked tiny. Quentin pointed his hands at them, then made left-right-left-right fists.

The dots banked down and to the right. He'd fired behind.

"Lead your target," Virak said. "Note the distance in the display, Quentin."

Part of his mind heard Virak's words and part ignored them because he'd already figured that out. He curled his fingers up and in, making the hash marks spread apart as his targeting area closed in tighter. At the same time, he twisted to the right, recentering on the two dots.

Stay calm, he told himself. *Stay in the pocket, do your job.*

Once he had centered his display on the arrows, they seemed to change angles — they shot straight for him.

"Strafing run," Virak said. "Quentin, they're coming right for you."

Stay in the pocket.

Quentin held both hands level, palms-down.

The arrows banked away from each other, then turned in, light-trails criss-crossing over their own paths.

BLINK

For just a moment, everything slowed. Quentin understood the fighters' tactic — they crossed in front of each other to throw off any leading. It was just like throwing a pass; he had to see the speed of the ball coming in, the angle, aim just in front of where the receiver would be.

Left-right-left-right-left-right.

One of the arrows flashed brightly, then blinked out.

"I got him!" Quentin said. "I got him!"

"Great, Quentin," Virak said. "Do not grow overconfident."

The second arrow flashed at Quentin's face, but this time he didn't flinch.

He should have.

A noise like the coming of High One himself raged in the gun cabin. Instinct threw his body to the deck. Sparks flew, things slammed into him, the room seemed to explode a dozen times all at once.

He became aware of a klaxon alarm blaring, hurting his head, making him wish that he'd go deaf. Then the voice of Captain Kate, fractured and highly amplified, even louder than the klaxon.

"Quentin! Get out of there!

And one more noise — a squeal of wind.

He rolled to his back and looked to the viewport. Bullets had ripped holes in the crysteel, torn the metal, bent the armor inward like a mag-can punctured by a screwdriver. Bits of wreckage flew to the holes as if the holes were supermagnets. Some of the debris clanged to a stop, too big to go through, while some of the smaller pieces shot out into the void at a million miles an hour.

Quentin's body slid toward the viewport. He put his hands and feet flat on the still-wet black platform, bracing himself as best he could, but his eyes never left the center of the viewport.

One fist-sized bullet had lodged in the clear material. A big bullet surrounded by cracks.

Cracks that were *growing*.

"Uh-oh," he said, then flipped to his hands and knees and started scrambling for the door.

He made it only a foot before he heard the crunching *crack* of the window giving way. He started to slide backward, yanked by the hand of a wind-god. Quentin threw his body forward as if he were Hawick diving for a pass. His fingers locked on the edge of the firing platform.

Hurricane wind lifted his feet up behind him, his body a straight line pointing right at the six-inch-wide hole. He couldn't breathe. If he let go, he'd slam into that hole. He was far too big to fit through — the pressure would pull on any soft part of his body exposed to the Void. His innards would *squish* out into space.

The klaxon.

The hissing.

Captain Kate yelling.

The gun cabin door clanged open. Quentin looked up, eyes watering from the air racing past his face and saw Mum-O, Crazy George Starcher right behind him, decompression wind making their clothes flap madly about their bodies.

Starcher put a foot on either side of the door and grabbed Mum-O's rear legs. Mum-O *compressed*, the accordion-like thing the Ki did just before they expanded and knocked the crap out of an opposing quarterback.

This is an odd time for a cheap shot. I hope Coach makes him run laps.

Mum-O expanded, shooting into the wreckage-strewn room. Multi-jointed arms reached out. Quentin had a blurry vision of the horror holos back home on Micovi, the ones that painted the Ki as murderous demons, then strong arms wrapped around his chest and shoulders and he was *flying*, but the *right* way toward the door and not into space.

Quentin felt the arms squeeze tighter. He hit hard against the corridor, heard a *slam* of a door closing, then the spin of an airlock wheel.

The wind vanished.

He felt the deck under his butt. He blinked, opened his eyes.

Crazy George Starcher. Right behind George, the five-eyed face of Mum-O.

George grabbed Quentin's shoulders and gave a little shake. "Quentin! Are you okay?"

Quentin's head bobbled.

George shook him again, harder. "Quentin!"

Quentin batted George's hands away. "Starcher, knock it off! I'm okay!"

"You're bleeding."

"What's new?" A deep gash ran the length of Quentin's thigh. His blood oozed out, ran onto the deck. "Uh ... can you guys help me get to Doc Patah?"

Mum-O pushed George aside. The twelve-foot-long Ki picked Quentin up and placed the Human on his back. Quentin felt a lurch, then wrapped his arms around Mum-O's chest and held on for dear life. The Ki tucked multi-jointed arms and legs to the side and slithered down the corridor like a giant snake.

"QUENTIN, SIT STILL," Doc Patah said. "Your injury is minor and I don't have time for this."

Quentin braced himself as Doc Patah applied two metal clamps to the five-inch gash in his left thigh. The Harrah put the pair of devices in place, then activated them both. The clamps pinched, pressing together the edges of Quentin's torn skin. Blood surged up as the clamps locked down, then the flow stopped. Doc reached a mouth-flap into his backpack, brought out a tube and squirted the contents on the cut.

"Nanocytes," he said. "The gel allows them to flow in around the clamps. The cut isn't deep enough to merit anything else. We just need to stop the bleeding."

With that, Doc flapped away, shooting across the room to a table that held Shun-On-Won, the backup offensive right guard. Black blood covered Shun-On's chest, with more flowing out every second. Doc's tentacles slid right inside the wound, wiggled for a moment. The trickle of black blood slowed, then stopped. Shun-On wasn't dead, but from the looks of things he wasn't that far away from it.

Quentin glanced around the infirmary. Hokor was there, unconscious on the table, wires connecting him to beeping machines. Why had Coach left the dining deck? Tried to help, like Quentin had? Doc Patah paid no attention to him, so Quentin assumed Hokor was fine.

A Human woman sat on a table, her left hand wrapped in a bloody blue bandage. Red blood stained her orange uniform. Quentin remembered her from his tour with Captain Kate. Sayeeda was her name, maybe. Something like that. Her eyes were squeezed tight, but she sat very still, bravely dealing with the pain while she waited her turn.

With a flash of guilt, Quentin suddenly realized why Doc Patah had stopped treating Shun-On long enough to check Quentin's thigh injury — prioritization. Shun-On was a backup lineman. He wasn't as important as the franchise quarterback. What if Shun-On *died* because Doc Patah stopped long enough to make sure Quentin's injury wasn't as severe? And Sayeeda, no matter what her injury, would have to wait until all of the football players had been treated.

Doc Patah's order of treatment was simultaneously abhorrent and perfectly logical. Even while under attack, while dying, the Ionath Krakens were about winning football games.

At least Sayeeda was alive. On another table, Quentin saw a Quyth Worker-sized body covered by a sheet. He hoped it wasn't Pilkie. And in the corner of the room, George Starcher sat on the floor, his head in his hands. Next to him was the trash can that held the remnants of Killik the Unworthy.

The klaxon alarms ceased.

"The last fighter has disengaged," said Captain Kate over the sound system. "We out-ran their support ship. However, we have suffered some engine damage, which we need to repair immediately. We can't go back the way we came, or we'll run into the same support vessel. We will have to tack back at angles to the Sklorno border. We'll move at full burn while we repair engines, but our tactical speed is down to about eighty percent of max. The punch-drive will not be recharged for another six hours. Hold for orders."

When she stopped talking, the ship sounded eerily quiet.

Mum-O-Killowe stood next to Shun-On's table, staring at his wounded Ki teammate, watching Doc Patah scramble to save a life.

Some of Captain Kate's words finally registered.

"Wait a minute," Quentin said. "We're tacking *back* to Sklorno space? If we're not in Sklorno space, where in the Void are we?"

George looked up. "The only other thing in this sector is Prawatt territory. So I guess we're there."

"You mean we're in Prawatt Jihad space?"

George thought, then nodded, then put his head back in his hands.

The speakerfilm crackled. Captain Kate was back.

"Barnes, Starcher, Mum-O-Killowe, Kimberlin, report to the bridge," she said. "All other footballers, get your damage-control assignments from Messal."

Quentin stood, tested out his leg. He knew he shouldn't be moving on it, but he'd played hurt enough times to know that didn't matter. He wasn't going to second-guess Captain Kate. She was probably the only reason they were all alive. Until this was over, he would run the plays that she called.

"Mum-O," Quentin said. "Come on, we need to go to the bridge. George, get up. Let's go."

Mum-O scuttled over. George stood and picked up the trash can.

"Uh, George?" Quentin said. "I think you need to leave Killik here."

George stared for a moment, then looked down, as if it surprised him to see he'd picked up the can at all. He lowered it gently, the bottom clinking slightly as it came to rest on the floor. Killik's foot was still sticking out of it.

"I knew you not well," George said to Killik's remains. "But if the spirits that guide the firmament are so inclined, the power of the Old Ones will let me mightily whip the asses of all that were responsible for this transgression."

George nodded once, then followed Quentin and Mum-O out of the infirmary.

• • •

QUENTIN, MUM-O AND GEORGE entered the bridge. The place radiated a lethal calmness. The seven sentients already here were focused on a life-and-death situation, where any mistake could be disaster.

The four bridge crew members sat at workstations below the large, holographic *Touchback*. They talked to each other, pointing to various parts of the hologram that glowed red. The crew's cool demeanor impressed Quentin — they were all probably excellent poker players.

Kate stood in the center of the bridge, talking to Michael Kimberlin and Messal the Efficient. Kimberlin held a message-board that showed a small holographic *Touchback*. Kate pointed and each time she did, Kimberlin nodded. The three of them struck quite an image — a towering, 8-foot-tall HeavyG, a normal-sized Human woman and a 3-foot-tall Quyth Worker.

She waved Quentin and the others over. Her eyes drifted down to his blood-soaked pants leg. "How bad is it?"

Not *are you okay?* Not *what happened?* Captain Kate only cared about one thing — could Quentin still get a job done?

He shrugged. "Does it matter? I'm here. What do you want us to do?"

She inclined her head toward Kimberlin. "He's going to walk you back to Gun Cabin 6."

"It's destroyed," Quentin said.

"Then make it un-destroyed," she said. "Whatever it takes, get the room repaired. The fighters didn't hit the cannon itself. The three of you are going to have to wear pressure suits. Seal off the corridor. Kimberlin will walk you through that process, then I need him on the engine decks. Starcher, you get in that gun cabin and figure out how to get the room re-pressurized."

George nodded. "Aye-aye, Captain."

"We're in a bad spot," she said. "We're pretty far past the Prawatt border. We have to get out of here." She was calm, but clearly worried. Her body language told Quentin there was more to the story.

"Do the Prawatt know we're here?"

"Probably," she said. "The only question is how long will it take them to reach us. We don't have military-grade sensors. We wouldn't even know they were here until they were right on top of us."

Something out past the bridge's large windows caught Quentin's attention. Something out there ... moving?

"Get the gun fixed," Captain Kate said. "There's a small chance the pirates will re-engage us before we can reach Yall and Creterakian protection. We may have to fight again. Messal, take that damage control list to the galley and make assignments as you see fit, got it?"

"A brilliant plan, Captain Cheevers, I doubt anyone could do better regardless of—"

"Cut the brown-nosing," she said. "Kimberlin, get back to the upper engine deck as soon as you can. We need a pair of smart hands up there."

Quentin stared. There *was* something moving out there. A dot of light? He squinted, trying to focus on it. Was it one of the fighters?

"I understand," Kimberlin said. "I'll do what I can."

One of the bridge crew stood up suddenly. "Captain! We're being jammed, random noise all across the spectrum. We're blind."

Kate ran to her chair. "We have to run for it. Correct course to go straight for Sklorno space."

There was a chorus of *yes captain*, but Quentin didn't really hear it. All his attention stayed locked on the thing out the window. The light. No, *multiple* lights. Almost as if the stars were ... moving.

"Uh ... Captain?"

"Not now, Barnes! Go fix that gun!"

"Captain, I don't think that will matter."

Kate looked at him. He just pointed out the bridge's wide window.

Kate saw, then sat back in her chair. "Crap," she said. "Well, that's it, folks. We're screwed. Boys, forget the long-range stuff, scan the damn thing that's right outside our window.

The moving lights grew a little larger, filled the entire view, blocking out the stars that stayed fixed in space. Quentin almost asked Kate why they didn't run anyway, but that was before the window flashed and holographic information danced across the crysteel. The info showed the other ship's distance and size.

"Uh … that's a really big ship, isn't it?"

Captain Kate laughed. She stood and walked to a workstation. She seemed to be in no hurry.

Kimberlin leaned in, talked quietly. "It is big, Quentin. As big as it gets. We're looking at something very few people see."

"Which is?"

"A Prawatt capital-class warship," he said. "The largest known vessels in the galaxy. If I were you, I'd enjoy it."

"*Enjoy* it? Why?"

Captain Kate reached the workstation and pressed a button. "Attention, all sentients on the *Touchback*. We have been overtaken by a Prawatt warship. If we're lucky, we will be boarded within moments. Everyone should stay where they are and make no effort to defend the ship. Our only chance is to pose no threat, hope we get a chance to explain ourselves. If we don't get that chance, well … it's been real shucking nice to know ya."

She released the button. She walked back to her chair, dropped into it. She reached beneath the chair and pulled out a glass bottle. Kate unscrewed the cap, then took a long sip of some brown fluid. She looked utterly defeated, resigned to whatever might happen next.

"Why enjoy the view?" Kimberlin said. "Because this is it for us."

He looked out the window to the sprawling mass of the Prawatt ship.

"History speaks for itself," Kimberlin said. "Sorry, Quentin, but I'm afraid that we're all going to die."

From *UBS Sports*

Tragedy mars title game as Themala takes GFL Championship

by PIKOR THE ASSUMING

VIRILLIVILL, YALL, SKLORNO DYNASTY — Deaths are a part of football, as we all know. For the second time in three seasons, the Grim Reaper plucked away a Jupiter star in the middle of the sport's biggest game.

Themala won its first GFL title with a 28-24 win over the Jacks at Galaxy Bowl XXVI, held at Tomb of the Virilli stadium. The team celebrated the win, as they should, but those celebrations lost some luster in the face of the death of Jupiter quarterback Shriaz Zia.

Zia led his team to a 21-0 advantage. It looked like a Galaxy Bowl shutout until midway through the third quarter, when Zia scrambled left due to pressure from the Dreadnaughts front four. Instead of sliding, Zia tried to pick up a few extra yards by taking on a tackle from linebacker Tibi the Unkempt. The hit severed Zia's C4 and C5 vertebrate. He was carted off the field and declared dead in the stadium hospital.

With Zia out of the game, the Jacks could not move the ball. To close the third quarter, Themala scored on a Galaxy Bowl record 88-yard run by running back Don Dennis.

The Dreadnaughts entered the fourth quarter down 21-7. Quarterback Gavin Warren hit wide receiver Keflavík for a 42-yard strike, then five minutes later, hit Dennis on a simple screen pass that turned into a 68-yard touchdown reception.

With the score tied at 21-all, Jacks returner Luxemborg ran the ensuing kick back to the Dreadnaughts' 11. Backup quarterback Steve Compton couldn't advance the ball any farther, so the Jacks settled for a field goal that put them up 24-21 with 2:17 left to play.

Following a touchback, Themala started on its own 20. The Dreadnaughts then proceeded to drive 78 yards for a first-and-goal on the Jupiter 2-yard line. With five seconds to play and no timeouts, Themala coach Smitty Halibut opted to go for the win instead of kicking the tying field goal.

> *"I'm mad as hell. We had that game wrapped up. Now my quarterback is dead and we have to start all over."*
>
> JT MANIS
> OWNER, JUPITER JACKS

"I said to my team, I said, *screw it*," Coach Halibut said. "We had the momentum."

The unexpected decision proved fortuitous. Warren dropped back and found fullback Zach Mann all alone in the end zone for the winning touchdown.

"I'm mad as hell," said Jacks owner JT Manis. "We had that game wrapped up. Now my quarterback is dead and we have to start all over."

The Jacks couldn't move the ball, true, but the Dreadnaughts did run roughshod in the second half of what will surely go down as the biggest defensive collapse in Galaxy Bowl history.

"Hey, their *defense* didn't die," Don Dennis said. "Those are the same guys who held us scoreless through two-and-a-half quarters. I'm sorry Shriaz is dead, but we scored twenty-eight points in the second half of the Galaxy Bowl. We owned them. We wanted it more and we took it. Vini, vidi, vici, we be the champs."

Themala finished the regular season at 9-3 for the second year in a row. Including playoff games, the Dreadnaughts are 22-7 over the past two seasons. ■

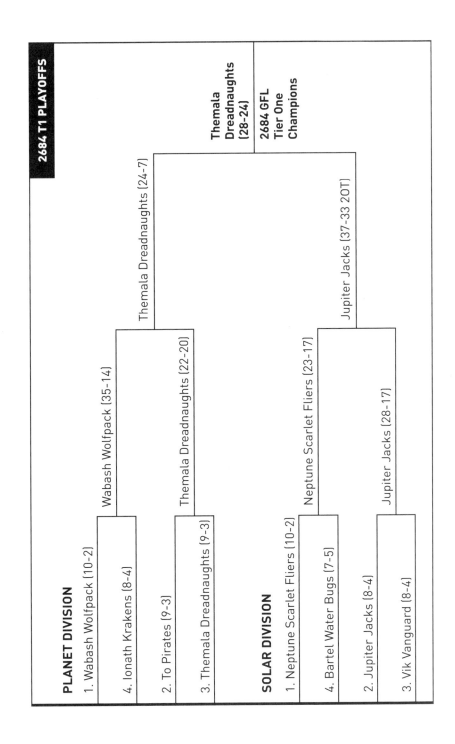

2684 T1 PLAYOFFS

Themala
Dreadnaughts
(28-24)

2684 GFL
Tier One
Champions

Themala Dreadnaughts (24-7)

Jupiter Jacks (37-33 2OT)

Wabash Wolfpack (35-14)

Themala Dreadnaughts (22-20)

Neptune Scarlet Fliers (23-17)

Jupiter Jacks (28-17)

PLANET DIVISION

1. Wabash Wolfpack (10-2)

4. Ionath Krakens (8-4)

2. To Pirates (9-3)

3. Themala Dreadnaughts (9-3)

SOLAR DIVISION

1. Neptune Scarlet Fliers (10-2)

4. Bartel Water Bugs (7-5)

2. Jupiter Jacks (8-4)

3. Vik Vanguard (8-4)

From the *Ionath City Gazette*

Krakens bus, entire team missing

by TOYAT THE INQUISITIVE

YALL, SKLORNO DYNASTY — The *Touchback*, team bus for the Ionath Krakens football franchise, has gone missing following an attack by an unknown force.

The ship had arrived in far orbit around the planet Yall in the Sklorno Dynasty. The Krakens players were there to attend Galaxy Bowl XXVI. Details are scarce, but reports indicate that an unknown fighter craft attacked the *Touchback* as soon as it came out of punch-space. Preliminary investigations seem to show that the *Touchback* fled this attack by crossing the Prawatt border.

"We are proceeding with caution," said the Creterakian Empire regional admiral. "We cannot go in after them. The Prawatt would consider that an act of war. We are trying to implement diplomatic communications, but so far our efforts have been ignored. The Prawatt remain in total communication blackout, as they have for decades."

Heightened tensions between the Prawatt and the Sklorno Dynasty have not helped efforts to find the *Touchback*'s whereabouts. Last year, a Sklorno vessel was destroyed near the border, killing 40,000 sentients. There is some suspicion that the perpetrators of that deed are also responsible for the attack on the *Touchback*.

GFL Commissioner Rob Froese reported the missing bus in a press conference. He said he is optimistic that the Krakens will be found.

"We haven't received a destruct signal," Froese said. "If the *Touchback* was destroyed, on-board sensors are eighty percent likely to send a signal. We are hopeful the ship remains intact. We can't say for certain if the team and the crew are alive, but if the ship is still in one piece it's a good sign."

As of yet, there has been no word from the *Touchback*. It is unknown if the team and crew are alive or dead.

"We will find them," said Ionath owner Gredok the Splithead. "No matter what it takes, we will find them. And I will find the sentients responsible for this, I assure you of that."

THE END